READER'S DIGEST

CONDENSED BOOKS

FIRST EDITION

Published by

THE READER'S DIGEST ASSOCIATION LIMITED
25 Berkeley Square, London W1X 6AB.

THE READER'S DIGEST ASSOCIATION SOUTH AFRICA (PTY) LTD.
Nedbank Centre, Strand Street, Cape Town

Typeset in 10 on 12 pt. Highland Lumitype Roman
and printed in Great Britain by Petty & Sons Ltd., Leeds

Original cover design by Jeffery Matthews A.R.C.A.

For information as to ownership
of copyright in the material in this book see last page

ISBN 0 340 185 341

READER'S DIGEST
CONDENSED BOOKS

EAGLE IN THE SKY
Wilbur Smith

STAY OF EXECUTION
Stewart Alsop

THE SALAMANDER
Morris West

THE BOY WHO INVENTED
THE BUBBLE GUN
Paul Gallico

COLLECTOR'S LIBRARY
EDITION

In this volume

EAGLE IN THE SKY
by Wilbur Smith (p. 9)

In David Morgan, wealthy, hot-headed air force ace, and in Debra Mordecai, the beautiful, courageous Israeli girl with whom he falls in love, Wilbur Smith has brought vividly to life two of his finest characters. He has produced an unforgettable story of their joy in one another, of the tragedies that so nearly destroyed them and of their victory against almost insurmountable odds.

THE BOY WHO INVENTED THE BUBBLE GUN
by Paul Gallico (p. 447)

Paul Gallico has a rare genius for gentle humour. He also has an affection and understanding for the young. In this exciting, engaging, and often hilarious story of a nine-year-old's escapades in the incomprehensible world of adults, he has written a book which will surely add many more admirers to those innumerable readers he has charmed so well before.

THE SALAMANDER
by Morris West (p. 277)

Some men perhaps are better dead – certainly if they have schemed the destruction of their own state – yet true servants of that state must, even at the risk of all they love, pursue the dead man's murderers. This is the dilemma of Colonel Dante Matucci, a man caught in a subtle and dangerous rip tide of events. Each moment in this brilliant novel brings new surprises, new suspense. And the climax offers a moving and startling irony – the true signature of a master storyteller.

STAY OF EXECUTION
by Stewart Alsop (p. 159)

The diagnosis was clear. The patient had perhaps one year to live. A leading journalist, a friend of statesmen on both sides of the Atlantic, a man of rare gifts and great influence, Stewart Alsop here spells out what this cataclysmic medical verdict has meant to him: the fear, the suspense of endless tests, the rise and fall of hope. An honest, remarkably vivid view of everyman's ultimate crisis, this is also a story – full of grace and humour – of one man's life: his eccentric relatives, his meetings with Mrs. Eleanor Roosevelt and Winston Churchill, his wartime experiences in England where he met and married his beautiful wife, a story that runs the gamut from hair-raising to hilarious.

Illustrated by Roger Coleman

Eagle in the Sky

a condensation of the book by

Wilbur Smith

Published by William Heinemann, London

David Morgan was a playboy: immensely rich, vain, bored. The purpose his life needed was not to be found in Europe's gilded pleasure domes. He needed opportunity to give rather than always to receive: to give himself to a person, to give himself to a cause.

A chance meeting on the dusty roads of Spain, a broken-down car, a lift given, and suddenly this need was filled. The person was Debra Mordecai, daughter of an Israeli Air Force general; the cause, Israel's fight to remain free.

For the first time in his life David was completely happy. By day, high in the hot still desert air, he flew strikes against Israel's enemies; by night he lay in the arms of his beautiful Israeli love. Soon he and Debra were to be married. Their future stretched golden before them. But it was a happiness that could not last. The terrible two-edged tragedy that struck was bred in the random violence of war. It shattered the young couple's hopes, threatened the very substance of their love.

This powerful story moves inexorably from beleaguered Israel to a haunting climax in the African wilderness. Its subject is the courage that transcends all suffering, and the love that transcends all fear.

> *" . . . Three things are too wonderful for me,*
> *Four I do not understand,*
> *The way of an eagle in the sky,*
> *The way of a serpent on a rock,*
> *The way of a ship on the high seas,*
> *And the way of a man with a maiden."*

Proverbs, 30, 18–20

THERE WAS SNOW ON THE MOUNTAINS behind Cape Town, and the wind came off them, whimpering like a lost animal. The instructor stood in the doorway of his tiny office and hunched down into his flight jacket, thrusting his fists deeply into the fleece-lined pockets. He watched the black chauffeur-driven Cadillac coming down between the iron-clad hangars, and he frowned sourly. For the trappings of wealth Barney Venter had a deep gut-envy.

The Cadillac swung in and parked in a visitors' slot against the hangar wall, and a boy sprang from the rear door, spoke briefly with the coloured chauffeur, then hurried towards Barney.

Barney's envy curdled as he watched the young princeling approach. He hated these pampered darlings, and it was his fate that he must spend so much of his working day in their company. Only the very rich could afford to instruct their children in the mysteries of flight.

At the age of forty-five he was reduced to this by having failed, two years previously, the strict medical test on which his position of senior airline captain depended. He growled at the child before him. "Master Morgan, I presume?"

"Yes, sir, but you may call me David." The boy offered his hand.

"Thank you, David. And you may continue to call me 'sir'."

He knew the boy was fourteen years old, but he stood almost level with Barney's five-foot-seven. David smiled at him and Barney

9

was struck by the boy's beauty. It seemed indecent that hair should curl and glow so darkly, that skin should be so satiny and delicately tinted, or that eyes possess such depth and fire. The total effect was almost unreal, theatrical.

Barney turned away abruptly and led the way through his office with its nude calendars and handwritten notices carrying terse admonitions against asking for credit.

"What do you know about flying?" he asked the boy as they passed through the hangar where gaudily coloured aircraft stood in long rows, and out again into the bright winter sunshine.

"Nothing, sir."

"But you want to learn?"

"Oh, yes sir!" The reply was emphatic and Barney glanced at him. The boy's eyes were almost black. Only in the sunlight did they turn deep indigo blue.

The aircraft was waiting on the concrete apron. "This is a Cessna 150 high-wing monoplane." Barney began the walk-around check with David following attentively, but when he started a brief explanation of the control surfaces, he became aware that the boy knew more than he had owned up to.

"You've been reading," Barney accused.

"Yes, sir," David admitted grinning. The smile was irresistible. Despite himself, Barney realized he was beginning to like the boy.

"Right, jump in."

Strapped into the cramped cockpit, shoulder to shoulder, Barney explained the controls, then led into the starting procedure. "Master switch on." He flipped the red button. "Right, turn that key."

David leaned forward and obeyed. The prop spun and the engine fired. They taxied down the apron with David quickly developing his touch on the rudders, and paused for the final checks before swinging onto the runway.

"Right, aim for an object at the end of the runway, and open the throttle gently." The machine buzzed towards the far-off fence markers. "Ease back on the wheel." And they were airborne, climbing swiftly away from earth.

"Gently," said Barney. "Don't freeze on to the controls."

10

Instantly, through his own controls, he felt David's death-grip on the wheel relax.

"That's it, David." He glanced at the boy, and felt a flare of disappointment. He had felt deep down that this one might be bird, one of the very rare ones like himself whose natural element was the blue. Yet here in the first few moments of flight the child was wearing an expression of frozen terror.

"Left wing up," he snapped, trying to shock him out of it. The wing came up and held rock-steady.

"Throttle back." The boy's right hand went unerringly to the throttle. Once more Barney glanced at him. His expression had not altered, and with a sudden revelation Barney recognized it not as fear, but as ecstasy.

"He is bird." The thought gave him vast satisfaction.

They skirted the harsh blue mountains with their mantles of sun-blazing snow, and rode the tail of the wild winds that came down off them.

"Wind is like the sea, David. It breaks and swirls around high ground. Watch for it." David nodded, his eyes fixed ahead savouring each instant.

They turned north over the bleak bare land, the earth stripped by the harvest of its golden wheat. Then south again, following the Atlantic coastline towards the great flat mountain that marked the limit of the land.

"Let's try a steep turn now," Barney said. Down went the wing and boldly the nose swept around holding its attitude to the horizon. They ran in towards the airfield.

"O.K.," said Barney. "I've got her." He took them in for the touchdown and taxied back to the apron. They sat silent for a moment, both of them aware that something important had happened. "O.K.?" Barney asked at last.

"Yes, sir," David nodded, and they unstrapped and climbed down.

Without speaking they walked side by side through the hangar and office. At the door they paused.

"Next Wednesday?" Barney asked.

"Yes, sir." David started towards the waiting Cadillac, but after a dozen steps he stopped, and turned back. "That was the most beautiful thing that has ever happened to me," he said shyly. "Thank you, sir." And he hurried away leaving Barney staring after him.

"I TAUGHT HIM GOOD," thought Barney, sprawled in the co-pilot's seat of the Lear. As he watched David fly, he felt warm affection for the boy. Barney had been chief pilot of the Morgan group for three years now, and he knew well to whose intervention he owed the post. He had put on weight since eating Morgan food and the beginning of jowls bracketed his wide down-turned mouth.

Today, Paul Morgan himself had sent him to fetch David from the family's holiday home at the foot of the Outeniqua Mountains. Paul Morgan wanted a pow-wow with his nephew who, with high school completed, had many roads open. Barney knew that the road David had chosen would draw violent opposition.

The golden beaches of Africa streamed beneath them, punctuated by rock promontories and tiny resorts and fishing villages. From Cape Agulhas they turned inland, climbing steeply over the mountain ranges. Then David eased back on the throttles and they sank down beyond the crests towards Cape Town, nestled under its mountain.

As they walked towards the hangar, Barney looked up at David, who now topped him by six inches. "Don't let him stampede you, boy," he warned. "You've made your decision. Stick to it."

David took his M.G. over De Waal Drive, and from the lower slopes of the mountain looked down at the Morgan Building and the other tall monuments to power and wealth. He enjoyed its appearance, clean and functional like an aircraft's wing—but he knew that the soaring freedom of its lines was deceptive. It was a prison and fortress.

He drove to the building and parked in its underground garage. When eventually he entered the executive apartments on the top floor, he passed the desks where the secretaries, hand-picked for their looks as well as their skill with a typewriter, sat in a long row. Their faces opened into smiles as David greeted them. Within the Morgan building he was treated with the respect due to the heir apparent.

12

Martha Goodrich, in her own office that guarded the inner sanctum, was business-like. "Good morning, Mister David. Your uncle is waiting—and I do think you could have worn a suit."

"You're looking good, Martha. I like your hair like that." It worked, as it always did. Her expression softened.

"Don't you try buttering me up," she warned him primly. "I'm not one of your floozies."

Paul Morgan was at the window looking down over the city.

"Hello, Uncle Paul. I'm sorry I didn't have time to change. I thought it best to come directly."

"That's fine, David." Paul Morgan turned to greet David. His eyes flicked over David's floral shirt, wide, tooled-leather belt, white slacks and open sandals. On him it all looked good, he admitted reluctantly. "It's fine to see you." He smoothed the lapels of his own dark, conservatively-cut suit. "Come in. Sit down by the fireplace." As always, he found that David standing emphasized his own lack of stature. Paul was short and heavily built, with a thick muscular neck and square, thrusting head. His hair was coarse and wiry and his features squashed and puglike. All the Morgans were built that way. David's exotic appearance was from his mother's side.

"Well, David. First, I want to congratulate you on your final results. I was most gratified," Paul could have added "—and mightily relieved." David's scholastic career had been tempestuous. There had been the business with the games master's young wife. Paul had smoothed it over by donating a new organ to the school chapel and arranging a teaching scholarship for the games master at a foreign university. Then David had won the coveted Wessels prize for mathematics, and all was forgiven—until he decided to test his housemaster's new sports car, without that gentleman's knowledge, and took it into a tight bend at ninety. The housemaster's prejudices had finally been overcome by the replacement of his wrecked car with a more expensive model.

The boy was wild, Paul knew it well, but he knew also that David possessed all the attributes that he wanted in his successor: the verve and confidence, the quick mind and adventurous spirit— but above all, the aggressive attitude, the urge to compete that Paul defined as the killer instinct.

13

He stood before the picture windows, so that the daylight back-lit him. It was an old trick of his to put the other person at a disadvantage. "And now we must consider your future," he said. David remained silent. "The choice is wide," Paul continued, and then went on swiftly to narrow it. "Though I do feel business science and law at an American university is what it should be. With this goal in mind I have had you enrolled in my old college—"

"Uncle Paul, I want to fly," said David softly.

Paul's expression changed fractionally. "We are making a career decision, my boy, not expressing preferences for recreation."

"No, sir. I mean I want to fly—as a way of life."

"Your life is here, within the Morgan group."

"I don't agree with you, sir."

Paul crossed to the fireplace. He selected a cigar from the humidor on the mantel, and while he prepared it he spoke softly. "Your father was a romantic, David. He got it out of his system by charging around the desert in a tank. It seems you have inherited this romanticism from him." He made it sound like some disgusting disease. "Tell me what you propose."

"I have enlisted in the air force, sir."

"You've signed? For how long?"

"Five years. Short service commission."

"Five years—" Paul whispered. "Well, David, I don't know what to say. You know that you are the last of the Morgans. I have no son. I wonder what your father would have thought of this—"

"That's hitting low, Uncle Paul."

"I don't think so, David. I think you are the one who is cheating. Your trust fund is a huge block of Morgan shares and other assets given to you on the understanding that you assume your duties and responsibilities. Anything else is cowardice, self indulgence—" The Morgan group, thought David fiercely, was reaching out its tentacles, to suck him in. "We can have your enlistment papers annulled—"

"Uncle Paul," David almost shouted. "My father joined the army."

"Yes, David. But it was different then. And when it was over he came back and took his rightful place here. We miss him now, David. I have always hoped that you might fill the gap he left."

"But I don't want to spend my life in here," David said, gesturing at the mammoth structure of glass and concrete that surrounded them. "I don't want to spend each day poring over piles of paper—"

"It's not like that, David. It's exciting, challenging—"

"Uncle Paul," David raised his voice again. "What do you call a man who fills his belly with rich food—and then goes on eating?"

"Come now, David." The first edge of irritation showed in Paul's voice. "I expect that you would call him a glutton."

"And what do you call a man with many millions—who spends his life trying to make more?"

Paul froze. "You become insolent," he said.

"I did not mean to. You are not the glutton—but I would be."

Paul turned away and went to his desk. He sat in the high-backed leather chair and lit the cigar at last. "You'll have to get it out of your system," he sighed. "But how I grudge you five wasted years."

"Not wasted, Uncle Paul. I will come out with a Bachelor of Science degree in aeronautical engineering."

"I suppose we'll just have to be thankful for little things like that. But after five years, David, I want you." Then he smiled slightly. "At least they will make you cut your hair."

FOUR MILES ABOVE the warm flesh-coloured earth, David Morgan flew the heavens with a rapt, almost mystical expression. Five years with the air force had not dulled the sensation of power and isolation that flight awoke in him.

Today's flight was tempered by melancholy. Tomorrow at noon his commission expired and if Paul Morgan prevailed he would become Mister David—new boy at Morgan Group. He thrust the thought aside, and concentrated on these last precious minutes.

"Zulu Striker One, this is Range Control. Your target-markers are figures eight and twelve. Commence your run."

The horizon revolved abruptly across the nose of the Mirage, as the wing came over and he went down, purposeful and precise as the stoop of a falcon.

David's right hand moved swiftly across the weapon selector panel, locking in the rocket circuit. The earth flattened out ahead, speckled with low bush that blurred past his wing-tips as the

15

Mirage sank lower. At this height the awareness of speed was breathtaking, and as the first marker came up it seemed at the same instant to flash away below the silvery nose.

Five, six, seven—the black numerals on their glaring white backgrounds flickered by. A touch of left rudder and stick, and ahead was the circular layout of the rocket range, the concentric rings shrinking in size around the bulls-eye—the "coke" of flight jargon.

David's Mach meter was recording a speed that was barely sub-sonic, but the shrieking machine achieved her correct, slightly nose-down attitude for rocket launch at the precise instant that the white blob of "coke" was centred in the reflector sight.

David pressed the trigger. The hiss of the rocket launch was almost lost beneath the howl of the jet. Certain of a fair strike, David pushed his throttle to the gate and waited for the rumbling ignition of his afterburner, giving him power to climb out of range of enemy flak.

"What a way to go." He grinned to himself as he lay on his back with the Mirage's nose pointed into the bright blue.

"Hello, Striker One. This is Range Control. That was right on the nose. Give the man a coke. Sorry to lose you, Davey."

On the ground, an orderly was waiting for him. "C.O.'s compliments, sir, and will you report to him right away."

Colonel Rastus Naude was a dried-out stick of a man, with a wizened monkey face, who wore his uniform and medal ribbons with a casually distracted air. He had flown Hurricanes in the Battle of Britain, Spitfires in Palestine and Sabres in Korea. He was too old for his present command, but nobody could muster the courage to tell him that, especially since he could out-fly most of the young bucks on the squadron. "So we are getting rid of you at last, Morgan," he greeted David.

"Not until after the mess party, sir."

"*Ja*," Rastus nodded. "You've given me enough hardship these last five years. You owe me a bucket of whisky." He gestured to the chair beside his desk. "Sit down, David."

David lowered himself into the chair, clumsy in the constricting grip of his flying suit. Rastus took his time filling his pipe. Then, puffing thick rank clouds of blue smoke, he slid a sheaf of documents across the desk to David.

"Read and sign," he said. "That's an order."

David glanced rapidly through the papers, then looked up and grinned. "You don't give in easily, sir." One document was a renewal of his service contract for an additional five years, the other was a warrant of promotion—from captain to major.

"You have been given an exceptional talent, and we have spent a great deal of time and money developing it until now you are —I'll not mince words—one hell of a pilot!"

"I'm sorry, sir," David told him sincerely.

"Damn it," said Rastus angrily. "Why the hell did you have to be born a Morgan. All that money—they'll clip your wings."

"It's not the money," David denied swiftly. "It's hard to explain, I just feel that there is something important that I have to find out about—and it's not here. I have to go look for it."

"All right then," Rastus said. "I had a good try. You and I will get drunk together this night—for both of us are losing something, I perhaps more than you."

IT SEEMED THAT DAVID had inherited his love of beautiful and powerful machines from his father. Clive Morgan had driven himself, his wife, and his brand new Ferrari into the side of a train on an unlit level crossing at a speed the police estimated to be one hundred and fifty miles an hour.

Clive Morgan's provision for his son was detailed and elaborate. The eleven-year-old child became a ward of his uncle, Paul Morgan, and his inheritance was arranged in a series of trust funds.

On his majority he was given access to the first of the funds which provided an income equivalent to that of a highly successful surgeon. On that day the M.G. had given way to a powder-blue Maserati. On his twenty-third birthday, control of the sheep ranches in the Karroo, the cattle ranch in South West Africa and Jabulani, the sprawling game ranch in the Sabi-Sand block, would pass to him.

On his twenty-fifth birthday the number-two fund interest would divert to him, in addition to title in two massive urban holdings— office complexes, and a housing project. From then onwards, every five years until he was fifty, further funds would open. It was a numbing procession of wealth that stretched ahead of him.

David drove southwards with the Michelin metallics' hissing savagely on the road surface. He thought about all that wealth and the prospect of becoming its prisoner appalled him. He pushed the Maserati harder, finding comfort in the rhythm and precision of driving very fast. It was still daylight when he let himself into Mitzi's apartment on the cliffs that overlooked the clear green Atlantic.

Mitzi was Uncle Paul's daughter. Her apartment was chaos. She kept open house for a string of transitory guests who drank her liquor, ate her food and created a spectacular shambles. David removed a forest of tights and feminine underwear that festooned the bathroom and drew himself a bath. As he settled into it the front door burst open and Mitzi came in like the north wind.

"Where are you, warrior? I saw your car in the garage—so I know you're here!"

"In here, coz," he called, and she stood in the doorway and they grinned at each other. Metal-framed spectacles sat on the end of her little nose, while her hair fuzzed out at unexpected angles. She had put on weight again, he saw.

"You're beautiful," Mitzi cried, coming to kiss him and getting soap on her sweater as she hugged him. "Drink or coffee?"

"Coffee will be great."

She brought it to him in a mug and perched on the toilet seat. "Tell all!" she commanded.

They chatted until Mitzi said suddenly, without preliminaries, "Papa is waiting for you. I ate with them Saturday night and he must have brought your name up one zillion times. It's going to be strange to have you sitting up there on Top Floor, in a charcoal suit, being bright at Monday morning conference—"

David suddenly threw up his arms, cascading suds and water over the edge of the bath. "I'm not going!" he said.

"But you have to! You promised Daddy that you would when you finished with the air force."

"No," David said, "I made no promise. When you said a moment ago—being bright at Monday morning conference—I knew I couldn't do it. I guess I've known all along."

"What you going to do, then?"

"I don't know. I'll find my own road to go!"

Mitzi was enchanted by this prospect of open defiance. "Yes, you'd shrivel and die up there."

David came out of the bath. He pulled on a bathrobe and Mitzi followed him through to the bedroom, eagerly nodding her encouragement as David made his formal declaration of independence. Then she spoiled it.

"What are you going to tell Daddy?" she asked. The question halted David's flow of rhetoric. "He's not going to let you get away again," she warned. "Not without a stand-up, knock-down fight."

"I've told him once," David said, "I don't have to tell him again."

"You're just going to cut and run?" Mitzi asked.

"I'm not running," David replied with frosty dignity. "I am merely reserving the right to determine my own future." He crossed to the telephone and began dialling.

"Who are you calling?"

"The airline."

"Where are you heading?"

"The same place as their first flight out."

"I'll cover for you," declared Mitzi loyally, "You're doing the right thing, warrior."

DAVID CAME OUT INTO THE impersonal concrete and glass arrivals hall of Amsterdam's Schiphol Airport. As he paused to gloat on his escape, there was a touch at his elbow, and he turned to find a tall, smiling man quizzing him through rimless spectacles.

"Mr. David Morgan, I think?" and David gaped at him. "I am Frederick van Gent. I have the honour to act for Morgan Shipping Lines in Holland. It is a great pleasure to make your acquaintance."

"God, no!" David whispered wearily. "I'm sorry. It's nice to meet you." He shook the hand with resignation.

"I have two urgent telex messages for you, Mr. Morgan." Van Gent produced them with a flourish.

The first was from Mitzi who had sworn to cover for him. "Abject apologies your whereabouts extracted with rack and thumbscrew stop Be brave as a lion stop Be ferocious as an eagle stop Love Mitzi."

David said, "Traitor!" and opened the second. "Your doubts

understood, your action condoned stop Confident your good sense will lead you eventually onto path of duty stop Your place here always open affectionately Paul Morgan."

David said, "Crafty old bastard," and stuffed both messages into his pocket.

"Is there a reply?" Van Gent asked.

"Thank you, no. It was good of you to take this trouble."

"No trouble, Mr. Morgan. Can I help you in any way?"

"No, but thanks again." They shook hands and Van Gent left.

David went to the Avis counter and the girl smiled brightly at him.

"Good evening, sir."

David slipped his Avis card across the desk. "I want something with a little jump to it, please."

"Let me see . . . we have a Mustang Mach I?" She was pure blonde with a cream and pink unlined face.

"That will do admirably," David assured her, and as she began filling the form he said, "They tell me Amsterdam's the city with the most action in Europe, is that right?"

"If you know where to go," she murmured.

"You could show me?" David asked.

"Please sign here, sir. If you have any queries on this contract, you can contact me at this number—after hours. My name is Gilda."

Gilda shared a flat with three other girls who showed no surprise when David carried his suitcase up the steep staircase. However, the action that Gilda provided was in a series of discotheques and coffee bars where lost little people gathered to talk revolution and guru babble. In two days David discovered that pot tasted terrible and that Gilda's mind was as bland as her exterior. She showed no visible emotion when he said good-bye.

With the heaters blasting hot air into the Mustang, David sent it out of the wintry north towards Madrid. He had read Hemingway and much of the other romantic literature of the bullring, and he wanted to evaluate its beauty and excitement in the great Plaza De Toros.

He reached the city in two days and checked in at the Gran Via with its elegance now faded to mere comfort. The porter arranged a ticket to the following day's bullfight, and David, tired from the long drive, went to bed early.

The next day he found his way out to the ring and took his seat. The excitement of the crowd was intense, and the music goaded them on. The late arrivals were finding their seats. Two of them climbed the stairs of the aisle near David. They were a striking young couple in their early twenties, but what first drew David's attention to them was the aura of companionship and love that glowed around them, setting them apart.

They climbed arm in arm, taking seats a row behind and across the aisle from David. The girl was tall. She wore dark slacks and an apple-green suede jacket that was not expensive but of good cut. In the sun her shoulder-length hair glittered like newly cut coal. Her face was broad and sun-browned, not beautiful, for her mouth was too big and her eyes too widely spaced, but those eyes were the colour of wild honey, dark brown and flecked with gold. Her companion was also tall, dark and strong-looking. They leaned their heads together and spoke secretly, and David glanced away, his own loneliness accentuated by their closeness.

In the pause following the parade round the sunlit ring, David looked at the couple again. He was startled to find that they were both watching him. The girl was leaning on her companion's shoulder, her lips almost touching his ear as she spoke and David felt his stomach clench under the impact of those honey-golden eyes. She dropped her gaze, but her companion held David's eyes openly, smiling easily, and it was David who looked away.

Below them in the ring the bull came out at full charge, head down, and hooves skidding in the sand. He was beautiful and black and glossy, the muscles in his neck and shoulders bunching as he swung his head from side to side, and the crowd roared. The *banderilleros* took him on a circuit of the ring, letting him show off his high-stepping style, the perfect sickle of his horns.

Then the trumpets ushered in the horse—a scrawny wretched nag, with eyes blinkered so he could not see the fearsome creature he was going to meet. He looked clownish in his padding, seeming too frail to carry the picador on his back. They led him out and placed him in the path of the bull—and here any semblance of beauty ended.

The bull went into him head down, sending the gawky animal reeling against the *barrera*. The picador leaned over the bull's back and drove his lance into the bull's hump. Raging at the agony of the steel, and with blood pouring out in a slick tide, the bull butted at the protective pads that covered the horse's flanks.

The crowd roared again as the quivering horse was finally led from the ring.

When the *banderillero* placed his darts in the bull, reducing it from a magnificent beast to a hulk of sweating and bleeding flesh, David was frozen by guilt for his own part in this obscene ritual. He sat on in silence until the bull stood alone in the centre of the ring, his head down, the blood and froth dripping from his nostrils and gaping mouth. David found he was whispering aloud. "No! No! Stop it! Please, stop it!"

Finally, the matador in his glittering suit of lights came to end it. The sword struck bone, the blade arched then spun away in the sunlight, and the bull heaved and threw thick droplets of blood. The matador picked up his sword and again his thrust was deflected.

At last David screamed: "Stop it! Stop it!"

The bull finally fell of its own accord. The *puntillero* killed it where it lay, with a dagger in the back of the neck, and they dragged it out with a team of mules—its legs waggling ridiculously in the air.

Stunned by the cruelty, David turned to look at the girl. She was shaking her head slowly, in a gesture of incomprehension, and her honey-coloured eyes were wet with tears as her companion helped her to her feet, and gently led her down the steps.

David's heart went out to the weeping girl. He followed her out of the arena. He wanted to speak to her, to tell her that he shared her desolation, but when he reached the car park they were already climbing into a battered old Citroën and although he broke into a run, the car pulled away—blowing blue smoke and clattering like a lawnmower.

David watched it go with a sense of loss, but he saw it again two days later, when he was heading northeast towards Barcelona.

The Citroën, looking even sicker than before, was parked at a filling station on the outskirts of Zaragoza, and David pulled off the road and parked beyond the pumps. An attendant in greasy overalls was filling the tank of the Citroën under the supervision of the young man from the bullring. David looked quickly for the girl—but she was not in the car. Then he saw her.

She was in a *cantina* across the street, haggling with the elderly woman behind the counter. Her back was turned but David recognized the mass of dark hair now piled on top of her head. She wore a short floral dress which left her back and shoulders bare, and her feet were thrust into open sandals. Acting on impulse, David crossed the road and went into the shop.

When she completed her purchases of dried figs, she turned smiling and recognized him instantly. The smile faded and she stood very still looking at him, her lips slightly parted, her eyes soft and golden.

"I saw you in Madrid," David said, "at the bullfight."

"Yes," she nodded, her voice neither welcoming nor forbidding.

"You were crying."

"So were you."

"No," David denied it.

"You were crying," she insisted softly. "You were crying inside." And he nodded in agreement. Suddenly she proffered the bag of figs.

"Try one," she said and smiled again. He took a fig and bit into the sweet flesh as she moved towards the door, somehow conveying an invitation for him to join her. Across the street, the girl's companion was leaning against the Citroën, lighting a cigarette. He looked up and evidently recognized David also, for he straightened up quickly and flicked away the burning match.

There was a soft whooshing sound as fire flashed across the concrete from a puddle of spilled gasoline. In an instant the flames had closed over the rear of the Citroën, and were drumming hungrily at the coachwork.

David sprinted across the road. "We have to get it away from the pumps!" he shouted. He got the handbrake off, and he and the driver pushed the car into an open parking area while a crowd materialized to scream hysterical encouragement.

They managed to rescue the baggage from the rear seat before the flames engulfed it entirely—and belatedly the petrol attendant arrived with an enormous fire extinguisher. To the delighted applause of the crowd, he drenched the pathetic little vehicle in a great cloud of foam, and the excitement was over. The crowd drifted away, leaving the three of them to regard the blackened shell of the car.

"I suppose it was a kindness really—the poor old thing was very tired," the girl said at last.

"Are you insured?" David asked.

The girl's companion laughed. "You're joking—who would insure that?"

They assembled the rescued possessions, and the girl spoke quickly to her companion in a foreign, slightly guttural language which touched a deep chord in David's memory. He understood what she was saying, so it was no surprise when she said to him, "We've got to meet somebody at Barcelona airport by seven. It's important."

"Let's go," said David.

They piled the luggage into the Mustang and the girl's companion squeezed into the back seat. His name was Joe, she was Debra, and surnames didn't seem important. She sat in the seat beside David. With one sweeping glance, she assessed the Mustang and its owner's silk shirt and slim gold Piaget watch.

"Blessed are the poor," she murmured, "but still it must be pleasant to be rich."

David enjoyed that. He wanted her to make a few comparisons between him and the muscular young man in the back seat.

He drove quietly through the city. Debra looked over her shoulder at Joe. "Are you comfortable?" she asked in the guttural language she had been using earlier.

"If he's not—he can run behind," David told her in the same language, and she let out a small exclamation of pleasure.

"Hey! You speak Hebrew!"

"Not very well," David admitted. "I've forgotten most of it," and he had a vivid picture of himself as a ten-year-old, wrestling unhappily with the strange and mysterious language.

"Are you Jewish?" she asked.

David shook his head. "No, I'm raised and reared in the Protestant tradition."

"Then why did you learn Hebrew?"

24

"My mother wanted it," David explained, and felt the stab of an old guilt. "It didn't seem important after she was killed."

"Your mother—" Debra insisted, leaning towards him "—she was Jewish?"

"Yeah. Sure," David agreed. "But my father was a Protestant."

Debra turned around to Joe. "Did you hear that—he's one of us."

"Oh, come on!" David said, laughing.

"Come and see us in Jerusalem sometime," said Joe.

"You're Israeli?" David asked, with new interest.

"Sabras," said Debra, with a note of pride. "We're both native born." Then she changed the subject. "Is this the fastest this machine will go?"

There was a relaxed feeling between them now. "Kindly extinguish cigarettes and fasten your seat belts," David said. They were out of the city now and he let the Mustang go.

She sat very still with a small rapturous smile on her face and David was moved to know that speed affected her the way it did him. Once when they went twisting down into a valley in a series of tight curves and David's hands were darting from wheel to gear lever, she laughed aloud with the thrill of it.

They bought cheese and bread and a bottle of white wine at a cantina and ate lunch sitting on the parapet of a stone bridge while the water swirled below them. David's thigh touched Debra's as they sat side by side, and she made no move to pull away.

David was puzzled by Joe's attitude. He seemed to be completely oblivious of David's dogging his girl, and he was deriving a child-like pleasure out of tossing pebbles at the trout in the waters below them. David wished he would put up a better resistance. He wanted to test himself against Joe. He was big, and strong, and David was not fooled by his lazy grin—the eyes were quick and sharp.

"You want to drive, Joe?" he asked suddenly.

A slow smile spread on Joe's face. "Don't mind if I do," he said, and David regretted the gesture as he found himself hunched in the narrow back seat.

For the first five minutes Joe drove sedately, touching the brakes to test for grab and pull, flicking through the gears to feel the travel and bite of the stick. Then he nodded to himself and Debra whooped as he shifted down to get the revs peaking. He slid the car through

25

the first bend and David's right foot stabbed instinctively at a non-existent brake pedal and he felt his breathing jam in his throat.

When Joe switched off the engine in the car park outside the airport at Barcelona, all of them were silent for a few seconds and then David said softly, "Son of a gun!"

Then they were all laughing. David felt a tinge of regret that he was going to have to take the girl away from Joe, for he was beginning to like him.

They were an hour early for the plane and they found a table in the restaurant overlooking the runways. David ordered a jug of Sangria, and Debra sat next to Joe and put her hand on his arm while she chatted, a gesture that tempered David's new-found liking for him.

A private plane landed as the waiter brought the wine, and Joe looked up. "One of the new executive Gulfstreams. They tell me she is a little beauty." And he went on to list the aircraft's specifications in technical language that Debra seemed to follow.

"You know anything about aircraft?" David challenged him.

"Joe is in the air force," Debra said proudly.

"So is Debs," Joe laughed, and David stared at them. "She's a lieutenant in signals."

"Only the reserve," Debra demurred, "but Joe is a fighter pilot."

"A fighter pilot," David repeated stupidly. If he was an Israeli flier—then he would have flown a formidable number of operations. "What squadron are you on?"

"You ever heard of a Mirage?" Joe asked.

David blinked, and nodded. "Yeah, I've heard of them."

"Well, I fly a Mirage."

David began to laugh, shaking his head.

"What's wrong?" Joe demanded. "What's funny about that?"

"I do too," said David. "I fly Mirages." And it was Joe's turn to stare, then suddenly they were all talking at once.

Halfway through their second jug of Sangria, David interrupted the talk which had been exclusively on aviation. "Who are we meeting, anyway? We've driven across half of Spain and I don't even know who the guy is."

"This guy is a girl," Joe laughed, and Debra filled in.

"Hannah," she grinned, "Joe's fiancée. She's a nursing sister at Hadassah Hospital, and she could only get away for a week."

"Your fiancée?" David whispered.

"They are getting married in June."

"Your fiancée?" David asked again.

"Why do you keep saying that?" Debra demanded. Then she realized and gasped. She covered her mouth with both hands, her eyes sparkling. "You mean—you thought—? Oh, no," she giggled. "Joe's my brother. Joseph Israel Mordecai and Debra Ruth Mordecai—brother and sister."

Hannah was a rangy girl with bright copper hair and gold freckles. She was only an inch or two shorter than Joe but he swung her off her feet as she came through the customs gate and then engulfed her in an enormous embrace.

It seemed completely natural that the four of them should stay together, and by a miracle of packing they got all their luggage and themselves into the Mustang.

"We've got a whole week," said Debra. "What are we going to do?"

They agreed on a seaside village near the border. They had no trouble finding pleasant rooms at a small hotel off the winding main street. That night the girls shared, but David insisted on a room of his own. He had certain plans for Debra that made privacy desirable.

The next morning, they went to the beach.

Debra's bikini was blue and brief, hardly sufficient to restrain an exuberant bosom. Her skin was satiny and tanned to a deep mahogany. She was a strong swimmer, pacing David steadily to a rocky islet half a mile offshore.

They had the tiny island to themselves and they found a flat smooth rock out of the wind and full in the sun. They lay side by side with their fingers entwined and talked away the day, learning about each other.

She talked about her land and the people in it. Her father had been one of the youngest colonels in the American air force during World War II, but afterwards he had gone on to Israel. He had been there ever since, and was now a Major-General. They lived in a five-hundred-year-old house in an old part of Jerusalem.

She was a senior lecturer in English at Hebrew University in Jerusalem and, she said shyly, she wanted to write. A small volume

27

of her poetry had already been published, but that was merely a beginning. She was going to write a novel about being young and living in Israel.

David looked at her with a twinge of envy. She was so certain of where she was from and where she was going. Beside her he felt insignificant and without purpose.

She reached up suddenly, squinting a little in the sunlight, and touched his cheek.

"You are very beautiful, David. You are the most beautiful human being I have ever seen."

Slowly he leaned forward and placed his mouth over hers. Her lips were warm and soft and tasted of sea salt. Her arms came up around the back of his head and folded around him. They kissed until he reached behind her and unfastened her bikini top. Immediately she placed her hands on his shoulders and shoved him with such force that he lost his balance and slid down the rock, grazing his elbow and ending in a heap at the waters' edge.

David scrambled angrily to his feet as Debra took a shallow dive off the rocks. Surfacing she called back to him, "I'll race you to the beach."

David would not accept the challenge and followed her at his own dignified pace. As he emerged unsmiling from the surf, she grinned. "When you sulk you look about ten years old," she told him, and David stalked back to his room.

He was still aloof that evening when they discovered a disco-theque named "2001 A.D." on the seafront. They crowded into a table at which there were already two British air hostesses and a couple of raggedy-looking beards. When the two hostesses gazed at David with awe Debra forsook her attitude of cool amusement and suggested to David that they dance. Mollified by this feminine by-play, David dropped his impersonation of the Ice King.

They moved well together, executing the rhythmic movements with a grace that drew the attention of the other dancers. When the music changed, Debra pressed her body against his. David felt some force flowing from her that seemed to charge every nerve of his body. When the record ended they left Joe and Hannah huddled over a carafe of red wine and went out into the silent street and down to the beach.

They took off their shoes and walked along the sand as the surf hissed and coughed. They found a hidden place in an angle of the cliff, and stopped to kiss. David mistakenly took Debra's new soft mood as an invitation to continue from where he had left off that afternoon.

Debra pulled away again, and said angrily, "Damn you! Don't you ever learn? I don't want to do that!"

"What's the matter?" David was immediately furious. "This is the twentieth century. The simpering virgin is out of style!"

"And spoilt little boys should grow up before they come out on their own," she flashed back at him.

"Thanks!" he snarled. "I don't have to stay around taking insults."

"Well, why don't you move on then?" she challenged him.

"Hey, that's a great idea!" He turned his back on her and walked away up the beach. She had not expected that, and she started to run after him—but her pride checked her.

Next morning, David carried his bag down to the proprietor's office and paid his bill.

Debra came out of the breakfast room with Joe and Hannah. They were gay and laughing until they saw David.

"Hey!" Joe challenged him. "Where are you going?"

"I've had enough of Spain," David told them. "I'm taking some good advice, and I'm moving on," and he felt a flare of savage triumph as he saw the quick shadow of pain in Debra's eyes. Both Joe and Hannah glanced at her, and she smiled then, a little too brightly and stepped forward, holding out her hand.

"Thank you for all your help, David. I'm sorry you have to go. It was fun." Then her voice dropped slightly and there was a tiny quaver in it. "I hope you find what you are looking for. Good luck."

She turned quickly and hurried away to her room. Hannah gave David a curt nod before following Debra.

"So long, Joe."

"I'll carry your bag," Joe said and took it out of David's hand. He carried it out to the Mustang, and dumped it on the rear seat. "I'll ride up to the top of the hill with you and walk back. I need the exercise."

David drove swiftly, and they were silent until Joe said, "I don't know what went wrong, Davey, but I can guess."

Still David was silent, not giving him any help.

"She's a pretty special sort of person, Davey, and I think you should know about her."

They had reached the top of the hill above the town. David pulled onto the verge but kept the engine running.

"She was going to be married," said Joe softly. "He was a nice guy. They worked together at the University. He was a tank driver in the reserve and he took a hit in the Sinai. He burned with his tank." David's expression softened a little. "She took it badly," Joe went on. "These last few days were the first time I've seen her truly happy and relaxed since then." He shrugged. "Sorry to give you the family history, Davey. Just thought it might help." He held out a huge brown hand. "Come and see us. It's your country also, you know. I'd like to show it to you."

David took the hand. "I might do that," he said.

"*Shalom.*"

"*Shalom,* Joe. Good luck."

THERE WAS A SCHOOL for aspiring racing drivers near Ostia, on the road from Rome, but after the first week David knew it was not what he wanted. The physical limitation of the track was constricting after flying, and even the snarling power of a Tyrell Ford could not match the thrust from the engine of a jet interceptor.

In Athens he investigated the prospects of buying a motor yacht and running it out on charter to the islands, but he quickly realized that charter work was merely running a sea-going boarding house for a bunch of bored, sunburned and seasick tourists.

The American Sixth Fleet had dropped anchor in the bay of Athens. David sat in one of the beach-front cafés and drank *ouzo* in the sun, while he studied the aircraft carriers through his binoculars. On the great flat tops the rows of Crusaders and Phantoms were grouped with their wings folded. Watching them he felt a need that was almost spiritual. He laid the binoculars aside, and looked up into the sky. The clouds were a brilliant silver against the blue. David picked up the glass of *ouzo* and rolled its sweet liquorice taste about his tongue. "East, west, home is best."

He spoke aloud, and had a mental image of Paul Morgan sitting in his high office of glass and steel. What the hell, I could still fly Impalas as a reserve officer, he thought, and there's always the Lear —if I can get it away from Barney.

David drained the glass and stood up abruptly. He flagged a cab and was driven back to his hotel.

In his room, he placed a Cape Town call. It came through with surprising speed. "Mitzi," he laughed. "How's the girl?"

"Where are you, warrior? Are you home?"

"I'm in Athens, and it's a drag. How are you?"

"I'm in love, Davey, and I'm going to be married." David was jealous of the happiness in her voice.

"That's great, doll. Do I know him?"

"Cecil Lawley, you know him. He's one of Daddy's accountants." David recalled a pale-faced, bespectacled man with a serious manner.

"Congratulations," said David and he felt very much alone again.

Mitzi prattled on for fifty dollars' worth before hanging up. David lay on the bed and thought about his dumpy soft-hearted cousin and her new happiness. Then he made the decision which had been lurking at the edge of his consciousness ever since leaving Spain. He picked up the phone and asked for the porter's desk. "I should like to get on a flight to Israel as soon as possible," he said. "Will you please arrange that?"

THE SKY WAS FILLED with a soft golden haze that came off the desert. The 747 came down through it, and David had a glimpse of dark green citrus orchards before the solid jolt of the touchdown. Lod was like any other airport in the world but beyond its doors was a land like no other he had ever known.

He had to fight for a seat in one of the big black *sheruts*, communal taxis plastered with stickers and hung with gew-gaws, but once aboard it was as though the passengers were all on a family outing. On one side of him a paratrooper with an Uzi submachine-gun slung about his neck offered him a cigarette; on the other a big strapping lass also in khaki uniform offered him a sandwich of unleavened bread and balls of fried chick-peas, the ubiquitous *pita* and *falafel*.

Then they climbed into the Judaean hills, and David felt a sense of nostalgia as they followed the winding highway through pine forests and pale slopes shining with white stone. It was so familiar and yet subtly different from those fair hills of the southern cape. There were flowers he did not recognize, crimson blooms like spilled blood, and bursts of sunshine yellow blossoms. Suddenly he glimpsed the flight of chocolate and white wings amongst the trees, and he recognized the crested head of an African hoopoe—a bird which was a symbol of home.

David felt excitement building within him as he drew closer to the woman he had come to see—and to something else of which he was as yet uncertain.

"There was fighting here," said the girl next to him, pointing to the burned-out trucks and armoured vehicles strewn along the roadside, preserved as memorials to the men who had died on the road to Jerusalem.

David studied her face, and he saw again the strength and certainty that he had so admired in Debra. "Will there be more fighting?" he asked.

"Yes," she answered without hesitation.

"Why?"

"Because—if it is good—you must fight for it," and she made a wide gesture that seemed to embrace the land and all its people, "and this is ours, and it is good," she said.

So they arrived in Jerusalem with its tall, severe apartment blocks of custard-yellow stone, standing like monuments upon the hillside. David had reserved a room at the Intercontinental Hotel. From its window he looked across the garden of Gethsemane at the Old City, at its turrets and spires and the blazing golden Dome of the Rock—centre of Christianity and Judaism, holy place of the Moslems—and David felt a sense of awe. For the first time in his life, he recognized that portion of himself that was Jewish, and he thought it right that he had come.

IT WAS EARLY EVENING when David paid off the cab at the University and submitted to a perfunctory search by a guard at the main gate. Body search was a routine that would soon become so familiar as to pass unnoticed. He was surprised to find the campus almost

33

deserted, until he remembered it was Friday—and that the whole tempo was slowing for the Sabbath.

The Judas trees were in full bloom around the main plaza and the ornamental pool as David crossed to the administration block and asked for Debra at the inquiries desk. The porter said she was in a students' tutorial, so he waited for her on the terrace in the warmth of the spring sun. He wondered if he had much cause to expect a hearty welcome from her.

He was uncomfortably exploring his behaviour during their last meeting when Debra came out on the terrace. She carried books under her arm and a sling bag over one shoulder. Her hair was pulled back severely at the nape of her neck, and she wore no make-up. She was in deep conversation with two students and did not see David until he stood up. Then she froze into that special stillness he had first noticed in the cantina at Zaragoza.

David was surprised to find how awkward he felt. He grinned and made a shrugging, self-deprecatory gesture. "Hello, Debs."

"David—" She started towards him, then stopped, glancing at her students. Sensing her confusion they melted away, and she turned back to him. "David—" she repeated, and then her expression crumbled into utter desolation. "Oh, and I haven't even a shred of lipstick on."

David laughed with relief and went towards her, spreading his arms, and she flew at him and it was all confusion with books and sling bag muddled.

"David," she murmured, "what on earth took you so long? I had almost given you up."

Debra had a motor scooter which she drove with murderous abandon. Perched on the pillion David clung to her waist and remonstrated with her gently as she overtook a solid line of traffic and then cut smartly across a stream coming in the opposite direction. "I'm happy," she explained over her shoulder.

"Fine! Then let's live to enjoy it."

She went down a twisting road into the valley of Ein Karem as though she were driving a Mirage, and called a travelogue back to him as she went. "That's the Monastery of Mary's Well where she met the mother of John the Baptist—according to the Christian tradition in which you are a professed expert."

"Hold the history," pleaded David. "There's a bus around that bend."

The village of Ein Karem was timeless amongst the olive trees, with its churches and monasteries and high-walled gardens, while the skyline above it was cluttered with the high-rise apartments of modern Jerusalem. From the main street Debra scooted into a narrow lane, and braked to a halt outside a forbidding iron gate.

"Home," she said, and wheeled the scooter into the gatehouse.

They entered the gate and came into a large garden courtyard enclosed by high walls lime-washed to glaring white. There were olive trees in the garden, and grape vines climbed the walls.

"My father is a keen amateur archaeologist," Debra said indicating the Roman and Greek statues and *amphorae* that stood amongst the olive trees, and the ancient mosaic tiles which paved the pathway. "It's strictly against the law, of course, but he spends all his spare time digging around in the old sites."

Debra's mother greeted them in the cavernous kitchen. She was a tall slim woman with a quiet manner. The family resemblance was striking and David thought with pleasure that this was how Debra would look at the same age. Debra announced that David was a guest for dinner.

"Please," he protested quickly, "I don't want to intrude." He knew that Friday was a special night in the Jewish home.

"You don't intrude. We will be honoured," Debra's mother said. "This house is home for most of the boys on Joe's squadron, we enjoy it."

Debra fetched David a Goldstar beer and they were sitting on the terrace when her father arrived. His uniform was casually cut, and open at the throat. He was slightly round-shouldered, probably from cramming his lanky body into the cramped cockpits of fighter aircraft. His head was brown and bald with a monk's fringe of hair and he had a fierce spiky moustache and a gleaming gold tooth. His nose was large, the nose of a biblical warrior, and his eyes were dark with the same golden lights as Debra's. They subjected David to a rapid, raking scrutiny.

David stood respectfully to shake the general's hand.

He learned that his host was nicknamed "The Brig" as a shortened version of "The Brigand", a name the British had given him before 1948 when he was smuggling warplanes and arms into Palestine for the *Haganah*. Everyone, even his children, called him that and only his wife used his given name, Joshua.

"David is sharing the Sabbath meal with us tonight," Debra explained to him.

"You are welcome," he said, and turned to embrace his womenfolk.

When Joe arrived, he was also in uniform, and he enfolded David in a bear hug, laughing over his shoulder to Debra, "Was I right?"

"Joe said you would come," Debra explained.

"It looks like I was the only one who didn't know," David protested.

At dinner, the candlelight gleamed on the polished wood of the huge refectory table and on the silver Sabbath goblets. The Brig, wearing a satin and gold embroidered *yamulka*, said a short prayer, then filled the wine goblets murmuring a greeting to each of his guests. Hannah was there, as well as two of the Brig's brothers with their wives and children. The talk was loud and confusing as the children vied with their elders for a hearing and the language changed at random from Hebrew to English. David was content to sit quietly beside Debra and enjoy the sense of belonging in this happy group. He was startled then when one of Debra's cousins said to him, "This must be very confusing for you—your not being Jewish, and not understanding Hebrew."

All conversation stopped abruptly. David was aware of Debra staring at him intently, as if to will words from him.

He smiled at the cousin and shook his head. "I understand Hebrew, though I don't speak it well. You see, I am Jewish also."

Debra exchanged a quick glance of pleasure with Joe.

"Jewish?" the Brig demanded, and David explained. When he was through it seemed that the Brig's manner had thawed a little.

"Not only that, but he is a flier also," Debra boasted.

"What experience?" the Brig demanded brusquely.

"Twelve hundred hours, sir, almost a thousand on Mirages."

"Mirages? What squadron?"

"Cobra Squadron."

"Rastus Naude's bunch?" The Brig stared at David.

"Do you know Rastus?" David was startled.

"We flew the first Spitfires in from Czechoslovakia together—back in '48. We used to call him Butch Ben Yok—Son of a Gentile—in those days. He must be getting on now? How is he?"

"He's as spry as ever, sir," David answered tactfully.

"Well, if Rastus taught you to fly—you might be half good," the Brig conceded. He picked up the wine bottle and carefully refilled David's goblet.

As a rule the Israeli Air Force would not use foreign pilots, but here was a Jew with all the makings of a first-class fighter pilot. . . .

Debra watched her father as he began to question David searchingly on his reasons for coming to Israel—and on his future plans. She knew precisely how the Brig's mind was working, for she had anticipated it.

She lifted her goblet to David and said, "*Lechaim!* To life!" and he echoed the toast.

THE TELEPHONE BESIDE HIS BED woke David in the dawn, and the Brig's voice on the line was crisp and alert. "If you have no urgent plans for today, I'm taking you to see something," he said.

"Of course, sir." David was taken off balance.

"I will fetch you at your hotel in forty-five minutes."

The Brig drove a small nondescript car with civilian plates, and he drove it fast and efficiently. They took the main highway west and the Brig broke a long silence. "I spoke with your old C.O. last night. He assured me that you can fly, and I want to see if he was telling the truth."

David looked at him quickly. "We are going to fly?" He felt a deep excitement when the Brig nodded.

"We are at war here, so you will be flying a combat sortie, and breaking just about every regulation in the book. But you'll find we don't go by the book very much."

As they turned southwards towards Beersheba and the desert, he quietly explained his own view of Israel's struggle, and David remembered particular phrases he used.

"—We are building a nation, and the blood we have been forced to mix into the foundations has strengthened them—"

"—If our enemies lose a battle, they lose a few miles of desert, if we lose one we cease to exist—"

A plantation of eucalyptus trees grew as a heavy screen alongside the road, and the Brig slowed at a sign that proclaimed in Hebrew and English: "Chaim Weizmann Agricultural Experimental Centre."

They turned into a gate in the barbed-wire fence and drove through the plantation to a second fence and a guard post. A guard checked the Brig's papers briefly. Then they drove on, emerging between neatly laid-out blocks of grain crops. The roads between each field were long and straight and paved with concrete that had been tinted to the colour of the surrounding earth.

The Brig, seeing David's interest in these smooth, two-mile long fairways, nodded, "Yes," he said, "runways."

They reached a giant concrete grain silo and the Brig drove through the doors of the barnlike building that abutted it. David was startled to see lines of buses and automobiles parked inside.

There were guards here again, and when the Brig led David to the silo, he realized suddenly that it was a dummy. The Brig explained that it was a massive bomb-proof control tower and operations centre housing all the sophisticated communications and radar equipment for four full squadrons of Mirage fighters.

They descended in an elevator, and the Brig led David along an air-conditioned underground tunnel to the pilots' dressing room. The orderly fitted David out in overalls, boots, flying-suit, gloves and helmet.

The Brig dressed from his own locker and they went into the briefing room where he outlined their patrol, and checked David out on aircraft identification and other details.

"All clear?" he asked at last, and when David nodded, he went on, "Remember what I told you, we are at war. Anything we find that doesn't belong to us we hit it, hard! All right?"

"Yes, sir."

The Brig picked up his helmet and map case, then fixed David with his fierce brown eyes. "It will be clear up there today, and you will be able to see our country from Rosh Hanikra to Suez, from Mount Hermon to Eilat. You will see how small and vulnerable it is. You said you were looking for something worthwhile—I want you to consider whether guarding the fate of three million people might not be a worthwhile job."

They rode on a small electric cart down a long passage, and entered the bunker situated at one point of a great concrete star whose centre was the silo. Six Mirages stood in a row, sleek and needle-nosed. They looked vaguely unfamiliar to David in their drab desert camouflage with the blue Star of David insignia on the fuselage.

The Brig signed for two machines, grinning as he wrote "Butch Ben Yok" under David's numeral.

"As good a name as any to fly under," he grunted.

David settled into the familiar cockpit. Moments later, in the confined space of the bunkers the jet thunder assaulted his eardrums. The Brig gave him the high sign. He returned it and reached up to pull the clear plastic canopy closed. Ahead of them, the steel doors rolled upwards.

There was no taxiing to take-off areas; no needless ground exposure. Wing-tip to wing-tip they came up the ramp out of the bunker. Ahead of them stretched one of the long brown runways. David pushed open his throttle to the gate and ignited the afterburner. Down between the fields of green corn they tore, and then up, and once again David experienced the euphoria of flight.

They levelled out at a little under forty thousand feet. David placed his machine under the Brig's tail and eased back on the throttle. His eyes swept every quarter of the sky as he weaved the Mirage to clear the blind spot behind his own tail.

They flew north over the ridge of Carmel and the flecked white buildings of Haifa with its gold beaches. Then they turned together sinking slowly to patrol altitude at twenty thousand feet as they passed the peak of Mount Hermon where the last snows still lingered. Then they boomed down the valley of the Jordan, over the Sea of Galilee enclosed by the thickets of date palm, losing altitude as the land forsook its gentle aspect.

On the left rose mountains, hostile and implacable, but beneath them Jericho was a green oasis in the wilderness. Ahead lay the shimmering surface of the Dead Sea. The Brig dropped down, and as they thundered so low across the salt-thickened water that the jet blast ruffled the surface behind them, the Brig's voice chuckled in David's earphones, "That's the lowest you are ever going to fly—twelve hundred feet below sea level."

They were climbing again as they crossed the mineral works at the southern end of the sea, and faced the deserts of the south.

"Hello, Cactus One, this is Desert Flower." David recognized the Operations Centre of Air Force Command.

"Hello, Desert Flower," the Brig acknowledged, and immediately the exchange became informal, just two old friends chatting.

"Brig, this is Motti. We've just had a ground support request in your area." He gave the coordinates quickly. "A motorized patrol is under low-level attack. See to it, will you?"

"*Beseder*, Motti, O.K. Cactus Two, conform to me," he told David, and they turned together onto the new heading.

"No point trying a radar scan," the Brig grumbled. "He'll be down in the ground clutter, so keep your eyes open."

"*Beseder*." David had already picked up the word. The favourite Hebrew word in a land where very little was really "O.K."

David spotted it first, a slim black column of smoke rising slowly against the dazzling cobalt blue of the horizon. "Ground smoke," he said into his microphone. "Eleven o'clock low."

The Brig squinted ahead and then grunted. Rastus had been right in one thing at least. The youngster had eyes like a hawk.

"Going to attack speed now," he said, and David acknowledged and lit his afterburner. The Mirage went shooting through the sonic barrier.

Near the base of the smoke column, David made out a tiny shape, flitting swiftly as a bird, its camouflage blending into the backdrop of desert.

"Bandit turning to port of the smoke," he called.

"I have him," said the Brig. "Hello. Desert Flower, I'm on an intruder. Call strike, please."

The answering voice was laconic. "Hit him!"

Swiftly the details of the drama below sprang into comprehension. Along a dusty road three border police vehicles were halted, camouflaged half-tracks, tiny as children's toys in the vastness of the desert.

One of the half-tracks was burning. The other vehicles were pulled off the road, their crews crouching amongst the scrub and rock. Some of them were firing with small arms at their attacker who was circling for his next run.

David knew instantly that it was a Russian MiG 17 of the Syrian Air Force. The high tailplane and the green, white and black roundels were unmistakable.

As the MiG levelled off for its strafing, the Brig lined up to attack in classic style from behind and above, while David dropped back to press in a supporting attack if the first failed.

The Syrian's cannon bursts blazed and another truck exploded in smoke and flame.

"You bastard," David whispered as he saw the havoc that was being wrought amongst his people. It was the first time he had thought of them as that, his people. He locked in his cannons-selectors and flicked the trigger forward out of its recess in the grip of the joystick. The soft green glow lit his gunsight as it came alive and he squinted through it.

The Brig was rapidly overtaking the MiG, when David saw the Syrian drop one wing in a slide towards the earth below. The Brig was committed and loosed his salvo of cannon fire. But the Syrian ducked under it like a boxer avoiding a punch. Then the Brig was through, having missed with every shell.

The MiG turned steeply away to port, no more than a hundred feet above the bleak desert earth. David hit his air brakes and dropped his own wing-tip ·to follow. The Syrian, slower and more manœuvrable, was turning inside him and David could not bring his sights to bear. Ahead of the two circling aircraft rose a steep and forbidding line of cliffs. In a desperate attempt to shake off pursuit, the MiG selected a narrow pass through the hills and went into it like a ferret into its run.

The Mirage was not designed for this type of flying, and David felt the urge to ride up over the jagged fangs of rock—but to do so was to let the MiG escape. He followed the Syrian into the pass, the walls of stone seeming to brush his wing-tips on either side. The gully turned sharply to starboard and David dropped his wing. The stall-warning device winked amber and red as he abused the Mirage's delicate flying capabilities.

Ahead of him the MiG clawed its way through the tunnel of rock, tantalizingly off-centre in David's gunsight. Now the valley turned again and narrowed, ending abruptly against a solid purple wall of rock.

The Syrian was trapped. He climbed steeply upward, his flight path dictated by the rocks on each side and ahead. David pushed his throttle to the gate and lit his afterburner again, and the mighty engine thrust him up under the Syrian's tail. The enemy plane filled his gunsight.

He pressed the cannon trigger and the MiG disintegrated in a gush of silvery smoke. The ejected pilot was blown clear of the fuselage. For an instant his body was outlined ahead of David's screen, arms and legs thrown wide, clothing ballooning in the rush of air. Then it flashed past the Mirage's canopy as David climbed swiftly up out of the valley and into the open sky.

The soldiers by their vehicles, looked up as David flew back low along the road. He could see their strong young faces clearly as they cheered him, waving their thanks. My people, he thought, and he felt a fierce elation. He lifted one gloved hand in salute before climbing up to where the Brig circled, waiting for him.

THE ARTIFICIAL LIGHTS of the bunker were dim after the brilliance of the sun. David crossed to where the Brig was already in conversation with the flight controller.

As David came up the Brig turned to him with his wintry smile and lightly punched his arm. "You'll do," he said.

David was late to fetch Debra for dinner that evening, but she had already learned the reason from her father.

They went to a restaurant in the Old City, where the Arab proprietor served moussakha chicken, with nuts and spices on a bed of *kouskous*.

They ate the excellent meal almost in silence, Debra quickly recognizing that David was in the grip of post-combat *tristesse*, the adrenalin hangover of stress and excitement. Over thimble-sized cups of Turkish coffee, however, she dared ask him: "What happened today, David?"

He sipped his coffee before replying. Then he told her the details, ending lamely, "I killed a man, yet I felt only satisfaction at the time. A sense of achievement."

"And now?" she prompted him.

"Now I am sad that I had to do it."

"My father has always been a soldier. He says that only those

43

who do the actual fighting can truly know what it is to hate war. And yet it is necessary. We must fight—there is no other way."

"There is no other way—with the sea at our backs and the Arabs at our throats."

"You speak like an Israeli," Debra challenged him softly.

"I made a decision today—your father has given me three weeks to brush up my Hebrew and complete the immigration formalities."

"And then?" Debra leaned towards him.

"A commission in the air force. I held out for the equivalent rank I would have had back home and he gave in at last. Acting Major, with confirmation of rank at the end of twelve months."

"That's wonderful, Davey, you'll be one of the youngest majors in the service." She smiled. "And I'll help you with your Hebrew."

They left the restaurant and strolled through the Christian quarter past open stalls loaded with exotic clothes, leather work and jewellery. The smells of spices and stale humanity were almost solid in the narrow lanes.

They left the Old City through a gate in the great wall and found a stone bench amongst the olive trees of the Moslem cemetery. The night was warm and there was half a moon in the sky, silver and mysterious.

"You can't stay on at the Intercontinental," Debra told him. They both looked up at its lighted silhouette across the valley.

"Why not?"

"You aren't a tourist any more. So you can't live like one."

"What do you suggest?"

"We could find you an apartment."

"Who would do the housework and the cooking?"

"I would," said Debra firmly, and her voice quavered. "That's if you want me to."

David was silent for a moment. "See here, Debs. Are you talking about living together?"

"That's precisely what I am talking about."

"But—" He could think of nothing further to say. The idea was novel, breathtaking. "Do you want to get married?" His voice cracked on the word, and he cleared his throat.

"I'm not sure that you are the finest marriage material in the market, my darling. You are as beautiful as the dawn, and fun to

44

be with—but you are also selfish, immature and spoiled. So I am about to throw all caution aside and become your mistress. The one condition is that we wait until we have our own special place."

"Does this mean that you *don't* want to marry me?" David found his mortal terror of matrimony fading under this slur on his potential marriage worth.

"I didn't say that," Debra demurred. "But let's make that decision when both of us are ready. And now, Major Morgan, you may kiss me."

A long while later, they drew apart and a sudden thought made David frown. "My God," he exclaimed, "what will the Brig say?"

"I'll lie to him graciously, and he'll pretend to believe me. Let me worry about that."

"Beseder," he agreed readily.

"You are learning," she applauded. "Let's just try that kiss again—but this time in Hebrew, please."

"I love you," he said in that language.

"Good boy," she murmured. "You are going to make a prize pupil."

DAVID DISCOVERED THAT the acquisition of an apartment in Jerusalem was like the quest for the Holy Grail. The waiting-lists for the new blocks that were being thrown up with almost reckless energy were endless, but an occasional apartment in one of the older buildings fell vacant.

After viewing several of these offerings, Debra's determinedly bright smile cracked. "Oh, David, we are never going to find a place!"

"Right," David said as he rubbed his hands together briskly. "It's time to send in the first team."

The Managing Director of Morgan Group in Jerusalem was a mournful-looking gentleman named Aaron Cohen who was overcome to discover that one of the Morgan family had been in Jerusalem without his knowledge. David told him what he wanted, and in twenty hours he had it. The price David must pay for this service was that Paul Morgan would have on his desk the next morning a full report of David's transaction, present whereabouts and future plans—but it was worth it.

Above the Hinnom valley, facing Mount Zion with its impressive array of spires, the Yemin Moshe quarter was being rebuilt by an entrepreneur. All of it was clad in the lovely golden Jerusalem stone, and the designs of the houses were traditional. However the interiors were lavishly modern with tall cool rooms, mosaic-tiled bathrooms, and ceilings arched like those of a crusader church. The one that Aaron Cohen procured for David was the pick of those that fronted Malik Street.

Debra stood bemused in the central room that opened onto the private terrace.

"David! David! How much is this going to cost? It's too beautiful. We can't afford it."

"It's paid for already."

"Paid for?" She stared at him. "How much, David?" Then she clapped her hands over her ears. "No, don't tell me. I'd feel so guilty I wouldn't be able to live in it."

"Even if I said a million Israeli pounds Debs, what difference would it make? It's only money. Now, what are we going to do about furniture?"

"Furniture?" Debra repeated. "I hadn't thought that far ahead."

"For what I have in mind, we'll need at least one king-size bed."

"Sex maniac," she said, and kissed him.

No modern furniture looked at home so they began to furnish from the bazaars and antique shops.

Debra discovered an enormous brass bedstead in a junk yard, they polished it until it glowed, fitted it with a new mattress, and covered it with a cream-coloured lace bedspread. They purchased woven woollen rugs from the Arab dealers in the Old City, and scattered them thickly upon the stone floors, with leather cushions to sit on and a low olive-wood table, inlaid with ebony and mother-of-pearl.

Both the bed and the table were enormously heavy, so they called Joe for help. David had expected Joe to be a little reserved, after all it was his baby sister that was being set up in a fancy house, but Joe was as natural as ever and fell to work enthusiastically, while Hannah helped Debra in the kitchen.

That night David left the terrace lights burning, and they shone through the slats of the shuttered windows, so the bedroom was softly lit. He lay on the bed and watched Debra undress slowly. She was conscious of his eyes upon her and shy.

She came and stretched out beside him on the lace cover. They lay on their sides facing each other. She sighed then, with happiness and contentment, like a traveller reaching the end of a long, lonely journey.

"I love you," she said for the first time, and, twining her fingers in his hair she drew him tenderly to her breast.

AARON COHEN TRACKED DOWN a Mercedes-Benz 350SL, a rare sports car in a country where extravagance was out of place. Debra, returning from the University, took one look at this glorious machine and stormed onto the terrace.

"David Morgan, you really are absolutely impossible! How much did you pay for it?"

"Ask me another question, doll. That one is becoming monotonous."

"You are really—" she searched frantically for a word of sufficient force "—decadent!"

"You don't know the meaning of the word," David told her gently as he rose from the cushions. "However, I am about to give you a practical demonstration of my decadence!"

She ducked behind the olive tree as he lunged, and her books spilled across the terrace. "Leave me! Hands off, you beast."

He faked right, and caught her as she fell for it. He picked her up.

"David Morgan, I warn you, I shall scream if you don't put me down this instant."

"Let's hear it. Go ahead!" and she did, but not so as to alarm the neighbours.

Joe, on the other hand, was absolutely delighted with the car. The four of them took it on a trial run down to the shores of the Dead Sea. The road challenged the car's suspension and David's driving skill, and they whooped with excitement through the bends. Debra overcame her disapproval.

They swam in the cool green waters of the oasis of Ein Gedi. Hannah had her camera and photographed Debra and David sitting together on the rocks, Debra half-turned to laugh into David's face, he smiling back at her, his face in profile and the dark sweep of his hair falling onto his forehead.

Hannah had a print made for each of them, and later those squares of glossy photographic paper helped to remind them of the joy of that day.

In the last few days while David waited to enter the air force, he loafed shamelessly, frittering the time away having his uniforms tailored, or doing small tasks around the house. One afternoon he began digging around in some crates stored in the unfurnished second bedroom. Debra had her books in them, fiction and biography, history and poetry, softbacks and leather-bound editions —and a thin green-jacketed volume which he almost discarded before the author's name caught his attention. *This Year, in Jerusalem*, a Collection of Poems by Debra Mordecai.

He carried the book through to the bedroom, remembering to kick off his shoes before lying on the lace cover—she was very strict about that—and he turned to the first page.

There were five poems. The first was the title piece, a patriotic tribute to the land where the two-thousand-year promise of Jewry "Next year in Jerusalem" had become reality. It was good, really good, and David felt a strange proprietory pride.

The last poem was the shortest of the five; it was a poem to someone dearly loved who was gone—and David found himself shivering at the haunting beauty of the words.

He lowered the book onto his chest, remembering what Joe had told him about the soldier who had died in the desert. A movement attracted his attention and he saw Debra watching him, leaning against the jamb of the door.

He sat up on the bed and weighed the book in his hands. "It's lovely. Why didn't you show it to me before?"

"I was afraid you might not like it."

"You must have loved him very much?" he asked softly.

"Yes, I did," she said, "but now I love you."

48

DAVID'S POSTING FINALLY CAME through and the Brig's hand was evident in it. He was ordered to report to Mirage squadron "Lance" which was a crack interceptor outfit based at the same hidden airfield from which he had first flown. Joe was on the same squadron, and he spent the evening briefing David on squadron personnel, from "Le Dauphin" the commanding officer, a French immigrant, down to the lowest mechanic.

The following day the tailor delivered David's uniform, and he wore it to fetch Debra at the University for their last evening together. He was surprised to find how the dress affected the strangers he passed on the street—the girls smiled at him, the old ladies called "Shalom", even the guard at the University gates waved him through.

Debra hurried to meet him, and then, after circling him with her head cocked at a critical angle, she tucked her hand proudly into the crook of his elbow and took him to eat an early dinner at the staff dining-room in the rounded glass Belgium building.

While they ate, David said casually, "I'll probably not get off the base for the first few weeks, but I'll write to you at Malik Street—"

"No," she said quickly, "I won't be staying there."

"Where then? At your parents' home?"

"No, they think I am staying at the hostel here at the University. I told them I wanted to be closer to the department—"

"You've got a room here?" He stared at her.

"Of course. I have to be a little discreet. I couldn't tell my relatives and friends to contact me care of Major David Morgan."

For the first time David began to appreciate the magnitude of Debra's decision to come to him. "I'm going to miss you," he said. "Let's go home."

"Yes," she agreed, "I can eat any old time."

As they were leaving Debra exclaimed with exasperation: "Damn, I have to have these books back by today. Can we go by the library? It won't take a minute."

They passed the brightly-lit plate-glass windows of the Students' Union Restaurant, and went on towards the square tower of the library. They had climbed the library steps when a party of students came pouring out, and they were forced to stand aside.

Suddenly the dusk of evening was lit by the fierce glare of an explosion, and the windows of the restaurant were blown out in a glittering cloud. The blast swept across the terrace, a draught of violence that shook the Judas trees and sent David and Debra reeling against the pillars of the library veranda. Then the sounds reached them, through their ringing eardrums, the small tinkle and crunch of glass, the platter and crack of falling plaster and shattered furniture.

David caught her to him. As they stared, a soft white fog of phosphorus smoke billowed from the gutted restaurant and began to drift across the terrace.

A woman began to scream, and there were shouts and running feet. One of the students near them cried, "A bomb. El Fatah have bombed the café."

Debra began to tremble. "The murdering swine," she whispered.

"Come on," grated David, "we must help." And they ran down the steps together.

The explosion had brought down part of the roof, crushing at least twenty-three students. Others had been hurled about amongst the tumbled furniture, broken crockery and spilled food, like the toys of a child in tantrum. David and Debra worked in a frenzy helping the injured and carrying the bodies of the dead onto the lawns beneath the Judas trees. Ambulances came, and the police cordoned off the site.

Afterwards David and Debra would learn that two young female members of El Fatah had enrolled in the University under false papers, and they had daily smuggled small quantities of explosive onto the campus. When they had accumulated sufficient they left it in a suitcase with a timing device under a table.

Finally David and Debra left. They drove in silence to Malik Street, and showered off the dust and blood. Then they drank coffee sitting side by side in the brass bed.

"So much that was good and strong died there tonight," Debra said.

"The dead were not the worst of it. It was the torn and broken flesh that still lived which appalled me. The dead have dignity, but the maimed are obscene."

She looked at him with almost fear. "That's cruel, David."

"In Africa there is a beautiful and fierce animal called the sable antelope. They run together in herds of up to a hundred, but when one of them is wounded, the lead bulls drive him from the herd. I remember my father telling me about that. He would say that if you want to be a winner, you must avoid the company of the losers for their despair is contagious."

"God, David, that's a terribly hard way to look at life."

"Perhaps," David agreed, "but then, you see, life *is* hard."

When they made love, there was for the first time a quality of desperation in it, for it was the eve of parting and they had been reminded of their mortality.

In the morning David went to join his squadron, and Debra locked the house in Malik Street.

EACH DAY FOR SEVENTEEN DAYS David flew two, and sometimes three, sorties. In the evenings, if they were not flying night interceptions, there were lectures and training films, and after that not much desire for anything but a quick meal and then sleep.

David and Joe flew together, and quickly they developed into a formidable team. Joe was the wingman without personal ambition for glory whose talent was to put David into the position for the strike. David was the gunfighter, in a service where the gunfighter was supreme.

The Israeli Air Force had been the first to appreciate the shortcomings of the air-to-air missile, and to rely heavily on the classic type of air combat. A missile could be induced to "run stupid". For every three hundred missile launches in air-to-air combat, only a single strike could be expected. However, if you had a gunfighter coming up into your six o'clock position with his finger on the trigger of twin 30 mm. cannons, capable of pouring twelve thousand shells a minute into you, then your chances were considerably lighter than three hundred to one.

At the end of those seventeen days, David's service dossier, like that of every officer, passed over the Brig's desk. The Colonel, Le Dauphin, had flown one sortie with David. He was a small man with a relaxed manner and quick, shrewd eyes. He had made his judgement quickly. "Morgan is a pilot of exceptional ability. Recommended that acting rank be confirmed and that he be placed on fully operational basis forthwith."

The Brig scrawled "I agree" at the foot of the report.

That took care of Morgan, the pilot. He could now consider Morgan, the man. Debra's sudden desire to leave home almost immediately after David arrived in Jerusalem had been too much of a coincidence. It had taken him two days to learn that Debra was merely using the hostel room at the University as an accommodation address, and that her real domestic arrangements were more comfortable.

The Brig did not approve. Although he spent much of his time with young people, he found the new values hard to live with—let alone accept. Yet he knew that his daughter had inherited his own iron will. "Well, at the least she has the sense not to flaunt it, not to bring shame on us all." He closed the dossier firmly.

Le Dauphin called David into his office and told him of his change in status. He would go on regular "Green" standby, which meant four nights a week on base. Also David would now have to undergo his paratrooper training in unarmed combat in case he were downed in Arab territory.

After the interview, David phoned Debra at the University. "Warm the bed," he told her, "I'll be home tonight."

He and Joe drove up to Jerusalem in the Mercedes, and he wasn't listening to Joe's low rumbling voice until a thumb like an oar prodded his ribs.

"Sorry, Joe, I was thinking. What did you say?"

"I was talking about the wedding—Hannah and me."

David realized it was only a month away now. Debra's letters had been filled with news of the arrangements.

"I would be happy if you will stand up with me and be my witness. You fly as wingman for a change, and I'll take on the target."

David accepted the honour with proper solemnity.

The wedding would be a traditional affair. It was to take place in the Brig's garden, for Hannah was an orphan. Also rigorous security precautions could be enforced within the secluded garden with its fortress-like walls.

"At the last count we have five generals and eighteen colonels on the guest list," Joe told him, "to which add most of the cabinet. Even Golda has promised to try and be there. Since

Hannah has asked to have as few guards as possible in the garden, it's going to make a juicy target for our friends in El Fatah or Black September. If it weren't for Hannah, I would just as soon go down to a registry office."

"You are fooling nobody." David grinned. "You are looking forward to it."

He dropped Joe outside the Brig's house. Then raced home.

The terrace door stood open in welcome, and she was waiting for him, dressed in a honey-coloured silk kaftan. "David!" she cried and he caught her up and spun on his heels.

She led him proudly about the rooms and showed him the additions that had turned it into a real home during his absence. They had chosen the furniture together but there was one article David had never seen before—a large oil painting that Debra had hung unframed on the wall facing the terrace. It was a desert scene which captured the soul of the wilderness. The colours were hot and fierce and seemed to pour through the room like the rays of the desert sun itself.

Debra held David's hand and watched his face anxiously for a reaction as he studied it. "Wow!" he said at last.

"You like it?" She was relieved.

"It's terrific. Where did you get it?"

"A gift from the artist, Ella Kadesh. She's an old friend. We are driving up to Tiberias tomorrow to have lunch with her."

"What's she like?"

"She's one of our leading artists. I can't begin to describe her. All I can do is promise you an entertaining day."

Debra had prepared a dish of lamb and olives and they ate it on the terrace under the olive tree. The talk turned to Joe's wedding, and in the midst of it David said abruptly, "Let's get married, Debs."

"Yes," she nodded. "That's a splendid idea."

"Soon," he said. "Soon as possible."

"Not before Hannah. I don't want to steal her day."

"Right," David agreed, "but immediately afterwards."

"Morgan, you have got yourself a date," she told him.

It was a three-hour drive to Tiberias so they rose at dawn.

"Ella is the rudest person you'll ever meet," Debra warned him as they set out. She looked like a little girl with her hair piled on top of her head and secured with a pink ribbon. "The greater the impression you make on her, the ruder she will be, and you are expected to retaliate in kind. But please, David, don't lose your temper."

"I promise," he said.

They drove to Jericho, and then turned north along the hot barren valley of the Jordan, following the high barbed-wire fence of the border with its warning notices for the minefields.

As they came into the fertile basin of kibbutzim below Galilee, the smell of orange blossom was strong on the warm air. At last they saw the lake flashing amongst the date palms, and Debra touched his arm. "Slow down, Davey. Ella's turn-off is just ahead."

It was a track that led down to the shore and it ended against a wall of ancient stone blocks. Five cars were parked there already.

"Ella's having one of her lunch parties," Debra remarked and led him to a gate in the wall. Beyond was a small ruined castle. The tumbled walls formed weird shapes over which grew flamboyant creepers of bougainvillaea. Part of the ruins had been restored to make a picturesque home, with a wide patio and a stone jetty. Across the green waters of the lake rose the dark smooth whale-back of the Golan Heights.

"It was a crusader fortress," Debra explained. "Ella's grandfather bought it, but it was a complete ruin until she did it up."

The care with which the alterations had been made was a tribute to Ella Kadesh's artistic vision, which was completely at odds with the woman herself. She was enormous; her hands and her feet were huge, her fat fingers were clustered with rings and her toenails through the open sandals were painted crimson, as if to flaunt their size. The tent-like dress that billowed about her was covered with explosive designs, enhancing her bulk. She wore dangling gold earrings and a wig of flaming red curls. She removed the thin black cheroot from her mouth and kissed Debra before she turned to study David. Her voice was gravelly, hoarse with smoke and brandy.

"I had not expected you to be so beautiful," she said. "I do not

54

like beauty. It usually hides something deadly. No, I prefer ugliness."

David smiled at her. "Yes," he agreed, "having met you, I can understand that."

She let out a cackle of raucous laughter. "Well now, at least we are not dealing with a chocolate soldier." She placed a huge arm about David's shoulders and led him to meet the company.

They were artists, writers, teachers, journalists, and David enjoyed the amusing conversation and the gargantuan *alfresco* meal until Ella attacked him again.

"A pox on your patriotism and courage—" she indicated him with a turkey leg "—It is all sham, an excuse for you to stink up the earth with piles of carrion."

"I wonder if you would feel the same when a platoon of Syrian infantry break in here to rape you," David challenged her.

"My boy, I should pray for such a heaven-sent opportunity." She let out a mighty hoot of laughter and her wig slipped forward. She pushed it back into place and turned towards Debra. "Have you written a word since you took young Mars to your heart? What of the novel we discussed on this very terrace a year ago? Have your animal passions swamped all else?"

"Stop it, Ella!" Debra's cheeks were flushed.

"Yes! Yes!" Ella tossed the bone aside and sucked her fingers noisily. "Ashamed you should be, angry with yourself—"

"Damn you," Debra flared at her.

"Damn me if you will—but you are damned yourself if you do not write!" She sat back and the wicker chair protested at the movement of her vast body. "All right, now we will all go for a swim. David has not seen me in a bikini yet—much he will care for that skinny little wench when he does!"

They drove back to Jerusalem in the evening and Debra snuggled close up against David.

"She's right, you know." David broke a long contented silence. "You must write, Debs."

"Oh, I will," she answered lightly.

"When?" he persisted.

"One of these days," she whispered as she made her head comfortable on his shoulder.

"One of these days," he mimicked her. "Stop being evasive, and don't go to sleep while I'm talking to you."

"David, my darling, we have a lifetime—and more," she murmured. "You have made me immortal. You and I shall live for a thousand years, and there will be time for everything."

Perhaps the dark gods heard her boast.

ON SATURDAY, JOE AND HANNAH came to Malik Street for lunch. Afterwards they decided on a tourist excursion for David.

They entered the Old City through the Zion Gate and joined the stream of worshippers flocking to the Wailing Wall. David looked up at the wall of massive stone blocks. Thousands of worshippers had written their prayers on scraps of paper and wedged them between the blocks, and around him rose the plaintive voices of spoken prayer. It seemed to David that a golden beam of prayer rose from this holy place.

That evening the four of them sat together on the terrace. The talk turned to God and religion and David glimpsed for the first time the vast body of his religious heritage. "I would like to learn a little more about it all," he admitted later.

Debra said nothing but when she packed for him that night she placed a Jewish history book on top of his uniforms.

He read it and when he next returned to Malik Street, he asked for others. This led to a desire to explore the land. They began with the hilltop fortress of Herod at Masada where the zealots had killed each other rather than submit to Rome, and from there they moved to the lesser-known historical sites. They were the happiest days that David had ever known. They gave point and meaning to the weary hours of squadron standby, and when each day ended there was always the house on Malik Street with its warmth and laughter and love.

THE DAY BEFORE THE WEDDING, Joe and David arranged leaves of absence from the base and drove to Jerusalem. They found the Brig's garden decorated with palm leaves and coloured bunting. In the centre stood the *chuppah*, a canopy worked with religious symbols in blue and gold—the Star of David and the grapes and ears of wheat, the pomegranates and other symbols of plenty.

Beneath it, the marriage ceremony would take place. Tables set with bowls of flowers and dishes of fruit were arranged beneath the olive trees. There were places for three hundred guests, an open space for dancing, a raised stand hung with flags for the band. There was professional catering and the menu would have two high points—an enormous stuffed tuna and a lamb dish in the bedouin style served from enormous copper salvers.

To David, Hannah had never been particularly attractive, she was too severe in body and expression. However, on her wedding day, in her white bridal dress, she was transformed. She seemed to float upon the billowing white skirts, and her face was softened by the happiness in her green eyes.

Joe, handsome in his air force tans, went forward eagerly to meet her at the garden gate, and to lower the veil over her face in the ceremony of *bedeken di kale*.

Joe then moved to the *chuppah* where the Chief Rabbi of the army waited with a *tallit*, a tasselled woollen shawl, over his shoulders. The Rabbi chanted a blessing as the bride and party of festively dressed women, each carrying a burning candle, circled Joe seven times, which, in olden times, served to ward off evil spirits.

At last bride and groom stood side by side, and the Rabbi spoke the benediction over a goblet of wine from which they both drank. Then Joe turned to Hannah and placed the plain gold ring upon her right forefinger. "Behold you are consecrated unto me by this ring, according to the law of Moses and Israel."

Then Joe broke the glass under his heel and the sharp crunch was a signal for an outburst of music and song and gaiety. David left Joe and worked his way through the crowd to Debra.

She wore a yellow gown and had fresh flowers in her dark hair. David smelled their perfume as he hugged her and whispered, "You next, my beauty!" and she whispered back, "Yes, please!"

Joe led Hannah to the improvised dance floor. The band began with a bouncy tune and all the younger ones flocked to join them. Yet amongst all the gaiety, almost every second man wore uniform, and at the garden gate and the entrance to the kitchens were paratrooper guards with Uzi submachine guns.

David and Debra danced together and, when the band paused

for breath he led her to a quiet corner where they discussed the other guests in the most disrespectful terms until Debra giggled at some particularly outrageous remark. "You are terrible." She leaned against him. "I'm dying of thirst, won't you get me something to drink?"

"A glass of cold white wine?" he suggested.

"Lovely," she said, smiling up into his face, and suddenly David felt a terrible premonition of impending loss.

"What is it, David?" She tightened her grip on his arm.

"Nothing." Abruptly he pulled away from her, trying to fight off the feeling. "I'll get you the wine," he said and turned away.

So he was cut off from Debra when a procession of three white-jacketed waiters came in through the iron garden gate. Each of them carried a huge copper salver from which rose the aroma of meat, fish and spices. There were cries of appreciation from the guests.

The procession passed close to David, and suddenly his attention was drawn to the face of the second waiter in line. It was shiny with sweat. Droplets clung in the man's moustache and slid down his cheeks. His white jacket was sodden at the armpits.

Their eyes met for an instant and David realized that the Arab was in the grip of some deep emotion—fear, perhaps, or exhilaration. Suspicion began to chill David as the three figures climbed the stone stairs to the high table. The waiter glanced again at him, and then said something out of the corner of his mouth to his companion.

Wildly David looked about for the guards. There were two on the terrace behind the waiters, and one near him beside the gate. David shoved his way desperately towards him, at the same time watching the three waiters and so he saw the horror begin.

It had obviously been carefully rehearsed, for, as the three waiters placed the salvers on the table to the applause of the guests in the garden below, they drew back sheets of plastic on which the display of food had been thinly arranged. From the deadly load beneath, the brown-faced waiter lifted a machine pistol and he turned swiftly to fire point-blank into the two paratroopers behind him. The clattering thunder of automatic fire was deafening. The first waiter, a wizened monkey-faced man, also lifted a machine pistol from his salver, and fired a burst at the paratrooper by the gate, who had cleared his Uzi and was trying to aim as a bullet hit him in the mouth. The machine-gun flew from his arms as he fell, and it slid across the tiles towards David. David dropped flat as all three Arab gunners turned their pistols on the wedding crowd.

A security agent fired twice and hit the monkey-faced gunman, who reeled against the wall. But he stayed on his feet and returned the agent's fire, knocking him down and rolling him across the paving stones.

The yard was filled with a screaming mob panic-stricken beneath the flail of the guns. Two bullets caught Hannah in the chest, smashing her backwards over a table. Blood spurted from the wounds, drenching the front of her white wedding gown.

The dark-faced gunman dropped his pistol as it emptied. He stooped quickly over the salver and came up with a grenade in each hand. He hurled them into the throng and the double blast was devastating. The deafening screams rose louder.

All this had taken only seconds. David rolled swiftly across the flags to the abandoned Uzi, and came up on his knees, holding it at the hip. The wounded gunman turned towards him but David fired first. The gunman slumped down leaving a glistening wet smear of blood down the white wall behind him.

David swivelled the Uzi on to the centre gunman who was poised to throw his next grenade. David hit him with a full burst. The Arab dropped the grenade at his feet and doubled over clutching at his broken body. The grenade exploded almost immediately, engulfing the dying man in a net of fire. The same explosion mortally wounded the third assassin at the end of the terrace, and David charged up the steps. He crouched at the head of the stairs and fired at the dying Arab, but his Uzi was empty, the pin falling with a hollow click.

David stood frozen as he watched the blank eye of the Arab's machine pistol seek him out. Then the Arab suddenly grinned murderously as he saw David in his sights. His finger tightened on the trigger.

David began to move but he knew it was too late. The Arab was at the instant of firing, when a shot crashed out at David's side.

The Arab was flung backwards, his death grip on the trigger emptying the machine pistol into the grape vines above.

Dazedly David turned to find the Brig beside him, the dead security guard's pistol in his fist. Then the Brig walked to the fallen bodies of the three Arabs. Standing over each in turn he fired a single shot into their heads.

David went down the stairs into the garden. The veils of smoke and dust could not hide the terrible carnage. The garden was drenched in blood; there were puddles of it everywhere. The wounded and dazed survivors crawled over a field of broken glass and crockery. They swore and prayed, and groaned and called for succour.

David's feet moved without his bidding, his body numbed. Joe was standing below an olive tree, the bark of which had been torn off in slabs by flying steel. He stood like a colossus, his powerful legs astride, and his face turned to the sky, but his eyes were closed and his mouth formed a silent cry of agony—for he held Hannah's body in his arms.

David could not watch Joe in his anguish; he walked on across the garden, in terrible dread of what he would find.

"Debra!" he tried to raise his voice, but it was a hoarse croak. His feet slipped in a puddle of blood, and he stepped over the unconscious body of a woman in a floral dress who lay, face down. He did not recognize her as Debra's mother.

He saw her then, at the corner of the wall where he had left her. He felt his heart soar. She seemed unhurt, kneeling below one of the marble statues, her head bowed as though in prayer. Her dark hair hung forward and she held her cupped hands to her face.

"Debra." He dropped to his knees beside her, and touched her shoulder. "Are you all right, my darling?" She lowered her hands slowly. A great coldness closed around David as he saw that her cupped hands were filled with blood.

"David," she whispered, turning her face towards him. "Is that you, darling?"

He saw her blood-glutted eye sockets.

"Is that you, David?" she asked again, her head cocked at a blind listening angle.

"Oh, God, Debra." He stared into her face.

"I can't see, David." She groped for him. "Oh, David—I can't see."

And he took her sticky wet hands in his, and he thought that his heart would break.

THE BRIG, JOE AND DAVID kept vigil that night upon the hard wooden benches of the hospital waiting-room. A security agent came to whisper reports to the Brig as more was learned of the planning of the attack.

One of the assassins was a long-term employee of the catering firm, and the other two were his "cousins" who had been employed as temporary staff on his recommendation.

The Prime Minister and her cabinet had been on their way to the wedding when the attack was made, delayed fortunately by an emergency session. She sent her condolences to the relatives of the victims.

At ten o'clock, Damascus radio reported that El Fatah claimed responsibility for the attack by members of a suicide squad.

A little before midnight, the chief surgeon came from the main theatre, still in his theatre greens. He told them Debra's mother was out of danger.

"Thank God." The Brig closed his eyes for a moment. Then he looked up. "My daughter?"

The surgeon shook his head. "They are still working on her in the small casualty theatre."

The dead totalled eleven so far. Four other guests were on the critical list.

In the early morning the undertakers arrived and Joe went with them to arrange the details of Hannah's funeral.

In the late morning the eye surgeon came out to David and the Brig. He was a smooth-faced, young-looking man in his forties. "General Mordecai?" The Brig rose stiffly. He seemed to have aged ten years during the night. "I am Doctor Edelman. Will you come with me please?"

David rose to follow them, but the doctor paused and looked to the Brig. "It might be best if we spoke alone first, General."

"But I am her fiancé—" David began, and the Brig squeezed

his shoulder briefly, the first gesture of affection that had ever passed between them.

"Please, my boy," and David turned back.

In his office Edelman sat on the corner of the desk and lit a cigarette. "Neither of your daughter's eyes is damaged," he began, but quickly held up a long, slim hand to forestall the expression of relief on the Brig's lips. He turned to the plates on the X-ray scanner. "The eyes were untouched, and there is almost no damage to her facial features. However, there is damage *here*—" he touched a hard outline in the grey swirls of the X-ray. "That is a steel fragment, almost certainly from a grenade. It is no larger than the tip of a lead pencil. It entered the skull through the right temple, severing the large vein which accounted for the haemorrhage, and it travelled obliquely behind the eyeballs without touching them. Then, however, it cut through the optic chiasma, before lodging in the bone sponge beyond." Edelman drew heavily on his cigarette. "Do you understand the implications of this, General?"

The Brig shook his head wearily and the surgeon returned to the desk. He pulled a scrap pad towards the Brig and sketched an optical chart, eyeballs, brain, and optical nerves, as seen from above. "The optical nerves, one from each eye, run back into this narrow tunnel of bone where they fuse, and then branch again to opposite lobes of the brain."

The Brig nodded, and Edelman slashed his pencil through the point where the nerves fused. Understanding began to show on the Brig's strained and tired features. "Blind?" he asked.

Edelman nodded. "I'm afraid so."

The Brig bowed his head. "Permanently?"

"All indications are that the nerve is severed. There is no technique known to medical science which will restore that."

The Brig sighed, and looked up slowly. "Have you told her?"

"I was rather hoping that you would do that."

"Yes," the Brig nodded, "it would be best. Can I see her?"

"Yes, I'll take you to her now." He stood up. "We won't attempt to remove the fragment. That would entail major surgery."

Debra lay on the high bed, a bandage covering her eyes.

"Your father is here, Miss Mordecai," Edelman told her.

She turned her head swiftly towards them. "Daddy?"

"I am here, my baby." The Brig took her hand, and stooped to kiss her. Her lips were cold, and she smelled strongly of anaesthetic.

"Mama?" she asked anxiously.

"She is out of danger," the Brig assured her, "but Hannah—"

"Yes. They told me," Debra stopped him, her voice choking. "Is Joe all right?"

"He is strong," the Brig said. "He will be all right."

"David?" she asked.

"He is here."

Eagerly she struggled up on to one elbow. "David," she called, "where are you? Damn this bandage!"

"No," the Brig restrained her with a hand on her arm. "He is outside, waiting," and she slumped with disappointment.

"Ask him to come to me, please," she whispered.

"Yes," said the Brig, "in a while, but first there is something we must talk about—something I have to tell you."

She must have guessed what it was for she went very still. Her tense hand in his was the only indication that she heard what he told her.

When he had done she asked no questions and they sat quietly for a long time. He spoke first. "I will send David to you now," he said, and her response was swift and vehement.

"No." She gripped his hand hard. "No, I can't see him now. I have to think about this first."

The Brig went back to the waiting-room and David stood up expectantly. The Brig took David's arm. "No visitors. You will not be allowed to see her until tomorrow."

"Is something wrong?" David tried to pull away but the Brig steered him towards the door.

"Nothing is wrong. She will be all right—but she must have no excitement now. You'll be able to see her tomorrow."

THEY BURIED HANNAH that evening in the family plot on the Mountain of Olives. It was a small funeral party attended by the three men and a handful of relatives, most of whom had others to mourn from the slaughter.

An official car took the Brig away to a meeting of the high command. Joe and David climbed into the Mercedes and sat silently.

"What are you going to do now?" David finally asked.

"We had two weeks," Joe answered him. "We were going down to Asheklon—" his voice trailed off. "I think I'll go back to base. They are flying night interception exercises tonight."

"I'll come with you." David said. He could not see Debra until tomorrow, and suddenly he longed for the peace of the night heavens.

The moon was a brightly curved Saracen blade against the darkness of the sky. They flew high, above the earth, remote from its grief and sorrow, wrapped in the isolation of flight and in the concentration on the surrounding velvety blackness.

David reached the hospital just as the sun lit the hills with its pink and gold rays. The sister at the desk was brusque. "You shouldn't be here until visiting hours this afternoon."

David smiled at her with all the charm he could muster. "I have to rejoin my squadron this morning."

The sister was not immune either to his smile or the air force uniform, and she consulted her lists. "You must be mistaken," she said at last. "The only Mordecai we have is Mrs. Ruth Mordecai."

"That's her mother," David told her.

The sister flipped the sheet on her clipboard. "No wonder I couldn't find it," she muttered irritably. "She was discharged last night. I remember her now. Her father came to fetch her. Pretty girl with eye bandages—"

"Yes," David nodded. "Thank you." He ran down the steps to the Mercedes, his feet light with relief. Debra had gone home. Debra was safe and well.

The Brig let him into the silent house. His uniform was rumpled, and his eyes bloodshot from sorrow and lack of sleep.

"Where is Debra?" David demanded eagerly, and the Brig sighed and waved him to a chair in his study, a large bare room with monastic furnishings of books and archaeological relics.

"I couldn't tell you yesterday, David, she asked me not to."

"What is it?" David was alarmed now.

"She had to have time to think—to reach a decision." The Brig began to pace, pausing every now and then to touch a piece of statuary, caressing it absently as he talked. David listened quietly, occasionally shaking his head, as though to deny what he was hearing.

". . . So you see, David, it is permanent, without hope. She is totally blind. She has gone into a dark world where nobody can follow her."

"Where is she? I want to go to her," David whispered.

"No, David. That was her decision. You will not see her again. Her words were: 'Tell him I am dead'."

David jumped to his feet. "Where is she, damn you?" His voice was shaking. "I want to see her now." He crossed swiftly to the door.

"She is not here."

"Where is she?" David turned back.

"I cannot tell you. I swore a solemn oath to her."

"I'll find her—"

"You might, if you search carefully, but you will forfeit the love she has for you," the Brig went on remorselessly. "Again I will give you her exact words. 'Tell him that I charge him on our love that he will not come looking for me.'"

"Why, but why does she reject me?" David demanded desperately.

"She knows she can never be your wife now. You are too young, too vital, too arrogant—" David stared at him "—she knows that it will begin to spoil. In a week, a month, a year perhaps, it will have died. You will be trapped, tied to a blind woman—"

"Stop it," David shouted. "Stop it. That's enough." He stumbled back into the chair and buried his face in his hands.

"She asked me to make you promise—" the Brig hesitated, and David looked up at him, "—to promise that you would not try to find her."

"No," David shook his head stubbornly.

The Brig sighed. "If you refused, I was to tell you this—she said you would understand, although I don't—she said that in Africa there is a fierce and beautiful animal called the sable antelope, and sometimes one of them is wounded."

The words were as painful as the cut of a whiplash. "Very well," David murmured at last, "if that's what she wants, then I promise not to try and find her."

"Perhaps it would be best if you left Israel," the Brig told him. "Perhaps you should go and forget all of this ever happened."

David paused, considering this a moment before he answered, "No, all I have is here. I will stay."

"Good. You know you are always welcome in this house."

"Thank you, sir," said David and went out to his car.

He let himself into the house on Malik Street, and saw instantly that someone had been there before him. In the living room the books and the Kadesh painting were gone. All Debra's toilet articles had been removed from the bathroom, and her cupboard was empty, every trace of her swept away, except for the lingering scent of her perfume and the ivory lace cover upon the bed.

He went to the bed and sat upon it, stroking the fine lacework, remembering how it had been. There was the hard outline of something upon the pillow, beneath the cover. He turned back the lace and picked up the thin green book.

This year, in Jerusalem. It had been left there as a parting gift. The title swam before his eyes. It was all he had left of her.

IT SEEMED AS THOUGH the slaughter at Ein Karem was the signal for a fresh upsurge of violence throughout the Middle East, as the Arab nations rattled their oil-purchased array of weaponry and swore once more to leave not a single Jew in the land they still called Palestine. The provocations were bold, directly aimed at the heart of Israel: border infringements, commando-style raids, shellings, and a massing of armed might along the frontiers of the tiny land.

Then the Syrians began a policy of provocative patrols, calculated infringement of Israeli air space. As the interceptors raced to engage they would swing away, declining combat, and move back within their own borders. The tactics were designed to wear on the nerves of the defenders, and in all the interceptor squadrons the tension was becoming explosive.

The anger that David and Joe shared seemed doubly to arm them, and their vengeance was all-consuming. Soon they joined the select strike teams that undertook the most delicate of sorties. Again and again, month after month, they were ordered into combat, and each time the confidence Desert Flower command had in them was strengthened.

While on "Red" standby, they would sit in their cockpits, dressed from head to foot in their constricting full-pressure suits, breathing oxygen from their closed face masks. With the statter lines plugged ready to blow compressed air into the compressors and whirl the great engines into life, and the ground crew lounging beside the motor, the Mirages were ready to be hurled aloft in a matter of seconds.

David had lost count of the weary uncomfortable hours he had sat thus cramped with only fifteen-minute checks to break the monotony, but there were four red, white and black miniature roundels painted on the fuselage below his cockpit—the scalps of the enemy.

DAVID AND JOE spent much of their leisure time together and often Joe slept at Malik Street, for his own home was a depressing place. The Brig was seldom there and his mother was so altered by her terrible experience that she was grey and broken. The bullet wound in her body had closed, but there was other damage that would never heal.

Now Joe sat opposite David in the crew-room, a worried expression creasing his forehead as he studied the chessboard. Three or four other pilots had hiked their chairs up and were concentrating on the game also.

David had been stalking Joe's rook for half a dozen moves and now he had it trapped. Two more moves would shatter the kingside defence, and the third must force a resignation. David grinned as Joe reached a decision and moved a knight out.

"That's not going to save you, dear boy," David hardly glanced at the knight, and he hit the rook with a white bishop. "Mate in five," he predicted, as he dropped the castle into the box, and then—too late—he realized that Joe's theatrical expression of anguish had slowly faded into a beatific grin.

"Oh, you sneak," David moaned.

"Check!" Joe gloated as he put the knight into a forked attack, and David had to leave his queen exposed to the horseman. "Check," said Joe again as he lifted the white queen off the board. "And mate," he sighed, just after the harassed king had taken the only escape route open to him. "Not in five, as you predicted, but in three." There was an outburst of applause from the onlookers and Joe cocked an eye at David. "Again?" he asked, and David shook his head.

"Take on one of these other patsies," he said. "I'm going to sulk for an hour." He vacated his seat and crossed to the coffee machine, moving awkwardly in his G-suit. He drew a mug of the thick black liquid and found a seat in a quieter corner of the crew-room beside a slim curly-headed young kibbutznik who was reading a thick novel. "*Shalom*, Robert. How you been?"

Robert grunted without looking up from his book, and David sipped the sweet hot coffee.

"What you reading?" David leaned forward to see the cover. The picture on the dust jacket was a desert landscape of fierce colours. Two distant figures, man and woman, walked hand in hand through the desert and the effect was haunting. David realized that only one person could have painted that—Ella Kadesh.

Robert lowered the book. "I tell you, Davey, it's beautiful. It must be one of the most beautiful books ever written."

David took the book out of his hands and read the title, *A Place of Our Own*. Robert was still talking. "It was only published last week, but it's got to be the biggest book ever written about this country."

David stared at the writer's name below the title. "Debra Mordecai."

He ran his fingers lightly over the glossy paper of the jacket, stroking the name. "I want to read it," he said softly.

"I'll let you have it when I'm finished," Robert promised.

"I want to read it now!"

"No way!" Robert almost snatched the book out of David's hands. "You wait your turn, comrade!"

David looked up. Joe was watching him from across the room, and David glared at him accusingly. He started to go to him, but

70

at that moment the tannoy echoed through the bunker. "All flights Lance Squadron to Red standby."

David snatched up his helmet and joined the lumbering rush for the electric personnel carrier. He forced a place for himself beside Joe.

"Why didn't you tell me?" he demanded.

"I was going to, Davey. I really was."

"Yeah, I bet," David snapped sarcastically. "Have you read it?" Joe nodded, and David went on, "What's it about?"

"I couldn't begin to tell you. You'd have to read it yourself."

"Don't worry," David muttered grimly, "I will." He jumped down as they reached their hangar.

Twenty minutes later they were airborne and hastening out over the Mediterranean to answer a Mayday call from an El Al airliner that was being buzzed by an Egyptian MiG 21.

The Egyptian raced for the protection of his own missile batteries as the Mirages approached. They let him go and escorted the airliner to Lod.

Still in his G-suit and overalls, David stopped off at Le Dauphin's office and got himself a twenty-four-hour pass.

Ten minutes before closing time he ran into a bookshop on Jaffa Road. There was a display of *A Place of Our Own* on the table in the centre of the shop.

"It's a beautiful book," said the salesgirl as she wrapped it.

When he reached Malik Street, he opened a Goldstar beer and kicked off his shoes before stretching out on the bed. It was a thick book, and he read slowly—savouring every word, sometimes going back to re-read a paragraph.

It was their story, his and Debra's, and he laughed aloud with the pleasure and the joy of it. Then at the end, he choked on the sadness as the girl lies dying in Hadassah Hospital, half her face torn away by a terrorist's bomb, and she will not let the boy come to her. Wanting to spare him that, wanting him to remember her as she was.

It was dawn when David rose from the bed, light-headed from lack of sleep, and filled with a sense of wonder that Debra had captured so clearly the way it had been.

He bathed and shaved and dressed in casual clothes and went

back to where the book lay upon the bed. The jacket caught his eye and he turned to the flyleaf for confirmation. It was there. "Jacket design by Ella Kadesh."

He drove fast, the road almost to himself, into the rising morning sun. Even the whisper of the wind against the Mercedes seemed to urge him. "Hurry, hurry."

He parked the car and went through into the garden on the lake shore. Ella was sitting on the patio before her easel. She wore a huge straw hat adorned with plastic cherries and ostrich feathers, and her vast overalls, stiff with dried paint, covered her like a circus tent. Calmly she looked up from her painting. "Hail, young Mars!" she greeted him. "Why do you bring such honour on my humble home?"

"You know damn well why I'm here, Ella."

"So sweetly phrased. Would you like a beer, Davey?"

"No, I don't want a beer. I want to know where she is."

"Just who are we discussing?"

"Come on, I read the book. I saw the cover. You know, damn you."

She was silent then, staring at him. Then slowly the ornate head-dress dipped in acquiescence.

"Yes," she agreed. "I know."

"Tell me where she is."

"I can't do that, Davey. You and I both made a promise. Yes, I know of yours, you see." She watched the bluster go out of him. "How about that beer now, Davey?" She heaved herself up and brought him a tall glass with a head of froth.

They sat at the end of the terrace in the mild winter sunlight. "I've been expecting you for a week now," she told him. "Ever since the book was published."

"That book was us—Debra and me," David told her.

"Yes," Ella agreed, "it's beautiful and it's true, but it does not alter Debra's decision."

"But I love her, Ella—and she loves me," he cried out.

"She knows that she can never keep pace with you now. You are beautiful and vital and swift. She would hold you back, and in time you would resent it." He began to protest, but she gripped his arm powerfully to silence him. "You would be

72

shackled, you could never leave her. She loves you so much, David, that for your sake she will deny that love."

"Oh, God," he groaned. "If only I could see her, if I could touch her and talk to her for a few minutes."

Ella shook her massive head. "She would not agree to that. She knows that if you came near her, she would waver."

They sat silently together. David drank the rest of his beer, and revolved the glass slowly between his fingers. "Will you give her a message from me, then?" he asked. Ella nodded. "Tell her that what she wrote in the book is exactly how much I love her. Tell her that it is big enough to rise above this. Tell her that I want the chance to try. Tell her—" he paused, then shook his head. "No, that's all. Just say I love her, and I want to be with her."

"All right, David. I'll tell her. Where can I reach you?"

He gave her the number of the telephone in the crew ready-room at the base. "You'll ring me soon, Ella?"

"Tomorrow," she promised. "In the morning."

"Before ten o'clock. It must be before ten." He stood up, and leaned forward to kiss her. "Thank you," he said. "You are not a bad old bag."

"Away with you!" She sniffed moistly. "I think I'm going to cry, and I want to be alone to enjoy it."

When she heard the Mercedes pull away slowly up the track, she crossed the terrace, and descended the steps towards the jetty and its stone boathouses which were screened from the house by the ancient wall.

She went to the farthest boathouse and stood in the open doorway. The interior had been painted white. The furniture was simple. A large bed was built into a curtained alcove in the wall beside the fireplace. On the opposite wall stood a gas stove above which hung a number of copper pots. A door beyond led to a bathroom which Ella had recently added. The only decoration was her painting from the house on Malik Street, which hung on the wall facing the door.

Debra sat at a work table, listening to her own voice speaking in Hebrew from a tape recorder. Then she switched off the machine and turned on a second recorder and began to translate the Hebrew into English. It was for an American publisher who had purchased the English language rights of *A Place of Our Own.*

Ella left the doorway and moved silently closer to the desk, studying Debra's eyes as she so often did. There was no hint that the eyes could not see. Rather their calm level gaze seemed to penetrate, to see all. The scar on her temple was V-shaped, like a child's drawing of a seagull in flight, and no bigger than a snowflake.

Debra switched off the recorder, and said without turning her head, "Is that you, Ella?"

"How do you do it?" Ella demanded with astonishment.

"I felt the air move when you walked in. Do you want some coffee?" Debra stood up and crossed to the gas stove. Ella knew better than to offer her help, though she gritted her teeth every time she watched Debra working with fire and boiling water. The girl was fiercely independent, determined to live her life without assistance. She could do her own housework, prepare her own food, work steadily, and pay her own way.

"Now," she said, "you can tell me what is keeping you fidgetting by the door," she smiled towards Ella, sensing the surprise. "You have got something to tell me, and it's killing you."

"Yes," Ella said after a moment, "you are right, my dear." She took a deep breath and went on. "He came, Debra. He came to see me, as we knew he must."

Debra's face was expressionless. "How is he, Ella? How does he look?"

"He is still the most beautiful man I have ever seen."

Debra nodded smiling. "What did he say? What did he want?"

"He had a message for you," and Ella repeated his exact words. When she had finished, Debra turned away to face the wall above her desk. "Please go away now, Ella. I want to be alone."

"He asked me to give him your reply tomorrow morning."

"I will come to you later—but please leave me now."

Ella left the boathouse. Behind her she heard the girl sob, but she did not turn back. She went up to the terrace, picked up her brush and began to paint, her strokes broad and angry.

74

DAVID WAS SWEATING in the stiff pressure suit and he waited anxiously beside the crew-room telephone. He and Joe would go on high-altitude "Red" standby at ten o'clock, in seven minutes' time, and Ella had not called him. Suddenly it rang.

"I'm sorry, David," Ella's voice was scratchy and far away. "I tried earlier but the exchange here—"

"Sure, sure," David cut her short. "Did you speak to her?"

"Yes, Davey. Yes, I did. I gave her your message."

"What was her reply?" he demanded.

"She said—" Ella hesitated, "—and these are her words—'the dead cannot speak with the living. For David, I died a year ago'."

He held the receiver with both hands but still it shook. He broke the silence at last. "That's it, then," he said.

"Yes, I'm afraid that's it, Davey."

Joe called from the doorway. "Hey, Davey. Time to go."

"I have to go now, Ella. Thanks for everything."

"Good-bye, David," she said, and even over the scratchy connection he could hear the compassion in her tone. It heightened the anger that gripped him as he rode beside Joe to the Mirage bunker.

He felt trapped and restless waiting in the cockpit, and it seemed hours between each of the fifteen-minute readiness checks. At last there was a click in his earphones and the distinctive voice of the Brig.

"Red Standby—Go! Go!"

With the driving thrust of the afterburner hurling him aloft David called, "Hello, Desert Flower, Bright Lance airborne and climbing."

"Hello, David, this is the Brig. It looks like another teaser from the Syrians. They are approaching our border at twenty-six thousand. We are going to initiate attack plan Gideon. Your new heading is forty-two degrees and I want you right down on the deck."

David immediately rotated the Mirage's nose downwards. Plan Gideon called for a low-level stalk so that the ground clutter would obscure the enemy radar and conceal their approach until they were in position to storm-climb into an attack position above and behind the target.

They dropped to within feet of the ground, so low that herds of black Persian sheep scattered beneath them as they shrieked east-ward towards the Jordan.

"Hello, Bright Lance, this is Desert Flower—we are not tracking you." Good, thought David, then neither is the enemy. "Target is now hostile." The Brig gave the coordinates. "Scan for your own contact."

Almost immediately Joe's voice came in. "Leader, this is Two. I have a contact. Range figures nine six nautical miles. Parallel heading and track. Altitude 25,500 feet."

"Beseder, Two. Lock to target and go to interception speed."

They went supersonic. David saw thunderclouds rearing up ahead. They were sculptured into wonderful shapes with the deep crevasses between them bridged in splendour by rainbows. Above these great blazes of colour the sky was a dark unnatural blue, out of which the sunlight poured down on the two speeding warplanes.

David looked at his radar screen. The target was flying parallel to them, twenty miles out on their starboard side. It was high above them and moving at a little more than half their speed. "Turning to starboard now," he warned Joe, and they came around together, crossing the target's rear. "Arm your circuits."

David activated the two air-to-air sidewinder missiles that hung under each wing-tip, and immediately heard the soft electronic tone cycling in his earphones. The tone indicated that the missiles had not yet detected an infra-red source to excite them. When they did they would increase the volume and rate of cycle. He selected his cannon switch, readying the twin 30mm. weapons in their pods just below his seat.

A moment later he saw the Syrians. There were five of them, and they appeared suddenly out of cloud high above. "I have target visual," he told Joe. "Five MiG 21s." Now at last his anger had something on which to fasten.

It would be another fifteen seconds before they had completed their turn across the enemy's stern. David saw that a huge tower block of cloud was perfectly placed to screen his climb into the sun.

"Target is altering course to starboard," Joe warned him suddenly. The Syrians were turning back. They had flaunted the colours of Islam, and now were making for safety.

David felt the anger in his guts sting sharper, and only with an effort waited out the last few seconds before making his climb. Then he called to Joe, "Two, this is leader, commencing climb."

"Two conforming."

They went up in a climb so vicious that it seemed to tear their bowels from their bellies. Almost immediately, Desert Flower picked up the radar images as they emerged from the ground clutter. "Both units Bright Lance. We are tracking you. Show friend or foe."

David and Joe punched in their IFF systems. Identification Friend or Foe would show a distinctive bright halo around their radar images on command plot, identifying them positively even while locked with the enemy in a dogfight.

"Beseder. We are tracking you in IFF," said the Brig, and they went plunging into the pillar of cloud.

"Target is increasing speed and tightening starboard turn," Joe intoned, and David compensated for the enemy's manœuvre. He was certain that they had not detected his approach, the turn away was coincidental.

A glance at his screen showed that he was now two miles off their quarter above them, with the sun at his back. It was the ideal approach.

"Turning now into final leg of attack pattern," he alerted Joe. The target centred dead ahead and the gunsight lit up, glowing softly on the screen. The sidewinder missiles caught the first emanations of infra-red rays from their victims, and began to growl softly in David's earphones.

Suddenly the planes burst out of the thick grey cloud. Ahead and below opened a deep trough of space, a valley between cloud ranges in which the five MiGs sparkled in the sunlight. They were in loose V-formation, and David assessed them in fleeting seconds. The four wingmen were pupils. They flew with an indefinable sloppiness. They were easy pickings. However, it did not need the three red rings about the leader's fuselage to identify him as a Russian instructor. Some leery veteran with hawk's blood in his veins, tough and canny and dangerous.

"Engage two port targets," David ordered Joe, reserving the MiG leader and the starboard echelon for his attack. In David's headphones the missiles were howling their eagerness to kill. He

78

switched to command net. "Hello, Desert Flower, this is Bright Lance on target and requesting strike."

Instantly the voice came back. "David, this is the Brig—" he was speaking rapidly, urgently, "—discontinue attack pattern. I repeat, disengage target. They are no longer hostile."

Shocked by the command, David glanced down and saw the long brown frontier valley of the Jordan falling away behind them.

"We are going to hit them," David said and he closed command net and spoke to Joe. "Two, this is leader attacking."

"Negative! I say again negative!" Joe called urgently.

"Remember Hannah!" David shouted into his mask. "Conform to me!" and he curled his finger about the trigger. The nearest MiG seemed to balloon in size as he shrieked towards it.

There was a heartbeat of silence from Joe, and then his voice strangled and rough. "Two conforming."

"Kill them, Joe," David yelled and pressed the trigger. There was a soft double hiss, and from under each wingtip the missiles unleashed. They skidded and twisted as they aligned themselves on the targets, leaving dark trails of vapour. At that moment the MiGs became aware, and the entire formation burst into five separate parts. But one of the sidewinders followed the rearmost Syrian's turn and united with him in an embrace of death.

The second missile had chosen the leader, but the Russian had pulled his turn so tight that the missile slid past him in an over-shoot. David saw the missile destroy itself in a burst of greenish smoke.

The Russian was in a hard righthand turn, and David followed him. He could see every detail of the enemy: the scarlet helmet of the pilot, the Arabic identification markings—even the individual rivets that stitched the metal skin of the MiG.

David pulled back with all his strength against his joystick, for gravity was tightening the loading of his controls. It had hold of David also. Its insidious force sucked the blood from his brain so that his vision dimmed, and he felt crushed down into his seat. About his waist and legs his G-suit tightened brutally like a hungry python. David tensed every muscle in his body, straining to resist his brain's loss of blood, and took the Mirage up in a sliding, soaring yo-yo, trying once more for the advantage of height.

His vision narrowed to the limits of his cockpit where the stall indicator blinked, changing from amber to red, warning him that he was courting the disaster of supersonic stall.

David filled his lungs and screamed with all his strength. The effort forced a little blood back to his brain and his vision cleared briefly, enough to let him see that the MiG had anticipated his yo-yo and had come up under his unprotected flank and belly.

David rolled the Mirage out left and went into a tight climb, his afterburner thundering at full power.

Neatly and gracefully, the Russian followed him. David saw him coming up into an attack position in his rear-view mirror and his rage turned gradually to despair as each of his efforts to dislodge the Russian were met and countered.

For an instant they flew wing-tip to wing-tip; David saw the man's face. Just the eyes and forehead above the oxygen mask—the skin pale as bone and the eyes deeply socketed like those of a skull—and then David was turning again, screaming against gravity, screaming also against the first enfolding coils of fear.

He rolled half out of the turn and then reversed the roll. The Mirage shuddered with protest and his speed bled off. The Russian saw it and came down on him from high on his starboard quarter. David ducked under the blast of cannon fire, and the Mirage went down in a spiralling dive. His blood was now flung upwards through his body, filling his head and his vision with bright redness, the "red-out" of inverted gravitational force. A vein in his nose popped under the pressure and his oxygen mask filled with blood.

The Russian followed him into the dive, lining him up for his second burst. David hauled back on the stick with all his strength, the nose came up, and again the blood drained from his head. He saw the Russian following him up, drawn by the ploy. At the top David kicked out in a breakaway roll and the Russian swung giddily through David's gunsight.

David let fire an almost impossible deflection shot that sluiced cannon shells wildly across the sky. Then he rolled and turned out, coming around hard and finding the Russian still hanging in the circuit, but losing air space, a feather of white vapour streaming from below his cockpit canopy.

I've hit him, David exulted. He fired a second burst and saw the shells lace into the fuselage.

The Russian came out of his turn, in a gentle dive, probably dead at his controls. David fired a two-second burst, and now the MiG went down vertically like a silver javelin. David watched the MiG burst in a tower of smoke that stood for long seconds on the brown plains of Syria.

David shut down his afterburner and looked at his fuel gauges. They all showed only a narrow strip above the empty notch, and David realized that his last dive had taken him down to an altitude of five thousand—in range of both flak and ground missiles. Expending precious fuel, he began to climb at interception speed.

"Leader, this is Two," Joe's voice came to him. "I have you visual. In the name of God, get out of there! We are fifty miles within Syrian territory."

"How did you go?"

"I took out one of mine. The other one ran for it."

Sweat was pouring down David's forehead and his mask was sticky with blood. "I got two," he said, "One for Debra, and one for Hannah."

"Shut up, Davey," Joe's voice was tense. "Concentrate on getting out of here."

"I'm low on fuel. Where are you?"

"Six o'clock high at 25,000." As he answered Joe leaned forward to watch the tiny wedge shape of David's machine far below. Two long, slow minutes would see them clear.

Joe almost missed the first missile. It streaked in from behind David, closing rapidly with him.

"Missile! Break left," Joe yelled. "Go! Go! Go!" and he saw David begin his turn instantly, side-stepping steeply.

"It's lost you!" Joe called, as the missile continued its crazy career through space, yawing from side to side before bursting in self-destruction.

They both saw the next one leave the ground. There was a nest of these "Serpents", the latest Soviet surface-to-air missiles, on a rocky ridge above a sun-blasted plain. This one slid off the rock and climbed rapidly towards David's machine.

"Break right! Go! Go! Go!" Joe yelled and David twisted violently aside. The Serpent slid past him, but came around to attack again, its seekers locked to David's machine.

"He's still on you," Joe was screaming now. "Try for the sun, Davey," and the Mirage pointed its nose upwards.

"He's on to you, Davey. Flip out now! Go! Go! Go!"

David flicked the Mirage out of her climb, and fell like a stone—while the Serpent fastened its attention upon the vast infra-red output from the sun and streaked on towards it, losing the Mirage.

"You've lost it. Get out, Davey, get out!" Joe pleaded with him, but the Mirage was helpless. In her desperate climb she had lost manœuvring speed. She was still wallowing clumsily when the third missile became airborne.

Joe did not consciously realize what he was going to do until he had commenced his dive. He came down at twice the speed of sound, and he levelled across David's tail, cutting across the nose of the oncoming Serpent.

The Serpent saw him with its little cyclops radar eye, and it sensed the heat of his exhausts—fresher, more tantalizing than David's, and it accepted him as an alternative target.

David saw Joe's aircraft flash past his wing-tip, and a second later, the Serpent. He realized instantly that Joe had deliberately pulled the missile off him.

He watched with fascinated horror as the missile followed Joe out of his dive and towards the sun. At the last instant Joe flipped out of the climb—but this time the Serpent was not deceived. It swivelled as Joe dropped and in a burst of flame, Joe and his Mirage died together.

David flew on alone, his Mirage once more at manœuvring speed. Ahead of him he saw the Jordan. "It should be you that's going home, Joe," he said aloud, his throat dry with horror and grief.

Then he saw the last missile coming in on him. It was just a small black speck far behind, but it was watching him hungrily with its wicked eye. As he saw it gaining on him, he knew beyond doubt that this one was his. The attacks he had evaded so far had worn his nerves and strained his judgment, and he felt a sense of fatalistic dismay as he gathered his reserves for a supreme effort.

The missile was almost upon him when he hurled the Mirage into the turn, but he had misjudged it by the smallest part of a second.

As the missile slid close past him its photo-electric eye winked at him and the missile exploded. The blast sent the Mirage tumbling. The cockpit canopy was penetrated by flying steel and a piece struck David's armoured seat glancing off and striking his left arm above the elbow, snapping the bone cleanly so that the arm dropped uselessly and hung in his lap.

An icy wind raged through the torn canopy as the Mirage hurled itself downwards. David was thrown against his straps, but held himself upright as he reached over his head and caught hold of the handle of the ejector mechanism. He expected to be hurled free of the doomed Mirage—but nothing happened.

Desperately he strained forward to reach the secondary firing mechanism under the seat. He wrenched it and felt despair as there was no response. The blast had damaged some vital part of the seat. He had to fly the Mirage out and with only one arm.

The earth was very close before he felt the first hint of response on the controls. Gently, he wooed her and she was flying straight and level again. But the missile had done mortal damage. He could feel the rough vibration of the engine, and he guessed that the compressor had thrown a blade and was out of balance. Within minutes or seconds she would begin to tear herself to pieces.

The vibration increased and he could hear the screech of rending metal. He wasn't going to make it home to base and there was insufficient height to parachute. He must fly the Mirage in.

He looked ahead, and saw a low ridge of rocky ground. Disaster lurked for him there—but beyond it were open Israeli fields, ploughed land, orderly blocks of orchards. Holding the stick between his knees, he let down his landing gear.

He skimmed over broken rocks, sucking in his belly as though to lift the Mirage bodily over the granite, and ahead lay the fields. He could see women in the orchards, turning to look at him, surprise and apprehension on their faces. A man on a tractor jumped to the earth as David passed only feet above his head.

All fuel cocks closed, master switch off—David went into the final ritual for crash-landing. Ahead of him lay the open brown field. He might just be lucky enough, it might just come off.

The Mirage was losing flying speed: 200 mph, 190, 180, dropping back to her stalling speed of 140. . . .

Suddenly David realized that the field ahead of him was latticed with deep concrete irrigation channels. They were twenty feet wide, and ten deep, a hazard deadly enough to destroy a centurion tank.

There was nothing he could do to avoid their gaping jaws. He flew the Mirage in, touching down smoothly. "Even Barney would have been proud of me," he thought bitterly, aware that all his skill was unavailing now. The Mirage was still travelling at ninety miles an hour when she went into the irrigation ditch.

The landing gear snapped like pretzel sticks and she nosed in. The far bank of concrete sent the fuselage cartwheeling across the field with David still strapped within. The wings broke away and the body slid across the soft earth, coming to rest at last, right way up like a stranded whale.

The whole of David's left side was numb. For many seconds he was unable to move or think. Then he smelled it, the pervasive reek of Avtur jet fuel from the ruptured tanks and lines.

With his right hand he grabbed the canopy release lever and heaved at it. He wasted ten precious seconds for it was jammed solid. Then he lifted the steel canopy breaker from its niche below the lever. He lay back in his seat and attacked the dome above his head. The stink of jet fuel was overpowering, and he could hear the tinkling sound made by white-hot metal.

His left arm hampered him, but he tore at the opening in the dome, and as he worked to enlarge it, a ruptured pressure line somewhere in the fuselage sprayed a jet of Avtur high in the air. It dribbled through the hole David was cutting and fell into his face, icy cold on his cheeks and stinging his eyes, and he began to pray. For the first time in his life the words took on meaning and he felt his terror receding.

"Hear O Israel, the Lord is our God, the Lord is one." He prayed aloud, striking up at the canopy and feeling the soft rain of death in his face. "Blessed be his name, whose glorious kingdom is for ever. . . ."

The opening was large enough. He hauled himself up in the seat, and found himself caught by the oxygen and radio lines attached to his helmet. He could not reach them with his crippled left arm.

"You shall love the Lord your God with all your heart . . ." he whispered, and with his right hand he tore loose the chin strap and let his helmet drop to the floorboards. The Avtur soaked into his hair and he thought about the flames of hell. " . . . For the anger of God will kindle against you. . . ."

Painfully he dragged himself out through the opening and crawled across the slippery wing root and fell to the ground. He lay there for a moment, exhausted. ". . . Remember all the commands of God. . . ."

He lifted his head and saw the women from the orchard running towards him across the field. They were speaking Hebrew. He knew that he was home. Steadying himself against the shattered body of the Mirage, he came to his feet.

"Go back!" he tried to shout to them, but his voice was a croak, and they ran on towards him. Their dresses and aprons were gay spots of colour against the dry brown earth. He staggered to meet them.

Within the battered Mirage a puddle of Avtur had been heated to flash point by the white-hot shell of the jet compressor, and a dying spark from the electronic equipment ignited it. With a dull but awful roar, the Mirage bloomed with dark crimson flame and sooty black smoke and the wind ripped the flames outwards in great streamers and pennants that engulfed all around them. David staggered onward in the midst of the roaring furnace. He held his breath—if he had not the flames would have scorched his lungs. He closed his eyes tightly and ran blindly. His body was protected by the fireproof pressure suit—but his head was bare and soaked with jet fuel. As he ran it burned like a torch. He did not believe such agony was possible.

The women from the orchard were forced back by the wall of heat and smoke that rose up in front of them.

Then abruptly a freak of the wind blew an opening in the smoke, and out of it stumbled a dreadful thing with a scorched and smoking body and a head of flame. They stared in horror, frozen in silence, and it came towards them.

Then a strapping girl with a mane of dark hair raced to meet him. As she ran, she stripped off her heavy thick woollen apron and when she reached David she swirled it over his head, smothering

the flames that ate into his flesh. The other women followed, using their clothing to wrap him as he fell.

Only then did David begin to scream. He was still screaming when the doctor from the kibbutz slashed open his pressure suit and pressed the morphine needle into his arm.

THE BRIG SAW THE LAST radar image fade from the plot and heard the young officer report formally, "No further contact."

He stood hunched over the plot and his fists were clenched at his sides. His face was expressionless, but his eyes were terrible.

It seemed that the frantic voices of his two pilots still echoed from the speakers above his head, as they called to each other in the extremes of mortal conflict. And now his son was missing. He wanted to cry out. He closed his eyes tightly for a few seconds, and when he opened them, he was in control again.

"General alert," he snapped. "All squadrons to Red standby." He knew they faced an international crisis. "I want air cover over the area they went down. They may have ejected. Also I want helicopters sent in immediately with medical teams—"

Command bunker moved swiftly into general alert procedure.

"Get me the Prime Minister," he said. He was going to have to do a lot of explaining, and he spared a few vital seconds to damn David Morgan roundly and bitterly.

THE AIR FORCE DOCTOR took one look at David's charred and scorched head and swore softly. "We'll be lucky to save this one." Loosely he swathed the head in Vaseline bandages and they hurried the blanket-wrapped body on the stretcher to the Bell 205 helicopter waiting in the orchard.

The Bell touched down on the helipad at Hadassah Hospital and a medical team was ready for him. One hour and fifty-three minutes after the Mirage hit the irrigation channel David was in the special burns unit on the third floor of the hospital, a secluded little world where everybody wore masks and long green sterile gowns.

Pain was an endless ocean. There were times when the surf ran high and each burst of it threatened to shatter his reason. Again there were times when it was low, almost gentle in its throbbing rhythm and morphine mists enfolded him. Then the mists would part and a brazen sun would beat upon his head, and he would writhe and cry out, until suddenly there was the beloved sting of the needle, and the mists closed about him once more.

Then David became aware of a smell. It was the rotting of his own flesh as streptococcus bacteria attacked the exposed tissue. They fought the infection night and day with drugs, but now the pain was underlined with fevers and terrible burning thirsts.

With the fever came the nightmares to goad him even further beyond the limits of his endurance. "Joe!" he cried out in agony, "Try for the sun, Joe! Break left now—Go! Go!" And then he was sobbing from the ruined and broken mouth. "Oh, Joe! Oh God, no!"

They changed the dressings every forty-eight hours under general anaesthetic, for the entire head was of raw flesh, an expressionless head, like a child's drawing. The remaining flesh of his eyelids had contracted, exposing the eyeballs to the air. They filled the eyes' sockets with a yellow ointment to soothe them, and to keep out the loathsome infection that covered his head.

Eventually it was time for the knife. The contracted eyelids were reshaped and stitched. Then they lifted a long flap of skin from his belly, leaving it still attached at one end, and rolled it up. They strapped his good arm to his side and stitched the free end of the rolled flesh to his forearm, training it to draw its blood supply from there. They brought him back from theatre and left him trussed and helpless.

The head was eventually cleansed of infection, and became glistening and bright red. There were two twisted flaps for ears; a double row of startlingly white teeth where the lips had been eaten away; and a stump for a nose with nostrils like the double muzzles of a shotgun.

Then it was time for the knife again. They freed the roll of flesh from his belly and it dangled from his arm drawing blood and sustenance. Then they grafted the flesh, fashioning a crude lump of a nose, and taut, narrow lips. They opened his chest and robbed his fourth rib of a long sliver of bone and they grafted this to his damaged jawbone.

After nine months the last area of raw flesh was closed beneath the patchwork of skin grafts and stitches. David was no longer a high-infection risk and he was moved from the sterile environment.

"You'll be allowed visitors now," said the consultant. He was a distinguished-looking young surgeon who had left a highly paid post at a Swiss clinic to head the burns and plastic surgery unit.

"I don't think I will be having any visitors," David said.

"Oh, yes, you will. We've had regular inquiries on your progress from a number of people." The surgeon began to move on.

"Doctor," David called him back. "I want a mirror." They were all silent, immediately embarrassed. This request had been denied many times over the last months. "Damn it," David became angry. "You can't protect me from it for ever."

"All right, David," the surgeon agreed gently. "We'll find you a mirror. You must understand that how you are now is not how you will always be. I have been able to make you functional again. There remains much that I can still do. But let me be truthful with you. The delicate muscles of expression, around the eyes and mouth have been destroyed. I cannot replace those. The hair follicles of your lashes and brows and scalp have been burned away. You will be able to wear a wig, but—"

David took his wallet from the bedside locker and drew out a photograph. It was the one which Hannah had taken so long ago of Debra and David sitting at the rock-pool in the oasis of Ein Gedi. He handed it to the surgeon.

"Is that what you looked like, David? I never knew." The regret showed like a quick shadow in his eyes.

"Can you make me look like that again?"

"No. I could not even come close."

"That's all I wanted to know," David took the photograph back. "You say I'm functional now. Let's leave it at that, shall we?"

"You don't want further cosmetic surgery?"

"Doctor, all I want now is a little escape from pain."

"Very well," the surgeon agreed readily. "It is not important that we do it now. You could come back at any time." He walked to the door. "Come on. Let's find a mirror."

There was one in an empty room at the end of the passage. The surgeon stood in the doorway as David crossed towards the mirror and then halted abruptly as he saw his own image.

He gasped aloud and the gash of a mouth parted in sympathy.

It was a tight, almost lipless mouth, like that of a cobra, white-rimmed and harsh. Drawn by the awful fascination of horror, David drew closer to the mirror. His dark hair had concealed the peculiar elongation of his skull. He had never realized that it jutted out behind like that. The skin and flesh of his face was a patchwork, joined by seams of scar tissue drawn tightly over his cheekbones. His eyes were round and startled, with clumsy lids and puffed flesh beneath. His nose was a shapeless blob, and his ears were knarled excrescences.

The gash of a mouth twisted briefly in a horrid rictus, and then regained its frozen shape.

"I can't smile," said David.

"No," the surgeon said. "You have no control of your facial expressions."

That was the truly horrifying aspect of it. The frozen features seemed long dead, incapable of human warmth or feeling.

"We'll have those last few stitches behind your ears out tomorrow, and then you can be discharged. Come back to us when you are ready."

Next day one of the nurses told him that a visitor was waiting for him in the hospital superintendent's office. He was a major from the military provost marshal's office, a lean grey-haired man with cold eyes and a tight hard mouth. He introduced himself without offering to shake hands and then opened the file on the desk in front of him.

"I have been instructed to ask for your resignation from the Israeli Air Force," he started, and David stared at him. In the long pain-filled nights, the thought of flying had seemed like paradise.

"I don't understand," he mumbled.

"If you refuse, we shall convene a court martial and try you for dereliction of duty, and refusing in the face of the enemy to obey the lawful orders of your superior officer."

"I see," David nodded heavily. "It doesn't seem I have any choice."

"I have prepared the necessary documents. Please sign here."

David bowed over the papers and signed.

"Thank you." The major gathered his papers, and placed them in his briefcase. He nodded at David and started for the door.

"So now I am an outcast," said David softly, and the man stopped. His cold grey eyes became ferocious.

"You are responsible for the death of a brother officer, for the destruction of two warplanes and for bringing our country to the brink of open war. You have embarrassed our international friends, and given strength to our enemies." He paused and drew a deep breath. "The recommendation of my office was that you be brought back to trial and that the prosecution ask for the death penalty. It was only the personal intervention of Major-General Mordecai that saved you. In my view, you should consider yourself highly fortunate."

He turned away and his footsteps cracked on the stone floor as he strode from the room.

David was suddenly struck by a reluctance to walk out into the spring sunshine. He went and sat for a long time in the hospital synagogue. The stained-glass window, set high in the wall, filled the air with shafts of coloured light, and the peace and beauty of that place gave him courage when at last he walked out into the square and boarded a bus for Jerusalem.

He found a seat at the rear and as the bus ground slowly up the hill he became aware that he was being watched. He lifted his head to find a little girl of four or five standing on the seat in front of him facing backwards, with one thumb thrust into her mouth. She was studying David's face with total absorption and David felt a sudden warmth of emotion for the child, a longing for the comfort of human contact. He leaned forward in his seat, trying to smile, reaching out a gentle hand to touch the child's arm. She removed her thumb from her mouth and shrank away, turning to her mother and hiding her face in the woman's blouse.

At the next stop David climbed down from the bus. The episode had distressed him terribly.

A taxi dropped him off at Malik Street. The front door was unlocked. Puzzled and alarmed he stepped into the living room. It was as he had left it so many months before, but somebody had cleaned and swept, and there was a vase of gaily coloured dahlias on the olive-wood table.

David smelled food, hot and spicy and tantalizing after the bland hospital fare.

"Hello," he called. "Who is there?"

"Welcome home!" There was a familiar bellow from behind the kitchen. "I didn't expect you so soon," and Ella Kadesh appeared. She wore one of her huge kaftans and an apple-green hat, the brim pinned up at the side by an enormous jade broach and a bunch of ostrich feathers. Her arms were flung wide in a gesture of welcome, and her grin persisted long after the horror had dawned in her eyes.

"Hello, Ella."

"Oh God. What have they done to you, my beautiful young Mars—"

"Listen, you old bag," he said harshly, "if you start blubbering I'm going to throw you down the steps."

She made a huge effort to control her tears as she hugged him to her bosom. "I've got a case of beer in the refrigerator—and I made a pot of curry for us. You'll love my curry, it's the thing I do best—"

David ate with enormous appetite, washing down the fiery food with cold beer as he listened to Ella talk. "They would not let me visit you, but I telephoned every week. The sister let me know you were coming today. So I drove up to make sure you had a welcome—" She tried to avoid looking directly at his face, but when she did the shadows appeared in her eyes. When he finished eating at last, she asked. "What will you do now, David?"

"I would have liked to go back and fly, but they have forced me to resign my commission."

"There was nearly open war. You and Joe did a crazy thing."

David nodded. "I was mad. I wasn't thinking straight that day—after Debra—"

Ella interrupted quickly. "Yes, I know. Share another beer?"

David nodded distractedly. "How is she, Ella?" It was the question he had wanted to ask all along.

"She is just fine, Davey. She has begun a new book."

"Her eyes? Is there any improvement?"

Ella shook her head. "She has come to terms with that now, just as you will come to accept what has happened—"

David was not listening. "Ella, when I was in hospital, every day I hoped—I hoped to hear from her. A card, a word—"

"She didn't know, Davey."

"Didn't know?" David demanded. "What do you mean?"

"After Joe was killed, the Brig was very angry. He believed that you were responsible. He told Debra that you had left Israel, and gone back home. We were all sworn to silence—and that's what Debra believes now."

David nodded, the blank mask of his face concealing his guilt.

"You still haven't answered my question, David. What are you going to do now?"

"I don't know, Ella. I guess I'll have to think about that."

A WARM WIND came off the hills and ruffled the surface of the lake. It caught Debra's hair and shook it out in a loose cloud as she stood on the battlements of the crusader castle, leaning both hands lightly on the head of her cane.

Ella sat on a fallen block of masonry watching Debra's face intently.

"I agreed to keep the truth from you, because I did not want you to torture yourself."

"What has happened to change your mind? What has happened to David?" Debra demanded.

"Yesterday David was discharged from Hadassah Hospital."

"Hospital?" Debra was puzzled. "You don't mean he has been in hospital nine months? He must have been terribly hurt." Debra's initial anger had changed to concern. "How is he now, Ella?"

Ella was silent a moment, and Debra took a pace towards her. "Well?" she asked.

"David's plane flamed out and he was very badly burned about the head. He has completely recovered, but—"

Ella hesitated again, and Debra groped for her hand and found it. "Go on, Ella! But—?"

"David is no longer the most beautiful man I have ever seen. Any woman who sees him now will find it difficult to be near him, let alone love him. He is alone, cut off from the world by the burned mask he wears—"

Debra's eyes had misted, and Ella went on gently. "But there is somebody who will never see that mask. Somebody who remembers only the way he was before." Debra's grip tightened on Ella's hand, and she began to smile.

"He needs you, Debra," Ella said softly. "Will you change your decision now?"

"Fetch him to me, Ella," Debra's voice shook. "Fetch him to me as soon as you can."

DAVID WALKED DOWN the steps from Ella's studio. She had sent him to find Debra who was down on the jetty. It was a day of bright sunlight and he wore open sandals, light silk slacks and a short-sleeved shirt. A wide-brimmed straw hat guarded him from the sun and softened his face with shadow.

A gaudily coloured towel and beach jacket were spread upon the jetty and a transistor radio blared out a rock tune. Far out in the bay Debra was swimming alone. She stopped to tread water and he could see that she was listening for the radio. Then she began to swim again, heading directly towards the jetty.

She came out of the water, and her tread was confident as she walked up the steps and picked up her towel.

David stood near and watched her avidly, seeming to devour her with his eyes. He moved slightly, and the gravel crunched softly under his sandals.

Instantly the lovely head turned towards him, the eyes, wide open and expressive, looked slightly to one side of him. "David?" she asked softly. "Is that you, David?"

He tried to answer her, but his voice failed him and his reply was a small choking sound. She ran to him swiftly, her face lighting with joy. He caught her up, and she clung to him fiercely. "Oh, David, you'll never know how I have missed you," she cried.

She broke from him at last, leaning back to run her hands over his face, feeling its new contours. She felt him begin to pull away, but she stopped him. "My fingers tell me that you are still beautiful—"

"You have lying fingers," he whispered, but she ignored his words, and gave a breathless little laugh.

"Come with me, please, sir." Holding his hand, she ran lightly up the path, dragging him after her. He was amazed at her agility and confidence. She drew him into her cottage and down onto the bed.

The two beautiful young bodies meshed hungrily. Even in the

intervals between their acts of love they clung together desperately; and in their sleep, they groped drowsily but anxiously for each other if they separated.

It was two days before they left the sanctuary of the cottage and walked together along the lake shore. When Ella looked down at them from the terrace and waved, David asked, "Shall we go up to her?"

"Not yet," Debra answered quickly. "I'm not ready to share you with anybody else. Just a little while more, please, David."

And it was another three days before they climbed the path to the studio.

ELLA HAD LAID ON ONE of her gargantuan lunches. They ate beneath the palm trees and drank wine, laughing and talking without restraint. The change in Debra was dramatic, Ella thought, all the reserve gone, the armour in which she had clad her emotions. She was laughing with delight at David's sallies, touching and caressing him as though to reassure herself of his presence.

It was disquieting to see the lovely dark face against that mask of ruined flesh, and yet it was also strangely moving. "For once I did the right thing," Ella decided.

She took up her wine glass. "I give you a toast. I give you David and Debra—and a love made invincible by suffering." And they drank the toast together in golden yellow wine, sitting in golden yellow sunlight, then the mood resumed and they were gay once more.

In the days that followed, David and Debra drew even closer together. The blind girl taught David to see for both of them. He learned to describe colour and shape and movements accurately and incisively. In turn, David, whose own confidence had been shattered, taught confidence to the girl. Her world had shrunk to the small area about the cottage and jetty within which she could find her way surely. Now with David beside her, she was free to move wherever she chose.

Yet they ventured out together only cautiously at first, wandering along the lakeside or climbing the hills towards Nazareth, and each day they swam in the green lake waters. Then one day, they borrowed Ella's speedboat, and planed along the lake to Tiberias.

They moored in the tiny harbour of the marina at Lido Beach and walked up to the town to do their shopping.

David carried a plastic bag that grew steadily heavier until it was ready to overflow. Then they went down the hill to the square and found a table near the harbour wall, beneath a gaily coloured umbrella. They sat touching each other, drinking cold beer and eating pistachio nuts, oblivious to everything and everybody about them even though the other tables were crowded with tourists.

When the sun was low they went to the speedboat, David started the motor and pushed off from the wall, steering for the harbour mouth with Debra sitting close beside him and the motor burbling softly.

A big red-faced tourist looked down from the harbour wall and, thinking that the motor covered his voice, nudged his wife. "Get a look at those two, Mavis. Beauty and the beast, isn't it?"

Debra felt David's arm go rigid under her hand. "Let's go, Davey, darling. Leave them, please."

When they were alone in the cottage, David was silent and Debra could feel his tension. She could think of nothing to say, for the careless words had wounded her as deeply. Later she lay silent and unsleeping beside him. He lay on his back, his arms at his sides and his fists clenched.

He broke the silence at last. "I want to go away from people. We don't need people—do we?"

"No," she whispered. "We don't need them."

"There is a place called Jabulani. It is deep in the African bushveld, far from the nearest town. My father bought it as a hunting lodge thirty years ago—and now it belongs to me."

"Tell me about it." Debra laid her head on his chest, and he stroked her hair, relaxing as he talked.

"There is a wide plain on which grow open forests of mopani and mohobahoba. The grass is yellow gold. At the end of the plain is a line of hills, they look blue in the distance, and their peaks are shaped like the turrets of a fairy castle. Between the hills there are pools. My father named them 'The String of Pearls', and that's what they look like. They give Jabulani its special character, for they provide water for all the wild life of the plain."

"What does Jabulani mean?" Debra asked.

"It means the 'place of rejoicing'," he told her.

"I want to go there with you," she said.

"What about Israel," he asked. "Will you not miss it?"

"No,"she shook her head. "I will take it with me—in my heart."

ELLA WENT UP TO JERUSALEM with them, to help Debra select the furniture they would take with them. David left the women at Malik Street and drove out to Ein Karem.

The Brig was waiting for him in his study. When David greeted him from the doorway he looked up coldly, and there was no warmth or pity in the fierce warrior eyes. "You come to me with the blood of my son upon your hands," he said, and David froze at the words. After a few moments the Brig indicated a chair and David crossed stiffly to it and sat down.

"If you had suffered less, I would have made you answer for more," said the Brig. "But vengeance and hatred are barren things —as you have discovered."

David dropped his eyes to the floor, and the Brig sighed heavily. "Why do you come to me?" he asked.

"I wish to marry your daughter, sir."

"You are asking me—or telling me?" the Brig demanded, and without waiting for an answer he went on. "You abused the power I gave you, and in doing it you killed my son and brought my country to the verge of war. If you abuse this also, if you bring my daughter pain or unhappiness, I will seek you out. Depend upon it."

THE SYNAGOGUE AT JERUSALEM UNIVERSITY is a gleaming white structure, shaped like the tent of a desert wanderer. The Judas trees were in full bloom and the wedding party was larger than they had planned, for apart from the immediate family there were Debra's colleagues from the university, some of the boys from the squadron, Ella, Doctor Edelman, the eye surgeon who had worked on Debra, and a dozen others. After the simple ceremony, they walked through the university grounds to a reception room. It was a quiet gathering with little laughter or joking.

Before he left, Dr. Edelman drew David aside. "Watch for any sign of atrophy in her eyes, any complaints of pain, headaches. And if you have any questions, no matter how trivial, write to me."

"Thank you, doctor."

They shook hands. "Good luck," said Edelman.

Debra, her mother, and Ella all broke down simultaneously at the airport. The Brig and David stood by, stiff and awkward, until the first warning broadcast gave David an excuse to draw Debra gently away.

They climbed the boarding ladder into the waiting Boeing without looking back.

IT WAS NECESSARY to spend some time in Cape Town before they could escape to Jabulani.

David took a suite at the Mount Nelson Hotel, and spent ten days there with the accountants who managed his trust funds.

One evening Mitzi and her husband, Cecil, came to see them, but the visit was not a success. They were both very reserved and at first David thought that his disfigurement was worrying them. Then, halfway through the evening Mitzi gave a eulogy on the strides that Cecil was making at Morgan group, and Cecil asked innocently, "Are you thinking of joining us at the Group? I'm sure we could find something useful for you to do—ha, ha!"

David assured them quietly. "No. You won't have to worry about me, Cecil. You take over from Uncle Paul with my blessing."

"Good Lord, I didn't mean that," Cecil was shocked, but Mitzi was straightforward.

"He really will be very good . . . and you never were interested, were you?"

After that evening they did not see the couple again, and since Paul Morgan was away in Europe, David had fulfilled his family obligations and could concentrate on the preparations for the move.

Barney Venter spent a week with them in choosing a suitable aircraft to handle the bush airstrip and yet give David the type of performance he enjoyed. At last they decided on a Piper Navajo, a six-seater with two big 300 h.p. Lycoming engines.

On the last day David and Debra drove to a farm near Paarl. The owner's wife was a dog breeder and when they went down to the kennels one of her labrador pups walked directly to Debra and placed a cold nose on her leg. Debra squatted and fondled him for a few moments.

"He smells like old leather," she said. "What colour is he?"

"Black," said David. "Black as a Zulu."

"That's what we'll call him," said Debra. "Zulu."

"You want us to choose this one?" David asked.

"No," Debra laughed. "He chose us."

When they flew northwards the next morning the pup was indignant at being placed in the back seat. He leaped over Debra's shoulder and took up position in her lap. "It looks like I have competition," David muttered ruefully.

JABULANI WAS ONE OF A BLOCK of estates that bounded the Kruger National Park—the most spectacular nature reserve on earth. It had once been a family hunting estate but little use had been made of it in the last fifteen years. David's father had been an enthusiastic sportsman, and many of David's school holidays had been spent there. However, after his father's death, the visits to Jabulani had become shorter and farther apart. It was seven years since the last visit, when he had brought up a party of brother officers from his squadron. Then it had been immaculately run by Sam, the black overseer, butler and game ranger.

"Where is Sam?" was the first question David asked of the two servants who hurried down from the homestead to meet the aircraft.

"Sam gone."

"Where to?" And the answer was the eloquent shrug of Africa. Their uniforms were dirty, and their manner uninterested.

"Where is the Land-Rover?"

"She is dead."

They walked up to the homestead and David had more unpleasant surprises. The buildings were dilapidated, the interiors filthy. The mosquito gauze, that was intended to keep the wide verandas insect-free, was breaking away in tatters. The grounds were thick with rank weed, and not only the Land-Rover had died. No single piece of machinery on the estate—water pump, toilet cistern, electricity generator, motor vehicle—was in working order.

"It's a mess, a frightful mess," David told Debra as they sat on the front step and drank mugs of sweet tea. Fortunately David had thought to bring emergency supplies with them.

"Oh, Davey, I am sorry, because I like it here. It's so peaceful."

"Don't be sorry. I'm not. These old huts were built by Gramps back in the twenties—and they weren't very well built even then. It's a fine excuse to tear the whole lot down, and build again." David's voice was full of a determination that Debra had not heard for so long.

They flew into Nelspruit, the nearest large town, the following day. With an architect they planned the new homestead, taking into consideration all their special requirements—a large airy study for Debra, workshop and office for David, a kitchen laid out for a blind cook, and finally a nursery. The hutment for the servants would be a quarter of a mile away, screened by trees and the shoulder of the rocky kopje that rose behind the homestead.

David bribed a building contractor from Nelspruit to postpone all his other work and bring his workmen out to Jabulani. While they worked on the main house, David was busy resurfacing the airstrip, and repairing the machinery.

Within two months the new homestead was habitable. Debra set up her tape recorders beneath the big windows overlooking the shaded front garden, where the afternoon breeze was cool. Soon she had trained the servants to replace each item of furniture in its exact position and could move about the house with confidence. Always Zulu, the labrador pup, moved like a glossy shadow beside her. He had decided that Debra needed his constant care.

David set up a large bird bath under the trees outside Debra's window, so her tapes had as background the chatter of half a dozen varieties of wild birds. She soon recognized each individual call and would pick out a stranger immediately. "David, there's a new bird. What does he look like?"

And he described not only its plumage, but its mannerisms and its habits.

Debra had discovered a typist in Nelspruit who could speak Hebrew, and David took tapes to her whenever he flew to town for supplies and the mail, and he brought typing back for checking.

They worked together on this task, David reading aloud to her and making the alterations she asked for. He made a habit of reading almost everything, from newspapers to novels, aloud.

"Who needs Braille with you around," Debra once remarked.

In time all the building was completed and the furniture from

100

Malik Street arrived, making Jabulani truly their home. The olive-wood table was placed under the window in Debra's workroom, and David hung the Ella Kadesh painting above the fireplace. The great brass bed was set up in the bedroom, and covered with the ivory-coloured bedspread.

DURING THE MONTHS OF PREPARATION they had not left the immediate neighbourhood of the homestead, but now the rush and bustle was over.

"We have eighteen thousand acres and plenty of four-footed neighbours—let's go check it all out," David suggested.

They packed a cold lunch and climbed into the Land-Rover with Zulu relegated to the back. The road led them to the String of Pearls, the focal point of all life upon the estate.

They left the Land-Rover amongst the fever trees and went down to the ruins of a thatched summer house on the bank of the main pool. David dug a thick earthworm and threw it into the clear shallows. A dark shape half as long as his arm rushed out of the depths.

"Wow!" David laughed. "There are still a few fat ones around. We will have to bring down the rods."

As they wandered along the edge of the reed banks David reminisced about his childhood, until gradually he fell into silence, and Debra asked, "Is something wrong, David?"

"There are no animals." His tone was puzzled. "Birds, yes. But we haven't seen a single animal." He stopped at a place that was clear of reeds, where the bank shelved gently. "This used to be a favourite drinking place." He stooped to examine the ground care-fully. "Hardly any spoor, just a few kudu and a small troop of baboon. Let's go and see the rest of the estate," he muttered, "there is something very odd here."

The leisurely outing became a desperate hunt, as they scoured the thickets and the open glades in the Land-Rover.

"Not even an impala." David was worried and anxious. "There used to be thousands of them."

A little before noon they emerged abruptly on the fire-brake track, the eastern boundary between Jabulani and the National Park. The Park was larger than the state of Israel, five million acres of virgin wilderness, and home for more than a million wild animals.

David stopped the Land-Rover, and began to swear.

"What's made you so happy?" Debra demanded.

"Look at that—just look at that!" David ranted.

"I wish I could."

"Sorry, Debs. It's a game fence!" It stood eight feet high and the uprights were hardwood poles thick as a man's thigh, while the mesh of the fence was heavy-gauge barbed-wire. "The National Park's people have cut us off! No wonder there are no animals."

As they drove back to the homestead David explained how there had always been an open boundary with the Park. It had suited everybody, for Jabulani's sweet grazing and its pools helped to carry the herds through times of drought and scarcity.

"The wild animals have become very important to you," Debra said.

"Yes. When they were here, I guess I just took them for granted —but now they are gone, well, now they are very important." He laughed bitterly. "I'm going to get them to pull that fence out. I shall get hold of the head warden right away."

David remembered when Conrad Berg had been the warden in charge of the southern portion of the park, but not yet the chief. There was a body of legend about him, and two of these stories showed clearly the type of man he was.

Caught in a lonely area of the reserve after dark with a broken-down truck, he was walking home when he was attacked by a full-grown male lion. In the struggle he had been terribly mauled, yet he had managed to kill the animal with a small sheath knife, stabbing it repeatedly until he hit the jugular. He had then walked five miles with a hyena pack following him expectantly.

On another occasion one of the neighbouring estate owners had poached one of the Park's lions. He was a man high in government and he had laughed at Berg. "What are you going to do about it, my friend? Don't you like your job?"

Ignoring pressure from above, Berg collected his evidence and issued a summons. The pressure increased as the court date approached, but he never wavered. The important personage finally stood in the dock, and was sentenced to a thousand pounds' fine or six months at hard labour. Afterwards he had shaken Berg's

102

hand and said to him, "Thank you for a lesson in courage." Perhaps this was one of the reasons Berg was now chief warden.

He stood beside his game fence where he had arranged over the telephone to meet David, clenched fists on hips, epitomizing the truculent male animal guarding its territory. He was a big man, with thick muscled arms still scarred from the lion attack, and a red, sunburned face. He wore the uniform and slouch hat of the Park's service, with the green cloth badges on his epaulets. Behind him was his brown Chevy truck with the Park's emblem on the door, and two black game rangers seated in the back. One of them holding a heavy rifle.

David parked close beside the fence and he and Debra climbed down and went to the wire. "Mr. Berg. I am David Morgan. I remember you from when my father owned Jabulani. I'd like you to meet my wife."

Berg's expression wavered. Naturally he had heard all the rumours about the new owner of Jabulani, yet he was unprepared for this dreadfully mutilated young man, and his blind but beautiful wife. With an awkward gallantry he doffed his hat, then realized she would not see the gesture. He murmured a greeting and when David thrust his hand through the fence he shook it cautiously.

Debra and David turned their combined charm upon Berg, whose defences slowly softened as they chatted.

"Isn't that Sam who used to work on Jabulani?" David pointed to the game ranger in the truck who held Berg's rifle.

"*Ja*," Berg was guarded. "He came to me of his own accord."

"He wouldn't remember me, of course, not the way I look now. But he was a fine ranger, and the place certainly went to the bad without him to look after it." Then David went into a frontal assault. "The other thing which has ruined us is this fence of yours. Why did you do it?"

"For good reason. Your daddy was a *sportsman*." Berg spat the word out. "He used to parade donkeys along the boundary to tempt my lions out."

David opened his mouth to protest, and then closed it slowly. It was true. He remembered the donkeys and the lion skins pegged out to dry behind the homestead.

"So that's why you put up the fence."

"No."

"Why then?"

"Because for fifteen years Jabulani has been under the care of an absentee landlord who didn't give a good damn what happened to it. It became a poachers' paradise and when Sam here tried to do something about it, he got beaten up. When that didn't stop him somebody set fire to his hut at night. They burned two of his kids to death—"

David felt his soul quail at the memory of flames on flesh. "I didn't know," he said gruffly.

"No, you were too busy making money or whatever is your particular form of pleasure." Berg was angry. "So at last Sam came to me and I gave him a job. Then I strung this fence."

"There is nothing left on Jabulani. I want the animals back."

"Why?" Berg scoffed. "So you can fly your pals down from Jo'burg for the weekend to shoot my lions?"

"Look here," said David. "If you pull your fence out, I'll have Jabulani declared a private nature reserve—"

Berg had been about to say more, but David's declaration dried the words.

"You know what that means?" he asked at last. "You place yourself under our jurisdiction, completely."

"Yes. I know. But there is something more. I'd undertake to fence the other three boundaries to your satisfaction, and maintain a force of private game rangers—all at my own expense."

Conrad Berg lifted his hat and scratched pensively at the long sparse grey hairs that covered his pate. "Man," he said mournfully, "how can I say no to that?"

"I think the first thing we should work on is the poachers," David suggested. "Let's snatch a couple of those and make a few examples."

For the first time during the meeting, Berg's big red face split into a happy grin. "I think I'm going to enjoy having you as a neighbour," he said.

"Won't you come to dinner with us tomorrow night. You and your wife?" Debra asked with relief.

"It will be a mighty great pleasure, ma'am."

"I'll get out the whisky bottle," said David.

"That's kind of you," said Conrad Berg seriously, "but the missus and I only drink Old Buck dry gin, with a little water."

"I'll see to it," said David just as seriously.

JANE BERG WAS A SLIM WOMAN of about Conrad's age. She had a dried-out face, lined and browned by the sun. Her hair was sun-bleached and streaked with grey, and she was probably the only thing in the world that Conrad was afraid of.

"I'm talking, Connie," was enough to halt any flow of eloquence from her spouse, and a significant glance at her empty glass sent him with elephantine haste for a refill. Conrad had a great deal of trouble finishing any story or statement, for Jane had to correct the details during the telling.

At dinner Conrad ate four steaks with unreserved pleasure although he spurned the wine. "That stuff is poison. Killed one of my uncles," and stayed with Old Buck gin.

Afterwards they sat about the cavernous fireplace with its cheer-fully blazing logs and Conrad explained, with Jane's assistance, the problems that David would face on Jabulani.

"You get a few of the black poachers coming in from the north—"

"Or across the river," Jane added.

"Or across the river, but they are no sweat. They don't kill that much, and they are just amateurs."

"Who are the professionals?"

"Where the dirt road from Jabulani meets the big national high-way, about thirty miles from here—"

"At a place called Bandolier Hill," Jane supplied the name.

"—there is a general dealer's store. The owner has been there eight years now, and I have been after him all that time, but he's the craftiest bastard—I'm sorry, Mrs. Morgan—I have ever run into. Catch him, and half your worries are over."

"What's his name?"

"Johan Akkers," Jane said. "Old Sam suspects it was Akkers who arranged to have him beaten and to burn his hut."

"How are we going to get him?" David mused. "There isn't anything left on Jabulani to tempt him."

"No, you haven't got anything to tempt him right now," Berg

105

said, "but about the first week in September the marula trees down by your pools will come into fruit, and my elephants are going to flatten my fence to get at them. A lot of other game are going to follow, and you can lay any odds that our friend Akkers will know within an hour when the fence goes."

"This time he may get a surprise," David said softly. "I think that we might run down to Bandolier Hill tomorrow and have a look at this gentleman."

"One thing is for sure—" said Jane Berg indistinctly, slightly owl-eyed by gin, "—a genelman, he is not."

THE TRADING POST AT BANDOLIER HILL was four or five hundred yards from the road junction, set back amidst a grove of mango trees. It was an unlovely building of mud brick and corrugated iron roof, the walls plastered thickly with advertisements.

David parked the Land-Rover in the dusty yard beneath the raised porch. At the side of the building was parked an old green Ford one-ton truck. In the shade of the porch squatted a dozen or so potential customers—African women, dressed in long cotton print dresses, timeless in their patience and showing no curiosity about the occupants of the Land-Rover.

Set in the centre of the yard was a thick pole, fifteen feet tall, topped by a wooden structure like a dog kennel. David exclaimed as a big brown furry animal emerged from the kennel with a chain buckled about its waist. It descended the pole in one swift action.

"It's one of the biggest bull baboons I've ever seen." Quickly he described it to Debra, as the baboon ruffled out its thick mane, moved out to the chain's limit and sat down in a repellently humanoid attitude, regarding them through small, brown, close-set eyes.

"A nasty beast," David told Debra. He weighed ninety pounds, with a long dog-like muzzle and a jaw full of yellow fangs. After the hyena, he was the most hated animal of the veld—cunning, cruel and greedy, all the vices of man and none of his graces.

While David's attention was on the baboon, a man came out of the store and leaned on one of the pillars of the veranda. "What can I do for you, Mr. Morgan?" he asked in a thick accent. He was of middle age, tall and spare with close-cropped greying hair and deep set eyes. His teeth were badly fitting with pink plastic gums.

"How did you know my name?" David asked.

He grinned. "Could only be you, scarred face and blind wife."

The man took from his pocket a clasp knife and a stick of biltong —black wind-dried meat—and cut a slice as though it were a plug of tobacco, popping it into his mouth and chewing noisily. "Like I asked—what can we do for you?"

"I need nails and paint." David climbed out of the Land-Rover.

"Heard you did all your buying in Nelspruit." Akkers studied David's ruined face with calculated insolence.

"I thought there was a law against caging or chaining wild animals." David's resentment showed in his tone.

Akkers grinned again, still chewing. "I got a permit—you want to see it?"

David shook his head, and climbed the steps to the veranda, leaving Debra in the car. "What about the nails and paint?"

"Go on in," Akkers was still grinning. "My nigger helper will look after you."

David hesitated and then walked into the store. It smelled of carbolic soap and kerosene and maize meal. The shelves were loaded with cheap groceries, patent medicines, bolts of cloth and hundreds of other items. He found the African assistant and began his purchases.

Outside Debra climbed from the Land-Rover and leaned against the door. The labrador scrambled down after her and sniffed about on the veranda.

"Nice dog," said Akkers.

"Thank you." Debra nodded politely.

Akkers glanced cunningly at his pet baboon, and a flash of understanding passed between them. With a leap and bound the baboon shot up the pole and disappeared into the kennel.

Akkers carefully cut another slice of biltong. "You like it out at Jabulani?" he asked Debra, and at the same time he offered the scrap of dried meat to the dog.

"We are very happy there," Debra replied stiffly. Zulu sniffed the titbit, and his tail beat like a metronome. He gulped it eagerly. Twice more Akkers fed him the scraps, and Zulu's muzzle was damp with saliva.

The women were watching with lively interest now. They had seen this happen before with a dog. Debra stood blind and unsuspecting.

Akkers offered a larger piece to Zulu, but when he reached for it Akkers pulled his hand away and walked down the steps with Zulu following eagerly.

At the bottom he showed the dog the biltong once more. "Get it, boy," he said softly and threw the meat at the base of the baboon's pole.

Zulu bounded forward, still slightly clumsy on his big puppy paws. The baboon came out of his kennel like a grey blur and dropped fifteen feet through the air, his limbs spread and his jaws open in a snarl. He hurled his ninety pounds at the unsuspecting pup.

Zulu went down and over, rolling on his back with a startled yelp, but before he could find his feet or his wits, the baboon had pinned him with his powerful legs and buried his long yellow fangs deep into his belly.

Zulu screamed in dreadful agony, and Debra ran forward. Akkers shot out a foot and tripped her, sending her sprawling on her hands and knees. "Leave it, lady," he warned her, still grinning. "You'll get hurt if you interfere."

Again the pup screamed, and Debra rolled blindly to her feet. "David!" she cried wildly. "David—help me!"

David came running out of the building. He took in the scene at a glance and snatched up a pick handle from the pile by the door.

The baboon saw him coming and released Zulu. He leaped for the pole, racing upwards to perch on the roof of the kennel, his jowls red with blood, as he shrieked and jabbered, bouncing up and down with excitement.

David gently carried Zulu to the Land-Rover, and ripped his bush jacket into strips as he tried to bind up the torn belly.

"David, what is it?" Debra pleaded with him, and he explained in a few terse Hebrew sentences.

"Get in," he told her and he laid the injured labrador in her lap.

Akkers was back at the doorway of his shop laughing. "Hey, Mr. Morgan, don't forget your nails!"

David swung round to face him. His face felt tight and hot, and

his dark eyes blazed with anger. He started up the steps, his fists clenched at his sides.

Akkers stepped backwards and reached behind the shop counter. He lifted out an old double-barrelled shotgun and cocked both hammers. "Self-defence, Mr. Morgan, with witnesses," he pointed out with sadistic relish.

David paused at the top of the steps. Debra called anxiously from the Land-Rover, "David, hurry—oh, please hurry." The pup was squirming weakly in her lap.

"We'll meet again." David's anger thickened his tongue.

"That will be fun," said Akkers, and David turned away.

Akkers watched the Land-Rover swing into the road before he set the shotgun aside. He went out into the sunlight, and the baboon scrambled down to meet him. It jumped up and clung to him like a child. Akkers placed a sweet tenderly between the terrible yellow fangs. "You lovely old thing," he chuckled.

CONRAD BERG CALLED to sample the Old Buck gin, and to tell David that his application to have Jabulani declared a private nature reserve had been approved and that the necessary documentation would soon be ready. "Do you want me to pull the fence out now?"

"No," David answered grimly. "Let it stand. I don't want Akkers frightened off. The man is a threat to us and to all we are trying to build at Jabulani. I'm going to get him."

"*Ja,*" Conrad agreed. "We have got to get him." He called Zulu to him and examined the scar where a veterinary surgeon had worked for over two hours repairing the torn belly. It was ridged and shaped like forked lightning. "We'll both get the bastard," he muttered, and then glanced guiltily at Debra. "Sorry, Mrs. Morgan."

"I couldn't agree more, Mr. Berg," she said softly, and Zulu watched her attentively when she spoke. Like all young things, he had healed cleanly and quickly.

The marula grove that ran thickly along the base of the hills about the String of Pearls came into flower and soon the green plum-shaped fruits began to turn yellow as they ripened. Their yeasty smell was heavy on the warm evening breeze.

The elephant herd came up from the south, forsaking the lush reed beds for the promise of a marula harvest. They were led by two old bulls, who for forty years had made the annual pilgrimage to the String of Pearls, and there were fifteen breeding cows with calves running at heel and many adolescents. They moved slowly, sailing like ghostly grey galleons through the bush, until they reached Conrad Berg's fence.

For reasons of pachyderm prestige, or perhaps merely for mischievous delight, each elephant selected his own concrete-embedded fence pole, and snapped it. They flattened over a mile of the fence and used the broken poles like tightropes, to avoid treading on the barbed-wire. Once across, they streamed down to the pools to spend a night feasting on the yellow berries. At dawn they moved back across the ruined fence into the safety of the Park.

Conrad Berg and Sam met David at the remains of the fence. Conrad shook his head as he surveyed the destruction, chuckling ruefully. "It's old Mahommed and his pal One-Eye, I'd know that spoor anywhere. They just couldn't help themselves—the bastards—" He glanced quickly at Debra in the Land-Rover.

"That's perfectly all right, Mr. Berg," she forestalled his apology.

Sam had been casting back and forth along the brake road and now he came to where they stood.

"Hello, Sam," David greeted him. It had taken a lot of persuasion to get Sam to accept that this terribly disfigured face belonged to the young *nkosi* David whom he had taught to track and shoot.

Sam saluted David with a flourish. He took his uniform very seriously and conducted himself like a guardsman now. It was difficult to tell his age, for he had the broad smooth face of a Nguni—the aristocratic warrior of Africa—but David knew that he had worked at Jabulani for forty years before leaving. Sam must be approaching sixty.

He made his report to Conrad, describing the animals which had crossed into Jabulani. "There is also a herd of buffalo, forty-three of them," he concluded. He spoke in simple Zulu that David could follow.

"That will bring Akkers running—the sirloin of a young buffalo makes the finest biltong there is," Conrad observed dryly.

"How long will it be before he knows the fence is down?" David

111

asked, and Conrad fell into a rapid-fire discussion with Sam that lost David after the first few sentences.

"Sam says he knows already," Conrad explained. "All your servants buy at his store and he pays them for that sort of information. Sam is dead keen to help us grab Akkers—and he has a plan of action all worked out."

"Let's hear it."

"Well, as long as you are in residence at Jabulani Akkers is going to restrict his activities to night poaching. He knows every trick there is and we will never get him."

"So?"

"You must tell your servants that you are going to Cape Town on business for two weeks. Akkers will know as soon as you leave and he will believe he has Jabulani to himself. Sam will remain on one of the kopjes near here with a two-way radio. The height will let him watch the whole estate. . . ." For an hour more they discussed the details of the plan, then they shook hands and parted.

After lunch the next day David loaded his and Debra's bags into the Navajo. He paid the servants two weeks' wages in advance. "I shall return before the end of the month," he told them.

He parked the Land-Rover in the hangar facing the open doorway, ready for a quick start. He took off and kept on a westerly heading, passing directly over Bandolier Hill, until the hill sank from view below the horizon. Then he came around on a wide circle to the south and lined up for Skukuza, the main camp of the Kruger National Park.

Conrad Berg was at the airstrip to meet them, and Jane had placed fresh flowers in the guest room. Jabulani lay fifty miles away in the northwest.

IT WAS LIKE SQUADRON "RED" STANDBY AGAIN, with the Navajo parked under a shady tree at the end of the Skukuza airstrip, and the radio set switched on, crackling faintly on the frequency of Sam's transmission, as he waited patiently on the hill.

The day was oppressively hot, with the threat of a rainstorm looming up out of the east. Debra, David and Conrad sat in the shade of the aircraft's wing. They chatted in desultory fashion, but always listening to the radio crackle.

112

"He is not going to come," said Debra a little before noon.

"He'll come," Conrad contradicted her. "Those buffalo are too much temptation. Perhaps not today, but tomorrow or the next he'll come.

Suddenly the radio set throbbed and hummed. Sam's voice carried clearly to where they sat.

"I see him, Nkosi."

"Red standby—Go! Go!" shouted David, and they rushed for the cabin door. He grabbed Debra's arm and guided her to her seat.

"Bright Lance, airborne and climbing," David laughed with excitement and then the memory of Joe stabbed him. But he shut his mind to it and banked steeply onto his heading, staying at tree-top level.

Conrad was hunched in the seat behind them, his face even redder than usual. "Where is the Land-Rover key?" he demanded anxiously.

"I left it in the ignition. Have you got your walkie-talkie?"

"Here!" It was gripped in one of his huge paws, his double-barrelled .450 magnum in the other.

They flashed over the boundary fence and ahead of them lay the hills of Jabulani.

"Get ready," David told Conrad, and flew the Navajo into the airstrip, taxiing up to the hangar.

Conrad jumped down and raced to the Land-Rover. Immediately David opened the throttle and swung the aircraft around, lining up for take-off.

As he climbed, he saw the Land-Rover racing across the airstrip, dragging a cloak of dust behind it. "Do you read me, Connie?"

"Loud and clear," Conrad's voice boomed out of the speaker.

David followed the grey ribbon of the public road, flying five hundred feet above it, and searched the open parkland until he saw a green Ford truck. A thicket of wild ebony concealed it from observation at ground level.

"Connie, he's stashed the truck in a clump of ebony about half a mile down the bank of the Luzane stream. Your best route is to follow the road to the bridge, then go down into the dry river bed and try and cut him off before he gets to it."

"O.K., David."

"I'm going to try and spot the man himself—chase him into your arms." David turned towards the hills, sweeping and searching. From the highest peak, a tiny figure waved frantically. "Sam," he grunted. "Doing a war dance." He altered course slightly to pass him closely, and Sam stabbed with an extended arm towards the west. David acknowledged with a wave, and turned.

Ahead the plain spread, dappled like a leopard's back with dark bush and golden glades of grass. He flew for a minute before he saw a black mass, moving ahead, dark and amorphous against the pale grass.

"Buffalo," he told Debra. "On the run. Something has alarmed them." She sat still and intent beside him.

"Ah!" David shouted. "Got him—with blood on his hands!"

In the centre of a large clearing lay the body of a dead buffalo. Four men stood around it, obviously about to begin butchering the carcass. Three of them were Africans. The fourth man was Johan Akkers. There was no mistaking the tall gaunt frame. He wore an old black Fedora hat on his head, strangely formal attire for poaching, and he carried a rifle in his right hand. At the sound of the aircraft he swung round and stared into the sky, frozen with the shock of discovery.

"You bloody swine," whispered David. "Hold on!" he warned Debra, and flew straight at the man.

The group around the dead buffalo scattered, but David selected the lanky galloping frame of Akkers and bore down on him. The tips of his propellers clipped the dry grass, as he swiftly lined up to cut him down.

As David braced himself for the impact Akkers glanced back and his face was grey with fright. He saw the murderous blades merely feet from him, and he threw himself flat into the grass.

The Navajo roared over his body, and David pulled the plane into a steep turn, with the wing-tip brushing the grass. As he came round he saw that Akkers was up and running, and only fifty paces from the edge of the trees. David sped across the clearing, but the lumbering figure reached the sanctuary of a big leadwood trunk, whirled and raised the rifle to his shoulder.

"Down!" David shouted, pushing Debra's head below the level of the windshield.

114

He pulled open the throttle and climbed steeply away but even above the bellow of the engines, he heard the heavy bullet clang into the fuselage of the aircraft.

"What was that, David?" Debra pleaded.

"He fired at us, but we've got him on the run. He'll head back for his truck now, and find Conrad waiting for him."

Circling above the trees David caught glimpses of Akkers trotting back along his escape route.

"David, can you hear me?" Conrad's voice boomed.

"What is it, Connie?"

"We've got trouble. I've hit a rock in your Land-Rover and knocked out the sump. She's had it."

"How far are you from the Luzane stream?" David demanded.

"About three miles."

"God, he'll beat you," David swore. "He's only two miles."

"You'll see. I'll be there waiting for him," Berg promised.

"Good luck," David called, and the transmission went dead.

Below them Akkers was skirting the base of the hills, his black hat bobbing along amongst the trees. Suddenly, a movement caught David's eye on the hill above Akkers. For a moment he thought it was an animal, then with an intake of breath he realized that he was mistaken.

"What is it?" Debra demanded, sensing his concern.

"It's Sam, the damned fool. Connie told him not to leave his post—he's unarmed—but he's haring down the slope to try and cut Akkers off."

"Can't you stop him?" Debra asked anxiously.

"Hold on," David told her. Then, looking down, he saw that Akkers had become aware of the running figure also. He stopped dead, and half-lifted the rifle, perhaps he shouted a warning but Sam kept on down, bounding over the rocky ground towards the man who had burned his children to death.

Akkers lifted the rifle to his shoulder and Sam's upper torso was flung violently backwards by the impact of the heavy bullet. His body rolled down the slope and came to a sprawling halt in a clump of scrub.

"Connie," David spoke hoarsely into his handset, "Akkers has just killed Sam."

CONRAD BERG RAN HEAVILY over the broken sandy ground. He had lost his hat and sweat poured down his face, stinging his eyes and plastering his lank grey hair to his forehead.

He looked up and saw David's aircraft circling ahead of him, marking Akkers's position. Clearly Conrad was losing ground in the desperate race, and he was burning the last of his reserves.

Suddenly the earth seemed to fall away under him, and he pitched forward down the steep bank of the Luzane stream, to finish lying on his back in the white river sand. The radio was digging painfully into his flesh and he dragged it out from under him. "David—" he croaked. "I am in the bed of the stream—can you see me?"

The aircraft was directly overhead now, and David's answer came back immediately. "I see you, Connie, you are a hundred yards downstream from the truck. Akkers has just reached it, he'll be coming back down the river bed at any moment."

Gasping for breath, Conrad dragged himself to his knees—and at that moment he heard the whirl and catch and purr of an engine. He unslung his rifle, pulled himself to his feet, and staggered into the centre of the dry river bed. It was fifteen feet wide at this point and made a good illegal access road into Jabulani. The tracks of Akkers's truck were clearly etched in the soft sand. Suddenly, the truck reached a crescendo as it came skidding wildly around the bend, and raced down towards him. "Stop!" Conrad shouted. "Stop or I shoot!"

Akkers began to laugh, and there was no slackening in the truck's rocking charge.

Conrad lifted the rifle and sighted down the stubby double barrels. At that range, he could have put a bullet through each of Akkers's eyes. But Berg was essentially a gentle person. His whole thinking was centred on protecting and cherishing life and he could not pull the trigger.

With the truck fifteen feet away, he threw himself aside, and Akkers swung the wheel, deliberately driving for him.

He caught Conrad a glancing blow with the side of the truck, hurling him away. The truck slewed out of control, hitting the bank farther down the stream, but Akkers got the truck under control again, and went roaring on down the river bed.

As the truck had hit him, Conrad had felt his hip shatter like glass, and now one leg was twisted at a grotesque angle. With difficulty he dragged himself to his radio. "David," he whispered into the microphone, "I couldn't stop him. He got away."

David picked the truck up as it came charging up the river bank and onto the road. It raced westwards towards Bandolier Hill and the highway, dust boiling out from behind, marking its position clearly for David as he turned two miles ahead of it.

The road ran arrow-straight, hedged in with thick timber. As David completed his turn he lowered his landing gear and touched down lightly, taking the Navajo along the centre of the road under power but holding her down. He had speed enough to lift off if Akkers chose a collision rather than surrender.

Ahead was a hump in the road, and as they rolled swiftly towards it the green truck suddenly burst over the crest, not more than a hundred yards ahead.

Akkers saw the terrible spinning discs of the propellers and wrenched the wheel hard over. The truck skidded, rocketing off the narrow road. The front wheels caught the drainage ditch and the truck cartwheeled twice, smashing the windows and bursting the doors open. She ended on her side against a tree.

David shut the throttles and braked. "Wait here," he shouted at Debra, and sprinted back along the road towards the wreckage of the truck.

Akkers saw him coming. He had been thrown clear and now dragged himself shakily to his feet beside the truck. David was close, leaping the irrigation ditch, and Akkers groped for the hunting knife on his belt. It was eight inches of Sheffield steel, honed to a razor edge, and he hefted it underhanded, in the classic grip of the knife-fighter.

David stopped short of him, his eyes fastened on the knife, and Akkers began to laugh, a falsetto and hysterical giggle. The knife weaved in a slow mesmeric movement and caught the sun in bright points of light. David crouched and circled, screwing up his nerve to go in against the naked steel.

Akkers feinted swiftly, leaping in, and when David broke away, he let out a fresh burst of high laughter. Again they circled, and slowly Akkers drove David back against the body of the truck, cornering him there. He charged and the knife drove upwards for David's belly.

David caught the knife hand at the wrist, forcing it down. They were chest to chest now, face to face. They swayed and shuffled, panting, grunting, straining, until they fell, still locked together, against the bonnet of the truck.

David was holding onto Akkers's knife arm with both his hands when he felt Akkers's free hand groping for his throat. He ducked his head down, pressing his chin against his chest but the steel hard fingers probed mercilessly forcing his chin up, and beginning to squeeze the life out of him.

David's vision starred and then began to fade. The smashed windscreen of the truck was beside his shoulder and, with one last explosive effort, David dragged Akkers's knife arm around onto the jagged shards of glass.

Akkers's strangling grip relaxed as David sawed back and forth, slashing and ripping the arm so that the knife dropped from the lifeless fingers and Akkers screamed.

David shoved him away. Akkers fell to his knees and David massaged the bruised flesh of his throat, gasping for breath.

"I'm dying! I'm bleeding to death!" screamed Akkers, holding the mutilated arm to his belly. "You've got to save me—don't let me die."

David pushed himself away from the truck and swung his right leg into a flying kick that took Akkers cleanly under the chin and snapped his head back.

MR. JUSTICE BARNARD of the Transvaal division of the Supreme Court found Johan Akkers guilty on twelve counts under the wild-life conservation act, sentencing him to three years hard labour. He found him guilty on two counts of assault with intent to do grievous bodily harm, and sentenced him to eight years imprisonment. On the final charge of murder he found Akkers guilty and said in court, "In considering sentence of death on this charge, I am satisfied that the accused was acting like an animal in a trap, and that there was no element of premeditation." The sentence was eighteen years' imprisonment, and all the sentences were to run consecutively.

118

As Conrad Berg said from his hospital bed with one heavily plastered leg in traction and a glass of Old Buck gin in his hand, "Well, for the next twenty-eight years we don't have to worry about that bastard—I beg your pardon, Mrs. Morgan."

"Twenty-nine years, dear," Jane Berg corrected him firmly.

IN EARLY SPRING the American edition of *A Place of Our Own* was published, and it dropped immediately into that bottomless pool of indifference wherein so many good books drown. Bobby Dugan, Debra's new literary agent in America, wrote to say how sorry he was.

The rejection hurt and Debra felt the urge to write wane. Now when she sat at her desk with the microphone at her lips, the words no longer tumbled and fought to escape. For hours at a time she just listened to the birds in the garden below the window.

David sensed her despair, and tried to help her through it. When the hours at the desk proved fruitless he would insist she leave it and come with him along the new fence lines, or to fish for the big blue Mozambique bream in the pools.

David was busy at this time recruiting and training a force of African rangers. Already a herd of the rare and shy nyala antelope had settled around the String of Pearls. When David first saw them his excitement was feverish. Nyala antelope had never been seen on the estate before, not even in his father's time. There were nine hornless females, delicate chestnut and striped with white, dainty-stepping and suspicious. The two bulls were purplish black and shaggy. Their horns were thick and corkscrewed, tipped with cream.

David called Conrad, who arrived still using a stick and limping heavily as he would for the rest of his life. He watched the herd with David and Debra from a hide. Back at the homestead, he gave his opinion. "You're getting a nice bit of stuff together here, Davey—another few years and it will be a real showplace. Have you got any plans for visitors? Five-star safari at economy prices—"

"Connie, I'm too selfish to share this with anybody else."

Shortly after Conrad left, a call came through for Debra. It was Bobby Dugan.

"Wonder girl," he shouted over the line. "Big Daddy has got news that will blow your mind! *Cosmopolitan* ran an article on you two weeks ago. They did you proud, darling, full-page photo—"

Debra laughed nervously and signalled David to put his ear against hers to listen.

"—the mag hit the stands Saturday, and Monday morning was a riot at the bookstores. They sold seventeen thousand copies of *A Place of Our Own* in five days, and you jumped straight into the number five slot on the *New York Times* bestseller list. Darling, we are going to sell half a million copies of this book. Doubleday are already reprinting—"

There was much more, Bobby Dugan shouting plans and hopes, while Debra laughed weakly and kept saying, "No! I can't believe it!"

They drank two bottles of champagne that night, and a little before midnight Debra fell pregnant to David Morgan.

IT SEEMED AS THOUGH the fates, ashamed of the cruel pranks they had played upon them, were now determined to shower Debra and David with gifts.

As Debra sat at her olive-wood table, growing daily bigger with child, once again the words flowed as strongly as the spring waters of the String of Pearls. She decided that this second novel would be called *A Bright and Holy Thing*.

Conrad Berg came to her secretly to enlist her aid in his plan to have David nominated to the Board of the National Parks Committee.

"Yes," Debra decided. "It will be good for him to meet people and get out a little more. We are in danger of becoming recluses."

"Will he do it?"

"Don't worry," Debra assured him. "I'll see to it."

Debra was right. David gathered increasing confidence with each subsequent journey to Pretoria where the Board met. Debra would fly up with him and shop with Jane Berg while they were at their deliberations.

However, by November Debra felt too big and uncomfortable to make the long flight, especially as the rains were about to break. "I'll be perfectly all right here," she insisted. "I've got a telephone, six game rangers, four servants and a fierce hound to guard me."

David argued for days before the meeting and only agreed after he had worked out a timetable. "I will be back here by six-thirty at the latest," he told her.

In the dawn there were thunderclouds the colour of wine and flame towering high above the aircraft. David flew the corridors of open sky alone and at peace.

At the airport, a car was waiting for him, and he spent the journey into Pretoria reading the morning papers. When he saw the prediction of a storm front moving in he felt uneasy. Before he entered the conference room he asked the receptionist to place a telephone call to Jabulani.

"Two hour delay, Mr. Morgan."

"O.K., call me when it comes through."

When they broke for lunch he asked her about the call.

"I'm sorry, Mr. Morgan. The lines are down."

His uneasiness became alarm. "Please call the meteorological office for me."

The official reported that rain was heavy throughout the area and the cloud was solid to above twenty thousand feet. The Navajo had no oxygen or electronic navigational equipment.

"How long until it clears?" David demanded.

"Hard to tell, sir. Two or three days."

"Damn!" said David bitterly, and went down to the canteen. Conrad Berg was at a table with two members of the Board, and when he saw David he jumped up and limped across the room.

"David," he took his arm, and his face was deadly serious. "I've just heard—Akkers broke jail last night. He killed a guard and got away." David stared at him, unable to speak. "You'd better fly back right away to be with Debra."

"The weather—they've grounded all aircraft in the area."

"Use my truck!" said Conrad.

"I need something faster than that."

"Do you want me to come with you?"

"No," said David. "If you aren't at the meeting this afternoon, they won't approve the new fencing allocations. I'll go on my own."

DEBRA WAS WORKING at her desk when she heard the wind coming. She switched off her tape recorder and went out to the veranda with the dog following her closely.

121

She stood listening to the roar of the wind building up, the branches of the marula trees beginning to thrash and rattle.

Zulu whimpered, and she whispered, "There, boy. Gently. Gently." The wind banged the screen of the veranda with a snap and Debra ran back into her workroom; the window was swinging open and she went to close it and was running to latch the other windows when she bumped into one of the servants.

"Madam, the rain will come now. Very much rain."

"Go to your families, all of you," Debra told him and they streamed away through the swirling dust to their hutments. Debra groped her way back to her room and locked herself in.

The wind passed soon and in the utter silence that followed, Debra felt a sudden fall in temperature.

The first thunder broke with a crackling explosion and she cried out aloud. Then the rain came. It drummed and roared, battering the windowpanes.

Debra crouched on her daybed, clinging to Zulu for comfort. She wished she had not allowed the servants to leave. Finally she could stand it no longer. She groped her way back into the living room and lifted the telephone to her ear. Immediately she knew that it was dead, but she went on calling desperately into the mouthpiece, until finally she let it fall and dangle on its cord.

She began to sob as she stumbled back to her workroom where she fell upon the daybed and covered her ears with both hands.

THE NEW NATIONAL HIGHWAY as far as Witbank was broad and smooth, and the rented Pontiac peaked at a hundred and thirty miles an hour. David kept his foot pressed down hard as he remembered how Johan Akkers had shouted as the warders led him to the cells, "I'm going to get you, Scarface. If I have to wait twenty-nine years, I'm going to get you."

After Witbank the road narrowed. The rain was a grey bank of water that filled the air and flooded the road. David switched on his headlights and drove as fast as he dared.

By the time he reached the bridge over the Luzane stream, he had been driving for six hours and it was a few minutes after eight o'clock. Darkness had already fallen.

David's headlights cut across the mad brown waters to the far bank a hundred yards away. The bridge was submerged under fifteen feet of fast moving water and the trunks of uprooted trees dashed downstream on the flood.

He climbed out of the car and walked to the water's edge. The rain had stopped abruptly; directly overhead the stars showed mistily. But the water was still rising. He judged that the respite in the weather would not last much longer.

David reached a decision and ran back to the car. He reversed well back onto the highest ground and parked it with the headlights directed at the river edge. He stripped down to his shirt and underpants, pulled his belt from his trousers and buckled it about his waist, and then tied his shoes to the belt. He felt his way slowly down the bank. Within a few paces he was knee-deep and the current plucked at him as he waited, staring upstream.

He saw a tree trunk coming down fast, its roots sticking up like beseeching arms. He lunged for one of the roots and instantly was whisked out of the car's headlights into the roaring fury of the river. The darkness was filled with the rush and threat of raging water, and he was buffeted and flogged by its raw strength, grazed and bruised by rocks and driftwood.

Suddenly the log bumped against an obstruction, then swung out into the current again. Gambling that the obstruction was the far bank, David released his grip on the log and struck out sideways across the current. His overarm stroke ended in the branches of a thorn tree hanging over the storm waters. Thorns tore his palm as his grip closed over them, but he dragged himself out of the flood and up the bank, coughing the water from his lungs.

His shoes had been torn from his belt, but he staggered forward into the darkness. By the feeble light of the stars he made out the road, and began to run, gathering strength with each pace. It was very still now, with only the dripping of the trees and the occasional far-off mutter of thunder to break the silence.

Two miles from the homestead, David saw an abandoned automobile on the side of the road—a late model Chevy. The doors were unlocked and David switched on the interior lights. There was dried blood on the front seat, and a bundle of clothing. David recognized the coarse canvas suiting as regulation prison garb. He stared at it stupidly for a moment, and then he began to run.

THREE HOURS EARLIER JOHAN AKKERS had driven the Chevy across the Luzane bridge with the rising waters swirling over the guard rail. The closer he had got to Jabulani the more reckless he had become.

During the long months that he had laboured and languished in prison, vengeance had become the sole reason for his existence. He had planned his prison break to give himself three days of freedom—after that it did not matter.

He had infected his own jaw with a filthy needle and they had taken him to the dental clinic as he had planned. The guard had been easily handled, and the dentist had co-operated with a scalpel held to his throat. Once clear of the prison, Akkers had used the scalpel, leaving the dentist slumped over his steering-wheel in a plot of waste ground. Then, wearing the dentist's white laboratory gown over his prison suit, he had waited at a set of traffic lights.

The shiny new Chevy had pulled up for a red light and Akkers had opened the passenger door and slid in beside the driver. He had been a small man, with a pale face and soft little hairless hands. He had meekly obeyed Akkers's instructions to drive on.

Akkers had rolled the man's body, clad only in vest and shorts, into a clump of thick grass beside a disused secondary road. Helped by the news flashes on the radio, he had groped his way carefully through the police net. The infection in his jaw had ached intolerably despite the shot of antibiotics the dentist had given him, and his crippled claw of a hand had been awkward and clumsy on the gear lever—for the severed nerves and sinews had never knitted again.

Once on Jabulani land, and he could restrain himself no longer. He hit the mudhole at forty and the Chevy whipped and spun, slewing her back end deep into the mud.

He left her there and went on swiftly to the kopje behind the Jabulani homestead. He lay there for two hours peering into the driving rain, waiting for the darkness.

DEBRA WOKE IN THE SILENCE. She had fallen asleep in the midst of the storm. Now she listened intently and there was nothing but the soft sounds of water in the gutter and the screeching of a night-jar that told her night had fallen. She got up from the bed, shivering with the cold in her loose, dark blue maternity blouse and slacks. She pushed her feet into her ballet pumps.

She had started towards her dressing-room for a sweater, when she heard Zulu barking at the door leading to the front garden. She went out onto the veranda and let him out. Moments later she heard Zulu's growling and the scuffling of bodies. She stood silently, uncertain of what to do. Then she heard the sound of a heavy blow. It cracked on bone, and she heard the thump of a body falling. Zulu's growls were cut off abruptly. Now she was completely alone in the silence.

No, not silence. There was the sound of breathing. Debra hurriedly locked the door and shrank back against the veranda wall, listening and waiting.

She heard footsteps coming through the garden towards the verandah door. Now the intruder was climbing the steps. A hand brushed against the wire screening, and then settled on the handle, rattling it softly.

"Who is that?" Debra called in a high panicky cry.

Instantly the sounds ceased. She could imagine the intruder standing on the top step, peering through the screening of the veranda, trying to make her out in the gloom. Suddenly she was thankful for the dark blouse and slacks.

She waited motionlessly, listening. The silence went on for a long time, and she knew she could not stand it much longer.

Then suddenly there was the sound of a man giggling. Her legs went weak under her for she recognized it—the sick insane sound was graven upon her mind.

A hand shook the door handle, jerking and straining at it. Then a shoulder crashed into the narrow frame of the door and Debra screamed, a high ringing scream of terror, and it seemed to break the spell which held her. She whirled and ran into her workroom, slamming the door and locking it. Then she crouched beside the door, thinking desperately. She knew that as soon as he broke into the house Akkers need only switch on a light. Her only protection was darkness, and darkness was in the forest. She must get out of the house and try to reach the servants' quarters.

She ran to the kitchen at the rear of the house, grasped her cane and slipped open the door latch. At that moment she heard the front door crash open and Akkers charge heavily into the living room. She closed the kitchen door behind her and started across the yard.

She tried not to run, she counted her steps. Her first landmark was the gate in the fence that ringed the homestead. She was slightly off in her direction and she ran into the barbed-wire fence. Frantically she began to feel her way along it. Above her head she heard the crackle of the electricity in one of the arc lamps that lined the fence. Akkers must have found the switch, and Debra realized that she must be bathed in light.

She heard him shout behind her, and knew that he had seen her. She found the gate, and with a sob of relief tore it open and began to run.

The track forked. She took the righthand path to the hutments, and ran along it counting her paces. She tripped over the rock marking the next fork, and fell heavily, barking her shins.

She stumbled to her feet. She had lost her cane, but could not waste precious seconds looking for it. Fifty paces and she knew she was on the wrong fork. This path led down to the pumphouse and she was not familiar with it. She missed a turn and ran into rank grass that wrapped about her ankles and brought her down again.

She was winded and lost, but she knew she was out of the arc lights. She tried to control her sobbing breath, and to listen.

She heard him then, pounding footsteps that seemed to be coming directly to where she lay, and she shrank down against the wet earth.

At the last moment the footsteps ran past her. She felt sick with relief, but the footsteps ceased and he was so close she could hear him panting.

He was listening for her, and he stayed like that for what seemed an eternity. At last he giggled. "Ah! There you are. There you are. I can see you."

Her heart jumped with shock. She almost leaped up to run again— but some deeper sense restrained her.

"I can see you hiding there," he repeated. "I'm going to catch you and hold you down and—"

She quailed in the grass, listening to the awful obscenities that poured from his mouth. Then suddenly she realized that he had lost her, and was trying to make her betray her position.

His sadistic threats ended in silence again. Something loathsome crawled over Debra's arm. The thing, scorpion or spider, moved up to her neck and she knew her nerves would crack within seconds.

Suddenly Akkers spoke again. "All right!" he said, "I'm going back to fetch a torch. We'll see how far you get then."

He moved away, noisily, and she wanted to strike the insect from her cheek and run, but again, some instinct warned her. She waited five minutes, and then ten. The insect moved up into her hair.

Akkers spoke again near her. "We'll get you yet," and she heard him move away. This time she knew he had gone.

She brushed the insect from her hair, shuddering with horror. When she stood up she felt the child move within her body. She must find a safe place for the child's sake. Then she thought of the hide by the pools.

How to reach it? For she was now completely lost. Then she remembered David telling her about the rain wind out of the west. She turned her back to the next gust and set off with hands held out ahead to prevent running into one of the tree trunks.

As the cyclonic winds at the centre of the storm turned upon their axis, so the rain wind swung, changing direction constantly. Debra followed it faithfully, beginning a wide aimless circle through the forest.

AKKERS FOUND THE GUN cabinet in David's office, and ransacked the desk drawers for keys. He found none, and swore with frustration. He saw a sealed-cell electric lantern on a shelf, took it down and thumbed the switch. The beam was bright, even in the overhead lights. He paused in the kitchen to select a long carving knife before hurrying across the yard to the gate and along the path.

In the lantern beam, Debra's footprints showed clearly in the soft earth. He followed them to where she had blundered off the path, and found the mark of her body where she had lain.

"Clever girl," he chuckled and went on through the forest. Every few minutes he paused to throw the beam of the lantern ahead of him. Suddenly he saw something move at the extreme range of the lamp.

He held it in the beam, and saw Debra's pale strained face as she moved forward slowly and hesitantly. She went like a sleepwalker, arms extended ahead of her. She was coming directly towards him.

Akkers stood quietly, letting her come closer, enjoying the fierce thrill of having her in his power. When she was five paces from him, he giggled.

She screamed, her whole face convulsing, and she whirled like a wild animal and ran blindly into a branch of a marula tree. She fell back, collapsing to her knees and sobbed aloud clutching at her bruised cheek. Then she scrambled to her feet, and cocked her head for the next sound.

Silently he moved close behind her, and giggled again.

She screamed and ran, witless with terror. Akkers moved leisurely and silently after her. He was enjoying himself and he wanted it to last a long time.

DAVID RAN BAREFOOTED in the soft earth. As the road rounded the shoulder of the hill and dipped towards the homestead he stopped abruptly, and stared at the lurid glow of the arc lights. He felt a fresh flood of alarm, and sprinted down the hill.

He ran through the empty, ransacked rooms shouting her name. When he reached the front veranda he saw something moving in the darkness, beyond the broken screen door. "Zulu!" He ran forward. "Here, boy! Where is she?"

The dog staggered up the steps towards him. His jaw had been broken and he was still stunned. David knelt beside him.

"Find her, boy, find her."

At the back door Zulu picked up the scent and started resolutely towards the gate. David saw the footprints in the floodlights, Debra's and the big masculine prints which ran after them. He turned back into his office. The lantern was missing from its shelf, but there was a five-cell flashlight near the back. He shoved it into his pocket and grabbed a handful of shotgun shells. Then he unlocked the gun cabinet, snatched a shotgun and loaded it as he ran.

JOHAN AKKERS HAD FINISHED playing with his prey. He came up behind the running figure and took a twist of her thick dark hair in his crippled claw hand, wrapping it quickly about his wrist, but she turned upon him with a strength and ferocity he had not anticipated.

He went over backwards with her on top of him, and he dropped the knife and lantern into the grass to protect his eyes, for she was tearing at them with long sharp nails.

At last he freed his claw from the tangle of her hair, and he drew it back, holding her off with his left hand, and struck her. It was like a wooden club. It hit her across the temple and knocked all the fight out of her. He came up on his knees, holding her with his good hand and with the other he clubbed her mercilessly.

At last he let her drop, and stood up. He went to the lantern and played the beam in the grass. The knife glinted up at him. He picked it up and set down the lantern so the beam fell upon Debra's supine figure.

Akkers giggled and wiped the sweat from his face with his arm. A movement in the shadows caused him to glance up. He saw the black dog rush silently at him, and he threw up his arm to guard his throat. The furry body crashed into him and they rolled together.

Akkers stabbed up into the dog's rib cage, finding the heart with his first thrust. Zulu yelped and collapsed. Akkers pulled out the knife and he was crawling back to where Debra lay when David came up.

Akkers started to his feet but David thrust the barrels of the shotgun into his face and pulled both triggers. Akkers dropped into the grass, his legs kicking convulsively, and David hurled the shotgun aside and ran to Debra.

He knelt over her and whispered, "My darling, oh my darling. Forgive me, please forgive me. I should never have left you." Gently he picked her up and carried her, still unconscious, up to the homestead.

Debra's child was born in the dawn. It was a girl, tiny and wizened and too early for her term. If there had been skilled medical attention available she might have lived, for she fought valiantly. But the homestead was cut off by the raging river.

At three o'clock that afternoon, Conrad forced a passage of the Luzane stream, and three hours later Debra was in Nelspruit hospital. Two days later she came conscious once more.

NEAR THE CREST OF THE KOPJE above the homestead there was a natural terrace which overlooked the whole estate. It was a remote and peaceful place and they buried the child there. One Sunday morning after visiting the grave, Debra and David walked down the hill, put a picnic basket in the Land-Rover and drove to the pools.

They lay together on the rug beneath the branches of the fever trees, and drank white wine cold from the icebox. It was two months since Debra had left hospital, and the African spring was giving way to full summer, filling the bush with bustle and activity. The weaver birds were busy upon their basket nests, tying them to the bending tips of the reeds, hosts of yellow and bronze and white butterflies lined the water's edge, and the bees flew like golden motes of light to their hive in the cliff. The water drew all life to it, and a little after noonday David touched Debra's arm. "The nyala are here," he whispered.

They came through the grove on the far side of the pool, timidly pausing to stare about them with huge dark eyes, striped, dainty, beautiful, they blended with the shadows behind them.

"The does are all belly now," David told her. "They'll be dropping their lambs within the next few weeks."

When the nyala had drunk and gone, and while a white-headed fish eagle chanted its weird and haunting cry high above them they made love in the shade beside the quiet water.

David studied her face. Her eyes were open, and he looked down into their gold-flecked depths. The pupils were huge black pools but as a beam of sunlight broke through the canopy of leaves above them they shrank rapidly to black pinpoints.

David was startled by the phenomenon.

"What is it, David?" Debra asked, "Is something wrong?"

"No, my darling. What could possibly be wrong?"

"I feel it, Davey. You send out the strongest signals."

He laughed almost guiltily. He had imagined it perhaps, a trick of the light, and he tried to dismiss it from his mind.

131

A week later, however, he at last brought himself to write the following letter:

Dear Dr. Edelman,

We agreed that I should write to you if any change occurred in the condition of Debra's eyes, or her health.

Recently Debra was involved in an unfortunate accident, in which she received several blows about the head. I have since noticed that her eyes have become sensitive to light.

I have tested my observations and there can be no doubt that under the stimulus of a strong light source, the pupils of her eyes contract normally.

It seems possible that your original diagnosis might have to be revised, but I do not wish to awaken any false hope in her. For your advice, I would be most grateful.

Cordially yours, David Morgan.

David sealed and addressed the letter, but when he returned from the shopping flight to Nelspruit the following week, the envelope was still in the top pocket of his leather jacket.

The days settled into their calmly contented routine. Debra completed the first draft of her new novel, and received a request from Bobby Dugan to carry out a lecture tour of five major cities in the United States. *A Place of Our Own* had just completed its thirty-second week on the best-seller list, but Debra refused the tour.

"Who needs people?" David agreed with her, knowing that she had made the decision for him. He knew also that Debra would have been a sensation, and a tour would have launched her into the super-star category.

One evening, they drove down to the pools, and walked hand in hand to the water's edge. They found a fallen log screened by reeds and sat quietly together.

As the sun sank to the treetops the nyala herd came stepping fearfully through the shadows.

David nudged Debra and whispered. "The old bulls seem to be on the verge of a nervous breakdown this evening. There must be a leopard lurking along the edge of the reed bed—" he broke off, and exclaimed softly, "Oh, so that's it!"

"What is it, David?" Debra tugged at his arm insistently.

"A new fawn! Oh Debra! His legs are still wobbly and he is the palest creamy beige—"

Debra's grip on his arm tightened. Perhaps she was remembering her own infant. "I wish I could see it," she said. "Oh God! God! Let me see. Please, let me see!" and suddenly she was weeping, great racking sobs that shook her whole body.

The nyala herd took fright, and dashed away among the trees. David took Debra and held her fiercely to his chest, cradling her head—and he felt the icy winds of despair blow across his soul.

The next morning, he flew into Nelspruit and posted the letter.

IT WAS FIVE WEEKS before David flew to Nelspruit again, and then only because Debra was anxious to learn news from her agent about the draft she had sent him of *A Bright and Holy Thing.*

He left Debra at the hairdresser's, and went directly to the Post Office. The box was crammed full and David sorted quickly through the junk mail and picked out three letters from Debra's agent, and two envelopes with Israeli stamps. One was addressed in a doctor's scrawl, and the writing on the second was unmistakable: it marched in martial ranks, each letter in step with the next.

David found a bench in the park under the purple jacaranda trees, and opened Edelman's letter first.

Dear David,

Your letter came as a surprise, and I have studied the X-ray plates once more. They seem unequivocal, and I would not hesitate to confirm my original prognosis.

Despite himself, David felt the small stirrings of relief.

—However, I can only accept that your observations of light-sensitivity are correct and I must also accept that there is at least partial function of the optic nerves—possibly due to the head blows that Debra received.

I would, of course, be all too willing to examine Debra myself. However, it will probably be inconvenient for you to journey to Jerusalem, and I have therefore taken the liberty of writing to a colleague of mine at Groote Schuur hospital in Cape Town. Dr. Ruben Friedman is one of the leading world authorities on optical

133

trauma, and I enclose a copy of my letter to him. I have also despatched to him Debra's original X-ray plates and a clinical history of her case. I have also shown your letter to General Mordecai, and discussed the case with him—

David folded the letter carefully—"Why the hell did he have to bring the old war horse into it?" He opened the Brig's letter.

Dear David,

Dr. Edelman has spoken with me. I have telephoned Friedman in Cape Town, and he has agreed to see Debra.

For some years I have been postponing a lecture tour to South Africa which the S.A. Zionist Council has been urging upon me. I have today written to them and asked them to make the arrangements. This will give us the excuse to bring Debra to Cape Town. Tell her I have insufficient time to visit you on your estate, but insist upon seeing her. I will give you my dates later—

It was in typical style, brusque and commanding. It was all out of David's hands now, there was no turning back. On the reverse side of the letter he drafted a dummy letter from the Brig for Debra setting out his plans for the forthcoming tour.

Debra was ecstatic when he read it to her later in the park and he experienced a twinge of conscience at his deceit. "It will be wonderful seeing him again, I wonder if Mother will be coming out with him—?"

"He didn't say, but I doubt it." David read the American mail to her.

Dugan wrote that United Artists wanted to film *A Place of Our Own* and were talking impressively heavy figures. Indeed, if Debra would go to California and write the screenplay, Bobby Dugan felt sure he could roll it all into a quarter-million-dollar package. He urged Debra to accept.

"Who needs people?" Debra laughed it away quickly, too quickly—and David caught her wistful expression.

"Let's think about your going, Deb," he said.

"What's to think about?" she asked. "This is where we belong."

"Let's wait a while before replying until—let's say, until after we have seen the Brig in Cape Town."

"Why?" She looked puzzled. "Why should it be different then?"

"No reason. It's just that it is an important decision.

"Beseder!" she agreed readily. "I love you."

"I love you," he said.

The Brig's arrangements allowed them three more weeks before the rendezvous in Cape Town, and David drew upon each hour to the full.

There was, however, one incident during those last happy days that saddened them both. One morning, they walked four miles northwards beyond the hills to a narrow wedge-shaped plain on which stood a group of towering leadwood trees.

A pair of martial eagles had chosen the tallest leadwood as their mating ground. The female was a beautiful young bird but the male was past his prime. They had begun constructing their nest, but the work was interrupted by the intrusion of a lone male eagle, a big young bird. David had noticed him several days earlier lurking about the borders of the territory, carefully avoiding over-flying the airspace claimed by the breeding pair.

Now, as David and Debra sat on an outcrop of rock overlooking the plain, David could see the old bird at the nest, a dark, hunched shape with white breast and head set low on the powerful shoulders. David looked for the invader with his binoculars, but there was no sign of him.

Then suddenly the old eagle launched into flight, striking urgently upwards. He opened his yellow beak and shrieked a harsh challenge.

David, turning quickly in the old fighter pilot's sweep of the sky, saw the cunning of the younger bird immediately. He was towering in the sun, a flagrant trespasser, daring the old eagle to come up at him. David's sympathy was with the defender as he climbed slowly on flogging wings.

Quickly and a little breathlessly he described to Debra how the young bird calmly circled, watching his adversary's approach. "There he goes!" David cried, as the attacker began his stoop.

"I can hear him," Debra whispered, as the sound of his wings carried clearly to them both, rustling like a bush fire in dry grass as he dived on the old bird.

"Break left! Go! Go! Go!" David called. The old eagle seemed almost to understand him, for he closed his wings and flicked out of the path of the strike. The attacker hissed by with talons reaching uselessly through air. Then the old bird streaked down after him. In one stroke of skill he had wrested the advantage.

"Get him!" yelled David. "Get him when he turns! Now!"

The young bird was plummeting towards the tree tops, and he flared his wings to break his fall, turning desperately to avoid the lethal stoop of his enemy. But the old eagle reached forward with his talons and hit him without slackening his speed. The thud of the impact carried clearly to the watchers on the hill.

Locked together by the old bird's killing claws, they tumbled, wing over tangled wing, until they struck the top branches of a leadwood tree, and came to rest at last in a high fork.

Debra and David hurried down the hill to the tree. "Can you see them?" she asked anxiously, as David focused his binoculars on the struggling pair.

"They are trapped," David told her. "The old fellow has his claws buried to the hilt in the other's back."

Screams of rage and agony rang from the hills, and the screeching female eagle sailed anxiously above the leadwood.

"The young bird is dying." David studied him through the lenses, watching the carmine drops ooze from the gaping yellow beak. "And the old bird will never get his claws loose. They lock as soon as pressure is applied."

"Isn't there anything we can do to help him?" Debra pleaded.

"Yes," he answered quietly. "We can come back in the morning and bring a gun with us."

In the dawn they returned to the leadwood tree. The young bird was dead, hanging limp and graceless, but the old bird was still alive, linked by his claws to the carcass of the other, weak and dying but with the furious yellow flames still burning in his eyes.

David stared up at the old eagle. "Not you alone, old friend," he thought, and he lifted the gun to his shoulder and hit him with two charges of buckshot.

David felt as though he had destroyed a part of himself in that blast of gunfire, and the shadow of it was cast over the last few days before he flew Debra to Cape Town in the Navajo.

136

THEY STAYED IN THEIR SUITE at the Mount Nelson Hotel until the Brig's arrival, for David had found the inquisitive glances and murmurs of pity that followed him hard to stomach.

The Brig knocked on the door of the suite and entered with his aggressive stride. After he and Debra had embraced, he turned to David and it seemed that he looked at him with new calculation in the fierce warrior eyes.

While Debra bathed and dressed for the Zionist Council's Dinner, he took David to his own suite, gave him a glass of whisky, and began to discuss the arrangements he had made.

"Friedman will be at this evening's reception. I will introduce him to Debra and let them talk for a while, then he will be seated next to her at the dinner table. This will give us the opportunity to persuade Debra to undergo an examination later—"

"Before we go any further, sir," David interrupted. "I want your assurance that at no time will it be suggested to Debra that there is a possibility of her regaining her sight. Even if Friedman determines that surgery is necessary, it must be for some other reason."

"I don't think that is possible," the Brig snapped angrily. "It would not be fair to Debra—"

It was David's turn for anger. "Let me determine what is fair. I know her as you never can. If you offer her a chance of sight, you will create for her the same dilemma I have had since the possibility arose. I would spare her that."

"I do not understand you," the Brig said stiffly.

"Look at me," David said softly, and the Brig did look at David —perhaps for the first time truly seeing the terribly ravaged head. His eyes dropped and he turned to replenish his whisky glass.

"If I can give her sight, I will do it." David felt his voice trembling. "But I believe that she loves me enough to spurn the gift if she were ever given the choice. I do not want her ever to be tortured by that choice."

The Brig lifted his glass and took a deep swallow. "As you wish," he acquiesced, his voice husky with emotion.

"Thank you, sir," David set down his glass. "If you'll excuse me, I think I should go and change now." He moved to the door.

"David!" the Brig called to him and he turned back. The Brig smiled an embarrassed but gentle smile. "You'll do," he said.

THE RECEPTION WAS IN THE BANQUETING ROOM at the Heeren-gracht Hotel and as David and Debra rode up together in the lift, she seemed to sense his dread, and she squeezed his arm.

"Stay close to me tonight," she murmured. "I'll need you." He knew it was said to distract him, and he was grateful.

It was an elegant gathering, women in rich silks and jewellery, the men dark-suited, with the poise which advertises power and wealth. The Brig brought Reuben Friedman to David and Debra and introduced them casually.

Reuben was a short heavily built man. His grizzled hair was cropped close to the round skull, but David found himself liking the bright bird eyes and the readiness of his smile.

As they went in to dinner, Debra asked David what he looked like, and laughed with delight when he replied, "Like a koala bear."

Somehow the fact that Reuben was a doctor seemed to set both David and Debra at their ease. Debra remarked on it when the conversation turned to their injuries and Reuben asked solici-tously. "You don't mind talking about it?"

"No, not with you. Somehow it's all right to bare your self in front of a doctor."

Marion Friedman, a slim girl with her husband's forthright friendly manner, joined the conversation. "Don't do it, my dear," she cautioned. "Not in front of Ruby anyway—look at me, six kids, already!" And they laughed.

Ruby was refilling Debra's glass when he paused and asked her. "How long is it since your eyes were last checked, my dear?"

David's nerves snapped taut, and he listened intently.

"Not since I left Israel—though they took some X-rays when I was in the hospital."

"I suppose they could strike me off, drumming up business, but I do think that you should have periodic checks."

"I hadn't even thought about it." Debra frowned slightly.

David felt his conscience twinge as he joined in the conspiracy.

"It can't do any harm, darling. Why not let Ruby give you a going over while we are here? Heaven knows when we will have another opportunity."

"Oh, David, I know you are itching for home—and so am I."

"Another day or two won't matter."

Debra turned to Ruby. "How long will it take?"

"A day. I'll give you an examination in the morning, and then we'll shoot some X-ray plates in the afternoon."

"How soon could you see her?" David asked, his voice unnatural, for he knew that the appointment had been arranged five weeks ago.

"Oh, I'm sure we could fit her in right away—tomorrow—even if we have to do a little juggling."

David looked across to Debra. "O.K., darling?" he asked.

"O.K., David," she agreed readily.

A moment later, the master of ceremonies rose to introduce the speaker, and David found it an intense relief to know the ordeal was drawing to a close.

At last, when they reached the sanctuary of their own suite, they sat close together on the couch and Debra nestled against him. "David, do you remember once I told you that you were spoiled, and not very good marriage material?"

"I'll never forget it."

"I'd like to withdraw that remark formally," she said softly, and he moved her gently away so that he could study her face. "I fell in love with a spoiled little boy who thought only of fast cars and the nearest skirt—but now I have a man, a grown man, and I like it better this way."

He drew her back to him and their lips met in a lingering embrace before she sighed happily and laid her head back upon his shoulder.

RUBY'S CONSULTING ROOMS were in the Medical Centre that towered above the harbour and looked out across Table Bay. The receptionist could not control the widening of her eyes as she looked at David's face. "Dr. Friedman is waiting for you both. Please go through."

Ruby's greeting was warm as he took Debra's arm. "Shall we let David stay with us?" he asked her in mock conspiracy.

"Let's," she answered.

Ruby directed light deep into the body of her eyes. Then he attached electrodes to her arm and swung forward a complicated-looking piece of electronic equipment. "It's a little invention of my own. I'm quite proud of it, but in reality it's only a variation on the old-fashioned lie-detector. We are going to flash lights at you, and see just what sort of subconscious reaction you have to them."

"We know that already," Debra told him, and they both heard the edge in her voice now.

"It's just an established routine we do," Ruby soothed her, and then to David. "Stand back here, please. The lights are pretty fierce."

David moved back and Ruby adjusted the machine. A roll of graph paper began running slowly under a moving stylus which settled almost immediately into a steady rhythmic pattern. On a separate glass screen a green dot of light began to repeat the same rhythm. Ruby switched out the lights, plunging the room into darkness, except for the pulsing green dot.

"Are we ready now, Debra? Eyes open, please."

Soundlessly a brilliant burst of blue light filled the room, and David saw the green dot on the screen go haywire for a beat or two then settle again into its old rhythm. Though Debra was unaware of it, the pulse of light had registered on her brain.

The testing went on for another twenty minutes while Ruby adjusted the intensity of the light source and varied the transmission. At last he was satisfied, and turned the lights on.

"Well?" Debra demanded brightly. "Do I pass?"

"You did just great," Ruby told her. "David can take you to lunch, but this afternoon I want you at the radiologist's. Here's the address." Ruby scribbled on his prescription pad and handed the note to David:

See me alone *tomorrow 10 a.m.*

The Brig joined them for lunch in their suite. Sensing that his help was needed, he had both of them laughing with stories of Debra's childhood, and David was grateful to him, for the time passed so quickly that he had to hurry Debra to her appointment.

The radiologist was a grey-haired man with big hands and heavy shoulders like a professional wrestler.

"I am going to use two different techniques on you, my dear—" David wondered why all males over forty referred to

140

Debra as though she were twelve years old. "First we will do five
of what we call police mug shots, front, back, sides and top. After
that, we are going to clamp your head to keep it still and the
camera is going to take a moving shot of the inside of your head,
focused on the spot where all the trouble is. It's a technique called
'tomography'."

It was a long tedious business, and afterwards when they drove
back to the hotel, Debra leaned close to David and said, "Let's
go home, as soon as we can?"

"Soon as we can," he agreed.

The Brig insisted on accompanying David on his visit to Ruby
the following morning. David had lied to Debra, telling her he
was meeting with the Morgan Trust accountants, and he had left
her in a lime-green bikini lying beside the hotel swimming pool.

Ruby seated them opposite his desk. "Gentlemen, we have a
hell of a problem. I am going to show you the X-ray plates first."
He swivelled his chair and switched on the scanner. "Here are
the plates that Edelman sent me. You can see the grenade fragment." It was stark, a small triangular shard of steel lying in
the cloudy bone structure. "Edelman's original diagnosis—based
on these plates—seems to be confirmed. The optic nerve is
severed." Quickly he unclipped the plates, and fitted others to
the scanner. "Now here are the plates taken yesterday. Notice
how the grenade fragment has been encapsulated and encysted."
The stark outline was softened by the new growth of bone
around it. "That is good, and expected. But here in the channel
of the optic chiasma we find a growth of some sort. It could be
scarring, the growth of bone chips, or some other type of growth
either benign or malignant." Ruby arranged another set of plates
upon the scanner. "Finally, this is the plate exposed by the
technique of tomography, to establish the contours of this growth.
It seems to conform to the shape of the bony channel of the
chiasma, except here—" Ruby touched a small notch which was
cut into the upper edge of the growth, "—this little spot runs
through the main axis of the skull, but is bent upwards in the
shape of an inverted 'U'. It is just possible that this may be the
most significant discovery of our whole examination." Ruby
switched off the light of the scanner.

"I don't understand any of this," the Brig's voice was sharp.

"No, of course." Ruby was smooth. "I am merely setting the background for my conclusions. There can be absolutely no doubt that part of the optic nerve remains. It is still conveying impulses to the brain. It is possible that the grenade fragment cut through part of the nerve. Such damage is irreversible. However, it is also possible that the optic nerve has suffered little damage, or none at all, please God."

Ruby paused. The two men opposite him watched his face intently.

"I believe that the notch in the outline of the chiasma is the nerve itself, twisted out of position, pinched like a garden hose by bone fragments and the metal fragment so that it is no longer capable of carrying impulses to the brain."

"The blows on her temple—?" David asked.

"Yes. Those blows may have been sufficient to alter the position of the nerve, so as to enable the passage of a minimal amount of impulse to the brain—like the garden hose, movement could allow a little water to pass through but once the twist is straightened the full volume would be restored."

They were all silent then, each of them considering the enormity of what they had heard.

"How could you find out—I mean, what steps would you take next?" David asked at last.

"There is only one way. We would have to go to the site of the trauma."

"Open Debra's skull?" The horror showed in David's eyes.

"Yes," Ruby nodded.

"Her head—" David's own flesh quailed in memory of the ruthless knife. "Her face—" His voice shook now. "No, I won't let you cut her. I won't let you ruin her, like they have me—"

"David!" The Brig's voice cracked like breaking ice.

"I understand how you feel," Ruby spoke gently, his voice in contrast to the Brig's. "But we will go in from behind the hairline, there will be no disfigurement."

"What are the chances?" David looked for help in the agony of his decision.

"That is impossible to say," Ruby chose his words with care.

142

"Let me put it this way—there is a possibility that she may regain a useful part of her sight. And there is a remote possibility that she may regain full vision. The worst that can happen is there could be no change."

"You know what the choice must be, David," the Brig said.

"All right," David surrendered. "But on one condition. Debra must not be told that there is a chance of her regaining her sight—"

"How will you get her to the hospital if you don't explain it to her?" Ruby asked.

"We'll tell her that you've discovered a growth—that it has to be removed. That's true, isn't it?"

"No." Ruby shook his head. "I can't deceive her."

"Then I will tell her," said David, his voice firm and steady now. "And I will tell her when we discover the result—good or bad—after the operation. Is that understood?"

After a moment the two others murmured their agreement.

DAVID HAD THE HOTEL chef prepare a picnic basket, and the service bar provided a cool bag with two bottles of champagne.

He rejected the impulse to fly with her—though he craved the feeling of height and space, he needed to concentrate all his attention on Debra. So instead they took the cableway to the top of Table Mountain and there, hand in hand, they followed a path along the plateau, to a lonely place on the cliff's edge where they could sit together high above the city and the ocean.

The sounds of the city came up two thousand feet to them, the horn of an automobile, the clang of a locomotive shunting in the train yards.

David gathered his resolve. "I saw Ruby today," he said abruptly, unable to find a gentler approach. She went still beside him in that special way of hers.

"It's bad!" she said at last.

"Why do you say that?" he demanded quickly.

"Because you brought me here to tell me—and because I can feel that you are afraid for me."

"It's not true," David tried to reassure her. "I'm a little worried, that's all."

"Tell me," she said.

"There's a small growth. It's not dangerous—yet. But they feel something should be done about it. . . ." He stumbled through the explanation he had so carefully prepared. When he ended she was silent for a moment.

"When will they operate?" she asked.

"Tomorrow you will go in, and they'll do it the next morning."

"So soon?"

"I thought it best to have it over with."

She nodded, trusting him completely—then she smiled and squeezed his arm. "Don't fret yourself, David, my darling. It will be all right. You'll see, they can't touch us. We live in a private place where they can't touch us."

HE WOKE IN THE NIGHT knowing that she was not beside him. Quickly he went to the sitting room and switched on the lights.

She heard the click and turned her head away, but not before he had seen the tears on her cheeks. He went to her quickly. "Darling," he said.

"I couldn't sleep," she said.

"That's all right." He knelt before the couch on which she sat, but he did not touch her.

"I had a dream," she said. "There was a pool of clear water and you were swimming in it, looking up at me and calling to me. I saw your dear face clearly, beautiful and laughing—" David realized with a jolt that she had seen him in her dream as he had been, not as the monstrous ravaged thing he was now. "Then suddenly you began to sink, your face fading and receding—" Her voice caught and broke, and she was silent for a moment. "It was a terrible dream. I cried out and tried to follow you, but I could not move and then you were gone down into the depths."

"It was only a dream," he said.

"David," she whispered. "Tomorrow, if anything happens—"

"Nothing will happen." He almost snarled the denial, but she put out a hand to his face, finding his lips and touching them lightly to silence them.

"Whatever happens," she said. "Remember how it was when we were happy. Remember that I loved you."

144

THE HOSPITAL OF GROOTE SCHUUR sits on the lower slopes of Devil's Peak. Below it lie the dark pine forests and open grassy slopes of the huge estate that Cecil Rhodes left to the nation. Herds of deer and antelope feed quietly in the open places.

The hospital is a massive complex of brilliant white buildings, all roofed in burnt red tiles. Ruby had secured a private room for Debra, and the sister in charge of the floor was expecting her. They took her from David and led her away. When he returned that evening she was sitting up in bed surrounded by banks of flowers which he had ordered.

"They smell wonderful," she thanked him. "It's like being in a garden."

"They have shaved your head." David said as he looked at the turban around her head. He had not expected that she must sacrifice that lustrous black mane.

She did not answer him and instead told him brightly how well they were treating her. "You'd think I was some sort of queen," she laughed.

The Brig was with David, gruff and reserved, and his presence cast restraint upon them. It was a relief when Ruby arrived.

"When do I go to theatre?" she asked him.

"We've got you down bright and early. Eight o'clock tomorrow. I am tremendously pleased that Billy Cooper is the surgeon. I will be assisting him, and he'll have one of the best surgical teams in the world backing him up."

"Ruby," Debra said, "you know how some women have their husbands with them when they are confined—"

"Yes." Ruby looked uncertain, taken aback by the question.

"Well, couldn't David be there with me tomorrow?"

"With all due respect, my dear, you are not having a baby."

"But couldn't you arrange for him to be there?" Debra pleaded.

"I'm sorry," Ruby shook his head. "It's impossible—" then he brightened. "But I tell you what. We have a closed-circuit television relayed to the students' room and David could watch from there."

"Oh, yes!" Debra accepted immediately. "We don't like being parted from each other." She smiled at where she thought he was, but he had moved aside and the smile missed him. "You will be there, David, won't you?"

Though the idea of watching was repellent to him, David replied lightly, "I'll be there."

THERE WERE ONLY TWO medical students in the small lecture room with its padded chairs circling the small television screen— a plump woman with a pretty face and a tall young man with a pale complexion. After the first startled glance they ignored David, and they spoke together in knowing medical jargon.

"The Coop's doing an exploratory through the parietal."

"That's the one I want to watch—"

David kept looking at his watch. At last the screen shimmered into a high view of the theatre, the surgeon's voice was picked up by the microphones. "Are we on telly?"

"Yes, doctor," the sister answered him.

David felt a sick sensation in the pit of his stomach as the surgeon spoke for his unseen audience. "The patient is a twenty-six-year-old female. The symptoms are total loss of sight in both eyes, and the cause is suspected damage of the optic nerve. This is a surgical investigation by Dr. William Cooper, assisted by Dr. Reuben Friedman." As he spoke, the camera moved in on the table. Sterile drapes covered all but Debra's shaven skull.

"Scalpel please, sister."

David leaned forward in his seat as Cooper made the first incision, and then drew back the skin. David's flesh crawled as the surgeon took up a drill that resembled a carpenter's brace and bit. Cooper's voice continued its impersonal commentary as he pierced the skull with four holes, each set at the corners of a square. "Periosteal elevator, please, sister."

The surgeon slid the gleaming steel introducer into one of the holes and manœuvred it until its tip reappeared through the next hole in line. Using the introducer, a length of sharp steel wire saw was threaded through the two holes and lay along the inside of the skull. Cooper sawed this back and forth and it cut cleanly through the bone. He carried out the procedure four times, cutting out the sides of the square, and then opening a trapdoor into Debra's skull.

146

As he worked David had felt sweat cross his forehead, but now as the camera peered through the opening he felt his wonder surmount his horror, for it seemed to be looking into the core of her being. What part of it contained her writer's genius, he wondered, and where was her love for him buried?

David was aware of new tension in the surgeon's voice as he moved slowly and expertly towards his goal. "Now this is interesting, can we see this on the screen, please? Yes! There is very clearly a bone deformation here—"

The voice was pleased, and the two students beside David leaned closer as Cooper scratched through tissue to the grenade fragment, a dark speck lodged in the white bone.

"We will go for this, I think. Do you agree, Dr. Friedman?"

"Yes, I think you should take it."

Delicately the long steel instruments worried the fragment, and at last Cooper drew it out. David heard the metallic ping as it was dropped into a waiting dish. Cooper plugged the hole left by the fragment with beeswax to prevent haemorrhage. "Now we will trace out the optic nerves."

They were two white worms, David saw them clearly, converging at the opening of the bony canal into which they disappeared.

"We have got extraneous bone growth here, clearly associated with the foreign body we have just removed. It seems to have blocked off the canal. Suggestions, Dr. Friedman?"

"I think we should excise the growth and ascertain just what damage it has done to the nerve in that area."

"I agree." Cooper worked on the white bone growth carefully removing each piece as it came away, gradually revealing the white worm of the nerve beneath.

"Now this is interesting. Can we get a better view here, please?" The camera zoomed in closer. "The nerve has been forced upwards, and flattened by pressure. It has been pinched off—but it seems to be intact."

Cooper lifted another piece of bone aside, and now the nerve lay fully exposed. "This is remarkable, a one in a thousand chance. There appears to be no damage to the actual nerve, and yet the steel fragment passed so close to it that it must have touched it. I think we can confidently expect good recovery of function.''

Despite the masked features, the triumphant attitude of the two surgeons was easily recognized, and watching them, David felt his own emotions at war. He watched Cooper replace the portion of Debra's skull that he had removed. Then the image on the screen changed to another theatre and the fickle interest of the watching students changed with it.

David waited in the visitors' room on Debra's floor until two nurses trundled Debra's stretcher down the corridor to her room. She was deadly pale, with dark bruised-looking eyes and lips, her head swathed in a turban of white bandages. A whiff of anaesthetic hung in the corridor after she was gone.

Ruby Friedman came then, changed from theatre garb into a suit. He looked delighted.

"You watched?" he demanded, and when David nodded he went on exuberantly. "My God, something like this makes you feel that if you never do another thing in your life, it was still worthwhile.''

"When will you know?" David asked quietly.

"I know already, I'll stake my reputation on it!''

"She will be able to see as soon as she comes around from the anaesthetic?'' David asked.

"Good Lord, no!'' Ruby chuckled. "That nerve has been pinched off for too long, it's going to take time to recover. When she wakes she's going to see colours and shapes as though she is on a drug binge; it's going to take time for the nerve to settle down—two weeks to a month, I would guess.''

"Two weeks," David said, and he felt the relief of a condemned man hearing of his temporary reprieve.

"You will tell her the good news, of course," Ruby gave a buoyant chuckle.

"I won't tell her yet," David answered. "I will find the right time.''

"You will have to explain the initial hallucinations. They will alarm her.''

"I will just tell her that they are the normal after-effect of the operation.''

"David, I—" Ruby began seriously, but he was cut off.

148

"I will tell her!" The voice shook with fury. "That was the condition. I will tell her when I judge the time is right."

OUT OF THE DARKNESS a tiny amber light glowed, pale and far off. She watched it split and become two, and each of those split and split again until they filled the universe in a great shimmering field of stars. The light throbbed changing from amber to an endless cavalcade of colours, blending, fading, flaring in splendour.

Then the colours took shape. They spun like mighty Catherine wheels, and soared and exploded in rivers of flame. At last she could bear it no longer and she cried out. Instantly there was a strong familiar hand in hers.

"David, David." She sobbed as new torrents of colour poured over her.

"I'm here, my darling. I'm here."

"Colours," she cried. "Filling my whole head. I've never known it like this. What's happening to me, David?"

"It's the result of the operation. It shows that it was a success. They removed the growth."

"I'm frightened, David."

"No, my darling. There is nothing to be afraid of."

"Hold me, David. Hold me safe."

And in the circle of his arms the fear abated, and slowly she came to accept the waves of colour, and at last to look upon them with wonder.

"It's beautiful, David. It's wonderful. . . ."

DAVID WAS ALONE IN THE SUITE, and it was after midnight when the call that he had placed to New York came through.

"This is Robert Dugan. To whom am I speaking?" Bobby's voice was crisp and businesslike.

"It's David Morgan. Debra Mordecai's husband."

"Well, hello there, David." The agent's voice changed, becoming expansive. "It's sure nice to talk to you. How is Debra?"

"That's why I am calling. She's had an operation and she's in the hospital at the moment."

149

"No! Not serious, is it?"

"She's going to be fine. She'll be up in a few days. Meanwhile I want you to set up that scriptwriting contract for *A Place of Our Own*."

"She's going to do it?"

"She'll do it. Just write her a good contract."

"Depend on it. That little girl of yours is a hot property."

"How long will the job last?"

"About six months," Dugan guessed. "You coming with her?"

"No," David answered carefully. "She'll be all right on her own."

"Hope you are right," Dugan was dubious.

"I'm right," David told him abruptly. "Just keep her busy. Don't give her time to think."

"I'll keep her busy." Then as though he had detected something in David's voice, he asked, "Is something bugging you, David?"

"I don't want to talk about it. You just look after her."

"I'll look after her," Dugan's tone had sobered. "And David— I'm sorry. Whatever it is, I'm sorry."

David's hand was shaking as he ended the conversation. He went out into the night and walked until just before dawn when he was weary enough to sleep.

THE EXPLOSIVE BURSTS OF COLOUR settled to calmly moving patterns. After the grey shifting banks of blindness the new brightness and beauty filled Debra with a wondrous sense of well-being. It was as though subconsciously she was aware of the imminent return of her sight.

Each day David waited for her to show that this knowledge had reached her conscious mind. He hoped for and at the same time dreaded this awareness—but it did not come. He spent as much time with her as hospital routine would allow, and her ebullient mood was infectious. He could not help but share the warm excitement as she anticipated their return to Jabulani.

Gradually David began to believe that their love and happiness were immortal and that Debra could weather the shock of seeing him. Yet he was not sure enough to tell her.

150

One evening Ruby and the Brig were waiting for him when he returned to his suite, and they came swiftly to the point.

"You have already left it too long. Debra should have been told days ago," the Brig told him sternly.

"I'll tell her soon," David muttered.

"David," Ruby was placatory, "it could happen at any time now. She has made strong progress."

"I'll do it," said David. "Can't you stop pushing me? I said I'll do it—and I will. Just get off my back, won't you."

"David." The Brig was brisk now. "You've got until noon tomorrow. If you haven't told her by then, I'm going to do it."

"All right," David said, all the fight had gone out of him. "I will tell her tomorrow morning."

IT WAS A BRIGHT WARM MORNING, and the garden below his room was gay with colour. David lingered over breakfast in his suite, drawing out the moment. He dressed with care afterwards, in a dark suit and a soft lilac shirt, then, when he was ready to leave, he surveyed his image in the full-length mirror of the dressing-room.

"It's been a long time—and I'm still not at ease with you," he told the figure in the mirror. "Let's pray that somebody loves you more than I do."

The Brig was waiting for him in the visitor's room on Debra's floor. He came out into the corridor, tall and grim.

"What are you doing here?" David demanded.

"I thought I might be of help. Would you like me to be with you?"

"No." David turned away from him as he spoke. "I can manage, thank you," and he set off along the corridor.

"David!" the Brig called softly.

David hesitated and then turned back.

"What is it?" he asked.

For a long moment they stared at each other, then abruptly the Brig shook his head. "No," he said. "It's nothing," and watched the tall young man with the monstrous head turn and walk swiftly towards Debra's room.

Debra sat in her chair by the open window, and the warm air

151

wafted the scent of the pine forests to her. She felt quiet and deeply contented, on the downy edges of sleep.

David found her like that, her face lit by the sunlight. He stood before her chair studying her, her face beneath its turban of white bandages was pale, but the bruises below her eyes had cleared. Tenderly he leaned forward and laid his hand against her cheek. She stirred drowsily, and opened her eyes. They were beautiful, and vague, and misty—then suddenly he saw them change, the look was sharp and aware. Her gaze focused, and steadied. She was looking at him—and seeing him.

Debra had been roused from sleep by the touch upon her cheek. She opened her eyes to soft golden clouds, then suddenly the clouds rolled open and she looked beyond to the monster's head that swam towards her, a head that seemed from the halls of hell itself, a head so riven with livid lines and set with such crudely worked features that she flung herself back in her chair, cringing in terror from it. She lifted her hands to her face and screamed.

David turned and ran from the room, slamming the door behind him.

The Brig heard him coming and stepped into the corridor.

"David!" He reached out a hand to hold him back, but David struck out wildly, a blow that caught him in the chest throwing him back against the wall. "David!" he called. "Wait!"

But David was gone, his footsteps clattered up from the well of the stairs. The Brig turned and hurried to his daughter where the hysterical sobs rang from behind the closed door. She looked up from her cupped hands when she heard the door open. He went to her quickly and took her in his arms. "It's all right," he told her, "it's going to be all right."

She clung to him, stifling the last of her sobs. "I had a dream, a terrible dream." Then suddenly she pulled away. "David," she cried, "where is David? I must see him."

The Brig stiffened.

"You have already seen him, my child," he replied heavily.

For many seconds she did not understand, and then slowly it came to her. "David?" she whispered, her voice catching and breaking. "That was David?"

The Brig nodded, watching her face for the revulsion.

152

"Oh dear God," Debra's voice was fierce. "What have I done? I screamed when I saw him. I've driven him away."

"So you want to see him again?" the Brig asked. "Even the way he is now?"

"More than anything else on this earth. Find him for me," she ordered. "Quickly, before he does something stupid."

"I don't know where he has gone," the Brig answered.

"There is only one place he would go when he is hurt like this," Debra told him. "He will be in the sky."

"Yes," the Brig agreed readily.

"Go down to Air Traffic Control, they'll let you speak to him." The Brig turned for the door and Debra's voice urged him on. "Find him for me, Daddy. Please find him for me."

THE NAVAJO SEEMED TO COME around to a southerly heading under its own volition. It was only when its nose settled on course, climbing steadily, that David knew where he was going Behind him, the flat-topped mountain with its glistening wreaths of clouds fell away. This was the last of the land and ahead lay only the great barren wastes of ice and cruel water.

David glanced at his fuel gauges. The needles registered a little over the halfway mark on the dials. Three hours' flying perhaps. He saw clearly how his suffering would end. He would continue to bore for height. When at last his engines starved and failed, he would push the nose down into a dive and go in fast, like the stoop of a maimed and dying eagle. It would be over swiftly, and the metal fuselage would carry him down to a grave that could not be more lonely than the desolation in which he now existed.

The radio crackled into life. Air Traffic was snarling his call sign through the static. He reached for the switch to kill the set when a well-remembered voice stayed his hand.

"David, this is the Brig." The words transported him back to another cockpit in another land. "You disobeyed me once before. Don't do it again."

David's mouth tightened and again he reached for the switch.

"David," the Brig's voice softened. "I have just spoken to Debra. She wants you. She wants you desperately."

David's hand hovered over the switch.

153

"Listen to me, David. She needs you—she will always need you." David blinked, for he felt tears scalding his eyes. "Come back, David. For her sake, come back."

Out of the darkness of his soul, a small light grew and spread until it seemed to fill him with its shimmering brightness.

"David, this is the Brig." Again it was the voice of the old warrior, hard and uncompromising. "Return to base immediately."

David grinned, and lifted the microphone to his mouth. He thumbed the transmit button. "Beseder! This is Bright Lance leader, homeward bound," and he brought the Navajo around steeply. The mountain was blue on the horizon, and he let the nose sink gradually towards it. He knew that it would not be easy—that it would require all his courage and patience, but he knew that in the end it would be worth it all. Suddenly he needed desperately to be alone with Debra in the peace of Jabulani.

ABOUT EAGLE
by Wilbur Smith

The seeds of *Eagle in the Sky* were planted long before I published my first novel, and before it appeared as a Reader's Digest Condensed Book.

In 1946, when I was twelve years old, I went with my father to buy cattle for the ranch, and I met a young man who had been a Hurricane pilot during the Battle of Britain. He had been shot down in flames over the Channel, and my childish horror still remains with me when I remember how he looked.

He was living alone on a remote ranch for reasons which were clear once I thought about it, which I did often.

I wondered how such a man might find happiness, and the solution occurred to me. When I became interested in writing I thought about it as a short story – the mutilated airman and the lovely blind girl. Now I know that the story was not ripe at that time, and I am glad that I waited so long to tell it.

When at last I started on the necessary research for the book, my wife and I visited Israel, and the deeper we went into Judaism the more intrigued I became. We spent months exploring that incredible land, but always we were drawn back to the golden city of Jerusalem, sitting on its many hills, wrapped in the folds of history. Within days of our going it was plunged into the holocaust of Yom Kippur war and I wonder how many of those cheerful youngsters, who crowded happily into the rear seat of the Volkswagen when we picked them up beside the road, now lie in some lonely desert grave.

Although I have flown light aircraft since I first took instruction at the age of sixteen, I had to research modern jet interceptors and this was not an easy task. An almost neurotic veil of security hangs over most airforce bases – but at last I found amongst the closed ranks people who had read and enjoyed my previous books.

Even they were reluctant to allow me actually to fly one of their beloved Mirage fighters, and I saw the reason later when I was seated in the earthbound flight simulator faced by the bewildering array of instruments and performing what I believed were a few masterly evaluations.

I remember the voice of the flight controller in my earphones. "Mr. Smith, you are now approaching Mach two. You are in a vertical dive, and you are three hundred feet above the ground. What are you going to do?" I solved the problem by raising the canopy and with great dignity stepping out of the cockpit. I faced the controller with the terse command. "Take over, major."

There is much else in the story that has very personal associations. I remember my eighteen-month-old son tottering into the circle of bare earth commanded by a fully grown chained baboon. I reached the child one hundredth of a second before the animal, but his shirt was torn from him and the baboon's claws raised long red scratches across his chest as I snatched him away. The baboon had not been chained by me. The captivity of any wild animal I find completely repellant.

My wife and I try to make a safari into the bush every year, but there are no guns on our safaris. When I was fourteen I shot my first lion – but I have not aimed a rifle at a living thing since I turned twenty-one. The abhorrence that I have for poachers dates also from about that age when I saw the work they had done on a cherished herd of the rare and lovely Roan Antelope that had the run of my father's ranch.

Eagle in the Sky then is a very special book for both my wife and myself. Much of it was actually lived and all of it was deeply felt.

STAY OF EXECUTION

A Sort of Memoir

a condensation of the book by
STEWART ALSOP

Illustrated by Isa Barnett
Published by The Bodley Head, London

To face the prospect of one's own imminent death
is obviously no light matter. Courage is required,
and a special sort of wisdom. A book on such a
subject might easily be morbid, even self-pitying.
Yet Stewart Alsop's "sort of memoir" is triumphantly
neither. It is a book suffused with quiet sincerity
– courageous, and uniquely wise.

On July 6th, 1971, Alsop – a busy and successful
American journalist – was told by the experts that
he had a kind of leukaemia that would probably kill
him within the year, and almost certainly in two.
Writing movingly, but without sentiment, he
describes what it means to live with a terminal
cancer. "One thing I discovered in the first ten days.
A man can't be afraid all the time. . . ."

As well as being a memoir of his full and happy
life – his army service, his days in England where he
met his wife, his career as a writer – his book is also
a suspenseful tale of medical detection, for his
disease still remains mysterious and deeply puzzling
to his doctors. Today their diagnosis has been
amended: his form of leukaemia may not be rapidly
fatal. In March 1974 he was back at work in the
Washington offices of *Newsweek*. "I have now
gained fifteen pounds. I can only say I feel
surprisingly well."

He has received a stay of execution.

PART ONE

I

At about nine thirty on the morning of July 19, 1971, I suddenly
knew that something was terribly wrong with me. I was standing
on top of an old stone wellhead that we use as a dump at our
country place in Maryland, which is called Needwood Forest.
July 19 was a Monday, and I was going back to work after a fine
three-week vacation. My four-year-old son, Andrew, brought out a
couple of cardboard boxes to throw in the dump, and I carried a
plastic pail filled with the weekend's rubbish. We clambered up the
sides of the dump, which are steep and slippery, and Andrew threw
in his boxes and I threw in the contents of the pail. Andrew shouted,
"Come on, Daddy," and scampered for the car. I couldn't move.

I had been feeling a bit tired lately, and I'd had trouble with
shortness of breath. But I had never felt quite like this before. I
was gasping like a fish on a beach, and I could hear my heart
pounding furiously. It was all I could do, for a long moment, to
keep my feet. "Face it, Alsop," I said to myself. "You're in trouble."

Then I walked slowly to the car.

My wife, Tish, was at the wheel. She hardly ever lets me drive.
She has a theory that I begin to think about politics, or something,
and that then I let the car do the driving, which is dangerous.
Nicky, our number five child, and Andrew, number six, were in
the back seat. I said something about feeling lousy, and Tish said

159

it was lucky I had an appointment for a physical with Dr. Perry that afternoon, and we let the subject drop. As Tish drove us back to Washington, the gasping and the pounding eased.

I married Tish in London during the Second World War, when she was eighteen and I had just had my thirtieth birthday. One reason I had fallen in love with Tish, aside from the fact that she was beautiful, was that she was markedly undemonstrative. I found her tendency to say nothing at all for long periods of time oddly entrancing. She is still laconic, especially where matters touching the emotions are concerned, and so am I.

This was one reason we said so little about the way I felt. Perhaps there was another reason too. As a small boy I was sick a lot of the time, asthma and other unpleasant things. But from my college days until that day I stood on the dump I had hardly ever had even a cold, and, like a rich man who thinks the poor must all be stupid, I tended to the notion that sick people were just weak-willed. Anyway, I couldn't believe that I was *really* sick.

By the time we arrived home I felt better, and I drove my own car downtown to the *Newsweek* office. I dictated some letters to my very pretty, very nice, and very competent secretary, Amanda Zimmerman. Then I walked across Pennsylvania Avenue to lunch at the Metropolitan Club. I had a martini and a steak with two old friends—they both recalled later that I looked well and seemed merry as a grig. Then I walked the four blocks to Dr. Perry's office. Halfway there, I was again so dizzy and breathless that I had to wait on a corner through two light changes before walking on.

Dr. Perry, our family doctor, is an able and likable young man with a longish, faintly Lincolnian face. I had the usual tests and then sat in the waiting room until a nurse summoned me. Dr. Perry looked graver and more Lincolnian than usual.

"You're anaemic," he said. "*Very* anaemic. We've retested your blood six times, always with the same results. I want to get you into Georgetown University Hospital right away, this afternoon."

"Is it cancer?" I asked. I knew enough to ask that.

"That's not my first concern now," said Dr. Perry. But from his tone I could tell he had by no means ruled out cancer.

I walked to my car and drove the fifteen minutes to our Cleveland Park house. Tish was in the drive when I came in. "Perry says that

160

I'm very anaemic and that he wants to get me into a hospital right away."

When I said this Tish kissed me, suddenly and surprisingly. We hardly ever kiss in public and, unlike couples much less happily married, we never call each other darling, or even dear. Tish knows a lot more about medicine than I do. She knew enough to suspect strongly what I was suspecting only vaguely.

Tish drove me to Georgetown University Hospital, and as the admission forms were being filled out I spotted a slip with Dr. Perry's name on it and the notation: "Suspected aplastic anaemia." I asked the lady at the desk what aplastic anaemia was. She looked embarrassed, muttered something, and shuffled the slip under some other papers. Obviously I had not been intended to see it.

Upstairs, installed in a surprisingly comfortable room, I was visited by platoons of doctors, most of whom seemed to be in their twenties. They poked me, and pricked me, and drew blood out of me, and asked innumerable questions. Had I ever inhaled a lot of benzine? Did I swallow a lot of aspirin? Had I ever taken a drug called Chloromycetin?

The answer to all these questions was a tentative no. It was especially tentative in the case of the Chloromycetin. I remembered feeling very lousy indeed on a trip to Paris in 1969. I also remembered that the hotel's *valet de chambre*, a friendly fellow, had given me a tube of big white pills guaranteed effective against everything from *migraine* to *la grippe*. Three a day, he promised, would fix me up in a jiffy. So I had taken my three pills a day and soon felt better. Chloromycetin? Unlikely, but I know now what an ass I was to take any unidentified and unprescribed pills at all.

About nine that evening I had my first bone-marrow test. A young doctor asked me to roll over on my stomach, and gave me a shot of Novocaine in the flat bony area at the bottom of my spine. Before I knew what he was doing he had poked a needle into the bone and sucked some marrow out. It was very unpleasant—my legs jerked like a frog's in a laboratory experiment.

The doctor turned over the marrow to a technician, who smeared it on slides and looked at it carefully.

"Enough spicules?" the doctor asked. That question I was to

161

hear often, and always with a prayer that the technician would, as this one did, say yes. The marrow, the doctor said, would be analyzed and Dr. Perry would tell me the results in the morning.

"Will it show whether I have cancer?" I asked.

"Yes," said the young doctor confidently. "Whether you have cancer, and what kind." He didn't sound as though he had much doubt about whether. He went out and left Tish and me alone. I was afraid and reached out for her hand, which felt warm and comforting and very much alive. Tish spent the night on a cot beside my bed. Twice I woke up, despite the sleeping pill I had taken, and was afraid and reached for Tish's hand. Both times she was awake.

The morning hours dragged while we waited for Dr. Perry. We began telephoning the family to let them know what had happened. We started with my generation—my older brother, Joe, and his wife, Susan Mary; my younger brother, John, and his wife, Gussie; my sister, Corinne, who was also in a hospital after an operation for a breast cancer. Then we began calling the four eldest children. Number one, Joe, is twenty-six, an executive of a small computer company in Cambridge, Massachusetts. He wasn't in his office. Number two, Ian, twenty-four, was living in Katmandu, in Nepal, making a living selling Tibetan woodcut prints to tourists. Katmandu was not easily telephonable. So we called our daughter, Elizabeth, who is married to Peter Mahony, an able New York architect, and was working as a children's book editor. Elizabeth— "Fuff", she is called in the family, because when she was a very little girl Ian had pronounced Elizabeth as "Fuff-fuff"—sounded sensible and reassuring. Number four, Stewart, nineteen, was touring with friends and we were unable to reach him.

Then we tried son Joe again. Joe had gone to the Massachusetts Institute of Technology and then helped found this business of his called Intercomp, expecting to make a million right away. He hadn't yet, but a few months before he had done something better when he married Candy Aydelotte, a charming blonde from Texas. By the time we got him on the telephone I had developed a sort of formula. I said I was in a hospital, and when Joe asked what was the matter I said with an attempt at a laugh, "My blood seems to have turned to water."

There was no answering laugh, and quite a long pause. Then Joe said, "I love you, man."

Joe is perhaps the least demonstrative of our undemonstrative family. He is also anything but a fool, and he obviously knew that something must be very wrong. I suddenly felt like crying, and I hung up quickly.

My brother Joe and Susan Mary came in, bearing fresh fruit and words of good cheer. When they left, Tish left too, to do an errand, and I felt more lonely than I had ever felt in my life.

About noon Tish came back—still no Dr. Perry. The usual hospital lunch was wheeled in—curiously unappetizing. Tish made me a martini and it helped to paper over the panicky suspense I was beginning to feel. Soon after lunch Dr. Perry came. There was something in his face that smelled of bad news.

"I'm sorry," he said, and then I *knew* it was bad news. "But you have leukaemia. Acute myeloblastic leukaemia."

"Are you sure?" I was rather proud that my voice was steady.

"Ninety-five per cent sure," he said.

Then he explained that he had been promised a bed for me at the National Institutes of Health, in nearby Bethesda, Maryland, "where they know more about leukaemia than anywhere in the world." Georgetown also had excellent leukaemia specialists, and if I preferred I could stay right here, where I'd have a private room, and Tish could spend the night occasionally. At NIH there were only double rooms. In either case I would be given a course of chemotherapy to get rid of the malignant cells. This treatment could last for as short a time as two weeks, but it was likely to be longer, maybe a month or more.

I made the decision easily. I'd go to NIH. In retrospect I think it was partly what Dr. Perry had said—"where they know more about leukaemia than anywhere"—and partly the reputation of NIH, which, although I never paid any attention to such matters, I had unconsciously absorbed. A man who knows his life is in danger instinctively tries to better the odds. The decision almost certainly prolonged my life. Chemotherapy, I discovered later, is a Rubicon. It buys the leukaemia patient some time—if he is lucky, quite a bit of time—but it can also destroy whatever it is that enables the body to resist the leukaemic cells. In the end, death is almost certain. At

Georgetown I'd have been put into chemotherapy immediately. I probably would have at NIH too, if it hadn't been for Dr. John Glick.

The next day Tish drove me home to collect some clothes and books, and from there to NIH, a cluster of functional brick buildings, most of them built in the 1950s during the Eisenhower administrations. We took the elevator to the thirteenth floor, on which the leukaemia ward is inauspiciously located, and Dr. Glick was waiting. I got into bed in a small double room and he sat down to talk.

He seemed surprisingly young, but I was getting used to that—some of the doctors at Georgetown looked like college freshmen. He had a thin, sallow, interesting face and a quick, eager, intense manner. It was very soon clear that he was highly intelligent, highly competent, and—this can be even more important to a patient whose life is at risk—a nice man and a good man.

The reason Dr. Perry had been so late, Dr. Glick said, was that the Georgetown doctors had spent most of Tuesday morning arguing about my marrow slide. It was so unusual that he intended to give me another marrow test that evening.

The purpose of a marrow test, I was to learn, is to find what a leukaemic's malignant cells are up to—whether they are crowding out and killing the good cells or, one prays, decreasing. It is in the bone marrow that the cells of the bloodstream are produced.

The oddest thing about my Georgetown slide was that my marrow had so few cells of any kind, good or bad. "Hypocellular," Dr. Glick called it. Of the cells they did find, about forty-four per cent were abnormal. Dr. Glick added, with a candour I soon discovered was characteristic, that they were very ugly. Most of them looked like the cells of acute myeloblastic leukaemia, AML for short. But some looked like another kind of leukaemia, acute lymphoblastic leukaemia (ALL), and some like the cells of still another kind of marrow cancer, dysproteinaemia—not a leukaemia at all. And even the myeloblastic, or AML, cells ("blasts", I was going to learn to call these) didn't look *exactly* like AML cells.

I was, in fact, a puzzle altogether, Dr. Glick said. In typical acute leukaemia the malignant cells tend to fill the marrow almost to bursting, enough to make the shinbones ache, whereas in my marrow, cells of any kind were scarce; in the blood, usually, the white cell count is very high and abnormal cells are almost always present. But in my blood the white count was very low and there were no abnormal cells. These appeared to be only in the marrow.

For now, however, in spite of these oddities, the diagnosis was acute myeloblastic leukaemia. Dr. Glick told us he had been assigned to my case, and we would be seeing a lot of each other.

Then he gave me a head-to-toe physical examination, peering into my eyes and thumping me all over. He asked me all the questions I'd been asked at Georgetown plus a lot of new ones, and in the intervals I asked him some. How old was he? Twenty-eight. How long had he been in NIH? Only about three weeks. Was he married? Yes. Children? One on the way. He asked how long I had been feeling badly. I said I had had trouble with breathlessness and heart pounding at least since early spring, and maybe longer. Couldn't I pin down just when these symptoms had first appeared?

I told him about one time, in the late summer of the year before, when Tish and I had played tennis at Needwood against Rowland Evans and his wife, Kay. Evans is a friend and fellow columnist and a much better tennis player than I am. I've always wanted to beat him, and Tish and I almost won the first set. Then I sat under a beech tree, feeling breathless, dizzy, with my heart pounding furiously, wondering if I were going to die. At the time, I ascribed my symptoms to the sun, advancing age, and my disappointed ambition to beat Evans. I remembered another time, at the opening of the hunting season that September, when I'd set off with my old Winchester 12-gauge shotgun and had suddenly felt awful. I'd had to sit down and then turn back. I realized I'd been bothered with breathlessness during the winter. In the spring it was worse. What seemed particularly to interest Dr. Glick in all this was my left shinbone. I have played a lot of tennis since I was a boy, rather incompetently, but with a lot of competitive spirit. I like to claim that I have "the arrogant grace of the great natural athlete," but when I serve I often inadvertently hit my left shinbone with my racket on the follow-through, which great natural athletes don't often do. So my left shinbone looked like a battlefield, with many old scars healed over. There was one new and unhealed scar on my knee, which is higher than I usually hit myself.

165

How long had this been going on? Dr. Glick asked. Oh, I'd been hitting myself with my racket for a long time, I said. Only lately it had seemed to bleed a lot, I supposed because I had a new steel racket. How much did it bleed? Well, lately my left leg would be covered with blood. He explained why he was so interested in my left shinbone. Cells called platelets control bleeding, and a low platelet count, like a high white blood cell count, is characteristic of leukaemia. My platelet count was very low, so the bloodied shinbone might provide evidence of how long I'd had leukaemia.

That first day John Glick was very impersonal, but I liked him instinctively and so did Tish. Later, liking grew into affection and admiration and also into genuine friendship, a relationship not easily attained between a twenty-eight-year-old and a man twice his age. Even that first day it seemed to me that he was genuinely interested in my case, perhaps for the same reason that Sherlock Holmes found his difficult cases most stimulating. John has a good sense of humour, but when he is chasing after clues to a diagnosis he has the humourless intensity of a bloodhound on the trail.

He is at once kindly and candid, and for a doctor dealing with leukaemics that is an uncomfortable combination. I asked him what was likely to happen to me, and he told me—as Dr. Perry had— that I would probably be given chemotherapy to induce a remission. The chemicals are powerful, he said—"we call them poisons, and that is what they are"—killing the bad cells, but many of the good too. I remarked that one of the Georgetown doctors had said that treating leukaemia was like trying to kill the weeds without killing the grass. Dr. Glick said that was about right—during chemotherapy the red blood cells and the platelets can be maintained at safe levels by transfusions, but there is no sure way to maintain the white blood cells at a satisfactory level. Since they are the body's protection against infection, infection during chemotherapy is the main danger to a leukaemic's life.

That was why I'd probably end up in a laminar flow room. Such a room existed at NIH but not at Georgetown. In a laminar flow room the air flows only one way. It is pumped in from outdoors, through the room, and out into the hospital. On the thirteenth floor there is virtually no danger of infection from the outside air, whereas the hospital air is likely to contain sources of infection. The

166

patient never leaves the room until he is in remission and his white cells are back at a safe level. Doctors and nurses wear rubber gloves and treat the patient through a transparent plastic wall; everything is sterilized—sheets, clothes, medicine bottles, everything.

"Can you sterilize martinis?" I asked. The laminar flow room sounded horrible.

"Yes," Dr. Glick said with a smile. "But you won't feel at all well while you're under treatment, even with martinis. After every five days of treatment we give you a rest for a few days, and then you'll feel better." My hair, or most of it, would probably fall out during chemotherapy, and I'd lose a lot of weight. But the weight comes back during a successful remission, and as for the hair, "We have a fine collection of wigs at NIH."

What were the chances of a successful remission? Better than fifty per cent, he said. This gave me pause. Clearly, the other fifty per cent left the laminar flow rooms one way only, like the air. A person in remission could lead a normal life, Dr. Glick said. I could go back to my job, and I might even be able to play tennis again.

How long would a remission last?

"About fifty per cent of our patients with AML who go into remission last a year or more," he said, trying to sound cheerful.

How many died before two years?

Dr. Glick hesitated a moment. "About ninety-five per cent," he said, and briskly changed the subject.

For the first of the many marrow tests I have had at Dr. Glick's hands, I was led into a treament room wearing one of those hospital gowns, open at the back, which seem designed to make the patient feel as unhappy and humiliated as possible. There were a couple of nurses and a male technician in the room. I lay down on my stomach, and as Dr. Glick swabbed off my lower back he said, "This is the Novocaine. It will feel like a mosquito bite."

"Mosquito bite, hell," I said. "It's a bloody great wasp."

"O.K.," he said, "A wasp. Now here's another wasp, to get in a little deeper." This second needle, because of the Novocaine, didn't hurt so much. He waited a bit before he went in with a third needle. I could feel it go through the bone and into the marrow, and I could feel the pull as he drew some marrow out. Again, as at Georgetown, my legs jerked like a frog's.

There was a little delay as the technician did things with slides. "Sorry," the technician said, "no spicules."

Dr. Glick explained what spicules are: bits of marrow with fat in them, which give a representative sample of the marrow cells. Without enough spicules the slide may give a wrong picture of what is going on in the marrow. When the marrow was, as in my case, very thin in all kinds of cells, it was particularly important to get enough. Being marrowed—the noun is used as a verb—is not so much painful as somehow psychically demeaning.

"We'll have to go in again, with a bigger needle," said Dr. Glick. "This won't take a minute." I could feel the needle go in again, and this time it hurt more.

"It's pretty thin," said the technician, "but it may be enough."

Dr. Glick said we'd leave it at that; he'd do another in the morning. "We'll try to get a biopsy too," he said.

That night was a bad night. Tish went home about ten. Dr. Glick had prescribed a sleeping pill, and I sneaked another I had in my shaving kit and slept for about four hours. When I woke up the room was pitch-dark, and my room-mate snored lightly. I thought first about the marrow test next morning. Then about what Dr. Glick had told me. Would it really be worthwhile to spend a month or more cooped up all alone in a laminar flow room, losing my hair and my flesh, and then either to die in that room, or emerge a bald skeleton and wait for death? Would it not be more sensible to reach for Hamlet's "bare bodkin," in the shape of a bottle of sleeping pills?

And then the reality of death crowded in on me—the end of a pleasant life, never to see Tish or Andrew or Nicky or the four older children again, never to go to Needwood again, or laugh with friends, or see the spring come. There came upon me a terrible sense of aloneness, of vulnerability, of nakedness, of helplessness. I fumbled for another pill and at last dozed off.

I never again had a night as bad as that night, nor, I think, shall I ever again. For a kind of protective mechanism took over, after the first shock of being told of the imminence of death, and I suspect that this is true of most people. Partly it's an act of will—a decision to allot to the grim future only its share of your thoughts.

My brother John sent me *Uncle Fred in the Springtime* by

P. G. Wodehouse, and my brother Joe sent me *The Duke's Children* by Anthony Trollope. I'd read both before, but both are marvellously rereadable, and Uncle Fred and the Duke of Omnium got me through the next few evenings, after Tish left. I read till the sleeping pill they gave me began to take effect, and then dozed off.

The conscious effort to close off one's mind to the inevitability of death accounts for, I suspect, the oddly cheerful tone of most of what I've written in this book. But the protective mechanism is also an unconscious reaction. I've instinctively preferred to recall wartime episodes that had amused me, like my first meeting with Tish, rather than the times when I was unhappy or afraid. And the episodes I've remembered from my career as a journalist are rarely those to which profound meaning might be attached.

I remember seeing much the same process at work in combat. On my first day at the front in Italy I wandered down a path with Deering Danielson, another American in the British army. We looked up and saw a couple of planes manœuvring above us. I remember diving for a ditch as the bullets smack-smacked into the earth near us, and the sudden incredulous awareness that we, good old Deering and inoffensive Stew, were the targets of the bullets. But the incredulity soon wears off and a kind of unhappy inner stolidity takes over, coupled with a protective conviction that the shell will kill somebody else—not you.

In this way the unbearable becomes bearable, and one learns to live with death by not thinking about it too much.

II

My mother died on June 23, 1971, My sister, Corinne Chubb, had her breast cancer operation on July 3. I got my acute leukaemia diagnosis on July 20. Those were not good weeks for the Alsops.

My sister is married to a very able and successful insurance executive, Percy Chubb. Like me, she has six children, and she and Percy also have such pleasant appurtenances as a big place in New Jersey, a yacht, and half of a beautiful island in the Caribbean. She is the second oldest of the four of us. After Joe. To her brothers Corinne has always been "Sis".

Sis had been home from the hospital for a few days, and I was still in NIH when she telephoned me to tell me her theory of what was going on in heaven. Mother, Sis said, having been there almost a month, had asked for a little chat with God. She had told God that she did not want her son Stew or her daughter, Corinne, to join her yet; she would tell Him when the time had come. God, of course, had agreed to put off the reunion.

Sis's theory struck me as sound. Mother was not a pretty woman, but she had an amazing self-assurance and a lot of charm. The self-assurance derived from the charm, I think, because the charm made it possible for her almost always to get her way. The charm in turn derived from the fact that she was a woman much involved in life, with a deep interest in other people.

When we were young an old friend of Mother's told us the story of how, as a girl, Mother charmed Lord Dunsany, an Anglo-Irish aristocrat and man of letters, who was immensely tall, immensely distinguished, and immensely silent. My grandmother, who was a sister of President Theodore Roosevelt and a famous hostess of her era, gave Lord Dunsany a big dinner party in New York. A very pretty and highly intelligent girl on the playwright poet's right had been straining every nerve to get him to talk, but Lord Dunsany responded only with long silences. When Mother's turn came she shifted right round to face Lord Dunsany, put both elbows on the table, smiled worshipfully, and asked, "Where did genius begin?" Thereafter, it was impossible to stop the great man talking.

Whenever Mother expressed sympathy or interest a little too enthusiastically we would turn around, put our elbows on the table, and ask, "Where did genius begin?" This made her laugh and damped her down a bit, but not for long.

During her last year, when she was eighty-four, she had constant pains in her stomach, and the flame of her life flickered. Mother knew she was going to die and said more than once that she hoped it would be soon. It was a sad last year. Macbeth said of Lady Macbeth, "She should have died hereafter." Mother should have died herebefore. That is true, I suppose, of many old people. But until her last year or so the self-assurance and charm remained at full strength. Both were displayed in her relationship with her first cousin and childhood friend, Eleanor Roosevelt, and with her more distant cousin, Franklin Roosevelt.

170

I recall vividly—all too vividly—a wartime incident which illustrated that relationship. I volunteered to join the British army shortly before Pearl Harbor. This was not as idealistic as it sounds. I had been turned down by all three American services because of a history of asthma and occasional high blood pressure, and I was about to be reclassified as fit for limited service. I could see myself folding towels in some damnable camp in South Carolina while my friends were seeking a hero's reputation at the cannon's mouth and having a lot of fun. I had heard from my younger brother, John, that a British regiment, the King's Royal Rifle Corps, which had originated in colonial America as the 60th Royal Americans, was taking a few American volunteers. So I went to the British Embassy and asked to see the military attaché.

I was ushered into the office of a tall, thin major with an enormous moustache. I told him I had been turned down on medical grounds by our own services. "Eyes all right?" he asked.

I said they were twenty-twenty, and he told me not to worry about getting into the 60th Rifles—as the King's Royal Rifle Corps was called informally. He'd get me onto a freighter in a convoy soon. He had a bit of advice for me: "Be sure to take a dinner jacket, and a shotgun for the grouse season. And, if you can manage it, ship over a small runabout—very useful for weekends."

He was a bit out of touch, as I discovered some months later when I arrived at the 60th's training depot in Winchester. I slept on the floor on a straw mattress called a palliasse, ate cold porridge, and, as a mere rifleman, or private, had no use at all for a dinner jacket, a shotgun, or a runabout.

One day I was summoned from the parade ground to a telephone and was astonished to hear the voice of the American ambassador to England, John Winant. Mrs. Roosevelt, he said, had come on a visit to Britain, and my mother had asked her to be sure to look me up and report on my state of mind and health. Could I come to tea the next day at the Embassy?

I felt very humble at tea, surrounded by Ambassador Winant, various intimidating people with titles, and the President's wife. I was sitting in embarrassed silence when Cousin Eleanor handed me a cup of tea. As I reached to take it, the brass buttons on the fly of my trousers burst from their moorings and rolled across the floor. There was a dreadful moment as all eyes followed one button which continued to roll interminably. Then, in a kindly effort to cover my confusion, the President's wife asked me whether the British troops appreciated that horrid fake ham which was a major item of lend-lease. I blurted out the tactless truth—that they hated the stuff—and then retired, my hand held over my fly.

Mother thought nothing of asking her first cousin to do so small an errand for her—what were families for? Since she had made many anti-New Deal speeches, it took a certain brass for her to ask favours of F.D.R., but this didn't bother her. Twice during the war she called Pa Watson, one of his secretaries, and politely demanded a little chat with the President. Once was when she wanted to make sure that my brother Joe would be on the prisoner exchange list— the Japanese had captured him when they took Hong Kong. The other time was when the American army had refused to accept my transfer from the British. Both times Mother had her way. And both times the little chat went on for more than an hour. The President liked her, despite her politics, and he was sentimental about old times. I don't suppose he ever knew that when he was courting Eleanor, Eleanor's cousin Corinne always referred to him as "the Featherduster" in her diary and repeatedly expressed the hope that "darling Eleanor" would not marry him, with his "narrow shoulders" and "his eyes too close together."

When Sis and I got into trouble, therefore, it was natural to imagine Mother's asking for a little chat with God. After Sis told me her theory I got into the habit, when seized with the fear of death, of making a small prayer: "Please Mother, please God." Eventually, I added two more people in heaven I had loved, my father and my Scottish nurse, Aggie Guthrie, who nursed me through a sick childhood. The prayer became standardized: "Please God, please Mother, please Father, please Aggie."

III

"What are the counts?" Or, "Your platelets are holding up O.K., but your granulocytes are in the cellar." Or, "Your haemoglobin is around nine point five. But don't worry—if it goes below nine, we'll transfuse you and bring you back over eleven."

172

Before I got sick all this would have been gobbledegook to me, but after the first week or so at NIH I spoke this new language like a native. After I understood the meaning of the very frequent blood counts and the less frequent marrow tests, I would wait for the results—as all leukaemics do—with a fast-beating heart. For they can spell life, or death.

In retrospect, I am astonished at how little I once knew about the blood and the function of the marrow. A tiny drop of blood at the end of your finger can show quickly, under a microscope, how energetic you are, how you would bleed if badly cut, what defences you have against infection, and all sorts of other things.

Every morning, patients in Ward 13 of NIH would get a "finger stick" to provide that revealing drop of blood. A cheerful lady with faded blonde hair would come around at about eight and deftly jab a little needle into your finger. Next she would squeeze the blood into thin plastic tubes and from these onto glass slides. About four hours later, after the technicians had analyzed the blood, the patient would be told the counts. A patient with good counts would feel bucked up for the day. Bad counts were bad news—much worse news than the gloomiest newspaper headlines.

My counts when I entered NIH were: haemoglobin, 6.8; platelets, 18,000; white blood count, 1100 with 14 per cent granulocytes. I once asked John Glick what these figures really meant, and he went into details about cells per cubic centimetre and the like. I have never been able to balance my cheque book, and he soon lost me. The mathematics don't interest the leukaemic anyway. What matters to him is how far he is away from death. Although I'd played tennis the weekend before and had waded across the upper Potomac to fly-fish for smallmouth bass four days earlier, those first counts meant that I was quite close to being dead.

Haemoglobin supplies energy, *joie de vivre*. If you have a high haemoglobin count—lots of red blood cells—you're in a mountain-climbing or girl-chasing mood. *An inability to think, a strong desire to doze and drink* (G. K. Chesterton, or is it Hilaire Belloc?) sums up the way a person with a low haemoglobin count feels.

A man can carry on somehow—"to grunt and sweat under a weary life"—with a haemoglobin count of 10 or so. I suspect, and so does John Glick, that my haemoglobin count had been far below normal for as much as a year before I went to NIH. For years I have liked to have a brief snooze in the afternoon (so did Napoleon Bonaparte, Winston Churchill, Lyndon Johnson, and for that matter John F. Kennedy, who was younger than I). The year before I went to NIH my snoozes had become longer and longer—every afternoon I'd get almost unbearably sleepy, lie down on the couch in my office, and go into a catatonic state.

A normal haemoglobin count is between 14 and 16—and the closer to 16 the more *joie de vivre*. When a person's red blood count goes below 8 he is in danger of congestive heart failure. To supply sufficient energy-giving haemoglobin to the lungs and the rest of the body, the heart has to work overtime, and under sufficient stress just gives up, like a furnace that explodes or simply goes out when it can't meet the demands placed on it.

My breathlessness and the heavy beating of my heart before I went to Dr. Perry's office were outward and visible signs of a low haemoglobin count. With a count of 6.8 I was lucky I hadn't died on the tennis court or in the middle of the upper Potomac. But a low red blood count can be temporarily corrected in a few hours with a haemoglobin transfusion. John Glick stuck a needle in a vein the first night I was in NIH, hung a bag of blood on a metal rack called an IV—for intravenous—and fed it into my bloodstream. The bags vary, but they average about two pints. After four bags I felt full of beans—fuller of beans than I had for a good many weeks.

A doctor does not like to transfuse his patients any more than necessary, though. With every four bags of fresh blood there is about a one and a half per cent chance of hepatitis, a liver inflammation for which there is no specific cure. A patient who has had a lot of transfusions is lucky if he hasn't caught hepatitis, and a patient with both leukaemia and hepatitis is not at all a good insurance risk. Ways of screening out hepatitis are being improved constantly, but the screen is not yet one hundred per cent safe.

Red blood transfusions were first performed around the turn of the century; they were the first true body transplants. Since then techniques for matching blood precisely to avoid rejection have been perfected. Platelet transfusion, about which I shall have more to say later, is a much more recent technique. Platelets, as Dr. Glick explained when he was looking at the scars on my shin, are the cells

174

in your blood that cause clotting and prevent a man from bleeding to death if he is cut. Death from haemorrhage was the most likely exit for a leukaemic before platelet transfusion techniques were invented. Now it is rare.

Platelet counts vary widely. A low normal would be around 160,000, but some people have 400,000 or more; 20,000 is considered the danger point. My count was 18,000, so John Glick gave me two bags of platelets that first night too. The count briefly jumped to 34,000, then rapidly sank back to around 18,000. But those healed old tennis-racket scars luckily suggested that even with that low count I did not haemorrhage easily. I could manage with fewer platelets than most.

So, on that first day in NIH, July 21, my haemoglobin and my platelets were both in the danger zone. My white blood count— 1100 with 14 per cent granulocytes—was even more dangerously low. The white blood cells are the cells that fight off infection. It is their fierceness in attacking alien cells that makes organ transplants so difficult.

There are several kinds of white blood cells, but for a leukaemic the most important are granulocytes. These are the principal battlers against infection. So when a doctor asks for the WBC— white blood count—he expects not only the total count but the percentage of granulocytes within that total. A normal WBC would be 4000 to 10,000 white cells, with anywhere from 45 per cent to 75 per cent granulocytes. A count of 500 granulocytes is the minimum safety level. With a count of 500 the body can put up some sort of fight against infection. With less than 500 the body has very little fight left. When I entered the hospital my granulocyte count was about 150. My lack of fight soon became apparent.

I entered NIH on a Wednesday, and on Friday, after the blood and platelet transfusions and two marrow tests, John Glick made a difficult decision. He would not put me into chemotherapy; instead, for the time being, at least, he would do nothing—simply send me home and keep an eye on me.

Dr. Glick and Dr. Edward Henderson, the chief of the leukaemic section, and the other doctors agreed by a big majority that I had AML. But to John's intuitive medical eye there was something so fishy-looking about the abnormal cells in my marrow, and something so unusual about my case, that he decided to wait and see, rather than put me into the laminar flow room. There were risks involved, of course. The greatest risk was that I might die of infection because of my defenceless state. But such risks had to be balanced against a near certainty—that if I had chemotherapy I would die, probably within a year, almost certainly within two. I could, John Glick told Tish and me, go home the next day.

On the afternoon of that Friday—July 23—I convened a small business meeting in an anteroom of the hospital. My younger brother, John, who is president of the Covenant Group of Insurance Companies and is the businessman of the family, flew down from Hartford. My old friend and broker Philip Watts joined us, and the three of us conferred solemnly about the changed family financial prospects, given the statistical probability that I would be dead in a year or a bit more.

We were calm and businesslike as we counted up my assets and discussed the need for a new will, for selling my two houses (but not on a forced-sale basis), for reinvestment of my securities to produce maximum income rather than growth to provide adequately for Tish, and so on. It gave me an odd sense of unreality—it was hard to grasp that it was, after all, *my* death we were discussing. I had a feeling that we were three characters in a rather bad play. Then, as the discussion wound to an end and we poured Scotch and sodas, I began to have another feeling. It was midsummer and the anteroom was air-conditioned, but it seemed to me that somebody must have turned the air conditioning way up. I kept shivering, and asked a nurse for a blanket. By the time we had finished our Scotches I was shivering uncontrollably. I had a chill—my first chill, as far as I can remember, but not my last.

That night my temperature went to 102, and on Saturday morning to 104. By Saturday afternoon, instead of going home, I was attached via a vein in my right arm to two antibiotics, both very powerful—John Glick called them cidal antibiotics. Since my defence against infection was so inadequate (thanks to that meagre supply of granulocytes), the antibiotics must not only kill whatever infection was causing my fever, but ensure that it didn't recur. I would, therefore, have to be hooked up to antibiotics for ten days.

Why, I asked Dr. Glick, not give me a white cell transfusion, like the haemoglobin and platelet transfusions I'd already had? That was just the trouble, he said. White cell transfusions were difficult. They had been done at NIH, but it was very hard to match the cells, and the transfusions often fail because the existing white cells fight off the reinforcing cells as though they were invaders. The only reliable white cell transfusions, he explained, were between identical twins. The next best was a transfusion from a brother or sister with the same genetic inheritance. Even so, the effects didn't last more than a few days. So except *in extremis*, the cidal antibiotics were better weapons against infection.

My sudden fever abated soon after I went on antibiotics. Until that Saturday morning I had not felt especially sick. But when my temperature went up to 104 I was a sick man and knew it. After the antibiotics took effect I again felt pretty well, and perhaps as a distraction from fear, I wanted to see people. We would have daily picnics, complete with martinis or wine, in one of the two recreation rooms of Ward 13, to the surprise and occasional irritation of nurses and other patients. But, however I felt, John Glick kept that damned needle in a vein for the full ten days. And against the time when he might want to try a platelet transfusion or even a white blood cell transfusion from them, he asked for blood tests from my brothers. He ruled Sis out.

My brother John had an entirely different sort of blood from mine. Joe's turned out to be a perfect fit, but, John Glick remarked, "a bit old." Naturally I could hardly wait to repeat this remark to my older brother. Fortunately, so far, I haven't had to call on him for his elderly white blood cells, but his elderly platelets have proved very useful indeed.

IV

Journalists usually acquire bad habits—indolence and a tendency to drink too many martinis, for example. I am a slave to both habits, but I have managed to acquire one good habit as well.

Because I know how unreliable my memory is, I keep a notebook within easy reach at all times and I spend a lot of time scribbling in it. I feel naked without one, and, being a pack rat by nature, I keep them all.

The one I had with me when I was hospitalized was about half filled with the raw material a Washington columnist uses to make his livelihood. Towards the beginning there are notes about one of those "revolts" that go on in the State Department and never get anywhere: "Young Turks . . . Union? . . . Old Turks edgy . . ." Then at the top of a page there is the word "leukaemia".

I scribbled this the morning after Dr. Perry had pronounced my sentence. Then some more scribbles: "Amazing how nice almost everybody is. . . . God tempers the wind to the shorn lamb . . . old cliché . . . suddenly a vivid visual picture . . . *Horribilis mors perturbat me*. . . . *Perturbat* the right word . . . remission of sins . . ."

Then there are a few words that frightened me as much as I have ever been frightened by words. One morning several days after I had my chill and fever, and while I was still attached to the IV, Tish suggested that we go to the solarium on the floor above, to smell a bit of fresh air and see the sun. As I pushed my IV stand in front of me on its wheels, with the bottles of antibiotics dangling from it, we walked out into the open air. But the air was not all that open. The solarium was completely covered with a thick wire mesh, overhead as well as along the sides. The purpose, obviously, was to prevent suicides. It gave me a trapped feeling. Tish and I lay in the sun for a while on folding cots and I tried to read, but the sun was too bright. Restlessly I got up to do some exploring, pushed open a door, and found myself in the auditorium.

Then I saw the words that frightened me. There was a large placard on a stand, presumably for the indoctrination of doctors and nurses newly arrived at the National Cancer Institute of NIH. It was headed RULES FOR ADMISSION. There were ten or twelve of them. I read only the first two: ALL PATIENTS MUST HAVE INCURABLE CANCER. ALL PATIENTS MUST BE INFORMED FRANKLY OF THEIR CASE.

I turned around quickly and shut the door. I said nothing to Tish, except that I wanted to go back to the room. Somehow those printed words brought home the reality to me in a way that all John Glick's kindly candour had not, and inside me there was a dark pit of fear. I can't talk about fear when I feel it, even with my wife. I can talk about it only when it's over.

I suppose I first read the Latin tag scribbled in my notebook—

178

Horribilis mors perturbat me—in about third-form year at Groton school, where Latin was compulsory. I remember thinking that "perturbed" seemed a rather mild reaction to "horrible death." But it turned out to be, as I also scribbled, "the right word." Not that I wasn't afraid. I was, and I hated the idea of dying soon. After the initial shock of being told that I had a lethal form of cancer, though, the protective mechanism took over, so that for the most part perturbed rather than terrified is what I was.

"Amazing how nice almost everybody is." Ward 13, I discovered later, was not a popular ward with the nurses, and it was hard to keep it fully staffed. Taking care of leukaemics is a lot of work. They have needles in their arms a good deal of the time, and the needles are always getting clogged or coming unstuck. And leukaemics require a lot of care in other ways, especially those in the laminar flow rooms. Moreover, as one young nurse remarked to me, "Gee, this ward is just so *depressing*." So it is, but almost all the nurses did their very best to seem briskly cheerful. The patients most of the time felt too horrible to be very genial. But they too made an effort, at least at concealing despair. Cancer was hardly ever mentioned, death never.

"Remission of sins"—the phrase tantalized my memory. It was suggested, of course, by the remission, alas temporary, which with luck followed chemotherapy—but I couldn't remember where it came from until Tish supplied the rest—"remission of sins, resurrection of the dead, and life everlasting." The Creed, of course.

Leafing through that notebook brings back to me vividly bits and pieces of that first stay at NIH. Tish would come in every day at about eleven, go out in the afternoon to do errands, and then come back for dinner, bringing agreeable titbits to vary the hospital diet. At first her devotion made me feel a trifle guilty, since when she had been in the hospital, usually with a new baby, I had rarely been able to force myself to spend more than an hour with her, hating hospitals as I do. But I soon got used to her being with me most of the day and resented it when she left me alone. I more than resented it—I feared it. Under the word "leukaemia" I had scribbled, "Tish left briefly this afternoon and suddenly I was alone with an awful loneliness." Those words tell something about what it is like to have a killing cancer, especially at first.

You become terribly dependent on other people, on their physical presence. Ordinarily I rather like being alone. During those days at NIH I hated it. But when Tish asked me if I wanted Nicky and Andrew to visit me, I said I didn't. There is something demeaning about being in pyjamas in daylight, hooked up to an IV, surrounded by nurses and sick people, and I didn't want my children to see me demeaned. Such dependence infuriated me. I have fought being dependent all my life. Perhaps it's in the genes.

I found out a bit about my genes in 1968. In that year, as its demise approached, the dear old *Saturday Evening Post* started a series on American families, in a futile attempt to recapture some of the old *Post* readership. The editors asked me to do a piece about my family, and I agreed.

It wasn't a very good piece. The cast of characters ranged from a couple of Presidents to the family thief and a collateral murderer, and it was too complex. But I got an unexpected pleasure out of finding out about my ancestors. It gave me a comforting sense of being part of a continuum, of something that had started a long, long time before I was born and would go on for a long, long time after I was dead. And I found out some interesting facts.

For one thing, not one of my direct forebears, on either my mother's side or my father's, had ever taken any part in any war. During the Civil War, Theodore Roosevelt's father, who was my great-grandfather, had been appointed to something called the Sanitary Commission, which was an elegant draft dodge. Perhaps that was why T.R. was so much the warrior. On the Alsop side, Joseph Wright Alsop III had "sent a man in his place" during the Civil War. Joseph Alsop I did the same in the Revolution.

For another thing, not one of my ancestors had worked for any length of time in a position of salaried dependence. I think these two characteristics were related. It was not that my ancestors were cowards, though no doubt some of them were. They just hated the idea of being in a subordinate and dependent position—and nothing is more dependent and subordinate than an army recruit.

I suspect that I joined the 60th Rifles because of my genes. I had an irrational feeling that in a foreign army I would be more my own master, and if it turned out to be intolerable I could just resign. My genes, I think (plus some small tax advantage), also

180

explain why my contracts with the *Post* and *Newsweek* have been as an independent contractor rather than a salaried employee. This provision has given me the wholly illusory feeling of being my own master, free to come and go as I please.

In any case, genes or no genes, the condition to which being seriously ill reduced me was repugnant. I was dependent on the nurses. If I wanted a sleeping pill, or to have my bedclothes changed (I had the sweats every night), I had to ask a nurse. If a nurse woke me up to weigh me, I had to get up and get weighed. It was like being a private all over again.

I was dependent for my very life on John Glick, and it was he, not I, who decided when I could have my IV removed, whether I could go home, and what I could do when I got there.

I was dependent above all on Tish, not only for edible and palatable titbits, books, and the like, but for the squeeze of a warm hand in a season of darkness and fear. Knowing how I resented my state, the emotional sustenance she gave me was always unspoken. And in time I got used to it. I even came, in a way, for the first time in my life to enjoy it.

I FIRST MET Tish in the summer of 1942, when I was an officer cadet in the King's Royal Rifle Corps. The training unit was stationed in the lovely old cathedral town of York. There were five other Americans also in the unit, one a very handsome recent Harvard graduate, George Thomson, who was later best man at my wedding.

George, a man of great charm, was the social manager of the Americans in the 60th Rifles. He had a genius for getting to know people, and within months knew half of England, especially the fraction that owned the stately homes. Somehow he had got an introduction to the premier baron of England, whose stately home was Allerton Castle, near York. The premier baron is the baron whose ancestors were barons before any other baron's ancestors. The premier baroness had written to George, asking him to come for the weekend and bring a friend.

We wangled some petrol and drove to the castle. It was an architectural disaster. A nineteenth-century premier baron, disenchanted with the Tudor castle, had torn the whole thing down and replaced it with a monstrous fake which looked like those the

American robber barons used to build on the Hudson or Long Island.

We approached the monstrous pile cautiously. There was no sign of life. No one answered our knocks. Then the door was flung open and there stood the premier baron himself. With bulging eyes and baronial nose, he was straight out of P. G. Wodehouse.

"Who are *you*?" he asked, not very hospitably.

George started to explain, and the baron, noting his accent, interrupted. "Are you Americans?" he asked accusingly.

George said we were. "Good God!" said the baron, profoundly moved. "Always had a rule here, back to my grandfather's time. No motorcars. No Americans." He paused for a moment. "However," he said briskly, "here you are. Might as well come in."

Inside we found a party in progress. A huge table in the banquet hall groaned with grouse, fruit, vegetables from the garden, and the best claret and port from the cellar. In a comfortable sitting room we had very cold martinis and a pleasant surprise—two pretty girls, both wearing a lot of lipstick and swilling martinis with enthusiasm. What with the lipstick and the gin, George and I thought they must be nineteen or twenty, a respectable age for us, since George was twenty-four and I was twenty-eight. One of them was a Saxon blonde and clearly the daughter of the premier baron. The other—introduced as Tish, real name Patricia—had mouse-coloured hair and attracted me strangely. As I later wrote to the family, she looked like a Trollope heroine, one of the really nice ones.

I sat next to her at dinner. My hair had been cut very short—the British army's idea, not mine—and her first remark to me was, "You look like a criminal." This seemed an intriguing start, but after that I could hardly get her to say more than "Please pass the salt," which intrigued me still more, since I had been brought up among girls with a noticeable tendency to babble.

As a result of gin, claret, and port, the party picked up steam. Emboldended by it all, I inveigled Tish into the rose garden and kissed her, a gesture which she returned with gratifying warmth. Unfortunately the premier baroness caught us. Later I learned that she had that very night written a letter to Mrs. Hankey, Tish's mother, in London, warning in strong terms of the dangers inherent in Tish's "hot Spanish blood." Tish, it turned out, had been brought up in Gibraltar, where her English grandfather had married a beautiful Spanish girl. The beautiful Spanish girl had produced Tish's mother.

I also later discovered something else—that Tish, despite the lipstick and the martinis, was only sixteen when I met her. Even so, that night in the rose garden I had fallen in love with her, and though she has always denied it, I still think she had fallen in love with me. We were married two years later, just after D day, in a Catholic chapel in London. A buzz bomb above us ran out of fuel as we were saying the marriage vows.

V

I never did get to know the other sick people in the leukaemia ward. Most of us spent most of our time in bed. Passing each other occasionally in the corridors, trundling our IVs in front of us, we would nod and smile with an effort. The patients in the laminar flow rooms were, of course, invisible.

Aside from Tish I had plenty of company. There was a telephone in my room and there were a good many calls outgoing and incoming, including one from President Nixon. He remarked that he hoped to visit me at NIH. I could hardly say so, but I rather hoped he wouldn't. Emmet Hughes had recently denounced me in *The New York Times Magazine* as a presidential toady, and a presidential visit would be taken as proof of the charge. More important, since neither of us is good at small talk, and I would be lying in bed hooked up to an IV, it would be an embarrassing occasion.

Fortunately he never came, but I had a lot of other visitors. Joe and Susan Mary came most days, and there were usually two or three other people at our noonday picnics. Quite often we achieved a certain gaiety.

We got into trouble with a head nurse one day when Joe came in ostentatiously waving a bottle of Scotch. "This is a federal reservation," she said sharply. "No liquor is allowed." We mumbled something and hid our glasses. We were enemies. I thought of her as the battle-axe or the sergeant major and I'm sure she thought of me in equally uncomplimentary terms. But by the time I left NIH she was my favourite of all nurses. She knew her business, and when you are in fear of death a nurse who knows her business is a pearl beyond price. Some kind of routine or discipline is, moreover, necessary in a hospital.

I spent a lot of time reading—nothing profound, since I was in a mood for escape. When I had had enough of Wodehouse and Trollope, I turned to *The Day of the Jackal*, the best seller about an attempted assassination of de Gaulle. I was enjoying it thoroughly when one character told another that his daughter had "Luke-something." I closed the book hurriedly, sure that the girl would die. I'm told she didn't, but I never finished the novel.

When I wasn't reading I spent a lot of time trying to remember quotations. I have a small store of them in my head, mostly from school and college days, and I almost always get them wrong. I have, in Byron's phrase, "just enough of learning to misquote."

There was the bit from T. S. Eliot's eternal Footman scribbled in my notebook:

> *I have seen the moment of my greatness flicker.*
> *I have seen the eternal Footman hold my coat, and snicker.*
> *In short, I was afraid.*

I had it just a little wrong, of course. And then there were snatches of nonsense verse. I've always had a fondness for Hilaire Belloc's *Cautionary Tales*, like this one:

> *The chief defect of Henry King*
> *Was chewing little bits of string.*
> *At last he swallowed some which tied*
> *Itself in ugly knots inside.*

> *Physicians of the utmost fame*
> *Were called at once; but when they came*
> *They answered, as they took their fees,*
> *"There is no cure for this disease."*

I found it oddly comforting to dig into my memory for such snippets. It was a way of papering over misery. I'd always liked the story about Winston Churchill doing the same thing when, as a subaltern in the Boer War, he had to spend a couple of days hiding from the Boers in a dark hole. It is at least a better way to spend the time than fearing death.

I also found comforting, and amusing, a note which arrived with a very pretty flower from Alice Roosevelt Longworth—"Cousin Alice," as I've always called her. (She is T.R.'s daughter and my first cousin once removed.) It was written on a yellowed calling card which looked as though it dated from the 1920s, and it read, "Stew—what a nuisance—love from your aged coz."

Acute leukaemia—a nuisance? The note is a nice example of Mrs. Longworth's highly idiosyncratic style, which shapes her rather macabre humour. She has had two mastectomies and likes to refer to herself, preferably before the most easily shockable audience, as "Washington's topless octogenarian." She also likes to call herself "Washington's only perambulatory monument."

The day after Cousin Alice's flower arrived, Susan Mary, my charming sister-in-law, paid a visit while Joe was tied up on some journalistic chore. She had bad news. Tommy Thompson (Llewellyn Thompson, twice ambassador to Moscow and a very old friend) had entered Georgetown Hospital because of his ulcer the day before I had. The doctors, Susan Mary said, had opened him up and found inoperable cancer. Tish and I had seen him the night we both spent in Georgetown Hospital. We'd met wandering in the corridor, both in bathrobes, and chatted for a bit. Tish and I said nothing about my diagnosis—it seemed pointless. I wonder if Tommy knew what was wrong with him and also said nothing.

There were times when the inescapable reality of my own situation suddenly overcame me. One such time was just before I was sent home from NIH. Dr. Henderson (John Glick's boss) had come in for a talk. He is a shy man, in his thirties, rather dour, but

185

his obvious competence is more encouraging to a sick man than any bedside manner. One compensation for being ill with a puzzling disease is that everybody talks about *you*, and after a few minutes of this I asked him a question which had been on my mind.

"Is there any chance I have aplastic anaemia?" Aplastic anaemia is a serious marrow disease, but it is not malignant.

Dr. Henderson hesitated for a moment. "No," he said.

"Then I do have some form of cancer, AML or something else?"

"Yes," he said quietly.

He left, and I started writing to thank Kay Halle for sending me an anthology of Winston Churchill's sayings that she had edited. I wrote my letter as a takeoff on Winston's famous speech of defiance on June 4, 1940. "We will fight amongst the platelets," I wrote. "We will fight in the bone marrow. We will fight in the peripheral blood. We will never surrender."

Having written this, I began, for the first time in about fifty years, to cry. I was utterly astonished, and also dismayed. I was brought up to believe that for a man to weep is the ultimate indignity, a proof of unmanliness. Only my room-mate was there, and he hadn't noticed, but I ducked into our bathroom, closed the door, sat down on the toilet, turned on the bathwater so that nobody could hear me, and cried my heart out. Then I dried my eyes with toilet paper and felt a good deal better.

I suppose this sudden unmanliness resulted from the combination of Dr. Henderson's monosyllables and Churchill. When Dr. Henderson said no to my first question and yes to my second, a light went out, a light of hope that I might not have cancer after all.

As for Churchill, of all the public figures I have known he is my only enduring hero. Perhaps an incurable anglophilia influenced my admiration for him, perhaps also a nostalgia for a time that will never come again—wartime London, wonderful parties at Rosa Lewis's Cavendish Hotel, falling in love with Tish. But what impressed me most was his genius for recognizing the obvious. (I think, but am not sure, that the phrase was his own.)

He displayed that genius when he recognized that Hitler really did intend to conquer Europe, a notion pooh-poohed by almost all fashionable and intelligent people in the 1930s; and he showed it again even more clearly in the late 1940s and early 1950s, when he was supposedly in decline, and made speeches examining the essential problem facing Western nations—the problem of living in the same world with both Soviet-style communism and the nuclear weapon. Recognizing the obvious, he concluded that the very horror of the nuclear weapon might offer the divided world a long period of peace—"a peace of mutual terror." But the essential condition was that the terror be truly mutual. Churchill's peace of mutual terror is the peace we have been living with all these years. It is at least very much better than a nuclear war. But his condition remains essential.

I met Churchill only once, but that occasion remains vivid in my memory. It was in the summer of 1950, and I was on a reporting tour of Europe. In Rome I ran into Randolph Churchill, the great man's son, who was writing pieces (when he was sober and the mood was upon him) for the Beaverbrook press.

Randolph and I decided to have a look at Soviet-occupied Austria, to which we travelled by train via Florence and Trieste. We were joined by Culbert Olson, who had been a Democratic governor of California during the early 1940s. He was handsome, about seventy, with a flat midwestern accent and a hyena laugh.

Randolph insisted that we all stop in Florence to inspect "the ancient glories of this great city" and also to renew his acquaintance with Mrs. Violet Trefusis, who had a villa outside the town. Violet Trefusis, Randolph explained, was known as "Mrs Trefusis, Never Refusis". She was the daughter of the famous Mrs. Keppel, who had decidedly not refused Edward VII, and she was thought to have royal blood in her veins. She turned out to be a woman of a certain age and great charm, which she exercised with startling effect on Governor Olson, who fell briefly but passionately in love with her. I do not know whether she lived up to her name.

We had a bibulous dinner in Florence (every dinner with Randolph tended to be bibulous) and then we set forth to view the ancient glories. Randolph and the governor staged a fine scene.

"Know what I'd do, if I was governor here?" the governor asked in his flat, nasal twang as he viewed the twilit splendours of the cathedral. "I'd tear the whole place down. Lay down a modern sewage system. Build some good, modern public housing. Then you'd have a city fit for people to live in."

"*Tear Florence down?*" howled Randolph. "Destroy this ancient monument of Western civilization? Replace the gilded splendours of this great city with public housing?"

"Yessir," said Governor Olson. "I'd tear the whole goddam place down." Then he cackled his hyena laugh, driving Randolph to paroxysms of eloquent fury. It was a great show, a classic Anglo-American vaudeville performance. We were joined by a crowd of ragged Italian kids, who hooted at the mad Englishman and the crazy American, and the show lasted the better part of an hour.

Governor Olson fell in love again in Trieste and left us. Randolph and I pushed on into Austria, and by the time we parted we were friends. Randolph was not easy to be friends with. When drunk he could be intolerable. And yet he was a man of great qualities—intelligence, courage, and a certain unexpected sweetness. Above all, it never occurred to him to be anything but himself—except very rarely, when he foolishly tried to be Winston Churchill.

When I got to London, a week or so after we parted in Austria, Randolph called me at my hotel and invited me to lunch at Chartwell the next day. The party consisted only of the old man, Randolph, and me, and at first it was a most uncomfortable affair. Mr. Churchill was dressed in a siren suit and looked like an angry old baby. He responded to my shy greetings with an angry *harrrumph*.

The first course was a delicious soup, which we ate in near-total silence, interrupted only by an occasional slurping noise. With the fish course a bottle of excellent champagne was served; Mr. Churchill and I consumed it between us, since Randolph was officially on the wagon. Then there was another bottle of champagne. The effect on Mr. Churchill was like that of the morning sun on an opening flower. He began to talk, and the talk was good. Very good —wise and witty and malicious by turns.

I recall saying something about a member of the Attlee Labour Cabinet whom I had interviewed the day before. Mr. Churchill's response was very much that of the grandson of the Duke of Marlborough. "I wouldn't have him for a gardener." He paused. "I wouldn't have him for an *under*gardener."

I think it was Randolph who introduced the name of Anthony Eden into the conversation. Churchill was leader of His Majesty's

188

opposition at the time, and Eden was his number two, as he had been for years and would remain for still more years.

"Ah, yes, Anthony," he said. "Dear Anthony. When there is a debate scheduled in which I do not greatly wish to take part— about sewer systems, or the like—I telephone Anthony. I tell him, 'This is a great opportunity for you, my boy, an opportunity for you to make a great name for yourself. *You can lead the debate*'." The old man smiled the smile of a naughty, happy child.

Towards the end of the luncheon, vaguely aware that I was an American, he began to talk about America. He made a ringing rhetorical tribute to "your great country" and concluded with a peroration in ripe Churchillian style. "America," he said musingly. "America. A great and powerful country. Like some strong horse pulling the rest of the world up behind it out of the slough of despond, towards peace and prosperity." He fixed his old blue eyes on me accusingly. "But will America stay the course?" he asked.

I said rather weakly that I was sure it would, and Mr. Churchill led the way outdoors. He led us first to a rather muddy pool. A secret service man, who knew the routine, produced a tobacco tin filled with grubs, and Mr. Churchill began to drop the grubs in the water. Large fat goldfish instantly appeared.

"See that one?" Mr. Churchill said. "Worth fully four pounds, I daresay. I paid only ten shillings for him." He pointed out several others, estimating with satisfaction his profit on each. Then he led us to another pool. In the middle was what appeared to be a bicycle tyre, with mirrors attached to its rim. Mr. Churchill pressed a button and the tyre began slowly to revolve. The contraption, he said proudly, was his own invention. The mirrors reflected the rays of the sun, thus frightening off the marauding birds that stole his fish. Just as he finished his explanation it began to rain. "Unfortunately for my invention," said Mr. Churchill, his tone bordering on the tragic, "on this small island the sun hardly ever shines."

He gave us then a guided tour of his painting studio and proudly displayed a handsome brick wall he had built. When I left, late in the afternoon, he was using another of his inventions, a peculiar contraption of counterweights and pulleys with which he was attempting, unsuccessfully, to uproot a small tree.

Throughout he displayed a kind of childishness—there is no

189

other word for it. His pride in his inventions was completely unfeigned. He was what Mark Twain once called Andrew Carnegie, "the human being unconcealed." The carapace, or outer shell, which people grow to protect themselves from other people had somehow never grown on him. This was, perhaps, one secret of his charm. He was the most undisappointing public man I have ever met.

At least one thing Churchill said at the lunch table has proved right. The Korean war had just started and the international horizon looked very dark. "And yet, you know," the old man said, "as soon as Hitler took power, I *knew* a great world war was coming. I felt war in my bones. I do not think a great world war is coming now. I do not feel war in my bones."

That was over two decades ago, and the feeling in Mr. Churchill's bones has so far proved accurate. Indeed, as of this writing, a third world war seems a lot less likely than it did in 1950 at Chartwell. The essential reason is, I suppose, that so far the terror has continued to be mutual. It begins to seem at least possible, bar madness or miscalculation, that this "peace of mutual terror" will prevail, even unto the third and fourth generation.

At any rate, after I had wept that day on the thirteenth floor of NIH, I consoled myself with the thought that Mr. Churchill too used to weep, when moved, quite publicly and shamelessly.

DURING my first stay in NIH—from July 21 to August 6, 1971—I lived on two levels. One level concerned what was going on in my mind, the other what was going on in my marrow and my blood. The second was a lot more mysterious than the first.

A great debate, John Glick told me, raged at NIH. Because my case was so peculiar I had visits three or four times a day from one staff doctor or another (I never did get all their names straight).

In the beginning most of the specialists believed that I had some form of AML. Dr. Harvey Gralnick, the chief morphologist, did not agree. He suspected some atypical form of dysproteinaemia, a marrow cancer, not a leukaemia. Dysproteinaemia, John Glick explained, had a longer average survival time than AML, and the chemotherapy was milder. There was also a minority view that I might have some unusual form of Hodgkin's disease, a related

190

lymphatic disorder. This would be good news, since Hodgkin's disease is now sometimes curable. In my notebook: "Imagine hoping you have Hodgkin's disease!"

After my temperature subsided I began to feel well enough to take part in the debate, sometimes a bit more than my part. John Glick and I took to referring to me as Dr. Alsop.

Someone remembered the marrow slides of a certain Mrs. Y, whose case had John Glick so tensely fascinated that he reminded me again of Sherlock Holmes. As a matter of fact, he looks like Sherlock Holmes—or would, with a deerstalker, a cloak, and a pipe.

Mrs. Y was a housewife who was diagnosed as having AML and given chemotherapy for that disease. The diagnosis, it turned out later, was incorrect. She had had, instead, a form of dysproteinaemia. She died, three and a half years after her chemotherapy, of pneumonia. She might have been saved if she had been treated immediately with antibiotics, but she was a gay and rather feckless lady, and she didn't report to NIH until it was too late.

Mrs. Y's marrow looked like mine—a fact which seemed to support Dr. Gralnick's theory. John Glick marked my marrow slide ALSOP and hers Y, and then transposed the labels. None of the specialists could tell for certain which was which.

In my notebook: "Every little helps. If Mrs. Y lasted three and a half years, then I might too, and that at least is beating the odds." A man clutches at straws.

Towards the end of the first week Ed Henderson came in with John Glick to talk, as usual, about me, and Henderson dwelt on how few cells of any sort, normal or abnormal, I had in my marrow.

"It sounds to me," I said, "like the end of some great battle, in which the slaughter has been intense, and both sides are so exhausted that all fighting has stopped."

"No," said Dr. Henderson. "The battle is still going on."

It is a curious feeling to have the inside of your bones a battlefield. I amused myself by trying to think of military analogies. Gettysburg? The victory of Pyrrhus over the Romans at Asculum? ("One more such victory and I am lost.") Perhaps Vietnam, for both sides the most unwinnable war in modern history.

John gave me several marrow tests—more than would have been necessary if I had been a classic case—and one biopsy. The biopsy meant getting a bigger hunk of me, for more detailed observation. This is done with an instrument that looks like miniature sugar tongs. I have unusually hard bones, and John twisted two of these instruments all out of shape before he got into the bone.

A marrow test is unpleasant, a biopsy more so. But neither is nearly so unpleasant as waiting for the results. Every time I had a marrow test there would be that hour or so of suspense filled with the fear of fulmination of the abnormal cells. A fulmination would be followed by chemotherapy, the laminar flow room, and the near certainty of death in a year or two.

But the abnormal cells (Thank you God, thank you Mother, thank you Father, thank you Aggie) did not fulminate. The percentage even dropped off a bit. Above all, the malignant cells, the myeloblasts, were still only in the bone marrow. This, John Glick explained, gave him leeway. If I had had blasts in the peripheral blood he'd have had to put me into chemotherapy. Otherwise, the blasts would have crowded out the life-giving cells in the blood, ensuring death in a matter of weeks. But John repeated with his characteristic candour that "those weirdos, the bad cells in your marrow, look *really* ugly."

I find another note, written after the biopsy: "Maybe I am not lucky my case is so peculiar. Maybe I am very unlucky. Maybe it would have been better if I had had a classic AML, and I had been put into chemotherapy right away, before I knew what had happened to me. I would surely have died, but sometimes this suspense is hardly bearable."

This unhappy scribble bears on a question which obviously concerned John Glick deeply: how much to tell a cancer patient. He talked about it often. He told me that certain leukaemia specialists, known as nihilists, believe that AML patients should be told nothing whatever about their disease and be left to die without chemotherapy. According to this school, a person newly diagnosed as an acute leukaemic should be told only that he has anaemia, and given occasional haemoglobin and platelet transfusions to keep him going until the time comes—usually in less than four months—when he will die of infection for lack of granulocytes to protect him. Meanwhile, having been told only that he is anaemic and that the anaemia is being treated, he is not hopelessly unhappy. To be hopeless is to be unhappy, and the AML patient who is told the truth is hopeless and therefore unnecessarily unhappy.

Many doctors, according to John, half accept this argument. "Treatment of AML is often unaggressive, since in any case the patient is likely to die." John made this remark during my first week at NIH and it was a bit hard to take, since my official diagnosis was still AML. The remark was typical of NIH policy, as exemplified by those rules of admission I had come across on the fourteenth floor. No doubt there is a lot to be said for this total candour, but my own view falls somewhere between the NIH view and the nihilists'. In my notebook: "A man who must die will die more easily if he is left a little spark of hope that he may not die after all. My rule would be: Never tell a victim of terminal cancer the whole truth—tell him that he *may* die, even that he will *probably* die, but do not tell him that he *will* die."*

On August 6, seventeen days after I entered NIH, Ed Henderson and John made up their minds. My diagnosis was no longer officially AML, even though about seventy-five percent of the abnormal cells in my marrow looked like myeloblasts. As long as there were no blasts in the blood, there was no rush to treat me. "Pancytopenia of unknown etiology" was the diagnosis, which, translated from medicalese, means, "This patient has damned few cells, normal *or* abnormal, but we don't know why."

They decided to do nothing—to send me home and keep an eye on me. I'd come in for a blood test every week, a marrow every other week. John Glick gave me his home and office telephone numbers. I was to call him right away if my temperature went over 100, or if I experienced a chill, unusual pain anywhere, an atypical cough, fast or painful urination, an earache, a sore throat, since I had so few granulocytes to protect me from infection. "But there are more sources of infection here than in your own house," he said, "so there's no reason not to send you home."

*John Glick, reading this paragraph, reminds me that when I was admitted to NIH he was almost as much a new boy as I was. After two years of experience at NIH he still believes in telling a patient the basic facts of his situation. But he says, "I am much less clinical," and he agrees in substance with the sentences I scribbled in my notebook.

I asked for his best guess about what would happen to me. He just didn't know, he said. "We can only wait for the nature of the disease to declare itself." He paused thoughtfully. "I don't want to mislead you. It is barely possible that whatever you have will just go away. But spontaneous remissions are very, very rare. It's a lot more likely that when the disease does declare itself, we will put you into chemotherapy to induce a remission."

"And after you've induced a remission, I'm certain to have a relapse. Right? The bad cells will certainly come back?"

"Almost certainly," said John Glick.

"Why? Why do they come back?"

"If we knew that," he said, "we'd know what caused them to proliferate in the first place—we'd be on the track of a cure. Whoever answers your question wins the Nobel Prize."

VI

On August 6, Tish drove me home to our house in Cleveland Park. It is set in over an acre of woods, and there's a tennis court carved out of the side of a hill. We bought the place in 1950, when our Georgetown house became too small. The house is comfortable and I have enjoyed myself in it, but I have no feeling for it as a house. It reminds me of Winston Churchill's remark when a waiter set before him a large and tasteless pudding. "Waiter," he said, "pray remove this pudding. It has no theme."

Our Washington house has no theme, no individual quality. It's roomy and convenient and characterless. When we talked about selling it in anticipation of my death, the thought aroused no pain; but the thought of selling Needwood Forest was almost as painful as the notion of selling my daughter, Elizabeth, might have been.

There are some things in the house, though, that mean a good deal to me, or at least amuse me. We Alsops are thing-oriented— we like objects, especially if we inherited them, more especially if they are valuable. We like money too, though no Alsop has ever been really rich. Among the objects I inherited was a gravy boat with the letters REVERE cut into the bottom. I assumed the REVERE was the mark of the Revere Copper & Brass Company, a Connecticut firm whose plant I remembered seeing near Hartford.

We used to leave the gravy boat casually on the sideboard. Then an insurance assessor told me it was an authentic product of "the patriot" ("One if by land, two if by sea")—the Revere named Paul —and that the last such piece had sold for eighteen thousand dollars. We hastily put the thing in a bank vault, but since it was doing us no good there we eventually sold it, for a lot more than eighteen thousand dollars. There were plenty of things, including the tennis court, that we wanted more than a silver gravy boat.

Still on the sideboard and scattered elsewhere in the dining room are various pieces of china with an oriental version of a federal eagle painted on them. Before I did my piece on the family for *The Saturday Evening Post* my attitude towards these bits of china was that they were rather pretty. But after I'd done the research for the *Post* piece, the china meant something more to me. For in the eighteenth and nineteenth centuries Alsops were in the West Indies trade, shipping rum north and ice south. And they were also in the China trade. Hence those china teapots, cups, and saucers, known variously as export china and Chinese Lowestoft.

It surprised me to discover how consistently reactionary all my ancestors had been. One early Alsop, a New York merchant known in the family as "John, the nonsigner," attended the Continental Congress as a member of the New York delegation, but refused to sign the Declaration of Independence on the grounds, he wrote, that the Congress had closed the door to "reconciliation with Great Britain on just and honorable terms." One suspects that his real reason was that he was horrified by the text of the Declaration itself, drafted by that young radical Thomas Jefferson—one can hear him muttering, "All men are created equal, indeed!"

An ancestor on my mother's side named Peter Corne was so uncompromising a Tory that he kept a life-size portrait of King George III in his cellar, to which every evening by candlelight he would usher his large brood and command them, "Bow down to thy master."

Perhaps I am even a bit of a Tory myself. Yet I have always thought of myself as a liberal. The first piece I ever wrote and got paid for was published by *The Atlantic* before the Second World War—like most youthful efforts, it is a bit embarrassing to reread now. In it I proudly described myself as a "Marxist liberal," having

196

at Yale dabbled very superficially in Marxism. But what I really was—and I suppose I still am—was a rather conventional New Dealer. I much admired my distant cousin Franklin Roosevelt, which irritated Father. He used to call the President "that crazy jack in the White House" and end dinner-table arguments about the New Deal by suggesting that if I didn't like it here I could "go back to Russia." Since those days, I have voted for every Democratic presidential candidate, including Hubert Humphrey in 1968, but not including George McGovern.

Father desperately wanted to be governor of Connecticut. Being an old-fashioned Connecticut Yankee, he thought of that governorship as the highest office in the land. In 1912 he was a leading Republican in the state senate and was thought to have had a good shot at it. Then Mother's uncle Ted split the Republican Party to run on the Progressive ticket for President. Father, a victim of the Roosevelt charm, headed the state's Progressive campaign organization, and that ended his gubernatorial hopes. The regular Republicans cast him into outer darkness. He never talked about it, but it was the one great disappointment of his life.

When I was in my teens my feelings about Pa were ambivalent, and I think that was true of Joe and John too. He was well over six feet tall, with a big head and a long, authoritative nose. He always sat very much at the head of the table. He insisted on our dressing for dinner, and he would shout at us in company when we leaned back in the dining room chairs. (I shout at my children when they lean back in the same chairs, but it is the most I can do to get the boys to wear ties sometimes.) It is normal for teenage boys to resist and on occasion to defy the domination of the male head of the family, but by the time Pa was an old man—he died at seventy-seven, which is old for an Alsop—I had great affection and admiration for him. Pa was very much his own man.

And he was not stuffy—he liked to shoot quail, to fish for trout, or play golf; and he enjoyed a good laugh and his martinis before dinner, and a brandy afterwards. But his political views seemed to his two older New Dealing sons (John was a conservative by instinct) stuffy in the extreme.

"Pa," I said once, "how did you get to be such a reactionary?"

"Goddammit, Stew," he roared in fury, "you don't seem to

197

realize I was the leading Progressive in this state in 1912, and I'm just as much a Progressive today as I ever was. How can you say I'm a reactionary, you crazy jack?" He was genuinely angry at me.

There is, I suppose, no escaping the genes. This is why I was relieved to discover that there was no blood relationship with the gentleman who was indirectly responsible for our dining room chairs—he was a relation by marriage. The chairs were carved in the Canary Islands during the First World War for a female cousin of Father's. She left them to Father, who passed them on to Joe, who passed them on to me. She was the last survivor of the branch of the family to which the famous Dr. Webster belonged.

Dr. Webster became famous when he murdered a Harvard professor named Parkman, to whom he owed large sums of money. He cut the professor into small pieces and shoved them into the furnace of the Harvard chemistry laboratory. Dr. Webster was duly hanged and his family moved to the Canary Islands. Whence our dining room chairs.

Curiously enough, objects like those chairs or the export china took on a new meaning for me after I was told that I had inoperable cancer. I suppose I took a new interest in my ancestors when I learned that I was likely to become an ancestor soon myself.

Although I like the things in it, the Washington house is, as I've said, a bore. The house I love—Tish loves it too—is Needwood Forest. As soon as John Glick sprung me from NIH I wanted to get to Needwood, to rest my soul, and Tish and I spent all the time we could there until I got sick again in September.

Tish had found Needwood Forest. But first she had found Polecat Park, which made Needwood possible. In 1950 we decided we wanted a weekend refuge for our growing brood—Joe, Ian, and Elizabeth were all small children then, with Stewart soon to arrive. Indefatigably, Tish searched, and eventually she came upon a property in Howard County, Maryland—a hundred and sixty acres at a hundred dollars an acre, with a house thrown in. The house was, strikingly unhandsome—poor farmhouse basic—but it had running water pumped up from a spring, and a bathroom of sorts which also served as a hallway between bedrooms. We christened it Polecat Park because we discovered, when we had the house rewired, that seven skunks had taken up residence in the basement.

198

I was thirty-six then, and Tish was only twenty-four, and the children were very young. For a long time we all loved Polecat Park, except perhaps for Elizabeth, who one summer, just as she was about to sit down, found a black snake coiled in the toilet, for relief from the heat. She never fully recovered from the trauma.

The pump kept breaking down, the heating was inadequate, and the termites got so bad by the mid-1950s that I put my foot through the living room floor. But we never regretted buying the place— and I especially had come to need it.

For twelve years, from 1946 to 1958, my brother Joe and I collaborated on a four-a-week column for the now defunct New York Herald Tribune Syndicate. Writing a political column is like climbing a ladder which has no end. When nothing very much is going on, it can be agonizing—you reach up for the next rung and there isn't any. During the two Eisenhower administrations there were many long, placid stretches when hardly anything at all was going on, and thus no rungs on the ladder to grasp.

Brother Joe, who had written a successful column with Robert Kintner before the war, was, of course, the senior partner. Since I'd never written a word for a newspaper, it was an act of remarkable generosity on his part to take me on. I have thoroughly enjoyed a quarter century as a political journalist, and I am eternally grateful to my brother for giving me the opportunity to become one, more or less overnight, without the gruelling apprenticeship most political journalists undergo. But Joe is a genius and, like most geniuses, not easy to work with. He seemed to feel a psychic need for at least one shouting, foot-stamping row per week. The tensions of our combative partnership, together with all those missing rungs on the columnist's ladder in the placid Eisenhower years, made Polecat Park a psychic need, a necessary refuge, for me.

By the early 1960s all that had changed. Joe and I had had an amicable divorce in 1958. I had become Washington editor of the dear old *Saturday Evening Post*, where I made more money and where there were few strains and tensions—too few for the magazine's good. Washington had become a much pleasanter place to live, at least for a political journalist. The Kennedy people were a great deal more agreeable and conversable than the Eisenhower people, most of whom were worthy but stuffy. And in John F. Kennedy's thousand days there was always plenty to write about.

For me, then, Polecat Park ceased to be a psychic necessity. For Tish, the primitive housekeeping that had been fun in her early twenties had become a bore and a chore. For the older children Polecat Park became less and less a fine place for messy living and muddy swimming, and more and more a tedious place where there were no contemporaries and nothing much to do. So we used it less and less. By February 1969, when Tish saw the ad for Needwood Forest in the *Sunday Star*, it sounded too good to be true: a completely modernized historic house with the original panelling and seven working fireplaces; thirty acres of land; a stocked pond. Fifty miles out, in Frederick County, Maryland. Price so reasonable that there must be something wrong. But it was a dreary Sunday afternoon and we had nothing to do, so we called the real estate agent and met him near Frederick.

We followed the agent over a low mountain range—the Catoctins, where Franklin Roosevelt built his Shangri-la, now Nixon's Camp David—and into a valley ringed by another mountain range, with a gap in the middle. The gap was the Harper's Ferry gap, where much history was made, with the Blue Ridge Mountains to the south and Green Mountain, of Civil War fame, to the north. The house was set in rich, rolling farmland. We approached it between two pillars topped by mossy stone squirrels, through ten acres of woods that had never been cut over (some of the oaks were certainly there when George Washington was alive). As for the house, Tish and I fell deeply in love with it even before we went in the front door. It is long, plain, and handsomely proportioned, a Georgian brick house built in 1808, with a tower at one end which lends oddness and originality. Inside, it was country comfortable: a big living room with two fireplaces, a big dining room, a nice little library, and behind, a huge kitchen, modernized. Upstairs we counted six bedrooms, including one enormous master bedroom with two fireplaces and a bath of its own. Out back there was a lawn and an overgrown garden and a pretty cottage.

We both knew right away that we wanted the place, but before making an offer we asked my brother Joe, who knows a lot more about old houses than we do, to have a look at it. Joe is very shrewd in most ways, but sometimes surprisingly undevious. On a previous occasion he kept saying in the presence of the agent that the place was a marvellous buy and that we ought to snap it up instantly. This precluded all hope of bargaining, of course, so this time we asked Joe to be sure to make no enthusiastic noises about Needwood Forest within the hearing of the agent.

Joe almost overdid it. He prowled about the place, making disparaging remarks and discerning much evidence of termites. But as soon as the agent was out of earshot he grabbed me by the arm and said, "Buy it, Stew, and don't haggle." I did haggle the price down a bit, and because of the real estate boom in Howard County, dear old Polecat Park turned out to be almost as good an investment as Polaroid or Xerox, so that there was enough left over for a tennis court and a plastic swimming pool.

VIII

When I was discharged from NIH on a wait-and-see basis on that Friday, August 6, 1971, my blood counts were low, very low, in all three vital categories, and all through August they sank lower. I was, in short, dangerously sick, but oddly enough I didn't feel it. When I came home, Andrew announced to Nicky that "Daddy is a little bit sick." A little bit sick was the way I felt. Sick enough not to want to play tennis, and to want to sleep a lot; sick enough to get to the office late, or sometimes not at all. But by no means sick enough to get into bed and wait to die.

It was a queer month, that month of August—a half-forgotten month, a half-alive month. I wrote a couple of columns for *Newsweek* and we spent several long weekends at Needwood. Outwardly, Tish and I and the children lived about as we had before. But there were inward differences. For one thing there was the temptation to let things slide, to say the hell with it. Why make an effort, especially since, with a low haemoglobin count, an effort is that much harder to make?

In this respect my friend and fellow columnist Rowland Evans was a great help. A columnist must be a reporter first, last, and all the time. Walter Lippmann wrote the best straight think pieces, or "thumb-suckers," as they are called in the trade, of any journalist of our time. Lippmann was able for long stretches to write perceptive and interesting columns from his place in Maine, far from the madding world. But even he was a reporter as much as a thinker, and when he was in Washington felt the need of extensive daily pulse taking in high places. For lesser journalists like myself, to see and talk with knowledgeable people is far more of a necessity than for a Walter Lippmann. All too often, when I try to do a thumb-sucker, I find my thumb empty of anything worth sucking. Throughout that August, as spirits and haemoglobin sank, I was constantly tempted to forget about reporting, to stay home and mope. That was where Rowly was such a help.

Once or twice a week he would summon me—and not take no for an answer—to reportorial lunches with people like Arthur Schlesinger and State Department intelligence chief Ray Cline; or with Senator Edmund Muskie's political manager, Jack English; or with Kissinger aide Winston Lord, or with other sources. Rowly Evans kept me journalistically alive, and I am truly grateful. Among his fellow journalists Evans has a well-earned reputation for competitiveness. This has never bothered me, since I am not uncompetitive myself. But that August I also discovered how *nice* he is. There is no other word for it. It may sound fatuous, but one compensation for getting really sick is the repeated discovery that people are nicer than they seem to be.

People are also curious about those known to be in danger of dying. Perhaps it's the "there but for the grace of God go I" syndrome. I looked healthy. My face is naturally pinkish, and not eating much had caused me to lose a lot of unnecessary weight. Friends would come up to Evans and me at one of our lunches, peer at me, and then, in a tone of mixed congratulation and surprise, tell me how well I looked. Obviously they had expected more outward and visible signs of moribundity. But although I looked well enough, there was an inward difference. As I waited for "the nature of the disease to declare itself," in John Glick's words, there was always a little pea of fear at the back of my mind. It was the fear of death. It was always present, like background music. Sometimes it receded almost into inaudibility, and then sometimes it would come blaring back: My God, I really *do* have cancer, I really am going to die. The fear leaps out, every fourth page or so, from my notebooks.

An old notebook is like an old diary. Sometimes it is surprising, sometimes baffling, sometimes embarrassing, and sometimes in a few words it brings back vividly what had been wholly forgotten. For example: "Nixon as peace President . . . an Ike type could have won hands down. . . . Basic weakness . . . Ike . . . cookout . . . the sleepers all favour Nixon." Obviously I was ruminating about a column. The phrase "Ike . . . cookout" was meant to recall an experience I had when I first began polling with Louis Harris back in the 1950s.

Walter Ridder, of the Ridder papers, and I had tried our hands at a little do-it-yourself poll taking in Minnesota and Iowa before the presidential election of 1952. We both got about the same result: Eisenhower, 6 per cent; Stevenson 3 per cent; Don't know, 20 per cent; Ain't agonna tell ya, 31 per cent; None of your damn business, 40 per cent. I recounted this sad tale to Harris, and he offered to show me the professional technique. It involved adopting the costume and manner of some minor bureaucrat, say a sewer inspector, and asking all the easiest questions first, in a no-nonsense, businesslike tone of voice. Ridder and I had tried to be too pally.

In 1956, after I had learned the sewer-inspector technique, I was polling in the suburbs of Chicago when I came on a jolly fellow raking leaves in his yard. I went through the softening-up questions, as taught by Lou Harris, and came to the crucial question—would he vote for Eisenhower or Stevenson?

"Oh, I'll go for Ike," he said. "I know he's been sick, and he goofs off a lot—sometimes seems like he's hardly minding the store. But he's the kind of guy I'd like to invite over for a cookout. Can you imagine inviting that Adlai for a cookout?"

Ever since, I've applied the cookout test to presidential aspirants. Nothing is more obvious than that Richard Nixon fails it even more abysmally than Adlai Stevenson did. His inability to arouse the kind of affection lots of voters felt for Dwight Eisenhower or John Kennedy was and is his greatest source of political weakness. But it was true that all the sleepers—the hidden factors, like the race factor—then favoured Nixon.

Lou Harris claimed that, using his polling technique, he never got a refusal, and he proved his point. In 1956 we went polling together in the Detroit area, and one day towards dusk we were in an upper-middle-income suburb—ranch houses, neat lawns. Following a rule that Lou had laid down for esoteric professional reasons, we were ringing the doorbell of every third house. We came to a house with a picture window, and through the window a couple—a burly man and a pretty girl—were eminently visible, in a passionate embrace on the sofa.

"Let's skip this one," I said.

"Certainly not," said Lou, and gave the doorbell a strong, demanding ring. Nothing happened. Lou rang again. The door opened and the burly man appeared, hair dishevelled, face pink with fury. Lou told me later that he recognized him as a famous professional football player. Adopting his incomparable sewer inspector's manner, Lou instantly started out on his no-nonsense, low-key spiel.

Slowly the pinkness left the football player's face and Lou had him answering every question. "Well, now, the way I see it . . ." Lou polled the pretty girl too, so we scored a double.

I became fascinated by polling as a reportorial tool. Then my brother Joe also became fascinated, and we did a great many—too many—polling columns. Polling is a serious business. It is a hard, footsore day's work to interview fifty people. As middle age and fallen arches crept ruthlessly upon us, both Joe and I became less fascinated by it. Nevertheless, in 1960, when John Kennedy and Hubert Humphrey were locked in dubious battle in the key Wisconsin primary, Joe and I went together to feel Wisconsin's pulse.

Joe is a journalist of commitment; he feels strongly about men and issues. He felt strongly about John Kennedy, whom he admired "this side idolatry." Joe is also an egregious fellow, in the true meaning of the word: *ex grege*, outside the flock. On that polling expedition he displayed both characteristics.

It was bitterly cold and still snowy in Wisconsin in early April. Joe had recently returned from a midwinter trip to Siberia, in preparation for which he had had an enormous fur hat made for him in Paris. For the polling expedition he donned this hat, together with a vast fur-lined cloak that had belonged to one of our grandfathers. He looked like an angry, large-nosed, bespectacled animal peering out from behind a bush. We trudged up through the snow to the door of our first house. Joe rang the bell and stood poised with his list of questions clamped to a clipboard. The door opened. An Irish-looking lady took one long, amazed look at Joe.

"Holy Mary Mother of God!" she cried, and slammed the door.

Joe turned to me, equally amazed. "What in heaven's name ails the woman, Stew?" he asked, honestly unaware of his own odd appearance.

The lady who answered our next ring was a native Midwesterner, to judge by her accent. She answered all the softening-up questions briefly; she had, it turned out, voted Democratic regularly. Then Joe came to the key question:

"In this primary election, madam, do you intend to vote for Hubert Humphrey or John F. Kennedy?"

"Well," she said, "I don't go too much for that Humphrey—he talks too much. But I guess we'll vote for him. We're Lutheran, you know, and we could never vote for a Catholic."

Joe coldly but courteously completed the interview and we turned to go. "Thank you, madam," he said. "I think you're a *goddam bigot.*"

As I say, Joe is an egregious fellow and a journalist of commitment. But the story of our polling expedition may suggest also why he is such good company, and why to a great many people there is an oddly endearing quality about him.

I RETURN, after a long digression, to the August notebook, with its peculiar mixture of notes about me and leukaemia, and notes about the nation and the world. Some of the notes are incomprehensible— one, for example, about wigs, which I can't decipher. I recall only that I had decided, if I lost my hair in chemotherapy, to wear a candid wig, possibly green or pink. Among the scribbles there is an ink outline of Andrew's hand. He likes to have his hand outlined, and his hand was small enough to get all but the tip of the thumb on a page of my notebook. On the facing page the pea of fear surfaces in a quotation: "Dreadful is the mysterious power of fate. There is no deliverance from it by wealth or by war, by walled city, or by dark, sea-beaten ships."

I went to the leukaemia clinic every few days for finger sticks or, more rarely, marrow tests. I became very used to the clinic, and I grew to hate the place. The leukaemics come on a regular schedule for blood tests, marrow tests, booster shots, and consultation with their doctors. There is a waiting space in the clinic, with rows of chairs with plastic seats, and coffee and cookies courtesy of the U.S. government. The leukaemics sit there, patiently reading, or chatting a little, waiting to be summoned for chemotherapy or to be told the results of their blood or marrow tests. I called us, the waiting leukaemics, the Nos Morituri ("we who are about to die") Brigade. The adults who had AML, at least, were all virtually certain to die, some very soon.

Most of the children had acute lymphoblastic leukaemia, or ALL, and there was something very hard to take about the small childish faces, often topped with wigs, and the wailing that was almost always going on, of children being given marrow or blood tests. And yet this is a genuine area of hope. ALL remains the greatest child killer of all diseases, but even since I got sick the survival rate has improved dramatically. About half the children with ALL now live for five years or more, and a high percentage of these are cured—their average life expectancy is as high as that of a normal child that age.

I am not a reporter for nothing, and by this time I knew John was expecting a fulmination of the abnormal cells, at which point the disease would "declare itself" as undoubted AML. On August 31, when Tish drove me in for blood and marrow tests, I suddenly knew what the results would be. On a corner about a hundred yards from the entrance to the clinic there is a well-tended little triangle of roses.

"Pretty," I said.

"Yes," Tish said.

There was a moment's silence. And I knew that I wouldn't see the roses next year. Today's marrow would show a sharp increase in malignant cells. John would tell me, in his kindest way, that I would have a course of chemotherapy and could then live a normal life. And I knew that I would have a relapse and die. I reached for Tish's hand. "I have just now run out of my small store of courage," I said. She squeezed my hand and said nothing.

As always, the results of the blood test came first. John tried to sound cheerful, but I could tell that he wasn't. The haemoglobin had sunk under 10 for the first time since my transfusion three weeks earlier, and the platelets were in the danger zone. The white count itself wasn't disastrous at 2000; but the percentage of life-saving granulocytes was so low that, for all intents and purposes, there weren't any. I was wholly defenceless against infection.

"Not too good, John," I said.

"Well, if you go too low on haemoglobin and platelets, we'll just transfuse you again—no problem," he said. "And we have the cidal antibiotics. But I do wish those granulocytes were better."

We went home. I didn't have the heart to go to the office and pretend I felt fine. Keeping up a bold front can be exhausting. Given the blood count, I expected the marrow to show the sharp rise in the malignant cells—the fulmination I dreaded. At about four thirty John telephoned.

His first words were, "Now don't get excited about this, it may mean nothing. It probably means nothing." But I could tell that *he* was excited. "Your abnormal cell count is down from thirty-eight to twenty-eight per cent. Stew, it just *could* be good news; though I don't know what it means."

I felt a sudden lifting of the fear that had gripped me near the roses and encompassed me like some damp and awful blanket all the hours since. No fulmination. For today, no sentence of death. I suddenly felt very gay.

My father always told me that a man who didn't drink till seven o'clock couldn't become a drunkard. (I used to apply his rule to before lunch too, but no longer.) It was only about five p.m. by this time, but I had a premature martini. Anyone who has ever jumped out of a plane with a parachute on his back and felt the chute open, and felt his feet hit the ground, and felt no bones broken, and all well, will know how I felt that afternoon.

A couple of days later, after the centrifuges and the computers had done their mysterious work, John called again. His own preliminary estimate had been right on the nose—twenty-eight per cent abnormal cells. But then he added something else. "I ought to tell you," he said. "The cells look a lot more like classic AML."

The background music blared high again for a moment. But then I put John's remark out of my mind—an essential art for one in fear of death—and it became again almost inaudible.

VIII

That Labor Day weekend we had a house party at Needwood. Kay and Rowly Evans and Kay Graham, publisher of the Washington *Post* and *Newsweek*, spent Saturday night, and we played aggressive bridge. On the Monday the Tommy Thompsons came for lunch (Tommy seeming much better), and so did John Glick and his sensible and entertaining wife, Jane. It was a pleasant weekend, with people coming and going, tennis, drinks, laughs— the classic country house party—and I enjoyed myself thoroughly until the late afternoon of Labor Day itself.

After lunch I played a couple of rubbers of bridge, and then I felt queer—enough so that I went upstairs and took my temperature. It was just a bit above normal. But that small fever signalled an experience that is still unexplained. I mentioned the temperature to John Glick before he and Jane left, and he told me to call him in the morning if it was still above normal. It was, and I did.

He told me to say in bed until afternoon, when I was due for a count at the clinic. The counts that day were all a lousy low, and the temperature persisted—38.8 degress Centigrade, meaning

101.9 degrees Fahrenheit. (NIH readings are always in Centigrade.) John sent me home to bed again.

From September 7 to September 27 I was sick—sicker than I knew. Later, John Glick and Ed Henderson said that in my defence-less state there was a one-in-three chance of an overwhelming infection every day, and that such an infection could have killed me within twenty-four hours. I didn't realize I was in that kind of danger. But I did know I was pretty miserable—for the first time in many years I had no impulse at all to scribble in my notebook.

My fever undulated between about 100 and 102. The night sweats started on September 8. I'd had them before, but nothing like this. After the first couple of nights I learned to take three towels to bed with me. I would wake up dripping wet, swab myself off, sleep for four hours or so, then wake up, and swab myself off again. The anorexia—lack of hunger—also started that week. I hadn't had much appetite since July, but this was different. It was all I could do to swallow one scrambled egg at breakfast and to pick a bit at lunch and dinner. Even my evening martini revolted me.

On the tenth, the thirteenth, and the fifteenth John tested my blood. The haemoglobin dropped steadily. The white blood count hovered around 1000, and the proportion of granulocytes went down to 12 per cent—virtually no protection at all. The platelets were consistently under the danger mark.

When I went to the clinic on September 13, John told me to stop taking allopurinol. This was a drug I'd been taking for high uric acid. Before I went into the hospital I was taking one tablet a day, and John had quadrupled the dose; this is routine for leukaemics, in order to prevent kidney stones. John now explained that he and Dr. Allen Rosenthal, an internist friend, had been discussing my case, and they both recalled rare instances when allopurinol had apparently been involved in causing very low blood counts. There was a risk involved in taking me off the drug, the risk of kidney failure—but John decided to take the chance.

On September 15 my blood was in the worst shape yet, with the haemoglobin at 8.3 and the other counts in the cellar, and I still had a low fever, about 101. John made another decision. He told me to come back into Ward 13. He would transfuse me, put me on cidal antibiotics, and give me a marrow test. I felt so awful that, for the first time, I was eager to go back to the hospital.

Then we had a conversation which caused me to scribble in my notebook again—about a "v. toxic treatment." John said he and the other doctors were all now virtually convinced that what I had was AML. If the marrow test confirmed their conviction, I would be given chemotherapy, not the kind originally planned, but, he said with his usual candour, "a very toxic treatment." It offered about a two-thirds chance of a remission, and it would not cause my hair to fall out. That was some recompense, but not much.

If the treatment induced a remission, he added, I could "lead a normal life for a year, maybe more." My case was so exceptional that there were some grounds for hoping that the length of remission might also be exceptional.

I re-entered NIH on September 16 and went down to the out-patient clinic for a three-bag haemoglobin transfusion. I am very allergic, and transfusions give me hives. Antihistamines are used to control the hives and they make me drowsy, so the hours I spend being transfused are long, sleepy, itchy hours.

I was into my second bag, and I had been dozing. I opened my eyes and saw a lady in a print dress lying on a bed catty-cornered across the room. She was attached to an IV through a vein in her right arm. I recognized her as Mrs. X, one of John Glick's favourite patients—he had pointed her out to me in the Nos Morituri Brigade. She had AML and had been in remission for almost two years. According to John, she lived a normal life, taking care of her husband and her children, visiting the beach, and going to the movies, living like any other housewife. She was his prime example of why it was worth having a course of chemotherapy.

Mrs. X looked healthy enough, and she was quite a handsome woman. She had pretty auburn hair (a wig, probably) and regular white teeth (also fake?). She was getting her regular booster shot of drugs, she said. We chatted in a desultory way, with long pauses as the chemicals dripped into her veins and the blood into mine. I was naturally wondering what it would be like to be in remission. Did she worry much about a relapse?

"Oh, no," she said, and there was a tone of genuine surprise in her voice. "The kids keep me too busy. I never even think about it,

210

except just when I have my tests." She was quite obviously telling the simple truth. Mrs. X was indeed leading a normal life, quite unbothered by the sword of Damocles she must have known was hanging over her.

Was she, I wondered, very brave? Or was she simply unimaginative? I was reminded of the war. The bravest men were rarely the most sensitive souls. But I did know one man during the war who was brave—and who was by no means unimaginative. After he had transferred from the British to the American army, Ted Ellsworth waged a one-man battle against a German company in France. He was put in for the congressional Medal of Honour, though he was eventually fobbed off with the Distinguished Service Cross. He was certainly the bravest of us Americans in the British army, and he proved he had a lively imagination when he spread the canard that my mother was an Indian.

I MET Ted Ellsworth in a shower room of a training depot of the King's Royal Rifle Corps near Winchester. It had been months since the British military attaché in Washington had advised me to bring my runabout, and the Japanese had attacked Pearl Harbor in the meantime. What with the inevitable delays, I didn't put on the uniform of the regiment until late spring of 1942.

When I arrived at the red brick Victorian headquarters of the 60th Rifles in Winchester, I was ushered into the officers' mess and received politely by four or five smartly dressed officers, most of whom were younger than I (I was twenty-seven). I was welcomed, proudly shown the regimental flags and the regimental silver, and offered a ceremonial glass of sherry. I began to think that my decision to join the 60th Rifles had been a shrewd one.

I was told that a truck had arrived to take me to the training camp. We said good-bye politely—handshakes all round—and that was the last I ever saw of that officers' mess. At the wheel of the truck was a long-jawed, handsome young man wearing a lance corporal's insignia.

"Hi, Yank," he said, jumping down and proffering a hand with a sweeping gesture. "You don't know what you got yourself in for."

Odd, I thought, the accent sounds midwestern American. No doubt an Englishman from the Midlands. I shook the hand.

"Those are my bags over there," I said. I thought he looked at me strangely, but he picked up the bags and put them in the truck. I climbed into the front seat beside him.

"I sure hope you've got some cigarettes," he said.

"Certainly," I said, and offered him one from my pack of Chesterfields. After that he seemed oddly uncommunicative, though I did manage to elicit the fact that his name was Tom Braden.

He stopped the truck about four miles outside of Winchester, beside a slatternly wooden barracks, and led the way inside. The place was buzzing with talk, mostly in cockney accents, but it stopped when we came in.

"This is where you sleep, Yank," said Braden.

"But where are the beds?" I asked.

He laughed a great cackle of a laugh and pointed to a bunchy bag of straw on the floor. "There's your beddy-bye," he said. "Want I should come and tuck you in?" He turned and departed, in what seemed to me an inexplicable huff.

The cockneys were nicer. They told me where to go for "char" which was the last meal of the day, and after that, since I wanted to clean up, they showed me where to go for a shower.

The showers—no hot water, of course—were in an unheated shed. There were a couple of cockneys in the shower room, plus Braden and a short man with black hair that stood up on his head like a Japanese doll's.

"Hey, Yank," said the short man, again in that puzzling accent. "I'm Ellsworth. Ted Ellsworth, from Dubuque, Iowa. Braden here is also from Dubuque. What's your name, and where you from?"

A great light shone. That had been no Midlands accent.

"Stewart Alsop," I said, pronouncing the name *All*sup—my father had insisted on the broad A. "From Avon, Connecticut."

"Alsop, huh?" said Ellsworth, with an A as in alley.

"No, no, *All*sup," I said, drawing out the A.

"Al Alsop from Avon," Ellsworth said loudly and firmly, matching the Al to *Al*sop, and Braden laughed that great cackling laugh.

For two and a half years thereafter, while I was in the British army, I remained Al Alsop. Long before those two and a half years had passed, Tom Braden and Ted Ellsworth had become, as they

212

remain, close friends, maybe my closest friends. It was together in London that we discovered Rosa Lewis's Cavendish Hotel in Jermyn Street, where we had more fun than most men ever find in wartime. Rosa Lewis had been both cook and mistress to Edward VII when he was Prince of Wales, as well as to other leading members of the prince's Marlborough House set, and the Cavendish had once been one of the world's great luxury hotels. It was still comfortable in a raffish way—it was furnished like a rather down-at-heel English country house—and Rosa herself, in her more lucid moments, was still wonderfully entertaining.

Five of us sailed together for Africa—Ellsworth smuggling a dog aboard—but there, alas, Braden and Ellsworth joined one battalion of the regiment, and George Thomson, Harry Fowler (another American), and I joined another. We were sent as infantry platoon commanders to Italy, and none of us enjoyed it, but we all emerged unscathed. Except for Harry, we all transferred to the American forces eventually.

Braden and Ellsworth and I did not become friends right away. I learned later that Braden had reported to Ellsworth that "this Alsop is a *real* horse's ass." It seems that my manner on the truck had somehow infuriated him, and Braden had been particularly incensed when I offered him *one* cigarette. There was a fierce tobacco shortage in Britain—though how I was supposed to know this I still don't understand—and Braden and Ellsworth had expected me to come to the rescue with at least a carton apiece. Anyway, the first impression I had made on them was not good.

Ellsworth's revenge started with that "Al Alsop," but it did not end there. I was thin in those days, and my cheekbones showed. I had spent a lot of time sunning myself on the deck of the freighter on the way over, and my face, naturally rubicund, was a coppery red. The rumour quickly spread in the training battalion that I had American Indian blood. A considerable delegation approached Ellsworth for confirmation of this interesting fact. "I say, Ellsworth," said an eighteen-year-old Etonian, who later reported the conversation to me. "Is it true that Al Alsop is a Red Indian?"

"Yes, it's true," said Ellsworth, his manner solemn. "But I wouldn't mention it to him, because he's kinda sensitive about it. Al's mother is an Indian, full-blooded. But she's not one of those fighting Indians, like an Iroquois, say, or an Algonquin. Al's mother is a squat Indian."

"A squat Indian?" said the young Englishman, surprised.

"Yeah, a squat Indian. Sometimes we call them mud Indians. These squat Indians, they make holes in the mud, and they do nothing—nothing at all, all day, except squat in the mud. Yeah. Al's mother is a squat Indian." Although Mother had a good sense of humour, she was not amused when, after the war, I told her about how she became a squat, or mud, Indian.

I did not realize, until I got sick, how much the war had meant to me. I am glad that none of my boys has been in a war. And yet they may have missed something. They may have missed some fun and some friendship. Wars can be a lot of fun, if you're lucky— plus a lot of boredom and misery, of course. And the friends you make in wartime are likely to be closer friends than any you make at other times. My children may also have missed finding out more about themselves, for a war is a good way to find out about yourself. They may have missed something else that is useful too. For to face the chance of death when you are young helps prepare you to face death when you are old. No young person really believes that this time will come. But it will.

IX

That evening, September 16, after my chat with brave Mrs. X, I was back in Ward 13. John hooked me up to the old IV, with two bottles of cidal antibiotics hanging on it, though with his accustomed candour he explained that he didn't think they would do any good. If I had had a bacterial infection, he said, I would have had a much higher temperature, so he was sure it was some sort of virus, and against a virus antibiotics are of no use. I had not known this. I asked him what new treatment there was for a virus. "Bed rest and plenty of liquid," he said. I remarked that medicine had not made any giant strides in this field since I was a boy.

That night, after Tish left, I slept, with the help of pills. But the next day I was scared again. John did a marrow test at about twelve thirty. Stilling the morning panic had been a problem. Waiting for the verdict was even worse. Please God, please Mother, please

Father, please Aggie. Then John came in, and I could tell right away that his news was at least not terrible news.

The blood counts were not good. The haemoglobin had responded less than he'd hoped to the transfusion—he'd give me another this evening. The platelets were in the danger area. The white count was "pretty lousy," with only 12 per cent granulocytes.

But—and here was the good news—there had been no fulmination of abnormal cells in the marrow. The proportion was just about what it was the last time I was marrowed—about thirty per cent. So no chemotherapy and no laminar flow room, at least for the time being. Also—and this was something not to count on, just to hope for—there seemed to be "increased megakaryocyte activity" in the marrow. Megakaryocytes, which manufacture platelets, had been "substantially absent" ever since I'd come into the hospital back in July. Now for the first time quite a few showed in the marrow slides. So this just *could* be good news.

"No news is good news," runs the old cliché. Most old clichés happen to be true, and none is truer than this one where a leukaemic is concerned. He soon learns to expect the worst, because the worst is sooner or later inevitable; so when the worst does not happen, that is a cause for rejoicing.

During this second go-around at NIH there were no picnics with friends, no martinis. My anorexia was almost total—and except for Tish and John Glick, people disgusted me almost as much as food and drink. Even when Joe and Susan Mary paid a visit—I had passed the word that I wanted to see no one else—it was a major effort to be polite, though I love them both.

It wasn't that I felt desperately ill physically, or even desperately depressed. I felt, instead, a kind of weariness, a vast difference. That low background music became a background cacophony—not exactly a headache, but a kind of murmuring unpleasantness. And a very bad thing happened—I could hardly read at all. After half an hour the page would blur, and the racket in my head would mount from a murmur to a shout. For want of anything better to do I watched television. It was the first time I have ever done so for more than a few minutes.

I was pretty sure by this time that my cause was hopeless, but this didn't bother me half as much as it had during my first stay at

NIH, when I still enjoyed reading, and laughing, and seeing my friends. Now I enjoyed nothing. I didn't want to die, but I didn't want terribly *not* to die. "Who would fardels bear, to grunt and sweat under a weary life," if the weary life consisted of being unable to enjoy friends or books or food or drink, and sweating like a pig every night?

Before I got sick I hardly ever thought about death. Since then I have had to think a lot about it, and I have learned something. And what I learned is something that most healthy people do not understand when they think about their own death.

If you are in good spirits and full of health, the thought of dying is not only utterly abhorrent, but inherently incredible. The inherent incredibility of death to a healthy young man acts as a protective mechanism. It helps, for instance, to keep a combat soldier sane. But the fear of death in battle is quite different from the fear of death on a hospital bed. It is, for one thing, much rarer. Most people do not die a violent death, whether on the battlefield or in the streets. Most people die in bed, because they are very sick or very old or both. But their sickness and their oldness also act as protective mechanisms. Sickness and age do not make death at all incredible. They do make it less than utterly abhorrent.

In short, for people who are sick, to be a bit sicker—sick unto death itself—holds far fewer terrors than for people who feel well. Both Cy Sulzberger of *The New York Times* and Bill Attwood of *Look* magazine wrote me letters in which they referred to death as the Greek god Thanatos, and I began to think of death as Uncle Thanatos. When I felt sick enough, I even felt a certain affection for Thanatos, and much less fear of him than I had before.

PART TWO

What I later came to think of as the *dies gloriae* (all those boring hours of Latin at Groton kept popping up again after forty years) started while I was still in the hospital with my mysterious undulating fever. At the time the days did not seem a bit glorious, only an apparently unending stretch of tedium.

As before, the faded blond lady would make her rounds every

216

morning pricking fingers, and by about lunchtime John Glick would come in with the readings. I felt a bit like a compulsive gambler waiting for news of how his nags had done at the track. For a while my nags were losing every race.

The low point came on September 19. My haemoglobin count was falling fast, platelets had scored a record low, granulocytes were almost nonexistent. The next day the platelets were suddenly back up, and by September 27 they had more than tripled. As, day after day, John Glick gave me the rising readings, he could hardly contain his excitement—he was at least as pleased as I was. The readings meant—they had to mean—that the marrow was again doing its job of churning out platelets.

John sent me home. I was to go back once a week to join the Nos Morituri Brigade for the eleven o'clock finger stick. It was at the first finger stick, on October 1, that the *dies gloriae* really began, for the counts showed that the marrow, all on its own, was manufacturing more than platelets. My haemoglobin was holding steady at 11.5. Red blood cells, like all cells, die and have to be replaced, so the haemoglobin count meant—it had to mean—that my marrow was churning out red blood cells fast enough to replace the dying cells. The platelet count was by then a handsome 54,000, up from the 14,000 of September 19. And for the first time there was really good news from the white cell front. The percentage of granulocytes was 16, meaning that I had almost 500, close to the safety line. It was the best white count I had had since the whole routine began.

Figures are boring, but these were not boring to me—they had a lovely, lyrical meaning. They meant that something strange and wonderful and inexplicable was happening to my blood. Having faced death, perhaps in a short time, I now faced life, perhaps for quite a long time. No one, I suspect, who has not experienced this sort of reprieve can wholly imagine what it is like. It induces, for a while at last, a special euphoria which no chemical can emulate and in which colours are brighter, life more interesting, and dear friends dearer than ever before. As the counts rose and I emerged from the slough of despond in which I had wallowed, I felt as though I wanted to feel life with my hands, and see it, and smell it, and taste it, and breathe it down deep inside myself.

217

On October 6 I got more good news. This time, instead of scribbling in my notebook, I put a sheet of paper in my typewriter when I got back to my office and began tapping away. Like scribbling in notebooks, this is an old journalistic habit. After an interesting interview I get to a typewriter as quickly as possible. I have a phonographic memory, but the record soon fades. In my mind's ear I can hear the person I have been interviewing talking, but only for a couple of hours or so. After that, silence.

Starting on October 6, I got into the habit of recounting my medical experiences on the typewriter when they seemed interesting. I came to think of those notes as my journal.

Sometimes, and increasingly often as time went on, instead of writing about my medical experiences I would sit down and tap out ideas or descriptions or recollections that had little or nothing to do with John Glick, NIH, or leukaemia. These essays, or maunderings, or whatever they are, were written as they appear in the journal, bit by bit, over a period of time. So some are not dated.

The journal is, as writing, markedly inelegant. The late Martin Sommers, a great editor and a most lovable man, who used to edit my articles for *The Saturday Evening Post*, had an annoying remark he would repeat ruthlessly: "You've got to put it through the typewriter one more time." Much of the journal needs another time through the typewriter. But aside from some judicious pruning I have left it as I wrote it, complete with inconsistent tenses and other inelegancies. In that condition it has at least the merit of spontaneity. The dated entries were written on the dates given, and without any foreknowledge of what was to come—although by the early winter of 1972 I obviously had some dark forebodings.

I started the journal on October 6 because I wanted to get down on paper an experience I still wish I hadn't had—the experience of looking through a microscope at the malignant cells in my own marrow.

October 6

Blood count at NIH. The count has broken all records. Platelets up. Haemoglobin steady. Genuine delight in John Glick's voice—granulocyte count the highest ever, 750, from a low of around zero less than a month ago.

At my urgent request John showed me some marrow slides, including my own, which was perhaps a mistake. He first showed me the slide of Mrs. X, the cheerful woman with the auburn wig who had been in remission for two years. Seen through the microscope at the first level of magnification, Mrs. X's marrow looked like Swiss cheese covered with caraway seeds. With maximum magnification the caraway seeds took on individual characteristics. The granulocytes were instantly identifiable; they looked like fat pink curly slugs. The megakaryoctyes, which make the platelets, were big angry-looking red blobs. The haemoglobin cells were neat little things like BB shots dyed purplish red. Then there were the myeloblasts (even normal marrows have some myeloblasts). Odd-shaped largish cells with little white spots, a bit like salami slices. Then Glick showed me the slide of a girl in relapse—sure soon to die. On this there were clusters of cells, mostly myeloblasts, and big empty spaces. John didn't like the slide, said there was certainly something very wrong-looking about it.

Finally my own last marrow, and there they were, the horrible little cells that are trying to kill me and, if one believes in the statistics, no doubt will. They were easily identifiable. Some looked like salami slices that had gone partly bad—pink but with whitish-rotten tails. Others, John said, looked like lymphoblasts; others looked like abnormal plasma cells.

"If I were Dr. Alsop," I told John, "I'd say this poor son of a bitch has three kinds of leukaemia all at once." He was not much amused and said that now I'd understand why my case was so hard to diagnose.

It is a strange feeling to look at the lethal cells crawling around in your own bones, big as golf balls under the microscope and, as John says, "obviously abnormal." Why, I asked John, don't the white cells, whose job it is to destroy enemy cells, recognize these easily recognizable monsters and kill them?

John shook his head and gave his stock reply, that whoever finds the answer to that question is a sure winner of the Nobel Prize. But he added that the evidence of my blood shows that something is preventing the uncontrolled proliferation of the abnormal cells—otherwise they would be crowding out the good cells, as in classic acute leukaemia.

I half wish now that I had not persuaded John to show me my own slide. A mental image of the malignant cells haunts me, and I suspect it will haunt me for a long time to come.

Wednesday, October 13

John called today's counts magnificent, and when he used that word his voice rose in excitement almost to the breaking point.

What is happening in the marrow? The question fascinates John. He theorizes that this sudden upsurge in the good cell count in all three categories could be a strong recovery from whatever virus I had—a kind of counterattack to the attack by the flu. Or a result of withdrawing the allopurinol. Or a combination of the two. Or something else. If the upspurt of the good cells in the blood means a significant decline in the proportion of abnormal cells in the marrow, it would be possible to begin to hope seriously for a total remission. John is obviously looking forward eagerly and hopefully to what he finds in the marrow on Monday. So am I.

Monday, October 18

Two p.m. John Glick gave me the long-awaited marrow test this morning. I ought to have gone to the office, but my mind is wholly on the glass slides that John is no doubt peering at now.

This is like final exams in school. If there's a marked drop in the percentage of abnormal cells, there really is hope for a cure—a word John used for the first time this morning. He is obviously hopeful—more hopeful than he likes to admit.

Four p.m. John calls. I say, my voice quivering with suspense, "What about the percentage of malignant cells?"

"Under ten per cent." This down from forty-four per cent at the start. "Marvellous," says John. "Almost miraculous." He had told Dr. Henderson that afternoon, and the usually dour Henderson's only comment was, "Wow!"

So what does it mean? What happened?

"We may never know. All we know is that something has happened to make you suddenly much better." And the marrow is not hypocellular—it has a normal cell disposition.

"How about those remaining cancer cells, though?" I asked.

"All we know is they're abnormal. They may not be cancer cells."

"So does it mean there is a serious chance of a genuine cure?"

"An exc—"

"You were going to say excellent, John, weren't you?"

"Let's say a good chance. You know, this is the kind of thing—well, if you have a bottle of champagne in your cellar, this is the night to get it out and drink it." This, mind you, from the doctor who told me in July that I had a fifty per cent chance of living a year, that it was twenty to one that I wouldn't last two years, and that the chance of a cure was statistically negligible.

I am not a religious man, but I think when nobody's looking I'll drop into a church tomorrow and say a prayer.

A COUPLE of days after this entry, walking back to the *Newsweek* office from a reportorial lunch, I came to the handsome old yellow stucco Episcopal church on Lafayette Square—"the Church of the Presidents." A door was open, and on impulse I went in and sat in a pew. With a certain sense of embarrassment I put my head down between my hands, as I used to do in chapel in Groton, and said the Lord's Prayer. I said it very rapidly, as I used to in the days when God was a big, bearded reality to me. I got as far as "Give us this day our daily bread. And forgive us our trespasses, As we forgive those who trespass against us."

Then I stopped. The faint sense of embarrassment persisted, the feeling I get when I am doing something that is not quite natural.

I wish I could say that this strange experience with leukaemia has given me profound spiritual insights. But it hasn't. I have been an agnostic since I was about eighteen. Agnostic, not atheist. I do not say there is no God—only that I do not know whether there is a God.

In a way we are all religious, whether we like it or not. That peculiar little incantation to God, Mother, Father, and Aggie is, I suppose, a manifestation of some sort of religion. I have developed another incantation. Reading Churchill's writings about America, I found a vintage Churchillism. When he was doing a lecture tour of the United States in 1931, he was hit by a taxi in New York and very nearly killed. He describes this experience in a plain, unadorned style. And then suddenly there it is: "For the rest, live dangerously; take life as it comes; dread naught; all will be well."

I find myself repeating this sentiment like a talisman—or, I suppose, like a prayer.

Wednesday, October 27

At NIH today, Dr. Rosenthal, the internist with whom John first discussed the withdrawal of allopurinol, came into the clinic. We went into one of the treatment rooms and had a long talk, John leaning against the high operating table, Rosenthal and I sitting on metal chairs. Glick and Rosenthal together seemed to be more conservative about a cure in my case than Glick alone had been. John has been talking about dismissal from NIH by Christmas or even by Thanksgiving, but today they agreed that there would be no final decision until February or even March.

John is one of nature's optimists—to him the glass is always half full, never half empty. Rosenthal is a cooler type, calm in manner and physically stocky, with a broad, humorous face. They plan a joint case report on Alsop's disease for some medical journal. They'll wait three or four months, until—or so one hopes and prays—two or three marrows have been normal. It is always possible, John says with uncharacteristic pessimism, that things could begin moving backward. But he clearly does not believe that this eventuality is at all likely.

He lists the variables—Atromid, which I had taken for high cholesterol; allopurinol; the virus attack—if it was a virus. There have been cases of a virus seeming to cause a spontaneous remission. But the odds against it are vast. Allopurinol remains the major suspect. But though allopurinol has caused a number of strange disorders, it has *never* been known to cause obviously abnormal cells, looking every bit as malignant as proven AML cells. The case study may thus have to record that the Alsop case is simply bizarre, wholly idiosyncratic, without any identifiable etiology.

Suppose it is definitely proved that allopurinol caused the problem. Will it be taken off the market?

Almost certainly not. Allopurinol, Glick and Rosenthal explain, is a very valuable drug, which has saved many lives. Doctors would still prescribe it, but carefully and more reluctantly, and would keep a close watch on subsequent blood counts. Chloromycetin is a valuable drug too, but doctors prescribe it with extreme care.

If allopurinol *is* the culprit, will this mean that I never had cancer at all? Probably. Then how explain the seemingly malignant cells? "We'd call them bizarre drug-affected cells," John says. "Dyspoietic is the technical word. We do see drug-affected cells in the marrows of patients in remission from AML."

THE NEWS that I was in NIH diagnosed as an acute leukaemic spread fast among my friends, and faster still when I wrote two pieces about the experience for *Newsweek*. I soon began to get a lot of letters. After my cousin Alice's "what a nuisance" note, perhaps my favourite letter came from Jock Whitney, whose sister, Joan Payson, owned the New York Mets:

Dear Stew:

A friend of mine was sitting next to my sister Joan at the opening of the Metropolitan Opera with Madame Callas, looking glorious, two seats away.

The programme began with the Star Spangled Banner, at the conclusion of which Joan settled into her seat with the audible statement, "Play Ball!" Mme. Callas cracked up.

With warmest wishes.   Jock

A perfect letter to a very sick man, since what a very sick man needs above all is to be cheered up, and nothing is more cheering up than a good laugh. I also had many thoughtful and moving letters from journalistic colleagues. I was touched when Teddy White (Theodore H. White of *Making of the President* fame) offered to act as my legman for the column, if I hadn't recovered "the full vigor to tackle the road in a presidential campaign." Journalism is a highly competitive trade, and, as any journalist will agree, it was a remarkably generous offer.

Another way to cheer up a sick man is to massage his ego. I got a number of ego-massaging letters from politician friends, including one from Ed Muskie. In the fall of 1971 Muskie seemed to have the Democratic nomination almost sewn up, and it was cheering up to get an ego message from a potential President. I also got one from Hubert Humphrey, who, ideology aside, has long seemed to me about the most humanly likable politician I have known.

Still another way to cheer up a man supposed to be dying is to suggest that he may fool the doctors yet and to produce substantiating evidence. John Roche, the columnist and Brandeis University professor, wrote an especially cheering letter:

Dear Stew:

I was terribly distressed to hear of your ailment, though glad to hear it has been tempered by ambiguity. Let me tell you a story: in 1948 my father was dragged into the hospital (he didn't believe in them, arguing that since most people died in hospitals they were places to avoid) and the wise men diagnosed terminal, inoperable cancer of just about everywhere from the belt down. They gave him up to 6 mos. and, unwisely, suggested to my mother that he not be told.

Ten years later—to make a long story short—he died of a heart attack, aged 72. When they did the post mortem, they discovered the cancer had simply died out. Of course, they went nuts trying to find out what he ate, drank, smoked, etc. . . .

Admittedly my old man was a hard case, but you have always struck me as being in the same general category. So fool the bastards. . . .   Yours, John

But the most cheering-up letter of all came from Dean Acheson, in response to the first column I wrote for *Newsweek* describing the experience of being told of death's imminent inevitability.

I had been worried about that column. A political columnist is supposed to write about politics, not about himself. I was afraid it would seem sentimental, self-pitying, mawkish. And curiously, what made me especially nervous was the thought that Dean Acheson would read it. I saw him quite often and he occasionally commented on a column, so I knew he read what I wrote.

224

I admired Dean Acheson very much. I admired him when, almost alone in terrified Washington, he stood up against Joe McCarthy, and I also admired him when in his old age he stood up against the post-Vietnam neo-isolationism of many of his fellow Democrats. He was sometimes wrong, of course, like everybody else, but there was never a man who so clearly had the courage of his convictions, right or wrong. I was also a little bit scared of Dean Acheson. He detested silliness, and he was justly famous for his putdowns. His letter is dated 29. VIII. 71, a way of dating letters peculiar to him:

Dear Stew,

You are one hell of a man. I am proud to know you and wish that I had half your guts. . . . May you go on to prove a miracle and live to write as wisely and sensibly as any man ever did.

Alice sends her love.

As ever, Dean

Dean Acheson died a few weeks later, on October 12, 1971. He died the way a sensible man should wish to die. Full of years and honours, he slumped forward on his desk, without a moment's agony or suspense. Something, I think, died with him.

It is hard to define what that something was, and many people, including highly intelligent people, are perfectly happy to see it die. I am not one of them, but then a man is a product of his conditioning as well as his genes, and I had very much the same kind of conditioning Dean Acheson had. It stemmed from what has come to be known as the WASP (White Anglo-Saxon Protestant) establishment, so many of whose sons (Roosevelts, Harrimans, Biddles, etc.) have had, until recently, so much to do with running the United States financially, administratively, even intellectually. Dean Acheson's sudden death symbolized the death of the WASP establishment, though it was a long time adying. To be sure, a lot of bad mistakes were made when policy was made by the WASP establishment, and a lot of people who thought of themselves as an elite were neither as able nor as disinterested nor as elite as they liked to think. Some of them were fools.

Yet they were at least generally incapable of the kind of sleaziness, the small-minded grubbiness, that has become so marked a

225

feature of the Washington political scene. This is why a small tear may perhaps be shed for the something else that breathed its last when Dean Acheson slumped forward on his desk.

Monday, November 8

Last week there was a mysterious dip in the blood counts, and John told me to come in today for a blood test and then, if things look wrong, a marrow test. He drew the blood, a bit extra since he had some esoteric tests in mind, and told me to come back in forty-five minutes, when he'd have the count.

I had had no breakfast, because the esoteric tests required an empty stomach. Tish and I wandered down to the basement cafeteria. Breakfast was no longer being served, so I had a detestable sweet roll and a cup of coffee. I was scared, for the first time in weeks, and I had trouble getting the roll down. I was scared of having a marrow and scared of what might follow if the bad cells had started up again. Tish and I sipped our coffee and watched the clock. At eleven the forty-five minutes had passed, and we went upstairs to the clinic.

There was a happy grin on John's readable face. "No marrow this time," he said. "If you went to a doctor with this count, he might tell you to come back in a few weeks for a checkup, but he'd be more likely to tell you to go about your business."

Wednesday, November 17

Finger stick and a marrow test this morning. Afterward, John Glick told me about a conference that had been held about my case. Last Friday, it seems, there was a national conference on acute myeloblastic leukaemia, attended by some of the leading specialists in the country, including—and one sensed a certain reverence as John pronounced his name—Dr. Bayard D. Clarkson of the Sloan Kettering Institute.

They had all had a look at my marrow slides, and most agreed that they would have diagnosed my case as an atypical AML—just as Drs. Henderson and Glick had done. After they had looked at the most recent slides, the ones with less than six per cent abnormal cells and a normal cell distribution, there was much mystification. Dr. Clarkson confessed himself as mystified as everyone else. But

226

he hazarded a guess—that I had had a harbinger, or warning signal, of some sort of atypical malignancy, perhaps a slow-growing cancer of the lymph glands. Someone else suggested an unusual lymphoma of some kind.

The result of the conference was a nasty shock I found in store for me. It had been decided, John said, to give me not only a routine marrow test, but a very thorough biopsy. As usual, after the thing was done and the holes in my back had been bandaged up, we chatted.

"Now suppose," I said, "that I had a series of normal blood and marrow tests, and that neither these nor the biopsies showed any evidence of cancer. Would you at some point pronounce me cured and tell me to go on about my business?"

"We won't pronounce you cured as long as we don't know what was wrong with you in the first place. We might keep you under observation for ten years or more, with periodic tests. But whatever happens, it's not going to be like three months ago, when you were under a sword of Damocles all the time."

TISH AND I GO into the waiting area, to join the Nos Morituri Brigade and wait for the results. As usual, there is the sound of children crying their hearts out—marrow tests hurt and small veins are hard to find. There are two little boys reading comic books. One is wearing a long black wig and the other a shorter blond wig. I scribbled in my notebook: "This place has saved my life, but I hate it with all my heart—I suppose because *Horribilis mors perturbat me.*" Then John comes in beaming. My blood test readings are high normal. A little later he gave us the marrow test news—still less than six per cent abnormal cells. Later still, he called us at home: all clear in the biopsy.

Thank you God, thank you Mother, thank you Father, thank you Aggie. I felt so well that I was convinced my troubles were over.

Christmas 1971

Ian and his friend, Jill Charlton, are back from Katmandu, and the house is rapidly filling up for Christmas with the other children. Ian looks dashing, if somewhat piebald. He has light blond hair, jet black eyebrows, a brown moustache, and a dark auburn beard, grown after the fashion of Nikolai Lenin. Tish and I had been a bit nervous about meeting Jill. Ian got to know her on the Far Eastern youth circuit, in New Delhi, where much hash is smoked and many pills popped, and we didn't know what to expect.

She turns out to be a small, charming girl, sensible and practical, with a tendency to wear dresses (if that is what they are called) that come down to her ankles, so that she looks like an illustration from *Punch*, circa 1880. She reminds me oddly of Sis at the same age—she has the same authoritative air.

About a year after I'd said good-bye to Ian in 1969 I wrote him one of those parental letters. Part of the letter was about the importance of hanging on to capital; Ian had spent a couple of thousand of the limited number of dollars he had inherited. This part of my letter he took in good part, I think. But then I couldn't forbear to add one of those snotty parental wisecracks: "As for the longer future, I think you must ask yourself whether you really want to spend the rest of your life as a Nepalese woodcut peddler."

This irritated Ian, and I confess I think he was right to be irritated. When I wrote the letter, he and Jill had just invented their unique business, which they have since greatly expanded. When the Dalai Lama fled the Communists in Tibet in 1959, many of his priests went to Nepal. They took with them, as well as many ancient artifacts, hundreds of traditional woodcuts, finely carved, from which black-and-white engravings with religious or symbolic motifs are made on rice paper.

Ian and Jill acquired some woodcuts, and began selling the prints on the streets of Katmandu, one of several fashionable Far Eastern gathering places for the liberated young. This venture, it seems, had a fantastic success, and Ian and Jill have two Nepalese employed helping them turn out the prints, which is hard work. Their purpose in coming here, aside from seeing the family, was to hold an exhibition in Georgetown and to try to start a print exporting business to the United States. Ian is serious about these prints and is well on the way to becoming a true expert in the rather arcane field of Himalayan art. As for his being a Nepalese woodcut peddler, he is a very successful Nepalese woodcut peddler. He and Jill live well, and he has not dipped into his small store of capital in a long time. Katmandu, it appears, is a lovely place—smiling

228

people and eternal spring. So why shouldn't he remain a Nepalese woodcut peddler as long as he chooses?

Joe and Candy have arrived, and Joe is very critical of my handling, if it can be called handling, of Nicky and Andrew. "Daddy," he will say, when one or the other is defying my feeble will or making himself obnoxious in some way, "how can you let them get away with that?" The truth is that I am a weakly permissive parent, but as I explained to Joe the other day, this is partly his fault. When he was about Andrew's age he had a passion for toy trucks. Until he was about six he retained an oddity of speech— the sound of the letters *tr* he pronounced as if they formed an *f*. This led to a major embarrassment.

Tish and I gave a large, pompous dinner party when Joe was about four. Cousin Alice Longworth was a guest, and so was the British ambassador, and there were a couple of Senators, fellow columnists, and the like. As the guests began to arrive, I told little Joe (who is now six feet three) to collect his toys and go on up to bed. He sensed that this would be a good time to test my will, and he went on playing with his toy trucks on the living-room floor. A little later I again told him to go to bed, in my best this-time-dammit-I-mean-it tone. He kept on playing.

I knew that it was now or never and grabbed him around the waist, while a hush fell on the party. The stairs leading to the second-floor bedrooms were open stairs, in the living room. By the time we got to them Joe was kicking like a mule and howling like a banshee. On the way up he grabbed a banister and hung on for dear life, and began to shout, "Give me my little trucks! Give me my little trucks!" Only that was not quite what he said. As usual, he pronounced *tr* with the sound *f*.

Nobody said anything about the incident; in those days the word Joe had been shouting was *never* used in respectable mixed company. But I think several of the guests, Cousin Alice especially, were secretly amused.

IN MY DAY, antiparental rebellion took the form of drinking too much, driving too fast, and getting involved with "unsuitable" girls. I got into trouble in sophomore year in college.

I shared an old Ford touring car with brother John. A friend

229

called Bob McCormick and I dropped in one night at an establishment called the York Athletic Club, where we met two young ladies. We suggested that we drive to Bridgeport in search of adventure; the girls agreed. One sat up front with me, and the other, whose name was Carla Something, sat with Bob McCormick in the back of the open Ford. I drove too fast, of course—I had been drinking bathtub gin and ginger ale—and when I passed a truck and just barely missed it, poor Carla began to scream. Her arm had been draped over the side of the touring car and the truck had scraped it.

We turned round and took Carla to the New Haven Hospital. Her two enormous brothers arrived, and we heard them asking for the names of the "Yale college punks," and threatening to "sue the bejesus out of them." While the hospital desk gave them our names, Bob and I scuttled back to the sanctuary of Yale.

When I woke up the next morning I knew what I had to do. I had to call Pa. The conversation was brief. "Father," I said (for this was too serious an occasion to call him Pa), "I'm in trouble."

"Oh, God, Stewart," he said. "What's her name?" I told him. "Oh, God!" he said, and hung up the telephone.

Afterwards Father was quite nice about the whole episode, even though the automobile insurance rates he had to pay were almost doubled. I think he was relieved that he had misjudged the kind of trouble I was in.

This small episode from my not very bright college days has a curiously musty air. Yale was very establishmentarian in those days, of course. Rebellion was not limited to drinking and driving too fast. It also took a political form. Most of my politically minded friends were left-liberal New Dealers, and a good many were, like myself, at least theoretical Marxists. But there were limits to rebellion. Among all my rebellious friends, I know of none who lived openly with a girl while not in a state of matrimony; a love affair in those days was a much more hole-in-corner business than it is today. Times have changed.

But only up to a point. Drink and fast driving and more or less Marxism have been replaced as symbols of rebellion by pot and long hair and public cohabitation and a strange variety of revolutionary doctrines. When Joe and Candy have children, rebellion will take some different form, but rebellion there will be. If they

230

have boys, I think I can confidently predict that the boys will rebel with special fury against son Joe, just because Joe has the kind of strong character male children always rebel against. I hope Candy can cope. I think she can, because she has, despite a pretty face and gentle manner, as strong a character as Joe.

Joe's business, Intercomp, has recently—and, as I thought, predictably—been broken by giant IBM as a butterfly on a wheel. Son Joe is undaunted, though. He is not easily dauntable. In fact he is mule stubborn, and although he may not be independently wealthy at thirty, as he hoped to be, I think he will be a genuinely successful man sooner or later. Maybe he is already. He is busy, deeply interested in what he is doing, healthy, and happily married. It is hard to think of a better definition of success.

Elizabeth—Fuff—and her husband, Peter Mahony, are here too, and the house is bursting at the seams. Fuff works at Harper & Row in the children's book department, and Peter works with an up-and-coming New York architectural firm, where he is doing, I gather, extremely well. Peter is a handsome young man. With his moustache and his wavy brown hair he looks a bit like the kind of young man Charles Dana Gibson used to draw, wooing one of his Gibson girls. Fuff is attractive, but she does not look like a Gibson girl. For one thing, she has too firm a jaw. Tish and I used to worry that Fuff, stubborn as she is, might dominate Peter. We worry no longer. Fuff used to swear that never, never, never would she live in New York City. When Peter got a promising job offer from the New York firm, she dug in her heels and ululated. Peter said nothing. Now they are sharing an apartment in Manhattan.

Every night, after she comes home from work and makes their supper, Fuff sits stubbornly down at a typewriter and starts tapping away. She is a professional writer, what is more—a writer who gets paid for what she writes. I am filled with admiration.

Stewart, nineteen and a freshman at Occidental College in Los Angeles, also has aspirations as a writer. He is currently at work on a long short story about his life at Groton. I read Stewart's story with fascination, because I disliked Groton very much, especially at first. Only one of my three oldest boys—Ian—graduated from Groton, and all three hated the place. All three seem to have decided, in their different ways, that the school was the enemy, and they either fought it or had as little to do with it as possible. Why? I think our generation was somehow conditioned to accept a degree of misery and discomfort—hard discipline, cold showers only, bad food, no girls—that our children are unprepared to accept. In any case, while Groton was a net plus for Joe and John and myself, it was clearly a net minus for Joe and Ian and Stewart. Neither Nicky nor Andrew will go there.

Stewart was much the handsomest of the children when he was a little boy. He was always cheerful, and not so long ago I especially enjoyed dandling him on my knee. He is now enormous—as tall as Joe, and over two hundred pounds. If I tried to dandle him on my knee, I too would be broken like a butterfly upon a wheel. I think Stewart can write. If he can achieve some of Fuff's self-discipline he might write really well.

I have always had a perhaps unhealthy obsession with my youngest child. I adored first Joe, then Ian, then Elizabeth, then Stewart. I began to stop adoring them—that much—at about seven or eight. That is when knee dandling becomes impractical. It is also the beginning of the end of innocence, the beginning of growing up. It is when a child's eyes become a little guarded, turn a bit opaque, and the child ceases, little by little, to be a child.

My obsession with Nicky, who was a postscript, seven years after Stewart, was especially powerful. This was partly because when he was very young Nicky was a rather sickly little boy, with a wandering eye. Finally he had an operation, but the bad eye had, and still has, only faint peripheral vision. Because of this Nicky had great trouble learning to read and write. This aroused my protective instincts and made me more permissive than ever.

Nicky is twelve now, and it is already clear that he is going to be even more enormous than Joe and Stewart. It is also clear that, being a determined fellow, he is going to be able to read and write properly, though the struggle has not been easy for him. He is getting to the age where his voice sometimes sounds like the cry of an adolescent alligator, and he can still arouse me to occasional purple-faced paroxysms. There are signs of the inevitable rebellion on the way, but he is full of vitality, and when he is not in full revolt we are friends.

My unhealthy obsession has been transferred to Andrew, who is almost five, and a sort of post-postscript, or do-it-yourself grandson, as Tish says. Andrew is a good-looking little boy and he has a wide, rather cynical grin which displays a missing tooth right in the middle of his mouth. He invariably amuses me and cheers me up. I may be a foolish, fond old man, but I even claim to discern in some of his remarks something very like conscious wit. For example, Stewart brought a pretty, tall, willowy girl friend home. As she sashayed through the living room, Andrew remarked, "I like the way she wiggles her things."

But the time is coming fairly soon when knee dandling will be impractical for Andrew too. There will be no post-post-postscript. So I wish the older children would get busy and supply us with some knee dandlers with unguarded eyes.

All this sounds a bit smarmy sentimental, but I am not at all sentimental about the children and neither is Tish. In fact, we shove them out of the nest as soon as they can flutter their wings, and although we like to have them about for holidays and week-ends, they are on their own. A neurotic emotional interdependence between parents and children, above all between mother and sons, has, I suspect, wrecked more lives than all history's wars.

The subject of my disease has hardly been mentioned between the children and myself. The line now is that "Daddy's much better," and the children and I leave it at that. As this suggests, there is a certain arm's-length relationship between us, a fear on both sides of invading the other side's privacy. To me, this seems a healthy relationship.

January 10, 1972
Bad news. Into NIH for a blood count. John asked me how I'd been feeling and I told him okay, but not so full of beans as in October and November, when my counts were zooming up.

Maybe, I said, it was just psychological, and John agreed—the euphoria of those early days of recovery certainly had something to do with my feeling of physical well-being. I also was having this flu-like stomach trouble, I said, a kind of queasiness, and it had lasted for a month. Maybe that had something to do with it too.

I had my finger pricked by the finger-stick lady and went back to the *Newsweek* office. John called. "I don't like the look of it," he said. "Your haemoglobin is fine, but your white blood count and your platelets are both down."

"What do you think it means, John?"

"I don't know, but you're leaving Wednesday for Georgia, aren't you? I think we'd better marrow you before you go."

"Okay. I'll pick up Tish and be there in less than an hour." It is better to know than not to know.

I pretty well knew that the results would be bad, partly because the counts so indicated, but mostly because I sensed what John expected. The question was: How bad? Waiting again. Tish seemed to be reading, but I don't think she was. I couldn't sit still. At last John came in, bad news on his face. But not terrible news.

"The proportion of bad cells is definitely up," he said firmly. "They look like about thirteen per cent. It hasn't galloped. But the megakaryocytes are definitely down—that accounts for your low platelets. The red cells are excellent. But there's no concealing that this is a setback. You've always been a realist, Stew, and you've realized that there might be more to this than just the allopurinol. Let's just suppose you have some unknown malignancy. This malignancy became much better. Why? We don't know. Then something happened to make it worse again. Why? Again, we don't know. Some diseases are cyclic. This is not anything like classic AML. But it could be some form of smouldering leukaemia."

"Have there been many cases of smouldering leukaemia?"

"No. It's rare—very rare."

"What's the prognosis?"

"It's so rare that you can't make any firm prognosis. But if you have smouldering leukaemia, you might live for years. You'd probably have doses of chemicals on an outpatient basis. All we do know is that the bad cells are up and the counts are down, and the two go together." So what should I do?

John says I should go to Georgia as planned. That would be better than "moping about Washington," and meanwhile there's nothing to do but watch the counts. "This is disturbing to me, and I know it is to you two. You'll be down in the dumps for a while, but you just have to learn to live with this uncertainty."

Strangely, it's less of a shock to me than I might have expected. I think I anticipated it, the way the stock market is supposed to anticipate ups and downs. The pea of fear has grown suddenly larger. But it has always been there, at the back of my mind.

Thomasville
Monday, January 17

John Glick gave me a To Whom It May Concern letter to deliver to a doctor in Thomasville, Georgia, where Tish and I are spending a luxurious quail-shooting week with the Jock Whitneys. Until yesterday I had pretty well managed to forget about the recrudescence, and since the quail shooting at Greenwood, the lovely Whitney place here, is the best in the United States, that makes the forgetting all the easier. My To Whom It May Concern letter had been delivered to a Dr. Mims, who had agreed to give me a complete blood count on Monday at ten in the morning.

I slept badly Saturday night. We had had a dove shoot Saturday and it had bothered me. When I was in close fear of Thanatos I had no desire to kill anything. The quail shooting didn't bother me. A quail is a miniature chicken, and there's surely nothing wrong with killing a chicken to eat. But doves are different. That night I had bad dreams—there was one terrible dream in which I shot at little Andrew and he flopped about on the ground like a hit dove.

The next day, Sunday, I felt lousy, my stomach was queasy, I could only nibble at the delicious food, and in the evening I played bridge badly and lost, deserving to lose. The next morning, at ten, Tish drove me to Thomasville. A nurse gave me a finger prick, and Dr. Mims told me to call about noon—he'd have the count by then.

Back in the Whitney guesthouse, a knot of fear in my belly kept me from working. I called Dr. Mims precisely at noon.

"Why, Mistuh Alsop," he said, "you have the blood of a perfectly normal man." Haemoglobin, 15.1; white count, 4500 with 40 per cent granulocytes; platelets, 151,000!

Loveable Dr. Mims. I called John. "A marvellous count," he said. My appetite came back with a rush and I felt absolutely dandy. Such is the power of mind over matter.

Monday, January 31

To NIH clinic. John has tragic news—Tommy Thompson has just been readmitted to NIH, and the cancer has spread. It seems unlikely that he will leave the hospital alive.

I get my finger pricked and leave for my office. John calls up as I am about to go to the White House for one of Henry Kissinger's lousy lunches. (The lunches sent up by the White House mess are almost inedible, but Henry is always interesting and amusing, though rarely very informative.) The platelets are down to 70,000, and the other counts are drifting downward. Maybe something's still in there gnawing busily away. Or else, as John suggested, something happened as a result of the allopurinol which has permanently affected my marrow and my blood. If so, he says, it is something I can live with, maybe indefinitely.

Wednesday, February 9

Tommy Thompson died. His funeral was at twelve today in the National Cathedral. Chip Bohlen made a fine funeral oration, and he used just the right word about Tommy—decent. Tommy was pre-eminently a decent man. Not that he was ever soft or silly—he was a tough and highly competitive man, as anyone who ever played cards with him can attest. But he also had an instantly recognizable integrity, and that, combined with good sense and vast experience, gave him a special personal authority. People, including Presidents, listened to what he said and believed him.

When I interviewed Bobby Kennedy on the Cuban missile crisis, I asked him which of the inner circle of presidential advisers had impressed him most during the crisis. He answered without hesitation, "Tommy."

Kennedy gave an example of Tommy's good sense. Khrushchev ordered the ships that had been sailing towards Cuba loaded with missile equipment to reverse course. The intelligence established that all the ships had done so—except one, which kept stolidly steaming towards Cuba. The hawks, especially the military, chose to regard this as a deliberate provocation, a test of will, and proposed to bomb the Russian ship out of the water. Tommy quietly argued that it would be better to wait and see. Maybe that one ship hadn't got the message—maybe the wireless operator had been drunk or asleep. The President agreed. In a couple of hours the ship awoke with a start, as it were, and hastily reversed course.

I went to see Jane Thompson yesterday. Tommy, she said, died without pain—rare in cancer of the pancreas—and in his lucid moments he was cheerful and even funny. He suddenly asked her, "Have you ever played millstone bridge?" and then went on to define millstone bridge as the kind of bridge in which your partner is a millstone around your neck.

She recalled one of Tommy's favourite Khrushchev stories. During the U-2 blowup at the Paris summit in 1960, Khrushchev came up to Tommy and stepped hard on his instep, and said, "Excuse me," in Russian.

"Why did you do that?" asked Tommy.

"Because in Russia when we do something like that, we apologize," said Khrushchev. "Why don't you apologize for the U-2?"

Tommy also loved the story about Jane and the dance at the Kremlin. During his first tour as ambassador, as the thaw began, he and Jane were asked to a party at the Kremlin, complete with dancing—something quite unknown in the Stalin era. A middle-level Soviet official approached Jane, whose Junoesque figure was much admired by the Russians, and asked her to dance.

"Do you waltz?" asked Jane.

"Naw," said the Russian. "I do not waltz. Is too old-fashioned. I fox. Sometimes I fox quick, sometimes I fox slow. All depends on what the lady likes."

I can hear Tommy, in my mind's ear, laughing his small, heh-heh-heh giggle at this story.* His death has moved me more than most, not only because I liked and admired him, but because we were both told we had inoperable cancer at almost the same time. And yesterday I played three sets of indoor tennis. His death serves as a reminder, an intimation of mortality.

---

* Jane Thompson tells me I have the story all wrong. But I like it as it is.

ROBERT BURNS wrote of "man's inhumanity to man." Hardly anybody writes about nature's cruelty to man. But nature's cruelty is, at its most horrible, more horrible than man's.

Leukaemics are lucky in some ways. Most die of fungal or bacterial infection, pneumonia being also a much used exit, although there are occasional deaths by haemorrhage when platelet rejection has occurred. These are all relatively painless ways of dying. Some cancers impose on their victims monstrous and unimaginable suffering before they are allowed to die. This suffering is, after all, the work of dear old Mother Nature.

There have always been "nature fakers," in Theodore Roosevelt's phrase, but never more so than now. The Mother Earth myth has led a lot of people, young people especially, to suppose that Mother Nature is wonderfully benign. In fact, nature is cruel, inherently and unchangeably cruel. The idealistic young who refuse to recognize this reality are courting a painful disillusionment.

I remember a talk I had with a very tall, very handsome young man in 1969, at the height of the Vietnam war. He was just out of law school and had joined an antiwar commune, and intended to devote all his time to defending enlisted men who got into trouble with the military for anti-war activities.

He seemed to be a most impressive young man. He held forth on the iniquities of the capitalist-imperialist system, and although this was old stuff mostly, familiar since freshman year at Yale, he was articulate and sincere.

What system, I asked, should be substituted? Perhaps some form of Marxism? No, he said, none of that; he had been to Russia and Eastern Europe, and he saw that people were even less free there than in America.

"What we want," he said, "is a society in which there is no government at all, and people live together in accord with nature, and love each other." Then he looked at me searchingly. "I can see in your eyes you don't believe in that."

"No, I don't," I said, and did not try to explain why. I wonder what's happened to that young man. Maybe a striving junior partner in his law firm, stepping on the faces of other junior partners in order to become a senior partner? Or maybe, "in accord with nature," he is writhing with bone cancer? Life will be cruel to him in the end, in any case. "Golden lads and girls all must, as chimney-sweepers, come to dust."

Perhaps it is just that Tommy's death has depressed me.

Tuesday, February 15

Noon. Blood and marrow tests. Feeling fine, filled with a secret hope that the percentage of bad cells would be nicely down. John will call us at home with the results.

Four p.m. John just called. The Damocletian sword has become a bit heavier, the pea is a bit bigger—seventeen per cent bad cells. There were also fewer megakaryocytes (so there will be fewer platelets in the blood) and less granulocytic activity in the marrow. The doctors all agreed that there should be no chemotherapy now. But there is, as usual, no agreement on what is wrong with me. Dr. Henderson, asked what he would guess if he had to, replied that he would have to guess that I had some form of wholly idiosyncratic leukaemia—"Alsop's leukaemia," in John's phrase.

What to do? For the present, learn to live with it. I felt fine this morning. Now I feel lousy. Did John have to tell me? A frightened man welcomes a certain blandness. I think I would be capable of a remarkable degree of self-deception, if only John would let me deceive myself.

Cheeha Combahee Plantation, South Carolina
February 20

Tish and I have been coming here for a week in the winter for fifteen years now, thanks to Mac Herter—more formally, Mrs. Christian A. Herter. Chris Herter, Secretary of State in the last Eisenhower years, died in 1967. Andrew Alsop's middle name is Christian, in his memory.

This place is very different from Greenwood, the Jock Whitney place. Greenwood is a handsome, pillared mansion. It has gardens of startling beauty, and every guest has a large bedroom and bath all to himself. The food is justly famous, and at dinner the wine is apt to be a Lafite '61 or a Margaux '49 or the like.

The house at Cheeha Combahee is a shooting lodge, built in 1929. It is a handsome but unpretentious one-story house with six double bedrooms in one wing and a dining room, kitchen, and living room in the other. The whole place is heated entirely by wood fires. There is one bathroom for the ladies and one for the men, each with a two-holer. Once, in 1959, when Tom Gates (then Secretary of Defence) was a fellow guest, I went into the bathroom and found both places already occupied, by the Secretary of State and the Secretary of Defence. I could not help but be impressed.

The house is surrounded by a bright green expanse of rye grass, with camellia bushes and live oaks bearded with Spanish moss. The food is delicious but simple—quail cooked outdoors in bacon fat for lunch, local shad or beef or ham for dinner. Chris Herter used to cook the luncheon quail. I have a vivid mental image of him fanning the frying pan with his hat to put out the fire when the bacon fat flared up.

Both places afforded a wonderfully pleasurable week-long house party to those lucky enough to be asked as guests, with lots of talk, lots of bridge, and lots of quail shooting.

Father used to be asked to various quail-shooting plantations every winter. My brother John and his wife, Gussie, are here this week, also making the quail-shooting rounds. In short, we Alsops are almost professional quail-shooting guests. I vaguely remember a scene, from a nineteenth-century English novel, I think, in which the duke and his duchess are discussing the guest list for the grouse shooting. The duke proposes Mr. So-and-so. The duchess objects: "But isn't he a bit of a cad?" The duke replies: "Of course he's a cad, but he's a good shot and he plays a decent game of whist." I tell John that we are asked every year for the same reasons.

Nonshooting friends of mine are mystified by my passion for shooting at quail. It is hard to explain. Granted that the little birds make delicious eating, is that any way for sensible grown-up people to spend hours at a time? You sit on an old horse as it plods through fields and through woods. Out front the dogs quarter back and forth, sniffing for quail, covering acre after acre like vacuum cleaners. The horse plods on, and you find yourself thinking in a way you don't often have time to think—lazily, at random, for pleasure. You remember a bit of poetry or a snatch of song, a girl you once liked very much and had almost forgotten, or something that happened long ago that amused or interested you.

My old Winchester double-barrelled 12-gauge I inherited from

Father. Pa's initials, JWA, are embossed on a little gold plaque on the stock. Seeing his initials winking in the sun, I began to think about Pa, two inches taller than I and heavier, plodding along on some now long-dead horse, waiting for the dogs to point, all those long years ago. Pa was about to go on a quail hunt when he died at seventy-seven, here in South Carolina, in 1952. He is dead, but there is still a lot of Pa alive in me, I thought. I have Pa's nose and forehead, and his legs, with big feet, round calves, and thin shanks.

And when I die, there will be a lot of me still alive in my children —probably more in Joe and Elizabeth than in the others, and least in Ian, or maybe Andrew, both very visibly Tish's children. Pa is alive in me in other ways too. For example, he infected John and me with the passion for shooting and fishing (it never took with Joe). Too bad that I have never been able to infect my children— they say they are against killing things, and perhaps they're right. But they miss something curiously exciting and pleasurable.

I found myself grinning suddenly. The duke and duchess and the cad reminded me of something that happened to me in the 1950s.

I was in London, on a reporting trip for Joe's and my column. I had an introduction to Lord Salisbury and interviewed him—he was a powerful figure in those days—and he asked me for the weekend to his country seat, Hatfield House.

I paid off the taxi and timidly rang a doorbell. To my surprise Lady Salisbury, a grey-haired lady with a strong ancestral face, answered the bell. With her was an enormous hound, which looked at me in a markedly unfriendly fashion and growled.

Lady Salisbury saw that I was nervous. "Don't worry," she said. "Bobo never bites a gentleman, only the lower classes."

At this point Bobo lunged forward and planted his teeth in my right calf. It was an embarrassing moment.

Wednesday, March 1

This morning I made a deal with John Glick. He agreed to it with surprising ease.

I had a wonderful time at Cheeha Combahee until the day before we came home. Good company, good talk, good shooting, and good eating. But on Friday I began to feel lousy. Queasy. Why? Because I was to have a blood test on Monday and, if the results were not good, a marrow test. John obviously suspected it was mainly psychosomatic. But the blood test was not good. Not at all good. Platelets and granulocytes are both sharply down. Something is going on. John theorized again that "Alsop's leukaemia," or whatever it is, may be cyclic; that allopurinol was perhaps not the key factor—in October, I just hit the up cycle. Now I am in a down cycle. Nothing to do but wait and see. He wants finger stick on Friday and, unless there's an improvement, a marrow on Monday.

I had a lunch date with Kay Graham at the Sans Souci. I called to tell her I couldn't quite face all those people, so she said to come to her house. We talked about my lousy news, and afterward I felt more cheerful. It was then that I made a decision.

John had told me that, bar some catastrophic fulmination, nothing would be done anyway. So why was it necessary to face all these prickings and probings, the Nos Morituri Brigade, and worst of all, the endless waiting for results? I discussed it with Tish that evening and decided to ask John for a one-month vacation from all tests of any sort. I am to call him if anything goes wrong. Otherwise no more probings until April.

I feel like a boy let out of school. No more lessons, no more books, no more teacher's dirty looks. No more blood tests, no more marrows, no more biopsies, no more clinic—at least for a month. I hadn't realized how all those prickings and probings had been getting me down.

Tuesday, March 21

Here we go again. Back to square one. Vacation ended early.

A toothache, very much like the toothaches I had last spring before I was diagnosed as a leukaemic, started on Sunday, and it got worse on Monday. I had it in mind to go to the dentist and get it fixed and say nothing to John Glick, but low platelets involve the danger of haemorrhaging, and Tish insisted on calling John. He said I had to have a blood count. I hated the idea. I didn't want to go back and I knew, somehow, that the count would be bad.

Tish drove me to NIH for the ten-thirty finger stick. Not at all good. Except for the haemoglobin, I'm back to the lousy counts of August. John's still sure I don't have AML. He still doesn't know what I do have.

I had two martinis at lunch, on the grounds that I deserved them. I played tennis, and pretty well, and we had a pleasant evening. But the pea is back. I remember a game we used to play in Avon as children. An object would be held over a child's head, and the other children would intone, "Heavy, heavy, what hangs over?" If the child guessed wrong, he was It, and all the other children would run away from him. There is something grim about the phrase "Heavy, heavy, what hangs over?"

Tuesday, April 4

This is Wisconsin primary day, and I've spent a good deal of time wondering about the outcome of the primary, and also wondering about whether I shall die soon.

This was the day agreed on with John Glick a month ago for the end of my vacation. I was prepared for bad news anyway before I went for my marrow test this afternoon. I was the more prepared because of what happened this morning. I got up feeling pretty spry, blew my large nose, and a nosebleed started. It refused to stop. I went back to bed and Tish brought up some ice in a plastic bag. I lay there freezing my nose until eleven. Then I got up, and the clot held. But I knew what the nosebleed meant—low platelets.

I'd meant to go to the office to do some preliminary telephoning for a Wisconsin piece, but with blood and marrow coming up at three, and my damnable nose still feeling as though it were about to bleed again, I called Amanda and told her I'd skip it.

I told John Glick that from now on I wanted to know only two things—if there had been a real turn for the better, or if there had been such a turn for the worse that some action had to be taken—a transfusion, for example, or chemotherapy. John agreed.

Less than half an hour after the marrow test John came into the room where Tish and I were waiting.

"Is the platelet count under twenty thousand?" I asked.

"You really want to know?" he asked, and I nodded. "Yes, it's under twenty thousand. But the news isn't all bad. Your granulocytes are actually up a bit, and your haemoglobin's normal." He confessed himself mystified all over again. "I can't account for this —platelets way down and haemoglobin steady—and your granulocyte count actually up. It just doesn't fit."

244

John called later to say there would be no transfusion and no chemotherapy. He is betting that the cyclic theory holds and that the counts will suddenly improve again. Please God, please Mother, please Father, please Aggie.

April 14

Today I called John to talk about yesterday's counts. He clearly expects the haemoglobin to follow the other counts down into the cellar. That's what I dread most—or, to be honest, second most. (What I dread most is getting very sick and dying.) You feel so lousy when your haemoglobin is low. And how am I to cover a presidential campaign if I can barely drag myself around?

It is full spring now, the lovely Washington April. But T. S. Eliot was right. April is the cruellest month.

MOST OF MY FRIENDS wrote me a letter when I first got sick, and thereafter, quite normally, left it at that. But there were a couple of exceptions.

Tom Braden, the lance corporal in the King's Royal Rifle Corps, is now, after a variegated career, a fellow Washington columnist. He is, I suppose, my best friend, and Tish and I see a lot of him and his famously charming wife, Joan. Joan is my second most assiduous correspondent. She wrote me every day when I was in the hospital, and when she is away—she and Tom are restless travellers—she always writes, which cheers me up.

But my most assiduous correspondent was—and still is—an interesting fellow called Peter B. Young. Pete Young has been more useful to me journalistically than a whole covey of Pentagon leaks handing out top secret papers by the bushel basket.

I met him in an odd way. Shortly after the Watts riot in Los Angeles in 1965, I went out and spent a long day of walking and talking in Watts. For the first time I sensed the depth of the bitterness of many blacks. As I wrote for my column in *The Saturday Evening Post:* "In Watts, for the first time, it began to seem to me that the racial problem in this country is wholly insoluble—that it is like some incurable disease, with which both whites and Negroes must learn to live in pain, all the days of our lives."

After the *Post* published my column I got a telegram: SO NOW

YOU'VE SEEN THE BLACK GHETTO. COME TO GREENE COUNTY NORTH CAROLINA KNOWN AS KU KLUX KLAN CAPITAL USA AND SEE THE WHITE GHETTO. SIGNED PETER B. YOUNG.

My curiosity was aroused. I phoned Young, who turned out to be a television newsman in Raleigh. He claimed to know the Klan better than any other non-Klansman. I owed it to myself and my readers, he said, to understand and describe the other side of the Watts coin—"the anguish and despair of the white ghetto."

I decided to accept Young's invitation. I also decided to invite Ted Ellsworth along. After the war Ted returned to the insurance business in Dubuque, but he is always ready for an adventure. Inviting Ellsworth turned out to be a brilliant idea. The Ku Kluxers found me a cold northern fish, but they immediately took to Ellsworth—they even offered him the Grand Dragonship of Iowa. They talked to him as they would never have talked to me.

Ellsworth came to Washington and we flew together to Raleigh. At the airport we met Peter Young and the Exalted Cyclops of the Greene County Ku Klux Klan. They were an odd pair. Young is a grandson of Brigham Young. Pete does not look a bit like a Mormon prophet. He is short, with close-cropped hair, and even at the age of thirty-three he was contending with a small pot. He is also, as we soon discovered, an entertaining fellow, with a unique talent.

The Exalted Cyclops also wore his hair cropped short, but in every other way he was as different from Pete Young as it is possible to be. He was a great, hulking brute of a man, with a slit of a mouth, a bullethead, and light, expressionless eyes. The three of us were immediately treated to the conversational style of the Exalted Cyclops.

"We believe a white man's got his civil rights too. I'll lay down my life for those rights, if I have to. These nigger civil rights, they're gonna end in the white man's bedroom. . . . When the Communists take over, they're gonna kill me quick. Well, you only got one time to die. . . ."

We spent four days rushing about in cars, inspecting the Klaverns —sad little Klan meeting halls built of cinder block—eating heavily fried food, and enduring the "nigger talk." All the Klansmen kept guns in their cars and on their persons. It was clear that to these people a gun is a phallic symbol, a proof of manhood.

246

In the end, it seemed to me that the Klansmen were more pathetic than evil. These farmers and gas-station attendants and small shopkeepers felt as excluded from the "white power structure" as the young blacks of Watts. Their guns and Klaverns and rituals and near-regulation service uniforms were pathetic substitutes for a grim or tedious reality. The trouble is, of course, that the guns of the Klan, like the guns in the black ghetto, are not play guns. They are real, and they are loaded.

The visit to the Klan, on the heels of the visit to Watts, gave me a foreboding sense of the fragility of American society, of the threat of violence that lies always close below the surface. So have many of the other expeditions with Peter B. Young.

Pete has led me to the black militant leaders in Harlem; to an army coffeehouse run by radical dissidents at the height of the Vietnam war; to draft dodgers and deserters in Toronto; to a kind of heroin speakeasy close to Central Park; to the South Bronx to examine the process that is causing the black slums to be physically destroyed; twice to Newark, for the smell of a city in full decay; and to other places I would never have visited on my own initiative. Every one of these expeditions has paid off, not only in good copy, but in my own understanding. Pete Young's unique talent, which I lack, is for making human contact with the alienated, the dissident, the angry, and the half mad, with all the diverse elements that ferment under the affluent surface of America. He little knows of England who only England knows, and he little knows of America who knows only the halls of Congress, the offices of the upper bureaucracy, and the other Washington externals of the American political scene. I am grateful to Pete Young.

Monday, April 24

I had a routine finger stick this morning. John decided I needed both a haemoglobin and a platelet transfusion. I lunched with Rowly Evans, and after I got back to the office John called to talk the situation over. The team of doctors at NIH and the outside specialists to whom they've shown the slides are more and more convinced that I have some form of marrow malignancy. Said John, "They always shake their heads. They don't like the look of those cells. But we don't know what they are." Thus I remain a medical mystery. A few months ago I rather enjoyed being a mystery. Now I could do without it. John talked about what drugs I might take. He is sceptical of steroids; although they make you feel full of beans for a while, you pay a very high price in side effects. This disappointed me. Remembering Jack Kennedy, who took steroids for adrenal insufficiency, I had envisaged myself filled with uncontrollable energy and happily horny. Too bad. I'd have enjoyed one last fling of feeling horny as an old goat.

I begin to feel like Webster in T. S. Eliot: *Webster was much possessed by death. And saw the skull beneath the skin.* . . . The trouble is that death has begun to seem banal. I sense that other people are becoming almost as bored with this old disease as I am.

Gloomy. Maybe tomorrow, after I get three bags of good rich blood into my veins, I'll feel better.

Wednesday, May 3

A queer day today. A marrow test at ten. Lunch with Henry Kissinger and Joan Braden at the Sans Souci. A column to write.

The marrow test was the worst ever. John had to go in several times before he got enough for a good reading. He said he'd call me after lunch, but I was pretty sure what his news would be.

John's news was much as I'd thought. Abnormal cells up to forty-four per cent, platelets in the cellar; haemoglobin wavering down below 13, since the transfusions; granulocytes at 300 and on the way down. What worried him most, he said, was that although I reacted well to the platelet transfusions, I couldn't hold the minimum platelet level. In all the slides from the marrow they'd seen only one single megakaryocyte.

Chemotherapy. After resisting it for so long, the thought fills me with dread. Perhaps the steroids alone will somehow "goose"— John's words—"the megakaryocytes back into action."

Whenever we drove home from NIH we passed the Home for Incurables. It has always seemed to me a peculiarly cruel name for a hospital, and it seems especially so to me now.

Back home after work, I was annoyed to find that Andrew was out—he cheers me up as no one else can. I love to see his hop when he runs out to meet me. All little boys develop their own hop, I suppose, but Andrew's is very special. I am too sentimental about children, especially mine, and, as I've said, especially the youngest.

Tish and I fly to Hartford on Friday for the family conclave, to divide the furnishings of the Avon house and to decide what to do about the property. Joe and Susan Mary will be there, and John and Gussie, and Sis and Percy Chubb. I enjoy my family, but I'm not looking forward to this. The occasion is a melancholy one, and I'm not feeling well—not sick unto death, but uneasy, unwell.

Monday, May 8

The Avon weekend was tolerable as long as we were all pretty squiffed, which was a good deal of the time. But it was somewhat intolerable in between times. I went up there with a kind of window shade drawn over my mind—no sentimental memories. But the shade kept popping up, and I would see Ma exercising her formidable forehand on the tennis court, or talking and laughing in her accustomed place before the fire in the living room, telling her funny familiar stories with her funny familiar gestures.

Or I would catch a sudden glimpse of Pa holding forth over the brandy and cigars. Pa was the First Selectman of Avon for thirty-three years, and I found myself remembering him presiding with genial tyranny over town meetings or the Republican caucuses in the old town hall, always with his hands in his back pants pockets. The Italians used to call him something that sounded like "Signor Gioffa." We children proudly thought it meant something like The Big Chief." We learned later it just meant "Mr. Pockets."

I especially remembered Aggie Guthrie, who came to Avon at eighteen when Joe was born in 1910, and nursed me through a sick childhood, and stayed till she died at seventy, of cancer. Aggie had a broad Scots accent, and since, when we were small children, we saw more of her than of our parents, when John and I went to school in Hartford we pronounced moon as "mum," and bird as "birrrd," which amused the other little boys. Aggie was a brilliant letter writer, though she never punctuated or capitalized. She wrote me much the best letters I got during the war. I saved them in the bottom of my trunk, as well as a lot from pre-war girl friends. They all disappeared after I arrived back in Avon. I suspect Aggie disposed of them, because she didn't want Tish, whom she instantly took to, to see either the girl friends' letters or hers.

The Avon house, we agreed, is to be emptied of all objects, which will be divided equally between us, and then the house will be sold in a package deal with the rest of the real estate. The house is no thing of beauty. It is big, comfortable, and utterly undistinguished—almost as undistinguished as my Washington house.

Yet it is hard to wander about rooms in which you played as a little boy, which hardly have changed at all, and of which you have a mental map that can never be erased, and realize that it really is for the last time—that it's all over. We were smart enough to get a professional to appraise the contents and divide them into equal lots. At least there was no bickering, and we are to get some objects I have always liked. But that is no compensation for breaking up that the end of Avon symbolizes. This has been a tough year.

Needwood
Sunday, May 14

On Thursday all the top specialists at NIH—Dr. Henderson, Dr. Gralnick, and others, as well as John—had a morning meeting to decide on an Alsop diagnosis and an Alsop treatment.

The diagnosis is smouldering leukaemia—smouldering, subacute, aleukaemic leukaemia. John said there had been only about ten cases under the same heading in the history of NIH. Therefore, treatment and prognosis were both difficult. Because I had had a near remission in the fall, John is hopeful that I will be especially responsive to drugs. And the prognosis is certainly more hopeful than if I had had AML. Almost anything is more hopeful.

I am to have a marrow on Wednesday, May 17 (my fifty-eighth birthday—nice birthday present), and if the bad cells are still increasing (which John obviously expects) I am to have a one-week course of steroids, tapering off thereafter.

Somehow, it is a relief to get a diagnosis, however ambiguous, and to have the prospect of treatment, however chancy.

Needwood
June 4

My birthday test was good. Bad cells were down to twenty-four per cent, a sharp drop. The marrow test encouraged John's optimistic suspicion that my disease may be cyclic, and that the up cycle (or down—depends on how you look at it) is now beginning.

Then we spent the weekend of May 20 at Needwood, and I suffered the Bluegills' Revenge. It has sometimes occurred to me that one day the thousands of small birds and fish I have killed might get their revenge. They got it that weekend. I went down to the pond with my fly rod and pulled out about a dozen bluegills. I vaguely remember a sharp back fin pricking one of my fingers.

At the office on Tuesday, Amanda noticed an angry red spot on my finger and said she thought it looked infected. I was going anyway to NIH that afternoon for a platelet transfusion, and Dr. Miller (John was in California on a business trip) took a swab from the finger. The next day I was back on the hated thirteenth floor for a ten-day course of gentamicin, a powerful antibiotic. Thus did the ghosts of all those little fish—cheered on, no doubt, by the ghosts of great piles of little birds—get their revenge. It was a damned unpleasant revenge: chills, fever, platelet rejection, malaise, anorexia, two marrow tests, and other ills that man is heir to, including boredom and fear.

While I was in the hospital I sensed that a debate was going on about what to do with me, and that there was considerable psychic pressure on Ed Henderson and the other doctors to do *something*. I only hold a platelet transfusion for a couple of days.

PART THREE

After I wrote the sentence with which the June 4 entry in my journal abruptly ends, I had an experience most of us have had at one time or another. I got bored with the sound of my own voice— or, in this case, my own typewriter. Suddenly I realized that no sensible reader of this book could fail to be bored by this sad little fact about my damned platelets, and what was more, I was bored myself. So I stopped writing the journal.

After the Bluegills' Revenge, though, I did have some odd medical experiences, interesting enough to recapitulate.

The gentamicin took care of the bluegill's infection, but the infection left me in bad shape. I had to have a platelet transfusion twice a week. I was up and about, writing the column, playing tennis, spending pleasant summer weekends at Needwood. But I was skating on very thin ice. The doctors knew it, of course. I knew enough about my disease to know it myself.

I had had no treatment at all, except transfusions to maintain me, and it was now a year since I'd been diagnosed, generally speaking, as leukaemic. My current diagnosis—smouldering, or aleukaemic leukaemia—was, I suspect, a way of saying that the doctors still didn't know just what was wrong. Doctors are unwilling to admit that they are puzzled—almost as unwilling as political writers. But I was right in suspecting that there was a lot of psychic pressure to give my disease, whatever it was, some kind of treatment.

So the question remained: What to do about Alsop? One doctor wanted to give me a marrow transplant, using my brother Joe as a donor. A marrow transplant is a nasty, complicated business. The implication was that I would soon die if I didn't have one, though the doctor didn't exactly say so. I replied that I'd think it over and let him know what I decided. Thereafter my reportorial instincts reasserted themselves sufficiently to ask a couple of other doctors (John Glick was still away) about the results of marrow transplants in NIH up to that point.

There had been, it turned out, twelve transplants. The patients had all been young, preteens to early twenties. Several had died in the laminar flow room, and those who survived the initial transplant lived, with one exception, only for a few miserable months, during which they were constantly sick almost unto death. The exception was a boy in his teens, but he was plagued by infections and other disorders. It was not difficult for me to decide firmly that, whatever happened, I would not have a marrow transplant.

Chemotherapy in the laminar flow room was another possibility. But to this I was passionately opposed, and so were most of the doctors concerned with me.

Finally a treatment John Glick had candidly described as highly experimental was decided upon. The general belief now was that it was the mysterious September virus, rather than the withdrawal of allopurinol, that had almost cured me. Therefore, the doctors reasoned, why not induce in me a sort of controlled artificial viraemia? The instrument was at hand, in a medication known as poly I:C. Animal experiments had suggested that poly I:C, injected

252

into the veins, tended to reduce abnormal cells. There had also been a few cases in which the injections appeared to have induced partial remissions in human leukaemics, apparently by heightening resistance to the leukaemic cells. It was decided to try me out on a course of poly I:C.

It was an interesting experience (though one could wish one were not so personally involved). After lunch on June 9, Tish drove me to NIH. I got into bed and John came in, stuck a needle into my right arm, and hooked me up to a bottle filled with what looked like plain water. It dripped into my veins in about forty minutes. John removed the needle at three p.m. Just before six I began to shiver, and by ten minutes past, I was shaking so uncontrollably that the whole bed shook with me. Then the chill began to abate, and for about ten minutes I lay under my pile of blankets, luxuriating in the warmth. Then the warmth became altogether too warm, and in a few minutes more my temperature shot up to 103. But the fever had almost disappeared by midnight, and next morning I felt well enough to eat breakfast and go to the office.

That was the first day of a peculiar three-week routine. After lunch every Monday, Wednesday, and Friday I would show up at NIH, take the poly I:C into my veins, and wait for the chill and the fever. By morning I always felt well enough to go to work.

John had told me that the purpose of the treatment was to prod or shock my marrow into doing its cell-producing job again. I told him it sounded like trying to badger a lazy, sick old bird dog, who just wanted to doze by the fire, into getting out into the field looking for birds. There were small signs that the bird dog was at least stirring in his sleep. My counts improved a bit, but after a few more weeks the bird dog snoozed off again—the counts went back down to where they had been. John decided on a second course of poly I:C.

Poly I:C did not induce the hoped-for remission. No one knows, or ever will know, whether these chills and fevers did me any good. At least they did me no harm.

By September of 1972, for whatever reason, I was fully operational again. Henry Kissinger was scheduled to make a trip to Moscow to wrap up the details of the agreements reached during the first Nixon-Brezhnev talks there in late spring. Kissinger has occasionally been infuriated by something I have written, but most of the times we are friends. He can be very tough, as some of his subordinates gladly attest. But there is also a thoughtfulness about the man—one is almost tempted to use the word sweetness—that is endearing, and that perhaps helps to account for his success with the ladies.

Henry asked for a résumé of my case to take with him to Russia; perhaps the Russians, who had made important advances in the treatment of leukaemia, would have some brilliant new ideas for treating me. John Glick agreed to write the summary. It seemed oddly naïve of Henry to suppose that the Russians would risk proposing some bold new treatment. What if I promptly died? Their response was almost laughably ambiguous, saying, in effect, that NIH had done just the right thing. But Henry told me that the high-level official who gave him the memorandum volunteered that they had treated cases similar to mine at the Soviet Institute of Experimental and Clinical Oncology, and that several had remained stable for a long time—in one instance, for ten years.

John says my marrow slides have become positively boring—each slide looks like the last, and the abnormal cells, still unidentifiable, look tediously the same. He too speculates that this stable condition might last for years—even for ten years.

I find that I am oddly ambivalent about this possibility. When I began to write this book I accepted John's odds, twenty to one against more than two years of life. Suppose I last much longer? I can imagine rude whispered comments: "Isn't that old creep the man who wrote a book about how he was dying of cancer?" Curious, the prospect of being embarrassed to be still alive.

To a leukaemic who has got used to thinking as a leukaemic, ten years is a very long time. I think I would be willing to settle for less, as long as the exit is quick, sudden, and painless. If I survive, I shall be sixty in May 1974, and after sixty the trail is all downhill.

Meanwhile I am glad I am still able to write a column, play tennis, and enjoy life. For months now a pleasant young man who does not want his real name used—call him Bob Park—has made it possible for me to do these things. He may have saved my life. To understand why, it is necessary to say more about platelets.

One of the reasons the doctors decided they had to do *something*

254

about patient Alsop was the shape my damned platelets were in. They tried several donors, but none of them gave me what is known in the trade as "a good increment." My platelet count would rise only to the modest level of 30,000 or so, and in three or four days it would sink again.

When I first began to try to understand the basic facts about leukaemia, I had gathered from John Glick that the only danger from platelet transfusions was from hepatitis—and that if a patient was lucky enough not to get hepatitis, transfusions could continue indefinitely. But nothing is simple about leukaemia. For one thing, producing the small plastic bag of platelets that will keep a leukaemic alive for a few days requires hours of work and a lot of professional expertise. It is also a boring business for the donor.

He sits in a high reclining chair with a needle in his arm for upwards of three hours. Four large plastic bags of blood are withdrawn from his body. An elaborate machine separates the platelets from the four bags by a centrifugal process, and the blood, now sans platelets, is reinserted in the donor's body. A healthy marrow quickly replaces the missing platelets in his blood.

The haemoglobin is then separated from the platelets, which are now almost pure. This is done so that a donor can give platelets to a patient with a wholly different blood type. Otherwise the recipient would have a reaction, perhaps a violent one, and reject both the blood and the platelets. The end result of all this trouble is a small plastic bag of a yellowish milky fluid, still with a faint trace of pink; it is transfused into the leukaemic's bloodstream, and thus he is permitted to go on living for a few days more.

How does the patient feel when his platelets are low? I feel a sort of malaise, a constant sense of uneasiness.

Until recently, leukaemics with a low platelet count were transfused with "random platelets," as I was originally. But almost always, transfusions from random donors can continue for only a couple of months. By that time the recipient's white cells have come to recognize the transfused cells as alien to the body, and they fight and kill the life-giving invaders.

This is where HL-A matching—and Bob Park—come in. Everybody inherits two human leukocyte antigens (HL-A) from his mother and two from his father. The technique of typing and matching these antigens in the blood is new—Dr. Ron Yankee, until recently the platelet specialist in NIH, had a lot to do with perfecting it. The work has been carried on by Dr. Robert Graw. If it were not for Dr. Yankee and Dr. Graw I might not be alive at all. I certainly would not be playing tennis or writing a column.

That I am still doing both is largely due to Bob Park, a technician with NIH and a very nice man. Bob's HL-A's are not a perfect match for mine and, theoretically, my body ought to make antibodies to fight his antigens. For mysterious reasons it never has, and my increments from a transfusion by Bob have actually increased, rather than the other way about.

My brother Joe bravely stood in three times for Bob when Bob went on vacation in August 1972, and I had a good increment every time. Joe's antigens are a carbon copy of mine. But given Joe's age, and some small indications of heart irregularity, John Glick does not want to use him as donor any more than necessary. Once John tried a transfusion from my son Joe, but within an hour I was spotted with hives and got a very modest increment. Finally, on the day after Christmas, 1972, John tried my son Stewart, and it worked—well enough.

It was a nice post-Christmas present. Bob Park is young and healthy. But it is a nervous feeling, all the same, to live from week to week dependent for life itself on the cells in another man's blood. It is nice to have brother Joe and Stewart as backups.

As I have seen more and more of NIH, I have been reminded increasingly that the place is, after all, a government bureaucracy, and not immune to the abuses to which bureaucracies are heir. And yet I owe a lot to NIH and to the people who inhabit the place. For one thing I owe it my life, which it has saved, or at least prolonged, repeatedly. In October 1972 NIH performed this life-saving function once again. While my life was being saved, I had an experience that haunts me still.

On Friday, October 13, playing tennis in the late afternoon, I began to feel a rawness in my chest. I finished the game and climbed up to the house to change for a dinner date. I told Tish I felt a bit rocky, but not rocky enough to beg off. But by ten o'clock I knew something was wrong. I began to shiver gently. We made our excuses, and by the time I got home I was having a severe

chill. I got into bed and Tish took my temperature—it was just over 100. Not enough to worry about, I thought.

The next day I was back in the same room I had occupied more than a year before, this time with lobar pneumonia, and this time in the privileged bed beside the window. The bed near the door was occupied by a muscular young man with brown skin, curly black hair, and a huge grin.

His name was Lekoj Anjain and he was from the Marshall Islands. He had been one year old in 1954, when we Americans tested our first deliverable hydrogen bomb on Bikini, one of the Marshall group. As it happened, I had done a lot of reporting on the bomb. It had been much more powerful than scientists had anticipated. The force of the blast churned up great mounds of earth below the explosion point and turned them into heavily irradiated dust, which followed the wind patterns until it fell out of the skies. Some of it fell on Rongelap, Lekoj's native island.

I am still haunted by a mental image of Lekoj as a cheerful brown baby playing in the sand under the palm trees as the sky lit up from the great explosion on Bikini and the dust of the fallout settled around him. The cheerful brown baby was now nineteen and he had, John Glick told me, acute myelogenous leukaemia, a particularly vicious variety. There was no doubt at all that the bomb and the leukaemia were cause and effect. Lekoj was the first case of leukaemia from the fallout of a hydrogen test.

The Atomic Energy Commission had flown his father out from Rongelap to be with him. The father, much smaller than Lekoj, would sit by his son's bedside for hours at a time, saying nothing at all. Once in a long while he would reach out and touch Lekoj's hand, and sometimes Lekoj would mutter something and grin.

Lekoj spoke hardly any English, so there was not much communication between us. Every morning I would smile and he would smile back—his teeth were perfect—and I would ask, "How you feel?"

"Fine. Fine," he would reply. But towards the end of the fourteen days we spent together he would be more likely to say, "No good. Feel deezy." He was being given chemicals in an attempt to induce a remission, and he was nauseated. But he remained remarkably cheerful. I wondered if he knew how sick he was.

258

He was a heavily built young man, and his muscles rippled under his skin. But there was a curiously gentle quality about him, a softness, a kind of endearing childishness—it was very easy to imagine him as that baby in the sand under the sudden glare.

One morning Lekoj was taken to the operating room for a marrow test, and when he came back I asked, "Marrow hurt bad?"

He replied enthusiastically, "Marrow hurt *bad*."

Then I had a marrow, and the same exchange took place in reverse. We both had haemoglobin transfusions. I said, "Blood make you feel good."

He enthusiastically agreed again. "Yes, blood feel *good*."

On October 27, at long last, John took the needle out of my arm and pronounced the pneumonia under control. One last time, I asked Lekoj how he felt, and this time he said again, "Fine."

About ten days afterward Lekoj was dead—of pneumonia.

He could have picked up whatever virus or bacteria had made me sick. John Glick told me not to worry, that chemotherapy had failed, that poor Lekoj was terminal anyway. But his death deeply depressed me for a while. There was the feeling, hard to shake off, that I had somehow been responsible for it. There was the further feeling, just as hard to shake off, that we Americans had killed Lekoj with our bomb. And, finally, there was the feeling of the desperate, irrational unfairness of the death of this gentle, oddly innocent young man. For some time I found a line (I think from T. S. Eliot, though I can't find it) going through my mind: *The notion of some infinitely gentle Infinitely suffering thing.*

Before Lekoj died, I had long believed in my mind that the nuclear bomb was an insane weapon, suicidal, inherently unusable. Now I knew it in my heart.

AT THE START of this peculiar book I remarked that when I found myself on top of the dump at Needwood, gasping like a beached fish, I said to myself, "Face it, Alsop. You're in trouble." That was the second time I had had to face the fact that I was in trouble. The first occurred in the summer of 1944.

I was still serving in Italy with the King's Royal Rifle Corps in late 1943 when one December day my cousin Ted Roosevelt, a brigadier general in the U.S. Army, appeared at battalion headquarters. He told me that it was about time to get into my own army, and I agreed. George Thompson, who was in the same battalion, also wanted to transfer. Ted Roosevelt wrote a To Whom It May Concern note recommending us for transfer. Armed with this and another note from our battalion's commanding officer, George and I set off for General Eisenhower's headquarters in Algiers. We proudly produced our handwritten notes for perusal by a colonel in charge of personnel.

"You two guys sure as hell are out of channels," he muttered. Then he leafed through great mounds of papers.

"Either of you guys happen to be a veterinarian?" he asked.

We both shook our heads.

"You're not Methodist ministers, by any chance?" he asked.

Again we shook our heads.

"Sorry," he said. "We got slots for a veterinarian and a Methodist minister. Other than that, the orders are no more transfers of American citizens from the foreign armies. Orders straight from Washington. Sorry."

We thus found ourselves in a kind of military limbo. The KRRC was over-officered, and as soon as we'd left Italy our old platoons had been taken over by others. To return to our battalion as supernumeraries—unemployed officers—would have been most shaming (in the British army, a supernumerary is expected to find his own spot). Besides, George and I agreed, there must be some better way of making a living than getting shot at all the time for forty-two dollars a month, then a British subaltern's pay.

We rented a room in Algiers, and one evening in the Club Interallié, George, who was very good at running into people, ran into Lady Hermione Ranfurley, an aide and confidante of General Jumbo Wilson, the British general who was second-in-command under Ike. George described our desperate situation and she offered to wangle us into "quite a good parachute outfit—behind the lines, *coup de main*, all that sort of thing." It was run, she said, by an old friend of hers, a Colonel Sterling. The outfit, called the Special Air Services, or SAS, consisted of a couple of battalions, each commanded by one of the Sterling brothers, both of the Scots Guards. So, with an assist from Lady Hermione, we joined the SAS.

The SAS was quite different from the King's Royal Rifle Corps.

260

Most of the SAS officers were in the Guards (the snobbiest of the British regiments). They were an eccentric lot. Colonel Sterling had a thing about hats. Somebody in London ordered that all combat parachutists were to wear pink berets. To Colonel Sterling the pink berets were as a red rag to a bull. The thought of discarding his Scots Guards peaked cap was utterly abhorrent to him, so he flew off to London to persuade his friend Winston Churchill to rescind the order.

In the end he succeeded, but in his absence discipline was pretty loose. Training consisted largely of a Guards-style battalion parade at the sensible hour of ten in the morning, after which the officers would retire to the officers' mess to drink Algerian brandy. When time hung heavy on their hands, they would agree that it was time to have a "bash". They would call a nearby American fighter squadron and invite all those interested. The American pilots and the British parachutists would drink more Algerian brandy, in a spirit of international amity, and then the bash would begin, a tremendous Anglo-American brawl.

George and I got our orders to sail to Britain in the late winter of 1944. We arrived in Scotland, where SAS had a base, in April, and immediately applied for London leave—I to pursue Tish, George to pursue pleasure. During his pursuit George again ran into somebody useful—Hod Fuller, a dashing U.S. marine lieutenant colonel in the Jedburghs, an outfit run jointly by the Allied secret services. The mission of the Jeds, Fuller said, was to provide arms and liaison for the Maquis, the French resistance group. Jed teams, consisting of one American or English officer, one French officer, and a radio operator, were to parachute into occupied France, where they would join the Maquis.

Partly because we hankered to be with Americans again, George and I eagerly agreed to Hod Fuller's suggestion that we transfer to the Jeds, and with help from him we ended up with them. (Hod Fuller's suggestion may have saved my life, since the SAS squadron to which I belonged was later badly cut up in France.) The American Jeds were an interesting and uninhibited lot. They played poker for enormous stakes, swore a great deal, and were as randy as young goats. They had one curious custom that astonished the English and the French.

261

The rather stiff British colonel who ran the Jedburgh base camp, at a handsome pile called Milton Hall, scheduled speakers once or twice a week. When the speakers were experienced behind-the-lines operatives they were heard with respectful attention. But occasionally they were pompous blimps or civilians in uniform. Once an American OSS man—one of those of whom it was said that "OSS was the last refuge of the well connected"—made a long, self-important, and tedious speech: "I wish with all my heart that I could be with you boys in the field, but direct orders from General Donovan keep me, unfortunately, chained to my desk."

An American in the back of the room murmured, "Fifty-five."

Another followed, more loudly, "Fifty-six."

In a rising crescendo the American Jeds all shouted, "Fifty-seven, fifty-eight, fifty-nine, *bullshit!*"

The OSS man retreated in confusion, while the Americans laughed and the more circumspect and better-disciplined French and British looked on in mixed admiration and amusement. Towards the end of the training period they all joined in the chant.

I took an eight-jump parachute course in May and found a French partner, a big, handsome, brown-eyed Saint-Cyr captain whose *nom de guerre* was Richard Thouville—under his real name, René de la Tousche, he is still a good friend. Together we enlisted an American radio operator, nineteen-year-old Norman Franklin, who was a whiz with Morse code. Then, in early June, 1944, just before D day, Thouville hurt his ankle in a motorcycle accident, so we couldn't jump into France for at least two weeks.

The Jedburghs were generous about leaves, and I had pursued Tish assiduously, and successfully enough so that by May her parents had agreed in principle to our getting married. One evening in June, after a couple of whiskies, I telephoned Tish at her parents' flat on Pont Street and suggested that we get married right away, while Thouville was *hors de combat*. I thought there was very little chance that Mr. and Mrs. Hankey would agree—after all, my future was uncertain, and Tish was only eighteen. I could hear Tish arguing with them as I put sixpence after sixpence into the pay telephone in the officers' mess at Milton Hall.

Tish is strong-minded, and she prevailed. "Mummy and Daddy say we can get married Tuesday," she said into the telephone.

"My God!" I heard myself saying. "Trapped like a rat."

Despite this tactlessness, we were duly married on June 20, with George Thomson as best man. It had previously been impossible to get an hotel room anywhere in London, but the buzz bombs started just before we were married and all the hotels emptied swiftly. Armed with a cheque for a thousand dollars from brother-in-law Percy Chubb, I hired a magnificent suite for us on the top floor of the Ritz.

The honeymoon was notably gregarious. My brother John had come to England and volunteered for OSS too. He had been taking a parachute course when Tish and I were married, but he came to London a day or so later. Liquor was available in unlimited quantities at the Ritz—at four pounds per bottle, but Percy Chubb's cheque took care of that. A continuous revel went on in our honeymoon suite, attended by John, George Thomson, Reeve Schley (who was to jump into France with John), Rosa Lewis of the Cavendish, Rosa's Scottie dog, Kippy, and assorted eccentric Cavendish guests.

At one point Tish rather timidly asked whether we couldn't have one evening alone.

The question amazed me. "Good God, woman," I said. "Don't you realize I'm on leave?" There are those who wonder how Tish has put up with me all these years.

When our honeymoon ended, Thouville's foot had healed and we were put on standby alert. The ranks began to thin at Milton Hall as teams were sent into France, and discipline became virtually nonexistent. I went AWOL every weekend to see Tish, with my shaving kit and a change of shirts in my gas-mask pack. In mid-July, Jed Team Alexander—Thouville, Franklin, and I—was put on full alert, and we left for London, to be ready to go on a couple of hours' notice. By special dispensation, as a newly married man, I was allowed to stay at the Cavendish with Tish.

By this time we had been thoroughly briefed on our mission. We were to be dropped with an O group—*coup de main* specialists, whose mission was to blow up an important bridge—to a well-established Maquis band in the area of Aubusson and Guéret. Both towns were held by the Germans, but lightly; this was before the Allied breakthrough at Avranches, and most of the German troops

263

were, of course, on the Normandy front. The countryside was Maquis territory.

I had applied repeatedly for a transfer to the U.S. Army, and my transfer at last came through, no doubt as a result of Mother's little chat with Franklin Roosevelt. I borrowed a uniform from brother John. It fitted badly and it was not nearly so dashing as my KRRC uniform. Moreover I had just proudly pinned on my third pip—I had been made a temporary acting captain in the British army—and the transfer came through for Lieutenant Alsop. I consoled myself with the thought that an American lieutenant's pay was about three times a British captain's.

When we were alerted, Tish went with me in a taxi to the bus station. Thouville and Franklin and the O group were on the bus. At the airfield we were trussed into our jump suits, complete with a slung carbine and an entrenching tool for burying our parachutes, and bundled into a Lancaster bomber, one of a flight of three bound for central France. On our plane a last-minute crisis occurred —the jump master assigned to our drop was nowhere to be found. An RAF corporal was hastily assigned to substitute, and we took off with a roar. It was a bright moonlit night in midsummer.

As we crossed over the Normandy battlefield the plane began to buck wildly, and there were loud banging noises and great flashes of light. I realized that the Germans were shooting at us. I glanced around the dimly lit plane and saw that, in a futile but instinctive gesture, every man had his hands clasped protectively over his crotch. The flak stopped and we droned on. The word was passed back from the cockpit that we had lost contact with the other two planes because of the anti-aircraft fire, but with the help of his navigator the pilot would try to find our designated drop zone on his own.

After about an hour the RAF corporal opened the jump hole—a square opening in the bottom of the Lancaster—and told us to take jump positions. I was number one, by choice—I have always hated to wait in line. I sat with my feet through the hole, feeling the pressure of the rushing air. Thouville sat with his legs around my bottom, then Franklin, then the O group. I glanced down, and there, beautiful in the light of the full moon, was occupied France.

We were circling. Obviously the pilot and the navigator were having trouble finding the drop zone. *"J'ai une trouille noire,"* Thouville muttered into my ear. Scared stiff, he was. I was glad he was in a little black hole too. I certainly was.

So was the RAF corporal who was supposed to act as jump master. "Look, chaps," he said nervously, over the roar of the motors. "I've never done this before, and I don't want to get it wrong. The pilot will light a red light when we're over the drop zone. So just as soon as you see a light, Number One, off you go, and the rest of you chaps follow as quick as you can. All right?"

The plane circled more steeply—apparently we couldn't find the prearranged pattern of fires with which the Maquis reception committee was supposed to light our drop zone.

My feet dangled in the chilly air. My hands were on the back of the hole, tensed to push when I saw the light. We flew on and on and on. Then, right in front of me, a light flashed on, and I pushed hard with both hands.

I felt the sudden rush of the prop wash. I turned over in the air and my parachute opened and I began to sway down through the moonlit night. I looked up and saw the plane disappearing in the night sky and knew instantly that something was wrong. I could see no friendly parachutes following me down. Below, there were no welcoming fires. And the light, I suddenly remembered, had not been red—it had been white. (Later I learned that the nervous corporal, desperate for a cigarette, had lit a flashlight to look for one, and when I jumped he stopped the others.) Even before I reached the ground I realized two things—that I had been a damned fool, and that I was all alone in occupied France.

My landing was a marvel. I landed so lightly that my toes barely touched the ground. I looked up and saw why. My parachute was neatly draped over a small tree, which happened to be just the right height to give me a soft landing.

I punched the release, freed myself from the chute, and grabbed the risers to pull the chute free and bury it. I pulled hard. The chute held fast. There was no way to free it from the tree, and by dawn it would be a beacon advertising where I had landed.

I went to the top of a little knoll and sat down behind a bush and tried to think sensibly. I took a healthy swig of brandy from the pocket-sized flask thoughtfully provided by the British army for such occasions. (I still have the flask—I regard it as a talisman and never travel without it.) I cupped a cigarette in my hands (for might there not be Germans about?) and puffed hungrily (I had one pack—only nineteen to go) and thought about what to do next.

In the moonlight I could make out a village in a valley a few hundred yards away. I would go to the village, I decided, knock on a door, and ask for help. I took another pull at the flask and started off toward the village. As I approached it a dog barked, then another. Soon what sounded like a hundred-dog chorus broke out.

Kee-rist, I thought, how can the Germans help hearing that noise? I retreated to my now familiar bush, and the canine cacophony slowly faded. I finished the brandy in my flask, cupped another cigarette in my hands (eighteen to go), and considered my situation. I was entirely alone in occupied France. I was in American army uniform. I had no idea where I was.

"Face it, Alsop," I said. "You're in trouble."

I started walking in the direction the plane was taking when it disappeared—I could think of nothing better to do—when I saw three trucks winding along a road near the dog-filled village. Gestapo? Then I heard someone call my name: "Stewart, Stewart!" I thought, My God, the Gestapo is efficient—they know my first name already. Then I recognized Richard Thouville's voice.

Thouville, Franklin, and the O group had parachuted about ten miles south of where I had so foolishly jumped. The Maquis reception committee boasted three trucks, and Thouville had organized a search party. By dawn's early light we were all happily ensconced in the basement of a small château, drinking lots of red wine and being embraced by pretty girls.

We spent a couple of months with the Maquis thereafter. We assisted in the liberation of several towns, ending conveniently in Cognac, where we consumed vast quantities of *le vrai Napoléon*. There were a few moments of fear, exhaustion, and even some danger, but for the most part those weeks with the Maquis were a lot of fun—in some ways the best fun I've had in my life.

By September our Maquis was thoroughly motorized, but gasoline was a real problem, and as a few battalions of Germans still holed up in our area continued to justify our existence, I was sent north to beg some gas from the Americans.

When I first made contact with the U.S. Army I got into a spot of trouble. My strange request was referred to a rear-echelon lieutenant colonel. I saluted smartly, palm out, clicked my heels, and announced, "*Lef*tenant Alsop reporting, *sir!*"

This was the way I had been taught in the British army to greet a superior officer. The colonel gave me a lynx-eyed look, taking in brother John's ill-fitting and by this time bedraggled uniform. There had been reports of Germans being sent to France in imitation American uniforms to assassinate General Eisenhower and other key men.

"*Loo*tenant," he said, emphasizing the first syllable, "how come you got your bars the wrong way round?"

"Do I, sir? Sorry, sir," I said.

"And how come you got your crossed rifles upside down?"

"Sorry, sir," I said again, nonplussed. The colonel lifted a field telephone and asked for counterintelligence. I had visions of being stood up against a wall, offered a last cigarette, and shot as a German spy. But some phone calls later my bona fides as "one of those goddam OSS screwballs" was established, and I even got some gas to take back with me to the Maquis. So that trouble, like other troubles I have had from time to time, faded away.

But I *was* in trouble, real trouble, that night when I found myself alone in occupied France. A few weeks after I got back home I received in the mail a handsome scroll awarding me a Croix de Guerre with Palm, marked—in type—*Signé, Charles de Gaulle*. The citation accompanying my Croix de Guerre, I must modestly note, was written by Thouville (I tried to get him an American decoration, but as a new boy at OSS I failed). It reads, in part: "*S'est trouvé de nombreuses fois dans les situations les plus périlleuses d'où il s'est toujours sorti avec un calme édifiant et une volonté galvanisant les énergies de tous ceux qui l'entouraient.*"

I cannot boast that my calm is edifying or my will galvanizing, but my situation is undoubtedly again a bit perilous. I came out of that peculiar experience all in one piece, and maybe I will again. Even if my stay of execution turns out to be short, I have reason to be grateful—for a happy marriage and a reasonably long, amusing, and interesting life. I even have some reason to be grateful for the experience I have had since that July day when I climbed to the top of the dump at Needwood and realized that I was again in trouble. There have been times when I have been, like Thouville that night over occupied France, in a little black hole. But there have been useful lessons to be learned from the experience.

It is useful, for example, to learn that most people are nicer than they seem to be. It is also useful to know, although it can be very hard at first, that in time one becomes accustomed to living with Uncle Thanatos. One comes to terms with death.

THIS IS being written in late May, 1973, in one of NIH's drearily familiar hospital rooms. I came here, on John Glick's orders, a week ago, on May 19.

On Friday, May 18, young Joe and Candy flew down from Boston for a Needwood weekend. Ian and Jill, who are back from Katmandu with a treasure trove of Himalayan artifacts to sell, were to join us on Sunday. On Saturday, Joe drove us to Needwood in Tish's station wagon, with me in the front seat and Tish and Candy and Nicky and Andrew squeezed into the back. Andrew was supposed to sit in front, but he is deeply in love with Candy and insisted on sitting on her lap all the way to Needwood.

I felt queer on the way out. In fact, I had been feeling queer for some two months. Since mid-March I had been having those familiar, unexplained, atypical symptoms—night sweats and low-grade fevers—I had had in September 1971 and have experienced intermittently since. But I felt especially queer on Saturday, so when we got to Needwood I went to bed. About five in the afternoon I woke up feeling really sick. My temperature was over 104. We called John Glick and he ordered me into NIH. By eight that night, after thumping my back and peering at a chest X-ray, he had made his diagnosis—pneumonia again.

In the two months of night sweats and fevers my blood counts had sunk inexorably. But the worst of my counts was the granulocyte count. For weeks it had been 100 or less. Statistically and medically I was an easy mark for a galloping infection, the kind that can kill a leukaemic in a matter of hours.

I felt very sick on Saturday night, and I had a feeling—quite a strong feeling—that this time I would not leave NIH on my two feet, that this was what the Bible calls *the end of the days*. Given my counts, this was not at all an irrational feeling. But I seem to have been wrong. As this is written, a week later, I have had no temperature for forty-eight hours, for the first time in more than eight weeks, and John Glick reports that the pneumonia is contained. He is very complimentary about my granulocytes, which, though few in number, seem to be brave and resourceful. I seem to have had yet another stay of execution.

John Glick can make no prognosis about what may happen next. Perhaps I shall drift back into the fever-and-night-sweats routine. Perhaps, as after my earlier bout of pneumonia, I shall make a half-way comeback, with no fever and feeling reasonably well as long as I get my haemoglobin and platelet transfusions. And just perhaps—although miracles, like lightning, rarely strike twice in the same place—I shall have another remission, as I had after my first bout of flu in the autumn of 1971.

In any case, one contrast strikes me. At the beginning of this book I described the trapped and desperate feeling that came over me after I had been told that I would die quite soon. Last Saturday night, when I felt so sick, I felt rather sure that I *would* die quite soon, perhaps very soon, within the next day or so. I did not at all welcome the prospect, but it filled me with no sense of panic. I kissed Tish a fond good-night at ten, took some Benadryl, and went easily off to sleep. Why the difference?

Perhaps the state of the nation has a little something to do with the difference. For weeks I have been haunted and depressed by a sense that the American system, in which I have always believed in an unquestioning sort of way, the way a boy believes in his family, really is falling apart; by a sense that we are a failed nation, a failed people. The thought has occurred to me quite often in recent weeks that perhaps this is a good time to bow out. No doubt it was the state of Alsop, far more than the state of the nation, that caused it to occur so often. The fact is that I *have* been depressed, not only because I have been feeling lousy, but also because John Glick, on whom I have become excessively dependent, leaves soon to take up a new post in California.

Since the fevers and the night sweats began in mid-March I have written my column for *Newsweek* and worked on this book and driven downtown to dictate letters to Amanda, make telephone calls, and make dates for business lunches. Tish and I have gone out to dinner several times a week and talked and laughed with friends. I have lived, in short, what John Glick calls a normal life.

But it has not been altogether normal. It is not normal to wake up every night just before dawn with a fever of 101 or so, take a couple of pills, and settle down to sweat like a hog for four or five hours. It is not normal to feel so weak you can't play tennis or go trout fishing. And it is not normal, either, to feel a sort of creeping weariness and a sense of being terribly dependent, like a vampire, on the blood of others. After eight weeks of this kind of "normal" life, the thought of death loses some of its terrors.

But the most important reason why I felt no panic fear last Saturday was, I think, the strange, unconscious process which I have tried to describe in this book—the process of coming to terms with death. A dying man needs to die, as a sleepy man needs to sleep, and there comes a time when it is wrong, as well as useless, to resist.

In his extreme old age Sir Winston Churchill visited his old school, Harrow, and the headmaster asked him to say a few words to the boys.

"Never give up," Churchill said. "Never. Never. Never. Never." There is no doubt that the old man lived beyond his allotted span by a tremendous effort of a tremendous will. He lived so long because he never gave up. But to what good end?

I saw Churchill once again after that luncheon at Chartwell. A year or so before he died I was in the visitor's gallery of the House of Commons when Sir Winston unexpectedly appeared on the floor. There was a hush as the old man waddled feebly towards his accustomed seat, hunched over and uncertain of every step. He sat down heavily and looked around the House, owlishly, unseeing, as if for some long-vanished familiar face, and then, as the debate resumed, his big head slumped forward grotesquely on his chest. He was an empty husk of a man, all the wit and elegance and greatness drained out of him by age. Like my mother, he should have died herebefore.

There is a time to live, but there is also a time to die. That time has not yet come for me. But it will. It will come for all of us.

270

Stewart Alsop

This is a peculiar book. I had two reasons, or excuses, for writing it. First, I have myself quite often wondered what it would be like to be told I had an inoperable and lethal cancer, and I suspect that a lot of other people have wondered the same thing. If a writer has had an unusual experience likely to interest a good many people, he has an instinct, and perhaps even a duty, to write about it.

Second, after I had been told my remaining span of life would be short, I began to think back quite often about the life behind me. This is in no sense an autobiography. But neither is it just a clinical record. This book is peculiar partly because my disease is peculiar, partly for another reason. It was all written by me, but it was written

John Glick, Stew, and Tish, at Needwood

by different me's: a me lying in the leukaemia ward at NIH in late July 1971, waiting for a treatment which might buy me a year or so of life; a me released in August with a question mark for a diagnosis, feeling rotten, but not rotten enough to stop writing for *Newsweek;* a me sick unto death in September; then, only a few weeks later, a euphoric me suddenly feeling better than I had for years and confident—almost—of a final cure. And part of it was written by me now writing—faced with a recrudescence of the mysterious disease and again a fear of an unwilling expedition to that "undiscover'd country from whose bourne no traveller returns."

This is, in short, a mixed-up sort of book. But I have led a mixed-up sort of life, and no experience in it has been more so than the peculiar hell-to-heaven-to-purgatory existence I have had since I was first diagnosed as an acute leukaemic. In a way, no experience has been more interesting than living in intermittent intimacy with the gentleman I have come to think of as Uncle Thanatos, and sometimes, when I have been feeling very sick, as dear old Uncle Thanatos. Death is, after all, the only universal experience except birth, and although a sensible person hopes to put it off as long as possible, it is, even in anticipation, an interesting experience.

Needwood, 1973. Andrew driving. Nicky behind.

Christmas, 1971. Candy, Joe, Tish, Elizabeth, Nicky, Daddy, Andrew, Peter Mahony, Stewart, Jill, and Ian.

The Salamander

A CONDENSATION OF THE BOOK BY

MORRIS WEST

ILLUSTRATED BY GUY DEEL

Published by William Heinemann, London

A high-ranking Italian general is found dead.
Suicide? Or murder?

An artfully wrought card depicting a
salamander – the legendary beast that lives in
fire and symbolizes man's survival – is discovered
near the corpse.

Colonel Dante Matucci of the Service of
Defence Information sets in motion a thrilling chase
through the dark underworld of Italy, through its
fashionable society, through politics and high
finance. As he exposes a dangerous plot to convert
a democracy into a dictatorship, Matucci must
determine the personal price that he must pay, as
the servant of a modern state. If, like the
salamander, he can survive the flames himself, can
it only be at the cost of his own honour and the
respect of the girl he loves?

BETWEEN midnight and dawn, while his fellow Romans were celebrating the end of Carnival, Count Pantaleone, general of the military staff, died in his bed. A bachelor in his early sixties, a soldier of spartan habit, he died alone.

At seven in the morning his servant, a retired sergeant of cavalry, found him lying on his back, fully clothed, gape-mouthed and staring at the coffered ceiling. The servant crossed himself, closed the dead eyes with two fifty-lire pieces and telephoned the general's aide, Captain Girolamo Carpi.

Carpi telephoned the Director. The Director telephoned me, Dante Matucci, colonel of carabinieri—the national police—attached for special duty to the Service of Defence Information.

The service is usually called by its Italian initials, SID (Servizio Informazione Difesa). Like every other intelligence service it spends a huge amount of taxpayers' money perpetuating itself, and somewhat less in scavenging information to protect the republic from traitors, spies and saboteurs. You will gather I am sceptical about its value, as men who work in it tend to become. However, that's a digression. . . .

Count Pantaleone was dead. I was appointed to stage a clean exit for the corpse. The army supplied me with a senior medical officer and a military advocate. We drove together to the general's apartment. Captain Carpi received us. So far, so good. No neighbours on the landing. No relatives yet informed. I had no great respect for Carpi, but I had to commend his discretion.

The medical officer made a cursory examination and decided that the general had died from an overdose of barbiturates, self-administered. He wrote a certificate, countersigned by the military advocate, which stated the cause of death as cardiac arrest. It was not a false document. The general's heart had stopped.

When an army ambulance had removed the body, I remained in the apartment with Carpi and the servant, who made us coffee. While we drank it, I questioned him. His answers established a series of simple facts.

The general had dined out. He had returned twenty minutes before midnight and retired immediately. The servant had secured doors and windows, set the burglar alarm and gone to bed. Visitors or intruders? None. The alarms had not been triggered. Telephone calls? No way to know. The general had a private line in his bedroom. The general's demeanour? Normal. He was a taciturn man. Hard to know what he was thinking at any time. That was all.

I dismissed the servant to the kitchen. Carpi then poured us two glasses of the general's whisky.

"What do we tell his friends—and the Press?" he asked.

"You saw the death certificate: cardiac arrest."

"And the autopsy report?"

"My dear Captain, for an ambitious man you are very naïve. There will be no autopsy. The general's body has been taken to a mortuary where it will be prepared for a brief lying-in-state. We want him seen and mourned as a noble servant of the republic. Then we want him forgotten. You can help us."

"How?"

"Your patron is dead. You did well for us. You deserve a better appointment. I'd suggest something far away from Rome—perhaps Sardinia. You will find promotion a lot quicker there."

"I'd like to think about it."

"No time, Captain Carpi! You pick up your transfer papers this morning. You deliver them, signed, by five this afternoon. You will have a new posting immediately after the funeral. You

278

are in a delicate position, you will remember. You agreed to spy on a superior officer. SID is grateful, but your fellow officers would despise you. Any indiscretion would therefore damage your career and expose you to great personal danger."

"I understand."

"Good. You may go now. Leave me your key, please. *Ciao!*"

Carpi was one of those weak, handsome fellows who always need a patron, and who will always betray him to a more potent one. I had used him to report on Pantaleone's political activities. Now he was a nuisance. He left me sitting with my whisky, trying to set my thoughts in order.

The Pantaleone affair had all the makings of a political time bomb—although not one in a thousand citizens would recognize his name; and of those who did, not one in ten would understand the magnitude of the conspiracy which had been built around it. The Director understood; so did I. I had dossiers on all the principal participants, and had been chafing at my impotence to do anything about them. They were not criminals—at least not yet. They were all high men—ministers, deputies, industrialists, service officers, bureaucrats—who looked to a day when the confusions of Italy—unstable government, industrial unrest, a faltering economy and a very frustrated people—would bring the country to the brink of revolution. On that day, which was closer than many people imagined, the conspirators hoped to seize power and present themselves as saviours of the republic. If a handful of Greek colonels had done it, they reasoned, why couldn't a larger and more powerful group of Italians do it better.

Their figurehead had been that passionate patriot, General Massimo Pantaleone. Now the general had removed himself from the scene. Why? Was there someone new in the wings? If so, when would he reveal himself? I would have to answer these questions, and the margin for error was very slim. Even a hint that an investigation was in progress, let alone that the army had notarized a dubious document, would be headline news and split the country apart. Conspiracy has been endemic to Italy since Romulus and Remus; but if the dimensions of this plot were made known—there would be blood in the streets, maybe also mutiny in the armed services, whose political loyalties were deeply divided between Left and Right. I had made no idle threat to Captain Carpi. If he tried to sell his information, an accident would be speedily arranged for him.

Meantime, I had my own work to do. I began to comb the apartment for papers. I went through drawers and cupboards and pockets. I shook out every book in the library. I removed the blotter from the desk pad. I tested everywhere for secret places. I lifted ornaments and peered into vases. Even so, I nearly missed the card.

It was lying on its edge against the skirting-board, behind the bedside table. On one side was a drawing, done by hand in Indian ink—a salamander with a coronet on its head, couched in a bed of flames; on the other, an inscription written in perfect copper-plate—*Un bel domani, fratello.*

"One fine tomorrow, brother." A very Italian phrase. Was it a vain hope, a promise of reward, a threat of vengeance, or a rallying cry? The word "brother" was ambiguous, too, and the salamander made no sense at all. I decided to refer it to the specialists. I took a clean envelope from the desk, sealed the card inside it and put it in my pocket.

It was time then for a private chat with the servant. I found him in the kitchen, a dejected old man ruminating over an uncertain future. I consoled him with the thought that the general had probably remembered him in his will and that, at least, he was entitled to severance pay. He brightened and offered me wine and cheese. As we drank together he became garrulous, and I was happy to let him ramble. "He didn't have to be a soldier, you know. The Pantaleones always had money. Lands in the Romagna, apartment buildings in the city, the Frascati estate, the villa on Ponza. Of course, she's got the villa now."

"Who has?"

"You know—the Polish woman. The one he had dinner with last night. Anders. She's been his girl friend for years. Although he never brought her here. He didn't want people to think he was enjoying himself. I knew about her, of course. Good-looking woman . . . Someone ought to tell her what's happened."

"I'll do that. Where does she live?" The question was a blind. I knew the answer and a great deal more about Lili Anders.

"Parioli. The address is in the general's notebook."

"I'll find it."

"Hey! You're not taking any of the general's stuff away, are you? I'm responsible. I don't want any trouble."

"I'm taking his papers. We can't leave confidential documents lying around. Anything that doesn't belong to the army we'll return to his lawyer. I'll give you an official receipt. All right?"

"If you say so. Wait a moment! Who *are* you?"

"Matucci. Carabinieri."

"Carabinieri! There's nothing wrong, is there?"

"Nothing at all. Normal procedure with an important man."

"Who's going to make the arrangements, tell his friends?"

"The army."

"So what do I do? Just sit around here?"

"People will telephone. Take their names and numbers and we'll arrange for someone to call them back. You'll still be paid, don't worry. Tell me, where did the general dine last night?"

"At the Chess Club."

"Thanks. I'll be on my way." I scribbled a receipt, shoved the documents into a valise of the general's and walked out into the sunshine. It was ten minutes after one. The alleys were busy with Romans going home for lunch and siesta.

I have to tell you frankly, I don't like the Romans. I'm a Tuscan, and these people are first cousins to the Hottentot. They are the worst cooks in Italy, devoid of the most elementary graces. They have seen everything and learned nothing. They have known imperial grandeur, papal pomp, war, famine and plague; yet they will bow the knee to any tyrant who offers them an extra loaf of bread and a free ticket to the circus. Yesterday it was Benito Mussolini, drunk with rhetoric, haranguing them from the balcony of the Piazza Venezia. Tomorrow it might be another—and my job was to discover where that one was now.

I shook myself out of my reverie, walked half a block to my car and drove to the office. I might have saved myself the trouble. My two senior clerks were out at lunch, number three was flirting with the typist, and the data bank was out of action because the power supply had been interrupted by a two-hour strike. There was a message from the Ministry of the Interior, under whose jurisdiction the SID comes, requesting "immediate contact on a most urgent matter". When I called I was told that my man was entertaining some foreign visitors and might possibly be back at four o'clock. "Urgent"—these Romans!

I dumped the bag of documents on my desk and shouted for number three clerk to sort and collate them. Then, because the strike had put the elevator out of action, I climbed three flights to the forensic laboratory, where there had to be someone alive. As usual it was old Stefanelli, who according to local legend slept every night in a bottle of formaldehyde and emerged fresh as a marmoset at sunrise every morning. He was a tiny wizened fellow, easily ten years past retirement age, who managed by a combination of patronage and talent to hang on to his job. Because what other technicians burst their brains to learn, Stefanelli knew. Sprinkle a speck of dust in his palm and he would name you the region and even make a reasonable guess at the village from which it came. Give him a drop of blood, two nail clippings and a lock of hair, and he would build you the girl who owned them. He was a tetchy and troublesome genius who would spit in your eye if you crossed him, or slave twenty-four hours at a stretch for a man he trusted. When I came in, puffing and sour-faced, he greeted me exuberantly.

"Eh, Colonel! What have you got for Steffi today?"

"Troubles, Steffi." I handed him the salamander card. "I want a full reading on this fast: paper, penmanship, the meaning of the symbol and any prints you can lift."

Stefanelli studied the card intently for a few moments. "The card is of Japanese stock—fine-quality bonded rice. I can tell you who imports it by tomorrow. The penmanship is fantastic! So beautiful it makes you want to cry. I haven't seen anything like it since Aldo the Calligrapher died in 1935. The design obviously is a salamander, the beast that lives in the fire. But what it means here I don't know. It could be a trademark, or a member's card for a club. It could be adapted from a coat-of-arms. I'll show it to my old friend, Solimbene. Knows every coat-of-arms in Europe."

"Good. How about doing some copies of it before the others get back from lunch? I'll need one for my own inquiries."

"Where did you get this, Colonel?"

"In General Pantaleone's bedroom. He died last night."

"Pantaleone? That old *fascista!* What happened to him?"

"Natural causes. We've got a notarized certificate to prove it."

"Very convenient! Suicide or murder?"

"Suicide."

"Eh! That smells bad."

"So, Steffi, this is between you and me and the Director. Dead silence until I tell you."

Stefanelli grinned. "I don't like Fascists any more than you do, Colonel. And if we don't get a stable government soon, we'll get a *colpo di stato,* a military takeover of the government with a Fascist in the saddle. Then civil war—Left against Right, North against South. I can smell it and I'm scared. I don't want my children to suffer as we did."

"Nor I, Steffi. So we have to know who steps into the general's shoes. Call me the minute you have anything. *Ciao.*"

Now I was at loose ends. I could make no sense of the Pantaleone documents until they were collated with the general's dossier. The Director, who was the only man I could talk to freely, was not in the office. I decided to find Lili Anders.

Her apartment was on the third floor of a new condominium, all aluminium and glass, with a porter in livery and an elevator panelled in walnut. Lili Anders must be living at twice the scale on which she was taxed. I was mildly resentful by the time an elderly housekeeper dressed in black bombazine opened the door. She confronted me like a true Roman, laconic and hostile: "Yes?"

"Matucci. Carabinieri. I wish to see the Signora Anders."

"You have an appointment?"

"No."

"Then you'll have to come back later. The *signora* is asleep."

"I'm afraid I must ask you to wake her. My business is urgent."

"Do you have any identification?"

She looked at my card, swept me into the hall like a pile of dust and left.

I waited, grim and dyspeptic. Then Lili Anders made her entrance. For a woman who had just been sleeping she was beautifully turned out; every blonde hair in place, no wrinkle in dress.

She was polite but cool. "You wished to see me?"

"Privately, if that is possible."

She led me into the living room and closed the door. She prayed me to be seated and then stood by the mantel under an equestrian portrait of Pantaleone. "You are from the carabinieri."

"I am Colonel Matucci."

"And the reason for this visit?"

"A painful matter, I'm afraid. I regret to inform you that General Pantaleone died early this morning."

She stared at me, wide-eyed and trembling, holding on to the mantel for support. I moved towards her to steady her, but she waved me away. I crossed to the buffet, poured brandy into a goblet and handed it to her. "If you want to cry, go ahead."

"He was kind to me and gentle, but I have no tears for him."

"There is something else—he died by his own hand."

She spread her hands in a gesture of defeat. "There were too many dark places in his life; too many secrets, too many people lying in wait for him."

"Did he tell you that?"

"No. I knew."

"Then perhaps you know why he chose last night to kill himself. Why not a week ago, or next month?"

"I don't know. He had been moody for a long time, but whenever I asked him what was troubling him, he put me off."

"And last night?"

"One thing only. During dinner at the Chess Club a waiter brought him a message. He went out for about five minutes. He told me it had been a telephone call from a colleague. Nothing more was said. When he brought me home I invited him in. Sometimes he stayed, sometimes he didn't. This time he said he had work to finish at home."

I handed her the copy of the salamander card. "Have you seen this before? Or anything like it? Or heard those words?"

She studied it. "Not that I can remember. I'm sorry."

"You must in no sense reproach yourself. You have had a grievous shock. And now I have to distress you still further. I must warn you that you stand in grave personal danger."

"I don't understand."

"You have been for a long time the mistress of an important man. Even if the general told you nothing, others will believe he told you everything. Inevitably, therefore, you will come under surveillance, under pressure, possibly even under threat."

"From whom?"

"From extremists of the Right and of the Left, from foreign agents operating in the republic, even from officials of our own public security. As a foreigner residing here on a sojourn permit, you are especially vulnerable."

"But I have nothing to tell! I lived a woman's life with a man who needed comfort and affection. His other life, whatever it was, I did not share. You must believe that." She was shaken now. Her face seemed to crumple, her hands fumbled restlessly.

I leaned back in the chair and admonished her. "I wish I could believe you. But I know you, Lili Anders, chapter and verse. I know you from your first birthday in Warsaw to your recent dispatch to one Colomba, a bookbinder in Milan, identifying yourself as 'Falcone'. You are all called by bird names, are you not? You are paid by Canarino from an account in a Zurich bank. You see, Lili, we Italians are not as inefficient as we look. We are good conspirators ourselves. I admire a good professional. But you are a problem. Another brandy? I'll have one myself, if you don't mind. *Salute!*"

She drank, clasping the glass in both hands as if it were a pillar that would support her. "What happens to me now?"

"Eh! That's a question, Lili. I could take you into custody on espionage charges. That means a long interrogation and a stiff sentence. Or I could leave you free, on certain conditions. Which would you prefer?"

"I'm tired of the game, Colonel. I'd like to be out of it."

"You can't get out, Lili. You can only change sides."

"Which means?"

"Full information on your network, and a contract with us."

"As a double agent, you mean. Can you protect me?"

"As long as you're useful, yes. Let's try some more questions. Who arranged your first meeting with the general?"

"The Marchesa Friuli. Her code name is Pappagallo."

"Parrot! The old girl looks it. What was your directive?"

"To give early warning of any attempt at a *colpo di stato* by neo-Fascist groups, and of actions designed to provoke it."

"Such as?"

"Acts of violence planned against police or carabinieri during labour demonstrations, bomb attacks that could be attributed to Maoist or Marxist groups, signs of disaffection in the armed services, any changes of political groups in the high command."

"Had there been any such changes recently?"

"No—at least not to my knowledge."

"Then why was the general depressed?"

"I was trying to find out. I had the feeling that it was personal rather than political. He had a habit of dropping cryptic remarks, then shutting up like a shellfish. The other night, for example, he said: 'There is no simple future for me, Lili, because my past is too complicated,' and then he quoted from the Bible: 'A man's enemies are the men of his own house.' But he wouldn't explain."

"Anything else?"

"I'm trying to remember—Oh, yes, when we were in Venice, we went to the opera at the Phoenix Theatre. He was talking about the phoenix, the fabulous bird that rose alive from its own ashes; then he said there was another fabled creature, more remarkable and more dangerous—the salamander that lived in fire and could survive the hottest flames. Wait! That's your card."

"So it is, Lili. Did he say more about the salamander?"

"Some friends joined us. The subject was dropped."

"Well, there will be other times and other questions. You'll now be under constant surveillance. Here is my card with day and night numbers. I'd like you to be at the funeral."

"Please, no!"

"Please, yes! I want tears and grief and black mourning. You will not move back into society until I tell you. No new boy friends until you are out of mourning. Then, when you find one, I'd like to check him out."

She managed a weak smile. "Check him or me, Colonel?"

"I can't afford you, Lili. Still it's a thought to keep. One fine tomorrow . . . ? Be good now. And there's a prize for every tear at the requiem."

Half an hour later I was seated on the Via Veneto, with a sandwich and a *cappuccino*, scanning the afternoon papers. The general's death was reported only in the late bulletins, in identical terms, directly quoting the army announcement. The bloodhounds would not be in full cry until morning. By that time the general would be safely lying in state in the family chapel at Frascati.

THE OBSEQUIES OF Massimo, Count Pantaleone, made a splendid piece of theatre. The requiem was sung by Cardinal Dadone, the Bishop of Frascati. The panegyric was delivered in ringing tones by the secretary-general of the Society of Jesus. The mass was attended by the President, ministers of the council, members of both chambers, prelates of the Roman Curia, representatives of NATO and the diplomatic corps, relatives and friends. Six field officers carried the bier to the vault, which was closed and locked by the President himself, a gesture of respect, gratitude and national solidarity not lost upon the gentlemen of the press. Lili Anders was there, leaning on the arm of Captain Girolamo Carpi, who was visibly moved by the passing of his beloved patron.

I was among the mourners, too; but my concern was that my camera crew photograph every person there, from the cardinal to the florist. I hate funerals. I was glad when the rites were over.

At three-thirty I was back in the forensic laboratory with Stefanelli. The old fellow was jumping like a grasshopper. "I told you Solimbene would recognize that card. The crowned salamander is the emblem of Francis the First. It recurs in arms derived from the house of Orléans, the duchy of Angoulême and the Farmer family in England. Solimbene is getting us a list of Italian families who use it. The pen work? Based on Aldo the Calligrapher, as I thought, probably executed by Carlo Metaponte, who forged papers for the partisans during the war and has been going straight ever since. The card is not Japanese—I was wrong there—but a passable imitation made by the Casarolis. They're giving us a list of their principal customers. The inscription makes no sense yet, but we're coming to it. How's that for forty-eight hours!"

"Great, Steffi. But we need more. How about fingerprints?"

"The only ones that we've been able to lift belong to the late lamented general. You didn't expect anything else, surely?"

"Try again, Steffi. I want miracles, and I want them yesterday."

"Everything takes time, Colonel. How was the funeral?"

"Beautiful, Steffi. I cried all through it!"

"*Requiescat in aeternum.*" Stefanelli crossed hands on his bony chest and rolled his eyes. "Have you seen the obituaries?"

"Now, when have I had time to read, Steffi?"

"I've got them here. They're worth a look."

They were. The Right wing was fulsome. The Centre was respectful and only mildly censorious of the general's Fascist period. The Left achieved a kind of poetry of abuse, culminating in a doggerel that worried me a little.

> *Uprooted today,*
> *The last of his line,*
> *Pantaleone,*
> *The rogue.*

This might simply mean that the Left had helped uproot him, and that happily no successor was in sight. It might also be the opening gambit of a campaign to vilify the general. But there was nothing I could do about it. At least not one of the obituaries questioned the official version of the general's demise, which was not to say they believed it but only that it suited all parties to accept it.

While I was leafing through the papers Steffi added a spicy commentary. "Now here's a pretty thing: 'The Principessa Faubiani presents her summer collection'! You know about her, don't you? Came from Argentina, married young Prince Faubiani, set him up with a boy friend and then petitioned for separation on grounds of his impotence. That way she kept her freedom, the title and a right to maintenance. Since then she's had a new protector every couple of years—old ones now, all rich. They finance her fashion collections. The last one was a banker. I hear she has a new one— I wonder who."

"And what's your interest in fashion, Steffi?"

"My wife has a boutique on the Via Sistina. High mode for rich tourists, decorative staff, interesting gossip. All that."

"You crafty old devil!"

"Lucky, Colonel. I married for love and got money as well.

288

Speaking of gossip, one of my wife's clients insists that Pantaleone
has a brother floating around somewhere."

"Not according to Central Registry. Old Massimo had two
daughters and a son. One daughter died in childbirth; the other
married a Spanish diplomat and lives in Bolivia. Our general, who
inherited the title, was the only male issue."

"Well, I admit the old Baroness Schwarzburg isn't the Central
Registry, but she knew the old count and she claims he bred himself a bastard from the girls' governess. He paid her off, and she
married someone who gave the boy a name, but the baroness
couldn't remember it. She's getting doddery, of course. . . . Anyway, it's a note in the margin, if you're interested."

"I'd be interested if you could tell me why Pantaleone killed
himself. . . . It's nearly five. The funeral photographs should be
ready. If they're not, I'll send you three heads for pickling. Keep
in touch, Steffi."

The photographs were not ready. After ten minutes of snap-
pish dialogue with the chief of photographic records I gave up
in disgust and went back to my own office. Here, at least, there
was some efficiency. The general's documents were indexed, and
number one clerk had made some discoveries.

"Brokers' notes, Colonel. The general has unloaded about eighty
million lire' worth of prime stock in the last four weeks. Question:
Where did the proceeds go? Not into his bank—there's his last
statement, issued only a week ago. Then here's a letter from an
estate agency pointing out that, though the Pantaleone property has been for sale for more than two months, there has been
no serious interest at the figure asked. They recommend withdrawing the property until the credit situation in Europe eases. . . .
Now comes this little piece—a handwritten note from del Giudice,
the art dealer in Florence: 'Strongly advise against any transactions
which involve you personally in a commitment to export works
from the Pantaleone collection. You offer the works for sale subject to the conditions of existing law. After that, full responsibility
for export rests on the purchaser'."

"So, he was trying to sell out. Any indication why?"

"Not in these papers."

"What else have we got?"

"No other surprises. But there's a key to a safe-deposit box at the Banco di Roma. I'd like to see the inside of that."

"We will—as soon as the banks open in the morning."

"His lawyer is howling for us to release the papers."

"I'll worry about him later. I'll also have a chat with the general's brokers about the stock sale. If you want me in the next hour, I'll be at the Chess Club. After that, at home."

THE CHESS CLUB OF ROME is a sacred institution. You enter it, as you hope one day to enter heaven, through a noble portico and find yourself in a courtyard of classic dimensions. You climb a flight of stairs to a series of anterooms, where servants in livery receive you with cautious deference. You tread softly, so as not to disturb the ghosts of kings and nobles who still inhabit the place. In the dining-room you are awed by the whispered talk of men who deal with great affairs, and daunted by the cold eyes of dowagers sour with the virtue of age. And you will look in vain for chess players, although it is rumoured that they do exist.

I was not coming to play chess. I was here to get myself put in touch—if the stars were in favourable conjunction—with those who had served Pantaleone on the eve of his death.

It was still only eight-thirty and the guests were sparse. The secretary was unusually urbane and presented me to the head-waiter. He, too, was helpful, and allowed me to explain my mission to the steward. Sometime during his last meal, I said, the general had been called to the telephone, and for reasons connected with military security I wished to trace the call and contact the person who had made it. Then I had my first surprise.

"No, Colonel." The headwaiter was definite. "The general was called from the dining-room, but not to the telephone. A senior member of the club had asked to speak with him in private. The steward conducted the general to him. They spoke for a few moments, the general returned to his table, the member left the club. I saw him leave."

"And who was this member?"

"The Cavaliere di Gran Croce Bruno Manzini from Bologna. He's in the club now. Came in about twenty minutes ago with the Principessa Faubiani."

290

"La Faubiani, eh?" I permitted myself a small grin of satisfaction—I was one up on old Steffi! "Would you give the gentleman my card and ask him to spare me a few moments?"

Manzini was an impressive figure. He must have been nearly seventy years old; his hair was snow-white, brushed back in a lion's mane over his coat collar; but his back was straight as a pine, his skin was clear, his eyes bright and humorous. He carried himself with the air of a man accustomed to deference. He announced himself with calm formality. "I am Manzini. I understand you wish to see me. May I see your official identification?"

I handed it to him and he read it carefully. "Thank you, Colonel. Now, your question."

"You were, I believe, a friend of General Pantaleone?"

"Not a friend, Colonel, an acquaintance. I had small respect for him, none at all for his politics."

"How would you define his politics?"

"Fascist and opportunist."

"And your own?"

"Private to myself, Colonel."

"I understand you had a conversation with the general here on the night he died. May I know the substance of it?"

"Certainly. Del Giudice, an art dealer in Florence, had told me that Pantaleone was about to sell the family collection. I was interested in certain items and wanted to negotiate with Pantaleone directly. It would save us both money. He said he would think about it and write to me soon."

"The Pantaleone collection is an old and important one. Why would the general want to disperse it?"

"I have no idea. May I know the reason for these inquiries?"

"At the moment I am not at liberty to disclose it, sir. And may I ask you to keep this conversation private?"

"You may not! I did not invite it. I stand upon my right to discuss it as I please, with whom I please."

"Sir, you know the organization which I represent?"

"The Service of Defence Information? I know of its existence. I am not familiar with its activities."

"You know, at least, that we deal with highly sensitive matters, both political and military."

"My dear Colonel, please! I'm an old man. I have no taste for spies, provocateurs or those who treat with them. I know that intelligence services can become instruments of tyranny. I know that they tend to corrupt the people who work in them. If you have no more questions, I trust that you will excuse me. Good evening!"

He stalked out of the room, and I let out a long exhalation of relief. This was a sturdy one. He looked you straight in the eye and gave you clean answers crack-crack-crack, knowing that you dared not dispute him.

But the important questions were still open. Why would Pantaleone, with suicide on his mind, embark on the long business of selling an estate? And why promise a letter he knew he would never write?

It was enough, more than enough, for one day. My head was stuffed with cotton and my heart full of envy for a seventy-year-old man who could afford expensive pets like La Faubiani. I drove reluctantly homeward to a hot dinner, a tepid hour of television and a cold bed.

I had a very troubled night. Shortly after ten a colleague from Milan telephoned with the news that a young Maoist being questioned in a bomb case had fallen to his death from the window of the interrogation room. There would be headlines in every morning paper. The Left would swear he had been pushed by the police. The Right would affirm that he had jumped. There would be troops on every street corner for a week, which would heighten the tension and polarize the factions even more. What a nightmare mess!

At eleven-thirty Lili Anders telephoned in panic. Her network contact had summoned her to a rendezvous at the Osteria dell'Orso at midnight. What should she do?

I told her to keep the rendezvous, rehearsed her in her story and then spent an anxious fifteen minutes rounding up my surveillance team to follow her.

I was just about to crawl back into bed when the telephone rang again. This was Captain Carpi's shadow. The captain was drunk and mumbling to a bar girl. What did I want done about it? Let him drink himself silly, then bundle him home.

AT NINE-THIRTY NEXT MORNING I sat in conference with a senior official of the Banco di Roma. He was courteous but firm. There could be no access to the late general's safe-deposit. The law demanded rigid performance of contracts between banker and client. Besides—he paused—the strongbox was empty. The general's lawyer had taken possession of its contents under an existing authority.

The brokers were more cooperative. They had indeed sold large parcels of the general's stock and had remitted the proceeds to his lawyer, Sergio Bandinelli. That ended their transaction.

Back in my office, I wrote a summons for Bandinelli to call on me within forty-eight hours. Then I settled down to examine the funeral photographs. At the end of an hour I had one small surprise. Bruno Manzini appeared in three shots, once with Cardinal Dadone, once with the Minister of Finance and the third time with an elderly peasant employed at the Villa Pantaleone. For a man who regarded Pantaleone as a Fascist and an opportunist, his presence at the funeral was a singular gesture. I wondered why he had troubled to make it. I telephoned a colleague for a copy of Bruno Manzini's dossier. Then I summoned Stefanelli.

Old Steffi was bursting with news. First, his wife had told him that La Faubiani's new protector was a certain Bruno Manzini, a Bolognese richer than anyone had a right to be—big in textiles, electrics, steel, even food processing.

"I know all that, Steffi."

"The hell you do! How?"

I told him. Then I showed him the photographs. "Now, Steffi. What's he doing at the funeral of a man he despised?"

"Easy. You may not like me, but you'll come to see me buried. How else can you be sure I'm dead?"

"Maybe . . . maybe. What else have you got?"

"The Casarolis sell rice paper to wholesalers only. Here's that list. But thousands of retailers sell the stuff."

"Body of Bacchus! Don't you have any good news, Steffi?"

"Solimbene called. So far he's found fifteen families in Italy who use the salamander in their coat-of-arms. Another paper chase, I'm afraid. . . . Did you read the headlines this morning?"

"I did."

294

"I'm scared, Colonel. Last night a suspect under questioning jumped or was pushed from a window. Why? Under what conditions? We have two thousand carabinieri on the streets of Milan this morning. Another thousand on extra duty in Rome. Cowing people. Stifling questions. We—the carabinieri and our colleagues in the police—are the real rulers of Milan at the moment. It's a terribly tempting blueprint, friend. We don't have to offer bread and circuses anymore, just public order, peace on the streets and buses running on time. Because we don't have a government; we have parties, factions, warring interests. And if things don't change soon, the man in the street is going to start shouting for a leader, a new *duce!*"

"What I'm trying to find out, Steffi, is who that would be."

"And when you do?"

"Say it, Steffi."

"You buried an embarrassing corpse yesterday—under orders. Suppose you stumble on another embarrassment, a live one this time—a man in our own service, for example. Suppose you're ordered then to close the file and keep your mouth shut. What will you do?"

"I'm damned if I know. Old Manzini was right. This job corrupts people. I don't know how much it's corrupted me."

"You may have to know very soon, Colonel. I'm a Jew, Colonel. You didn't know that? Well, I live in the old ghetto. In the synagogue we've got a list of names, eleven hundred people who were shipped out to Auschwitz on the Black Sabbath of 1943. Fourteen men and one woman came back. Do you know why I joined the service? So that I'd know in advance if it were ever going to happen again. . . . How old are you, Colonel?"

"Forty-two. Why?"

"You were only a boy then. But every time I see an election poster now, I get nightmares. I'm sorry if I've offended you."

"You haven't, Steffi. I'm glad you told me. Now, why don't you go play with your microscope, eh?"

But when the old man had gone, all the litter of photographs and memoranda on my desk suddenly seemed irrelevant. What was at issue was not the sordid power games of politics, but myself, Dante Matucci: who I was, and what price I would accept for my soul—if indeed I had one. To be a servant of the state was easy. The state was like God—you couldn't define it. You didn't have to ask questions about it. But I, Dante, was—or hoped I was—a person. How much of me did the state own? How far could it legitimately direct me? To toss a living man out of a window? To shoot a rioter? To stifle a citizen with papers so he couldn't even get up in the morning without a permit?

And then there was the other side of the coin: fifty million turbulent people locked in a narrow peninsula, poor in resources, rich only in sap and energy, easy prey to agitators. How did you stop them from tearing each other to pieces if you didn't break a few heads from time to time?

I was still chewing on that sour thought when the boys from the surveillance team came to report on Lili Anders. Their tapes of the nightclub meeting were almost unintelligible. I wanted to know why.

"No time to plant anything effective, Colonel. Anyway, they only stayed half an hour. We followed them back to Anders's apartment. The contact dropped her there and drove off. Giorgio followed him. I stayed to get a report from the lady."

"Who was the contact?"

"Picchio—Woodpecker."

"What did sweet Lili have to say for herself?"

"Woodpecker asked what the general died of. A heart attack, she said. Had she known he was sick? No, but he did have occasional chest pains that he called indigestion."

"Good for Lili. Go on."

"Who brought her the news? A colonel of carabinieri, Matucci. Had he asked any significant questions? Only about Pantaleone's movements on the night of his death. She had told him the truth. Who, Woodpecker asked, were the general's heirs? She didn't know. Did she know the general's lawyer? She did. She was ordered to cultivate him, and find out all she could about the estate. Had she ever met a Major General Leporello?"

"Impossible! He's one of ours."

"It shook me, too, Colonel."

"What did Lili say?"

"She'd never met him. Had the general ever spoken of him? Not

296

that she remembered. What was her next assignment? Sit tight, concentrate on the lawyer and await further instructions. That's it, Colonel."

"Anything from Lili's phone tap?"

"Nothing since her call to you, Colonel."

"Good. Now, let's hear about our little Captain Carpi."

"He passed out cold about three in the morning and I took him home. He's a bad drunk, Colonel."

"That's something new. Anyway, he'll sober up in Sardinia tomorrow. Thank you, gentlemen. Make sure you're fresh and sharp by eight this evening. You're still on night roster."

I grinned at their discomfiture as they slouched out. This was what the Americans called the name of the game. You walked your feet off, you knocked on doors, you waded through reams of useless information, until you came up with one item that began or completed a whole mosaic. I had one now: Why was Woodpecker, a Polish agent, interested in Marcantonio Leporello, major general of the carabinieri?

AS AN INVESTIGATOR I have many shortcomings and two special talents. I have a photographic memory. And I know how to wait. Comes a moment in every investigation when there is nothing to do but let the chemistry of the situation work itself out. If you try to hurry it, you make mistakes. The Italians love brouhaha. Sketch them a scene and in an hour they've built you an opera. I am a colonel at forty-two because I have learned to make a virtue out of the vices of my countrymen. But when a big thing came up, the trick was to create a zone of quiet and sit there, visible but enigmatic. It was a tactic that disconcerted my associates.

At that moment in time the Pantaleone affair was in suspension. The meaning of the salamander card was not yet deciphered. The general's lawyer had the contents of his strongbox. Manzini's presence at the funeral might mean nothing. He was simply a buyer of expensive art. There was nothing to go on, nothing—except that a Polish agent was interested in Major General Leporello. It seemed the time to have a chat with the Director.

The Director was a character in his own right. In the SID they called him Volpone—the old fox. To me he was a chameleon. One moment you saw him, the next you had lost him against the political undergrowth. He had the manners of a prince and the mind of a chess player. He had a sense of history and a conviction that it always repeated itself. He was inordinately rich, generous to those he liked and ruthless to those he did not. He insisted that I was one of those he liked. We clashed often. He had tempted me, more than once, but I had turned away with a grin and a shrug. I made no secret of my weaknesses, but I was damned if I would be blackmailed with them. And if the Director wanted to play games, I had a few of my own.

I was playing one now. Major General Leporello was a big man in the carabinieri. I wanted to know whether the Director was big enough to handle him. "Woodpecker is interested in Leporello," I said abruptly. "Why?"

The old fox sniffed the air. "Isn't it your job to tell me?"

"Leporello's dossier is marked 'Reserved to Director', sir."

"Forgive me, I'd forgotten. Let me see now. General Leporello has spent the last five months abroad. An official tour to study riot control and counter-insurgency."

"Do you know the general personally, sir?"

"Yes. He's a sound man."

"Vulnerable?"

"He's a patriot, a devout Catholic, a Christian Democrat and financially independent. I doubt he could be bought or frightened."

"Might he be seduced?"

"By what, Colonel?"

"The ultimate infirmity—ambition. The student of counter-insurgency might put it into practice."

"You're lost in fables, Matucci. What's your evidence?"

"Suggestive only. Woodpecker and his network have a commission which I quote: 'to give early warning of any attempt at a *colpo di stato* by neo-Fascist groups, or of actions designed to provoke it'. If Woodpecker is interested in Leporello, we have to be, too."

"I think not. But let me play with the idea. Anything else?"

"No, sir."

"Then permit me to offer you a compliment. I like your attitude to your work, careful and open-minded. That's rare in these times, you know."

"You are kind, sir. Thank you." I walked out a very pensive man. I had no wish to end my days in the dungeons of official disfavour. And yet . . . a military man who could control rioters and urban guerrillas might, one fine tomorrow, control the country, especially if he were a patriot, a good Christian and financially independent.

I was hardly back in my office when my secretary announced that Sergio Bandinelli was waiting to see me.

The lawyer was short, fussy and very irascible. "I am here to protest the illegal seizure of the papers from my client's domicile and to demand their immediate delivery into my hands."

"No problem. They're yours to take. As for the protest, what's the profit? You know that the SID works under the President's directive and to rather special rules. Of course, if you wish to press a complaint . . ."

"Well, under the circumstances . . ."

"Good! I am encouraged to solicit your assistance."

"I am happy to assist, Colonel, provided I may reserve my position in the event of conflict of interest."

"Of course. The general's death has political consequences which I am directed to study. All his activities are of interest. Why, to begin with, was he liquidating his estate?"

"I am not at liberty to say."

"His brokers informed us that the proceeds of his shares were transmitted to you. What were you directed to do with the money?"

"I cannot tell you that, either. Legal privilege."

"Before you invoke it, let me tell you that your late client maintained relations with a member of a foreign espionage network. You yourself are under surveillance by the same network."

"Is this some kind of threat, Colonel?"

"No threat—simple fact. When you refuse to disclose what has happened to large sums of money you put yourself in jeopardy. A threat to the security of the state is involved. You are answerable for your part in your client's affairs. I ask you again—what happened to the money?"

"I reinvested it in Switzerland and Brazil."

"And if the art collection had been sold, and the land?"

"I was instructed to do the same with the proceeds."

"Have you approval from the Ministry of Finance for export of funds?"

"Well, no . . . but the nature of the transaction—"

"Would involve intermediaries who have safe channels for currency export. Who charge five per cent, for which they guarantee immunity to the client. They can't guarantee that, and you know it. You can be charged with conspiracy to circumvent the law. So—why was Pantaleone exporting funds?"

"He was afraid. He had joined with the new Fascists as their military adviser and commander-in-chief in case of a *colpo di stato*. Their provocative tactics worried him. He felt they were not strong enough to risk a *colpo di stato* and that, if they tried, it would lead to civil war. So they began to lose faith in Pantaleone. They wanted to move him out in favour of a bolder man."

"Did Pantaleone know who that man was?"

"No. Only that it was a military man not now in the movement but who might be attracted into it when the time was right."

"Was the general frightened of a rival? Or of something else?"

"Action against himself. Some kind of revelation of his past. He had a chequered career and many enemies."

"Blackmail, in fact. Had he had any direct threats?"

"About a week ago he received a communication by messenger. It consisted of a very complete biography which, if it had ever been published, would have damaged his reputation beyond repair and banished him forever from public life."

"Was a threat of publication made?"

"I read it so."

"Read what?"

"A card, attached to the typescript."

I laid the salamander card on the table. "This card?"

"Yes, that's the one. Where did you get it?"

"In the general's bedroom. What happened to the biography?"

"He lodged it in his strongbox at the bank."

"Which you emptied yesterday. I want it."

"On a judge's order you may have it. Otherwise not."

"This card, what does it signify?"

"I don't know. The general mentioned something about Saint Martin's Day, but he wouldn't explain what it meant. I know only that in Spain pigs are usually killed on the Feast of Saint Martin."

"If you want to avoid your own Saint Martin's Day, I'll make a bargain with you. I'll forget the currency question. I'll send a man to your office with you now to list every paper you hold on the Pantaleone family. He will then seal them in your safe. Tomorrow I will go through them with you. Agreed?"

"I seem to have no choice. I agree."

"Good. My man will spend the night in your office."

"Why?"

"Protection. Politics is a risky business these days."

I meant it as an irony. I was the old-line professional patronizing a civilian. I should have known better. In this trade, in this country, you are always standing on a trapdoor with a hangman's noose around your neck.

The which being said, an explanation is needed. This republic of Italy is not a nation at all. We Italians are provinces, cities, countrysides, families, individuals—anything but a unity. Ask that fellow, that street cleaner, what he is. He will answer, "I am a Sard, a Calabrese, a Neapolitan." Never will he tell you he is an Italian. I myself am a Tuscan. I am paid to serve the nebulous public thing called the state, but my belonging is elsewhere—Florence and the Medici and the Arno and the pines on the graves of my ancestors.

Hence a kind of anarchy Anglo-Saxons can never understand. I can never say, "This is the enemy, destroy him!" I must say, "This is the enemy of the moment, but he comes from my country, his sister is married to my cousin and tomorrow we may need to be friends." I must comport myself so that the links are not broken, though the chain may be stretched almost to the breaking point.

Hence also a kind of order Anglo-Saxons can't understand. We have but one life, one opportunity to come to terms with it. We have to survive. So we try to negotiate. And if we are forced to accept a base bargain, we wait for a tomorrow when the contract may be annulled or improved by mutual consent. As you see, I know it all. So there is no excuse for the follies I began to commit that afternoon.

The first was my contemptuous bargain with Sergio Bandinelli, whom I judged to be a pliable, frightened man. I gave him for guardian one Giampiero Calvi, promising but young, who was to call headquarters every hour on the hour until I relieved him at nine the next morning. Then I called Lili Anders and told her that, in line of duty, I would call on her at eight-thirty for a cocktail and take her out to dinner afterwards. Finally, because I was—and am—too arrogant for my own good, I elected to play out my little testing game against the Director.

I had found out that Major General Leporello was here in Rome for conferences with senior service officers and was lodged at the Hassler. I telephoned him. The conversation was terse.

"General, this is Colonel Matucci, SID."

"Yes?"

"A very urgent matter. I should like to see you."

"I am busy until six. I can spare you half an hour after that. Call me from the lobby. Suite ten."

"Thank you, sir."

"The name again?"

"Matucci. Section E."

I put down the telephone and waited. If I judged my man right, he would check back. Within three minutes my phone rang.

"Who is this, please?" said Leporello's voice.

"Matucci, Section E."

"This is Leporello. We have an appointment, I believe."

"Yes, sir. Suite ten at eighteen hundred hours."

"Please be punctual. Good-bye."

I'd need some relaxation with Lili after half an hour with this hardhead. I made one more call, this time to a curious little office which provides information on the comings and goings of celebrities. My contact is a busty Dane. Her civil status is highly dubious, but her information is always accurate.

"Faubiani? Well, old Manzini's in town, so she's doing the rounds with him. Let's see . . . Tonight Fosco is displaying jewellery, and they will probably be there. It's a buffet supper at Fosco's, eight-thirty until the champagne runs out. If you want a ticket, I can let you have mine. I only get envious when I look at all that expensive junk."

"You're an angel, Inger."

"When am I going to see you, Dante?"

"When I pick up the card at seven-thirty. *Ciao, bambina!*"

After leaving two numbers with the night duty officer—Lili Anders's and my own—I was ready for grooming: a change of clothes, a trim, a shave, and a massage to tone up my sagging face muscles.

At six o'clock precisely I telephoned Major General Leporello from the front desk of the Hassler. He sent his aide to fetch me—a muscular young blood with red hair and freckles. I suspected that when he left me with the general he posted himself just outside the door. Leporello was a surprise. He was a tall man, blond and ruddy, more German than Latin. His chest was broad, his belly flat. His manner was brisk. He had no sense of humour at all. "Your identification, please." I gave it to him. "What do you wish to discuss, Colonel?"

"Matters arising out of the death of General Pantaleone."

"Such as?"

"This card, sir. It was found in the general's room, attached to a dossier which had just been delivered to him."

"What sort of dossier?"

"Incriminating documents of the general's past life."

"Blackmail?"

"We believe so."

"Where are they now?"

"In his lawyer's office, in custody of an officer of SID."

"What is this symbol?"

"A salamander."

"That's odd. During the war one of the most important of the partisan groups was led by a man called the Salamander."

"What was his real name? Did he use a card like this?"

"I don't know who he was. But I remember some talk of a calling card pinned to the chest of victims of the band."

"Did this group have Marxist connections?"

"Most groups in the North were reputed to have."

"Did you ever work with such groups, General?"

"I? Never. My loyalties were to the Crown. I disliked the Fascists, I loathed the Germans; but even for that I could not be a turncoat soldier. Today I am able to be both honest and proud."

"I am sure you are, sir. You are also a natural target for the terrorists of the Left. Which brings me to the real purpose of my visit—you are, sir, under surveillance by at least one network of foreign agents."

He gave me a thin smile. "That's hardly news, Colonel. I have always assumed surveillance—foreign and local."

"The news is, General, that this group regards you as a possible successor to General Pantaleone."

"In what capacity?"

"As leader in the event of a Right-wing coup."

"Which is nonsense, of course."

"Of course, sir. But it does make you vulnerable to blackmail or assassination."

I had thought to shake him, but he was hard and smooth as cemetery granite. "Blackmail, Colonel? Impossible. My life is an open book. As for attempts on my life, these have been foreseen and security measures arranged. I am more concerned by the suggestion that I might have political ambitions. I have none. I believe in hierarchy and order. I see myself only as a servant of duly constituted authority. Have you discussed this matter with your director?"

"I have."

"His opinion?"

"That no action is réquired by SID. I have, in fact, exceeded my brief by seeking this interview with you."

"Why did you seek it then?"

"We are members of the same corps, General, you and I. I felt that a point of carabinieri honour was involved. I decided to act on my own initiative and at my own risk. I am prepared to accept all consequences."

Leporello relaxed. He leaned back and surveyed me with grim approval. "You impress me, Colonel. If you need a friend, you have one in me. I shall instruct my staff that you may have instant access to me at any time."

"That is very generous, sir."

"Not at all. The security and stability of the republic is my business, and yours. Pantaleone was a dangerous fool. Today we need strong men who are prepared to risk themselves in public service. If ever you feel an inclination to join my personal staff,

I should be happy to have you. And—ah, Colonel—I have no intention of discussing this meeting with your director."

"Thank you, sir," I said as he shook my hand and ushered me out, commending me to the care of his aide, who escorted me downstairs and saluted as I drove away.

In the gardens of the Pincio I stopped the car and sat for twenty minutes trying to make sense of Major General Leporello. I have an instinctive fear of characters who act as if they were first cousins to God Almighty. Their certainty of rectitude never ceases to amaze me. They are dogmatists all, and have no hesitation about rewriting the moral code to suit themselves. Their passion for order sets them beyond reason or pity. In short, I'm more afraid of them than of all the crooks I meet in my trade. They make me afraid of myself, too, because they provoke me to anger and misjudgment and savage reaction.

Still there was a tenuous profit to the interview. Leporello was tempting me with a promise of friendship into an alliance; an alliance suggested a strategy—to what end? What would be the next ambition of a man whose current job was controlling ant-heap cities and their millions of volatile humans? Eh! It was too late and too early for Dante Matucci to read the future. I started the car and drove through the dappled alleys of the gardens to drink cocktails with Lili Anders.

THE APARTMENT HAD CHANGED since my last visit. The portrait of Pantaleone was gone. Things had been rearranged to produce an air of femininity. Lili herself was changed; her hair more softly swept, her clothes more modish, her manner more confident. When I commented, she smiled and shrugged. "I am perhaps a little more my own woman. What will you drink?"

"Whisky, please."

"You are changed, too. More human, less professional. How am I to call you, Colonel?"

"Dante. I'd like us to enjoy ourselves as friends tonight."

"That's hardly possible, is it? Because, Dante, in fact you own me. You direct me like a puppet. Your drink, master."

"Your health, Lili."

"Where are we dining?"

"We are guests at an exhibition and a champagne supper afterwards. Fosco is displaying his new season's jewellery."

"That should be interesting. Do you like jewellery, Dante?"

"I do—even though I can't afford it."

"If you would like to see mine, I'll show it to you when we come back. I presume you will bring me back after the supper?"

"You're being rough with me, Lili."

"No. I want you to know that I understand our relationship. I promised value for money and protection."

"I'm not a whoremaster, Lili."

"Then what are you?"

"I am self-indulgent and I like pretty women. Also I'm tired and I want to laugh. I'm puzzled and I want to stop thinking. I'm scared and I don't really want to ask why."

"You, scared?"

"Yes. This is the age of the assassins, Lili—fanatics who want a new world. They'll tear down twenty centuries of civilization to achieve it. They don't see that when they're sitting in the ruins the old gang will come back—the technocrats to build the factories, the police to bully people into order, even the city rat-catchers like me. It's a madness, Lili, and I'm at the centre of it. So are you. There's no escape for either of us. Now, please, may I have another drink?"

She gave it to me. Then she laid a cool hand on my cheek. "Even if you mean only half of it, I'll believe you."

I wasn't sure I believed myself; but I wanted to feel less like a pimp and more like a man who could face the sunlight without shame. I kissed her hand lightly. "Now, let's start again."

Twenty minutes later we were driving to Fosco's, and we joined the gathering, hand in hand, like lovers.

It was a gala occasion. The best titles in Rome staged a slow pavane around the showcases of Fosco's work. A master chef presided over the buffet. An army of waiters distributed champagne and canapés. It was a sophisticated social ballet, and Fosco directed it with charm and only a hint of contempt for the performers. He received us with vague courtesy and waved us into the concourse. We snared two glasses of champagne and a pair of catalogues and began our circuit of the exhibits.

It was immediately clear that Fosco had made a killing. Half the items had been made to order or optioned in advance to great houses—Bulgari, Cartier, Buccellati, Tiffany. His designs were original, his craftsmanship superb. He labelled every exhibit as if it were a museum piece, including whenever he could the name and title of the person who had commissioned it. We were halfway around the room when Lili tugged at my sleeve and pointed to Number 63 in the catalogue. The description read:

SALAMANDER. Brooch in the form of an heraldic beast. Emeralds in pavé. Crowned with brilliants and ornamented with Burma rubies. Adapted from a calligraphic design. Commissioned by Cavaliere di Gran Croce Bruno Manzini, Bologna.

It was not a gaudy jewel, but the craftsman had preserved the character and sweep of the calligraphy. There was no doubt that the design was identical with the one on the card. I drew Lili away from the showcase into the crush around the buffet. At the same moment Manzini entered the gallery with the Principessa Faubiani at his side. Fosco greeted them effusively and led them on a personal tour of the masterworks.

Somehow I must see Manzini before he left the gallery. I excused myself to Lili and made my way to the entrance, where a young man was hosting for Fosco. I flashed my card at him. "Carabinieri. Who is in charge of your security guards?"

"Over there, tall fellow with grey hair. There's trouble?"

"No, no. Just routine."

I drew the tall fellow into the shadows and showed him my card, too. "This is important. You will take me to Fosco's private office and escort there the gentleman to whom I'll give you a note. Then I'd like you to stay outside the door and let no one in while we're talking—clear?"

"Clear. There's no trouble, I hope."

"None. I've noted your security arrangements. First class."

He was happy then. In Fosco's office I scribbled my note.

Regret intrusion but have urgent and official communication. Please accompany messenger to office.   Matucci, SID

307

Manzini was with me in three minutes, cool and condescending. He demanded that I state my business and be done with it.

"Still General Pantaleone. Shortly before he died he received a communication—a dossier, in effect, of his past life."

"And what has that to do with me?"

"Attached to the dossier was this card. The design corresponds exactly with number sixty-three in the Fosco catalogue."

"So what do you want from me, Colonel?"

"At this stage, an informal discussion. Now, if possible, sir."

"Quite impossible. It is a long story and I am occupied with friends. But tomorrow, at nine in the morning at the Grand Hotel, my dear Colonel, I'll do my best to enlighten you. Now, may I be excused?"

"One question, sir. What does the salamander signify?"

"Survival. It was my code name during the war."

"And the inscription?"

"Pantaleone was my half-brother. Only he happened to be conceived on the right side of the blanket."

I stared at him open-mouthed, like an idiot. He smiled at my discomfiture. "Please! I am not trying to make theatre, only to show you that we do need time to be clear with each other. And now, Colonel, will you answer one question for me?"

"If I can, yes."

"Who killed Pantaleone?"

"The death certificate states that he died of cardiac arrest."

"But that's what kills us all. No other comment, Colonel?"

"None until tomorrow." Why didn't I hold him? Why didn't I hammer him with questions while I had him off-balance? Because this was a very special one, the best of the breed. He off-balance? Never for an instant. With him, I was the unsure novice groping for a handhold on a bare mountain.

Happy to leave, I carted Lili off to dinner at a place I knew in Trastevere, where the food was honest Tuscan, the wine honourable and the waiters proud to serve you. I have friends there: the cook whom I prized, and others whose talk, in front of the open fire in winter or under the arbour of vines in the summer, was as good as the food and drink. It was one place where I was myself— whoever that might be. I accepted everyone at face value. I used no one. I paid the score and was welcome in the house. Everyone needs a refuge. This was mine.

I tried to explain all this to Lili as we walked the last hundred metres through lanes hung with laundry. She seemed happy to listen, holding close to me as we stepped over spilled refuse while cats slunk back into the shadows. Sometimes, when the rare light fell on her face, she looked like a young girl. But I was not hunting now, I was simply glad not to be alone.

When we were settled at the table, she laid her hands on mine. "You look different now, Dante Matucci. At Fosco's you were tight, wary, like a fox. Now you are loose, free. You greet people like human beings. They, too, are glad to see you."

"This is Trastevere, my love. Across the river. These people refuse to belong to anyone but themselves."

"I like that. For tonight we, too, may do that. Please, may I have some wine?"

"I may get drunk and sing."

"I'll sing with you."

"And who will drive us back across the river?"

"Perhaps we won't go back—ever again."

It was a happy thought and we nursed it, from the antipasto to the dessert, to the tune of a guitar played by a plaintive fellow who sings there, sings the soul out of your body with the songs of the South. By one-thirty in the morning we were vaguely drunk. The waiters had begun to wilt, so we wandered back to the car. Lili said drowsily, "Do you know, I really don't want to go home. Home is yesterday. I want to forget it."

"So let's drive out to a place I know. . . . But I have to call my duty officer first. I left your number with him."

"There's no escape, is there? You have to telephone—"

"Please, Lili."

"Please, just kiss me. . . ."

The evening of liberty ended with that kiss. Headquarters told me our agent, Calvi, had not made his hourly call from the lawyer's office; the time was ten minutes after two. I ordered one car of the mobile squadron to pick up Steffi, another one to meet me at Bandinelli's. I put Lili into a taxi. Then I drove like a madman across the sleeping city.

WHEN I ARRIVED AT THE OFFICE on the Via Sicilia, one squadron car was already there. The second, carrying Steffi, hurtled around the corner seconds later. I gave a few sharp directions to the squadron leaders: this was a high-security matter; no police, no Press; two men to stand by the cars, one to stay with the porter, three to accompany Steffi and me. Then we rang the bell.

The porter, bleary-eyed, opened the door. We flashed our cards, left him grumbling and took the elevator to the fifth floor. Bandinelli's office was dark when I opened the door. I switched the lights on—to a curiously tranquil scene. The lawyer lay stretched on a leather settee. Our agent, Calvi, was seated in a chair behind the desk, head pillowed on his arms. Old Steffi sniffed the air and briefly examined the bodies. "Dead. Hydrocyanic-acid gas. Pistol or pressure pack."

I examined the safe. The seals were broken, the door was open—the Pantaleone papers were gone. I picked up the phone and called the Director's private number. He answered with surprising promptness. I told him, "We're in trouble. Documents missing, and two bundles of dirty linen for immediate disposal—one of them ours. As soon as the situation is tidy, I'll report in person."

"I'll expect you for breakfast—the earlier the better."

Steffi cackled at me like an ancient parrot. "When everything's tidy! So now we're in the miracle business!"

Steffi was right as usual. If I reported to the police, the Press would swarm. Finding the Pantaleone papers involved, they would ask about the general's hasty burial and handicap our search for the documents. We had, therefore, to get the bodies out. I sent Steffi down to question the porter in his cubbyhole—Steffi's talk would hypnotize a fighting cock.

The boys and I emptied Bandinelli's and Calvi's pockets, then bundled the bodies into the elevator and into the two squad cars. One drove Bandinelli to the casualty department of the Policlinico; the other deposited Calvi at the hospital of the Blue Sisters. In each case the story was the same: the mobile squadron had found a man lying, apparently unconscious, in an alley. They were consigning him to the hospital while they pursued inquiries as to his identity. Dead on arrival? Dear me! Then hold him in the mortuary while we trace him.

Meanwhile I examined the last entries in Calvi's notes:

24.00 hrs.   Telephoned duty officer HQ.

00.37 hrs.   Bandinelli telephoned. He wished stop by office for late conference with two clients. A police matter, he said. He would not disturb me, but would use outer office. Since my instructions referred only to custody of safe, I had no authority to refuse access to his own office. I agreed.

01.00 hrs.   Telephoned duty officer to report Bandinelli's request and my decision.

I called the duty officer. He confirmed the entries, which left me with a vital question: had Bandinelli come to the office under duress or as an accomplice who was liquidated when his usefulness was ended? Steffi, who came back at that point, was no help. The porter always went off duty at midnight; tenants had passkeys and came and went at all hours. "In fact anyone with a passkey could bring an army in here after midnight with no one the wiser," Steffi said.

"All right. So where was Bandinelli when he telephoned? Let's ring his house."

A surly major-domo finally answered. No, the lawyer wasn't there. Hadn't come home for dinner. The *signora*? She was in Naples. I thanked him and hung up.

Steffi grinned. "Which helps your little fiction about an unidentified body."

"But it doesn't tell me who killed him and took the documents."

"Does it matter, Colonel?"

"Steffi! What sort of question is that?"

"Look! This is a neat, simple, professional job. Do you want the killers or the people who paid them? This is not police work, friend; it's intelligence analysis. Start from the top and you halve the work and double your chances of solving it—believe me!"

"I do believe you, Steffi, but sometime in the next three hours I have to face the Director. What do I offer him?"

"Human sacrifice!" Steffi favoured me with a gallows grin. "So, Colonel, why don't you make me some coffee and we'll discuss the candidates."

THE DIRECTOR'S APARTMENT was the top floor of a sixteenth-century palace just off the Via della Scrofa. The revenues from the rest of the palace—dwellings and fashionable shops—would keep him in kingly state for a lifetime. His paintings and sculptures were a fortune in themselves, his library a minor treasure-house. The Director was resplendent in a brocaded dressing-gown. At six in the morning, grubby, unshaven and very unsure of myself, I was in no mood to appreciate the dramatic effect. He offered me a cool welcome and an English breakfast. I asked for coffee and pastry. He conceded the point with a smile and then proceeded to make a few of his own.

"You knew the Pantaleone papers were important, Colonel. Why did you not take immediate possession of them?"

"I needed a judicial order. I'd have had to appear against Bandinelli in the presence of a judge, which I thought unwise."

"So you made an arrangement which resulted in the death of our agent and of Bandinelli himself. Any excuse?"

"No excuse. I was trying to scare Bandinelli into further revelations. I thought the risk was minimal. I was wrong."

"Who else knows the facts at this moment?"

"Only SID. We had the place cleaned up by four this morning."

"And who has the Pantaleone papers? Right wing or Left?"

"Right, I think."

"Why?"

"The Left have a lot of dirt they haven't published yet. The Right have a lot of dirt they want to bury—I think last night was a funeral party."

"You don't convince me, Colonel."

"I'm not trying to, sir. I'm telling you what I believe. If you're thinking of Woodpecker, forget him. I had him pulled in at four this morning. I've worked on him for nearly two hours. I know his brief. Assassination is not part of it. Let's look at the other side of the coin. Bandinelli was far Right. He served Pantaleone. He could have sold out to a successor—"

"And been killed for his pains?"

"That, too."

"Name me a possible successor."

"Major General Marcantonio Leporello."

The Director set down his teacup with a clatter and sat staring at me with bleak and hostile eyes. At last he said quietly, "I presume you have evidence in support, Colonel?"

"Some. I interviewed the general yesterday at his hotel."

"You what?"

"I interviewed Leporello."

"In spite of my orders that no action was to be taken with that subject?"

"Yes, sir."

"And what did you tell him?"

"That he was under surveillance by a foreign network who had tipped him as political candidate for the Right. The whereabouts of the Pantaleone papers. And that I was acting against your orders."

"Oh! And what was his reaction to that?"

"He promised to keep the interview secret, and he offered me a job on his own staff."

"I'm tempted to make you immediately available, Matucci. You disobey orders, and that's dangerous."

"It was a risk. I think it paid dividends. I know who sent the card to Pantaleone. I've identified the Salamander."

That brought him up short. His piece of toast stopped halfway to his thin lips.

"And do you propose to tell me who he is?"

"Yes, sir. He's the Cavaliere di Gran Croce Bruno Manzini. He tells me he's the bastard brother of General Pantaleone. I have an appointment with him at nine o'clock this morning."

"Leporello, your military superior. Manzini, one of the most powerful financiers in Italy. You're flying high, my friend."

"And you can shoot me down now, if you choose."

"What if I let you go on?"

"I want a free hand and access to the Leporello file."

"Can I trust you, Matucci?"

"You can, but you'd rather not."

314

"Do you trust me?"

"With reservations. I know what you are commissioned to do as director of SID. What I don't know is how you interpret your commission and to what secret ends you direct SID activities."

"Do you have any right to know?"

"Legally, I suppose not. Personally? If you'd asked me that a week ago I'd have given a nice, complaisant answer. This morning it's different. I'm tired, I've lost a good man because I didn't think straight, and I don't want to be manipulated any more. I want to know where I'm being directed and why. If I don't like it, I'll go back to police work."

The Director walked to the window and stood a long time looking out at the tumbled rooftops of Rome, gold and umber and crimson in the early light. When he turned, the light was at his back and the contours of his face were in shadow. He began to talk, quietly at first, then with mounting passion and eloquence.

"You are a presumptuous fellow, Colonel. Yet I can forgive you, because I also presume—on wealth and family and myself as a product of all our history. In a way I am yesterday's man; but then Italy is yesterday's country as well as today's. We build our prosperity on ruins and the genius of our ancient dead. Our law is a confusion of Justinian, the Church, Napoleon, Mussolini and the founding fathers of the United States. We shout for federal republican democracy—yet a man's country is whatever miserable village he was born in. We exist in a precarious balance, and when it tips ever so slightly we are plunged into civil strife and beg to be delivered. We tried one dictator, and we made a shambles of democracy. Now the people don't know what they want. I don't even know what they will tolerate.

"So I manipulate things to hold a balance as long as possible. I don't want dictatorship. I don't want Marxism. But I think the kind of democracy we have is too unstable to last. So, come one or the other, I'll try to make it as tolerable as I can. Politics, they say, is the art of the possible. Mediterranean politics is the art of the impossible, and I understand it better than most. You're worried about Leporello, but you have no evidence against him and I'm not going to antagonize him just when we may need him. I do confess your Salamander makes no sense to me at all just now. You may have your free hand to investigate, but—understand me, Matucci—when I move I am king on the board and you are a pawn. Take it or leave it."

I gave him the answer without a second's hesitation. "I'll take it. And I'll give you an honest report. If we don't agree, I'll fight you, but I'll do it in the open."

"If you ever fight me, Matucci, you'll have to lie like a whore and cheat like a cardsharp, just to save your skin. By the way, you can't meet Manzini looking like that. My valet will show you to the guest room and find you a razor and a clean shirt."

AT EIGHT O'CLOCK on that same morning I joined Stefanelli as he strolled whistling down the Spanish Steps. The sun was bright, the air was crisp; every tread of the staircase blossomed with girls. I had been up all night, but I felt miraculously refreshed, and I could see the sap rising even in Steffi's withered trunk. At the foot of the Steps we bought him a carnation for his button-hole, then we turned into Babington's Tea Room, where he had promised to meet Solimbene for tea and English muffins. Solimbene was an amiable pedant who affected small eccentricities like velvet smoking-jackets, and nourished a passion for English manners. We found him enthroned in a corner of the tea room, clasping the hand of a waitress. He gave her up reluctantly for Steffi.

"My dear colleague! I have revelations for you!" He laid the salamander card on the table. "This is not heraldry at all, but calligraphy, a monkish art. At first I accepted a heraldic origin, and I chased salamanders across every escutcheon in Europe. Insanity! Finally I found this photograph, listed in our files under 'Curiosa and exotica.' There is your salamander. Only it is not a coat-of-arms at all. It is merely an artist's conceit. It belongs to no known family."

"If it means nothing, why show it to us?" Stefanelli said.

"Oh, but it means a great deal—fraud, fakery and scandals. In the year 1910, dear colleague, there lived not a stone's throw from here a notable lady of fashion who called herself the Countess Salamandra. She entertained only the noble and the wealthy— among them a certain opera singer, who was shot and killed as he

316

left her house one morning, presumably by a jealous rival. The lady fled to Nice. Police inquiries revealed that the Countess Salamandra was a young Scots lady named Anne Mackenzie, who, having fallen from grace in a noble bed, decided to enrich herself by the same means. She had this coat-of-arms forged for professional purposes."

"Is that all?"

"All?" Solimbene was outraged. "My dear Colonel. Miss Anne Mackenzie was once governess to Count Pantaleone's daughters. Pregnant by him, she married, in August 1900, one Luca Salamandra, a circus performer, who, two days after the wedding, fell from a high wire and broke his neck. The child was born a week later and baptized Massimo Salamandra. I offer certificates of marriage and birth and baptism, all dated 1900. In October of the same year the Countess Salamandra began to prepare her entry into Roman society. It is a reasonable guess that she was financed by old Count Pantaleone."

"And what happened to the boy?"

"His mother took him with her to Nice. Yesterday, at the Central Registry in Rome, I found that in 1923 a young man named Massimo Salamandra changed his name to Bruno Manzini. Now, gentlemen, do I get my money?"

He could have tripled the fee. When you are playing against the house, it pays to have a spare ace in your sleeve. Even that doesn't help, of course, when the deck is stacked against you.

THE CAVALIERE DI GRAN CROCE BRUNO MANZINI received me in a suite large enough to house an infantry division. His morning face was benign. "You're looking peaked, Colonel. A late night?"

"A long one. I haven't been to bed yet."

"My dear fellow, let's save time then. How much do you know?"

"That your mother was one Anne Mackenzie. That, as you told me last night, you are the son of the old Count Pantaleone. That you were baptized Massimo Salamandra in Rome in 1900. That your mother adopted a spurious title and a coat-of-arms to match it. In 1923 you changed your name—"

"And how did you come by all this information?"

"Some luck, some heraldry and the Central Registry."

"What else can you tell me?"

"That depends, sir, on how much you are prepared to tell me."

"Anything you wish to know."

"Why were you blackmailing your brother?"

"Blackmail? My dear Matucci, I could have bought and sold him twenty times over. I was threatening him with public disgrace if he persisted in his crazy politics."

"Instead you killed him."

"I beg your pardon?"

"He died of an overdose of drugs—self-administered."

"A fact which was not made public. Why?"

"For fear of scandal which might lead to civil disorder."

"Now I could make the scandal."

"Will you?"

"No. It would defeat my purpose, which I take it is the same as yours. To avoid political disruption and civil violence."

"Next question then. If the dossier you sent your brother fell into other hands, what use could be made of it?"

"Now that he is dead, very little. Why do you ask?"

"Because all his papers were stolen last night from his lawyer's office. Bandinelli and one of our agents were murdered."

"There was no news of this in the Press."

"Nor will there be, unless you choose to release it."

He stared at me in blank disbelief. "I can't believe that any intelligent man would put such a bomb in the hands of a stranger. I could blow up the country with it. You, a serving officer, have just admitted falsifying the records of a suicide and concealing two murders! What guarantee have you that I won't splash this news all over the place?"

"There are no guarantees in this dog's world. But I have to trust someone. Let's say I trust you because you despise the trade I'm in and make no secret of it. Now, can we go on?"

"You'll check my answers, of course?"

"As if I were the Grand Inquisitor himself."

"That's better. Please begin."

"What in the Pantaleone papers would be worth two lives?"

He pondered that. "In the family papers, very little. In my brother's personal papers? Well, as a soldier playing a political power game, he would have assembled dossiers on friends and enemies, and those might be valuable enough to the subjects, or to political rivals, to steal. But murder? Somehow I don't see it. There must be something else."

"For example?"

"Plans, more likely. The tactics and strategy of a coup. The political and military organization that must be ready to take over at a moment's notice. The list of participants, location of arms, and the disposition of available forces in sympathy with the plotters. Even your own service might murder for such things."

"In this case they didn't."

"So now, Matucci, we are at the heart of the artichoke. We have to decide whether we can trust each other. Whose move is next?"

"It's your turn, sir!"

"Before you arrived your director telephoned me."

I had that strange sensation of disembodiment that comes in moments of shock as I saw the trap opening under my unwary feet. Then I was back in my own skin, writhing at the irony of my situation. Manzini watched me gravely. "You are angry. You have a right to be. Your director is too clever for his own good and as vain as Lucifer. He wanted to display his cleverness to me and also, I think, to teach you a lesson for some delinquency."

"That's true, at least. Well, so now what?"

"Now I am going to give you information which your director does not yet possess. At eight o'clock yesterday evening I signed, on behalf of one of my companies, a procurement contract with the government. The contract calls for the urgent supply of great quantities of riot-control equipment. The specifications were drawn up by Major General Leporello, and the equipment will be used by troops under his command. You may care to hear what conclusions I draw from this."

"Please!"

"If I were a Fascist looking for a new leader, I'd be very ready to bargain with Marcantonio Leporello."

"Perhaps the bargain has already been struck."

"No, Colonel. Leporello would not commit himself until Pantaleone's papers were safe in his own hands."

"And he has them now?"

319

"I believe so."

"You are, it seems to me, rather more than a businessman."

"I'm a salamander, Colonel—a perennial survivor. You?"

"A servant of the state. Except that I'm not sure what the state is today, and I'm scared of what it may be tomorrow."

"That makes us allies."

"In a lopsided league."

"Does that frighten you?"

"Yes, that frightens me."

"Then let me offer you a small reassurance. I shall give you a name and an address. If you go there you will hear part of the truth about me. If it satisfies you, come to see me in Bologna."

On the back of a business card he wrote the name—Raquela Rabin; the address, a street near the Theatre of Marcellus. We shook hands. "Advice from an old campaigner, Colonel. Always walk close to the wall. I hope we meet again soon."

When I hit the street the church bells were tolling ten o'clock. All of a sudden I was maudlin tired, rocking on my feet. I drove in a perilous daze to Lili's apartment and almost fell into her arms when she opened the door. She asked no questions but led me into the bedroom and let me collapse into sleep.

That sleep was a journey to the underworld. I woke, sweating and trembling, with the sheets knotted about me like a shroud. The smell of my body offended me. It was the odour of dammed-up fear. I was marked now—by the Director as an intransigent, by Leporello as a man who must be bought or seduced, by Manzini as a collaborator, useful one moment, dispensable at the twitch of an eyebrow. I was in danger because I knew too much and could do too little.

Lili could be picked off, too. With Woodpecker's network broken, she'd be marked for liquidation. If her own people did not get her, the Director would arrest her, if only to teach me a lesson. I looked at my watch. Siesta-time. I lifted the bedside phone and called Stefanelli's house.

"Steffi? Matucci."

"Don't you ever sleep?"

"Steffi, the roof's falling in. Have you got a spare room? I have to store a very sensitive package."

"Miserable swine! I've had two hours of bad sleep and I'm still in my pyjamas! Eh-eh-eh! Where do I collect it?"

"I'll bring it to you. Go back to sleep."

"Thank you for nothing, dear friend."

I had just put the phone down when Lili came in, frowning and solicitous. "I thought you were talking in your sleep. Earlier you were shouting and groaning."

"I had bad dreams. Lili, listen to me. It's condition red for you. I want to get you to Switzerland, but that needs time and planning. I'm taking you to a safe house. You stay there until I'm ready to move you. Yes or no?"

I saw the suspicion in her eyes. "If I say no . . . ?"

"You get killed by your own people or jailed by mine."

"I don't believe it. Last night—"

"That was a million years ago. While you and I were singing, two men were murdered—one of mine and Pantaleone's lawyer. I arrested Woodpecker at four this morning. You're compromised. I can't protect you for more than a few days."

"Why should you risk it at all?"

"To prove to myself I'm not a whoremaster. Will that do? You have fifteen minutes while I dress. Then you're on your own."

"Please! Hold me. I'm frightened."

"I want you frightened, Lili. I want you to do exactly as I tell you. Understand?" She nodded. "Pack an overnight bag. Take your jewellery, your chequebooks, cash—"

At that moment the doorbell chimed. I laid a finger on Lili's lips and whispered, "The housekeeper?"

"Out. Her day off."

I crept into the hallway. A letter had been thrust through the mail slot.

I bent to pick it up and then drew back. No self-respecting postman would be on the streets at siesta-time. I went back into the bedroom.

"Lili, can you get me a spatula or something?"

While she rummaged in the kitchen, I dressed. Then, duly armed, I lifted the letter by sliding a fish-slice under it and gingerly laid it on the coffee table in the living room. The address was typed. The stamp was Italian. But it had not been stamped by a post office. I snapped at Lili to finish packing and telephoned a friend in the security section of the Post and Telegraph Office.

He gave me the cheerful news that a normal letter bomb contained enough explosive to kill the man who opened it and maim anyone else in the room. He promised to have an expert on the doorstep in thirty minutes. I told him I couldn't wait that long. He told me to call the police and put a man on guard until the expert arrived.

Lili locked the apartment after us, and then, avoiding the elevators, we walked down four flights of stairs. The street was lined on both sides with parked vehicles. My car was jammed beautifully between a Mercedes and a Fiat 600. I went back to the lobby and dialled Pronto Soccorso, the police emergency service.

Five minutes later a squad car pulled up, and the crew came in at a run. The *brigadiere* was cool and efficient. The explosives squad would handle the letter as well as check my car for booby traps. Meantime, if I would give him a deposition . . . ? My card convinced him he could wait for that. I needed his car and his driver to deliver the lady and myself to the Excelsior Hotel.

In a few minutes we were dropped across from the hotel. We waited five minutes, window-shopping at Rizzoli's bookstore, then took a taxi to the Theatre of Marcellus and, when I was satisfied we were not followed, walked through the maze of alleys to Steffi's house.

Steffi received us with characteristic flourish. He clucked over Lili, insisted on settling her into her room himself and then stormed downstairs to give me the rough edge of his tongue. "Matucci, you're a madman! That little baggage upstairs is dangerous! When the Director hears of this—and he will, sooner or later—you'll be cooked, screaming, like a lobster."

"Steffi, have you got any whisky?"

"For you, hemlock and soda."

"Then pour me a big one. Now, who is Raquela Rabin?"

"Why do you want to know?"

"I have an introduction to her."

He sat down heavily, cupped his hands around his glass and stared into it, an old man ravaged by time and history. "Fifteen came back from Auschwitz, Colonel. Raquela Rabin was the only

322

woman. In the ghetto, when you say that name you say it with respect. She did not have to go to the camp; she had powerful protectors. But when the trucks came she was here, standing in the *piazza*, waiting like a daughter of David. Everything that should not happen to a woman happened to her, but she is still sane and splendid as the evening star. You will be gentle with her. You will not mix her in this stinking business of ours, understand? And what she tells you, believe without question. I'll take you to her, but I want you humble, because this is a great woman. Tell me, who gave you this introduction?"

"Bruno Manzini. He said that if Raquela Rabin spoke well of him I might be prepared to trust him. I'm on the auction block, Steffi. The bids will be high and tempting, and I'm not sure I can resist them. A strong friend might lend me courage. I need that, Steffi. I don't know what to believe anymore. I don't even know who I am."

He brightened at that, as if I had told him the best news in the world. "So you don't know who you are? Who does? But sure as breathing, you'd better see what's being done to you."

"I see it. I don't understand it."

"Because you refuse to come to terms with yourself. You don't want to decide what you are—a patriot or a mercenary."

"Hard words from a friend!"

"True words, because I am your friend. Today you might have been killed. Tomorrow the risk is bigger. When you stake your life like this, what are you staking it for—or against?"

"Maybe for a dream, Steffi. I don't know. Maybe against a madness I smell in the streets. The land is the centre of it somehow. The vines greening on the terraces, the white hills and the river with the mist on it. The people, too, are part of the dream; I see a woman bursting like a grape with love; I am served by a peasant who greets me and offers me wine and bread and salt as if I were his brother. These are the good things, Steffi, and this is home. I don't want it trampled by jackboots or desecrated by mindless mobs. . . . Now, let's leave it, eh?"

"I can leave it, friend. You can't. You're the man who knows the underside of politics, the cogs in the power machine. You have to decide how you will use that knowledge."

"I'm not paid to use it—only to collect it."

"But you filter it, too. You suppress, you emphasize, you collect. To what end?"

"Dammit, what do we all want? A quiet life. Some dignity in our living and dying."

"Not enough! Not half enough! Look—"

"Be quiet, old man!" Lili challenged him from the doorway, cold and angry. "Let him find his own answers in his own time."

"He has no time." Steffi was brusque and brutal. "He robbed himself when he gave it to you."

"I am here to give it back. May I sit down, please?"

She sat between us, holding herself erect. "You two are friends. I am the outsider. I accept to be here because I am afraid. I don't want to be killed. I don't want to spend the rest of my life in a Roman prison. But I am not a beggar, Dante. I can pay."

"You were not asked to pay."

"This morning you held my life in your hands. You did not bargain. Neither did your friend. So I will tell you what I did not tell last night. Massimo Pantaleone did not leave all his documents in the bank. He left microfilms and maps in the villa on Ponza. He took them there on our last visit—a week ago."

"But you didn't tell Woodpecker or any of your own people?"

"No. Because if Woodpecker had stolen the stuff, it would have finished me. Only Massimo and I could possibly have known the hiding place."

"Could you describe it to me?"

"No. I would have to take you there."

"I'll arrange it. You wait here, Lili. If there are any callers, don't answer. Steffi and I have a visit to make. We'll be back in an hour or so."

"I may never come back," said Steffi mournfully. "I may drown myself in the Tiber. I do not want to be alive when you try explaining this madness to the Director."

STEFFI DID NOT drown himself. He withdrew, quite deliberately, into his own yesterdays and forced me to withdraw with him, as if it were some rite I must undergo before I met Raquela Rabin. As we strolled through the alleys of the old ghetto he conjured ghosts out of every doorway, many of them friendly ghosts. But some were traitors and some were nightmare enemies.

"I would like to forget them all," said Steffi moodily. "But God keeps the key to memory in his own hands. Now I will present you to Raquela Rabin and then leave. You will come directly to the point with her and not stay too long. She is very frail."

She was frail indeed, white-haired, almost transparent. Only her eyes were alive, dark and lustrous, and strangely pitying. She sat listening in silence while I explained why I had come. I felt humbled, diminished—an ignorant neophyte in the presence of a woman who had seen and suffered everything. And when she spoke—she was very gentle with me—there was a quality of ageless wisdom in her tone that humbled me still further.

"Do you know why Bruno sent you to me?"

"No, madam."

"We were lovers for a long time. The love is still there. And he is still fighting those who took me to Auschwitz. He believes in forgiving, but not in forgetting. Strange . . ."

"Can I trust Bruno Manzini, madam?"

"To be what he is, yes. Which is a man who has built himself, cell by cell, from nothing. He is very strong, very faithful. Each year, on the anniversary of the Black Sabbath, he sends me a card. Get for me please the leather folder in that desk drawer."

When I gave it to her, she spread it open on her knees and handed me two cards—salamander cards like the one in Pantaleone's bedroom. Only the inscriptions were different.

HANS HELMUT ZIEGLER
São Paulo—3 January, 1968

EMANUELE SALATRI
London—18 August, 1971

"What do these mean, madam?"

"They are the names of men connected, each in his own way, with what happened to me and to others in 1943. I have fifteen so far. There are nine to come. Bruno Manzini traced them all, and sent each man a card and a dossier on his past."

"What do the dates mean?"

"The days on which they died."

"Who killed them?"

"They killed themselves."

"Are you happy with Bruno Manzini—a man who plays God?"

"He does not judge. Every man, he says, must be allowed to judge himself, but he must not be allowed to bury the evidence."

"And you agree, madam?"

"I do, Colonel. I hate no one now. But the terror has come again—in Vietnam, in Brazil, in Africa, here in Europe. Is not that why you have come to me—because you, too, are afraid?"

"Yes, madam, I am very much afraid."

"Then trust my Bruno, but not blindly, because then he would have no respect for you. Argue with him, fight him. You may even end as adversaries, but he will never, never betray you."

"Thank you, madam."

"Thank you for coming. I wish peace on your house and in your heart." I was grateful for the blessing, but I walked out into the sunlight a very pensive man.

I could understand Manzini and his conviction that tyrants should not be allowed to flourish; the Director and his willingness to settle for balance, however precarious; even Leporello and his fanatic belief that order at any price was cheaper than chaos. But I did not understand myself.

On the way back to Steffi's I stopped in a bar and telephoned Manzini to tell him I had seen Raquela Rabin and would like to see him. It was agreed I should go to Bologna as soon as I could.

Then I called the Director, and suppressed a sigh of relief when his aide told me he had been summoned to an urgent conference at the Ministry. No, no message I could leave him on an open line, except that there were new developments that would keep me out of contact for forty-eight hours. I knew I was only putting off the bad day; but if I could lay my hands on those files at Ponza, I might still cheat the headsman.

I was faced now with a problem in space and time. To get to the island of Ponza means a road journey south from Rome and a three- or four-hour sea trip by ferry from Anzio, Formia or Naples. But I must at all costs avoid public transport. If the

Director should have reason to send out a panic call for me, I would be as conspicuous as a wart on the Mona Lisa. Also, whoever had the stolen papers would know by now that they were incomplete, and might come looking for Lili Anders at the villa she had shared with Pantaleone. I needed help in a hurry.

By the time I got back to Steffi's, it was five-thirty. I put through a priority call to Colonel Carl Malinowski at NATO headquarters in Naples.

Malinowski is an agreeable American I'd managed to help out of an embarrassing situation involving his girl friend and a Russian agent. He owed me a favour. I needed it now, in the shape of the big Baglietto, the motor cruiser which he used for drinking parties and seduction and which could do twenty-five knots in any reasonable sea.

Malinowski was happy to oblige. He had a new girl friend who would appreciate the outing. If we cared to come to Naples tonight, he would feed us dinner and offer us a bed. Two hours later Lili and I were heading south in an unidentifiable hired car.

COLONEL CARL MALINOWSKI of the United States Marines was all brawn and muscle, with ham fists and a big laugh. He was a tonic for our spirits. His apartment was a bachelor's paradise, with a view across the Bay of Naples, a bewildering liquor cupboard, and piped music in every room. His new girl was a Swede, culled from the summer crop of tourists and blooming after the transplant. He took one look at Lili and shouted his approval to the neighbourhood.

"*Bella! Bellissima!* Dante, my boy, your taste's improving. Helga, why don't you get Lili settled while Dante and I build some drinks." He clamped an iron fist on my shoulder. "Tell me now, Colonel, is this business or pleasure?"

"Business, Carl. We've got to get to Ponza and back, fast."

"In this weather it's three hours each way—more if the wind freshens. How long do you want to stay?"

"Two hours should do it."

"O.K. We leave at six in the morning. Expecting trouble?"

"An outside chance."

"What's with you and Lili-belle?"

"Some business, some pleasure. Too much of one, not enough of the other."

"I get you. So tonight we drink and make merry!"

We did. We dined like kings on caviar, steak and Neapolitan ice cream. We drank wine and brandy. We told bawdy stories. And sometime after midnight we paired off and went to bed.

It was a good night for Lili and me. We pleased each other. We were glad, we were grateful and, for a while, not solitary. We slept deeply and we did not dream at all.

I have told it badly. I might have used the same words for a dozen encounters, because I am a man who has been fortunate in his women. But this time there was a difference, a sense of consequence if not yet of commitment. There was another difference, too. I was disposed to be sentimental afterwards, while Lili would have none of it.

She told me so bluntly, as we stood on the Baglietto's deck and watched the green cone of Ischia fade against the dawn.

"*Caro*, sometimes you treat me as if I had no brains at all. I know what's at stake. If the material at the villa is important, it puts power into your hands. You think it will also buy me a free passage out of Italy."

"I hope it will."

"I don't need you to get me out of Italy, Dante. I could hire any fisherman on Ponza to run me into Corsica tomorrow."

"What are you trying to say, Lili?"

"That you need me, as much as you need the Pantaleone records, for a bargaining card. Let me go, and you rob yourself of your ace in the hole. I understand that. But you insult me when you try to dress the thing up. Your friend Steffi was right. You refuse to come to terms with yourself. Now can we go inside, please? I'm cold."

It was cold. The wind was freshening from the northwest, whipping up an uncomfortable sea, and Malinowski was driving the boat hard. We settled ourselves in the Baglietto's saloon and I tried with some desperation to salvage the argument. "Let's have it clear, Lili. I made a treaty with you. So far I've honoured it. You're free and protected. Now you want to change it. You want me to turn a blind eye while you make a run for Corsica."

"No! I want you to be sure what kind of treaty you are making with other people, and what it will do to you in the end."

"And why the hell should you care?"

"Poor Dante! So many women and you've learned so little!"

"At least I don't have any illusions."

"Let's not argue. You write the script, you say the words, you pull the strings, and when the play's over, Lili, the puppet, is packed up in her box. Just so we know, my love."

"So that's the way you read it. Let's go up on the bridge."

"I'd like to be alone for a while."

"This is business, Lili."

"At your service, Colonel."

Malinowski welcomed us and spread out a map of Ponza. The villa was on its eastern shore, noted as a landmark for mariners: "a large square building of grey stone, due east of which the pillars and arches of a Roman ruin are clearly visible. In winds W to NW the southern inlet offers fair shelter to small vessels."

I asked Lili, "If we put in there, can we get to the villa from the beach?"

"Yes. There's a rough path that goes up to the ruins."

"The villa itself. Any servants?"

"No. Out of season it's closed up. But we don't have to go near the villa. What we want is in the ruins."

"Can you overlook the ruins from the house?"

"Only the top of them. Our domain is walled all the way round. The ruins are outside the walls, on government land."

"Better still. How close in can you anchor, Carl?"

"Let's see . . . for safety, a cable's length."

"Which will be visible from the house?"

"On the approach, yes. When we're anchored, probably not. I don't understand your problem though. The shoreline's public terrain. Anyone can land from the sea."

"I'm not worried about trespassing, Carl. Lili owns the villa anyway. Let's say I'm concerned with hostile intruders."

"Those, Colonel, we can take care of nicely." He opened a cupboard and brought out an automatic rifle. "While you and Lili-belle go ashore, I watch for hostile intruders. O.K?"

"No. I can't have an American officer involved in an Italian domestic drama. So, if you don't mind, I'll take the gun with me."

"Just as you like. Switch on the radio, will you? I'd like to catch the news and the weather."

The news was the usual mixture, until the terse postscript: an Arab had been shot dead outside the Libyan embassy. He was the Roman representative of El-Fatah, the Palestine guerrilla organization. The police assumed it was a political crime, probably organized by Israeli agents. The item made my hair stand up; this was a personal disaster. I was the SID expert on Arab-Israeli affairs. The Director *would* be pressing panic buttons and combing the country for me. If I could deliver the Pantaleone papers and Lili Anders before he found me, I might just escape the rack and thumbscrew. But if I got back empty-handed, he would rend me limb from limb and feed me to the lions in the zoo.

We reached Ponza in a driving rain, visibility terrible. At least any watchers in the villa would see nothing either. Lili and I draped ourselves in oilskins, Carl handed me the rifle and we drove the dinghy to the beach.

The path which led to the ruins was steep. We scrambled up on hands and knees. Breathless and irritable, I was convinced that either Pantaleone was mad to have hidden the documents in such a place or Lili had deliberately led me on a fool's errand. I said as much. She took me by the hand and led me through a mouldering archway into a vault which had somehow withstood the ravages of the centuries. The outer walls were stone, but the inner ones were brick. The floor was paved with marble, cracked and sagging but mostly intact. Lili threw back the hood of her oilskins and surveyed the shadowy interior.

The brickwork of the walls revealed nothing. I tested the floor for hollow spaces. Again nothing. Lili grinned. She moved to a small sunken patch of floor where the rain driving in through the archway had created a puddle. She knelt down and with her bare hands eased up a piece of marble about the size of my palm. "Like a bath plug, eh, Dante? You didn't walk in the puddle, but even if you had, the floor would have sounded solid. Massimo was not as stupid as he looked."

She plunged her fingers into the aperture and drew out a long aluminium tube, sealed at both ends with black adhesive tape.

"It is exactly as we left it. The maps and the microfilms are inside."

"There's nothing else?"

"Nothing." She replaced the marble piece.

"Let's go. You carry the tube."

"Not even a thank-you for puppet Lili?"

"Thank you, puppet Lili. Follow me out of here. Then on the beach track you go first."

I released the safety catch on the rifle and stopped to scan the narrow vista framed by the archway. All I could see was the rise of the land and the base of the wall surrounding the villa. So far, so good. I moved closer to the entrance so that the vista widened and the top of the wall became visible. Then I heard a shout, amplified and distorted by a bullhorn. "You, in there! Come out with your hands up. This is the carabinieri."

I snatched the tube from Lili. "Stay close. Say nothing." And holding the rifle and the tube high above my head, I walked through the archway with Lili at my heels. Twenty yards away, just outside my last field of vision, there were five men. Four were in uniform and armed with submachine guns. The fifth, with the bullhorn, was in civilian clothes. I recognized him immediately: the freckle-faced redhead I'd seen at the Hassler, aide to Major General Leporello. He recognized me, too, and the expression on his face gave me a singular pleasure.

The troops began to close in, guns cocked. I let them come to within five metres before I halted them in my best parade-ground style. Then I said, "I will identify myself in proper form. I am Dante Matucci, colonel in the Service of Defence Information. The person with me is Lili Anders, in my custody and assisting me in highly secret investigations. Now we shall lower our hands, and the officer in command will approach to check my documents and explain the situation."

The shaken young man found voice and gave me a tentative salute. "Captain Matteo Roditi, aide to Major General Leporello. Your papers, please, sir?" He made a great play of reading them, then handed them back. "Thank you, sir. The situation, sir, is as follows. I am under orders from General Leporello to maintain surveillance of the Villa Pantaleone and its environs, and to inhibit any attempt to remove property from the premises. In pursuance of these orders I am empowered to call upon the assistance of local units."

"May I see those orders, please, Captain?"

"Certainly, sir."

I took a little longer than I needed to study them. Then I quizzed him, loud enough for the local boys to hear. "It would appear, Captain, that you have misread these orders."

"Sir?"

"The orders refer exclusively to, and I quote, 'the villa and the domain dependent thereon which is called the Villa Pantaleone'. You will note that the land on which we are now standing and the ruins at my back are outside the domain and are, in fact, public property. Therefore you have exceeded your orders. You have placed a senior officer of SID and the person in his custody at considerable risk. One incautious move by your troops might have caused a fatal accident. You do see that."

"Respectfully, I submit the danger was minimal."

"No doubt that submission will be considered at the proper time and place. Anything else, Captain?"

"No, sir."

"My compliments to General Leporello. I shall telephone him on my return to Rome. Dismiss! Come, Miss Anders."

It is hard to make it down a slippery path in the rain, carrying a rifle and a long tube of documents. In point of fact, we slid the last thirty feet and floundered into the dinghy like seals.

By the time we reached the Baglietto, I was sweating from every pore and Lili was retching. Helga hauled us aboard; Carl had the anchor up and was charging seaward before I had poured our first brandy. Lili lay on the settee while I forced the liquor between her chattering teeth. She stared at me as if I were a stranger. "They were going to kill us!"

"They didn't, Lili. And they can't touch us now."

"Not now. But tomorrow, the day after . . ."

"Finish your drink. Relax now . . . relax."

"I don't know you at all, Dante. Your face changes all the time. I can't tell which one is yours."

"I'm a bad actor, that's all: Trust me, *bambina*."

"I have to. There's no one else."

She lay quiet then, and the surge of the sea made her dozy. I stripped the seals from the metal tube. I found a set of overlay maps on transparent paper, each labelled with the name of a city and references to standard ordnance maps, and half a dozen metal capsules, each containing a spool of microfilm. The maps showed the positions of police posts, military installations, communications centres, traffic control points, military and civilian airfields. The microfilms were impossible to decipher without projection equipment. However, with the boat's chart enlarger I could see that they consisted of documents, letters, lists of figures and of names. I had no doubt these supplied motive enough for the murders in the Via Sicilia. They were, in fact, the blueprints of a *colpo di stato*. It would need an expert to interpret them—and a very wise statesman to decide how to use them. I went up on the bridge to talk to Carl.

"How much fuel have you got? Enough to get us to Ostia?"

"Ostia! That wasn't on the schedule at all! Why?"

"Because I've just identified a murderer, and we could have been murdered ourselves. I've got to get to Rome fast."

"So we go to Ostia. Take five while I lay me a course."

While he was playing with his slide rule I sent a coded message to the Director by ship-to-shore radio. I'd need a car and armed escort from Ostia, an emergency conference immediately on our arrival at Rome, and a guard for Lili Anders. Forty minutes later I had the Director's answer:

"Communication acknowledged. Arrangements agreed."

We have code words for thanks and commendations. He didn't use them. Under the circumstances I could hardly blame him.

THE DIRECTOR was extremely civil, if a little frosty at first, but he thawed like ice in whisky when I handed over the maps and the microfilms. He lodged Lili Anders, with protection, at the Grand Hotel and took me to dinner at his apartment. He commended me for my imagination, my finesse, my courage in risking my career and perhaps my life to conclude an important investigation. He saw good sense in my suspicions of Leporello, although he was not yet ready to pass judgment. He sat with me through a screening of the microfilms, and he read the maps. At the end of the session, which lasted until midnight, he ordered fresh coffee, brought out his best brandy and offered me the rewards of virtue.

"This Lili Anders—I agree with your estimate," he said. "She has done us a service. She is no longer a security risk. She could be an embarrassment. Let's get her out of the country—tomorrow."

"Very good, sir."

"As to your own future, Matucci, how much leave have you accumulated?"

"About four months."

"I'd like you to take it, now. After you return I propose to detach you for extended studies with agencies abroad. You will have the best possible introductions, a flexible schedule, and your pay and allowances will be supplemented by a generous grant from the funds of this service. How does that sound?"

"Like an obituary notice."

The Director smiled and spread his elegant hands in a gesture of deprecation. "My dear Matucci! You will not be dead, just buried for a while enjoying yourself till resurrection day."

"No alternatives?"

"There are always alternatives, my friend. I could retain you on the Leporello investigation, in which case you would be a prime target for assassination. Or I could return you to your own corps of carabinieri, under the direct authority of General Leporello. He knows you for a nuisance. He may consider you a threat."

"I see what you mean."

"You see everything except the core of the apple."

"Which is?"

"You know too much. You lack the authority and—forgive me— the experience to make use of the knowledge."

"And . . . ?"

"And you would be very unwilling to make a deal with political conspirators, however high they stood."

"Exactly."

"So, because I respect you and want to be in a position to recall you at an appropriate time, I immobilize you. I offer you as a propitiatory victim to powerful people—and so buy myself time to deal with them."

"I couldn't ask for a more stylish funeral."

"Excellent. Some more brandy? As of this moment you are on vacation. You will escort Lili Anders to Zurich tomorrow morning. The service has no further interest in her, provided she does not attempt to re-enter the republic. Your flight has been booked. A reservation has been made for you at the Hotel Baur au Lac. You yourself will remain outside Italy for at least a month. It's all a little rushed, but I am sure you will find the financial arrangements more than generous. . . . Questions?"

"No. Just a minor worry. I'd hate to spend a long vacation waiting for a bullet in the back. I'd much rather stay on duty where there's a certain amount of protection."

"The whole purpose of this tactic is to demonstrate that you are no longer a threat to Leporello or anyone else, and that action against you would violate your very useful neutrality. . . . There is a danger period, however: from the moment you leave this house until you take off for Zurich. So I've assigned a two-man team to cover you. They've already packed your clothes and delivered the suitcases to the Grand Hotel, where your room adjoins Miss Anders's. You will leave the hotel together at eight-thirty. Now . . . two air tickets, ten thousand Swiss francs and an order on the Union Bank in Zurich for another twenty thousand. That's a bonus, with my personal thanks. Your salary will be credited in the normal way to your bank account. . . . That's all, I think. My car is waiting for you. I wish you a pleasant vacation. *Sogni d'oro*, Matucci—golden dreams."

We parted with a handshake, firm and fraternal. I was escorted from his door to the Grand Hotel like a visiting potentate.

It was after midnight. The foyer was deserted. Two Sicilian bodyguards installed me in my bedroom, checking inside cupboards and under the beds and pointing out that the key to the *signora's* room was on my side of the communicating door. Then they bade me good night and retired like lackeys from the presence of a prince.

Perhaps they were right. I was the Director's man, bought and paid for. His brand was on my head, his money in my pocket, his gift sleeping next door. Still, give the devil his due, he was a rare specimen. Never once had he suggested that I was making a slave's bargain. He knew it, of course. So did I. Which is why I could not go to Lili, but instead lay dressed and wakeful, scheming revolt.

At dawn I abandoned the futile exercise and went to Lili Anders. The Director had told her nothing, so at six o'clock in the morning I was forced to explain the whole complicated play. She was so delighted to be going to her liberty in Switzerland, and to be going with me, that I had no heart to tell her the price. From the moment I left Italy I would be, in effect, an exile.

Our exit from Italy was impressive. Limousine, VIP lounge at Fiumicino Airport, escorts all the way to our first-class seats. Airborne then, and in the care of the Swiss, we held hands and made foolish jokes and toasted each other with champagne.

At the Baur au Lac we were accommodated in a three-room suite, compléte with flowers, fruit, liquor, a welcome note from the management and a telegram from the Director. Second Samuel Seven One, it said. I deciphered his joke, from the Bible on my bedside table: "The Lord gave him rest from all his enemies."

By that evening the joke was becoming too bitter. I had to make an end of it and tell Lili the truth.

The moment of telling had a curious quality about it. We had decided to dine in the suite. I was mixing drinks, feeling very domestic, remote, as if I were recovering from a long illness. I heard myself speak as if I were listening to another man.

"Everything the Director says is true and yet it all adds up to a lie. He conjures you into a world that doesn't exist and makes you believe it—shows you another self and makes you believe it's you. 'You lack authority, Matucci. You lack experience. You are not dead, just buried for a while.' But I knew, the moment I stepped on that plane, I was dead; because he has all my files now and he can reprocess history in any way he chooses. Suppose he wants to conquer, to play Fouché to Leporello's Napoleon and like that opportunist chief of police betray and succeed his superior? I've given him all the weapons he needs, and he paid me for them—with this long holiday."

"Why did you accept it, Dante? Because I was part of it?"

"No. I believe he'd have let you go anyway, might have worked to set you against me—he spins the web so fine. I don't know . . . but last night, working with him on the documents, I enjoyed him and respected him—because he respected me. So when he gave me his reasons for my stepping out, I had to respect those, too. But after I had agreed, he had to show me how clever he was; how he was so certain of my consent that he had arranged everything in advance—even to the roses in your bedroom. Suddenly I was not a man anymore, I was—"

"A puppet, my love. It's a bitter experience, isn't it?"

"The joke of the century! Dante Matucci, the clown puppet! That's his final triumph, don't you see? He's probably spread the news all over the service."

"I'd like to see how it ends."

"This *is* the end, Lili. Don't you understand that?"

"It's the end he wrote. I think there's a better one."

"I'd love to hear it."

"The puppet becomes a man, scrapes off the clown's paint and rides out to confront his enemy."

"It's a fairy tale, Lili."

"No! It's a truth. Remember that salamander card? 'One fine tomorrow, brother.' Telephone Bruno Manzini, my love. Now."

The idea was seductive. But I was still gun-shy and suspicious. True, there was Raquela Rabin, his proof of good faith. Manzini had invited my trust. But if he betrayed me, then I was truly lost beyond redemption. The jurisdiction of money is universal.

I argued this with Lili—the new Lili who had flowered overnight into another woman, serene, mature, wholly confident.

"What have you to lose?" she said. "Nothing. What have you to gain? At best a powerful friend; at least an alliance of interest that you can dissolve at will. Most important of all, you will have begun to fight."

To put the call through to Bologna was easy. To get Manzini on the line was only less difficult than having a Sunday chat with the pope. Finally I took a risk and used the magical name of the service. It worked. I told him the story of Ponza, of the records I had delivered to the Director, of the current situation.

There was a moment's silence, then a series of brusque questions.

"Have you yourself examined the records?" Manzini began.

"Yes."

"Important?"

"As you suggested in Rome."

338

"Do you know what will happen to them now?"

"Only what might happen. There are several possibilities."

"Which you can no longer control."

"Precisely."

"Do you need assistance, financial or otherwise?"

"I need the man Raquela Rabin recommended, provided, of course, he is still available."

"He is. He will be at the Dolder Grand in Zurich tomorrow evening. Are you in good health?"

"Our mutual friend assures me I have nothing to fear."

"He would know, of course."

"Yes. But he never tells all he knows."

"Remember it, my friend. Walk close to the wall."

"Thank you, Cavaliere. . . . Good night."

When I put down the phone I was trembling. I was truly afraid now. The old man's parting words had demolished the last frail illusion of security. I was a stranger in a foreign land, a member of a legal underworld, suspect everywhere and nowhere loved. I could be shot down on any street corner with no fuss. In that moment I tasted the full, fine Florentine flavour of the Director's revenge. Lili held me close while she whispered over and over, "One fine tomorrow, brother . . ."

Tomorrow was a gift of God: no wind, no cloud, the lake dazzling under the spring sun, snow on the uplands, the lower meadows ankle-deep in spring grass. I hired a car and we drove into Graubünden, aimless and happy as a honeymoon pair. Lili sang, clowned, played word games and love games and built dream houses. And for the first time I really saw her: the honey colour of her hair, the high Slavic cheekbones flushed with wind and excitement, the little flecks of gold in her eyes, the half smile that haunted the corners of her mouth, even the first faint touch of time in the texture of her skin. She was no girl, this Lili. She had lived too strangely for too long. But I was no boy either; and I was tired of baby talk and lovers' lies.

We lunched in a mountain inn on cheese soufflé and a thin, sparkling wine. We talked of the future and Lili assessed her own without resentment.

"I am on file now. Any policeman can harass me like a street-walker. So I have to be careful. If I live modestly and soberly, I may be able to live in peace in Switzerland for a long while. If I married, it would be different. I would have a new civil status and a new life. So I have to think of that . . . but not yet. I have enough money for two years of simple living. And I can sell the villa on Ponza. Massimo told me he had provided for me, but even if his will is found I can base nothing on it, as I can never return to Italy. Still, I am very lucky. Lucky in you, too, my love. I did not believe you would have so much concern for me."

"I didn't believe I'd ever need a woman in this way. To be calm, to prove nothing, just to be glad she's in the room. What would you say if I asked you to spend this month with me?"

"I would say yes, but I would also say let it be as it is now—one hour, one day at a time."

"One day at a time. Good."

"And when you go away, as you must, and find yourself lonely, come back. You must be very free now. You have to begin to know the man who lives in your skin."

"I'm afraid of him, Lili."

"So one day you must confront him in the mirror. After that, please God, you will be able to be happy."

"I hope so. But there is something that must be said, Lili. If a day should come when you have to choose between me and yourself, consider your own interest first. I would want that."

"I don't understand."

"Listen, *bambina!* We are not lodged here by people who want us to be happy. We are to become so tied to each other that a threat to one could be used as pressure on the other. The Director may be convinced he has bought me, but he also buys insurance against my cheating on the contract. You see?"

"I do. And I want you to cheat him. Tell me—you never name this man, the Director. Why?"

"A rule of the game that has become second nature. But there is another reason. This is a very attractive man. He can seduce you with a smile, a handshake, a show of confidence and infinite good sense. That talent was bred into him through twenty generations. I envy it, I am awed by it, and I have grown afraid of it. So I force myself to think of him not as a man, but as a function, like the pope or the president. That way I can cope with him."

"Perhaps the day will come when you will be able to name the two in one breath—the man who lives in your skin, and the other of whom you are still afraid."

"Am I so great a coward, Lili?"

"There is one fear that makes each of us a coward."

"And what is yours?"

"The little room, the light shining in my eyes, the questions and the blows that come from nowhere. You saved me from that, and there is nothing I would not do to repay you."

"We're both rewarded, *cara*. Today is enough. We should go back now. It's an hour and a half to Zurich."

THAT EVENING Bruno Manzini received me in his opulent suite at the Dolder Grand. His greeting was warm, but from the moment I entered he was reading me by stance and attitude and intonation. "You are changed, Colonel."

"How so, Cavaliere?"

"You are more loose, more forthcoming. I would guess you had found yourself a good woman and a new crop of courage."

"Both true."

"A drink?"

"Whisky, please."

He served me himself, and I noticed that he drank very lightly. He raised his glass in a toast. "Health, money and love—"

"And time to enjoy them, sir."

"That above all, Colonel. Now, tell me all that has happened since we met in Rome."

I told him all—up to and including my arrival in Zurich with Lili Anders and the relationship which had begun to mature between us. As I did so his eyes never left my face. There was a long silence before he began the questions. "So, you are convinced that Major General Leporello has allied himself with the neo-Fascists?"

"I am convinced that he is a candidate for such an alliance."

"You infer, then, that he ordered the murders of the lawyer, Bandinelli, and your agent, Calvi, and the theft of the Pantaleone papers."

"There is a case to be investigated. Leporello knew, from me, where the papers were. Whoever had the papers would have seen instantly that they were incomplete, and he would take steps to trace the remainder. It was Leporello's aide who was on Ponza."

"What is the ground of dispute between you and your Director?"

"I asked for an investigation of Leporello. He deferred it. I disobeyed a direct order and made contact with Leporello."

"In effect then you may be responsible for two murders and the theft of vital documents."

"I believe I am responsible."

"So the Director is justified in having taken you off the case."

"If he did it on disciplinary grounds, yes."

"You suggest he had other reasons?"

"He stated them clearly: I lacked the authority and experience to deal with a complex political situation, and I was a convenient victim who would buy him time."

"Good reasons or bad?"

"Eminently sound."

"So what is your quarrel with him?"

"I have no quarrel, no valid objection. But I said it to his face and I say it still. I do not trust him. He said to me, 'I don't want dictatorship. I don't want Marxism. I'm sure the kind of democracy we have is too unstable to last. But, come one or the other, I'll try to make it as tolerable as I can'."

"A laudable ambition, surely?"

"That depends on the interpretation. He added, 'I am king on the board and you are a pawn'."

"You would prefer to be king, no doubt?"

"I would like to be a servant of an open society."

"But you joined a closed service, more subject than any to the corruption of secrecy. Why?"

"Because I think I have a talent for investigation."

"And a taste for influence without responsibility?"

"No. I like responsibility."

"And you resent the fact that you can no longer exercise it?"

"Yes. But what I resent most is that the man who can, at a whim, make me less than I am can also, if he chooses, bury, manipulate or trade information that may determine the political future of this country. My country, and yours."

342

"Can you be bought, Colonel?"

"I was, forty-eight hours ago."

"Can you be frightened?"

"I am frightened now. I know too much. And I'm isolated."

"And who would want to eliminate you?"

"The Director for one. Leporello for another. Or—and this is the real nightmare—both, working together. Acting in concert they could be very formidable very quickly."

"And what did you think I could do about this?"

"Advise me how to use what I know to prevent a *colpo di stato*."

"What knowledge do you have, Matucci?"

"I know every name on the Pantaleone microfilms, every document, every map. I have a photographic memory, Cavaliere."

"Does the Director know that?"

"Yes."

"Then he told you the truth. You are a natural victim."

"And you, Cavaliere?"

"I, too, told you the truth. We are natural allies. But you will have to accept that it will be—what did you call it?—a lopsided league. I have everything you lack—influence, money, friends, Also I'm old and obstinate. I hold the advantage."

"I understand that and accept it."

"There is one more condition. This Lili Anders is a danger to you, an embarrassment for me, since she was my brother's mistress. Pay her off and forget her."

"I can't do that, Cavaliere."

"I insist on it, if we are to work together."

"You offer me the same stale bargain as the Director. Submit and be safe. The market's closed." I rose. "And if you'll excuse me—"

"Sit down, man! The game is over."

"I beg your pardon."

"I offered you a shabby contract, my friend. Had you consented, I would have sold you myself to the assassins. Now, ring the bell, please. I think we are ready to dine."

THE MAN WHO SAT WITH ME at dinner that night was a phenomenon. He was in his seventies, yet he bubbled like champagne. He talked books, women, painting, money, fashion, religion, wine and the growing of roses. He enjoyed. He savoured. Between the fruit and the cheese he opened a new line of talk.

"We are all inheritors, Matucci, and we can no more shed our past than we can slough off our skins. You and I, for instance, have begun a friendship. But you will never understand me unless you remember that I was born in an attic above Zia Rosa's brothel, on the Feast of the Assumption of the Virgin, which is the day the acrobats came to town. You are curious? . . . I'm glad. I will tell you of my birthday.

"On that feast day in 1900, Matucci, my mother was in labour in that attic, with Zia Rosa's sister Angela—later my nurse—as midwife. Down in the *piazza*—and this I know, because Angela was watching—Luca Salamandra, the high-wire walker, was about to begin his pilgrimage across the sky. Dressed all in black, with plastered hair and curled moustaches, he climbed to the little platform on top of the pole and saluted the cheering crowds. He stepped onto the wire. The crowd fell silent. He moved slowly, testing the tension of the cable. Then halfway across he flipped into a somersault and landed upright on the swaying cable. He was, perhaps, five metres from the end of the wire when he stopped, staring straight into Angela's eyes. She remembers him smiling at her, beginning to walk towards her. . . . At which precise moment, Matucci, my mother screamed and I poked my reluctant head into the world and Luca Salamandra toppled into eternity.

"Ten days later a woman in deep mourning, with an elderly companion, presented herself at the registry office to deposit a set of notarized documents. The first was a certificate of marriage between Anne Mary Mackenzie and Luca Salamandra. The second was the surgeon's certificate of the death of Luca Salamandra. The third was a notification of the birth of Massimo Luca Salamandra. This extraordinary collection of documents was the result of a long discussion between Anne Mary Mackenzie and Zia Rosa, followed by three hours' hard bargaining among Angela, Zia Rosa and Aldo the Calligrapher, an elderly forger of legendary skill. The registry clerk accepted the documents without question, with the result that Anne Mary Mackenzie became a respectable Roman widow, and I was endowed with a spurious legitimacy.

"That is my story, Matucci. It is also a parable. I was sired by a

344

nobleman, fathered by a dead acrobat. I am, and always have been, a contradiction. And you, now, are the man on the tightrope. You want to save yourself and serve a very divided country and a very contentious people. You will need steady nerves, because you, too, will see monsters borning—and if you slip once, you are dead. I hope you understand that."

"I do. But where do we begin?"

"You are under orders not to return to Italy for a month. We use that month to take out some insurance of our own. Tomorrow morning at nine you and Lili Anders will check out of the Baur au Lac. A limousine will take you to a house in Liechtenstein which belongs to one of my companies. A converted hunting lodge, quite comfortable. There you will record everything you know of the Pantaleone affair, the microfilms, the maps—everything. This material will be copied and lodged in banks inside and outside Italy. During this same month you will receive other material from me which will prepare you for your return to Italy. We shall, of course, remain in close personal contact. You will have two of my staff on constant call as guards and couriers."

"And when I go back to Italy?"

"I shall offer you substantial fees as a consultant on economic intelligence. Of course, I shall make it my business to secure your Director's approval."

"Are you sure he will give it?"

"Why not? It will give him another possible means of compromising you. He will take it that you are, as he hopes, a venal man, easily bought and silenced. Under this cover you will continue to investigate Leporello's connection with the new Fascist movement. You will report your findings to me, and we will agree on a course of action. Does that make sense to you?"

"With one reservation. I have seen the Director write similar scripts. I do not believe he will buy this one."

"Nor I. But he will try to make us believe he has bought it. The real problem is rather different; we have to keep you alive."

THE HUNTING LODGE was built at the neck of a high valley, accessible only by a single road which ended at a massive pine gate slung between pillars of hewn stone. Inside the gate a paved driveway wound through tall trees to the lodge itself, a long, sandstone building, raftered with logs and roofed with zinc on timber.

Outside it looked unwelcoming, ready to withstand invasion or avalanche. Inside it was warm, with firelight gleaming on panelled walls and polished copper and peasant pottery. The house was kept by an elderly Tyrolese and his wife, and there were two other staff: Heinz, a taciturn fellow from Graubünden canton who was a deadly shot with a rifle, and Domenico, a swarthy young Varesino accomplished in pistol and karate. One of them was always on duty. Each evening the gates were locked and a complicated series of alarms was set. There was a telephone in the house, but we were warned not to use it. We could walk freely within the estate, but only with Heinz or Domenico in attendance.

For the first few days I felt caged and restless; but Lili scolded me into relaxation and a simple routine of work. Each morning I settled down to the task of reconstructing from memory the material on the microfilms. It was an exhausting job on which I could concentrate for only about four hours a day. The rest of the time I spent annotating the dispatches which arrived each day by mail from Bruno Manzini.

All the dispatches were posted from Chiasso, which is the frontier town of the Swiss canton of Ticino. The information was codified and covered everything from the organization and control of labour unions to the financial structure and principal directors of large companies; from investment holdings by foreign organizations to the private histories of prominent functionaries and a schedule of their visits to Greece and Spain; from the makeup of Marxist cells to the finances of the Vatican. I had been in the intelligence trade for a long time, but much of this was new even to me. I was impressed with the organization that must have collected it all, and, as I read, was more and more in awe at the complexity of Italian life. The tension was so high, the balance of forces so precarious, that no one could ignore the daily threat of disaster.

I understood vividly the frustration of the revolutionary who wanted to sweep the whole mess away and begin again. I understood the despair of the young who wanted to drop out and live in fraternal simplicity. I understood the seductive illusion of a dictator who could impose order and unity with a wave of his sceptre.

346

More slowly, I began to see the meaning of Bruno Manzini's belief that we were all prisoners of our genes and our history, and that our future was written by scribes long perished. And I was oppressed. What right had I to try to determine a single line of that future?

In those desert days Lili was an oasis of comfort. She refused to be put out by my snappishness. She lavished tenderness on me and shamed me back into sanity. "I know how you feel, my love. You and I will pass, and the horror of the world will still remain. But think of this—while we are still fighting, we hold it back, if only for a little while. If everyone gave up the fight, the barbarians would take over for another thousand years. Even if we are ignorant and misguided, the cause is still good. You must never let yourself forget that."

And our love was good; but it was haunted, too, by the thought that all too soon it must end. I was the cord that tied her to the past; the cord must be snapped before she could be wholly free. There was no hope for either of us in a daydream future, but the thought of lonely tomorrows weighed heavily on us both and our days and nights were the more precious because of it.

We had been at the lodge about two weeks when Bruno Manzini came to visit us. He took my notes and retired, joining us only for a drink before dinner.

"I've studied your notes, Matucci. Excellent! But very disturbing. Have you made any sense out of the stuff I've sent you?"

"Some, yes. I'd like to discuss it with you after dinner."

"That's why I'm here. We will shut you out, young lady, but you are going to forgive me in advance; because the more you know, the more you are at risk." He put his arm around Lili and toasted her with old-fashioned gallantry, then launched into a cascade of reminiscences that swept us from soup to coffee.

Afterwards, when we were alone, with the brandy warming in our hands, he said, "Things are bad, Matucci. Take this business last week of Bessarione. The police say he blew himself up while attempting to sabotage a power pylon. The Left say he was framed and assassinated by the Right. I knew him—a wealthy romantic and a very good publisher. What's the truth? Who knows? At least it should be open to public debate. Instead, we arrest journalists and students in the old Fascist dragnet: 'Spreading news calculated to disturb public order': Result? More division. More unrest. The Fascists blame the Marxists, the Marxists blame the Fascists. In the middle are the people—they can't get educated because we don't build enough schools, and when they're sick they're lined up three-deep in hospital wards. They can't get to work and back because of bus strikes, and they live on a dungheap when the garbage collectors are on strike.

"Even the markets are beginning to panic. If I told you how much money went out of the country last week, you'd weep, Matucci. And now I'm on notice to rush my deliveries of riot equipment. What I cannot make I am to buy, borrow or steal. So how does it add up? The Marxists can, and maybe will, disrupt the country, but they are not ready to mount a military coup. The Right could, given enough support from the Centre and from the Church.

"Your notes confirm all this, Matucci. But they tell more; my half-brother planned better than I knew. His strategy is valid, and—I've kept this till last—Leporello has made his deal. He has stepped into Pantaleone's shoes."

"And the Director?"

"Has joined him. They had a meeting last weekend at Prince Baldassare's villa."

"How do you know this?"

"I was there, too. The Director invited me because they wanted me to join the club. I agreed, of course. A natural union, when you come to think of it. Heavy industry, textiles, newspapers, banking, and a stable government pledged to law and order."

"Why had they never asked you before?"

"Pantaleone wouldn't hear of it then. And they needed him more than me. But now they knew all about my connection with my brother, so the time was ripe for a civilized arrangement. Don't you think so?"

"I think, Bruno Manzini, that I am going quietly mad."

"Not yet, please, Matucci. I need you very sane. I joined to be inside the conspiracy. I want this precious junta broken and brought down. I believe between us we can do it, by convicting Leporello of murder and the Director of conspiracy with a murderer. Could you do that?"

"I'd be willing to try. But I think we need a new script."

"We'll discuss that in a moment. Do you have any conditions?"

"Only that I conduct the affair in my own way, without interference. And with help from you as I need it. But I have one request, that's all."

"Name it."

"From the moment we leave this place I want Lili Anders protected. If I succeed in the job, I want amnesty for her, from the President, so she may be free to re-enter Italy if she chooses. Can you guarantee that?"

"No. But I'd break my back to procure it."

"That's all, then. Now let's talk about the script."

"My dear Colonel, did we not agree, in Zurich, on that?"

"We did. But the circumstances are different. Your being inside the club colours any public relationship I have with you."

"May I suggest that the colours make a better camouflage?"

"You may suggest what you like. I need proof."

"Let me try to give it to you. During the weekend at the Villa Baldassare your name was mentioned several times. The Director, with his usual delicacy, said you were a nuisance. Leporello used the words 'grave risk'. The Director said you were immobilized. Leporello said he required the risk eliminated."

"To which you replied?"

"That as a very intelligent senior officer you had probably taken certain precautions, such as lodging documents in a bank for publication in the event of your death. I suggested that an untimely accident might demoralize your colleagues in the service. I then ventured a small fiction and said that after your arrival in Switzerland you telephoned me and asked whether I could find a place for you in my organization, saying that you had been badly treated and were thinking of resigning your commission. I told the Director I had invited you here to discuss the matter and that it might be a good idea if I offered you temporary employment while he still retained you under his authority. In sum, I persuaded him that you were safer alive than dead, for the moment. Leporello did not agree. The Director overrode him—for how long I don't know. However, the arrangement depends on your consent. You may prefer to operate in secret and without any overt connection with me."

"If I work underground, I am constantly on the run. I prefer to work openly as your employee, but I might expose you to risk."

"I've faced that already. So tomorrow I telephone the Director that I want to employ you on trial and ask his permission to bring you back to Italy with me."

"So soon?"

"The answer's in your own notes. There is very little time."

"I haven't finished the notes yet."

"Finish them at my house near Bologna. I'll be lodging you."

"What do I tell Lili?"

"Whatever she needs to keep her happy. I'll instruct her on the security arrangements, you handle the love passages."

"Talking of love passages, Cavaliere—what is your exact relationship with the Principessa Faubiani?"

"And how the devil does that concern you?"

"I have to ask, Cavaliere. I've known several good men talked to death in bed."

He stared at me for a long, hostile moment. Then he smiled. "Let's say that I'm a wealthy patron who has visitor's privileges. But I take your point, Matucci. The lady does gossip. Perhaps I should introduce you and let you judge for yourself. I also have other relationships. Do you propose to intrude on them all?"

"If my life is involved, yes."

"We do snarl at each other! Well, I need an argument occasionally to keep me honest. Good night, friend!"

Later I told Lili, as she and I lay in the dark, the promises I had exacted to keep her safe and claim amnesty for her.

"No!" she exclaimed, to my surprise. "Don't you see? You tie me to the past. And to yourself in a way I do not want. When you come to me again—if you come—you will visit me in my house, drink my wine, eat at my table. I will not be empty-handed as I am now. I need that, my love. And you must be free, too, to choose other women. You'll be doing work you can't do with a divided mind. Now, please, let's not be tense and desperate."

SOMEWHERE, IN THE SMALL DARK HOURS, the alarm went off—an ear-shattering noise of bells and sirens. I ran to the window. The grounds blazed with floodlights, and I saw Heinz and Domenico loping towards the pinewoods. We threw on dressing-gowns and hurried downstairs, where we found Manzini, erect and calm, staring into the night. It was impossible to speak against the noise until, in about twenty minutes, Domenico hurried back and switched off the system and reset it.

"We got him, Cavaliere," he reported. "Up on the northern boundary. Heinz killed him with the first shot."

"Who was he?"

"Italian, I think. No papers, no identifying marks. He had grenades, plastic explosive, fuses and a Walther pistol."

"How did he get in?"

"He had to come over the mountain on foot. We might be able to trace his route when the sun comes up."

"Not worth the trouble. Bury him."

When Domenico had gone, Manzini poured three glasses of brandy and passed one to each of us. His hand was steady as he raised his glass in salute. "Like the old partisan days, Matucci, which you were too young to remember."

He meant it as a battle cry. To me it sounded like an epitaph.

WE DID not go directly into Italy, but drove by way of Salzburg, where Manzini wanted to discuss a lumber contract with an Austrian mill, and then down through the Brenner Pass and on to Mestre, where one of his companies was building a dry dock for small tankers. It was a tedious journey. Because of heavy snowfalls north and south of the Alps, the roads were a mess of churned snow and dangerous ice.

Manzini talked business. "You will stay for a few days at my place outside Bologna, Matucci. Then I suggest you establish yourself in my Milan apartment. You will need a bank account, credit facilities, and a cover story for your activities in my employ."

"I'll also need a list of safe houses and two or three sets of papers. The best forgeries."

"I know the best forger in the business."

"Yes. Carlo Metaponte, who engraved your salamander. He's on our files. Usable if you can control him."

"I can control him. Matucci, will you try to be generous with me? Your father was an old-line Socialist, exiled to Lipari. Mine was an old-line aristocrat who exploited the poor. But when you were thirteen years old, I was making petrol bombs in a barn. When you were fourteen, I was hung by my thumbs in a Gestapo cell in Milan. What I fought for then, you are trying to preserve now—a liberty, however precarious and imperfect. I cannot risk what you risk because I have only the tag end of a life. But I savour every second of it. This is—how can I tell it?—a plea that we should enjoy this fight. Go down, if we must; survive, if we can, singing and shouting. Can you understand that?"

"I can. I do. I'm grateful, Cavaliere."

"Please! I am Bruno now. And you are Dante. *Bene?*"

"Bene, grazie!"

"And I want you to develop some style, my Dante. New uniforms. New suits, too, the best fashion. And don't be mean with money; spread it like sauce on spaghetti. Good! That's the first time I've heard you laugh like a happy man!"

But he must still play the conjurer. Tonight, he announced, we would stay, not in Mestre but across the water in Venice, at the Gritti Palace—and the Director would join us for dinner. After all the charm he had spent on me, I had to take this trick with grace.

"You have to confront him sometime. Better with me than alone. Better in his own city, where he feels most a prince. You will be courteous, reserved, but not insensible of his magnanimity. He will goad you, you will fight back. He will ask you about Lili Anders. But you will shrug her off, a ripe peach tasted and thrown away. When you want to leave, say you have to meet a woman in Harry's Bar. You do, in fact. Ask the barman for Gisela Pestalozzi. She will be on your list of safe houses. You will say that the Salamander sent you. Clear?"

"Clear. Except how you manage it all."

"It's a game, Dante. One of the few I can still play well."

Domenico drove us to Venice in the early dark. He parked the car, and we took a gondola to the Gritti, where we were welcomed like mediæval cardinals and lodged in adjoining suites.

At dinner the Director received me like the prodigal son. "My dear Matucci! Delighted! Filthy weather, isn't it?"

I agreed it was; but Venice was still Venice after all.

Manzini asked him if he had invested in a little project he had recommended, and snorted when the Director replied he'd bought a Picasso instead. "You should have waited for the Pantaleone collection to come on the market," he said.

"If you are interested in painting, Matucci," the Director said, "take my advice. Collect the young ones. If you have a good eye, you can't fail to pick at least one in ten, and you'll still make a profit. Wouldn't you say, Bruno?"

"I want him interested in my profits first. That's the quickest way he'll make them for himself. He has already made some intelligent suggestions. If he can put them into action, I'll be prepared to bid very high for him."

"Provided, my dear Bruno, that the service is prepared to waive claims on his valuable talents. Still, I'm glad to see him have this opportunity. I owe you some thanks, Matucci. You behaved well in a difficult situation. We've made a few changes at headquarters since you left."

"Oh?"

"Gonzaga takes the Middle East desk. We've retired Stefanelli from forensics. He was getting too old and crotchety. . . . Ah, the menu! . . . What do you recommend, Bruno?"

"My dear fellow, I never recommend food, horses or women. By the way, have you recovered the Pantaleone will?"

"No. Which reminds me, Matucci. We were lucky about the lawyer, Bandinelli. It appears his wife was having an affair with a young singer. She was only too pleased to consent to a quiet funeral."

"I'm afraid I didn't handle that situation very well, sir."

"You were under a big strain. Let's order, shall we?"

I was glad of the respite and the small talk that came with the food. They were well matched, these two: the Director so entrenched in history that you had only to change his costume to set him back among the Council of Ten—rulers of mediæval Venice; Manzini, the technocrat, straddling past, present and future like a colossus in a business suit. I was content to listen. Then, without warning, the Director tossed a question to me. "Matucci, what happened to the Anders woman?"

"I took your advice, sir."

"Where is she now?"

"She was talking of going to Klosters for a while. And I think she has marriage in mind."

"Any prospects?"

"Not with me, I assure you. Which reminds me, if you gentlemen will excuse me, I have an appointment with another lady."

"Before you go, Matucci . . . this dual employment of yours. I'm glad to oblige my friend Bruno here. But you will be discreet about it among your service colleagues, won't you? You do understand?"

"Perfectly, sir. I'm very grateful. Good night, gentlemen."

"It's a dirty night," said Manzini. "Don't fall into the canal."

I TOOK THE WARNING seriously. I went up to my room, put on a top-coat and slipped a pistol into my pocket. I spent a moment in the lobby buying postage stamps and then stepped out into the alley. The alley opens into a *piazza*. To get to Harry's Bar you turn right and cross a bridge into the Calle Larga 22 Marzo, which brings you slap against the façade of the church of San Moise. Even by day it is a quiet route. That night, in fog, with every window shuttered, it was like a city of the dead.

I paused and heard a murmur of voices from the left; boatmen, probably. I began to walk, holding to the wall for direction, listening for footsteps. Nothing except the wash of the canal and the wail of foghorns. When I turned out of the *piazza* I thought I heard a faint *slap-slap* of rubber soles on the cobbles, but the sound was too muted to be sure. I walked on faster, though, towards the bridge. Then, from behind me, I heard a long, high whistle. I flattened myself against the wall, took out the pistol and slipped off the safety catch. Behind me was one man. Ahead, where the canal cut across the alley, there would be two. Before I reached the bridge they would close the trap and kill me inside it.

I began to ease myself slowly along the wall, feeling for a doorway. I heard a few swift, running steps. I saw a faint movement near the bridge, which might have been a man, but could just as easily have been a swirl of mist. Then my fingers slid off the wall

354

and groped in emptiness. It was an open archway into a courtyard. Thanks be to God! Now they would have to come for me. I slid down on one knee and peered out cautiously. It was perhaps ten seconds before they began to move, two hugging the wall on my side, the third moving down the opposite side of the alley. This was the one I must take first. Mercifully he made a run that brought him into range, but I could not see him clearly. I had to guess that he was between a barred window and the deeper shadow of a doorway. I fired. He did not fire back. He turned and ran. The others ran, too. I fired two more shots, wild into the mist. Then, because shutters were opening, I bolted for the shelter of Harry's Bar.

Luckily the bar was busy. My breathless entrance attracted no attention. I ordered a large drink, carried it to the telephone booth and called Manzini at the Gritti. "Thanks for the warning," I said. "I nearly did fall into the canal."

"What happened?"

"A well-laid trap. Three men. I fired shots. They got away."

"Where are you now?"

"Where you sent me. I haven't met the lady yet."

"Come to my room when you get back."

"How's our mutual friend?"

"Smug as a cat. I think I'll stir him up a little."

When I asked the barman about Gisela Pestalozzi, he grinned. "She's expensive, but she's got the best girls in town."

"How will I know her?"

"She sits in the far corner. Big redhead in her mid-forties. Wears lots of bangles, big earrings. You can't miss her."

I took my drink over to Gisela's corner and sipped it slowly. A few minutes later she came in, scattering greetings and perfume, and sat down beside me. She wore neck chains enough to moor the *Galileo*. Her hair was Titian red, her lips geranium and her voice like pebbles in a gravel-grinder. She ignored me for a full half minute, then announced, "This is my place, young man. You must be new here."

"And you must be Gisela? The Salamander sent me."

"Eh!" She collapsed like a vast balloon. "What do you need?"

"A safe house."

"For how long?"

"I don't know yet. Weeks, months."

"With or without?"

"With or without what?"

"A woman, of course. What else?"

"Without."

"Two rooms, kitchen and bath. Fully furnished, light, heat and telephone. Near Saint Mark's. Two hundred thousand lire a month. Suit you?"

"It's a murderous price."

"It's safe. Private entrance. No porter and two other exits."

"Where do I get the key?"

"From me. With a month in advance and a month's deposit."

"I'll think about it. How do I find you?"

"The Salamander has my number. Now move over, lover! This is working hours."

"*Ciao*, Gisela! We'll be seeing each other."

And that was it, pointless and unreal like everything else that was happening to me. I left my drink on the table and paid a sleepy boatman one thousand lire to deliver me two hundred metres down the canal. From the Gritti, I called Stefanelli. "Steffi, this is Matucci." In ten seconds it was clear I was not a welcome caller.

"I remember the name. Yes?"

"I'm in Venice, Steffi."

"Happy you. Happy Venice."

"Steffi, stop clowning. This is serious. Listen, please!"

"No! You listen. You sold out, little brother! You took a long leave, and now you're on the payroll of private industry."

"Where did you hear all this?"

"From the great talking horse himself on the day he retired me. I quote: 'Why don't you emulate your colleague Matucci and direct your talents to civilian occupation? I venture to suggest that Matucci will end a very rich man'. Do you want to hear any more?"

"No, thanks. But do me one favour, Steffi. Go talk to Raquela Rabin and ask her what we discussed when I saw her. Then, if you want, you can call me all the names in the book when I ring you again. Good night, Steffi."

After that I went up to Manzini's suite. I was surprised to see the Director still with him. The atmosphere was tense.

"What happened, Matucci?" Manzini asked.

I made it clear that someone had set me up like a clay pigeon and that I wasn't happy about it. Manzini cut me off. "I have told your Director what happened at the lodge. And our suspicion that both attempts were officially inspired."

"And I am shocked at the suggestion." He looked it, too. I caught a hint of real unease under the Director's sardonic mask.

"It had to be you or Leporello," I said. "You both knew where I was. Knowing the trade, it's not illogical, is it?"

"From my point of view, Matucci, it's madness. I have a vested interest in keeping you alive."

"I will not work with fools," said Manzini flatly. "You will talk sense into that upstart Leporello."

"Please, Bruno," said the Director softly. "No tantrums. I will deal with it." He rose. "Sleep well, Matucci."

When he had gone, Manzini surveyed me with ironic amusement. "Well, my Dante, what did you make of that?"

"I think he's telling the truth."

"I know he is. He's worried. If he can't control Leporello now, he'll never be able to afterwards. All profit, Dante! When thieves fall out, it's gold in the pockets of the godly." And he sat there chuckling like a spider who had just made a meal of a gadfly.

THERE WERE LIONS at the gates, supporting an illegible escutcheon. The gates were of black iron, scrolled, and twice the height of a man. A gravelled drive wound through an avenue of cypresses and opened into a fantasy of flower beds, beyond which a stairway of white marble led to the villa, a small jewel, light and beautiful even under the steady drenching rain.

This was Pedognana, country seat of the Cavaliere di Gran Croce Bruno Manzini, and he displayed it to me with pride.

"Home, my Dante! The one place where I am truly myself. My mother bought it in the good years and sold it in the bad ones. When I made my first real money I bought it back. The battered arms over the gate are the ones my mother invented for herself. I defaced the salamander in the partisan days, because this was my headquarters until the Germans arrested me. Come inside."

In the pillared entrance, under a resplendent dome, the

358

household was assembled to greet the master. Manzini saluted them all by name, and I had to repeat each salutation. By the time the ceremony was over I felt myself in the nineteenth century.

The housekeeper bustled me upstairs to a room whose splendour overwhelmed me—the blazing fire, the bookcase full of leather-bound tomes. Suddenly it was all too much, and I wondered irrationally whether this were not a Manzini tactic—to stifle me with grandeur and bind me like a serf to his service. Or was it another of his ways of testing me?

Later that evening, with maps and documents spread all over the table, we sketched the first plan of campaign. I marvelled again that so old a man could be so precise and so ruthless.

"State the purpose of the exercise, Colonel."

"To convict Major General Leporello of conspiracy to murder the lawyer, Bandinelli, and the agent, Calvi. To discredit the Director by showing him joined in the conspiracy."

"And where do you begin?"

"With three facts: Leporello knew the location of the Pantaleone papers and my arrangements to have Calvi guard them; his aide, Captain Roditi, appeared on Ponza with orders to claim the other documents; later the Director joined Leporello in a plot to establish military rule."

"Given those facts, where do you probe first?"

"At the weakest point. Captain Roditi."

"Next?"

"Leporello. We can build a dossier on him easily enough, but it will take time. What is your impression of him?"

"Cold, ambitious, more than a little paranoid. But put him on that balcony in the Piazza Venezia and many people would go mad for him. I'd like you to examine him in social circumstances. He's based in Milan, so we'd better install you in the apartment there as soon as possible. Which raises another question, Dante *mio*. Women!"

"Oh?"

"I suggest you put yourself in the marriage market."

"You must be joking!"

"Not at all. You're a good candidate for any woman's guest list. Use that. Now, your cover story. You are appointed as my personal adviser on all aspects of industrial security. You have free access to all plants and offices. You will be supplied with a company credit card and a car. When I am absent from the country, you will report to me in a code which I shall supply to you. My secretary will inform you of my movements. My banker arrives at ten tomorrow morning to open your account and establish a credit rating backed by me. Now, what else is on the list?"

"Personnel."

"Employ whomever you wish. But check with me before you use any of my staff. Next?"

"You've written here: 'The Church'."

"Oh, yes. This is a delicate one, Matucci. Mother Church is up to her neck in Italian politics. She's a very old and very shrewd lady, and she has friends of the Left and Right as well as Centre. Sometimes it's hard to distinguish them. If you find you're treading on a cassock, tread lightly until you know who's wearing it. Are you religious, by the way?"

"I was baptized, communicated and confirmed. Why?"

"It helps to know what a man thinks about dying—"

"I think about it as little as possible. I find that helps."

"My age makes a difference. I've lived the discord, but I think I hear a harmony. I hear it plainest in the old words and the old signs of grace. Maybe it's an illusion, but I'd rather die with it than without it. . . . I really must get you to a good tailor! That suit was cut by a pork butcher."

In the morning the banker came; in the afternoon a tailor, who measured me for more clothes than my father had worn in a lifetime. In the evening I called Steffi.

"So, I apologize," he said.

"Don't mention it. How would you like to work for me? Good salary, expenses, a little travel."

"I'll have to ask my wife."

"She can't wait to get you out of the house and you know it."

"Now, that's a great truth, little brother. How soon?"

"A week. Ten days at most."

"How much?"

"Your service salary."

"You've bought me."

"Good. One more thing. Do I have any friends left?"

"Still a few. Need something?"

"Yes. Any background you can get on Matteo Roditi, captain of carabinieri, aide to Major General Leporello."

"Should be easy enough."

"Thanks, Steffi. Soon, eh?"

I felt happier after that, and I typed a short note to Lili, who was staying at a small hotel in the Bernese Oberland. The note would be carried across the border by a courier and posted inside Switzerland. There is no official censorship of mails in Italy, but letters do get opened. I could not say very much because Lili might still be under surveillance and someone might go through her things. And it's hard to be passionate when you sign a letter Uncle Pavel. Still, she would know I was well and would be able to answer through Manzini's private Chiasso address.

For the next week I worked like a galley slave on notes and mnemonics, and had daily conferences with Manzini. He was a rough old pirate, but I was beginning to love him. He had so much talent, so much drive, that he made me feel like a clod. No detail was too small for his attention: the names I should use on my false papers, the decoration of the apartment in Milan, the clubs at which he might present me, whether I should play tennis or take a few lessons in golf, and even the make of car I should drive. He instructed me in the workings of the stock market, in the histories of the great families and the careers of the modern adventurers. He showed me where the money was—American, German, Swiss— and how the oil war was fought. "Think always in the frame of history, Dante," he would say over and over.

Then, abruptly, he would change the subject and take me out on a tour of the estate, reminiscing about his youth and about his father. "He was happy to profit from politics but refused to engage himself in it, being content with a public affirmation of loyalty to the Crown and a private manipulation of conflicting parties to the sole interest of Pantaleone. . . . I see you smile, my friend. You're right. I'm very like him. He was a good businessman, too. My mother fought him to make a settlement on me, and that was the foundation of what I have today. Have you no land of your own, Dante?"

"None."

"Then buy yourself a plot, however small. Plough and plant and love it. Every man needs earth he can call his own."

"Perhaps, after this is over . . ."

The rest of the thought remained unspoken, but we both understood the big *perhaps*. If things went wrong, I should have all the earth I needed: two metres long, a metre and a half deep— a grave in the churchyard.

THE APARTMENT IN MILAN was the penthouse of a new building built by Manzini. There was a terrace on three sides, planted with shrubs. The only access was by private elevator, whose entrance and interior could be scanned by closed-circuit television from inside the apartment. The servants had one key to the elevator. I had another. The doors of the apartment were equipped with double locks and chain bolts, and the windows with steel shutters. There were two independent alarm systems, each connected by telephone circuit to the headquarters of the mobile squadron.

Everything in the place was new and designed for a rich and social bachelor: deep leather furniture, a well-stocked bar, stereo and television, books, old and new. There were a typewriter, a Xerox copier, a tape machine, notepaper with my name on it and visiting cards. Concealed behind the bookshelves was a safe with an electronic locking device and an alarm. The telephone index on my desk listed not only tradesmen, doctor and dentist, but all the numbers I might need within Manzini's organization. He turned it all over to me with a smile of satisfaction.

"There, my dear Dante. All yours. Now you have nothing to do but work and divert yourself profitably. Let me introduce you to the servants."

There were two of them, twin brothers from Sardinia named Pietro and Paolo. They had served a prison term for banditry. Manzini had hired them for a season on his yacht, and then offered them permanent jobs. They were fiercely loyal and discreet.

We toasted the enterprise and blessed the house with a glass of champagne, and then Manzini did a touching thing. He put his hands on my shoulders and embraced me, cheek to cheek, as if we were brothers. Then he took from around his neck a thin gold chain which he slipped over my head. "It's the Saint Christopher I had all through the war. You don't have to believe. Just wear him for me, eh?" An instant later he was walking out the door, his old ironic self. "Good luck!"

The old man's spirit gave me the will to be up and doing. I telephoned Steffi to get to Milan fast. He said he had pulled the file on Captain Matteo Roditi, but there was nothing in it. So I'd have to start digging for myself.

There is a club in Milan called the Duca di Gallodoro that I used whenever I came to Milan. It was one of the few places where the food was reasonably good, the drinks were honest, and it was close enough to headquarters for carabinieri officers to drop in for a drink. It was about ten-thirty when I arrived. I perched myself in my favourite corner and made small talk with Gianni, the barman, who was kind enough to notice my new clothes and pay me what he thought was a compliment.

"Eh! Beautiful! English cloth, virgin lamb's wool. And the cut—perfect! What is this, Colonel—a legacy or a rich widow?"

"My life's savings, Gianni. I'm on leave. I thought I owed myself a present. What's going on in town?"

"The same, only more so. Strikes, students marching, police on every corner. People are scared. They're buttoning their pockets and staying home. All this violence! Maybe we need a new *duce* to pull things into line."

"Maybe."

"This new fellow's shaking things up, though. What's his name? Lep-something. That's it—Leporello. I hear your boys talking about him. They say he doesn't care how many heads get broken, so long as we have a quiet city. He's training new riot squads, they tell me. You must know him. Big fellow. The boys call him Old Iron Jaw."

"Good name. Do you know any of his staff?"

"Sure. Some of them come in here. Never on duty, though. He's stopped all that. Hello, isn't this a friend of yours?"

He sidled up to the bar, all six feet six and two hundred and sixty pounds of him: Giorgione, Big George, Major Marinello. When he saw me his sad spaniel eyes brightened a little. "Matucci! Good to see you. What are you doing in this town?"

"I'm on leave. Let me buy you a drink."

"Thanks, I need it. Old Iron Jaw's been snapping at my heels."

"Big changes, eh?"

"Changes? I tell you, Matucci, this Leporello is a one-hundred-per cent armour-plated bastard. He's bringing in brains, he says, computer boys and statisticians, even psychiatrists! But that's not all. He's building up a private group of musclemen. Something funny's going on. I wish I knew what. Ever see that Roditi fellow he's got running around?"

"I've met him. I don't know him."

"Well, he's a weird one. Big shot, big secrets. No friends, except among the new bunch. I wouldn't trust him far."

"Does he ever come here?"

"No, no! This is girl territory. Nothing here for our Roditi."

"*Finocchio*, eh? Is Leporello that way, too?"

"I wouldn't say so. He's married, got two kids. Goes to lunch with the cardinal archbishop. Very proper! Say, what's your big interest anyway?" He set down his glass and swivelled himself around to face me. "Come on, Matucci, give, eh?"

"How would you like to take a walk, Giorgione? Come on to my place; it's not far. It's quiet there, and the drinks are free."

"All right. But it won't get you off the hook. I want—"

"Shut up, or I'll make you pay for the drinks."

The walk gave me time to think. For all his vast bulk and shambling ways, Giorgione was as cunning as a badger. He was one of the mainstays of the division that dealt with fraud and corrupt practices. If I wanted his help, I had to give him enough of the truth to keep him happy and discreet. The apartment helped. He smelled money and power, and he had a healthy respect for both. So, when I judged Giorgione ready and relaxed, I gave him the story.

"For the record, Giorgione, I'm on leave. Four months. I'm working for a big company as security adviser. This place goes with the job. Everything else is off the record."

"Listen, Matucci, I didn't mean to—"

"I know you didn't. And you may be able to help me. I'm still with SID, active. All this is a cover for a job that's maximum security and dangerous. I've also been asked to check out Roditi while I'm here, without upsetting General Leporello. If Roditi is a homosexual, we don't want him in a sensitive post. If he's a disruptive influence, that's another good reason for moving him out. So I have to move carefully, but because of this other business I can't waste time. If you can help me, fine! If not, there's no harm done, provided you sit quiet, as I know you will. That's it, Giorgione . . . check?"

"Check. What do you want to know about this fellow?"

"The full sheet, Giorgione. What's his relationship with Leporello, and what, if anything, does he have to do with the musclemen? Any immediate thoughts?"

"Some, yes. Roditi's a bit of a muscleman himself. Works out every day in the gymnasium—weight lifting, judo, karate. Then he's doing some kind of recruiting job around the country, inside the corps, that is. They seem to be setting up some kind of commando group—real thugs, from what I hear."

"Where do they train?"

"That's one of the big secrets. I'll smell around a bit."

"Where does Roditi live?"

"I don't know that either, but it must be on file. I'll get Rita to dig it out. You remember Rita, you and she—"

"Please, Giorgione, don't tell her I'm in town! Now, you think Roditi's a *finocchio*. Any evidence?"

"Not really. But no girl friends and all this body-building stuff— it points that way, doesn't it?"

"How does Leporello treat him?"

"Oh, very formally, but like a man of confidence. You know the sort of thing. 'If you need any further direction, Captain Roditi will make himself available. . . . Captain Roditi will call you to arrange a conference. . . .' I know he visits Leporello's home."

"Where's that?"

"On the road to Linate Airport. Big villa with a high wall."

"Does Leporello have any women working in his office?"

"Three. Nothing for you there, Matucci. The secretary's a dragon and the two typists are straight from the nunnery."

"What about Leporello's wife?"

"Never seen her."

"Does his wife travel with him?"

"No. But Roditi did, by God! Yes, he did."

"It doesn't prove anything, Giorgione. What's the general feeling in the corps about Leporello?"

"Uneasy. Except the top group, the hard-nose, everything-by-the-book boys, they like Leporello. And he's good, very good. A lot of the things he's done are real improvements."

"But you don't much like him yourself, I take it?"

"I hate his guts. But that's natural. I'm good enough at my job, but I'm no great ornament to the service. And Leporello makes me feel it all the time. Hey! It's late. My wife will kill me! How do I get this stuff to you?"

"Phone me here. If I'm out, leave a message with the servants. Name a place and time, and I'll meet you or call you back."

He left me both pleased and worried. Roditi was unpopular, with a dubious reputation. Leporello was a hard-nose with an unhappy staff. There would be plenty of enthusiastic helpers to dig up the dirt. But the news about the strong-arm squads was disquieting. It was a new threat to privacy and personal rights. Italian law was already heavily loaded in favour of the state and against the individual. A man could be held almost indefinitely on a trumped-up charge. Our interrogation methods were brutal, and our prison system a public shame. I understood Manzini's anxious conviction that the twenty-third hour was already past and the minute hand was climbing to midnight.

I was restless now, itchy for action, so I flipped through my notebook in search of a night owl I could call. I settled on Patrizia Pompa, a lady of singular beauty who made a handsome living decorating the apartments of rich Milanese. To my knowledge, she never went to bed before three in the morning. I called her. She sounded faintly hostile. "Who the hell is this?"

"Dante Matucci, sweetheart. Did I interrupt something?"

"Nothing important. What do you want at this hour?"

"Information—and a little company."

"What sort of information?"

"Clubs for the gay boys. Know any?"

"A couple. Why?"

"I'm looking for a man."

"I didn't think you'd be looking there for a girl, lover."

"He's a nasty man. I think he killed a friend of mine."

366

"Oh! Then try the Alcibiade. It's open till four."

"Care to come along and hold my hand?"

"Why not? I'll be ready in twenty minutes."

I picked her up in the red Mercedes that Manzini had provided. When she saw my new rig she chuckled. "You didn't do all this on a colonel's salary, Matucci. Who's keeping you?"

"Sweetheart, you embarrass me."

"You'll be more embarrassed where you're going."

"About where we're going, listen, darling, and get the story straight. I'm an old friend and you're showing me the town. This is serious. If you get any telephone calls afterwards, stick to this story and don't play games. It could be dangerous."

"With a friend like you, Matucci, I need extra life insurance."

The Alcibiade was plush and expensively decorated. It was designed in a complete circle, with a bar on one side of the small round dance floor and a curved stage on the other. The stage, when we went in, was occupied by three youths in baggy gold pants and turned-up slippers, one playing a sitar and another tooting soulfully on a pipe while the third executed some kind of slow dance. The drinks cost an arm and a leg, but they were served in crystal goblets, with fresh canapés.

Patrizia purred. "Lover, I'm glad you brought me. Can you see your man?"

"Not yet. Wait till the act's over and the lights go up."

We waited a small eternity. The lights, when they were turned on, were dim, but they were bright enough to show me Captain Matteo Roditi seated with two other young men at a table on the edge of the dance floor. I whispered to Patrizia, "I've seen him."

"What do you want to do?"

"Talk to him, alone. Better you're not seen with me. It doesn't look it, but it's dangerous. Order another drink and make your own arrangements."

I pressed some notes into her hand and then wandered to Roditi's table. They did not notice me until I stood over them. "Captain Roditi, isn't it?"

He didn't recognize me for a moment, then he leaped to his feet. "Colonel Matucci! Forgive me, I didn't recognize you."

"Relax, Captain, we're not on parade now."

"What are you doing in Milan, sir?"

"Enjoying some leave."

"Forgive me, but I heard you were retired from the service."

"It's under discussion. I'm still on the active list. Won't you introduce me to your friends?"

"Oh, I'm sorry, sir. Franco Gozzoli, Giuseppe Balbo—Colonel Matucci."

"Are you gentlemen in the service too?"

He was quick, but not quick enough to intercept their swift looks of inquiry. "No, sir, no. They're both in business here."

"What sort of business?"

"Oh—er—architectural draughtsmen."

"How very interesting. Please sit down, gentlemen. Do you come here often, Captain?"

"Occasionally. It's a change. You, sir?"

"Oh, I just dropped in for a drink—cruising, you might say."

"Indeed?" He reacted instantly to the word, and a hint of conspiracy crept into his smile. "Will you be here long?"

"A few weeks. Come and have a drink one evening."

"I'd like that, sir."

"Good. I'll call you at headquarters. Please give my compliments to General Leporello. Tell him I hope to see him soon."

"I'll do that, sir, with pleasure."

"Good night, Roditi. Enjoy yourself."

I saw Patrizia Pompa deep in conversation as I walked past the bar. She gave me a farewell twitch of the fingers, letting me know it was too early for her to go home.

It was three in the morning when I got back to the apartment. I was desperately tired, but slept restlessly.

AT MIDDAY STEFFI ARRIVED, chirpy as a cricket. He brought me blessings from his wife, who, he claimed, was happy to be rid of him. He listened in silence while I told him what had happened to me since our last meeting. Then, sober and subdued, he gave me his own version of events in Rome.

"Look, a simple thing! When I arrived at the airport this morning the computer system had broken down. The airline officials went into hiding. And five thousand passengers didn't know

The Salamander

whether they were coming or going. We don't form a queue like the English. We shout and scream just for the merry hell of it. But there could have been a riot. For what? A blown fuse that cost maybe a hundred lire. That's the terror of it, Matucci. Nobody blames the fuse. Everybody wants a scapegoat to kick because the plane's late. They're daubing slogans on the bridges of Rome now: DEATH TO THE FASCISTS and DOWN WITH THE MARXISTS. And where I live, it's ZIONIST PIG. . . . I wonder if you understand what you're fighting."

"I wish I didn't, Steffi. This is a dangerous project. I don't want you too close to me. You work from the Europa Hotel. We're investigating murder at this moment, so it's old-fashioned detective work I want from you. On Leporello and Roditi first. I want to know what they eat for breakfast and what brand of toothpaste they use. If you've got any friendly colleagues at Milan headquarters, use them; but be careful."

"I should give you the same advice, little brother. The Director has a man writing a black book on you."

"I'm writing a black book of my own, Steffi."

"The big question for the big money—who gets into print first? One more item: Woodpecker has sold out his whole network. Lili Anders figures prominently in the transcript."

"The Swiss don't extradite for political offences."

"They do for criminal acts."

"There's nothing criminal in her dossier."

"There wasn't when you last looked at it. There may be now."

"Steffi, you make me feel like Job."

"So, bless the Lord for your afflictions and pray for His mercies. Also, don't underrate the Director. He wants you alive—but buried up to your neck in a mess. Get me a drink and I'll give you a few good words for a change."

"The words first, you old vulture."

"Remember the letter bomb that was posted in Lili Anders's flat? Well, the police reported that the prints on it belong to Marco Vitucci, age twenty-eight, wanted for larceny and robbery with violence. He also uses the name Giuseppe Balbo—"

"Say that one again."

"Giuseppe Balbo."

369

"One Giuseppe Balbo was with Roditi last night at the Alcibiade! If it's the same one, what a beautiful beginning! Steffi, the soup's beginning to cook!"

"So, please may I have my whisky?"

We talked it all over. We arranged codes, meeting places, a schedule of telephone contacts; then Steffi left to rest his aged bones and plot his own campaign of investigation. And he left me disturbed, in spite of the lead to Roditi.

Because once again I had lapsed into dangerous inattention, concentrating on only one issue and ignoring a whole complex of threats behind it. The black book was an ingenious perversion. The trick was to take a man's dossier and, by editing, emphasis and interpretation, distort it into a criminal caricature. For "bachelor" read "not interested in women", for "likes card games" read "known gambler", and you have the art in a nutshell. It's a filthy game, but it works.

I knew the game because I had played it myself. And I knew what an easy victim I was, a secret agent working always on the outer margin of the law. Lili Anders likewise. One telephone call from the Director to his counterpart in Switzerland, and she would be helpless as a leaf in a winter storm.

I had just finished transcribing Steffi's information onto tape when the telephone rang. It was Major General Leporello, brisk and cordial. "Welcome to Milan, Colonel. Captain Roditi delivered your message. I should be delighted to see you."

"I simply wanted to pay my respects, sir," I said. "I know how busy you are."

"Dinner on Thursday. How would that be?"

"Fine, sir. I'm free on that night."

"My house at eight-thirty. I'll send you directions. Informal—a family foursome. Is there someone you would care to bring?"

"No, sir."

"Leave it to my wife, then—she's the party girl. You and I can have a private chat over the coffee. By the way, have you thought about my offer?"

"Yes, sir, I have."

"Let's talk about it again. Until Thursday, then."

I had expected some approach, but this was out of all proportion.

Two weeks ago he wanted me dead; now he wanted me to dinner. This was not necessarily a contradiction. I was chewing on that sour thought when a courier arrived with messages from Manzini.

One was a note requesting me to dine with him this night at the Bankers' Club, in order, as he put it, "to meet money and see whether it smells or not". The other was a letter from Lili:

My dear,

I am sitting on my balcony, bathed in sunshine, with a marvellous vista of snow-covered peaks and valley farms like dolls' houses. I am enjoying it all, my dear, in a way I would never have thought possible. I walk. I read. I chat with the other guests, pleasant people. There are a honeymoon couple who make me envious sometimes, an elderly American professor who is writing a book, and a very dashing fellow from Lugano, an engineer here on a construction job, who keeps offering me whirlwind tours in his Maserati.

I worry sometimes, because I am still so transient and insecure; but my lawyer, Herr Neumann, reassures me. He says that I may be able to apply for political asylum. He has taken a lot of depositions and is seeking advice from colleagues in Zurich.

And you, my Dante, how are you? I love you and I miss you, but I dare not let myself depend on the loving, and I must get used to the missing. As I write, I am jealous of every woman you meet. I wonder if you are jealous of my engineer. I'd like to think so. Take care, my dear. Think gently of me.

One fine tomorrow, perhaps I'll be

Yours, Lili

I read it three times, then tore it and burned the shreds in the ashtray. I was jealous, and I had no right to be. If I wasn't in love, I was as near to it as I had ever been in my life. I couldn't risk the distraction. There were too many dangerous tomorrows to survive, and Lili's shining day might never come.

THE BANKERS' CLUB in Milan is only a whit less venerable than the Chess Club in Rome. It is, however, much more impressive because the focus of its power is clearer, and all its members are fluent in a single, international language—money. It is a religious language reserved to priests and acolytes—and as such, precise, flexible, subtle, and quite unintelligible to the profane populace. I was curious to know why Manzini had chosen so sacrosanct a place to present me to his world. I asked him as we sat over cocktails.

"Here everyone has money, Dante. Money imposes discretion. Discretion conduces to free speech. Here, therefore, there is free speech—quite a lot of it, in fact. There are six of us who meet for dinner once a month. We talk about everything under the sun. Any of us may bring a guest, provided he guarantees him as a safe man with a secret. Two of the men I particularly want you to meet. One is Ludovisi from the Banca Centrale. The other is Monsignore Frantisek, from the Vatican, one of the shrewdest bankers in the business. They can both be very useful to you."

"How?"

"They can tell you quicker than anybody where the big money is going and why. There's another reason, too. Ludovisi is the brother-in-law of your director." He chuckled and held up his hand. "No, don't be alarmed. They love each other like cat and dog. Ludovisi is suing for divorce. He blames his wife's family for the failure of the marriage. The rest of the men? Well, they're agreeable and well informed. One's a Liberal, others are Christian Democrats of varying shades. Paolini's an out-and-out Fascist, but on a personal basis he's so agreeable you can almost forgive him."

"And what do you expect me to do?"

"Whatever you like. Talk, listen, argue. Now, tell me, what have you been doing?"

He heard me out in silence and then gave a long, low whistle of satisfaction. "Good! Good! What do you propose to do now?"

"Wait until I get more evidence. I may lose Balbo, but if I hand him to the police now, I might lose Roditi and Leporello."

He frowned over that. "I hate the thought of losing a key witness. But premature action is a risk. Those riot squads worry me, though —and I do wonder why Leporello's asked you to dinner. He's in high favour with the businessmen just now. He gave a talk here last week on order and progress—very well received. Let's go in, shall we? The others should be here by now. We'll take soundings and see if there's any news floating around."

We were eight people at a round table so there was no question of precedence. Protocol was honoured by an opening grace from Monsignore Frantisek. Ludovisi was the wit of the group, a lean, grey-eyed dandy. The others, except for Paolini, were typical of their breed, eloquent about everything to do with money, agreeably cynical about any other human concern. Paolini I found an enigma. He radiated charm, but his mind was closed to every logic but his own.

"Look what happened in Greece," he said. "A few years ago you could hardly raise a dollar for investment. Now they've got some law and order, the money pours in. And the government controls the terms. That's a much better situation than we've got."

"Correction, old friend," the monsignore cut in with a tart reminder. "The colonels suspended law and imposed order."

"It's a proper distinction," said Manzini mildly, "but I wonder if it makes any difference to the man in the street. We've got so many laws we can't enforce that we end up with government by regulation. Did anybody hear Leporello's speech last week?"

"I did," said Paolini. "I thought he made excellent sense."

There was tepid agreement from everyone except Ludovisi, who groaned. "He was one long cliché! 'Liberty is not license; provocative elements; strong security measures'. Paolini, do you know this fellow personally?"

"I do. And I think he's the kind of man we need, resolute, clear-headed, absolutely incorruptible."

"Has anyone else met this paragon?"

I caught a faint signal from Manzini. "I have," I said.

Frantisek's eyebrows went up. "And your opinion of him?"

"I'd rather not make a judgment of him as a man. I will say I think he's embarked on a highly dangerous policy."

"What policy is that?"

"Surely you gentlemen know. He's recruiting special riot squads. It's a secret operation, and that worries me. Where the recruits are coming from worries me even more."

"Where do they come from, Matucci?"

"Resorts of known criminals and social delinquents."

"That's a serious statement." Paolini was visibly shocked.

"I know. I make it here in privacy. I shall be presenting evidence to General Leporello himself on Thursday."

"It sounds like the death squads in Brazil," said Ludovisi grimly. "A familiar pattern: pull the rowdies off the streets and set them breaking heads under legal sanction. If you're right, I'd say we were in for a very bloody mess."

"I think we're making a morbid prejudgment." Paolini was too bland to be true. "Why don't we change the subject? No offence, Matucci, but you don't know my colleagues. If you spread alarm like that, you'll rattle the market for a month. Eh, Bruno?"

"I hope not." Manzini chuckled like a happy child. "I'm coming into the market myself tomorrow. The English have just come out with an electron welder that will join two plates of steel—twenty-centimetre steel—in a single welding pass. I want to buy rights in it and finance a local manufacturer. Any of you interested? You'll come in, won't you, Monsignore? Just what His Holiness needs to repair the rifts in the Church."

They all laughed at that, and the tension relaxed.

As we moved from the dining-room to take coffee in the salon, Ludovisi laid a hand on my arm. "That was bad news, Matucci. Do you know where it's pointing?"

"Yes."

"How do you know?"

"I work for SID as well as for Manzini."

"Then you know my brother-in-law."

"Yes."

"Where does he stand in this matter? Before you answer—I don't like him. I think he's both devious and dangerous."

"As a serving officer, I couldn't comment. As a guest in your club, I would say that I agree with you."

"Thank you. Here's my card. If ever I can help, call me."

"Thank you, but I doubt you can help me with this mess."

"You keep an open mind. I'll keep an open door. Agreed?"

At eleven-thirty the guests dispersed, but Manzini held me for a final coffee. There were dark circles under his eyes. "That dinner tonight . . . Truly, I could go out and cut my wrists in a bathtub! You shoved a live grenade under their noses and only two had sense enough to see it. The others didn't want to see it. Have you thought, friend, that if you die one night in a back street, you'll be dying for men like these?"

"You must have thought about it, too."

"I have, many times. When the Gestapo had me in jail, Dante, my half-brother came to see me. He was Captain Pantaleone then, very chic, very general staff. He offered me a bargain. If I'd give him the list of the Salamander network, the Gestapo would release me and I could live out the war at the Pantaleone villa in Frascati. I was sick and tired, and I didn't spit in his eye like a hero. What I did was to tell him the story of my birth, and another story—of how his father, and mine, had had one of my mother's lovers murdered for threatening to tell the world whose son I was. I thought I was signing my death warrant, which would have suited me well at that moment. Instead I was handed back to the interrogators to be worked on for another month. Then, without warning, I was put into a car and driven to Frascati—house arrest at the villa.

"One day my half-brother told me why he had procured my release: he wanted to discharge his father's obligations to me! I'm afraid I did spit in his eye then; though, looking back, I think he meant at least half of it. That was the half that took me to his funeral. The other half? Well, you know what he was doing—the other half is what made me send him the salamander card. You see what I mean, Dante—motives for martyrdom are sometimes clear and simple, and sometimes they're very confused."

EARLY NEXT MORNING Giorgione woke me up with good news. He had discovered the location of a camp that could be where the riot squads were training. It was in Camerata, a small town in the mountains north of Bergamo, about an hour's drive from Milan. He had other information, too. He told me that Captain Roditi lived in a new apartment house with rents much higher than he could afford on a captain's pay. So either he had private income, or someone was subsidizing him.

After breakfast I rang Roditi's office to set our date for drinks. His sergeant told me Roditi would be in Turin with General Leporello until Thursday. By ten o'clock Steffi and I were on the expressway heading for Bergamo.

I explained my plan to Steffi. I still had my SID identification, which would procure me entrance to any maximum-security installation. The risk was that the commanding officer could insist on his right to check the document back to its origin before admitting me. I thought I could bluff my way through that. Nevertheless, I proposed to drop Steffi off in Bergamo with instructions to telephone Manzini if I were detained beyond a reasonable time.

Steffi was not enthusiastic. "You're crazy, Matucci. If they do check, you're up to your neck in trouble. What reason are you going to give them for this visit?"

"The best. I'm looking for a man named Marco Vitucci, wanted on charges of subversion and murder. We feel he may have slipped through the screening into a sensitive organization. Of course I won't find Vitucci. But if I do find Balbo, we're in big profit."

"Enough to buy you a beautiful tombstone, little brother."

"Relax, Steffi. I'll be back in a couple of hours. *Ciao*."

From Bergamo the road to Camerata wound upwards along the flanks of the Lombard hills. I drove into the town and stopped several times to ask directions. No one knew where the camp was. Security was obviously effective. Finally, I had to call on the local police and produce my card for the *brigadiere*, who drew me a map on a sheet of yellow paper. Even then I nearly missed the turn-off, a rutty road into a narrow pass which was closed off at the end by a stockade of logs surmounted by a watchtower with a searchlight and a machine gun.

Two husky guards halted me. I told them I wanted to see the commandant. One of them took my card and went to his box to telephone. I waited five minutes, and then they waved me through.

The place was grim: twin rows of log huts with a broad parade ground in between, and beyond, a vast basin, obviously the training area. I parked my car outside the commandant's office and went inside. A desk sergeant took my card, and it was five more minutes before I was presented to a bullet-headed major who looked as though he could straighten horseshoes with his bare hands. His desk was a mess of papers and he was quite self-conscious about it, fumbling with this sheet and that, as if he weren't sure what was written on them.

His greeting was uneasily cool. "Major Zenobio at your service, Colonel. I'm afraid I had no notice of your visit."

"There were good reasons, Major. General Leporello left for

Turin early this morning. I was still waiting for information from Rome, and I left as soon as it came. I am required to report to the general on his return. In fact, we're dining together tomorrow evening. If you feel the need to check that, please call his secretary immediately. I'd like to get down to business."

"And your business is?" His tone was one degree less frigid.

"I'm looking for a man. The police want him for attempted murder. We want him because he is a known subversive."

"And you hope to find him here, Colonel?"

"There's a certain logic in the idea. Your recruiting methods are, shall we say, unorthodox. Even social delinquents are acceptable, provided they can be retrained to certain essential skills. Correct? And the project is secret. A man who wanted to go underground might well present himself for enlistment."

"The project *is* secret. So how would your man know about it?"

"Ah, that's one of the matters I have to discuss with the general. It affects an officer who has been less than discreet. Take it for granted that the man would know and could present himself. Now, we're not interested in the police side, but an active Marxist agent inside this kind of group—well! You do see my point?"

"Too clearly, Colonel. What's the name of your man?"

"Marco Vitucci."

"Let's take a look at the roster."

"In a moment. What other records do you keep on your troops?"

"Each man has a record card, containing his personal details, a photograph, thumbprint and a list of distinguishing marks."

"Good. Now let's have a look at the roster."

It took him three minutes to find it under the mess on his desk. It took only a minute to establish that in a list of four hundred men there was no Marco Vitucci.

"Well, we do have one other alias." I thumbed through my notebook. "Here it is—Barone, Turi." That landed me among the B's. There was no Barone either; but I did light on the name Balbo, Giuseppe, and I pointed it out to the major. "Balbo, eh? Nothing to do with the case, of course. I was just wondering if he's any relation to General Balbo, who marched with the Duce?"

The major smiled for the first time. "I doubt it. But let's take a look." He opened a filing cabinet and handed me a card. The identification was clear. This was the same man I had met with Roditi in the Alcibiade. If the thumbprint tallied with the one on the police files, I had all I needed. I gave the card back to the major, who tossed it onto the littered desk.

"No connection, I'm afraid. The old general was a Ferrarese. This one comes from Gaeta. I wonder if I could ask you one favour. Could I have a cup of coffee?"

"Certainly." He yelled for the sergeant, and when there was no answer he went through the door at a run, and I heard him shouting across the parade ground. I slipped the Balbo card in my pocket and followed him. "Don't bother, please, Major. I'll be on my way. Just a reminder—this visit is strictly confidential."

"Of course, Colonel. Have a good journey."

He was glad to see me go, but not half so glad as I was to hear the gates of the stockade slam behind me. I drove fast and dangerously back to Bergamo, snatched up a plaintive Steffi and shot back to Milan. The prints on the Balbo card did match the prints from Rome. We made four copies and locked the original in the safe. Then we had Pietro bring champagne to celebrate this first real rape of the ungodly. It was a jubilant hour. But at four in the afternoon, sober but sleepy, we still did not know what to do with our evidence.

Steffi summed it up irritably. "Well, now! We could put one Giuseppe Balbo in prison for life. You don't want that. You want him here, singing like a lovebird, telling you all he knows about Roditi, the letter bomb and the murders of Bandinelli and Calvi. Then you want Roditi here, singing another song about General Leporello. And when you've got it all down, who's going to want to believe you? And much more important, who's going to do anything about it? Matucci, little brother, big woodenhead, you have to answer all those questions!"

"I know, Steffi, I know! I have to create doubt, confusion and panic among them. How far is it to Chiasso?"

"Less than fifty kilometres. Why?"

I grabbed the telephone and dialled Bruno Manzini's private number.

When he was on the line I said, "I want a courier, Bruno. To drive to Chiasso and post some letters. They have to be delivered in Milan with tomorrow's mail. And I need to see you, here at the apartment. It's very urgent."

He always ran true to form. The courier would be with me in fifteen minutes. He himself would join me at six. Steffi was looking at me as if I were a lunatic as I unlocked the safe, took out the Balbo card, rubbed it clean with a handkerchief and laid it on the desk. Then I asked Paolo for a pair of his white gloves.

"So, tell me, Matucci!" Steffi finally burst out. "Or do I just stand here and watch you make like Sherlock Holmes?"

"Step one. We make two fresh copies of this document, without our fingerprints all over the copy paper. Step two. We clip Balbo's thumbprint off each copy. Step three. I type two identical notes to accompany the thumbprints. Step four. Said notes and thumbprints are posted from Chiasso."

"And what will be in the notes?"

"Two names: Bandinelli, Calvi. A place: Via Sicilia, Rome. And the date on which they died."

"And who gets the notes?"

"General Leporello and Captain Roditi—at their homes."

"And how long will it take them to check the print?"

"Forty-eight hours at least."

"And how long to tie it all back to you through a stolen card?"

"Another twenty-four. Maybe a little longer."

"Then what, little brother?"

"Then there is the beautiful scene, Steffi. I think we'll get Fellini to film it. I, Dante, am standing solitary and noble in the middle of the Olympic Stadium. The stands are full. All the spectators look exactly like the Director. They all have guns and they're all pointing at me. What happens after that, I'm not sure."

"I'm sure, Matucci. I'm going home to Mother."

"Not tonight you're not. At ten o'clock we are going to visit the apartment of Captain Matteo Roditi. How does that sound?"

"Like madness. Like old-fashioned dancing madness!"

WHEN MANZINI heard of my day's exploits he was coldly and eloquently angry. "Matucci, you shock me! You have at least some sense of politics. So this children's game you have played today is an incredible and inexcusable folly."

"Now, listen—"

"No! You hear me first! You have set in motion a whole train of events for which we are unprepared. Have you learned nothing? This is high politics. We are talking of revolution, barricades in the streets, gunfire and bombs!' Yet you behave like some fly-brained agent from a comic book! Truly I despair!"

"You despair too quickly. First point. Locked in that safe is a document which can tie Roditi and Leporello to a conspiracy to murder. Next point. We agreed on a policy of doubt and confusion. I have begun to create it."

"Prematurely. Without foresight!"

"We are dealing with conjurers, sir. People who can make files disappear and silence politicians and buy perjurers—if we give them time. I'm trying to deny them time. You can sit with them, the movement, in the Bankers' Club and plan. I have to fight the street battles. I'm the opportunist because I have to be. . . . Eh! This is madness! Let's drop it!"

He stared at me for a long moment, bleak-faced and hostile; then he nodded slowly. "You are right and I am right. And we are both wrong. Let's see what we can salvage."

"No. Let's see what we can build."

A small reluctant smile twitched at the corners of his mouth. "You're a real woodenhead, Matucci. What am I to do with you?"

"Wear me, like a hairshirt, and give me some advice. We establish a case that involves Balbo as an assassin, and Roditi and Leporello as conspirators. But how do we present our case? And how do we tie the Director into it? He's got a perfect position. He can excuse anything he has done on the grounds that he was infiltrating a conspiracy that threatened the security of the state. He knows so many secrets that everyone's afraid of him."

"I'm not afraid of him, Dante."

"No. But neither have you the lever that will topple him."

"You, my Dante, may without knowing have provided both lever and fulcrum."

"I don't understand."

"I know you don't. And that is what makes me angry with you. In the heat of a new situation you slip out of gear. You lose sight of the main show. You chase the marsh light and forget the fires

381

burning on the hills behind you. Remember what happened at the lodge? In Venice? The same thing is happening now. This is why you are at the mercy of such a man as the Director. You have every talent he has, and some he lacks, but you cannot or you will not focus them. So, always until now, you have been a tool of other men's designs. I'm sorry if I offend you, but I have so much regard for you that I cannot bear that you do this to yourself. . . . Let me show you what I mean. First, when you left my brother's house on the morning after his death, you left the old servant weeping, and asked him to record telephone calls for you. He did that, but you never went back to him, never spoke to him again. I did, I went there to see to the wants of an old man who had known my father. Because he was afraid, he told me that he had lied to you. He was not awake when my brother came home from the Chess Club; he was drunk and snoring. He had lied because he thought he would be blamed for not having put on the alarms; they were off when he woke in the morning. . . . No, please don't interrupt. Let me embarrass you a moment longer. The night after my brother's funeral I had his body removed from the vault. An autopsy was performed in a private clinic. My brother had indeed taken barbiturates, but not enough to kill him. He was killed by an injection of air into the femoral artery. The mark of the syringe was clearly visible. You see what happened, Dante? You connived with the Director to hush up a suicide; by his will and your own blindness you were made an accomplice in murder."

"Why didn't you tell me this before?"

For a full minute he said absolutely nothing. When he did speak, his voice was frosty, remote, like the first chill wind of autumn. "To teach you a lesson, Matucci. Trust no one. Not even me. Don't believe that the old Adam is dead until you've screwed down the coffin and seen the gravedigger stamp the last sod on top of him."

He was right, of course. We are an illogical people, sometimes mistrusting our mothers but believing happily the most unprovable propositions. The old man was always right.

OUR VISIT TO Roditi's apartment began auspiciously. There was a party on the sixth floor; the lobby was busy with guests and the porter had lost count of the arrivals. Steffi and I rode with the

382

partygoers as far as the fifth floor and stepped out into a deserted corridor. We rang the bell of Roditi's apartment. There was no answer, so I opened the door with a picklock. It was as simple as shelling peas.

The interior of the apartment was a surprise. It was as impersonal and spotless as an hotel room. The furniture, Danish modern, glowed with recent polishing. The only pictures, arranged in a severe symmetry, were of soldiers in historic costumes. There were a cabinet for drinks and a stereo player with a few records of popular songs. The desk was bare, with a clean blotter and a leather cup full of ball-point pens and freshly sharpened pencils. Kitchen, dining-room and living room revealed nothing of any interest. We moved on to the bedroom. Roditi had ten suits and four uniforms, all made by an expensive tailor. His shirts were handmade and monogrammed. He was prolific in shoes, ties, scarves and costly accessories.

It was all unnaturally tidy—and like the rest of the place, as neutral as a showroom.

Then, in the right-hand drawer of the dressing-table, face down, I found a photograph in a silver frame. It was a professional portrait of a woman in her early thirties, inscribed in a bold, round hand: "To my dearest Matteo, for memory and for promise, Elena." Beside the photograph lay a bundle of letters, more than thirty of them, written in the same hand, signed with the same name. I passed them one by one to Steffi. They were love letters, lyrical, tender, and uninhibited in their celebration of passionate nights and days. I have thumbed through many letters in my time, but these moved me deeply, and I was filled with shame at my invasion of this unknown woman's privacy. There were no dates, but from the text it was clear that the last had been written no more than a week ago. Elena was married, unhappily, to an older man. Roditi, whatever else he was, was obviously a warm and thoughtful lover. There was no reproach in any of the letters, only yearning and gratitude and a vivid, sensual poetry.

Even old Steffi was awed. "Eh, Matucci! If you and I could move a woman like that . . ."

"It doesn't make sense, Steffi. A fellow like Roditi—"

"Now hold it, Matucci. Maybe you have to rethink this fellow.

You've seen him once, at the Alcibiade, and you've heard he's a physical-culture buff. That's all you've got. Hand me that photograph a minute." He slid it out of the frame and looked at the name on the back: A. Donati, Bologna, 673125. "Tomorrow I'll trace that print. Let's take one letter from the middle of the bundle and get out of here. I feel like a criminal."

"Which is exactly what you are, Steffi. But you bring me back the lady's name tomorrow and I'll pin a medal on you."

We left the apartment as pristine as we found it. In the lobby the porter was watching television. We could have been trailing a bloodied corpse and he would not have blinked an eye.

It was a little after eleven. The night was balmy and the streets were still lively with strollers and traffic. Steffi was tired, so I dropped him at his hotel. I was too restless to sleep. Bruno Manzini had taught me a rough lesson. My thinking stopped short of the point. My judgments were hasty. My actions were precipitate and dangerous. The Director, seeing this, had made me a facile actor in his sardonic dramas. Lili, too, saw my weaknesses, and would not commit herself to me until I had mastered them, if indeed I ever could.

The prospect of my solitary apartment daunted me, so I headed for the old Duca di Gallodoro, where I could share my loneliness at least. They greeted me warmly and gave me a table in a shadowy corner, where I sat morosely over a drink watching the shuffle of the dancers. I had been there for perhaps twenty minutes when I noticed two men come in and sit a few tables away from me. One was a big fellow with the battered face of a pugilist; the other was small, dark and dapper, with ferret eyes.

The small one I knew. Everyone in the corps knew him at least by name and reputation. They called him the Surgeon, because, they said, he would cut the brain out of a living man and dissect it for the last morsel of information. The suspect who had jumped or been pushed from a window had been under his studious care. The big fellow was obviously his bodyguard—and probably his assistant butcher. I sat back farther into the shadows lest he see me and I be forced to acknowledge him.

A few moments later the band stopped playing and the dancers drifted back to their tables. Then the lights went out, and there

384

were five seconds of darkness until a spot splashed in the centre of the dance floor and revealed a singer in a splendour of fishnet and sequins. She looked better than she sang, but the audience loved her, called her back for two repeats and sang the last chorus with her.

When the houselights went up again, I glanced across at the Surgeon. He was lying slumped across the table. His bodyguard was sprawled sideways on the banquette. Both had been shot in the head by a small-calibre pistol. I tossed some money on the table and made for the exit. I was halfway there before I heard a woman's scream and the commotion that followed it.

THE KILLING OF THE SURGEON made headlines in the morning press. The police announced a nationwide hunt for the assassins and appealed for information from the public, especially from anyone who had left the Duca di Gallodoro before the police arrived.

Manzini, who had telephoned me at breakfast to invite me on a tour of his factories, was gloomy. "A fellow like that is better dead, but fifty others are waiting to step into his shoes. So nothing is solved. The factions are polarized further, each suspicious of the next. Watch the tensions rise, Dante, the unrest and the fear. And tyrants look so much more attractive to a scared people. I've just had a call from Rome. The government is considering a new regulation that will give the police even wider powers of search and arrest. They talk of ninety-two hours' preventive detention on mere suspicion. That's madness! It puts us back forty years."

He was still dispirited when we had lunch with some of his plant managers. Afterwards, when we got into the car, he said, "Come now, I'll show you something a little more cheerful."

Ten miles or so out of the city we turned off the main road into a private parkland, all lawns and gardens, where twenty bungalows were grouped around a central building that looked rather like a clubhouse.

"A sop to my conscience, Dante. It's a home for mongoloid children who can't be cared for by their families. Institutional care of any kind is so often only destructive. Here we try to reproduce a family situation. Each house has six to ten children under the care of a married couple. The central building contains classrooms, a clinic, a recreation hall and staff quarters. And every week we learn something, some small revelation that makes it even more worthwhile."

To me, the greatest revelation was the old man himself. The staff adored him. With the children he was like a happy grandfather. He hugged them, squatted on the floor and played games with them. He swung one tiny mite on his shoulders and carried him around, while half a dozen others tugged at his coat-tails. There was nothing organized about the chanted chorus of welcome or farewell. He came and went as the patriarch of a frail family which without him would have remained ungathered and forgotten. The odd thing was that he seemed to need to justify it—and to me of all people.

"To me it's pure joy, Dante. I go back to the ant-hill changed, if only a little. I know that life is not all vendetta and woe to the vanquished. The mystery is that we must still fight to keep room even for so small a loving. If we didn't, they would hand those babies of mine over to the brutes of the world for anatomical experiments."

He spoke to me in a new vein as we drove back to town. "We are going back into the jungle now—you to see Leporello. You cannot afford illusions, Dante."

"What illusions, Bruno?"

"That the Salamander will always survive. That's a myth, a beautiful legend. I have a heart condition which will kill me, probably sooner than later. If I go before this is finished, you will be alone. What then?"

"I could go back to SID, an obedient servant. Or take the job Leporello will offer me tonight. Or emigrate to Australia and live happily ever after."

"There are no other possibilities?"

"Yes. There is one. Write me into your will, Bruno. Leave me the engraver's plate from which you print your cards. I'll set up in business as the Salamander. Who knows? I might write a new legend!"

He laughed. I laughed, too—at the wondrous spectacle of Dante Matucci, perched on his dungheap and crowing defiance at all the dark powers of this sunlit Latin world.

I GAVE GREAT CARE to the manner in which I dressed for Leporello's dinner. I must cut just the right figure. The general should know where the bidding started. Pietro flicked the last speck of fluff from my impeccable lapels, and swept me out into the car.

I drove carefully, because there were police and carabinieri at every intersection. The murder of the Surgeon was no small matter in this city of a million and a half people, restive under the twin threats of violence and repression. Two carabinieri checked my papers at the gates of Leporello's villa. There were two plain-clothesmen inside the grounds. One of them opened the door of my car and delivered me to the front door, where a maid took charge and led me into the living room.

Leporello was alone. His handshake was firm and welcoming. A servant offered drinks. We toasted each other. Leporello made a joking reference to the security men. I said I thought them a wise precaution. Then the ladies came in—and it was as if the roof had fallen on my head. The woman in Roditi's photograph was the wife of Major General Leporello.

I stammered a greeting and bent over her hand in a panic of embarrassment. It is one thing to look into a woman's cleavage when you know she has put it on show for you. It is quite another to look into her eyes when you have read her love letters.

Fortunately the other lady provided a diversion. Laura Balestra was a lively blonde with big, bedroom eyes, a little-girl smile and a talent for chit-chat. She loved dressy men. She hated stuffy soldiers. She had just come back from Austria, where she had almost fallen in love with a ski instructor. Didn't I love Elena's dress and wasn't this a beautiful villa? I was so grateful for her chattering I wanted to kiss her. Then she turned to Leporello and left me to my hostess.

Elena Leporello was a beautiful woman, with large, lustrous dark eyes and dark, straight tresses drawn back over her ears and braided behind the head. I wondered how a ramrod like the general had managed to marry her. She was wondering about me, too. "You're older than I expected, Colonel."

"I try hard to conceal it, madam."

"I didn't mean that. My husband likes to surround himself with very young officers."

"Oh? I've only met one member of the staff, Captain Roditi."

"Do you know him well?"

"Hardly at all. We've met only three times, very briefly."

"He's rather exceptional. He's been with my husband for seven years. My husband tells me you're to join his staff."

"The general has suggested it."

"You don't like the idea?"

"I have some reservations I'll be discussing with him."

"You're very discreet."

"In my business I have to be discreet."

"Oh, yes. You're something in intelligence, aren't you?"

"That's right."

"Do you like your work?"

"Not always. It destroys one's illusions too quickly."

"Do you have any left, Colonel?"

"Some. And you?"

"Ask me some other time."

Dinner was announced at that moment. If I guessed my lady right, she was playing a reckless game of spite-my-husband. At table she found a dozen subtle ways of flattering me and denigrating Leporello as he expressed his earnest wish to have me on his staff. I had the impression that he was afraid of her, and that she, knowing it, was prepared to push him to the limit of endurance. Tiring of their game, I began to devise one of my own. "By the way, General, did you know someone tried to kill me in Venice?"

He was a good actor. He choked on his wine, silenced the women's excited exclamations with a gesture and demanded a full account of the affair.

I shrugged it off. "Well, I'd just dined with the Director and Cavaliere Manzini. I was on my way to Harry's Bar to meet a girl, and three men waylaid me in an alley. I fired some shots, and they ran away."

"This worries me, Colonel. This kind of violence is becoming epidemic. You heard what happened in Milan last night?"

"I was there, General."

He was not acting now. He gaped at me, fish-eyed. I explained with elaborate discretion. "You won't find my name in your reports

388

because I slipped out before the panic started—to avoid embarrassing questions."

"And you saw nothing?"

"Only the bodies when the lights went up. It was obviously a professional job. I wouldn't push the inquiries too hard."

"That's an odd thing to say, Colonel."

"Not really, General. Both sides stand to gain. The Left have their victim, and you're rid of a discreditable nuisance."

Elena Leporello was quick to see the point and turn it against us both. "That sounds like a loaded proposition, Colonel."

"Not at all. It's a statement of fact—unless you want me to say that your husband approved of sadism in police interrogations. However, I agree it's not a thing one shouts in public."

Leporello brightened and nodded a vigorous approval. "Very proper, Matucci. Our public image is very important at this time."

"And what do you think of the image, Colonel?" Elena was persistent. "I get the impression it's rather tarnished just now."

"In some respects. But your husband's reputation is growing."

"His reputation for what, Colonel?"

"Firm policy, decisive action. I was at the Bankers' Club the other night, General. Your speech had made a big impression. These riot squads you are training—"

"Where did you hear about those, Colonel?"

"They're talked about in every bar in town, General."

"It's supposed to be a secret project."

"I assure you it isn't any more."

"Could you name me any places where you've heard this talk?"

"The Duca di Gallodoro, the Hilton bar, the Alcibiade . . ."

The general developed a sudden interest in the strawberry flan. Laura Balestra quizzed me pertly. "The Alcibiade? And what were you doing there, Colonel?"

"Just looking."

"Did you find what you were looking for?"

"Yes. I found a man I've been chasing for weeks."

"I didn't think you could find a man in that place."

"Indeed, yes. I was there. Captain Roditi was there."

"Matteo?" Elena addressed the question to Leporello.

"Don't ask me, my dear," said the general, smiling. "I wasn't there. . . . Now, if you don't mind, the colonel and I will take coffee in the library."

No sooner were we alone than his manner changed. He was every inch the soldier again, curt, decisive. "Matucci, why do you hesitate to join me?"

"Two reasons to begin with: I want to finish my leave, and I want to test myself in civilian employment with Bruno Manzini."

"Manzini's a dangerous rogue. He has blackmailed people into suicide. Before you leave this evening I shall give you copies of two dossiers to study and return to me. You will come to your own conclusions."

"You seem sure mine will agree with yours."

"We'll see. If you join me, you may finish your leave first."

"That's very fair."

"Now, as to the post itself. You would be required to set up a completely new section, subject only to me, for political intelligence in the widest sense. If certain events take place, your position would be one of considerable power. Interested?"

"So far, very. Can you specify the events, General?"

"I can, when I am sure of your political affiliation."

"Which should be of what nature, General?"

"I need a very conservative man."

"That could be a contradiction in terms. Intelligence deals both with the actual and the possible. I could quote the Director—"

"Would it help if I told you that the Director has become a very conservative man?"

"I already know that, sir."

"What do you know?"

"The meeting was held at the Villa Baldassare, was it not?"

"How the devil—"

"I told you I dined with the Director and Manzini."

"What did they tell you?"

"Let's say I was made aware of certain situations. For instance, that there had been a discussion as to whether I should be eliminated. There were two votes against, one for killing me—your vote, General. So you see, I'm rather puzzled by your offer."

I had thought to shake him. But as soldier and strategist he was impregnable. He reproved me quietly. "Why? You know the trade. We're all at risk. I voted yes. Then I changed my mind."

"Why?"

"I have always regarded the Director as a useful but fickle ally. After that meeting I concluded I needed a rival and an ultimate substitute for him. You, my dear Colonel. Simple, isn't it?"

"Too simple. Everyone carries life insurance except me. Manzini has wealth and influence. The Director has a presidential appointment. You have the rank of general in the carabinieri. Me? I'm out on the limb of the cherry tree."

"Join me and you will have my personal protection, Colonel."

"I was thinking of the Surgeon. He's dead."

"I wasn't protecting him. You said it yourself: the man was a discreditable nuisance. More brandy?"

"Thank you. Do you mind if I ask a few questions?"

"Please!"

"This aide of yours, Captain Roditi. Explain him to me."

I had touched him on the raw. He was suddenly tense and threatening. "I think you should explain yourself, Colonel."

"You want me to join you. But I am not prepared to come in blind. Roditi, I hear, is a court favourite. He is resented. Because of him you are resented, too. I want to know why."

He considered that. Finally he said, "Roditi is dispensable. You come, he goes, if that's what you want."

"What was he doing at the Alcibiade?"

"He recruits there."

"I'm curious to know why you're using these types."

"We need men without ties, with no ambition beyond money and the companionship of their own kind. They, too, will be dispensable, like mercenaries."

"General, if you were I, would you accept that answer?"

"If I were you, I should not expect to have all the words spelled out for me."

"Fair comment, General. However, you offer me patronage. I have to know where the power lies, and the weakness, too."

"I'm listening."

"Your marriage is obviously unhappy. You must be very lonely."

"I am. I confess that these are desert days for me, Matucci."

"So you lean on Roditi?"

"More than I should, perhaps. He's become like a son to me. But I need someone much stronger, much wiser. You, my friend."

"But you're still not prepared to trust me. Please, General, let's not play games. There's a dossier on you at SID. The Director knows what's in it. I don't, because he has always reserved it to himself. You want to set me up against him, but I'm impotent unless I know what weapons he can use against you. Why don't you think about that? If you still want me, we can talk again."

"You might decide not to join me after all."

"And you might decide to withdraw your protection. In which case I could end like the Surgeon. If that happened, there is a data bank in Switzerland which would immediately circulate a lot of information to the Press and other interested parties."

"Blackmail, Colonel?"

"No, General. Simply insurance. Look, I didn't ask for this job. If you're unhappy with my terms, let's forget it."

"Let's define them more clearly."

"Full disclosure on both sides?"

"Very well. I'll be in touch with you again in a few days. Meantime, you can study the two dossiers and judge Manzini's role. More brandy?"

"No, thank you. I should get home. It's been a long day."

"Not too unprofitable, I hope?"

"Far from it, General. I think we've come a long way."

"Good. By the way, would you mind dropping Laura in town?"

"Not at all. I'd be delighted."

"She's a cheerful soul and rich in her own right—and unattached. A word to the wise, eh?"

Cheerful she was, and she chattered like a featherbrain in the car. "You know, you were very naughty, Dante. You're the first man I've ever seen who could handle Elena when she had her claws out for Leporello. You don't really want to work for him, do you? With all those *finocchi* he has around him? Did you see Elena's face when you dropped that hot brick about Roditi at the Alcibiade? My dear man, everybody knows they're lovers—even the general. Matteo has to be the father of their five-year-old twins. . . . Why? Oh, come on, Matucci! Why do you think the old boy uses Matteo to do all his dirty work? Look, I know Elena! I'll make a bet with you. If she doesn't call you in the next twenty-four hours, I'll give you a night in bed myself."

"No bet. You're already invited. There's champagne and—"

"And Elena will hate me ever after. She's wild for you."

"You told me she was wild for Roditi."

"Oh, that's special. The others—and there have been a lot—are her revenge on her husband. If you join him, she'll get you to bed if she has to scream murder to do it."

"She sounds like a candidate for the madhouse!"

"Who wouldn't be, married to a middle-aged homo with delusions of grandeur? Now, tell me about *your* love life, Colonel."

As it turned out, three glasses of champagne put Laura out cold. I tucked her into bed, stuck a get-well note to the bathroom mirror and closed the door on her.

IT WAS NOW ONE in the morning in Milan, where, if her citizens are to be believed, money will buy you anything, day or night. My needs were essentially simple: an atomizer and a one-eyed notary, deaf and dumb and very greedy. Even with my contacts it took me an hour to find him and a hundred thousand lire to coax him out of his house.

At three-fifteen, armed and accompanied by said notary, I presented myself at the apartment of Captain Roditi. The captain was out. I entered, closed the notary in the bedroom to doze awhile, made myself a cup of coffee and settled down to wait. At three forty-five, not quite sober, Roditi came home. I pushed him against the wall while I patted him for concealed weapons. Then I sat him in the Danish armchair and perched myself on the desk, with the pistol and the atomizer beside me.

"Captain, you may be tempted to think I am playing games. I am not. If you don't give me truthful answers, I shall spray hydrocyanic-acid gas in your face, and you will be dead in four seconds. If you cooperate, I may offer you a way out of the mess you're in now. Clear?"

"Yes."

"In your bedroom there is a photograph of a woman and a bundle of love letters from someone called Elena. Who is Elena?"

"She's the wife of General Leporello."

"How long have you been lovers?"

"About six years."

"Are you the father of her children?"

"I believe so."

"Does the general know of your association?"

"Yes."

"And condones it?"

"Yes. It gives him a hold over both of us."

"Explain that."

"He is the legal father of the children. His name is on the registration of birth. He could remove them from Elena's custody."

"And what is his hold over you?"

"I have procured for him. I am therefore in legal jeopardy."

"Inside or outside the service?"

"Both. I have an apartment, near the cathedral, which he uses. I pay the people and make sure there's no trouble afterwards."

"How do you do that?"

"Threats mostly. Action, if necessary."

"You have people beaten up, that sort of thing?"

"Yes."

"Do you know Major Zenobio, the commandant at Camerata?"

"Yes."

"Have you heard from him today?"

"There was a message to call him. I haven't done it yet."

"Did you get a letter from Chiasso today?"

"Yes."

"Did the general get one?"

"Yes."

"What did you do about them?"

"I sent them to forensics to have the fingerprint and the typewriting checked."

"Did you know whose print it was?"

"It could have belonged to Balbo."

"Did he kill Bandinelli and Calvi?"

"Yes."

"Did he plant a letter bomb in the apartment of one Lili Anders?"

"Yes."

394

"Who gave the orders?"

"I did."

"Who gave you your orders?"

"The general."

"Where are the Pantaleone papers?"

"I gave them to Leporello."

"Where are they now?"

"I don't know. Possibly at his house."

"Where is Giuseppe Balbo?"

"I think he's dead. The general told me to take him to the Alcibiade tonight and make sure we left at two forty-five."

"Who was going to do the job?"

"I don't know. He didn't tell me."

"Did you ever think he may want to get rid of you one day?"

"Yes."

"Did you never take out any insurance?"

"Yes. I had the other apartment bugged. Elena has one set of tapes and photographs. I have another in a safe-deposit box at the Banca Centrale."

"I'll need the key to that box and an authorization for access."

"Very well."

"How do you feel about Elena now?"

"I love her. Why else do you think I've stayed in this rotten business?"

"Because you didn't want to get out. If Leporello brings off his coup, you'll be a very big man."

"What are you going to do now?"

"Not I, Roditi, you! You're going to write a deposition. There's a man in your bedroom who will notarize the document. Then we'll talk about what's next. Now, I'll dictate. You write."

It took us half an hour. I then sent the notary on his drowsy way, had Roditi write a letter to his bank, stuffed the documents into my breast pocket and settled down to chat. Roditi was sallow and trembling, so I let him have a whisky while I laid out the deal.

"You're going absent without leave, Roditi. You'll pack a bag. I'll drive you to a safe place in the country, and you'll stay there until I've built the last brick into my case against Leporello. You'll be interrogated. You'll make more depositions. But at least you won't be in jail, waiting for some cellmate to put a skewer in your back. Then, before the case breaks, you'll have twenty-four hours to get out of the country with Elena and the children. It's the best I can do. Take it or leave it."

"It's no good. It won't work."

"Have you got a better idea?"

"Yes. Leave me free until you've finished your case. I can feed you information. Things are going to happen fast now, Matucci."

"What sort of things?"

"I can't tell you yet. But I will as soon as I know."

"I'm sorry. I don't like it. Pack your bag now."

"I'm not going."

"Then you're going to tell me why."

"All right. You've been followed all evening. While your car was at the general's house, they fixed a bleeper on it."

"Which means they know where I am now?"

"Yes."

"So that's why it was all so easy, eh? They cut me down as I walk out the front door! Or they've taped the car with plastic explosive, and when I switch on the ignition it blows me sky-high. Now, which is it?"

"I don't know. I swear I don't know."

"Then let's find out." I dialled the SID office in Milan and spoke to the duty officer, quoting my identification number. "I am questioning a suspect. My car is parked outside the building. Red Mercedes with a Milan license. It has been bugged, and may be planted with an explosive device. It is also possible there may be an attempt to assassinate me as I go out. The suspect is an officer of carabinieri, so I'd rather not have them brought in. I don't care about the car, but I'll need another vehicle to use. When you're ready, send a man up to this apartment. Code word, Dragon. Hurry, please. Oh, for safety, check me back on this number as soon as I hang up."

He checked and told me the boys would be with me in thirty minutes. A lot could happen in that time. I switched off the lights and looked out of the window. It was already happening. Three police cars were parked outside the building, another was pulling in. The plot was clear: arrest and ninety-two hours' detention on

396

any charge in the book. I could think of two that would stick—breaking and entering, and withholding information on the killing of the Surgeon. By the time I got out, if ever, the deposition would have disappeared into thin air.

I hauled Roditi to his feet, thrust a wadded handkerchief into his mouth, poked my gun into his kidneys and prodded him up four flights of stairs to the roof. I locked the roof door from the outside; then I faced Roditi against it and chopped him hard on the back of the skull. He went down like a sack. I dragged him into the shelter of the water tanks and took the gag out of his mouth so he wouldn't choke. He had a lot more talking to do, if ever I could get out of this very neat trap.

A cautious circuit of the roof showed me that I could get across to the next two roofs and escape through the third building. But it would be impossible to take Roditi with me. So I left him, and a few minutes later I found myself in a deserted office block. There I waited until morning, wondering what had happened to Roditi and whether anyone had bothered to check the rooftop. When the workers began to arrive, I walked out into the crowded, sunlit streets and took a taxi to Steffi's hotel.

STEFFI IN CRISIS was a treasure. While I bathed and shaved he went out and made copies of the depositions on a coin-in-the-slot duplicator. He deposited the original document in the Milan office of his bank for safekeeping. After that he took one of the copies to Manzini and presented it to him with my compliments. The pair of them then came to the hotel for breakfast, chatting as if they had known each other all their lives.

Breakfast, however, was a sober meal. Manzini telephoned the editor of his newspaper, and came back with two stories which would be featured in the afternoon editions. One dealt with a gun battle in which Giuseppe Balbo, a suspect in the murders at the Duca di Gallodoro, had been killed while resisting arrest. The other was an account of a mysterious occurrence in a fashionable apartment building. Answering an anonymous telephone call, the police had visited the apartment of Captain Matteo Roditi, personal aide to Major General Leporello. The apartment was empty and in disorder. The captain, at press time, was still missing. The

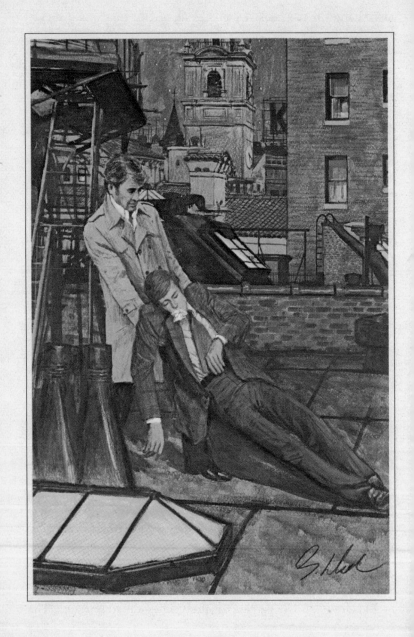

police had detained one man who was known to have visited the apartment in the early hours of the morning. They were seeking Dante Matucci, member of a government agency, whose car was parked outside the building and whose fingerprints were found in the apartment. There was a photograph of me.

"And that, gentlemen," said Manzini flatly, "disposes of our case. Balbo is dead. Roditi is dead or in protective custody. His deposition is worthless, because they will get out of your notary a signed counter-deposition proving duress. You, my Dante, are now a man on the run."

"You're forgetting something, Bruno. I have a key and Roditi's authorization to open his safe-deposit box at the Banca Centrale. If he was telling me the truth, what's in that box can finish Leporello."

Manzini was not cheered. "How do you plan to get to that box? You'd have to present identification, and an hour from now your description will be all over Milan. Which also means we've got to get you out of here fast."

"You have that authorization signed by Roditi to work with. You have a very good calligrapher in Carlo Metaponte, who did your salamander card. And you have your friend Ludovisi right in the Banca Centrale. Well, Bruno . . . ?"

"It depends on Ludovisi, doesn't it? I'll try him. Give me that authorization and the key. Now, Matucci, what are we going to do with you?"

"I'll have to go underground. I'll need the false papers which are in the safe at the apartment."

"I'll get them. Meantime, where do we put you?"

"Could you keep me at Pedognana for a couple of days?"

"Not in the house. I think we might have a visit from the carabinieri. On the estate, certainly, if you don't mind a little peasant living. What about Stefanelli here?"

"I'll stay in town, Cavaliere. This oaf needs an old hand more than he admits."

I thanked Steffi. "When I call, I'm Rabin. It should be a lucky name for us all."

Manzini ignored this. "What if Ludovisi won't play?"

"Then there's one last hope—Leporello's wife."

"When she reads that report, she'll think you killed or kidnapped Roditi."

"The report came from her husband. I don't think she'd believe him if he told her the day of the week."

"It's an awful gamble."

"I know a worse one," said Steffi somberly. "Leporello for *duce* and his bullyboys keeping order with truncheons."

I SPENT FOUR DAYS at Pedognana, lodged in the attic of the farm manager's house. The carabinieri prowled the estate all one afternoon; I was in a barn loft acquiring a dose of hay fever. On the fourth day Manzini arrived with my false papers and clothes to fit my new identity as one Aldo Carnera, a travelling salesman with a Manzini company. If anyone checked, the name and personal details were on file there.

He brought discouraging news, too. Ludovisi was in New York on his way to Mexico, and he was not expected back for ten days. Manzini was fretful. All his careful plans for me were now in ruins, and because of me he had fallen into some discredit with the movement. He was excluded from its inner councils. The Director had sent him a caustic note suggesting that he might confine his activities for now to financial contribution.

We dined together that night, and I tried to coax him into his anecdotal mood, but he refused to be drawn out until I mentioned the two dossiers Leporello had given to me, which I had not yet read. But I remembered the names: Hans Helmut Ziegler and Emanuele Salatri. He mused over them for a moment and then cast off his ill humour like a cloak.

"Eh! What is the past for, if not to renew our hope in the future? The Ziegler file. That story began in 1930. I was in Saõ Paulo then, spending my first big money. One night in a gambling club I was standing next to a Brazilian about my own age. By midnight he was cleaned out. He was so disconsolate I invited him to share a stake with me, and we won. We walked away, friends for life. He is now one of the biggest bankers in Brazil, Paulo Pinto. When he got his first directorship he sent me a souvenir of that night—an emerald. I had it set in a brooch for Raquela Rabin.

"The second part of the story is much later. Hans Helmut

Ziegler was the Gestapo man who worked me over in prison. After the war he disappeared. In 1965 my old friend Pinto sent me his daughter's wedding photograph. The man she had married was Hans Helmut Ziegler. It took me two years' work and twenty thousand dollars to build the dossier on him. I sent it to him with a salamander card. He drove himself over a cliff at high speed. When Pinto read the dossier, he thought the Israelis had killed him. He called in the Brazilian police, and they sent the dossier to Interpol. Eventually it was tracked to me, by way of the Italian authorities—which is, I suppose, how it came into Leporello's hands.

"That ought to be the end of the story, my Dante, but it isn't. In the days before the Black Sabbath the Jews of Rome believed they had a deal with the Germans to ransom themselves. A fund was set up to which everyone contributed gold, jewellery, whatever they had. But the Germans took the collection and the people as well. Raquela had given her emerald brooch to one of the collectors, a man called Emanuele Salatri. He vanished with the loot. In 1969 there was an auction of jewellery in Zurich. Among the pieces in the catalogue was that brooch. I traced it to a prosperous gem dealer in London, one Emanuele Salatri. I sent him a dossier and a card. He blew his brains out. Again the dossier was traced to me. Again I had committed no crime.

"Old history! Am I wrong to dig it up? I have thought so many times. Always though, I come back to the same question: why should the villains flourish while the victims still suffer the effects of their villainies? This is your question now, Matucci. It is possible that Leporello could wade through a whole ocean of crimes and still become a good ruler. But even if he did, should we still suffer him? Even if he came now in sackcloth and ashes, should we in one breath forgive him his crimes and consecrate him to power? I cannot see it."

IT WAS LATE when we went to bed that night. And I didn't sleep. I sat up, desperately lonely, and wrote to Lili; not from Uncle Pavel this time, but from Dante Matucci, fugitive.

My dearest Lili,
This letter is from your puppet-man, who has discovered, late

and painfully, how little he can control his own destiny. I tore up your last letter because I wanted to put you out of my mind until all this business was finished. It was no use. I cannot bear the empty room in my heart. I am jealous that you may have found someone to take my place in yours. I love you, Lili. There now! It is said. Will you marry me? Don't answer until you are sure; because when you are sure and I am free, I shall follow you to the last frontiers.

Things have gone badly for us, but there is still hope of a good outcome. Tomorrow I go back into the underworld, a man on the run looking for something left by a man I think is dead. If I find it, all will be well. If not, I'm likely to turn up in Switzerland sooner than you expect.

I am afraid, but not too afraid, because I am learning slowly to live with the man who lives in my skin. And I am learning from the Salamander the art of survival. . . . You will smile, but I never thought I could survive so long without a woman's company. Perhaps the truth is that my woman is never so far absent that I am without her utterly.

Strange how the words of that poet namesake of mine come back: 'She who makes my mind a paradise'. Old Dante said some very good things in his day. A pity he didn't write more about the body. That's very lonely just now.

> Always yours,
> Dante

I have the letter still, because it was returned to me in circumstances which belong later in this record.

I GOT IN TOUCH with Gisela Pestalozzi in Venice. The safe apartment was a little gem: with a front entrance on a quiet alley, a rear one from which you could step straight into a boat, and an attic window from which you could climb over the rooftops. I paid two months' rent in cash.

Then I began the approach to Elena Leporello. She was my last chance. If I lost on her, I might as well head for the Alps at once. Telephoning her in Milan was risky, but to write a note or have Steffi accost her in the street would be much more so. I decided to telephone. A maid answered.

"May I speak with the general, please?" I asked.

"The general is not home. I suggest you try headquarters."

"This is headquarters. Is the *signora* at home?" I waited a very long moment, and when Elena came on the line I talked fast and eloquently.

"Please, madam, do not hang up until I have finished. This is Dante Matucci. There is an order out for my arrest. I have been in hiding for several days. I do not know whether Captain Roditi is alive or dead. Can you tell me, please?"

"I can't tell you, not at this moment."

"The reports give the impression that I either kidnapped him or murdered him. Neither is true. If he is alive, I must find him. Are you willing to talk to me?"

"Yes."

"When?"

"Any day between ten and six."

"Thank you. Now listen, carefully. At ten-thirty tomorrow morning go to the Ambrosian Library. Say you want to look at Petrarch's *Virgil*. A friend of mine will contact you then and bring you to me in your own car. Are you being watched?"

"I don't know."

"If you think you are, don't keep the appointment. The same arrangement will stand for three days. My friend will ask, 'Are you Raquela Rabin?' You will answer, 'Yes!' Then do whatever he asks. Expect to be out of town all afternoon."

"I understand that. Thank you. Good-bye."

So far, so good; but how far is far when you are dealing with a woman practiced in intrigue? I called Steffi to tell him about my plan to get Roditi's tapes and photographs from Elena.

"Matucci, little brother," Steffi said dolefully, "hear what an old married man has to tell you. This woman is sick. Worse, she knows it and loves it. She needs a husband she can kick around and humiliate. If he's a big shot, so much the better. She needs—and has got—a lover of the same kind. Now you come waltzing to her party all done up like a wedding cake. You're new, you're male. She has to prove she can make you eat out of her hand, too. She's got something you want—even if it's not what she'd like you to want—and she's going to make you sit up and beg. And beg, and beg. And if you won't, she'll turn you in, just to show you who holds the whip."

"She has got something I want. How do I get it?"

"A woman like that, with a dirty story and pictures to match, isn't going to keep it to her lonely self. She has to tell it. Figure who shares it with her. Crack that source, and threaten Elena you'll tell her husband."

Laura Balestra, I thought. She might well know where the stuff was. But Elena would not react to such a threat by handing the stuff to me. "No, I don't buy that," I said. "You get Elena to Venice, buy her a sandwich in St. Mark's Square and leave when I turn up. Wait for me at the safe house."

At two o'clock the next afternoon, dressed in slacks and a green pullover and carrying the papers of Aldo Carnera, I walked to St. Mark's Square. Steffi saw me coming and left.

Elena gave me a frosty welcome. "I hope, Colonel, there is some sense in this sordid little drama."

"I hope so, too, madam. Have you heard from Captain Roditi?"

"Not a word."

"Does your husband know where he is?"

"No. He knows, from the notary, that you forced Matteo to write a false and incriminating document, then had him killed or kidnapped."

"Has your husband seen the document?"

"He hasn't said so."

"Would you like to see it?"

"Please."

I handed her a copy of Roditi's confession and watched her closely as she read it. The colour drained from her face. She trembled violently and I thought for a moment she was going to faint. By the time she had finished she was in control of herself again, and the sudden mastery of her emotions was frightening to see. She faced me, cold-eyed and contemptuous.

"That's a tissue of lies, Colonel, monstrous, horrible lies. Dictated by you—the notary heard you from the bedroom."

"Are you sure it's false? You and Roditi were not lovers?"

"Of course not."

"I read your letters, madam. I saw your signed photograph."

404

"There are no letters, Colonel."

"You mean they were removed on your husband's orders. Not all. I have one in my pocket now. The photograph was taken by Donati in Bologna. He made a copy for me. Let me tell you something else. Roditi was a friend of Guiseppe Balbo, who was killed by the police a few nights ago. I met them together at the Alcibiade. No, madam, I'm not lying. You are. Why? Are you afraid of your husband?"

"No, Colonel."

"Roditi told me you have photographs and tapes which prove against your husband all the charges in that document. He said they were your only insurance against your husband."

"I have no such material. And I need no insurance."

"Why? Because Roditi's dead? Or your husband's giving up his little games? What about you? What sort of woman are you?"

"I'll tell you the sort of woman I am, Colonel. If my husband is clever enough to handle this mess, he's clever enough to climb to the top of the tree. I want to be there, too. If he can't make it . . . Well, there's always another day for me."

"You can settle your future now, madam. There's a policeman over there, and two carabinieri in front of the cathedral. Call them. Tell them who I am and have me arrested."

"No, my dear Colonel, I'm not sure yet how clever you are and whether you're a match for my husband. It's a game, don't you see? I'm the privileged spectator. I could even enjoy an hour in bed with you now. No? Another time, perhaps. Which reminds me, did you hear about Laura?"

"Hear what?"

"She drove her car into a tree last night. She drinks too much, you know. She may live, but as no more than a vegetable. Pity! She was such a pretty girl. Good-bye, Colonel."

She offered me her hand. I could not take it. I watched her walk away, head high, hips swinging, jaunty as any girl on the beat. The pigeons rose in clouds as she passed, and the waiter, counting my change, sighed at the waste of so much woman.

IT WAS ALL DEFEAT and disaster. Steffi summed it up.

"Checkmate, little brother. Your last hope—and it's a slim one— is the safe-deposit box. I wish I could help you. I can't. I'm going home. Call if you need me. But take some advice. Leave this to Manzini, and you cut out to Switzerland. You're in a trap. I'm fond of you, Matucci, God knows why, and I don't want to see you lopped off before you grow up."

I called Manzini, and he, too, advised Switzerland. He sounded tired and spiritless, and I wondered about his health. When I put down the phone I found myself in the grip of a violent reaction. I slammed about Gisela's apartment in a frenzy of frustration. It was incredible that with so much evidence we could do nothing. It was monstrous that an individual could manipulate an arm of the law to make it an instrument of crime. It shamed me that an unprincipled man could turn me into a fugitive while his wife sat laughing. To hell with it! I would not be forced to flee like a criminal. I would stay!

How I was going to stay was another matter. I needed to think that one out over a meal and a bottle of wine, and I was not going to sit here afraid to poke my nose outside the door. I strolled out and found a simple place where the food smelled good. The night was balmy, so I sat outside. I ordered a risotto and a dish of seafood and a bottle of red wine. I was settling down to enjoy it when two carabinieri picked me up like an orange from a basket and carted me off to headquarters.

They took me straight to the commandant. He looked at my papers, and I assured him that I was indeed the Aldo Carnera, travelling salesman, described in them. Was I charged with some offence? He assured me I was not. It was simply a question of the green pullover. Had I been in St. Mark's Square that afternoon? I had. Ah! That was it.

I begged to know what was so special about a green pullover. He admitted that he could see nothing special in it. However, a woman who declined to give her name had telephoned them; she had identified a man wearing such a garment as one Dante Matucci, wanted for questioning in Milan. She had seen his photograph in the papers.

The commandant brought out a photograph of me and a set of fingerprints from the SID files. I smiled and he smiled, and we agreed it was the luck of the game. I asked whether I might make a telephone call. He produced an order stating that if Colonel

Matucci were apprehended, he should be held incommunicado. He was going to telephone Milan now. He hated to do this to a senior colleague. He begged me to make myself comfortable until he returned. A wink being as good as a nod, I used the telephone on his desk and dialled Manzini. He was out. His servant took the message. At least the old man would know what had happened.

The commandant was gone a long time. He came back looking grave and preoccupied. I was now, he said, formally under arrest. I must surrender all my belongings, for which he would issue a receipt. His orders were to detain me overnight, and to send me, in the morning, to Milan.

A *brigadiere* escorted me to the detention cell. A turnkey locked me in. About fifteen minutes later the *brigadiere* returned, accompanied by a guard and a man in a white coat carrying a kidney dish covered with a towel. He introduced himself as the police surgeon and asked me to roll up my sleeve for a sedative. I winced at the prick of the needle and began counting one, two, three . . .

Then all the lights went out.

I WOKE—or dreamed I woke—in absolute darkness and absolute silence. I was—or dreamed I was—floating in undetermined space in a timeless continuum. I was not sad; I was not happy; I was not in pain; I simply was. At first that was enough. Then I began to be uneasy, faintly at first, then more and more acutely. Something was absent. I could not define what it was. My mind was a swirl of mist and I was groping, without hands, into nowhere.

The mist dispersed slowly in drifts and eddies. I began to collect the scattered parts of myself. My thumb encountered my fingertips. My tongue met my palate. My eyelids blinked. Somewhere out in the fog my feet brushed one against the other. Then the parts became a whole, and I was aware that my body and I were still together. I was there, naked and lying on a hard, flat surface.

Then panic engulfed me. I was buried alive. I was blind. I was deaf.

I was dumb. When I cried out, no sound would issue from my parched, constricted throat. I broke out into a sweat of terror. Slowly the panic subsided until, mercifully, it was no longer a madness. Now at least I knew I had a mind and must, somehow, begin to use it.

First I directed my fingers to explore my environment. The slab on which I lay felt like marble. It terminated a few centimetres on either side of my body; above and all around was empty space. Below it my fingers encountered a floor, rough to the touch and colder than my slab. How far it reached I did not know. Enough that I had found a foothold in reality.

Now I must make a search of my inward self, testing for time holds and memory pegs. This was more difficult. At last one memory held: a woman walking through a cloud of pigeons, a man in a green pullover sitting at a table watching her. I could go on from that. I could go back from it. I found myself weeping quietly in the dark. The tears were good. They felt like oil on the panic waters. When they were spent, I knew that I was still a man. I knew what had happened to me and what would happen very soon.

Of all the intricate instruments of torture men have devised, none is so potent as darkness and silence. My namesake, Dante Alighieri, wrote a poem about hell which is one of the world's classics. I stand to witness that he didn't know what he was talking about. Hell is a dark and silent room. Damnation means to be locked inside it—alone.

I can tell you what happens because it happened to me. It was the subtlest vengeance any man could contrive against another. . . . You say to yourself, I know who I am. I know what they are trying to do to me. I will not let them. I will live inside my skull and hold fast to the facts I know. I know they will have to give me food, or at least water. Someone will come, if only to gloat; else why take all this trouble to torment me when it would have been so simple to put a bullet in my head.

Nobody comes. You discover in your first circuit of the walls that they have left three plastic demijohns of water, enough to keep you alive for a long, long time. You discover, too, that the world inside your skull won't stay in focus. You grasp for one memory and find another. You hallucinate constantly. If they came, you would not know whether they were real or not.

408

This is the trick of it, you see. They do come, but you do not know. They scoop you up from the floor and pump barbiturates into you to continue the hallucination. They drip enough glucose into your veins to keep you alive, and they feed you with enough new fears to derange you. I learned later that I was there fifteen days. When they brought me out I was blind for a while, and dumb and ataxic, shambling like an animal, bearded, and filthy. I was put under deep sedation for forty-eight hours, and when I came out of it I was sure I had died and arrived, by some cosmic mistake, in paradise.

THERE WAS SO MUCH LIGHT, I could only bear it for the shortest while. Always, when I opened my eyes there was a pretty nurse in the room. She told me her name was Claudia. Whenever the light began to fade I'd become fretful, scared that it would go out altogether. But it never did. Always another nurse came in and turned on the lamps, and even when I slept there was always a small light burning. The night nurse was not as pretty as Claudia, but she was gentle and patient. Sometimes I couldn't stop talking. At others I was morose and silent, unable to change the fixed and horrible trend of my thoughts.

Every day the doctor examined me and chatted for a while about my illness, a psychic disfunction which would cure itself, he told me, with patience, a little sedation and the simple therapy of human communication. When I asked where I was, he said simply that I was in his clinic. I told him I had difficulty remembering, and that I couldn't concentrate even on a page of print. This, he explained, was the natural response of an organism taxed beyond endurance. It simply refused to function until it was rested and ready. When I asked whether I was still under arrest, he smiled and told me that I was free.

Gradually I began to take hold of the realities around me, but distant realities were still vague. I thought about Lili and Manzini and Steffi, but I could neither grasp them as present nor regret them as absent. Leporello, his wife, the Director, were so vague as to be almost irrelevant. I knew only that in some fashion I had survived them.

When they allowed me out of bed for the first time, I was

409

astonished to find how weak I was. The short walk to the window left me dizzy and trembling. Even the view outside proved a shock. I saw it first in a single dimension. Then, quite suddenly, it fell into perspective. There was a terrace, set with cane chairs and bright umbrellas. Beyond were a lawn, flower gardens, and then a wall of cypresses, dark against a limpid sky. But it told me nothing. There were no people, no landmarks. After a few moments I was glad to go back to bed.

When I awoke, the night-light was burning and Bruno Manzini was standing at the foot of the bed. He came and took my hands between his own and held them a long time in a wordless greeting. Suddenly I was weeping. Manzini wiped the tears from my cheeks with his handkerchief. Then he perched on the bed and talked me back to composure.

"It's been a rough road, my Dante. But you've survived it. In a week or so I'm taking you to Pedognana. You'd like that?"

"I would. I feel so lost. What's the matter with me?"

"You've had your season in hell. It takes time to recover."

"I suppose so. Where is this place?"

"Near Como. It's a small psychiatric clinic. I finance it. . . . Oh, don't worry, you're quite sane; but you wouldn't have been if they'd held you much longer."

"How did I get here?"

"I brought you. It took me ten days and a lot of bribery to find you. Then I had to get a judicial order for your release, which was harder. You're on provisional liberty, of course. Charges still lie against you."

"I can't imagine why Leporello let me go."

"He was convinced you were broken beyond repair. And the movement would have lost a large cheque from me. He may still get you into court. Fortunately, we now have medical evidence of your treatment, and I don't think he wants that revealed just yet."

"Everything's in pieces. I—I can't put them together."

"You put it all together before this happened. We have in our hands your notes on the microfilms, the tapes and photographs from the safe-deposit in the bank. We can break Leporello now—and the Director after him."

"Do you know what happened to Roditi?"

"Yes. They put him through the treatment, too. He'll be no danger to Leporello now and no use to anyone else."

"I'm afraid I'm not going to be much use to you, either."

"Listen to me, my Dante. You are a lucky man, too lucky to have pity for yourself. You cannot surrender now. You will not, because if you do, you hand the victory to Leporello, and all you have suffered will be useless."

"I'm so tired. . . ."

"Try a little hating, my friend. It's the best stimulant in the world. Relax now. I'll see you again in a few days."

I was glad to see him go. I wanted to feel sorry for myself. I deserved a little pity, and this old man had none.

The next day I sat for an hour on the terrace. The day after, I made my first circuit of the garden with my nurse. Then I was walking in the garden every morning, ambling like a monk in meditation, soaking up the sun. I was beginning to be a man once more. I could read for perhaps an hour at a time. Newspapers were brought to me, but these I did not open. The news was a responsibility which I was not yet ready to shoulder.

Then Manzini came again. He brought champagne and caviar and we made a picnic on the terrace, but I was wary of him. I did not want him to disturb my precarious comfort. He did not disturb it. He shattered it. "There is something you must know, my Dante. Lili Anders is in prison in Rome."

"No . . . it can't be true."

"It is. The Director called me yesterday to announce the good news. He asked me to pass it on to you."

"But why? How?"

"It seems you called her back, by telegram."

"How could I? I've been out of action for nearly four weeks."

"That's the way the Director tells it. You telegraphed that she was free to return, that you would meet her in Bolzano, where you were arranging to get married. She produced the telegram from her handbag when the frontier police looked her up in the black book and questioned her."

"It was a trap!"

"Of course. But she walked into it."

"We've got to get her out."

411

"How, my Dante? You collected the evidence against her and broke the Woodpecker's network. You can hardly refute your own testimony, can you?"

"But the Director promised to let her go."

"He did. She came back. He's got her on illegal entry."

"What a stinking mess. I've got to get out of here, Bruno."

"If that's what you want, so be it."

We were halfway across the lawn when a thought stopped me in my tracks. I caught his arm and challenged him brutally. "Did you arrange this, Bruno?"

There was not a tremor in him. He stood straight and firm, staring me down. "Do you think me capable of it?"

"Yes, I do."

"Good. Then you have learned something."

"Did you do it?"

"I might have—if I had thought it useful. In fact, I did not. I think you fixed it yourself by your own talk, sometime in those fifteen days of disfunction. I know that you told things about me, because I've had to lie about them since—and we nearly missed the safe-deposit box. Leporello did get a judicial order to open it the day after we'd extracted the contents."

"Dear God! Oh, Bruno, I'm sorry!"

"Don't be sorry. Think about those who made a traitor out of you against your will."

"I'll kill the bastards!"

"Which is what they'll expect you to try—and if they take you a second time, there will be no escape. No, Dante, this time we'll do it my way. You're not setting foot outside the gate a minute before the doctor says you're ready."

The doctor was dubious. Under stress the disfunctions would again become acute. My memory would play tricks, concentration would lapse, I'd be subject to fits of depression and anxiety. He would let me go only if I understood the risks and would not force myself. It was easy to say I could handle it.

But with guilt for Lili's betrayal nagging at me, I lapsed into deep despondence the moment we drove out the clinic gates. Manzini let me brood for a while, and then he faced me with a blunt question. "How serious are you about this woman of yours?"

"I've asked her to marry me."

"When?"

"I wrote her just before I left Pedognana last time. I gave you the letter to mail through Chiasso."

"I thought you were supposed to be her Uncle Pavel."

"I wasn't when I wrote the letter."

"Wasn't that rather foolish?"

"On the face of it, yes."

"So you don't know whether she wants to marry you or not?"

"No. Why?"

"I merely wondered. There's something else more important. I think we know the date of the *colpo di stato*."

"When?"

"October thirty-first is being whispered among the initiates. And it checks with dates in the microfilms."

"That's five months ahead."

"Never count on time, Dante. It runs away too quickly. Leporello is a splendid organizer, and he's already intimidated or eliminated several important witnesses. As he thought he'd eliminated you. No, we have to move before summer."

"What do you want me to do?"

"For the moment, what the doctor ordered—rest. However, there is one thing you can do without prejudice to your health."

"What's that?"

"Entertain your friends. I assume you *have* friends of your own rank in the corps. Write a few letters. Make some phone calls. You've been ill. You'd like to see them sometime at Pedognana. We have plenty of guest rooms. There is riding and shooting. . . . They'll come."

"What are you looking for now, Bruno?"

"A praetorian guard. Ten men would be enough, so long as they were resolute and understood what was at stake. On your own showing, there's quite a bit of disaffection from Leporello and his policies."

"If you're asking me to stage a revolt of the armed forces, forget it. I'm not very bright at the moment, but that's madness."

"Who said anything about revolt? On the contrary, we need ten good men proud of the traditions of the corps, jealous of its honour and its oath; old-fashioned patriots who don't like seeing their fellow citizens kicked in the teeth and justice denied by perjured witness."

He would say no more then, and I was too tired to press him.

At cocktails that evening I discovered there was another guest at the villa: the Principessa Pia Faubiani. I was in no mood to lavish on this prima donna of Roman fashion the attention she very obviously demanded, but for Bruno's sake the least I could do was exert myself to be agreeable. I was amply rewarded. She was a witty and intelligent woman, with enough malice to survive in the rough world she exploited, and more than enough affection and good humour to spend on her friends. She was wearing the salamander pin from Fosco's exhibition, and when I commented on it she announced cheerfully, "It's a parting gift. This is my first and last season with Bruno. He's deserting me."

Manzini chuckled. "I've never deserted a woman in my life, and you know it. I'm just retiring from the field with honour. You're too young and I'm too old, my love, and I hate to be second best at anything. When do you open your show in Bologna, Pia?"

"Next Wednesday."

"And in Milan and Turin?"

"Each one ten days after the other."

"After that you're free. To do one last thing for me?"

"Not exactly free, darling. I have to go back to Rome, but . . ."

"I want you to hostess a party for me here for a couple of days. I've been promising to introduce Dante to people ever since he came to Milan. He's had a rough time, and I think he needs some diversion."

"Please, Bruno!" I said. "A party's the last thing I need."

"It may be the last one you'll get, Dante, if you go to trial. You'll do it for me, won't you, Pia?"

"You know I will."

"And if you see this fellow moping around like a barnyard owl, take him out, introduce him to your girls, seduce him yourself if you like, but bounce him out of his miseries, understand?"

"Your servant, Cavaliere."

"I wish you were, my love. Still, it's been fun, hasn't it?"

She laid a hand on his. "It's been fun, *caro*. I'm sorry about—"

414

"Enough, please! I'm tougher than they think. I've had a good life. And I'll tell you something—I've been in love, twice. That's more than enough for any man."

"I know about Raquela, darling. But who was the other one?"

"My wife."

We both stared. He gave us an odd, embarrassed little smile. "I've been thinking a lot about her lately, wondering if we'll meet again, and if we do will we recognize each other. I married her in Paris in 1934. She was nineteen. I was thirty-four. I had travelled all over the world and I thought she was the most beautiful creature in it. She fell in love with Pedognana at first sight. Ask some of the old ones, and you'll find how they still remember her. She was born to the land, and this place flowered under her hand in those two strange years.

"We were ludicrously happy. My affairs prospered, and Marie Claire became pregnant. For a man like me, who had never known a family life, this was like the announcement of the Second Coming. I was bubbling with wild plans for my son—because, of course, it had to be a son.

"In her fourth month Marie Claire fell sick and died within a week, of cerebro-spinal meningitis. She's buried in the chapel. You'd have seen the inscription, Dante, if you'd bent that stubborn neck to pray. Marie Claire, beloved wife of Bruno . . . long ago and far away. Let's have coffee in the study. It's cozier there."

But when the coffee was brought he announced abruptly that he was going to bed. Pia made a move to go with him, but he pushed her gently back into her chair and bent to kiss her on the forehead. His tone was very tender. "Stay here, my love. I'm very tired. We'll talk tomorrow. Good night, my Dante."

When he had gone Pia Faubiani kicked off her shoes, curled herself in the armchair and gave a deep sigh of contentment. "I'm glad it's ended this way. I would hate to have hurt that man. He is—God bless him—very special."

"I know what you mean."

"He loves you, Dante."

"I know. He's told me."

"How do you feel about him?"

"I admire him. I fight him often. Sometimes I wish I could

be like him. I never quite understand him. . . . How sick is he?"

"He's not sick, really. His heart is tired. He could go quickly. I think he's more afraid of lingering too long. His big regret is having no son. Wasn't that a sad little story?"

"Very. It's the shortest story I've ever heard him tell. What are you going to do now?"

"Me? The same, with someone else's money. Give me a little sun and I can grow anywhere. Tell me about yourself."

"What is there to tell? I am an intelligence man who thought he could break the system. Instead the system broke me."

"You don't believe that."

"I do. Look at my hands. I can't hold a glass steady. Do you know why? I'm scared to go to bed and switch off the light. I know it will pass, but I'm still scared."

"I'll make you a promise, Dante. You'll sleep well tonight."

And I did. Without nightmares.

Across the breakfast table Bruno blessed us with a grin and a Venetian proverb: "Bed is a medicine." Once again he was right.

I FOUND I COULD NOT WRITE LETTERS, so I made telephone calls all over the country to men who had once been friends. There were those who were delighted to gossip but were too busy to come, and others who said they'd come but found it hard to set a date. Only six of them expressed a care for an old friend and a concern about what they heard had been done to me. These would come, on various days of leave, to have a meal and chat with me. I wondered, with growing disillusion, why there were so few. As we sat in the study examining papers and photographs and tapes, Manzini gave me his answer.

"Cattle smell the wind, Dante. They turn their tails to it and wait for it to pass. Chaff blows away in the gusts and only the good grain settles. Be grateful, however small the harvest. I talked to Frantisek at the Vatican today. If you want, he will visit Lili, and if she wants to marry you, we can arrange for you to visit her and become betrothed in the prison. The regulations provide for that, but be sure you know what you are doing. You cannot live a lifetime on guilt and pity. And we may not get her out. Face it— for her, too—that there is nothing so destructive as a disappointed

416

hope. So think carefully before you lay new burdens on the girl."

I knew I must. I knew also that I could not determine myself to a lifetime of lonely fidelity. I was not proud to admit that. I tried to put this fact out of my mind and concentrate on the work in hand—the collation of all the material at our disposal to see if it added up to a case which would unseat Leporello and the Director.

There were problems. My notes on the microfilms from Ponza were third-hand material, collated from memory. Even the originals had represented Pantaleone's plans for a military coup, which would not be held to be legal evidence against Leporello. All we had against him, in fact, were the photographs and tapes of his sexual activities in Roditi's apartment in Milan. With these we could make a scandal, but the scandal could be suppressed in Italy because the law forbids the publication of obscene material. If we published it outside the country, we would be open to accusations of forgery and political chicanery. But this was a risk we might be forced to take.

Whether we could make a legal case out of this material was also problematic. Photographs can be forged very easily, and Roditi was not available as a witness to their authenticity. Then the defence could claim that the tapes had been edited and thus also constituted a forgery.

We decided to concentrate our case on the photographs and I settled down to study them with a magnifying glass. There was no doubt that we had Leporello. I was concerned to see if I could identify any of his partners. The problem was that we had only contact prints of thirty-five-millimetre size and each had to be examined minutely.

Finally I was lucky. In one frame I was sure I had Giuseppe Balbo. In another was a face which was very familiar to me. I groped vainly for the name, but my memory, jolted and jarred by my experience, failed me.

Manzini nevertheless was jubilant. "Balbo is all we need. A known criminal, probably a murderer, whom we can identify from a thumbprint and your testimony, and who was killed by Leporello's men in Leporello's zone of command. Yes, that would do it! The other one will come back to you. Now listen! This stuff is too explosive to let out of our hands. We'll have to bring all the printing and enlarging equipment we need into the villa. Can you do the job?"

"No, only the basics. This needs an expert. One we can trust."

"I'll call my people in Zurich. Your party may be a victory celebration after all, my Dante."

It was still an hour to lunchtime. I paced up and down the terrace trying to reason a way out for Lili. Wherever I looked, there was none. Escape was impossible. Acquittal was unthinkable. There was enough material to convict her twenty times over. The thing she feared most was a present reality: the small room, the lights, the questions that came from nowhere.

Manzini came out to join me, rubbing his hands with satisfaction. The equipment was being packed in Milan. His expert would fly in from Zurich tomorrow. When the news failed to cheer me he snapped at me. "Matucci, stop it! Your Lili is no child. She will survive if she wishes. So long as she survives, there is hope. You do her no service with self-torment. Now, have you put a name to that face?"

"Not yet."

"Keep trying. I have set the party for four weeks from now. It will be a gala affair. This old place needs some life put into it. So do I, for that matter—and you."

"Truly, Bruno, I don't see—"

"You don't see the nose on your own face! That's your problem. You think you can go back to the service? Never! Even if they wash you in the blood of the lamb. You have to start again. Where? As a street sweeper? Of course not. You want to begin as far up the ladder as you can. For that you need friends and recommendations. Hence we shall give the party, one that everyone will want to attend and will remember. I've left a book in your bedroom; you might find it instructive."

The book was the *Ricordi politici* of Francesco Guicciardini, and I found the gentleman entertaining company. Like me, he was Tuscan born, a Florentine, who by two Medici popes was named to high governing posts. He was utterly without mercy, but he knew how to govern and he loved women of all kinds and ages and conditions. The only man who could handle him was Cosimo de' Medici, who climbed to power on his shoulders and then kicked him into

418

retirement. But Guicciardini was a natural survivor. He retired gracefully, grew vines, wrote books and died peacefully. The *Ricordi* were his secret notes, a kind of diary of opinion and experience, which were published centuries after his demise. Manzini had marked and annotated several passages.

> To be open and frank is a noble and generous thing, but often harmful. . . . It is often indispensable to dissemble, because men are evil by nature. (So smile, my Dante. Show them you are a man who has no care in the world, because you have aces in your sleeve!)
>
> I do not blame those who, on fire with love of country, confront dangers to establish liberty . . . though I think that what they do is very risky. Few revolutions succeed and, even if they do, you find very often they didn't win what you hoped. (Which is why I draw back from public disorder and seek rather to seduce the ungodly in secret.)
>
> Do not take people too seriously when they prate the advantages of freedom. If they could find a good job in a tyrannical state, they would rush to take it. (I would go further. If they could be tyrants themselves, they would climb over a mountain of skulls to arrive.)
>
> The past illuminates the future; the world has always been the same. The same things come back with different names under different colours. (You and I, my Dante, are trying to change the course of history. But let's not expect too much. The river is still the same.)
>
> Nobody knows his subjects as little as their ruler. (This is what we are betting on, you and I. They think they have bought me. They know they have frightened you. They do not understand we have not yet begun to fight back.)

It was at that point that I laid down the book. I still could not turn out my light, but lay a long time staring at the ceiling.

NEXT DAY A VARIETY OF THINGS began to happen at Pedognana. The artisans of the estate converted an attic into a photographic studio, and the expert from Zurich, sworn to secrecy, set to work installing the equipment which had come from Milan. Early in the evening, Corrado Buoncompagni, the editor of Manzini's newspaper, arrived with Milo de Salis, the noted film director. Dinner that night, with those two, turned into a council of war, at which Manzini exposed for the first time the scope of his design. Now at last I saw him plain and was amazed at the subtlety and the audacity of his genius. He was quiet, dispassionate, and yet he held us as no orator could have.

"I ask no oaths of you, my friends. From this moment we are all conspirators, all at risk. We shall have to use other people. We shall give them only the information they need to carry out their tasks. For the rest, we shall lie, conceal, confuse and obfuscate, so that the true issue is clear only to us.

"I will define that issue. We are attempting to discredit and remove from power men who wish to impose by force, or threat of force, a government by dictation. We believe that this form of government is unacceptable to the vast majority of the people. We know, however, that with all the modern mechanisms of control it can be imposed—and could be held in power for a very long time. Therefore, we must abort the *colpo di stato* which we know is planned.

"Now, Corrado, commencing with Thursday's edition you will reverse the editorial policy of the paper. We are no longer Centrists but swinging to the Right. I want editorials that my Fascist friends will read. I want a big feature on Major General Leporello. The staff won't like it. It's your job to keep them happy. I don't want to lose either staff or circulation, but I want it known that I am prepared to support the Right—under conditions. I want them to invite me to lunch. Then I can invite them here instead.

"Milo, your job is more difficult, because of time and technical problems. Matucci has a mass of documents and notes, of which the most important are military maps and campaign plans. In addition we have a collection of obscene photographs and tapes. You have access to other material from film files and newsreels. You have three weeks in which to write, film and edit a ten-minute film based on all that material. The film will say that Major General Leporello is a deviate with his own troops, a murderer and a conspirator against the state. Matucci will edit the film with you. He will also appear as commentator and final accuser. As an actor, he needs much direction. I trust you will succeed where I have failed.

"Matucci, you will work with Milo. You will also recruit the praetorian guard we spoke of—senior officers who will agree to attend an official function and act with you if an expected crisis should arise. This is the riskiest point, because if they fail us at the crucial moment, we may all be brought low and the ungodly may survive stronger than ever.

"Now let me describe that crucial moment. I have just completed plans for one of the biggest ventures of my career, a chain of tourist hotels and marina developments around the southern coastline. Because it will bring tourists and tourist industries into the depressed South, this enterprise is of major interest to the government. A consortium of banks has now agreed to finance the whole project. I propose to announce that fact at a gathering in this house a little over three weeks from now. No Press will be invited, but Corrado will attend as my personal guest and as pipeline to the media. If we fail here to abort the *colpo di stato*, we shall, for our own protection, publish all the material we have.

"The guest list includes senior ministers and functionaries—among them Major General Leporello and his wife and the Director of SID. I believe that our new editorial tone will encourage them to attend.

"I am still not fully decided what will happen on that night. One thing, though, is clear. If we win, no one will thank us. If we lose . . . Eh! We'd better take the next plane to Rio!"

THE NEXT DAY I identified the second man in the Leporello photographs. It was Captain Girolamo Carpi—aide to the dead Pantaleone. This was a stunning surprise. It established a direct link between Leporello and Pantaleone. It also revealed a yawning hiatus in my own information on Carpi, since there was no hint of any deviate practices in his army dossier. I had hired him to work for SID, and I had arranged his safe exile to Sardinia. Now I had to arrange his return This was not going to be easy. I was no longer in a position either to get at army files or to make requests to army authorities.

I took the dilemma to Bruno. He frowned. "This could be our most important witness. We must get him here, question him, break him, get him on the film. How do we do that, without showing our cards to the army?"

"If we could get him posted to Bologna . . . You must have friends in the army high enough to swing a transfer."

"I have. The problem is how far I can trust any of them at a time like this. How did you come to use Carpi in the first place?"

"Let me see now. He had been aide to your brother for about six months when the Director suggested we enlist him as a domestic spy. He gave me Carpi's dossier, which showed that he was living way beyond his means. My proposition was that if he worked for SID, we would pay his debts and give him a monthly stipend as well. He leaped at it."

"The Director gave you his dossier. You hadn't sent for it yourself? What does that suggest?"

"That it could have been doctored before I saw it."

"Exactly. We need your Captain Carpi. Somehow I will get him. With him here, we may well prove murder."

"Murder—for what motive?"

"Profit—on every level. Pantaleone dies. Leporello replaces him as military leader. Since Leporello has organized the murder, the Director moves in as chief of state, just to keep the record pure. Don't you see? And Carpi, Dante—think of Carpi as an intimate of Leporello, as an emissary of the Director, as a man with free access to Pantaleone's apartment—and as the man who killed my half-brother."

"And think of myself as the man who employed him. That's very pretty!"

"Precisely. You told me the Director was preparing a black book on you. If we indict Carpi, you could be in trouble, too."

"Bruno, let's face it now. You can surround me with angelic choirs; I'm still up to my neck in the filth. I'm the man who started all this. I'm the man who must finish it. That's the way I'm constructing the film with Milo. If things go wrong, you must walk away from me."

He lifted his white head and gave me a small enigmatic smile. "Dante, son of my heart, never underscore the obvious. If we lose, I can't afford you. If we win, we shall both be very busy men. Too busy for dramatic gestures."

THE NEXT THREE WEEKS were a period of mounting panic, suppressed only by the calm generalship of Manzini. The ballroom was invaded by painters, decorators and electricians. A barn was transformed into a studio and cutting room for Milo and his crew. The guest list was filling up. The press campaign had been well received by the Right. Leporello and the Director had consented to come.

My friends from the corps came, one by one, to visit me, and I probed them like a confessor before I dared hint at our project. All of them were troubled by the situation of the republic. They were divided on the remedies. In the end there were only four in whom I felt confidence enough to make my proposition. To them I spoke as follows:

"You will be invited as guests to an official ceremony here at the villa. You will wear formal mess uniform. I guarantee you each a pretty girl to escort. Now, here's the reason. The place is going to be full of important people, ministers, functionaries, that sort of thing. There'll be the usual security men, but we don't want them in the dining room. That's why I want you there, looking like happy guests. We've been told something may happen on that night. I can't tell you what. I want you to trust me and come for friendship's sake, and maybe for the sake of all the things we've talked about. You are committed to nothing beyond attendance. Now, can you accept that or not? If you can, will you accept one other condition? That this is a state secret, and you'll have to keep it a secret."

They accepted, and I believed them. They were friends of the heart, close as family, which is the one thing on which you can depend in this troubled land of mine. When I told Manzini I had only four instead of the ten he'd wanted, he nodded. "Ten officers in full uniform would be impressive, yes. But I'd rather have only these four than risk a single waverer!"

I asked him about Carpi. He shook his head. "Nothing yet. Tomorrow I am flying to Rome to see a friend in the Ministry of Defence. There is risk involved and some very devious staff work, but I hope we shall get him here in time."

He was disappointed. On the day of the great event Captain Carpi had still not arrived.

AT THE FINAL COUNCIL OF WAR at three o'clock that afternoon it was decided that I should not appear at the function until its closing moments. My presence could prove an embarrassment to Leporello and the Director and introduce a dangerous note of uneasiness into a gathering whose success depended upon a careful contrivance of atmosphere.

After the meeting Manzini walked us around on a final tour of inspection. In the foyer the guests would be received by four of Pia's girls and led to the first reception room, there to be presented to Manzini and Pia and circulate for cocktails around an illuminated projection of his tourist hotel and marina development— models of the installations on a huge relief map of the boot of Italy.

After cocktails guests would proceed to the ballroom, which had been converted into a dining-room for the occasion. The place was ablaze with flowers, and the lighting was contrived to flatter the least beautiful of women. The seating was unusual: a series of small rectangular tables seating only three persons a side, so that the guests faced one another in a small closed community. At one end of each table was a silver bucket containing six gold-wrapped party favours; at the other, a small television set connected by closed circuit to a central control in an adjoining room. The host's table at the far end of the room was arranged as a horseshoe, with its own television receiver.

For each guest there was a programme card, illuminated by Carlo Metaponte and set, with impudent irony, in small silver holders in the shape of a salamander. The programme was simple: a toast to the President and to the republic, an opening address by the Minister of Tourism, a reply by Bruno Manzini and the showing of a short television film on the new development, produced and directed by Milo de Salis. Manzini pointed out other refinements, too: three television scanners, two focused on the tables where Leporello and the Director were to be seated, a third covering the room, so that all the proceedings could be monitored and recorded on tape. Leporello and the Director were to be at opposite sides of the room, out of each other's line of vision. One of my praetorians was seated at each of their tables, with another at the table next in line. What Manzini had spent in terms of money was staggering; in terms of imagination and ingenuity, unbelievable. When the tour was over he took me back to his study, poured brandy for both of us and made a last toast to the venture.

"I will not say good luck, my Dante. What has brought us to this point is believing and working and daring. What happens at the end, of course, is in the hands of God . . . and though you may not believe it, He has to have an interest in tonight's affair. Perhaps that should be my toast: I pray that He may hold you safe, my Dante, and bring you to a quiet harbour."

I said amen to that, and it was the closest I had come to praying for a long time. We drank and set down our glasses. Then Manzini sprang his last surprise.

"Dante, my friend, have you thought about tomorrow?"

"Tomorrow?"

"Yes. It will come, you know—unless we die in our sleep."

"So?"

"So if our strategy succeeds, you will have the Director and Leporello under arrest. How will you proceed from there?"

"By the book. Depositions by the arresting officer and the accused. Documents sent to the magistrate. Examination, indictment, submission of pleas by the defence, public trial."

"Which will, of course, make an international scandal?"

"Inevitably."

"With profound political consequences for which neither the government nor the people are yet prepared."

"True."

"Read me the consequences as you see them."

"We shall have aborted a Fascist coup. We'll have damaged public faith in the senior bureaucracy. We'll have given new strength to the Left. On the other hand, we shall have affirmed that the state is capable of purging and regulating itself to the benefit of the people."

"And the final outcome?"

"Potentially healthy. That's my best estimate."

"Which leaves us still at risk—grave risk. And the first risk is yours. You will make the arrest, prefer the charges, file the indictment. Is the case complete?"

"Against Leporello, yes. Against the Director, no. A good lawyer could win it for him."

"And then you would go to the wall. Are you ready for that?"

"I hope so."

"You could avoid it."

"How?"

"Accidents happen—fortunate accidents."

"I know. 'The prisoner was shot while attempting to escape'. 'The suspect suffered a cardiac seizure while under normal interrogation'. No, Bruno! Not for me. Not for you. Not for the President himself."

"Not for the people, either? Your people, my Dante."

"The people belong to themselves, not me. I am the only man who belongs to me. You taught me that lesson, Bruno."

He gave me a long, quizzical look, then grinned and went to his desk. From a drawer he brought out a small velvet box. "It's a gift," he said simply. "I hope you like it."

I opened the box and found, slotted in the velvet bed, a gold signet ring. The symbol engraved on the seal was a crowned salamander. My emotions were still unsteady, and I was deeply moved.

"The ring is a symbol, my Dante, not a talisman. The only magical thing about it is the love that goes with the giving. Remember that, when I leave you, as I shall, as I must. . . ."

IT WAS only twenty minutes to six, and I had a long wait ahead of me. The guests would not arrive until eight-thirty. They would not sit down to dinner until nine-thirty, when I would go down to the control room to watch the monitor. The moment Manzini finished his speech, I was to go into the ballroom, take up my post inside and lock the door. If Leporello or the Director should try to leave, I could then detain them. In the meantime I must rest. I set my alarm and lapsed into a deep sleep.

I woke refreshed and strangely calm. I shaved carefully, bathed and put on my new uniform. When I looked at myself in the mirror I saw a man I hardly recognized: a serving officer of a corps whose oath still had a ring of royalty about it, whose tradition of service, however besmirched by individuals, still carried a blazon of honour. I felt some pride and a small hesitant affection for the man inside my skin. Enough! It was time to go.

As I walked into the empty foyer the major-domo opened the

front door and let in Captain Carpi. For a moment he did not recognize me, and when he did he was nonplussed. He told me that he had been sent from Sardinia with urgent dispatches to be delivered personally into the hands of Major General Leporello. His plane had been delayed at Cagliari, and he had been forced to hire a car to bring him out to Pedognana. I told him the general was at dinner, but that I would take him in as soon as the function was over. I took him into the control room, fed him champagne and canapés, and drew Milo aside to warn him not to make any indiscreet comment. Then we settled down to watch the show, while I tried frantically to figure how I should make use of this very untimely arrival. By the time Manzini stood up to announce the presidential toast, I had made my decision.

The Minister of Tourism made an elegant and witty speech, aiming to impress the important people present—his colleague, the Minister of the Interior, among them. He praised the boldness of Manzini's vision, complimented the bankers on their confidence in the economy and the country's stability, assured all the participants of the benevolence of the government. He ended in a flourish of metaphor and sat down to polite applause.

Then Bruno Manzini began his own speech.

"I thank the minister for his confidence in our enterprise, which is itself an act of faith in the future of this beloved country of ours. This act of faith is the more sincere, because my colleagues and I have committed huge sums of money to Italian development at a time when, despite the optimism of my good friend the minister, the country is deeply divided. We are one people, under one flag, but we are also many peoples with many different histories. We have too many parties and too little consensus to achieve easily a government for the people and by the people. Too much wealth is concentrated in too few hands, my own among them. However, to attempt to reconcile these differences, as some seek to, by violent and sinister means is a dangerous folly that could negate all we have achieved since the war, all that we hope to build."

They applauded him then. This was a proposition they could all accept. Manzini hushed them with a smile and gesture.

"In the silver buckets at the end of each table you will find a number of packages. If the gentlemen will pass them around the tables, please? Don't open them yet. They will make no sense until you have seen the film, which is not, I must tell you, the one promised on your programme. The Press does not know of its existence. The public will never see it—only you, my friends and compatriots. Some of you, especially the ladies, may be discomfited. I beg you to be patient until the film justifies itself. Now, if you will turn your chairs a little, you should all have a good view of your television screens."

This was the cue. In the movement that followed, two of my praetorians stood up and leaned against the wall—a single pace would bring them to Leporello and the Director. Other men did the same, so there was an air of casual reshuffling. I hurried Carpi out of the control room, and we reached the dining-room just as the lights went down. I locked the door, put the key in my pocket and focussed on the nearest screen.

Milo de Salis had settled on a film method that was simple and devastating. It consisted of a series of direct and unqualified statements, in image and commentary.

"This is a photograph of General Massimo Pantaleone, who died in Rome this year, on Carnival night.

"This is the death certificate which states that he died of natural causes. In fact, he died of an injection of air into his femoral artery. He was murdered."

There was a gasp of surprise, a flurry of whispers, then silence, as the commentary began again.

"This is a photograph of the later autopsy report, signed by three very reputable physicians.

"This is a photograph of an office building in the Via Sicilia, where the general's papers were stored after his death. The papers were stolen and two men were murdered—the lawyer, Sergio Bandinelli, and Giampiero Calvi of the SID.

"This is the identity card of the man who murdered them, Giuseppe Balbo, a criminal who used a number of aliases.

"Among the general's papers were these military maps, which have since been altered in detail but not in substance. They show how, on the thirty-first of October of this year, a military junta plans to overthrow the legitimate government of the republic of Italy and establish a government by dictation.

428

"The maps and plans you have just seen are now in the possession of this man, Major General Leporello, who is here tonight."

Once again there was a stir as all heads were turned to identify Leporello. They could not see him in the dim light, so once again the image and the commentary commanded their attention.

"This is a recent photograph of General Leporello's aide, Captain Matteo Roditi, who is now under psychiatric care. He was tortured into insanity to prevent his giving testimony in court.

"This is another photograph of Giuseppe Balbo, murderer, who was shot down while resisting arrest by General Leporello's men.

"This is the Club Alcibiade, a resort of deviates, where Captain Roditi met often with Giuseppe Balbo, who was, strange to say, an enlisted member of the carabinieri, under General Leporello's own command.

"This woman is the wife of Major General Leporello.

"This is a love letter, one of thirty, which she wrote to Captain Roditi, her husband's aide and true father of her children. Their love affair was condoned by the general, for good reason."

Instantly Leporello was on his feet, his tall frame monstrous in the half-dark. He shouted, "This is an outrage against an innocent woman. I demand—" He demanded nothing. My praetorian was at his side with a pistol rammed into his ribs.

Manzini's voice rang like a trumpet blast from the rostrum. "Sit down, General! Ladies and gentlemen, I beg that you control yourselves. We are not here to insult a woman but to prevent an imminent bloodshed."

There was a gasp of horror which I could feel physically. They waited until Leporello subsided into his chair, then submitted in silence to the last brutal revelations.

"These next photographs will distress you, but I beg you to look at them carefully. This one shows Major General Leporello engaged in a sexual act with Giuseppe Balbo, murderer.

"This one shows him in another act with the man identified as the personal aide, and probable murderer, of the late General Pantaleone. His name is Captain Girolamo Carpi.

"This man, Major General Leporello, was chosen to lead the *colpo di stato*. He himself, however, would never have assumed power. There was another man behind him.

"This man—Prince Filippo Baldassare, Director of the Service of Defence Information—plotted the death of Pantaleone, hired Carpi to kill him and then arranged for Leporello to replace him."

Again the audience turned around in the darkness, looking for Baldassare. I was one of the few who could see him. The Director sat calm and unmoved, sipping brandy from a crystal goblet as the film went on.

"Who am I? I am Colonel Dante Matucci of the same service. I collected this information. I, too, was imprisoned and tortured to prevent my revealing it. I take full responsibility for the substance and presentation of this film. I depose it as true, and I shall offer to the appropriate authorities documents in support."

The screens went dark. The lights went up, and a hundred and fifty people sat there, dumb and ashamed to look at each other. I moved forward into the silent room with Carpi, like a sleepwalker, at my side. I had one moment of blind panic. Then I found the words.

"The officers present will place the general and Prince Filippo Baldassare under arrest."

I did pray then—Dear Christ, make them move, please! They moved. They placed their hands on the shoulders of the two men. The act was final and complete.

I heard myself say, "Ladies and gentlemen, I have here with me, under arrest, Captain Girolamo Carpi, who will testify in the proper place."

Then, from his own table, Bruno Manzini took command. "My countrymen! You have been shocked and shamed tonight. I will not apologize. I tell you only that it is a small price to pay to prevent the bloodshed of a civil uprising and the oppression of a new tyranny. Now, may I ask you to retire to the salon, where coffee and liqueurs will be served."

They got up slowly and moved away like automatons, each carrying the supper gift, which was a dossier of the damned, with a card from the Salamander. Elena Leporello passed me without a glance of recognition. Finally there was no one left but the praetorians and the accused and Manzini and the Minister of the Interior and myself.

Manzini and the minister stepped from the high table and walked slowly towards me. They faced me, bleak and expressionless. The minister said, "Thank you, Colonel. You will do what has to be done with those gentlemen. I shall wait here. You will report to me before you leave."

Bruno Manzini did exactly as he had promised. He walked away.

IT WAS AN EERIE MOMENT. Three prisoners with their jailers, silent among the debris of a rich man's feast. We were like actors, frozen on an empty stage, waiting for the Director to move us. Then I understood that I was the Director and that, without me, the play would neither continue nor conclude. I must speak. I heard the words as if they issued from the mouth of another man.

"Prince Baldassare, General Leporello, will you please remain seated. You other gentlemen, will you please conduct Captain Carpi to the control room and wait there till I call you."

The praetorians led Carpi, mute and unprotesting, from the room. When the door closed behind them I was, at last, alone with my enemies. I felt no triumph, only a strange sense of loss and a vague humiliation. Both men sat bolt upright, their faces averted from me. I went to Leporello first. I straddled a chair in front of him and found myself staring into a death mask.

"General, it is your privilege to be held under arrest in barracks, under custody of service officers, and you may elect to be tried under military law. If you waive this privilege, you become immediately subject to civil process. Which do you choose?"

He did not answer. He sat like a stone man, his lips locked, eyes blank as pebbles. His muscles were rigid; there was no twitch of recognition. Then I heard Prince Baldassare, cool and ironic.

"Classic fugue, Matucci. Total withdrawal. You'll get nothing out of him tonight—if ever. To cover yourself, I'd call a doctor."

I swung around to see him, calm and smiling, sipping a glass of brandy and puffing a cigar. He raised the glass in a toast. "My compliments, Matucci. Trial by television! I wonder why I never thought of that. It's very effective." He poured a goblet of wine and pushed it across the table towards me. "Sit down! Relax. I'm a co-operative witness. You can afford to be pleasant to me. You must be very satisfied. What's the next move?"

"You know the legal code as well as I do, sir."

"And I know the trade better, Matucci. You made your case against Leporello—though I doubt he'll ever stand to answer it. The man was always a psychotic. Tonight you pushed him over the edge. A good lawyer will plead him unfit, and the state will, in its own interest, concur. Against me, what have you got? Carpi will be frightened or eliminated before you get a line of decent testimony out of him. Still, it's your case, and you must make it, win or lose. Unless, of course . . ."

"What?"

"Unless you are open to a little lesson in statecraft. You were always weak in that discipline, as I told you."

"If you're proposing a deal, the answer's no."

"My dear Matucci! Do you think I would be so naïve as to propose a deal to a man both righteous and triumphant? On the contrary, I invite you to a mature consideration of realities. Statecraft has nothing to do with justice, relative or absolute. It is the art and craft of controlling large masses of people, of holding them in precarious equilibrium. All means are open to the statesman and he must be prepared to use them all—from the headman's axe to the circus holiday. Clemency for him is not a virtue but a strategy. You, Matucci, are still a servant of the state. You are not yet a statesman. Tonight you have the opportunity to become one." He broke off, sipped his brandy and smiled at me through eddies of cigar smoke. Then he began on a new tack.

"At this moment you are in a position of great strength. You have forestalled a military coup. In the minister you have an important patron, who is waiting for you to give him the right advice. What would you want if you were in his shoes? A discreet and well-managed triumph or a platter full of bleeding heads? One head is useful. You can display it for a warning to the populace. More than one is carnage. Which head would you select? In my view—which I admit could be prejudiced—the one with the fewest brains. You've got it, over there. Mine is worth much more to you and the minister if you leave it on my shoulders. I am discredited, so I can't do any harm unless you bring me to trial—when, my dear Matucci, I promise scandals that will be shouted from Moscow to the Golden Gate. On the other hand, if clemency were offered, I should respond to it gratefully. I would remove myself from the scene and leave a rich legacy of information to my successor. Do I make myself clear?"

I was ashamed for him then. For a moment he had been eloquent. Now he was merely plausible. I told him bluntly, "I have no authority to offer clemency."

"My dear fellow, I know that. Further, it would be dangerous for you to treat with me at all. You should and you must treat only with the minister."

"What are you asking of me then?"

"I want to speak to the minister privately, now."

"He may not want to speak to you."

"He will. And afterwards he will ask to see you."

"And?"

"All I ask is that you give him honest professional answers."

"Can you be sure I'll do that?"

"No. I hope you will. I would not blame you if you pressed your advantage to the limit. However, I've read you the lesson; make what you like of it."

"Give me a hand with Leporello. We'll get him to a bedroom, and I'll call a doctor. Then I'll talk to the minister."

THE INTERVIEW between Prince Baldassare and the minister lasted more than three hours. I was not present. I was closeted with Professor Malpensa, of the army's Psychiatric Unit in Bologna, who had been brought by helicopter to Pedognana. With him was Dr. Lambrusco, Manzini's personal physician. I had asked them to examine Leporello and render a joint diagnosis. They expressed it in writing: "A catatonic or pseudo-catatonic state, induced by guilt and shock. It is our joint recommendation that the patient be institutionalized for clinical observation. It is our opinion that the patient is at present incapable of rational communication, and that to submit him to interrogation or confinement would be pointless and dangerous. Prognosis, doubtful."

I accepted the document and signed the general into the hands of Professor Malpensa. Then I went to Manzini. I found him alone in the drawing-room, grey about the gills, but cheerful.

"Well, Matucci, we did it!"

"Yes. It's very quiet now."

"What did you expect? Garlands and a triumph?"

"Blessed is he who expects nothing, because he is sure to get it. I think I'd like a brandy."

"Help yourself." He gestured in the direction of the study. "Our friend Baldassare is trying to strike a bargain with the minister. Would it surprise you to know that I have recommended it?"

"In what terms, Bruno?"

"I have represented that without his co-operation we could never have staged this evening's drama."

"That's not true."

"I know it. You know it. The minister knows it. But it happens to be a fiction that fits the moment. Objections?"

"I don't approve. I can see why it's expedient."

"You're learning, my Dante."

"The hard way. Could you reach your editor now?"

"Of course. Why?"

"I'd like him to file a report to the wire services."

"What do you have in mind?"

"I can't tell you until I've spoken with the minister."

He gave me a swift appraising glance. "At last I can approve of you, Dante. For a long time I wondered how much of you was man and how much a confection of circumstance. Forgive me! How does one know whether a nut is sound until one cracks the shell? You are a man full of contradictions. You are coward and hero, wise and foolish, soft as putty and hard as iron. I do not know how you will end, but I have not wasted myself on you. I'll call my editor."

He had been out of the room perhaps three minutes when the minister came in and, seeing that I was alone, announced brusquely that he had questions to ask me.

"At your service, sir."

"The charges you made tonight. Are they true?"

"They are."

"Can you sustain them in court?"

"I can sustain those against General Leporello."

"Could you guarantee a conviction?"

"Guarantee, no."

"But you would be willing to proceed?"

"As an officer of public security, yes."

"You have qualified that statement. Why?"

I handed him the medical report on Leporello, and waited while he read it. He handed it back to me. "I repeat, Colonel, why did you qualify your last statement?"

"Because, sir, I am commissioned to act and advise as an officer of public security. I have not been asked to tender a political opinion."

"I now ask you to offer, without prejudice, a political opinion. We have, thanks to your efforts, averted a national crisis. How should we act to avoid a national scandal?"

"We have two important men under arrest, sir. One is incompetent. The case against the other is incomplete; and even if we could complete it, we should risk his making revelations prejudicial to public security. We should risk also divisive enmities both in the republic and between the republic and her allies. I would advise, with deference and respect, that Prince Baldassare be permitted to retire from public life and remove himself within twelve hours from the republic."

"Could that be done without raising a public outcry?"

"There would be a hostile comment, also political embarrassment. I would count that a lesser evil than a celebrated trial."

"What are your personal feelings about Prince Baldassare?"

"I admire his talent and have learned much from him. I disapprove of his politics and personal ambitions. I have very private reasons for wishing to see him brought down."

"What are those reasons?"

"He has imprisoned a woman, once a foreign agent, whom I love. He has damaged my career. He conspired to submit me to psychological torture, from which I am only recently recovered."

"But you would still recommend his release?"

"As a political expedient, yes."

"Would you arrange it and supervise it?"

"You mean, sir, will I accept personal responsibility? Thus absolving the ministry and the government, and placing myself in jeopardy?"

"You express it very accurately, Colonel. Would you like time to consider? Or a gift to sweeten the risk?"

"There is no time, sir. And I'm not for sale—not any more. I'll do it for my own reasons. I'll get him across the border tonight."

"Thank you, Colonel. I should like you to report to me as soon as possible in Rome."

"May I remind you that I am still subject to charges laid by General Leporello?"

"The charges will be withdrawn. You are now restored to active duty. Answerable to me. By the time you return to Rome I trust to be able to confirm your appointment as Director."

He meant it as an accolade—manna in the hungry desert of a bureaucrat's career. Instead it tasted like Dead Sea fruit, dust and ashes on the tongue. For a moment I had felt like a patriot; then, with this reward, he had made me a whore again. Still, I had no choice but to play the game or toss the cards back on the table. I bowed. "Thank you, sir. You do me a great honour."

"Thank you, Colonel. Good night."

IT WAS STRANGE sitting in the Director's chair. For a man so elegant he kept a very dingy office. The only symbols of power were the grey filing cabinets and the scrambler telephone and the intercom switchboard, which would bring twenty people running to attend me.

Old Steffi sat on the other side of the desk and cackled. "So, Matucci! How does it feel? Does your backside fit the seat of the mighty? And what now, what policy? Left, Right or Centre?"

"Middle of the road, Steffi. *Toleranza*. I think we all need to breathe a little."

"Until somebody tosses a bomb or the police fire on rioters, and the boys up top get panicky and scream for action. I wonder how tolerant you'll be then! Well, here's hoping!"

"Come on, Steffi, give me time!"

"I can give you time. But will they? And what about yourself?"

"Please, old friend!"

"So, my nose is twisted out of joint. I'm sorry. What do you want me to do?"

"The commandant at the prison is expecting you. You present the minister's letter and mine. Lili is released to you. You deliver her to her apartment. I'll be there when you arrive."

He stared at me as if I were some curious animal. There was

437

contempt in his eyes and a kind of wondering sorrow. "Why don't you fetch her yourself? What have you got in your veins, Matucci, ice water?"

I was angry then, desperately angry, and I poured out on him months of pent-up fury.

"I'll tell you what kind of a man I am, Steffi. I bleed like everyone else. And I'm sick and tired of all the smug bastards like you who think they can sum me up in a line. You want to know why I'm not going to the prison? I'll tell you! Because the first time Lili would see me I'd be in company with the commandant and a notary and a turnkey with a pistol at his belt. I'd look exactly the way they do, and I don't want her to see me like that, because that's not the kind of man I am—at least not to her. I'll want to take her in my arms and kiss her and comfort her, and I wouldn't be able to do that while a gallery makes a dirty joke of it and every little jack-in-office smiles behind his hand. I won't submit her to that. I asked you to go because I thought you were my friend. Instead you sit there and make jokes as if God gave you the right to be the conscience of the world. Now get the hell out of here! I'll find someone else."

He sat there, downcast, his lips working. Finally he faced me, and there was compassion in his look, and a new kind of respect. He said quietly, "I'm an old fool with a bird's brain. I'll be glad to go for you, little brother."

"Thank you."

"You're scared, aren't you?"

"Yes, Steffi, I'm scared."

"Softly, softly, eh! Take it very easy!"

I filled Lili's apartment with baskets of flowers. I had champagne cooling in a bucket, and canapés on a silver tray and a whole refrigerator full of food. I had documents ready to put up the marriage banns on Capitol Hill. I had even an emerald betrothal ring, especially designed by Bulgari. I still had to wait an hour and a half before Lili came home.

The ring at the door was like camel bells in the desert. When I opened it Lili was standing alone and very still. I swept her into my arms and was astonished at how light she was. I kissed and hugged her and wondered where all the passion had gone. I sat her in the armchair and served her like a princess. And then I looked at her. She was almost transparent, shrunk to skin and bone. Her clothes hung on her like scarecrow garments. Her mouth was pinched, her hands fluttered. Those eloquent eyes were glazed and dull as pebbles. She ate and drank mechanically, and when I laid my hands on her brow and her cheeks, she submitted but did not respond.

I knelt beside her and begged. "Tell me, Lili, what happened? What did they do to you?"

"Not much. Sometimes they questioned me. Mostly they left me alone.

"Lili, you know I didn't send the telegram."

She stared at me blankly.

"What telegram?"

"I was told you came back because of a telegram from me."

"There was no telegram."

"Then why did you come back?"

"I got your letter. I used to read it every night before I went to bed. One night it wasn't there. I thought I had mislaid it. The next day I was out walking. My friend from Lugano, the engineer, stopped and offered me a lift. I got in his car. Someone put a pad over my face. The next thing I remember, two men I didn't know were driving me to Rome. That's all. Except they told me you were in prison, too."

"Oh, darling, darling. I'm so sorry."

"It doesn't matter."

"Listen, sweetheart. I'm going to get you well, and we're going to be married. After that, no problems. You're under the personal protection of the Director of the SID forever and ever. How does that sound?"

"Most beautiful, Dante. But I don't want it."

As I stared at her, not understanding, I saw the first flush of life in her cheeks, the first dawning of emotion in her eyes. She told me, very gently, "Dante, I know you love me. Your letter was the most touching compliment I have ever read in my life, but I'm going to give it back to you. I couldn't bear to keep it. I don't want to destroy it."

"But you said the letter was gone."

"They gave it back to me in prison. They do strange things, cruel and kind; you never know which will be next. I love you, too, Dante—I suppose I always will—but not to live with forever and ever."

"Lili, please—"

"No, listen to me, Dante! I don't understand you Italians any more. You are so warm and kind; then, suddenly, you are devious and so cruel, it makes my blood run cold. You have no loyalties, Dante—only to the family and to today. Outside the family, after today, everything is doubt and calculation. Oh, Dante, I hate to hurt you, but I have to say it. You're the people who always survive, no matter what happens to you. That's wonderful, a hopeful thing. But it is also very terrible, because you will trample each other down to get the last drop of water in the world. Even you, my Dante! I can't face that. I want to live secure, with a little book that tells me what to do. I want to be sure that if I keep the rules, the rules will keep me safe—safer than promises, safer even than loving. In Switzerland I can do that. Not here. I cannot risk you any more."

What could I say? It was all true. The ring on my finger symbolized it: the fabulous beast that survived the hottest fire. And yet it wasn't true. Not the way she said it. The book of rules wasn't the answer. Not for us, the sun people. How could we believe in permanence who walked to the office over the bones of dead emperors? We couldn't trust tomorrow; we could only make do with today.

I knelt there a long time, my face buried in her hands, whose pores still exuded the stale smell of prison. I loved her, and I could find no words to comfort her or myself.

Then I heard her say, "Will you help me pack, please, Dante, and see if you can get me a flight to Zurich. I'd like to leave as soon as I can."

It was then I discovered how important it was to be the Director. I was able to command a first-class seat on an overbooked aircraft. I was able to park the car in a prohibited zone at Fiumicino. I was offered free drinks in the distinguished visitors' lounge. I was able to walk Lili all the way onto the aircraft and settle her in the seat and commend her to the good offices of the chief steward.

All that, because of a small piece of card in a black leather folder, stamped with the arms of the republic.

I drove back to Rome and telephoned Pia Faubiani. She wasn't at home; she had gone to Venice to open her show there. I called an agency and commissioned them to find me a larger apartment in a more fashionable district. I needed a better *figura*, a better image, now that I should be dealing with high men and large affairs. I dined at my old place in Trastevere, but found it suddenly cramped and provincial. Even the musician seemed to have lost his touch. I went home early and tried to read a little of my old poet namesake before I went to bed. I was too sleepy to concentrate on his ponderous imagery—and besides I didn't believe a word of him. No, that's not true. There were three lines I had to believe:

> *And she said to me: "There is no greater grief*
> *Than to remember happy times, in misery;*
> *And your teacher knows it, too."*

Morris West

Mr. West's childhood was not such as might perhaps be expected to foster the talents of a best-selling novelist. Born of poor Irish parents in a Melbourne slum, he spent the most formative twelve years of his life – from fourteen to twenty-six – as a postulant monk in a strict Jansenist monastery. His decision to leave before taking his final vows was made only slowly. "Perhaps the main reason was the loneliness," he says. "I felt a great need for human contact and affection, particularly for the company of women." Difficult also was the rigid watch the Brothers kept on his writings of this period. Gradually the constrictions of his life crowded in on him. "That whole time," he says of his years as a monk, "was special only to me. When I came out, at twenty-six, I did not even know how to knot a tie."

The year was 1942, and he was posted at once into Army Intelligence. When the war was over it was natural that he should turn to his writing as a means of livelihood. He took a job with a local radio station, where he learned to concoct episodes for serials at £2 a time. Over the next few years he travelled to Italy, then to England, continuing to write and publish his novels and with *The Devil's Advocate*, published in 1959, he made his breakthrough into best-sellerdom. Now, although he and his wife and four children live mainly in Sardinia, he has houses in England and Australia also. His work has made him famous, and with the fame has come fortune.

Traces of his contemplative beginnings still remain, however. He describes himself as a "novelist of the moral dilemma". In *The Devil's Advocate* (Condensed Books 1961) he dealt with the dilemma of a churchman who had lived a life ritually perfect but totally lacking in charity. In *The Shoes of the Fisherman* (Condensed Books 1964) the dilemma was that of a prominent cleric who retained his faith "even though its preservation involved the destruction of a man". In *The Salamander* also his hero – although no churchman – must come to terms with fundamental questions of belief and reconcile conflicting allegiances.

Serious though Mr West's themes may be, he claims no literary pretensions. "I'm in an honourable tradition," he says, "the tradition of the sailor spinning his yarn, and I'm proud of that."

The
Boy Who
Invented
The Bubble
Gun

a condensation of the book by Paul
Gallico

Illustrated by John McClelland Published by William Heinemann, London

Dear Mom, don't worry about me. I've gone to sell my invention. . . . P.S. Don't worry, I took some stuff for sandwiches.

Julian West stood just over three feet tall in his sneakers. At nine and a half years old, with carroty hair and steel-rimmed spectacles, he surely rated as the world's least likely successor to Hiram Maxim. Yet he carried in his pocket a weapon that was to startle the military establishments of the two most powerful nations in the world.

He was off to Washington. The bus fare there cost him over ninety-eight dollars of the money his Grandma had given him for his birthday. He didn't grudge the expense—his invention was going to earn him far more than that.

Clearly Julian West was an enterprising young person. Yet before his bus ride was over he would be called upon to show far more than mere enterprise. Courage would be demanded, and of the highest order. For the journey was to escalate somewhat, helped by—among others—a crazy cowboy and a Russian spy. It became, in fact, a wild and terrifying chase that looked like ending in catastrophe till Julian took a hand. . . .

With wry humour and genuine affection for the young at heart, Paul Gallico here spins a tale as enchanting as any he has written since his brilliant novel, *The Snow Goose*.

CHAPTER 1

The miracles of the moon walk had always remained, in a sense, remote to Julian as something taking place inside the box of the big colour television set. The visible, workable magic of the electric beam that operated the entrance doors to the San Diego Bus Terminal, however, was something so differently enthralling that it almost drove from Julian's head the enormity of the expedition which had brought him thus far to the terminal at half-past two in the morning.

A small carroty-haired boy peering through steel-rimmed spectacles, clad in jeans, sneakers, a T-shirt and a leather jacket, he was carrying a small cardboard suitcase containing two changes of underwear and socks, a clean shirt, a toothbrush but no toothpaste, a hairbrush and, sealed in glass jars or cellophane wrappings, the makings of tunafish salad and peanut butter sandwiches.

Aged nine and a half and a scientist himself, Julian was not unfamiliar with the theory of the electric eye, but encountering this phenomenon for the first time coupled wonderfully the mixture of the practical and the dreamworld that animated him.

The doors turned Julian into a magician with powers over inert objects. He was startled and enchanted the first time the portals swung open as he approached them. He passed through in a kind of daze and wonderment and they closed behind him. He turned about, advanced, the doors immediately made way for him and he found himself on the outside once more, the possessor of a new and captivating magical power. But now the scientific investigator came uppermost, and by discovering the source of the beam and edging forwards and backwards he determined the exact spot where the doors could be kept open. People had to make their way around him causing a disarrangement of entrance and exit which caught the eye of a huge special policeman clad in light blue with a silver badge, who strolled over to inspect what was holding up the works. His shadow fell upon Julian in sufficient time before his arrival to make the scientist-wizard realize that he was not there to explore the mysteries of the electric beam. Instead he was on his way to Washington, D.C. to patent an invention, having stolen away from his home in a well-to-do section of San Diego and the sleeping household, with his grandmother's birthday present to him of one hundred and fifty crisp dollar bills in his pocket. He was not running away from home, simply bringing to life a dream that had become imperative. But he had no desire to handicap himself by being interrogated by the law. He therefore picked up his suitcase and trotted inside the bus terminal to influence not only the lives of a number of people there but also two of the most powerful nations on the face of the globe.

Julian had never been inside a bus station and ordinarily it would have terrified him had he not been armoured by the importance of his mission. He had been a tinkerer ever since he could remember; every toy bestowed upon him he had taken apart and put together again. Now he had invented something. He had planned it, drawn it, machined some of the parts in the school shop, put them together, and it worked—well, except for one minor defect. His schoolmates had coveted it. And his father had laughed at him.

The bus station is the crossroads of the masses. It smells of them and the orange peels, banana skins and candy wrappers with which they litter the floor and of exhaust fumes drifting in through the gates. Its music is the shuffling of feet across stone floors, the shouts of children, the crying of babies against the antiphonal thunder of the engines of the big transcontinental vehicles and the metallic voices of loudspeakers bawling information, directions and warnings from on high like the voice of God.

448

Julian thus moved into this world where the neon tube turned night into day, where there appeared to be only a chaos of coming and going until one saw that it resolved itself into long benches on which sat men and women with resigned, expressionless faces or nodding with half-closed eyes, and an information booth, ticket offices, drugstores, news-stands, souvenir and candy stores.

Julian saw people of his own age travelling, accompanied it was true, but nevertheless reassuring. On one bench, there was even a mother with a brood of seven, four boys and three girls ranging in age from about six to fourteen and surrounded by luggage which the mother kept checking by counting on her fingers. She kept track of her family in the same manner as one always seemed to be running off, to be called back and slapped.

Julian went to the information booth where a bored girl in Greyhound uniform was manicuring her nails. Julian said, "I want to go to Washington, D.C., please."

The girl looked up from her manicuring. "Three-ten from Gate Sixteen. It'll be announced. The ticket office will open in ten minutes." And she nodded in the direction of an unoccupied window. Thereupon she returned to her cuticle.

Julian found a bench where he could keep the ticket window in view and sat down.

SAM WILKS was keeping a low profile off in a corner where he could watch the special policeman and the closed ticket window for the eastbound bus. He had not shaved or washed since he had fled from Carlsbad two days before after robbing and killing a gas station attendant. He was clad in worn Levis, a soiled shirt, leather jacket and a ten-gallon hat, a uniform not likely to attract too much attention in that part of the country. Yet he had the surly visage connected with the baddie and which led policemen almost automatically to stop him for interrogation. Once on the bus, with the two articles concealed about his person, he would be all right, but in the meantime he did not want to be jostled. He sat chewing a toothpick, his pale eyes never still, thinking hard about his plan.

Frank Marshall, with his square jaw, good brow, curly brown hair and clear blue eyes, looked like a movie actor or the All-American Boy except for the sardonic curl to his lips which were the weakest part of his features. He was clad in khaki trousers, a checked shirt and a garment which any army man would have recognized as a battle jacket except that all insignia had been removed.

The twist to Marshall's mouth was partially self-mockery. He looked upon the world with half-humorous derision. He was not embittered by the violent alteration of his life. When he had returned from Vietnam fourteen months previously with some three thousand dollars, he had thought it would be to pie in the sky, adulation and a job. Four months later he had removed the insignia which proclaimed him to a large part of his countrymen not a hero but a sucker. He could not remove the scar that ran from his wrist to above his left elbow, gashed by a Punji stick, but that did not show beneath his sleeve. As for jobs for veterans, that was a laugh. He had criss-crossed the West looking for any road to quick and easy money that was not criminal. His capital was depleted. He was twenty-five, too old to go back to school. Maybe he could get a break in the East. He knew a couple of fellows in Washington. He needed a stake of some kind.

With some time to kill he sauntered over to the news-stand and thumbed over the supply of paperbacks.

A man named Clyde Gresham was standing next to him watching him furtively. Gresham was softness itself, in the shape of his mouth and rounded chin, his skin texture and dark, moist eyes. He was elegantly over-dressed in a shirt, Givenchy tie, and suit in matching pastels. He carried his Panama hat to show thinning, silky grey hair, brushed back from his forehead. His hands were beautifully manicured but pudgy and somewhat shapeless.

When Marshall, fingering down an Agatha Christie from the rack, turned towards him, Gresham smiled warmly, "Going far?"

Marshall's cold eyes lingered on Gresham no longer than an instant before he turned, without replying, made his purchase and walked away.

THE HANDS OF THE CLOCK moved so slowly that Julian wandered over to the machine next to the drugstore. The deposit of twenty-five cents activated a movable crane in a glass case which players manipulated in hopes of getting the loose forks to latch onto a camera, radio or cigarette lighter embedded in jelly beans. A boy and a girl of high-school age whispering nearby stopped as he approached. Julian had some change in his pocket extracted from his savings bank. Twenty-five cents was a stiff tariff, but he coveted the camera.

He had his money in his fingers when he examined the affair more closely and his inquiring mechanical mind presented him with the sixty-four-dollar question. Why all those jelly beans? Drag. Weight and surface against which the crane would have to pull. And all the prizes had either squared or rounded corners, nothing on which the forks could get a solid grip. Julian put the coin back into his pocket and turned away, grinning at the two high-school students, but they did not smile back. When he had wandered back to his bench, the girl, whose name was Marge, whispered, "Oh, Bill, I'm frightened. I feel as though everybody is looking at us."

Bill was nervous too, a virgin himself, as was she, about to explore the mystery which would make of him a man. But he said, "Don't be scared, Marge." He fished a Woolworth's wedding ring from his pocket. "Here, put this on. Nobody'll think anything then." Marge slipped it on gratefully.

They were not eloping, only slipping out of town to end the tensions that had developed through their going together, but more to conform to the sexual pressures of the times.

Marge was plain but had a sweet expression, trusting eyes and a downfall of soft chestnut hair. She was sixteen. Bill, a year older, was tall, loosely put together, with the big hands and speed that won him his position of wide end on the San Diego High football team. The coach was an old square left over from the bygone thirties who preached that sex weakened your energies for the game. Elsewhere Bill was assailed by sex, sex, sex and a certain shame that at his age he had not yet participated. Also, opportunity had been a problem. This exciting adventure was tempered by apprehension.

BACK ON HIS BENCH Julian watched the woman with the brood of seven counting her luggage and children for the fifth time and wondered what it would be like to have brothers and sisters.

An olive-skinned, foreign-looking man with thick black hair passed by carrying an extraordinarily shaped case which would later be revealed to contain a Hurdy-Gurdy, a fifteenth-century Symphonia. But now, Julian could only wonder what was inside it.

Next his attention was attracted to the man sitting opposite him beside a fat, perspiring woman. A black, flat briefcase obviously belonging to the man was between them and at this point Julian became witness to an international plot going awry. He had no knowledge of the coming fiasco and his participation in it.

The man with the briefcase was Colonel John Sisson of the United States Army Ordnance, temporarily attached to Military Intelligence in liaison with the CIA. Tall, his short hair greying, he was in civilian clothes which could not conceal his commanding military bearing. One could not look at him without knowing that he was "somebody".

The drama got underway with the loudspeaker bawling, "Attention please. Will Colonel John Sisson please come to the Dispatcher's Office." The colonel waited until the repeat before he hurried off in the direction of the terminal offices. In his rush he apparently forgot his briefcase.

And now the action speeded up. A man whose false passport proclaimed him as Philip Barber, born in Waukegan, Illinois, and whose equally false papers identified him as a plywood salesman, arose from behind a newspaper whence he had been watching the colonel. His real name was Nikolas Allon and he was a Russian spy connected with the KGB and a sleeper, planted in the United States twelve years before for just this moment. He was small, with the toothbrush moustache of the travelling salesman, the type no one would look at twice. He was moving towards the vacated bench when the fat woman noticed the briefcase next to her, picked it up and hurried after the retreating colonel calling, "Mister, hey Mister, you forgot something." She was already ten feet away when Nikolas Allon arrived where the colonel had sat. To have walked off unobserved with the abandoned article would have been one thing. To initiate an incident now by snatching it from the fat woman was unthinkable. Nikolas Allon just kept on going.

Julian watched the fat woman catch up with the colonel and thought, "Grown-ups! Oh boy, if I ever forgot my school satchel like that."

452

The colonel, checked by the woman's cries hesitated, and was lost. Puffing and panting she caught him by the sleeve and handed him the briefcase. The colonel, who was from Louisiana, accepted it with Southern grace. "Why, thank you, ma'am. That's mighty thoughtful of you."

The fat woman toddled off. The colonel, clutching his briefcase, turned away. Nobody saw the look of baffled rage on his face or heard him grate to himself, "Damn busybody!"

The episode over, Julian reached into his pocket and pulled out a page torn from a popular science magazine. Briefly, he examined an article headlined "Anyone Can Patent An Invention" Suddenly he became aware of movement and looking up saw that the ticket seller had arrived and was preparing to open his window. Julian put away his article, and got up.

CHAPTER 2

When he reached the window there was already a line. The two high-school kids were at its head and then the colonel, the man with the toothbrush moustache and the dark foreigner with the strange case. Julian got behind them and behind him came other passengers, including Frank Marshall and Clyde Gresham.

The ticket seller queried Marge and Bill, "Where to?"

The phony wedding ring had given Marge confidence, but Bill, now faced with ultimate decision, lost his cool and was unable to reply. He looked in panic at Marge, then gulped, "Two. El Paso. Round trip." The ticket seller stamped and handed out the tickets.

Colonel Sisson appeared next at the window. "Washington, one way, please," he said. As he put his briefcase on the floor to reach for his wallet, Allon, directly behind him, twitched, momentarily so close to giving way to his impulse, that he broke into a cold sweat. He could have whipped up the case and been away in seconds, but a hue and cry was not part of his assignment. At the ticket window he had recovered sufficiently, once the colonel had departed, to say, "Washington, please. One way."

And then an incident occurred which did not either surprise or discomfort Julian since he accepted grown-ups pushing kids about

as a fact of life. Sam Wilks, the cowpuncher in the filthy dungarees and jacket, suddenly appeared out of nowhere and thrust himself in front of Julian. The action irritated Frank Marshall, three passengers back. He stepped out of line, strolled forward, picked up Julian by the elbows and set him down in front of Wilks.

Bewildered, Julian looked up to see a young, tall, handsome man with bright blue eyes confronting the ugly-visaged cowboy. A veteran of television conditioning, Julian knew that here they were in real life, a goodie and a baddie.

The goodie had a smile on his face behind which Julian was unable to read the hint of derision and challenge, but there was no mistaking the anger and truculence on the face of the baddie. Suddenly the special policeman appeared within corner-of-eye-sight, the fury went out of the baddie's face, and he became impassive.

"You're next, sonny." The goodie winked at Julian and went back to his own place in line.

The ticket seller, without looking up, intoned automatically, "Where to?"

"W-W-Washington, please. One way." Julian's stammer was a tribute to the overwhelming eminence and importance of his father who, as Sales Manager of the Dale Aircraft Company, president of the Rotary, and co-owner of the San Diego Bullets, the city's pro football team, was always being interviewed and having his picture in the papers.

The ticket seller said, "One way, ninety-eight, thirty-five," whereupon Julian handed over five brand new twenty dollar bills. The ticket seller snapped them into his cash drawer, stamped the ticket, shoved it with the change onto the counter and then, looking up was startled to see no one there. Or so it seemed until he observed the top of Julian's head and half of his bespectacled eyes just over the counter. Nothing in the company regulations forbade him from selling a ticket to anyone who could pay for it. But out of curiosity he inquired, "You all by yourself, sonny?"

Julian felt a surge of panic. Was this the end to the grand design? He looked about, caught sight of the mother with the family, and replied, "No, s-s-sir." He took his ticket and change and wandered over and joined the group of children. Satisfied, the ticket seller waited on Sam Wilks's impatient request for a ticket to El Paso.

Julian wanted to ask one of the boys where they were going, but the mother went into her count again and when, having included Julian, she reached the eighth finger, her countenance reflected such panic that Julian sauntered away.

Marge and Bill were waiting for the bus to be called when Marge queried, "Why did you say El Paso, Bill?"

Bill replied, "I had to say something. But we can get off any place." Then, after a moment's hesitation, "What did you tell your parents?"

"I said I was staying with Dottie. You?"

"I told mine I was going camping with Chuck."

All her doubts came back and Marge said, "What we're doing isn't right, is it?"

It was what Bill needed to bolster his own failing courage: opposition. He said, "I thought we talked all that out, Marge. Today nobody cares what you do. And it isn't like we just met."

Marge, relieved to find what seemed like strength, whispered, "All right, Bill. If you say so."

Bill looked down at the girl and felt stirred.

The bulletin board blinked their departure time and the loud-speaker confirmed, "Bus three nine six for Tucson, El Paso, Dallas, Memphis, Nashville, Knoxville and Washington, D.C., immediate boarding, Gate Nine."

The portals of Gate Nine now acted like a vacuum cleaner sucking in some twenty-nine passengers, including the *dramatis personae* whose lives Julian was to alter.

The special policeman wandered over and stood casually by the gate. Sam Wilks, one hand tucked inside his jacket, was the first one through. The next few seconds would tell one way or the other. But the special merely glanced at him, obviously a cowpoke on the bum. Wilks passed through the gate and removed his hand from his coat. Then his description had not yet been broadcast. But it might be at any moment. They would be looking for him at the Tijuana border, but once on the bus he could still pull it off.

Allon had pushed to where he was right behind the colonel and the colonel knew it. Now it would be difficult for the colonel to

456

accomplish his mission and he wondered and worried how to go about it.

Marge and Bill played the honeymoon couple to perfection. Bill had his arm about her waist and Marge glanced shyly at her wedding ring.

Frank Marshall went through with a jaunty swing of his shoulders. So long, California, hello, Washington. Here comes Marshall.

Julian hung back. The special policeman and the gateman frightened him. What would happen when he produced his ticket? At the back of his head was the worry that his mother might have come into his room in the night to see whether he was all right, found him missing and given the alarm. His fears were unrealized. The big cop smiled at him, the gateman punched his ticket and as he had already done some two dozen times, repeated, "Watch your step. All aboard, please."

The bus was clean and shiny and smelled of plastic, machinery and polish. Behind the driver was a well with eight seats, four on each side, with a view through the front windscreen. These were already taken, as were the front seats three steps up in the main body of the bus. The ill-smelling baddie was in one of them, and a few seats behind was the man who had forgotten his brief-case. Farther down, absorbed in his paperback, the young man who had protected Julian's place in line was sitting on the aisle next to another passenger. But across from him there was an empty seat next to a well-dressed man by the window, and Julian asked politely if he might sit there.

Clyde Gresham examined Julian. "Why sure, sonny, sit here by the window." He stepped into the aisle and stowed away Julian's bag as he settled into the window seat. Gresham occupied the other one and asked, "There, how's that?"

Julian replied, "G-g-great. Thanks."

Gresham smiled down at Julian with warm fondness, unaware that the young man across the way had lowered his book and was giving him a look that was not exactly pleasant.

The driver was already at his wheel when a Greyhound dispatcher appeared to make a last-minute passenger check. Was he being looked for? Alarmed, Julian slouched down in his seat, but the number of occupied seats tallied with the ticket count and the dispatcher was satisfied. It was all over in a second and the only one who noticed Julian's action was Frank Marshall, who wondered, then thought that there was nothing all that extraordinary in these times about a kid that age travelling by himself. He also thought that nobody ever got hurt minding his own business.

The dispatcher left the bus and the driver, working his lever, slid the hydraulic doors shut. He then picked up a microphone to communicate with company headquarters, "Three nine six, on time out of San Diego at three ten a.m."

In the company's huge dispatchers' office in Oklahoma City, where a constant check was kept on all buses on the road, an operator spoke into his own microphone as he noted the time and number on a pad, "O.K., three nine six, take it away, Mike."

The bus driver picked up another microphone for interior communication, "O.K., folks, we're off." He trod on his clutch, dropped smoothly into gear and moved his bus off into the night.

CHAPTER 3

The bus passed through the business district of San Diego, out past the factories and finally into the countryside lit by a waning moon which threw eerie patterns on the window through which Julian peered, still excited over his successful escape. Perhaps the most difficult part of his project had been realized. There was no way for his family to stop him now.

Thinking back he saw them as actors in an old silent film, moving hysterically about to piano and drum accompaniment in the wake of his defection. The interplay of light and shade upon the bus window turned it in Julian's mind into a screen on which subtitles flashed and whereby he reviewed the events leading up to his present situation.

The fact was that his father, Aldrin West, was a sports buff and successful businessman and was mildly upset because Julian did not follow his bent. He was over-worked by the demands of the era, with insufficient time for all his interests and his family. Ellen West, Julian's mother, tended to over-protect him which completed his thoughts as to his family. He felt neglected by the one and smothered by the other.

The film began with Julian watching himself enter his father's study where Aldrin West, in the striped trousers and cutaway coat of all important businessmen in the silent movies, was at a desk heaped with papers and speaking into two telephones at the same time. Julian was clutching the diagram of his invention and he now filled the bus window with the first sub-title. "Dad, can I speak to you?"

Even at his desk his father loomed large and menacing. He hung up the two receivers and glared at him. "Well, what do you want?"

Julian held out his diagram, "Look, I have invented a Bubble Gun."

Here Julian showed some technical knowledge for he now saw a close-up of his father's face looking angry and laughing sarcastically. "Ha-ha. What good is that?"

Julian cut in on his own face too, and in his mind the piano and drum hotted up. "I'm going to make a million dollars with it."

In the silents characters moved jerkily and there was no mistaking their emotions, so Julian's father first clapped his brow, tore his hair and then, to a crashing of chords and a long drum roll, arose and pointed dramatically to the door. "Come back when you've got the million dollars and stop bothering me. I'm busy."

Julian watched himself creep crestfallen from the room and dissolved now to the title, "Julian's Bedroom—Morning".

He listened with satisfaction to the excitement music (deedle deedle dum, deedle deedle dum, deedle, deedle, deedle, deedle, deedle deedle dum) as his mother entered in her dressing gown and then as she saw the bed unslept in and the note pinned to the pillow, registered anguish, fright and despair. Julian was not quite certain how to get the latter across so in addition to having her wave her arms about he used a title, "Scream".

As his pyjamaed father rushed into the bedroom, his mother pointed to the note which Julian reproduced as best he could remember: "Dear Mom, Don't worry about me. I've gone to sell my invention. I will make a lot of money. Dad only laughed at me about it. I've taken the money Grandma gave me for my birthday and some underwear. Love, Julian. P.S. Don't worry, I took some stuff for sandwiches."

His mother now pointed accusingly at his father, "You've driven our child from his home." She wrung her hands, "What will happen to him? He will starve."

His father pointed at the note. "He said he took some stuff for sandwiches."

His mother flung herself upon the pillow, "Julian, Julian. Oh my God, he's just a baby."

At this juncture Julian took some liberties with his father's character and had him go soft. He went to his wife to comfort her. "Don't worry, mother. Our brave boy will be all right. How I have misjudged him." And as his father and mother fell sobbing into one another's arms Julian dissolved to: "The Patent Office, Washington."

He was standing there with several important-looking men in morning coats and top hats, one of whom unrolled a large scroll decorated with seals and ribbons reading, "Patent for Bubble Gun Awarded to Julian West", and with a thrill, he read his final title, "There you are, my boy. This will make you a fortune," and fade out. With a contented smile in recollection of the final scene Julian leaned back and went to sleep.

THEY WERE DRIVING due east and the blinding yellow rays of the morning sun smote through the centre of the bus and began to wake the passengers who lifted their heads groggily through the stuffy atmosphere.

The bus was making time on a straight, uncluttered road and was swaying slightly when Julian awoke to a moment of overwhelming panic and loneliness. Why wasn't he in his bed in his room within reach of his ancient teddy bear? Then he remembered and a little of his fright drained away. He was on his way to Washington to patent his invention and show his father. To verify this he slapped the left pocket of his jacket, which returned a comforting crackle, and then withdrew the paper which he unfolded and studied lovingly.

460

There were two drawings: the exterior, showing a compact, blunt-nosed, automatic pistol, a replica of one sold in toy shops which squirted a stream of water when the trigger was pulled; the other showed the internal mechanism, Julian's adaptation and invention, a gun that when the trigger was activated shot forth soap bubbles.

All the parts had been numbered and labelled:

THE BUBBLE GUN

1. Soapy solution compartment.
2. Trigger-actuated soapy solution pump.
3. Soapy solution hose.
4. Bubble-making ring.
5. Soapy solution fill-up plug.
6. Air rubber bag.
7. Trigger-actuated air bag compressor.
8. Air nozzle.

OPERATION

Compressing the trigger the soapy solution will be drawn to the bubble ring. The air bag will be compressed releasing the air through the nozzle and this air will produce a bubble when going through the perforated bubble-making ring.

In the lower right hand corner was printed, "BUBBLE GUN, INVENTED BY JULIAN WEST, 137 EAST VIEW TERRACE, SAN DIEGO, CALIFORNIA, APRIL 25, 1973".

The tubing and rubber air bag had come from the medicine chest at home, and a game provided the ring that formed the soap bubbles at the muzzle, but the spring, compressors and plungers he had designed and manufactured in his school shop. He was still niggled by the Bubble Gun's occasional crankiness in operation for instead of the one large bubble, a stream of smaller ones sometimes emerged, giving a machine gun effect.

He thought back with delight to the day he had first shown it to his classmates and heard again their impatient clamour.

"Hey, Julian, lemme shoot it."

"He said I could next."

"Can you make me one, Julian?"

When he had patented it millions of kids would want one. Then his father wouldn't laugh any more.

"What have you got there, sonny?" The voice made Julian suddenly aware of the arid landscape whizzing by, the whine and rumble of the bus and the passengers yawning, stretching, adjusting their clothing and chattering.

The question had come from the man next to Julian, who exuded a flowery fragrance like scented soap or toilet water. Julian's hand had dropped instinctively over his diagram so that no one could steal it. But Gresham's dimpled face and pleasant smile boded no evil intentions. He then replied, "My B-B-Bubble Gun," but he did not remove his hand.

Gresham said, "A bubble gun, eh? What does it do?"

Julian replied, "It shoots bubbles."

Gresham's smile grew even sweeter. "You don't say. What a clever little boy."

Julian studied the man again and saw no further cause to distrust him. Besides the praise had pleased him. He said, "I'm g-g-going to Washington to p-p-patent it."

This extraordinary statement from the small, stammering boy across the aisle caused Frank Marshall to turn his head slightly to take in Julian and his scented companion. His fragrance had reached Marshall and suddenly caused his hackles to rise. He recognized the boy as the one that bum had crowded out of line. What kind of a crazy deal was this, a kid going to Washington to patent a gun that shot bubbles? And where did this fat fag fit in? He sat up and sharpened his listening faculties.

Gresham asked, "What's your name, sonny?"

Julian returned the diagram to his jacket pocket. "Julian."

Gresham smiled indulgently. "I mean your last name."

Julian did not reply, obeying the subconscious reflex of self-preservation. When his parents discovered he was gone they would call the police and if he, Julian, went around telling everybody his name they'd be able to find him.

His companion broke the silence. "My name is Clyde Gresham, but you can call me Clyde."

Julian remained silent but across the aisle Marshall shifted uneasily.

Gresham asked, "Where are your mommy and daddy?"

"Home." Julian nodded in the direction from which they had come and then added, "In San Diego."

"Isn't anybody with you?"

Marshall looked across to see Julian simply shake his head while Gresham asked, "You mean to say you're going all the way to Washington by yourself?" Julian nodded.

Gresham bent towards him, his back half-turned so that he was unaware of the mounting anger in Marshall's eyes. "You're quite a little man." His voice was so full of admiration that Julian looked again into the warm, friendly eyes. Praise and understanding from a grownup were rare.

Gresham succeeded in keeping the excitement out of his voice. "Well, now, it just happens I'm going a good part of the way. Would you like me to look after you?"

Julian saw nothing in the bland smile to intimidate him. What lay ahead was unfamiliar and being "looked after" might have its uses, particularly since there could be no question of this stranger having authority over him and so he replied, "O.K."

"Then we're friends," said Gresham, and he slid an arm about Julian's shoulder and squeezed it.

Julian reacted to this as he did to all adults not of his immediate family who seemed unable to be in contact with children without patting them or taking them onto their laps. He kept quiet and planned to get away as quickly as possible. These thoughts led to an unconscious wriggle and Gresham removed his arm. Across from him Frank Marshall balled his hands into hard, tight fists.

Looking out the window Julian saw that the dun-coloured lonely country had given way to a few green fields, some outlying barns, and then clapboard houses and adobe dwellings, indicating the outskirts of a fairly substantial town. The driver's voice came over the loudspeaker, "Folks, we're coming into Yuma, Arizona. Thirty-minute stop for breakfast."

The houses increased in number and soon the highway became the main street. Gresham slid his arm about Julian's shoulder again and said, "We'll have a wash-up and breakfast together." Although

463

he knew it was none of his business, Frank Marshall's anger was so intense that he got up and walked to the door as the bus halted at the Greyhound station.

CHAPTER 4

"We're coming into Yuma." Bill looked questioningly at Marge. "Here?"

Marge had awakened with all the trust of a sleepy-eyed child. Her face had been burrowed in the boy's shoulder and his comforting arm had been about her, but now sitting up and being asked again for a decision, she felt the panic that had beset her ever since leaving home. She searched for an excuse. "Someone might know us. Myra, a girl friend of mine, has an aunt in Yuma," and then it was her turn to inquire, "Are you sure you love me, Bill?"

The glib answer refused to come to the boy's lips. What *was* love, a feeling that demanded release? Or was it thinking about Marge when he ought to be doing his homework, remembering the texture of her hair, her fingers on his hand? He was content when he was near her but how could you tell whether that was love? If you said you loved someone, and didn't, just to make them go all the way, that was unfair. In exchange for three words a good kid like Marge would give away everything she had.

He looked at Marge again and there was the physical surge and, too, something in the curve of her lips, in the line of the young neck that was moving. If one looked too long tears could be dangerously close; unmanly tears. He said, "I dunno, Marge. I guess I must because when I look at you I want to bust."

This satisfied her for she snuggled closer to him. But it was Bill's own insecurity which led him to say, "If Myra's aunt lives here she might be around. We could have some breakfast and then go on to Tucson. Nobody'd know us there."

The bus station at Yuma was classic, mingling diesel fumes with frying eggs and bacon. There was a lunch counter on one side, a news-stand on the other, a few benches and at the far end lavatories. There was also a small Navajo trading post with blankets, baskets and badly-made turquoise jewellery.

464

Gresham apparently had had difficulty locating something in his luggage. He and Julian were the last to enter the waiting room and the majority of the passengers were already ordering breakfast or buying newspapers. Gresham, his arm still about Julian's shoulder, glanced about him. "Smell that bacon. I'll bet they've got pancakes too. Would you like some?"

Julian said, "Uh, huh, but I've got to . . .". At the far end of the room two of the passengers emerged from the door marked MEN.

"Sure," Gresham said, increasing the pressure on Julian's shoulder, "we'll do that first," and they moved off.

Gresham had miscounted the male passengers in the waiting room by one. Frank Marshall now stepped out from behind the corner of the news-stand and blocked their path. His expression was blank, almost disinterested, as he ignored Julian and in a conversational tone said to Gresham, "Take your arm off that kid."

Gresham's shock was total. The amazingly blue eyes of the young man who had ignored him so pointedly in San Diego seemed to take all of him in and at the same time not to see him at all.

Gresham loosed his grip upon Julian and huffed, "Who do you think you are? I'm looking after this little fellow."

Succinctly, Marshall said, "Get lost."

Julian moved a little away, thus disassociating himself from the pair, and gazed with curiosity from the face of one to the other. This was the second time that the man he had labelled as the goodie had intervened for him. Gresham had only been trying to be nice. True, he had been a bit icky but then a lot of grown people were. What was it all about?

The two faces were close together, one smiling easily and the other suddenly disintegrating before Julian's eyes. And the boy became aware of a feeling of mingled discomfort and relief.

Gresham made a last attempt. "You can't . . ."

This time Marshall made no reply whatsoever. He simply stepped on Gresham's foot, hard, and kept up the pressure as Gresham grimaced with pain.

Marshall said sweetly, "Sorry, dearie," and then allowed a grating note in his speech. "You're off the bus, too. If I see you again you'll really get hurt."

Julian felt a little frightened. Violence on TV was fun, but here so close by, it gave one a sickish feeling.

Gresham pleaded, "Listen, I've got to get to Memphis."

"There'll be another bus along. This is where we part company." Marshall removed the pressure from Gresham's foot and stood to one side. "Now get going," and without another word Gresham hurried out the exit. Whatever it was it was over and Julian was no longer frightened. If he felt a moment of pity for the stranger who had been destroyed before him it evaporated into admiration for the man who had accomplished it with such ease. He felt as though a shadow had been lifted from him. He asked, "What happened? Was something wrong?"

Marshall said, "Never mind. If you got to go in there," and he nodded in the direction of the men's room, "get on with it."

Julian went in and Marshall waited for him, berating himself as he did so. "Marshall, why can't you learn to mind your own business? You could get stuck with the kid."

Julian emerged from the men's room.

Marshall asked, "O.K.?"

Julian replied, "O.K."

Marshall said again, "O.K.," and sauntered off. He did not turn around to see whether Julian was following him for that was the surest way to make any stray come after you. Julian stood there watching him go neither hurt nor puzzled. Children are not apt to linger over events that are closed or the curious behaviour of adults.

He went over to the lunch counter and found a seat next to the dark-haired man with the strange-looking case, consulted the menu and ordered pancakes with little pork sausages. When they appeared he doused them with syrup and noticed that his neighbour had nothing before him but was sitting there unhappily hugging his instrument case. Julian asked, "What's your name?"

"Milo Balzare. You?"

"Julian. What have you got in there?"

Balzare said, "It is very ancient instrument. For music. But it very old from other times. Am coming here to America to learn your popping music." He looked hungrily at Julian's plate. "How you say that please? I like."

Julian told him, "Pancakes and little sausages," and signalled the counterman. From Balzare it came out, "Pon cakes and leetle sausage."

The counterman yelled through the kitchen hatch, "Toss one. Small porkers with."

The musician looked baffled. "Is so difficult language. What is coffee?"

The counterman shouted through the hatch, "Draw one," and a cup of coffee was served. Julian laughed. He was having a wonderful time.

Towards the end of the counter Marshall was drinking coffee and looking straight ahead. Julian thought if Marshall glanced over he might wave to him, but Marshall didn't.

CHAPTER 5

Boarding the bus after the break in Yuma, Colonel Sisson managed to stumble, drop his briefcase and spill the contents all over the aisle. Any film director watching this scene would have called for a retake but apparently none of the passengers blocked behind him thought there was anything extraordinary in this and only casually glanced at the papers which seemed to be mainly diagrams and blueprints. In great and obvious embarrassment the colonel attempted to cover up the nature of these papers as he scrabbled them up off the floor. While they waited Marshall said to the driver, "The little fat guy who was going to Memphis ain't comin'. He changed his mind."

The bus driver shook his head in disgust. "He might have said something before. Passengers." The hydraulic doors hissed shut. He picked up his short-wave microphone, "Three nine six on time out of Yuma."

When the aisle had cleared and the passengers settled, Julian found that his strange friend had pre-empted his window seat. He didn't resent losing his view. Children were there to be pushed around, but it might provide an opportunity to probe into the mystery of the vanished Gresham. He asked, "Please, can I sit next to you?"

Marshall looked at him without enthusiasm, then realized that he had taken the boy's seat, felt guilty and replied, "Sure, go ahead."

Julian slid down into the seat. Marshall looked out the window as the bus pulled away from Yuma. Julian waited until Marshall got bored with the scenery and turned for his book. Then he asked, "What's your name?"

Marshall thought, *Oh hell. Well, I asked for it.* Aloud he said, "Frank Marshall."

He looked to find his place in his book when Julian said, "Mr. Marshall?"

The man gave up. He said, "Just Marshall will do."

Julian then asked, "Why did you make that man go away?"

Marshall was aware that kids were a lot smarter than they used to be but he had the feeling that this boy had a peculiar kind of innocence and trust and probably had not known what that son of a bitch was up to. He therefore produced that completely phony voice used by adults when they are telling a thumping lie to the young. "Well, you see, kid, I recognized him as a—pickpocket."

Julian clapped his hand to his jacket where the Bubble Gun design reposed. He produced the folded diagram and said with satisfaction, "He didn't get my invention. After I p-p-patent it I'm g-g-going to make a lot of m-m-money with it."

The word 'money' startled Marshall and a slight change of expression came over his countenance. "Let's have a look at it."

Julian only said, "I g-g-got to work on it some more."

Marshall said carelessly, "O.K., so don't," which of course produced an immediate unfolding of the diagram. Marshall studied it, noting Julian's name and address, and then asked, "What's wrong with it?"

Julian replied, "Sometimes when you pull the trigger it shoots a lot of little b-b-bubbles instead of a b-b-big one."

Marshall said, "Why don't you ask the guy up front to help you, the one who spilled his papers? I had a look at 'em. That was ordnance."

"What's ordnance?"

"Guns and stuff. He's probably Army in civvies." He studied Julian for a moment. "Do your folks know where you are?"

Julian shook his head, ". . . but I left a note saying I was g-g-going."

Marshall's curiosity was past mild interest. "It doesn't make sense. What's the plot, kid? Come on, give."

"My d-d-dad thinks I'm a s-sissy and no g-g-good. When I showed him my invention and said I was going to m-m-make a million dollars he laughed at me and said to stop bothering him and to come b-b-back after I had made my m-m-million dollars. That's why I'm g-g-going to Washington."

A million dollars had a sweet ring in Marshall's ears but of course it was crazy. A kid going to Washington because his father had laughed at him. The printing on the diagram caught Marshall's eye again. "Hey! West! Is your pop Aldrin West, the guy who owns the San Diego Bullets? I'll bet you're a real football freak."

Julian shook his head. "I'm not. It makes dad mad. I think football's crazy."

Suddenly a vista opened for Marshall. A kid that didn't like football. He said, "What do you like?"

Julian shrugged. "M-m-making things."

Marshall glanced at the diagram more intently and then again at Julian. He said, "Your Pop's probably having a fit right now. Did you say in your note where you were going?"

Julian said, "No. Anyway, he wouldn't care."

Marshall sat back for a moment and wondered just how true this was. One did not know what to believe.

BUT, OF COURSE, Aldrin West did care, his concern intensified by a feeling of guilt and his wife's hysteria at the thought of her "baby" somewhere loose in the United States.

The repercussion of all this soon reached a corner of the Missing Persons Bureau of the San Diego Police Department where a bored sergeant in shirtsleeves took West's call. He repeated as he wrote, "Julian West, age nine and a half, reddish hair, wears glasses, has slight stammer . . . didn't say where he was going. O.K., Mr. West, that shouldn't be too difficult. We'll put it out on the radio and let you know as soon as we hear anything."

A short while later the police teleprinter was tapping out the alarm, "Missing from home, Julian West, age nineteen and a half, red hair, glasses, stammer. Thought to be wearing denims and T-shirt with leather jacket. Anyone seeing please contact their local police."

BY MID-MORNING Bus 396 had metamorphosed from a transcontinental transporter to a cozy social centre. Two men, chess fiends, had discovered one another and were engrossed in battle on a pocket set. Four other passengers, all strangers to one another, were playing gin rummy. There was so much going on that any fears Julian might have had at being by himself vanished.

Three seats to the rear of him the musician withdrew an odd-looking instrument from its case and began to tune it. Julian went over to have a look.

"What's that?" he asked.

Balzare said, "It is called 'symphonia', but also 'hurdy-gurdy'."

The instrument resembled a mandolin except that there was a handle which Balzare now turned causing the hurdy-gurdy to give forth a drone against which with a pick he plucked out a gay melody. A man across the aisle said, "Say that's great," and a group quickly gathered round.

Marshall had put his book by and was listening with interest to a small transistor radio which was not generally audible in the racket of the bus.

Julian wandered away from the musician, and climbed up into his seat to reach his suitcase on the rack. "I'm hungry," he said to Marshall. "Are you?"

Marshall said, "Not yet. I want to listen to the news." Julian took his suitcase, strolled down the aisle and addressed himself to Marge and Bill. "Hello."

Marge quickly withdrew her hand from Bill's and smiled at him. "Hello. What's your name?"

"Julian. Are you two on your honeymoon?"

Here Marge almost gave the show away by repeating "Honeymoon?" Then she recovered and said, "How did you know?"

Julian said, "Aw, I've been watching you. Would you like a tunafish sandwich?"

Marge exclaimed, "Would I." But small boys meant nuisance

470

to Bill. He said, "Come on, where are you gonna get a tunafish sandwich? Why don't you beat it?"

Julian said, "I'll make you both one," and knelt in the aisle opening his suitcase.

Curious now, Bill leaned over to look inside and saw a half loaf of white bread in cellophane, one jar each of tunafish, peanut butter, and mayonnaise, some lettuce leaves and a knife. Julian expertly whipped up three tunafish sandwiches, handing two of them to Marge and Bill, the latter saying, "Sorry, kid. These are great."

Julian said. "That's O.K.," reflected for a moment and then made a fourth sandwich which he took to Marshall, saying as he handed it to him, "I'll bet you'd like this if you tried it." He put his case beneath his feet, sat down and chomped contentedly.

Marshall regarded him quizzically, bit into his sandwich and said, "Not bad." When they were both close to their last bite and Julian was licking his fingers, Marshall said, "Did you know the cops were after you?" He indicated his now silent transistor. "I heard it after the news. General police alarm."

Wide-eyed with terror Julian asked, "Are you going to give me away?"

Marshall replied half truculently, "Why should I?"

Julian was miserable. "I don't want them to catch me until I get my patent."

Marshall said, "Keep your hair on. How old are you? Nine, nine and a half?" Julian nodded.

Marshall said, "Cheer up, the fuzz added ten years. They'll be looking for some nineteen-and-a-half-year-old dropout." Only half-meaning it he added, "If anybody asks you, you can say you're my kid brother."

Relief, wonder and admiration glowed in Julian's eyes as he gazed up at Marshall. "Say, can I?"

Marshall suddenly realized what he had let himself in for. "No, certainly not," and then at Julian's hurt look, "All right, all right, so you're my kid brother."

Julian felt a sudden thrill. He looked up at the man next to him and was comforted by the mantle of his protection and his last words repeated themselves delightfully in his mind. *All right, all right, so you're my kid brother.* Julian had often longed for a brother as confidant. With a big brother such as this, one could dare anything. And now his scrutiny was beginning to yield some clues. He asked, "Were you in Vietnam?"

A curious expression which Julian was unable to interpret came over Marshall's handsome face. "What makes you think so?"

Julian pointed to the khaki jacket across his lap which, folded inside out, showed Marshall's name followed by "SGT."

Marshall was irritated. Behind those spectacles the kid had eyes. He was going to be even more of a nuisance than he had foreseen. "Forget it, will ya."

Julian wasn't to be put off. "Does SGT mean sergeant?"

Marshall turned upon him angrily. "I said forget it. That's ancient history. I came out of school, they grabbed me, I went, I came out. Any more questions?"

Julian was not upset by this sudden attack for he had learned that adults only half meant what they said, and so he replied, "No, sir." And then inquired, "What are you doing n-n-now?"

Marshall was forced to repress a smile. Kids *were* hard to beat. He replied, "Looking for a score. Make me some money."

Julian asked, "What d-d-do you do?"

Marshall laughed. "You name it. I'm lousy at it." Julian laughed politely at the old joke.

Marshall said, "O.K., now I'll ask you one. That was a lot of crap, wasn't it, about your old man not caring about you?"

The question allowed Julian a glimpse of his life at home, and with it the perpetual pain that his father was disappointed in him. So Julian merely shook his head. What was the point in trying to tell?

CHAPTER 6

In the San Diego Police Headquarters office of a Lieutenant King, the sergeant who acted as his secretary was holding delicately between thumb and forefinger a telephone receiver from which enraged sounds were emerging. He said, "You'd better handle this, Lieutenant. Guy named Aldrin West. He's boiling."

The lieutenant picked up his extension. "Lieutenant King speaking . . . yes, Mr. West, I know who you are. . . . What? . . ." He covered the speaker with a palm. "Phil, let's see that alarm on the West kid."

The sergeant shuffled through a sheaf of papers. "Here it is. Runaway. It's being broadcast every hour."

The Lieutenant took one glance at the sheet, murmured, "Oh no," and then speaking into the telephone, "I'm sorry, Mr. West, we'll send out a correction immediately and notify all airports, terminals, state troopers' and sheriffs' offices in the vicinity. I'll give it my personal attention."

He put the receiver back on its hook and said to the sergeant, "That lame brain Cassidy sent out the wrong age on the kid. He's only nine and a half. Put out a correction right away."

JULIAN WAS HAPPY. Travelling by bus was like watching two movies simultaneously. There was the ever-changing one outside the window and the other with the hurdy-gurdy music and friendly people inside the bus. The tyres whined as they rolled through the wild, tumbled Arizona mesas, dry arroyos and rock formations like cathedrals. Marshall was deeply engrossed in his book.

Towards the front of the bus, fate, the eternal playwright, was preparing the first of the dramas it had decided to weave about the small boy with the red hair, steel spectacles and stammer.

Nikolas Allon, the Russian intelligence agent, was worried. He had had his instructions and through bad luck which had led to an attack of nerves he had blown two chances at the colonel's briefcase. A change of plan was called for.

The colonel was equally frustrated. Everything that had been so carefully worked out had gone wrong. Unless he could improvise he was in for a record-breaking chewing-out in Washington. He put his briefcase on his lap, took out one of the blueprints and a pencil and began to work over it, aware that he was partly visible to Allon in the driver's rear-vision mirror.

The seat next to Colonel Sisson, who was by the window, was empty. So was the one in front, but it cut off Allon's view of him just below the shoulders. However, in standing up to take his satchel from the rack, Allon saw that the colonel was working on one of the blueprints in which the KGB were vitally interested. The Russians would prefer the entire contents of the briefcase which were known to the KGB as details of a new type of weapon, but failing that, one clear picture of a significant blueprint and the ordnance experts would be able to reconstruct the rest. If Allon accomplished the latter without American knowledge he would certainly be decorated. He therefore opened his satchel, made certain preparations, then replaced it and sat back to await his opportunity.

In so doing he had missed the entrance of one of the principal members of the cast. Julian had strolled up the aisle and standing by the seat next to Sisson, had queried timidly, "Sir, c-c-could I ask you something?"

Sisson, looking up at the eager-faced boy, had replied, "Sure, sonny, sit down," and quietly slipped the diagram marked TOP SECRET back into his briefcase. The height of the seat in front of him made Julian invisible through the rear-vision mirror and the racket inside the bus covered his and the colonel's conversation. As far as Allon was concerned the colonel was still doing exactly what he had been.

The colonel queried, "What's on your mind?"

Julian said, "My Bubble Gun invention, sir. Marshall said that you . . ."

"Your Bubble Gun invention?" The colonel had not expected to be tackled on a subject connected with his own department—hardware. "And who is Marshall?"

Julian nodded towards the rear of the bus. "My friend back there said you'd know all about guns."

Again the colonel was startled. Then he remembered the ploy of his scattered papers. "What about your invention?"

Julian said, "S-s-something d-d-doesn't work right," taking the diagram out of his pocket to show him.

The colonel spread it out on his briefcase, his practised eye taking it in in an instant. A smile of interest and admiration touched the corners of his mouth. "You dreamed this up yourself? Ingenious." He examined the sheet more carefully and reached for a pencil as Julian explained the problem.

Allon stole another glimpse into the rear-vision mirror.

474

The colonel's shoulder movements and the angle of his head told him that his quarry was still working on a diagram.

Over the loudspeaker the driver announced, "We'll be in Tucson in twenty minutes, folks."

Allon had accomplices in Tucson, El Paso and Dallas, but the farther they moved from the Mexican border the more difficult became their assignment. The time to move was now. Conditions were right. The bus was barrelling along at some sixty-five miles per hour on a bumpy road. In walking to the lavatory he could clutch quite naturally at the seats to steady himself. As he made his final preparations, sweat poured from him, beading his brow and making the palms of his hands slippery. He wiped them dry carefully on a handkerchief.

At the rear of the bus Marshall had seen Julian slip into the seat beside the colonel. With an inward smile, he wondered what would be the reaction of an army ordnance bigshot when confronted with a gat that shot soap bubbles instead of bullets.

The smile died away as something niggled at him. What kind of colonel spilled blueprints and diagrams marked TOP SECRET all over the floor of a public conveyance? As he was reflecting he saw an unobtrusive little man several seats ahead of the colonel get up and march down the aisle of the swaying bus.

The colonel was telling Julian, "It's a matter of distance." He studied the diagram intently and then, tracing with his pencil, said, "The air rubber bag is too close to the muzzle for you to get the build-up for a large bubble every time you squeeze the trigger." And then he added, "Did you make a working model?"

Julian nodded and his hand stole to his right-hand pocket and yet he hesitated, ashamed to let the colonel see his mistake. But Sisson had not noticed. He sketched lightly over the diagram saying, "Move the rubber air bag back here, shorten your trigger action and lengthen your air compressor hose."

Stark with admiration Julian said, "Gee, I ought to have thought of that." Then he added, "But shouldn't I p-p-put another washer here?"

The colonel said, "Good for you. *I* should have thought of that." And he drew the washer in. "You're a pretty bright kid. What did you say you were going to do with this?"

Julian was exultant. "P-p-patent it in Washington."

The bus favoured Allon, for just as he reached the colonel it lurched violently, enabling the agent to throw himself against the seat. His quick eye registered the small boy next to the colonel and at the same time the extraordinary ordnance design on which Sisson was working. The Japanese mini-camera in his right palm took six pictures over the colonel's shoulder during the time Allon mumbled "Sorry," regained his balance and continued down the aisle.

Frank Marshall saw the splinter of light flashing from the unsteady passenger's hand but it didn't yet register. His mind was on the amount of time the colonel was giving Julian. Wouldn't it be funny if his invention really worked?

As the passenger teetered along Marshall saw that he was sweating violently and his right hand was clenched as though in a spasm. He thought, *The poor bastard's sick. I hope he makes it.*

The colonel studied the diagram a moment longer. How old could the kid be, nine, ten? He had been so engrossed in the simple ingenuity of the invention that he had not even looked up when a shadow had fallen athwart it and somebody apologized for stumbling against the seat. He had simply murmured, "That's all right," and continued with his examination. Suddenly he glanced at Julian. "Are you really going to patent this?"

"Uh huh." Julian fished forth the crumpled article from *Popular Mechanics.*

The colonel glanced through it. "Sure," he said, "anybody *can* patent an original invention, but there's a lot more to it than this. Are you travelling with this fellow Marshall?"

Julian nodded.

The colonel suddenly felt bewildered and began to wish he had not become involved. He said, "I see," and then was compelled to ask, "Do your parents know about this?" Julian, close to panic, nodded again.

Sisson said, "Have you got any money? Do you know anybody in Washington?"

The word "money" led to "grandmother" and "birthday present". Grandmother would do. Julian said, "My grandmother lives in Washington."

The colonel snorted. "Your grandmother will be a great help in the Patent Office."

Subliminally Marshall was aware of Allon emerging from the lavatory too soon to have been ill and marching past him up the aisle quite steadily, his hand no longer clenched, but, more interesting than that, Julian and the colonel were still chatting.

Marshall did not bother any more about Allon except to note that he was taking his satchel from the rack again and the bus was entering the outskirts of Tucson.

The colonel handed back Julian's diagram which he folded up and put in his pocket. He said, "This whole thing sounds cock-eyed to me, young man, but your engineering is sound. If you need any help in Washington, get in touch," and he took a card from his wallet, initialled it and handed it to Julian.

After he had been overwhelmed with "Gee, thanks," and Julian had departed, his mind turned back to his mission. He glanced ahead to where Allon was sitting and could not think of a thing to do beyond going up to him and handing him the blueprints. The next move would have to be Allon's.

Julian dropped into the seat next to Marshall as the bus slowed down through Tucson and excitedly produced the diagram. "He showed me what to do. See?"

Julian became aware that Marshall was not listening to him, and he looked up to see that Marshall was gazing in a puzzled manner towards the front of the bus.

He asked, "What are you looking at?"

Marshall replied, "Nothing." Nevertheless he continued to watch the little man who had looked sick and who was now standing, curiously tense about his neck and shoulders as if he was getting ready to leave the bus fast.

"Tucson, ten minutes, keep your seats please." The driver drew up to the station, the bus doors hissed open and several new passengers boarded.

Suddenly the subliminal that had so often helped Marshall in Vietnam to avoid grenades hung from trees, pressure mines that tore one to bloody shreds, the poisoned Punji sticks buried in the ground and all the other booby traps, brought everything into focus. And even as Allon was off the bus and running Marshall was down the aisle saying to Sisson, "I may be wrong, sir, but I think the guy that just got off took a picture over your shoulder. When he fell on you something flashed in his hand."

Fear settled in the colonel's stomach. He glanced at his brief-case, then gripped Marshall's arm, "When? Did you notice when he got the picture?"

Marshall said, "When you were talking to the kid."

The colonel yelled "Son of a bitch!" so loudly that it startled everyone in the vicinity, particularly the man named Wilks in the front seat. Beyond the offence of his appearance, Wilks's behaviour had been subdued ever since he had got on the bus; he hardly moved at all, as though concerned with not attracting attention, and did not get out during stopovers. He sat hunched by the window, hat pulled over his eyes, moodily observing the scenery as it flashed by and occasionally studying a roadmap. The seat next to him was unoccupied. Two passengers had tried it and been driven away by his unwashed fetor. These defections did not seem to upset the man.

But now as the colonel rushed out of the door, reaching inside his jacket for his shoulder holster, Wilks immediately arose, his hand movement duplicating the colonel's.

Marshall bumped Wilks as he dashed after the colonel, dis-tracting him just long enough for him to see that the sudden furor had nothing to do with him. He removed his hand from his clothing, mopped his brow and sank back into his seat.

Colonel Sisson and Marshall saw Allon at a distance halting a taxi. The colonel produced his gun, a black army .45, his back to the bus so the passengers could not see the gun. There was a moment of frozen tableau as Allon, his face a mask of fright, glanced at the colonel, the gun and Marshall. Then he nipped into a cab and was gone.

Marshall was unable to keep the contempt from his voice. "You could have had him, sir."

For the first time Sisson took in Marshall wholly, and recognizing an ex-soldier, reholstered his gun and said, "Thanks, but I didn't want him with holes in him." And suddenly he felt nine years old like the kid with the design and wanted to cry from sheer frustration. "What a foul up," he said bitterly. "They'll

478

have my chicken feathers for this. That crazy kid! Tell the driver I'm not coming back."

Marshall said, "I don't get it," but Sisson was already running for a second taxi.

As Marshall climbed back into the bus he told the driver, "They won't be back."

The driver was beginning to feel a sense of injury. He said, "What's the matter with my bus? That's three guys."

Marshall laid a hand on his shoulder. "Weirdos. Forget it."

The driver looked up into Marshall's face. *Smooth. If the guy knew something that was nobody else's business, so what.*

Marshall went back to his seat passing Wilks, who remembered him from the bus station episode and whose thoughts were somewhat different. *Dangerous! If that son of a bitch starts anything he'll get it between the eyes.*

As the bus moved off Julian asked, "What happened?"

Realizing that the boy was too bright to be fobbed off, Marshall whispered, "Secret agents."

Wide-eyed, Julian said, "Gee, honest?"

Marshall made the motion of closing his lip with a zipper and looking at the diagram in Julian's lap thought, *Now what did that scared little monkey want with a picture of that?* Aloud he said, "Did the colonel say this would work?"

Julian nodded, explaining the corrections. "Look, he gave me his address in W-W-Washington."

Marshall glanced at the card. The Pentagon Building. *And he had been right about the colonel being in ordnance. Then the boy really had something.*

Aloud he said, "When I was a kid I was always tinkering too. I was gonna be an engineer."

Julian asked, "What happened?"

Marshall touched the battle jacket on his lap and a look of anger flashed across his face as he picked it up and stuffed it down on the seat beside him. He replied, "Nothing," and then his countenance regained its usual bland expression as he added, "But you stay with your inventions, kid. You'll get somewhere."

He glanced at the drawing again and leaned back in his seat, his head tilted, his eyes staring in long, faraway thought.

CHAPTER 7

It was dusk. Lights had begun to come on in the small community of Indian Falls, New Mexico, at the foot of the pass that led over the Black Range Mountains to the Valley of the Rio Grande. No stop was scheduled there. Nevertheless, the bus had come to a halt at the other side of town at a road barrier where a sheriff's car and a confusion of people were gathered.

As the bus driver got out two state troopers on motorcycles came roaring down the road posted "Indian Falls Pass", dismounted and spoke to the sheriff, then briefly to the driver who returned to his bus and spoke to the dispatcher's office and then to his passengers. "Folks, there's been a washout twelve miles up the Pass and they say we can't get through until morning. So, we'll stay overnight here, motel and dinner on the company."

Marshall said, "A night in the sack suits me fine," adding hastily, "Can you look after yourself, kid?"

If Julian was disappointed at the question he did not show it. A motel room to himself was pretty exciting. There might even be a TV set and no one could tell him to turn it off and go to bed. He said, "Sure. I got my case."

"O.K., see you in the morning," and Marshall was off the bus.

As people were pressing down the aisle, Bill looked at Marge in sudden excitement. He put his arm about Marge's shoulder and whispered, "I guess here, maybe."

Marge nodded and leaned her head against Bill's cheek. Then, they retrieved their bags and joined the end of the line of passengers. Julian, too, lagged behind fascinated by the troopers' guns and shining cartridge belts.

The sign read INDIAN FALLS MOTEL, R. GRADY. PROP. and the name was repeated in coloured lights that blinked on and off. It was a fair-sized establishment since tourists coming through town at nightfall preferred to stay and run the twisting roads of the Pass in the morning. The cabins were gathered, U-shaped, around the forecourt, in which were flowers and cactus and yucca, with the office at one end and the dining room at the other.

R. Grady was known as Pop, his wife as Mom. Pop had been

dried out by the sun until he was as stringy as a slab of jerked deer meat. Mom, in the other hand, had blown up into a butterball with three chins and specs worn mostly on top of her head.

Behind the counter Pop booked the passengers in: Mom, billowing on a high stool, handed out the keys. At the end of the line Marge and Bill and Julian were waiting to be assigned rooms, Julian barely visible over the counter. Neither Mom nor Pop noticed him.

Pop looked queryingly at Marge and Bill, spotted Marge's ring and said, "Mr. and Mrs. . . ?" and when neither of them said anything, chortled, "Newlyweds." He turned to his wife. "Number twenty-five, Mom."

"Welcome, folks. Now, where did that number twenty-five get to?" Mom began to search for the missing key.

Suddenly Pop became aware of carroty hair, a forehead and half of a pair of steel-rimmed glasses. Julian was standing on tiptoe so that he would be noticed.

Pop said, "Well, hello, Buster. Where did you come from?"

Julian replied, "The bus. C-c-can I have a room, p-p-please?"

"Ain't you with nobody?"

Julian shook his head.

Pop glanced at the key rack. "Looks like we're fresh out of rooms. What do we do about this shaver, Mom?"

She leaned over to look at Julian. "By hisself, is he?" Suddenly she looked at Marge and Bill. "You two are a young married couple. You're gonna have to get used to kids sometime. How about taking him in with you? Number twenty-five's got a foldaway bed in it."

She had flipped her glasses down from the top of her head and from behind them her eyes glared at them. The boy and the girl could only exchange one miserable glance before Mom said, "Well?"

Marge said, "All right, you can put him in with us."

Mom said, "Well, that's right nice of you. Oh, for land's sakes, here's the key right in my pocket." She handed it to Bill and said to Julian, "You go along with them, sonny."

Bill moved Marge off to one side and muttered fiercely, "What the hell did you say yes for?"

Marge was anguished. "What could I do? They saw the wedding ring."

Julian moved over to them. "Is it all right for me to come?" He looked so anxious Marge put her arm about him. "Of course."

Pop said, "Number twenty-five's right next to the office. I'll show you how to work the folding bed."

IN A PHOTOGRAPHIC DARKROOM in a southwestern city three men were examining wet prints and conversing in Russian.

The technician held up a print. "Excellent. You have done well, Comrade Allon."

The courier, clad in black leather for a night motorcycle ride, inquired, "What is it?"

Allon replied, "Secret weapon. The plane will be waiting."

The technician studied the picture again, "What is this about soapy water and air bag?

Allon replied, "Code. The KGB will break it in a few hours."

The technician wrapped the finished work in plastic and then in waterproof linen. The courier stowed it inside his jacket and sealed the pocket with tape. Then all three men went out of the darkroom, the technician locked the door and they hurried down three flights of stairs to emerge from a shabby loft building in the industrial part of town.

The courier straddled the latest model giant Honda and kicked it into life. They shook hands and the technician and Allon merged with the passersby as the courier gunned his machine and shot off. When he reached the outskirts of the city he turned off his lights and became one with the darkness.

WITH THE FOLDING COT, the big double bed, a giant colour television, the chest of drawers and an overstuffed chair, there was hardly space in Room 25. As a matter of fact there was no path at all to the foldaway except directly across the double bed which it joined so closely that the mattresses touched.

After a generous supper Julian, on his best behaviour, had brushed his teeth and then appeared in his pyjamas. Bill slouched unhappily in the overstuffed chair, Marge sat on the arm. Julian gazed longingly at the big colour set. "C-c-can we look at TV?"

482

Marge began doubtfully, "Well . . ." Bill cut in curtly, "No, we can't," and then more placatingly, "Look, Julian, it's been a long day and we're all tired. You better get some sleep."

Julian hadn't expected to be allowed to watch the box. That had gone down the drain along with the dream of a room to himself. And so he said amiably, "O.K.," and studied the layout. There was no route to the foldaway except cross country. He leaped onto the double bed which turned out to be a kind of trampoline and took three bounces, each one higher than the last, to land with a chortle of delight on his bed where he cried, "Say, that's great," and settled himself between the sheets.

Marge could not look at Bill. Something deep inside of her wanted to laugh. She felt as though she ought to give Julian a good-night pat or kiss, but she was halted by two visions of herself, one bouncing across the bed to get to him, the other crossing on her hands and knees. The deeply buried laugh pushed harder. Marge pushed back and told Julian, "Good night. Sleep tight."

Julian answered, "Good night," removed his glasses which made him look extraordinarily young and vulnerable, put his head to the pillow and was off.

Bill got up and flipped the light and the room was now illuminated only by the reflection of the motel sign. The two sat on the edge of the double bed, but with distance between them and spoke in whispers. Marge looked over at the sleeping boy. "He's sweet."

Bill said, "He's a pest."

Marge said, "Bill, do you think . . . I mean, should we . . . ?"

"Ssshhhh. We'll wait until we're sure the kid's asleep."

Julian had dropped off immediately but now he stirred lightly and then was quiet. Bill looked inquiringly at Marge and reached for her hand, but she withdrew it, putting her finger to her lips.

The two sat waiting and watching the sleeping child.

TWO CARS ROARED UP to the loft building and disgorged Army Intelligence, three FBI men and Colonel Sisson, still hugging his unstolen briefcase. They stormed up the stairs and down a corridor to a door marked "Cosmo Co., Inc.". An FBI man said, "This is it," and tried the door.

Sisson ordered viciously, "Kick it in," and they burst into the deserted darkroom where the odour of developing chemicals had not yet evaporated.

The leader of the FBI men said, "We've had this place under surveillance."

Sisson remarked bitterly, "Some surveillance."

They went downstairs again and when they came out a third car was just drawing up. A young lieutenant of Army G2 hailed them. "We think they've got a small plane on the Brubaker farm."

"Well, come on then," Sisson said, and they piled back into their cars, the lieutenant leading, and drove off. In the FBI vehicle, the agents looked to their weapons.

THE MOTEL SIGN had been extinguished and the room was now in darkness except for a reflection from a street lamp. Marge and Bill had managed to get into their nightclothes and were standing facing one another tremulously.

"Gee, Marge, you look beautiful." The boy wasn't aware that he had opened his arms nor Marge that she had moved into them. For a moment they clung to one another, experiencing a surge of tenderness they had not known was there.

Then they parted, shyly and with curiosity and wonder. Bill got into bed nearest Julian hesitantly, and with a glance towards the child, Marge joined him. They pulled up the covers but not touching lay there side by side, afraid to move. Somehow the magic of the instant before was gone.

Bill was nervous again.

How did one open this game? He whispered nervously. "I love you, Marge."

The girl replied dutifully, "I love you too." And each still remained rigid.

Something had to give. Bill put out a tentative arm for Marge's shoulder but touched her breast. With a quick intake of breath, she whispered, "Bill, please. What if he wakes up?"

"He won't." The feel of soft flesh beneath her nylon gown made him bolder and he reached for her. Julian suddenly flung out an arm in his sleep and hit Bill across the ear. Bill, startled, yelled, "What the hell . . .?" And Marge, in panic, shifted to the edge of the bed.

Bill sat up, rubbed his ear, and turned Julian over so that his back was to them. The boy continued dead out. "It's O.K." Bill moved towards Marge. "You couldn't wake him with a cannon."

Marge made a tentative move to abandon the sanctuary of the far side but not a great one, wondering what she was doing there in bed with a boy she did not really know and, above all, why?

Bill was furious with frustration. He had managed to get over the hurdle of that first tremendous move and did not know how to gather himself to do it again. He was spared.

"Mom?" Julian sat up and looked about him confused. Marge put her feet to the floor. "What is it, Julian?"

"I've g-g-got to go to the bathroom."

Bill said, "Oh, for Pete's sake, why didn't you go before? Hurry up, then."

Julian did his trampoline act across the double bed and disappeared. Bill thought *Oh, my God, what if we were on our honeymoon?* But then he thought, too, that he wasn't, but only upon an exploratory voyage into the mysteries of sex which suddenly was making him both look and feel foolish.

Julian emerged from the bathroom and varied his act with a run, one bounce and a three point landing on his own bed. He said, "Thanks," and was asleep immediately.

Bill made another half-hearted attempt, whispering, "It's all right now. C'mon back to bed, Marge."

The girl took her feet from the floor but kept them curled under her as she said, "Oh, Bill, can't you see this isn't the way we wanted it."

He sat up, suddenly relieved. He had not failed and it was she who had let him off the hook. He looked at the unhappy girl. A ray from the street touched her brow and one eye and showed the shadow of her tumbled hair. She looked different by lamplight and strange. He said half-grudgingly, "O.K."

"You're not angry?"

"No. Honest."

Marge leaned over to kiss him on his temple but in the dark

486

she missed and caught the side of his nose. He kissed back and got an eye. "Good night, Marge. Sleep well."

Marge whispered back, "Good night," and then barely audibly, "And thank you, Bill."

Sleep was upon Marge within minutes. She had been let off from something she knew now she had not really wanted. By the grace of one small boy, the time to revalue had been restored to her.

Bill lay awake a moment longer and thought *Oh boy, if the gang ever finds out I went to bed with a girl and didn't do anything*, and then suddenly he felt younger even than the child sleeping next to him and he was filled with the sense of something found and then lost and knew it would be perhaps a long time before he were to find it again. He was too old to shed tears. Instead, he murmured bravely, "Oh, hell," rolled over and joined the other two in oblivion.

UNDER MOONLIGHT partially obscured by scudding clouds a light plane sat at one end of a long, neglected field bordered by trees. The pilot sat on a wing, smoked and listened. When he heard the distant throbbing of a motorcycle he glanced at his wristwatch, stubbed out the butt, leaned into the cockpit, and switched the machine into life. Right on time. Whoever the bastards were, they were efficient as well as good-paying.

The racket of the approaching motorcycle grew louder, then it came leaping across the field to the plane, the rider pulling a packet from his pocket even before he had dismounted. The pilot stowed it, climbed into the cockpit and said, "Pull those stones from under my wheels and get out of here quick. I see car lights."

The chocks removed, the pilot braked to give the courier time to duck out of the way, leap onto his cycle and drive off. Even over the hum of his propeller he heard the grind of fast cars and saw the glare of their headlights. He gave his ship full throttle.

The field was uneven and the little ship bounced and swayed. A stone fence at the end of the field rushed at him but by then he was able to yank her off the ground. He flew level for a moment to pick up power just as three cars roared up to the side of the field disgorging angry men. The pilot stayed even with the trees using them for cover to gain still more speed. Then he pulled her up, banked sharply and vanished into the night.

On the ground, Colonel Sisson watched helplessly and one of the FBI men released a burst of useless machine-gun fire. The young lieutenant, who saw himself wearing a single bar for the rest of his life, said, "I'm sorry I took you to the wrong field first, Colonel, but there wasn't anything too definite."

Sisson felt sorry for him. This was obviously going to be the pattern, lousy Intelligence, bad luck, always too late. He said, "Never mind. We've got to get in touch with the Air Force."

IN THE MORNING Marge was already dressed when Bill awoke and sheepishly climbed into his clothing. The sound of water and tremendous splashing came from the bathroom where Julian was showering. Distracted by the noise, Bill fell over Julian's suitcase, kicking it hard with his bare foot and yelling in pain.

He caught sight of Marge, who appeared to be in the grip of something extraordinary; it was the deep-down laugh of the night before which could no longer be controlled. At her first peal of laughter his own rage evaporated and they fell into one another's arms laughing until they were weak.

When they had parted, Marge regarded Bill with wry maturity. "Bill, do you mind? I want to go home."

Bill, too, had grown up. "Yeah, I guess you're right."

The bathroom door opened with dramatic suddenness and Julian, fresh and bright, shouted, "Hi, I'm ready!"

After breakfast the passengers emerged from the motel to see the sheriff's men removing the road barrier as a state trooper on a motorcycle appeared from the direction of the pass followed by a Greyhound bus displaying its destination sign, SAN DIEGO. It pulled up alongside Bus 396, the drivers exchanged a few words and the passengers streamed back on board. Marge, Bill and Julian were the last to appear, but only Julian climbed onto the bus. Marge came over, reached up and kissed him. "Good-bye, Julian and thank you."

Julian looked baffled. "What for?"

Bill held out his hand. "Be seeing you sometime," and he and Marge turned towards the San Diego-bound bus.

The driver called after them, "Hey, aren't you two going on?"

Bill called back, "We changed our minds."

The driver used the fingers of his right hand for counting, "That makes five. Of all the loony trips."

Marshall let Julian have the window seat as the bus moved off. "Sleep O.K. last night?"

Julian replied, "G-g-great. There weren't any more rooms and I had to g-g-go with Marge and Bill. There was an extra bed in a cupboard." He grinned in recollection. "I had to b-b-bounce over them."

Marshall studied Julian, half-amused, wondering exactly what had happened and whether Julian suspected as he himself did that this was not a honeymoon pair at all. He thought not. It was this innocence in Julian which somehow had touched him. He said, "What made them suddenly decide to go back to San Diego?"

"They didn't say."

"And you didn't ask?" Marshall laughed. "Kid, if you go on minding your own business like that you'll go far."

CHAPTER 8

The pilot of the light plane had just spotted the distant fringe of Pacific coast in the early morning light when the two searching army jets picked up his blips on their radar and soon eyed him flying at five thousand feet.

The first jet pilot tuned to the private commercial band. "Piper VN four-seven-three, do you read me?" He received no reply. "Land before we shoot you down. Those are orders."

The man in the cockpit of the Piper quickly noted his position, the coastline and a stretch of flat beach vacated by the tide. He also saw something which the pursuing jets would not think about. Their job was simply to get him out of the air. He picked up his microphone and tuned to the military frequency. "O.K., boys, I'm going down."

He kicked the right rudder, put his plane into a side slip and dropped like an express elevator while the two jets descended to the level he had vacated. With the ground looming he kicked the rudder again, yanked the stick back and fishtailed onto the strip of beach. The hovercraft waiting in the shallows sent up a spume of spray as it darted in shore and onto the beach.

The man in the Piper climbed out of his cockpit, ran to the hovercraft and handed his packet to the man waiting at the open door. He received an envelope in exchange. The hovercraft backed off and then, engines full out and propellers whirring, roared off. It was several minutes before the jets realized what had happened. The second pilot in a blaze of anger put his ship into a dive, prepared his rockets for firing and at a thousand feet got the hovercraft into his crosshairs.

The first pilot chased him down and shouted into his mike, "Cool it, Johnny. We're over Mexico. You gonna declare war all by yourself?"

THE COSY ATMOSPHERE aboard Bus 396 had temporarily spared Julian from the searching hand of Lieutenant King, for only Marshall seemed interested in the news broadcasts. Luck had also helped Julian, for when the dispatcher in Oklahoma had routinely warned the driver to keep his eye out for a child travelling alone, he was still mulling over the mystery of his defecting passengers and furthermore, he had never actually seen Julian alone. The fact that one of the kids on his bus had been with three different parties failed to register.

It was shortly after two o'clock that Julian's incognito was to become violently destroyed.

There had been a short halt at Lordsburg to buy lunch and Marshall had treated handsomely. They had changed seats again with Marshall by the window. Julian had a hamburger in one hand, a Coke in the other and on his lap a paper plate containing a cream puff and a Mars bar. Marshall was munching a ham and cheese on rye and washing it down with beer.

Julian finished his hamburger and got his nose into the cream puff. He said, "Say, this is great. I was all out of tunafish. Can I pay you for what you spent?"

Marshall said, "No, that's all right, this one's on me," and as Julian acquired a fetching cream moustache, Marshall regarded

490

him with curiosity and in spite of his desire for non-involvement, with growing affection. He said, "Look, Julian, this crazy caper of yours to Washington? How much money have you got?"

"Fifty dollars."

Marshall snorted. "You know how far that will go in Washington? I've got my last five hundred but if I don't connect with a job when I get there I'll be flat." He grinned suddenly at Julian. "I guess you and me are in the same boat. . . ."

Here Marshall cut off, for suddenly looking towards the front of the bus his subliminal sense of danger again warned him that something was not as it should be. He said, "Now, what the hell is going on up there?"

Sam Wilks was a thief and murderer, a psychopathic killer. By incredible luck he had avoided the police dragnet at San Diego where he had abandoned his stolen getaway car and vanished on an eastbound bus. There had been no known witnesses to his crime and no accurate description of him available and nobody had either expected or looked for him.

Hunched now in the front seat of the upper level of Bus 396, a map of the district in front of him, Wilks had the Godlike feeling of knowing he was master of life and death. He had gotten away and would vanish into Mexico until the heat was off. He carried two articles which practically guaranteed this, a .45 automatic and a highly explosive hand grenade of a new army mark from which Wilks always kept the pin half-pulled. He belonged to that breed of self-justified terrorists spawned in the seventies and like all of them was prepared to risk everything on a gamble.

His map showed that they were approaching Deming, about an hour from El Paso and Ciudad Juarez, Mexico. The authorities would not be looking for him coming from that direction and even if they were no one was going to stop him crossing into Mexico. He put away the map, having committed it to memory, and mopped his brow for only the briefest moment of nerves which he shed by thinking that he would enjoy killing that good-looking son of a bitch who had been interfering with him. His right hand closed around the .45, his left around the grenade. He turned around once for a last look at the passengers, glanced again at the bus driver, and then made his move.

JULIAN SAID, "Whats going on up there?"

Marshall said, "I dunno." But he thought he did for having half-risen he had seen the character in the dirty clothes and ten-gallon hat go forward and lean over the bus driver holding objects in his right and left hands which Marshall had no difficulty recognizing. He muttered, "The son of a bitch," and watched helplessly as the bus driver momentarily took his eyes from the road, stared at Wilks with incredulity and then with a shaking hand picked up the microphone connecting him with headquarters.

THE MAIN DISPATCHER'S OFFICE in Oklahoma City was a vast, soundproof chamber filled with receiving and sending apparatus and men and girls serving them as messages came pouring in from every corner of the country. At one end of the room there was a huge map of the United States into which boys stuck pins and flags as messages were relayed so that an overseer at a glimpse would know where every one of his vehicles might be within fifty miles at any given time. At the other end of the room the chief dispatcher sat at a high desk with earphones and a plug-in switchboard which could connect him with any of the circuits. The room was filled with the quiet hum of the voices livened by occasional interference crackling from weather.

At one of the receiving desks there was a bleep and then the muffled tone of a voice adulterated by electronics. "This is three nine six. Do you read me?"

The dispatcher yawned. "I read you, three nine six. What's cooking?" and then his eyes popped as a tense voice said, "We're ten miles west of Deming. I've got a guy with a gun on me. He wants us to cross the border at Juarez Oeste. And he says he wants half a million bucks or he'll blow us all up. He's got a bomb."

To the dispatcher it could be nothing more than a gag or maybe the driver had got loaded somewhere, but he pressed a button and spoke to the chief dispatcher, "Three nine six claims he's been hijacked," and then to the driver, "C'mon, cut out the clowning. Nobody hijacks a bus."

Fear distorted the bus driver's voice. "Listen, will you. He's letting me get through to tell you to keep the cops off and he ain't kidding. He says he wants the half a million in small bills and

492

to have it waiting at the U.S. Immigration Station at West El Paso."

The chief spoke into his microphone and said, "This is Chief Dispatcher Olson. Look here. . . ."

The driver's voice rose to a near hysterical pitch. "I don't care who it is. He says a cop comes within twenty yards of us and the grenade goes bang. Says it'll kill everybody on board. I got twenty-one adults and three kids."

The chief said, "O.K., we believe you. Keep cool. We'll do all we can to help," and the bus driver clicked off.

On the top step of the second level of the bus, the .45 in one hand, the grenade in the other, facing the rear but angled so that he could likewise threaten the driver as well as the passengers below him, Wilks was in complete control. He said to the driver, "O.K., bud, speak to the passengers."

One by one, in unbelieving horror, they had become aware of the man with the gun and the grenade. The driver picked up his interior microphone. "Folks, our friend here would like to jump the border at Juarez and if you'll stay in your seats and keep calm he says nobody ought to get hurt. We should be there in about an hour."

Speaking loudly so as to be heard over the roar of the big wheels on the tarmac, Wilks said, "That's about the straight of it, folks. Stay where you are and don't nobody try to get brave. See this here pin?" He held up the bomb so they could all see the clip pin at the side withdrawn from the ring holding it. "If this comes out the rest of the way, we all go," he laughed. "That's O.K. with me, so don't get any ideas that I ain't got the guts to do it," and he flipped the grenade in his hand.

The bus erupted with little cries of alarm and notes of incredulity.

"Oh my God, he's got a gun and a bomb."

"What is it? A hijack?"

Wilks laughed, "You might call it that. So, just keep nice and quiet on account of these here things are kind of nervous like."

One of the male passengers rose from his seat. "You can't get away with—"

Wilks levelled the .45. "Shut up." And his admonishment was unexpectedly followed by one from Marshall who cried sharply,

"Sit down! Can't you see the grenade pin is half-out?"

Wilks caught Marshall's eye and called out sarcastically, "Well, now, one of them *he*-roes. Tell the folks what happens when one of these things goes off."

Marshall rose and said placatingly, "Listen, fella, you got a gun on us. What about getting rid of that grenade. There are women and children on this . . ." His voice trailed off, for a sour expression had come to Wilks's mouth and the .45 was now levelled at Marshall's head.

Wilks said, "Don't try no *he*-ro stuff with me. You already been in my hair and I'm figurin' on putting a bullet through your skull before I get off this bus. Maybe I'll do it now."

Marshall went white and sweat appeared on his brow. He remained standing, but Julian, looking at him with surprise, saw that he was holding on to the seat in front of him. Wilks laughed loudly, "Yer scared, ain't you?"

Marshall did not reply and Julian regarded him with sudden and overwhelming disappointment, unaware that Marshall was within seconds of being killed by a psychopath.

As Wilks's trigger finger began to tighten the bus flashed by a crossroads and two state troopers on motorcycles roared out and onto the highway in pursuit. Wilks now relinquished the bead he had drawn on Marshall to concentrate on the discharge mechanism of the grenade and ordered the driver, "Tell your company if them cops come any closer this thing goes off."

A four-year-old girl sensing danger began to cry. Her mother hugged her and called out, "You beast!"

At once Wilks became transformed, replying with exaggerated courtesy, "Why, ma'am, I ain't no beast. I got kiddies of my own at home I wouldn't want to see no harm come to any more'n you would yours. I like kiddies and kiddies like me. You got nuthin' to be afraid of as long as nobody don't try nuthin' funny."

Again the bus driver: "He's asking what about the money."

The dispatcher quickly picked up the mike, "Tell him we're rounding it up."

Number 396 was approaching the road off to the right for Juarez Oeste. Two more motorcycle policemen, a sheriff's car and two state troopers' vehicles were at the side of the road, but they made no move. Wilks waved his gun to the right, and reluctantly the driver tugged at his heavy wheel and headed south. The troopers and police joined the cortège.

At police headquarters in Oklahoma City, a captain was snapping orders into the telephone. "I want outriders no closer than fifty yards in front to clear the road to the border. We've contacted the Mexicans at Juarez Oeste that they're coming through. There'll be a man in West El Paso with the money. . . . No, no, don't try anything! And tell the FBI if there's a shoot-out they'll have the blood of those passengers on their hands."

By this time some thirty motorcycles and state troopers' cars were following 396. Ahead, a squadron of troopers was waving traffic off the road. Above, three helicopters clattered.

Wilks could not keep from smirking at the size of the escort and its helplessness. The bus entered the town of Morellos. Nothing moved in the streets, and Wilks's smirk turned into amusement as they emerged from the other side of town. He said, "Them cops sure had that town fixed up nice. That's the way it's got to be all the way." He tossed the grenade into the air again then, grinning, looked at Marshall. "That's what got you scared, ain't it? Some *he*-ro. Yer nuthin' but a yellowbelly."

Wilks's satisfaction with the way things were going had made him forget that he had intended to kill Marshall, but Marshall, still visibly shaken, did not know this. With a sidelong glance he became aware of Julian's reproachful eyes, questioning him and waiting for him to do something. This increased his frustration to the point where it almost overcame his fear. But the man with the grenade was in command. Marshall had noted that when he flipped it he always caught it so that one finger was at the loop of the pin already half-pulled out. One twitch and the bomb would be armed.

CHAPTER 9

Curiously the fantasy that Julian was now entertaining had no beginning, no end, only a middle. In it the Bubble Gun became the classic long-barrelled Colt. He would beat the baddie to the draw and save Marshall and all the rest.

The thought was clouding his bewilderment over Marshall's strange behaviour. Julian had nothing against which to compare the gulf between the dream world of the idiot box, in which puffs of smoke issued from six-shooters, but somehow the good guys never got hit, and the cruelty of reality in which live people suddenly found themselves torn and suffering. He had no inkling of the speed with which a tragic situation can explode or of the mind of Wilks who, ill-favoured though he seemed, spoke to the woman in the language of reasonableness. "Why ma'am, I like kiddies and kiddies like me." Nobody had been hurt, there had been no violence and within that context Julian's scenario—BOY HERO SAVES HIJACKED BUS—would work.

However, to reach the middle part where this beautiful dream would be realized he had to get there and so Julian arose and stood in the aisle. Automatically, the .45 followed him, and Wilks said, "Where do you think you're goin', sonny?"

Julian glanced at Marshall who hissed, "Sit down," and then looked quickly away, for this frightened man was not the Marshall of his fantasy, his friend who had been looking after him and offered to be his big brother if he came to any trouble. Julian said, "I'm thirsty."

The fear Marshall had known for himself was nothing to that he now had for the child. Out of the corner of his mouth he said, "For Christ's sake, sit down. You want to get us all killed?" But he was careful not to move. There was no telling what could light the fuse to that filthy package of human explosive up front.

As it happened Wilks sneered, "Well now, mister, that ain't no way to talk to the little feller."

Blind anger suddenly replaced Marshall's fear and he lost his common sense. He said, "You're just looking for an excuse to kill someone, aren't you?"

It did seem that the more one accused Wilks of villainy, the more eager he became to exhibit the sweet moderation that lay behind the deadly weapons he wielded, and he whined, "Now, now, you got me all wrong," and to Julian, "Pay no mind to that yellow-belly. You just get yourself a drink."

Politely Julian said, "Thanks," and marched down to the water cooler where he pulled a paper cup out of the dispenser and took a long sip. The water cooler was just outside the lavatory. He asked, "Can I g-g-go in here a minute?"

Wilks laughed, "Sure, kid. When you gotta go, you gotta go. Ain't that right?"

Julian studied Wilks for a moment and then glanced again at Marshall, who was still sitting stiffly, staring straight ahead. He carried his cup of water into the lavatory and shut the door behind him. Inside, using a piece of soap from the basin, Julian did what was necessary to implement the glorious dream.

And all the while the bus was rolling down to Mexico with its helpless outriders front and rear and helicopters overhead, wires were humming far and near about the first hijacking of a transcontinental bus.

In the grip of euphoria, Wilks shouted to Milo Balzare, the foreign musician, "Play something to cheer the folks up," and he waved the .45 in his direction.

Music was indeed all that was lacking in that weird scene. Balzare took up his hurdy-gurdy and a melancholy melody rang through the bus as the door to the lavatory opened and Julian emerged, his right hand in his jacket pocket.

Wilks turned his attention to him, "Feel better, kid?"

The way Wilks talked made it somehow simpler to go on. "Uh huh. Thanks. Say, would you like to see my Bubble Gun I invented?" Julian was level with Marshall who noted the hand in his pocket, had a frightful prevision of what was coming and the results and breathed in anguish, "Oh God, Julian, don't."

But there was no Marshall for Julian then, only his own line to follow and he moved past him and produced his Bubble Gun, a replica in miniature of the .45 which now stiffened in Wilks's hand and again levelled at Julian's freckled forehead. Wilks shouted, "Hey!" and the smell of death filled the bus, though Julian was unaware of it as he pulled the trigger of the only existing model of the Bubble Gun. A large soapy sphere blossomed from the muzzle, floated away, caught a splinter of reflected light which turned it first gold, then blue and pink, after which it vanished in mid air leaving a single drop to fall into the aisle.

The anti-climax was as much a shock to the passengers held in terror as it was to the terrorist, as though the bubble had exploded with the roar of the grenade in the man's hand. Somebody laughed hysterically and Wilks, lowering his gun, said, "Whaddya know. You invented that? Lemme have a look at it," and Julian continued down the aisle.

How Wilks was enjoying the kindly figure he was cutting behind the ever-present threat of his weapons. They could all see that Sam Wilks loved children. He let the .45 hang from his trigger finger and held out his hand for the Bubble Gun. Close to him now Julian pointed it into Wilks's face and pulled the trigger for the second time and here fantasy did come to an end. Reality of an unexpected nature took over.

Instead of the fat, soapy sphere there came from the muzzle a stream of small bubbles like a flight of coloured bees which enveloped Wilks's face, momentarily blinding him. He yelled, "My eyes. I'll kill . . ." but that was as far as he got. The bus driver, ready with the big spanner he had managed to sneak to his side, leaped up and with a backhand stroke hit Wilks with all his force on the side of the head and, even as the hijacker was falling, the driver trod on the brake and jerked the bus to a halt.

And so for the end to Julian's fantasy it was still Marshall who saved the situation, for as Wilks toppled forward, the ex-soldier saw that the finger looped in the grenade pin had pulled it loose. He had ten seconds. He needed only seven to whip down the aisle, knocking Julian out of the way, dive frantically under the unconscious Wilks and come up with the grenade which he flung, from a sitting position, out of the driver's open window and into a cabbage patch where, with a shattering roar, it sent up a geyser of earth knocking two troopers off their motorcycles. Pieces of metal rattled against the bus, starring one of the shatterproof windows. A shower of dirt and cabbage leaves descended. And then it was over.

For the first few minutes, until Rangers and State Troopers regained control, there was hysteria within the bus, blows, the screaming of the women, and all in a swirl of dust invading the interior from the landing helicopter.

At the front, passengers piled up blindly and insanely trying to hammer at the unconscious hijacker. Law men crowded in the narrow doorway, weapons cocked. "O.K., O.K., break it up, break it up . . . where is he?"

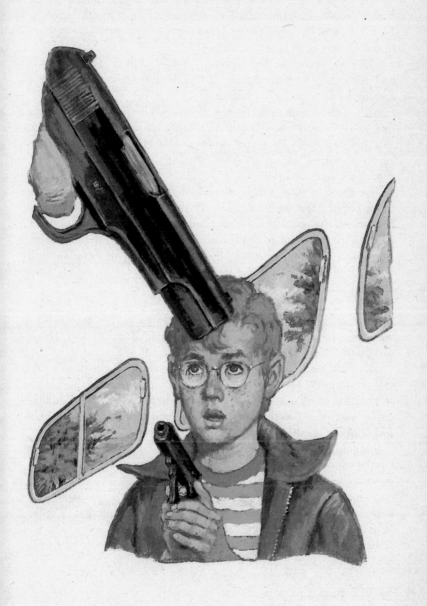

One by one they dragged off the hysterical passengers. At the bottom of the heap Marshall was protecting Julian with his body. Now he climbed slowly to his knees and Julian stirred, his glasses knocked awry, his expression dazed.

The driver pointed to the prone figure of Wilks. "That's the guy and his gun is under the seat. The kid squirted something in his face and I hit him with a spanner."

One of the troopers snapped cuffs onto Wilks's wrists, two more dragged him erect, and another, peering into his face, said, "Say, this guy's wanted. They just sent over a description of the guy who shot that filling station attendant at Carlsbad. A woman saw him but was scared to report it. . . ."

The swift, smooth action turned what had been chaos into the more orderly pandemonium of every one trying to tell how it had happened. In the hubbub Marshall and Julian were unnoticed. Marshall helped Julian up, brushed him off and put the Bubble Gun back in the boy's pocket. Then to his surprise he found himself saying, "If anybody asks, say it was a water pistol. You want to keep it secret until it's patented, don't you?"

Julian shook himself like a dog just out of water. "You got the grenade, didn't you?" His fantasies had evaporated. Reality was big brother Marshall who in the nick of time had grabbed the grenade and saved them all.

Marshall said, "Uhuh. But what was all that about you and those bubbles?"

There was no way Julian could tell him about his imaginings so he said, "I thought maybe if the man saw the bubbles he'd forget about shooting anybody."

Suddenly Julian seemed to levitate. A passenger seized him by the elbows and hoisted him up shoulder high, shouting, "Hey, everybody, here's the real hero!"

A reporter who had landed moments earlier in a press helicopter managed to squeeze into the bus and queried, "Who? What did he do?"

Julian looked down to Marshall for help but the latter only grinned at him, "Don't forget it was a water pistol."

There were plenty to give testimony:

"Bravest thing I ever saw."

"Walked right up to that murderer and squirted stuff in his eyes. He coulda been killed."

"Picked up the grenade and threw it out the window."

"What's your name, sonny? You ought to get a reward."

The troopers herded the passengers into a field to sort out what had happened. A king-size traffic jam had built up, drivers leaning on their horns, or abandoning their vehicles to see what the excitement was about. Photographers and reporters milled about cornering Julian in one group, the driver and his spanner in another.

Marshall hovered about keeping an eye on Julian. Nobody but the boy seemed to connect him with the episode of the grenade, which suited Marshall who did not like cops or newspapermen. He was still considerably shaken by what he had been through, but what was taking precedence in his thoughts was the boy's little black gun. The damn thing had worked.

"What did you say your name was, sonny?" a reporter was asking Julian.

Marshall had meant to warn him not to give his right name. Within him was the heartbreaking certainty that here was the finish of the boy's odyssey.

"Julian West."

"Where do you live?"

"S-S-S-S-San Diego, C-C-C-alifornia."

"Travelling all by yourself?"

Julian did not see Marshall's frantic signals. "Uhuh."

"Where were you going?"

Marshall spoke up quickly. "To visit his grandmother in Washington."

"Tell us how it happened!"

During the interview, two state troopers emerged from their radio car and stood watching and listening. One finally nodded to the other. "That's the boy, Buck," and then pushed forward with his companion to tower over Julian. A sickish feeling gripped Marshall—*There goes Julian.*

The trooper named Buck bent down and said gently, "I think your Daddy would like to know where you are."

Julian looked up at him miserably. Marshall turned and walked away.

ONE WOULD HAVE SAID that Aldrin and Ellen West had been turned to stone there by the telephone waiting in anguish for it to ring. When at last it delivered its signal, it took West three rings before he could unfreeze to seize it, fumble the receiver and face the news.

"West speaking . . . Thank God!" He turned to his wife, "They've found him, mother." The lieutenant's voice was still coming from the receiver. "Where did you say? New Mexico? On a bus . . . ?"

It was unbelievable, but the voice at the other end was firm. West shouted to Ellen, "He's a hero. Shot a hijacker or something. And he's O.K."

She began to cry. "Please, Aldrin, tell them to send him back. . . ."

The excited words tumbled from West. "Can they send him home? The fastest way. . . . Thank you, Lieutenant. And keep us posted. We'll be right here."

He hung up nearly sick with relief, but when he turned to his wife again there was a puzzled frown. "What did they mean he shot him with a water pistol? My God, Ellen, it must have been his Bubble Gun. . . ."

JULIAN AND THE TWO TROOPERS were over by the radio car. Within, the operator removed an earphone and spoke to one of the troopers who told Julian: "They've just been on to your home in San Diego, and your Ma was plenty worried about you. We'll have you started home in a jiffy."

The trooper had unwittingly edited the message of West's concern. Thus Julian's vivid imagination could picture his mother, but not his father. He supposed he would laugh at him again when he got home and probably take away his Bubble Gun as punishment.

A tall sheriff came up to the car, and drawled, "We have to get this road opened up. You two fellers better take charge. . . ."

Buck said, "O.K.," and to the operator, "Keep an eye on the boy 'til we get back."

In the field, troopers, sheriffs and FBI men were arguing over jurisdiction of the prisoner, now conscious and sullen. The

502

Press, eager to get to a wire and photo labs, had retired to their helicopter, as had the army, and their helicopters rose almost simultaneously, beating up dust that for a few moments shut off all visibility.

When it cleared, Julian was no longer beside the radio car. The operator wondered whether to notify Buck, but just then a bleep from his set called him. The kid wouldn't have got far.

Julian hadn't. He was just down the road fighting back tears and kicking viciously at weeds when Marshall appeared out of the settling dust, and saw him. "Hey kid, you all right? Don't you know you're a hero—picture in the papers?"

Julian took another savage kick at a tumbleweed. "The p-p-p-olice have talked with Dad. They say I've got to go home. I want to patent my Bubble Gun but what does Dad care?"

Marshall had just wanted to be sure. He patted Julian absently then said, "Let's see that thing again."

Julian fished into his pocket and handed him the Bubble Gun. No one was paying any attention to them. They were surrounded by whistle-blowing police, men shouting, motors revving up, and the still settling dust of the 'copters. Reflectively Marshall pressed the trigger. A single bubble emerged, turned to pure gold and borne aloft on a wave of hot air, twinkled for an instant and then, plop, it was gone.

Marshall looked down at the unhappy boy. "You wanna get to Washington?" Julian could only nod, not wanting to burst into tears.

Marshall said, "O.K. Keep your mouth shut and do as I say." He stowed the Bubble Gun back into the boy's pocket, took Julian by the hand and they strolled, unnoticed in the pandemonium, past assorted lawmen, past the bus with its passengers, then past the radio car and on down the line of stalled northbound traffic, past cars and transport vehicles. Marshall glanced at the drivers of the latter and then walked on until they came to a huge canvas-covered truck with a young, bored looking, short-haired pilot. Marshall said, "How 'bout a lift, Mac? Me and my kid brother got to get to Albuquerque."

The driver tapped the "no riders" sign on his cab and said lazily, "What's goin' on up front?"

Marshall replied, "They caught some crook hijacking a bus," and then, "You been over to Vietnam?"

The driver looked more interested and replied, "Ben Hoa. Thirty-first carriers."

Marshall said, "Oh brother."

The driver queried, "You?"

Marshall replied, "An Loc. But you guys really caught it."

The driver nodded, "You said it. O.K., get in. I go through Albuquerque."

Marshall looked around. No one was paying any attention to them. They quickly climbed into the cab, Julian in a state of bliss to be with his friend and on a new adventure, between Marshall and the driver. From up front came the shrilling of police whistles and the sound of engines starting up.

Marshall figured correctly that the cops would notify the bus driver that the boy was being sent home. As for himself turning up missing, Marshall thought that the driver would accept the loss of yet another passenger as fate.

The truck began to crawl. Marshall winked at Julian. "Your shoelace is untied," then said, "My God, it's hot," removed his jacket and held it in his lap as Julian bent down, carefully untied both laces and then tied them again. The young driver was staring stonily ahead. Traffic speeded up and then they were passing the scene of the action with troopers waving the vehicles through.

In a glimpse Marshall saw the bus ready to take to the road again, and the radio car now surrounded by troopers arguing agitatedly. Marshall quickly turned towards the driver. "That musta been where it happened. They sure got a lot of law around."

The driver looked squarely at Marshall and said, "I don't go much for cops," and then they were rolling up the road, every turn of the wheels putting distance between them and those left behind.

BACK IN SAN DIEGO, Lieutenant King of the Missing Persons Bureau was going through one of the most uncomfortable moments of his life trying to explain to a man with a thundering temper and a woman on the verge of screaming hysterics, that Julian and his Bubble Gun had vanished again.

504

AT EIGHT A.M. the truck drew up at an intersection in the heart of Albuquerque where a policeman was directing traffic and passersby were stopping at a corner news-stand for papers. The driver said, "O.K. bud, Albuquerque and watch out for the cop over there."

"What cop?"

The driver snorted. "While you were sacked out last night I heard on the radio that there's a five-state alarm out for your kid brother. Is this some kind of a caper?"

"Just hang onto that kid a sec." Marshall jumped down from the cab, bought a morning paper, and was back in again handing it to the driver. "Here, read this."

The driver stared at the headlines of the bus hijacking and photographs of Julian. "Well, for Pete's sake. This the kid?"

Marshall said to Julian, "Show him," and Julian produced the Bubble Gun and squeezed the trigger releasing a whole flight of coloured bubbles.

The driver goggled. "Well, whaddaya know?" then to Marshall, "So, where do you come in?"

Julian filled in: "He's my friend. He's helping me. I'm g-going to Washington to patent it and they're t-t-trying to stop me."

The driver grinned. "O.K. then, good luck. Get out on this side and the cop won't notice."

They shook hands and Marshall and Julian slipped from the cab. The driver crashed into gear, wheeled his truck around the corner and left the two on the busy intersection feeling naked and conspicuous. Marshall had to take a chance. He said to the newsvendor, "Excuse me, Mac, where's the bus station?"

The man didn't even look up. "Straight ahead, four blocks. You can't miss it."

Marshall looked in the direction indicated. There was the cop at the intersection and two blocks down a prowl car at the kerb. There were now several reasons why Marshall wanted to finish what he had started. If they picked up the kid, he would, of course, be sent home immediately but Marshall was uncertain as to what charges would be brought against himself.

Marshall noticed suddenly that they were opposite a J. C. Penney chain store and exclaimed, "Hey, wait a minute." He inspected the display window, then said, "C'mon, kid," and entered the store.

THE TWO CIA MEN had managed to elude the guards at the gate to the runway of Mexico City's International airport where the giant Russian jet was waiting.

The first CIA man said, "There's the guy," and Nikolas Allon emerged from the departure building surrounded by six tough-looking and obviously well-armed Russian bodyguards.

The second CIA man groaned, "And his pals. What do we do?" They both had their hands inside their jackets fingering their shoulder-holstered guns only to find themselves hypnotized by the methodical march of the group to the plane. The bodyguards were looking in every direction but if they noted the CIA men they gave no sign. The second CIA man said succinctly, "Kamikazes we ain't," and the hands of the two emerged from their jackets—empty.

Allon climbed the stairs, vanished inside the ship and the heavy door slid shut. Soon the plane was heading down the runway and the two men watched as the great silver bird heaved itself into the Mexican sky where for an instant it was framed against the snow on the peak of Popocatépetl. The second CIA man spat in disgust, "Next stop, Moscow."

MARSHALL AND JULIAN emerged from J. C. Penney's, Marshall in a different shirt, his battle jacket replaced by a leather windbreaker and on his head a ten-gallon hat.

But the greatest transformation had been worked upon Julian. He was practically unrecognizable in a shirt with "Buffalo Bill" across it, and fringed buckskin trousers and coat. His glasses had been removed and covering his carroty hair was a Buffalo Bill Stetson. To complete the illusion, glued to his chin and upper lip was a Buffalo Bill moustache and goatee. He was carrying a toy rifle, a new suitcase to replace the one left in the bus and around his middle was a leather belt and holster into which the Bubble Gun had been thrust. They were now prepared to make the test.

They passed the cop at the intersection and approached the corner. The policeman in the prowl car smiled at Julian's costume as they went.

Julian said, "Is this what Buffalo B-B-Bill really looked like?"

Marshall stopped so abruptly that Julian, who was still holding

506

his hand, was almost yanked off his feet. "Listen kid, that stammer of yours. If anybody got suspicious that's the first thing they'd nail you on. Do you have to do it?"

"I g-g-guess not—if you say so." He was already half-hypnotized by his worship for Marshall.

Marshall said, "Right. So, from now on cut out the stammer. Let's hear you say Bubble Gun."

"Bubble Gun."

"That's great. Now say ding-dong-dell, pussy's in the goddamn well."

Julian repeated, "Ding-dong-dell, pussy's in . . ." Marshall stopped him. "See, there you are."

Julian said, "O.K.," and then with the casualness of the child who is utterly finished with one subject went on to the next. "Where do we go now?"

Marshall said, "To the bus station. You've still got your ticket to Washington haven't you?"

"Sure."

Marshall said, "O.K., let's go."

CHAPTER 10

In a secret engineering laboratory somewhere in Moscow a Russian arms expert completed the object on which he had been working under heavy guard. He hefted it in his hand and laid it on the workbench before him. A red light flashed on a wall panel. Someone had begun the long routine of five passes and passwords to penetrate the laboratory. It would be someone properly indentified. Nevertheless, the man, as a precaution, threw a cloth over the object and waited.

The visitor wore the insignia of an army colonel, but he held even higher rank in the branch of Soviet counter espionage. He said. "Have you completed it, Comrade Vosnevski?"

"Yes, Comrade Veznin." The expert removed the cloth.

The colonel examined it then gave Vosnevski a long, hard stare. The latter, who was valuable enough and high enough in the party not to care, returned the look.

MARSHALL EXPLAINED the distant peaks of the Sangre de Cristo Range to Julian as a knife edge sharply dividing rainfall so that drops falling on one side ran eastwards while those dropping a few inches away headed west and wound up in the Pacific Ocean. He illuminated the endless plains of Kansas with the saga of "Bleeding Kansas", remembered from his high-school days in Abilene. Through his eyes Julian saw northerners, southerners, soldiers, pioneers in covered wagons and outlaws.

They crossed the Mississippi at its confluence with the Missouri at St. Louis and Marshall, who had once made a short trip on its broad, yellow waters in an old sternwheeler, pictured for Julian the days of the river gamblers and double-barrelled Derringers fired under tables when an ace too many made its appearance.

Marshall never talked down to Julian or attempted to impress him, probably because he was talking more to himself than the boy and trying to revive some of his own lost faith in his country and countrymen.

To Julian, those days and nights of rolling across the country were as close to heaven as any boy had the right to expect. He had earned the friendship and respect of an adult and had lived through the maddest kind of storybook adventure in which he had played a real-life hero, though curiously that incident left less impression on him than the joy of the trip with Marshall. For they lived during that time as men on the loose, washing when it was convenient and abusing their stomachs at all hours with dubious frankfurters, 'burgers, greasy chips, candy bars, and ice cream cones washed down with every variety of soft drink. For Julian it was sheer bliss.

And yet all the time and with growing impatience what he knew he would do was at the back of Marshall's mind, though he despised himself for it. Julian appealed to him because he was a dreamer with the courage to attempt to grasp the dream. He had few of the irritating traits of the small boy, he wasn't a cheeky or know-it-all, he didn't pry and could take no or shut up for an answer, besides which he showed complete faith in Marshall, as evinced by the instantaneous cure of his stammer.

This worship, this love, were painful for Marshall to contemplate, and had to be pushed back, no longer connected with what he intended to do.

508

So when at last the opportunity presented itself the intention which had lain dormant in Marshall's mind took over. It was one-thirty in the morning. A difference in the music of the tyres caused by a change in the roadbed awakened Marshall and through the window he saw the orange glow of Pittsburgh's furnaces. When he looked upon Julian curled up asleep with his head on his Buffalo Bill jacket it induced his sympathy and affection until he saw an edge of the diagram of the Bubble Gun showing from the pocket of his coat, far enough from the sleeping boy's head to remove it.

The bus driver's voice boomed over the intercom, "Coming into Pittsburgh, folks. Forty-five minutes refreshment break."

Through the announcement which brought the other passengers astir Marshall kept his eye on Julian but the boy never moved. He glanced around. No one was observing him. Then, with infinite care not to rustle the sheet of paper, he drew the diagram from Julian's pocket and put it in his own. What he needed would surely be available at the terminal.

But first he had to slip out of his seat without waking Julian. He let all the others disembark first to see whether their bustle and the noises from without would disturb him. But the boy only shifted position and thereafter was dead to the world.

The coin-operated photocopier was next to a stamp-vending machine. Marshall went over to it and taking the diagram from his pocket, flattened it out, then tore a square from an envelope, wrote on it and drew a heavy border around it. He positioned this on the diagram, slid it into the slot, inserted his quarter and waited for the machine to deliver his photocopy. He examined it with satisfaction and invested two more coins for additional copies, then retrieved the original diagram and removed the piece of envelope which he shredded into bits and dropped into a refuse basket. He pocketed Julian's drawing and once more carefully examined the photocopy. Where in the lower right hand corner it had read "BUBBLE GUN INVENTED BY JULIAN WEST, 137 EAST VIEW TERRACE, SAN DIEGO, CALIFORNIA. APRIL 25, 1973," it now read, "TOY BUBBLE GUN INVENTED BY .FRANK MARSHALL, 39 ORCHARD ST., ABILENE, TEXAS. APRIL 3, 1973." The border he had drawn had completely concealed the fact that a new address and inventor had been superimposed.

The photocopies he stowed in an inside pocket—but how to get the paper back into Julian's pocket unobserved? The sooner he got back to the bus the better. Marshall was sweating and quite ridiculously found himself tiptoeing to his seat, but Julian was still asleep and almost in the same position. The bus was half empty, and it was no problem at all to restore the diagram to his pocket exactly as it had been before. This done, he settled back and was actually asleep when they pulled away from the Pittsburgh terminal.

CHAPTER 11

The shaft of the Washington Monument in the distance poked its pencil point into the haze of the hot morning air, heavy with traffic fumes. Marshall and Julian stood there on the sidewalk transfixed by a sudden strangeness which separated them from the camaraderie of their trip.

It was ten o'clock when they had emerged from the bus, and marched through the bus station. Marshall had changed into his battle jacket, carried his sombrero and had attracted no notice with the small boy in the Buffalo Bill outfit. Thus Marshall and Julian passed unchallenged into the city of their destination.

The overwhelming presence of the Capital City had thrown Marshall into a state of confusion mixed with guilt and worry plus a sense of the passage of time as the large clock outside the terminal now showed ten-fifteen and he realized he had no fixed plan.

With Julian it was a matter of tact or perhaps more the fear of offending a grown-up. He had set out for Washington and now in Washington he was. But he was well aware that without Marshall and the truck ride to Albuquerque he would probably at that moment be back in San Diego. And then there had been the matter of the hand grenade. None of the Press had got straight what had happened, but Julian knew and remembered the roar and eruption of dirt, metal, and cabbage leaves.

Now with no more than a taxi ride separating him from the Patent Office and the realization of his dream he did not know how to show his gratitude or how to say good-bye; nor at that moment did Marshall.

It was Julian who gave Marshall the opening he needed. Fingering his flowing moustache and goatee he asked, "Should I keep these on?"

The question yanked Marshall's scattered thoughts back onto an orderly track. What he didn't want for at least twelve hours was a hullabaloo over Julian West and his invention and so he replied, "Yeah, you better. It got us past the cops, didn't it?"

Julian made a tentative trial at parting. "Well . . . thanks for everything . . . you were great. If you hadn't thrown away the grenade, we. . . ."

Marshall said, "That's O.K. If you hadn't distracted that looney cowpuncher I could be lying in a mortuary parlour. I was scared."

Julian looked at him and pulled at his lower lip. "For real?"

Marshall said, "Look, kid, after you've been around a while you learn that there are times to be scared and others not to be. But you can't always pick 'em. See?"

Julian was satisfied and Marshall now had to try to prepare the boy for what he was about to do to him. "Listen, do you know anything at all about how the Patent Office operates?"

Julian reached for the diagram. "Well, I show them this and the . . ." and here he patted the Bubble Gun in its absurd western holster.

Marshall said, "It isn't all that simple. They've got to make a search and maybe somebody else thought of it or something like it first."

Julian refused even to consider this, but Marshall was insistent on conditioning the boy for the catastrophe he was preparing for him. "A lot of people get ideas which are almost the same."

Julian said, "That's why I better hurry. I gotta get mine in first." And his gaze into Marshall's face was so straightforwardly innocent that the deviousness of Marshall's own mind at that moment forced him to wonder whether Julian actually suspected what he was up to, but the moment passed and he realized there was no guile in the purely practical statement. He said, "Look, you haven't got a grandmother here. Where are you gonna stay tonight?"

Julian shrugged. "Somewhere. I've got some money left."

Marshall had one more try. "Listen, Julian, oughtn't we to phone your old man?"

Julian shook his head emphatically. "He wouldn't care. He's too busy." Then he added, "I've got to go to the Patent Office."

Marshall's good impulses faded. He, too, had to get to the Patent Office and what was more, with a head start. And, he'd got to stop worrying about Julian. Sooner or later the cops would pick him up and send him home. He would come to no harm.

He said, "O.K., we'll get a cab and I'll drop you off there." Then Marshall began the perpetration of his black deed. "Hey, wait a minute. I gotta make a phone call. I'll be back in a sec," and he was off, leaving Julian on the sidewalk, uncertain as to whether he was upset by the delay or pleased that the total separation from Marshall was not yet to be.

Marshall wasted no time. He re-entered the station and exited the other side where he told an arriving cab, "The Patent Office," got in, shut the door, and was driven off.

After some twenty minutes of standing, a solitary and slightly absurd figure, outside the bus station, Julian realized that something had perhaps gone amiss, though the suspicion that he had been ditched never entered his mind. He decided to wait another five minutes and then go look. Now, further uncertain, he gave it ten and then went back inside where he found the public telephone booths, but none of them containing Marshall, and he then fell prey to the sudden panic that he might have missed him in the crowd or that Marshall had now returned to their rendezvous, so he ran to the door and looked out at where he had been standing, but there was no sign of his friend.

He wandered back into the terminal hoping to catch a glimpse of him, but as he threaded through the passing throng Julian suddenly became aware that people were turning to look at him. Intuition, plus some of Marshall's hard practical wisdom that had rubbed off on him during the voyage, caught him up. As long as he had been in the company of his "big brother", no one had paid him any attention, but now by himself in this outfit he was highly conspicuous.

Julian drifted out of the maelstrom of passengers and coming upon a corner where the cleaners kept their gear quickly stripped off his moustache and goatee and then the Buffalo Bill outfit which he stuffed into his suitcase, resuming his leather jacket and putting on his glasses again. The toy rifle was too long to fit into his bag, but he took off the cartridge belt and holster and restored the Bubble Gun to his righthand jacket pocket. Then he stood the rifle up with the mops and brooms, gave it a last regretful look and emerged from the cleaner's nook the same small boy who boarded Bus 396 in San Diego, California, so many ages ago. Well, not exactly the same. He found himself missing Marshall dreadfully, to the point where he was close to being frightened.

If there had never been a Marshall he would have wandered through his dream world untouched, following the line of least resistance but always moving towards his objective. But there *had* been Marshall, tall, handsome, laughing with those funny eyes that lit up as though there was a battery behind them. There had been the Marshall who had fed him, looked after him, treated him like a man and took him seriously. Now he was gone, leaving no address, nothing but a memory and Julian realized a void such as he had never felt before. His friend's disappearance had to be accepted as one of those things that happened. Kids got lost. Why shouldn't grown-ups? He thought of going to the information desk and having Marshall called over the loudspeakers and then said to himself, "Boy, that would be a great idea. Tell everybody where we are."

It wouldn't do to linger in that terminal with the police on the lookout. He pulled himself together, strode purposefully through the exit to the head of the cab rank where the driver was reading the morning paper, and asked, "Are you free?"

The driver, who was a young, pleasant-looking black with an

amused quirk to his lips looked up. The face of the small boy at his window gave him a shock as though he had seen him before and ought to be saying, "Why, hello there," instead of, as he did, "Sure. Where to, sonny?"

Julian replied, "The Patent Office, please."

The driver shifted to a more alert position. "The Patent Office?"

Julian replied, "I want to patent my invention."

Slightly startled, the man said, "Starting early, aren't you? That's about a three-dollar trip across the river. Don't get me wrong, kid, but I'm running a business. Have you got any money?"

Julian reached into his pocket and produced what he had left, some thirty-three dollars. The driver glanced at it, then smiled and said exaggeratedly. "Excuse me, sir. Get in. You got yourself a ride."

Julian said, "Thanks. Do you want it now or later?"

"Later will be fine," the driver said as he moved off.

Julian sat back and studied the driver's licence framed behind cellophane with his photograph, name, Meech Morrow, age thirty-eight, M for married and a number. He asked, "Is it far, Mr. Morrow?"

The driver replied, "About ten minutes," and then chuckled, "Mr. Morrow! That's a good one. What's your name?"

Julian had been on the verge of blurting it out but then remembered that this might be unwise and replied, "Herman."

"Well, Mr. Herman," Morrow said, "We'll have you there in a jiffy."

Julian nestled into a corner and gave himself up to the golden dream in which every child in every block would be wanting a Bubble Gun invented and patented by Julian West.

As Meech Morrow's cab edged through downtown Washington's mid-morning traffic in the direction of the Potomac Bridge, other events that were to affect the life and times of that same Julian West, inventor, were taking place.

AT CRYSTAL CITY, VIRGINIA, across the river from Washington, Frank Marshall emerged from the U.S. Department of Commerce Building where the Patent Office was located with a number of forms in his hand and an expression of brisk satisfaction on his face.

514

He glanced at his wristwatch, which registered eleven o'clock, consulted an address on a sheet of paper and walked quickly to a neighbouring building where he studied the lobby directory, which was three-quarters filled with the names of patent attorneys. The rest of the board was devoted to engineering, drafting and research firms concerned with assisting would-be inventors in meeting all the requirements of the Patent Office. He noted down the name of a drafting firm as well as that of a patent attorney and then headed for the elevator. With any luck and the investment of the last of his cash resources, he might be able to file at the Patent Office before closing time.

IN THE VAST COMPLEX of the Pentagon Building, the photograph of Richard Milhous Nixon was looking down from the wall of the conference room where Major-General Thomas H. Horgan was meeting two generals, three colonels, several CIA men and a pair from the FBI. Horgan was chewing out Colonel John Sisson, "You sure screwed this one up. What was it that was photographed anyway?"

Sisson was not easily cowed, but he replied inanely, "Well . . . er . . . a Bubble Gun. A pistol that shot bubbles."

Horgan's voice rose, "That shot what? You said there was a diagram? What kind of a diagram?"

Sisson could not have reproduced it at that moment if his life had depended on it. He blurted out, "Well, sir, I never really paid much attention to it. A kid was bothering me—something about a washer in the wrong place—and before I knew it. . . ."

General Horgan completed the sentence for him. ". . . the stupid bastard photographed it and made the American Army look like a pack of fools."

A general with one star less but from a different department came to the rescue of the unhappy Sisson. "Now wait a minute, Tom. The Russians put a set of phony rocket plans in our hands and we organized our own phony plans so they'll cut out the kidding and we can both stop wasting our time. What's the difference as long as they get the message?"

Horgan, still furious, snarled, "The difference is a foul-up and we don't know where we're at. Besides which, we've been saving up that Russian pigeon, Allon, for years and now we've got him to

515

blow his cover for nothing." He pointed at Sisson, "Listen, I don't care how you do it or where you get it, but I want that diagram before tomorrow. I want to know just what they've got."

The other general who had spoken up asked, "What became of the kid, John?"

Sisson replied miserably, "He just disappeared. Haven't you been reading the papers?"

The second general said, "Look, let's go back and get the whole thing from the beginning and maybe we can see daylight. John, this kid wouldn't have been in cahoots with Allon, would he?"

"A ten-year-old? No." And Sisson again launched into his story, racking his brain for every scrap that might bear on the subject. The men around the table listened silently. A glance of one of the CIA men drifted to the portrait of the President and a stab of light upon the glass over it gave him the impression momentarily of an eyebrow having gone up.

THE STEEL AND GLASS MOUNTAIN of the Department of Commerce Building jolted Julian into reality. "Anyone Can Patent An Invention" had been the headline which had seduced him into attaining that goal. But he wasn't "anyone". He was Julian West, age nine and a half, fifth grade, Elias P. Johnson Preparatory School, San Diego, California, with a messy diagram in one pocket and a dubiously performing Bubble Gun in the other, and San Diego was a million miles away.

Julian got out of the cab and stood on the sidewalk facing the building. The bus ride from beginning to end had been a fairy tale. How was anyone to understand the feelings of a small boy faced with his first real plunge into a world far removed from every security he had ever known?

But in a curious way Meech Morrow did, not so much because he had children of his own but because of the figure Julian cut. Not quite three feet tall from the soles of his sneakers to the top of his carroty hair, paper suitcase in his hand, one sock up and one sock down, head tilted slightly to look at the top of the building, he penetrated to Morrow's heart. Whether the whole thing was made up or the child actually believed he had created something patentable, the pathos of the moment was almost unbearable. Besides, something was niggling at Morrow. Where had he seen the boy before? Whatever, Morrow knew that to abandon him was unthinkable and so he said, "I'll wait for you."

Julian, startled, plunged his hand into his pocket. "Gee, I forgot for a minute but I wasn't going without paying, honest."

Morrow said, "You can pay me when you come out. Maybe you'll be needing another ride somewhere. I'll stop the clock."

Julian said, "You've got work to do," but some of the fear drained out of him. Somebody was standing by.

Morrow laughed. "That's all right, kid. Go ahead and tell 'em about your invention."

Julian said, "Thanks. I'll hurry." And he marched across the pavement and was whirled within by the revolving door.

Meech Morrow watched him go and scrabbled in the well at the side of his seat until he found a two-day old newspaper. He opened it, read the story again, looked at the photograph and began a chuckle that grew into a laugh. *Well*, he said to himself. *Ain't that Mr. Herman some kid.*

IN THE OFFICE of Atwell, Robbins and Taylor, Drafting Engineers and Patent Consultants, a young man, using a pen as a pointer was smiling at the diagram before him. He said, "That's amusing. Have you got a model?"

Marshall asked anxiously, "Do I have to have one?"

"Not really. They'd prefer it if you had, but your diagram is clear and you could put the model in later."

Marshall asked, "How long will it take?"

The draftsman smiled. "Not too long. The Patent Office closes at five. We could do it by four. In the meantime you could be filling out the forms. The filing fee is sixty-five bucks and the drawing's half a C."

Marshall said, "That's O.K.," and thought of the hole this would make in his capital. But if he got his patent . . . He asked, "You couldn't make it by three-thirty, could you?"

The draftsman said, "I'll try."

They were always in a hurry these inventors, even the ones with the craziest ideas were always terrified that someone might get ahead of them.

517

CHAPTER 12

After some twenty minutes Julian emerged from the revolving door clutching pamphlets and forms and as he slowly approached the cab Morrow said, "Well, Mr. Julian, how did you make out?" and was immediately sorry that he had called him by his right name for to the dazed expression on Julian's face now was added terror.

For an instant he thought the boy was going to run and Julian, his identity so easily pierced, had actually been minded to do so. Then he remembered that he had not paid the man and remained on the pavement, a picture of abject misery, clutching his sheaves of bumph.

Meech Morrow opened the front door of the cab and said, "Come sit here alongside of me and we'll have a little chat. You got nothing to be afraid of with Meech Morrow."

Julian got in and Morrow closed the door. The driver said, "Sure, you're the boy I read about in the paper, but we'll forget about that. Did you sure enough have an invention? What happened in there? They give you the run around?"

Julian shook his head slowly. "They were busy. A man asked if I'd researched it and if I hadn't I ought to." He was looking up at Morrow but his eyes were turned inward to the bureaucratic turmoil through which he had been whirled with the shortness that a small boy with a much folded and dirtied diagram might expect. He said unhappily, "It's gotta be in India ink on special paper with drafting instruments and I have to take it to a patent attorney. What's a patent attorney?"

Morrow said with a note of contempt, "Lawyers. I guess there's a lot of legal stuff about getting a patent." He thumbed through one of the pamphlets. "'Written document of petition', 'Oath of declaration', 'Drawing on pure white paper of the thickness corresponding to two- or three-ply Bristol Board', Brother, they don't make it easy."

A man stuck his head inside the window. "This cab free?"

Morrow replied respectfully, "No sir," flipped on his ignition and drove a way before stopping and saying to Julian, "Maybe you better get in back. Then nobody will ask me."

518

Julian did as he was told and relapsed into that helpless nightmare from which he was trying to wake.

Morrow looked back. "What do we do now?" As Julian drew his diagram from his pocket a piece of white pasteboard fluttered to the floor. He picked it up and with a sudden change of expression handed Morrow the card and said, "Could we go there?"

Morrow looked at the name and Pentagon address and whistled with astonishment. He asked, "You know him, boy?"

Julian nodded. "He helped me on the bus with my invention and said if I got into any kind of trouble. . . ."

Morrow whistled. "Kid, you got some uncle there. Want to go see him?"

"Yes, please."

Morrow said, "No charge for the waiting time, but that's a four-dollar trip. O.K.?"

Julian nodded and the cab pulled back into the stream of traffic.

Julian's invasion of the Pentagon was classic. The two marine guards at the portal didn't see him because they weren't looking for a small boy to march stolidly and unquestioningly between them and into the main entrance. He had left his suitcase in the cab, for when he had gone to pay Morrow had said simply, "Skip it, kid. I'll be here when you come out." Morrow had figured the boy would be ejected in minutes with nothing but the initialled card of a colonel in ordnance.

The lobby of the Pentagon presented the most efficient and complicated security check that could be devised by a nervous soldiery—counters, barriers, sergeants behind desks, marines and military police.

Julian approached the nearest desk behind which sat a naval petty officer and showing him the card said, "Please, sir, where can I find Colonel Sisson?"

The petty officer said, "Ask him, sonny," and indicated a corner of the lobby where everyone was khaki-clad.

Julian took his card to a sergeant at a desk and said again, "Please, sir, where can I find Colonel Sisson?"

Like a shuttlecock the name of Sisson was batted to and fro until it reached a corporal in front of a huge directory. He called back, "Southwest wing, corridor G. Second floor, room nine-three-four."

But by the time the answer wafted back to the original inquirer, Julian was no longer there. And then, as an important piece of brass with an overloaded briefcase interrogated the sergeant, he forgot about the boy. The two guards at the inner entrance, seeing him leave the desk with the guard apparently satisfied, made no attempt to stop him. And thereafter, Julian, with the wing, the corridor and the room number firmly in his mind, proceeded to penetrate the recesses of the most protected building in the world.

A guard asked, "Have you got a pass?" Julian showed him the colonel's card. The guard said, "O.K."

Another Cerberus asked the same question. Julian showed the card. The M.P. said, "You've gotta have a pass."

Julian said, "The sergeant at the desk said it was O.K."

"Billings? A fat guy?"

"Uh-huh."

"O.K., go ahead."

The third was more adamant. "Nix, sonny. Nobody gets through here without a badge."

Julian said, "But, Colonel Sisson's my . . ." He was going to say "friend," but the Marine finished it for him, grouching, "Oh, for Pete's sake. I wish the Brass would let us know when their kids are coming. Go ahead and see your daddy, but don't say I let you through."

The farther he went, the easier it seemed. Julian walked past two guards who never even questioned him and a third who seemed satisfied with his credential. He finally encountered two together who appeared impenetrable, for they wore sidearms and looked grim. But they were army and quite the easiest, for one said, "Hey, you got yourself in the wrong corridor, sonny," and he led the way to the outer office of Colonel John G. Sisson, Weapons Department, U.S. Army Ordnance, from whence Julian was ushered to the senior sergeant guarding the portals of Major Horgan.

The arguments around the conference table were still raging and had increased in scope, for Horgan, something of a safety-firster, had called in a member of the President's Advisory Committee in case the matter should call for diplomatic intervention and attention, and a pair of Russian experts.

The newcomers had not only solved nothing but had raised

General Horgan's temperature to the point where he blew off at them collectively and individually.

". . . And all you can think about are your own jobs. Don't you ever give a thought to your country? Sisson," he aimed a forefinger at the unhappy Colonel, "you're gonna find yourself on the retired list so fast. . . ."

At this point the general's sergeant, whose length of service entitled him to take liberties, entered, saluted, said "I beg your pardon, General," and handed Sisson a card. He said, "Colonel, excuse me for busting in, but there's a kid outside who knows you and says he has to see you on something important. He got right through to your office without a pass and I thought maybe. . . ."

Sisson took the card, mechanically turned it over and when he saw his initials in his own handwriting a chill slid down his back as he remembered the boy and his diagram. He thought, *That's impossible. It's only in the movies that the marines arrive in the nick of time*, then asked, "He wouldn't be a four-eyed kid with red hair and a stammer, would he?"

The sergeant said, "He didn't have no stammer I could see."

In icy fury General Horgan addressed them. "If you two are through discussing family matters, will you oblige me, Sergeant, by getting out of here?"

The sergeant did, but Julian entered as though on cue, looking about him anxiously at the beribboned officers and grim civilians around the long table until he located Colonel Sisson. He went directly to him and said, "Excuse me, sir . . . I thought this was your office and you said, sir, if I . . ."

Before he could finish Sisson leaped out of his chair and seized him by the shoulders. "Julian! Have you still got that diagram?"

Julian replied, "Is it all right, sir? I mean, you said if I was in trouble I should . . ."

The words came tumbling from Sisson, "That's exactly what I said and you were perfectly right to come. You see, they'd all like to look at your invention."

It bewildered Julian but he took out the grubby drawing of the Bubble Gun which Sisson unfolded and placed dramatically on the centre of the table.

General Horgan swallowed. "What the hell is that?"

Sisson announced, "This, sir, is the kid, and that's his diagram," and then to Julian, "Have you got a working model?" Julian produced the gun and Sisson put it on the table too.

The articles lay there hypnotizing an entire section of the intelligence and diplomatic service of the United States of America until General Tom Horgan, a huge, ex-football-playing figure, arose to scrutinize the diagram. Then the assemblage waited in silence while the general reached forward and picked up the Bubble Gun, weighing it first in his palm and fitting it to his grip. He held it up, examined it closely. Then holding it at arm's length, he squeezed the trigger.

Before the fascinated eyes of the experts, a soap bubble began to form at the muzzle, expanding until it was the size of a grapefruit at which point it detached itself, became exquisitely iridescent and ascending, drifted straight for the watching portrait of the President where it burst silently leaving a tiny damp stain on the glass of the frame.

"Ha!" burst from the lungs of General Horgan. None of them knew whether this was the beginning of another bellow until it was followed by similar explosions. "Ha Ha Ha Ha Ha!" The general was laughing! He squeezed the trigger again and a whole stream of bubbles emerged.

And now the hypnotic spell was broken. They had all been bursting to let go and now raised the roof with their merriment as the General pounded the table with his fist in hysteric guffaws and began to find words. "Wait until the sons of bitches try to figure this one out. This is the funniest damn thing that ever happened. John, you're a hero. I'll get you a gong for this if it's the last thing I do. Oh, brother, I'd give my retirement pay if I could be over there when they get a load of this."

The conference disintegrated, the friendly general slapping Sisson on the back. It wasn't only in the movies. The marines sometimes did arrive in the nick of time.

Julian thought they were all crazy.

IN A CONFERENCE ROOM in Moscow, there was high tension as General Barzovsky, his staff and experts from the KGB and allied intelligence, espionage and counter-espionage units awaited

the revelation of photographs and a Soviet-reproduced model of what had been hinted at as America's newest and most secret weapon. The spy planted in the United States twelve years before to be available for that one moment, had succeeded in photographing it, a brilliant technician of the Soviet State had succeeded in making a model.

The conference room was extraordinarily like the one in the Pentagon, except that there were two photographs instead of one, Lenin, of course, and then the dour visage of the Premier. The other difference was that the frame holding the photograph of the Premier was so constructed that the top could be removed and another photograph substituted in a matter of seconds. General Barzovsky, who appeared just as massive and formidable as General Horgan, looked up as there was a stir at the door, murmurs, heel clicks, the sound of passwords. Then a major in his greatcoat and epaulettes entered with Comrade Vosnevski, still in his laboratory overalls, and behind him Comrade Allon, flanked by two members of the counter-espionage group.

"Well?" rumbled General Barzovsky.

"Proceed," ordered the major.

Comrade Vosnevski threw a scrutable look at the major, then produced an enlarged photocopy of a diagram of the interior construction of a pistol and likewise, made up from the diagram, in gun metal and about the size of a .38 automatic, a model of the gun itself. These, he laid in the centre of the conference table.

General Barzovsky examined both articles. "And what may I ask is that?" he said indicating the diagram.

The major clicked off the reply. "It is a photograph of the diagram of the latest secret weapon of the Department of Ordnance of the United States Army obtained by Comrade Allon."

"And that?" inquired the General.

"That," replied the major, "is a working model of the secret weapon itself achieved by the skill of Comrade Vosnevski and with the aid of the obviously coded instructions to be found on the photograph. Our decoding department broke the code by discovering that it was not a code at all, but actual instructions for manufacture of the weapon thus bringing to naught the brilliance of the American scheme to confuse us."

524

General Barzovsky regarded the diagram once more, looked over the silent assemblage, then took the gun in his right hand and holding it at arm's length, squeezed the trigger. A grapefruit-sized bubble formed faithfully at the nozzle, detached itself and floated away and then another and another as the general kept squeezing. They were all the same size, for the engineer had constructed the model from the corrections made by Colonel Sisson, and were even more beautiful than those that had entertained the Pentagon group, for the bubbles caught up the colours of the room's magnificent crystal chandelier and floated away to burst here and there before the horrified gaze of the onlookers.

It was as though the general was under a spell, for he could not seem to stop squeezing the trigger until one of the bubbles which had settled on his hand, where it reflected himself expanded five-fold, blew up quietly and broke the spell. He then put the gun back on the table, sat down and thundered one ham of a fist upon the wood while from his massive chest there burst a tremendous, "Ho!"

Comrade Allon slid to the floor in a faint. There was nothing for him but the firing squad. Thus he missed the general's second and third "Ho's!" and the tears streaming from his eyes. General Barzovsky was laughing his head off. Then it was permitted for everyone to laugh, and yells and bellows went up from the gathering to join the hilarity of a Russian general with a sense of humour until the last of the bubbles exploded into nothingness.

CHAPTER 13

In Sisson's office Julian asked, "What happened?"

The sergeant at his table was still grinning and the colonel at his desk, the diagram and Bubble Gun before him, likewise smiled. "It's too complicated, Julian," he replied. And then feeling that this was on the short side, said, "Often when men get into a panic they do something silly in the hope that what is worrying them will go away."

Julian, in his straight-backed chair, the soles of his sneakers barely meeting the carpet, stared.

The colonel continued. "Thanks to you, something sillier than usual happened and everybody is very pleased with me, and I shall be eternally grateful to you."

"Me?" Julian cried. "What for?"

The colonel did not reply immediately. Then, he said gravely, "As I told you, it's difficult to explain, but I want you to promise me to keep your lip buttoned about anything you saw or heard in that room," and here the colonel extracted from his desk a rubber stamp and ink pad, applied the former to the latter and carefully pressed the stamp first upon Julian's diagram and then upon the back of the boy's hand. In glorious purple ink it read, "TOP SECRET".

Julian looked at the mark on his hand as though it were the Congressional Medal and without realizing it, raised it to his cheek where it made a faint purple smudge. Then he whispered, "I won't say anything to anyone, ever," and once again he felt the sweet thrill of having participated in something important, even dangerous in the world of grown-ups, but this time it was too tremendous even to be talked about.

The colonel asked, "How did you make out at the Patent Office?"

The exquisite feeling drained from Julian's breast, and he was back once more in the world of trouble. He would have been glad to have relieved himself in tears but not in front of Colonel Sisson or the sergeant. Instead he simply shook his head and produced a pamphlet from the Department of Commerce entitled, "Patents and Inventions, An Information Aid for Inventors".

The colonel sighed, "I know it practically by heart," and opening the booklet at random began to mutter aloud the long extract of instructions.

When he had finished he looked over at Julian, who was regarding him miserably. "Did they tell you about researching and recommend that you acquire a patent attorney?" Julian nodded.

"Did you see an examiner?" But the colonel answered his own question. "No, you wouldn't until you'd filed your drawing and claim and paid the fee." The boy's lips and chin were trembling now and Sisson said, "Look Julian, it isn't as bad as it sounds. Anyway, we can fix you up with your first step, the drawing. I'll have one of my draftsmen get on it right away and you can file it tomorrow morning and see what happens."

"Gee, sir, would you?" But immediately after his face clouded over. "I haven't got the filing fee. I spent almost all my money getting here."

Sisson nodded gravely. "Hmmmm, I see. Would you let me . . ."

Julian was positive and immediate. "I couldn't, sir. I wanted to use my own money to show my dad. He didn't think my invention would work."

The colonel, reflecting for a moment, said, "Would you let me lend it to you? You could pay me back with royalties from your patent."

Julian looked doubtful.

Sisson smiled. "Here, I'll fix up a note," and he took a pen and a sheet of paper, speaking as he wrote, "I, Julian West, of—what was your address again?" Julian gave it to him. "Promise to pay Colonel John Sisson, on demand, the sum of sixty-five dollars." He counted out the money from a billfold and handed it over, along with the Bubble Gun. "Now sign this and it's legal."

"That's terrific, sir. Thank you very much. What time do you think the drawing will be ready tomorrow?"

"Say, ten."

Julian said, "I'll come back for it."

The colonel looked up. "Then you've got a place to stay?"

Julian said nothing. He didn't wish to burden the colonel any further. The cab driver could help him find a cheap room.

The colonel glanced over the diagram again, left for a word with his assistant and returned minutes later to find his sergeant alone in the office. He asked, "Where's the boy?"

The sergeant replied, "He said he'd be back in the morning."

The colonel looked puzzled, then glanced at the note that Julian had signed and said, "Get me a Mr. West at 137 East View Terrace, San Diego, California on the phone."

The sergeant balked. "You ain't gonna give him away, are you, sir? That's the kid who was in the papers with the hijacker on the bus. I recognized him."

The colonel said, "Well, if you read the papers, you ought to realize his parents must be frantic. By the time his father gets here, the kid will have his drawing and be at the Patent Office. Mission accomplished."

It had been a good hour since Julian had vanished into the Pentagon. Meech Morrow had slumped into his seat and was talking to himself. "You're sure one smart cab driver. They must be holding the kid to send him home and you got about nine dollars worth of nothing on the clock besides wasting half the day. Meech Morrow, the great philanthropist. . . ." At this point Julian emerged from the doorway, ten feet tall and beaming."

Morrow sat up blinking. "What happened?"

Julian said, "The colonel was O.K. They're gonna make me the design. I gotta be back for it at ten in the morning."

Meech Morrow liked things to make sense. This did not. But then nothing had since he had encountered Julian, including his own behaviour. He said, "Come on, now, quit kidding."

Julian began, "The colonel said . . ." whereupon he remembered, "I'm not allowed to say," and exhibited the back of his hand to Morrow.

The cab driver grinned. "Top Secret, are you? Well, you won't be for long with every cop in town looking for you. What are you going to do now?"

Julian stared at Morrow without replying. He hadn't thought.

Morrow said, "You better come home with me or you won't be making it to any Patent Office in the morning. To keep it strictly business let's say you pay me off now. That'll be nine and a half."

Julian handed him a ten. Morrow asked, "O.K. I keep the tip?" Julian nodded. Morrow said, "Right! Now get up front here with me. From now on, Julian, you're my guest."

AT TWO-THIRTY THAT AFTERNOON Julian was finishing lunch with the Morrows and, at exactly the same hour Frank Marshall was opening the door of the drafting firm, Atwell, Robbins and Taylor, to find the draftsman waiting with his drawing.

When Marshall exhibited the completed forms, the draftsman asked, "You getting a patent attorney?"

Marshall said, "Can't afford to. I'm down to my last five C's."

The draftsman tapped the beautifully inked design. "You can't afford not to. They'll run you ragged over there if you try to push this through yourself. Go to Shine, Williams and Burdett on the eighth floor and ask for Jim Williams. Say I sent you. They're

528

reasonable." He scribbled a few words on a card and gave it to Marshall.

Jim Williams was a fat, little man with alert, intelligent eyes and a brisk manner.

". . . I'm in a hurry," Marshall began.

Williams said, "Yes, yes, I know," and glanced at his watch. "Two hundred bucks retainer. If the patent is denied it won't cost you any more. If it's granted, another three hundred. You'll want to get this in before closing." And he was on his way out of the office with Marshall trooping after him.

Two hundred dollars was steep, but at least Williams was a hustler. At twenty-past four they were in the office of an examiner and Frank Marshall's papers had been dated, time-stamped as well as given a registry number and Marshall had been relieved of his filing fee. Williams told Marshall, "There's some more processing before we start the search, but it's too late this afternoon. We can get it done tomorrow morning. Anyway, you're registered now, so you can sleep tonight."

Walking to the exit Frank Marshall found himself wondering whether he could.

CHAPTER 14

At ten-fifteen the following morning Julian emerged from the Pentagon accompanied by Colonel Sisson. Meech Morrow's cab was faithfully drawn up at the kerb behind a black limousine belonging to a one-star general. A sergeant sat at the driver's wheel. Sisson said, "There you are, young man. A general's car. How does that suit you?"

Julian thought he would die of excitement. "For me? How did you . . . ?"

Colonel Sisson said smoothly, "Borrowed it. He was only too delighted. The driver will look after you."

In his cab Meech Morrow grinned and wondered whether Julian would remember.

He did. Julian suddenly cried, "Excuse me," and ran over to the cab. "Look, Mr. Morrow, I'm going in a general's car."

Morrow nodded. "You're in good hands. I guess you won't be needing me anymore."

Julian was aware of the colonel standing beside them and said, "Mr. Morrow here looked after me last night."

The colonel said, "I wondered where you were. That was kind of you, Mr. Morrow."

Morrow said, "He's a great kid. We were glad to have him."

Julian held out his hand. "Thanks, Mr. Morrow and thank Mrs. Morrow again too, please."

Morrow held the small hand for a moment, then eased into gear. "Good luck, kid. Let me know how things turn out."

Julian said, "I will." And it wasn't until the car turned the corner that he realized he had not asked Morrow for his address.

An hour later Julian sat in a straight-backed chair in the office of an examiner in the United States Patent Office. On the desk lay an expert drawing of the Bubble Gun plus the filled out forms, including the receipt for the filing fee. Julian was at the end of his quest, at least the part which had come to mean the most, the patenting of his invention.

The examiner leafed through the papers, picked them up and laid them once more on his desk. He looked at Julian sharply. "You did say this was original?"

Julian replied, "Yes sir. It's my invention, but the drawings were made by Colonel Sisson, a friend of mine in the Pentagon." He reached into his pocket. "Here's my diagram."

The official compared it with the work done by the draftsman. He asked, "What's this 'Top Secret' stamp on it?"

Julian had a moment of alarm. He replied, "I'm not allowed to say."

For a moment the examiner found himself bewildered. But the immediate escape hatch from what seemed to be some kind of nonsense was the return strictly to business. He therefore said to Julian, "Actually, young fellow, a duplicate set of these drawings passed through my office late yesterday. They're probably being processed right now. Let me have a look." He got up and went into the corridor and Julian followed, his heart thumping violently.

As they emerged from the office a door about three down from them opened and to his astonishment Julian saw Frank Marshall accompanied by a fat little man and an official who was saying, "That's all O.K. Now go to the third floor, second office on the right. They'll look after you."

Julian's lips formed the word, "Frank", but no sound issued and he was suddenly horribly frightened. His examiner was saying to the other official, "Wait a minute, Fred. I've got an identical set of plans for that same invention presented by this kid as his own. Can we have a look?"

The official said, "Sure." The two groups moved closer.

The unexpected appearance of Julian's friend had set up not only an inexplicable fear but bewilderment. It *was* Frank Marshall, his pal. There was the handsome figure, the worn battle jacket and those unforgettable eyes. Julian was suddenly flooded with relief. Of course. They had lost one another in the terminal and Marshall knew that he, Julian, would be at the Patent Office and had come to find him. He said, "We got lost, didn't we? I looked for you in the station but couldn't find you."

Frank Marshall did not reply. Now Julian noticed that those bright blue eyes were stony cold.

Julian's examiner said to Marshall, "Do you know this boy?"

Marshall replied, "Never saw him before."

One stricken cry emerged from Julian, "But . . . Marshall!"

Marshall turned his back while the examiner glanced at the papers and said, "That's right, they're duplicates," and handed them back.

The official said, "We processed them this morning."

The fat man took back the papers. Marshall said, "O.K.?"

The official nodded and Julian watched them go off down the corridor. He felt sick. Distantly he heard the examiner say, "Suppose we go back to my office for a chat, sonny."

Numbly Julian followed him and then he was once more propped up in the straight-backed chair where he sat, like one paralysed, his thoughts ranging far in search of the answer to the impossible. How could Marshall, his friend, have done this? Why? The diagram had never left his pocket until he handed it over to Colonel Sisson. Where? When? How?

He half-remembered then. Pittsburgh. He had been asleep and a shadow had fallen across him and a touch and then he had slept more peacefully because it would have been the comforting pressure of Frank Marshall's hand.

The distant voice was saying, "I'll accept this application if you like, but the one you saw go down the hall is time-stamped yesterday and the serial number is twenty-seven ahead of yours. If the research proves it patentable, it will have priority. If there is any funny business with that young man I suppose you could sue. What about your family?"

He looked at Julian and then at the papers again. Julian was unable to reply. The chill at his feet moved up, gripping his middle.

The examiner said, "Wait a minute. Did you ever make a model of your invention?" Julian nodded.

"Well, that's something. Where is it?"

"I gave it to the taxi man's baby. The one where I stayed last night."

It seemed to Julian as though part of him had turned to ice, yet in his mind he heard again the baby's gurgle of delight as the stream of bubbles emerged from the Bubble Gun and sailed about the Morrow apartment sticking on bits of furniture, even on the baby's nose. When he had reached for it, it had disappeared leaving him with the mystery of a droplet in his palm.

The baby's name was Matthew, he was a year and a half old and sat in a high chair. Julian had had the most fabulous dinner: ham steak with candied yams and peas and apple pie and cheese.

There was Della, the daughter, aged twelve and Tom, the boy of fifteen, and Abbie, Mrs. Morrow, who had the most beautiful face of anyone Julian had ever seen, and who, when she looked at him made him feel good all the way through, and happy.

After the fabulous dinner Julian had had to re-enact the shooting of the hijacker. Tom acted as the driver, Matthew screamed with delight, Della and Abbie Morrow had applauded and looked upon Julian with admiration.

Afterwards, Julian had been bedded down on the living room couch and Mrs. Morrow had covered him with a blanket and dropped a featherlike kiss upon his cheek. Morrow had looked in and ordered, "Now, you go to sleep. Don't worry, I'll get you to the Pentagon at ten."

And in the morning Julian had filled the soapy water compartment of the Bubble Gun for the last time and presented it to the baby as the only thank-you gift he felt he could leave behind. And as he went out the door he saw a bubble floating across the room and heard Matthew's laughter.

The examiner, suddenly on the verge of losing his temper, said, "What are you talking about, boy? What taxi man? Where was all this?"

The part of Julian that was still able to function replied, "I don't know, sir, I didn't get his address."

The examiner recovered his temper, for something of Julian's state of mind had managed to penetrate to him. There was more behind this curious mix-up and the strange encounter in the hall. But, whatever it was, the official wanted to be quit of it. With a sigh of resignation, he said, "I'm afraid I can't help you. It's up to you now, my boy. Do you want to take the drawings or leave them?"

Julian, feeling that something inside him had died, arose from the chair and without taking the papers, turned and went out.

He found his way down the corridor to the lobby where he sat on a bench, his back against a pillar, dry-eyed and staring at nothing, in his hand the grubby original diagram of the Bubble Gun which the examiner had returned to him.

He did not see Frank Marshall as he emerged from the elevators, but Marshall caught sight of the small figure dwarfed even more by the pillar and kept on going. He had snatched no more than a glimpse of the child's face and did not wish to be reminded of Julian's look of bewilderment earlier in the corridor when he had denied him. And yet he knew that it was necessary to be tough. In today's jungle you had to look out for Number One!

As he made for the revolving door, and his exit forever from the life and times of Julian West, inventor, Marshall felt himself yanked to a stop as though someone had flung a lasso about his shoulders. He slowly turned about for one last look. He had not thought that it would be so shattering. He had expected tears or abject misery but not the look of one whom disillusionment had robbed of every aspect of childhood.

To his surprise, his feet turned away from the door and brought him before Julian. The child did not look up. The two legs before him meant nothing.

Marshall squatted down, his face level with that of the boy. He heard himself say "Julian," and realized that he was still under the spell that had seized him at the door. Julian turned so that Marshall was confronted with the full force of the white, stricken face.

Marshall said in a voice he hardly recognized, "O.K., kid, so I'm a rat."

Julian stared at him, a flicker of life returning to his eyes, but he remained silent.

Frank Marshall had to explain and drive that terrible look of a beaten man from the face of the boy. He said, "Look, I guess you won't understand and it's tough when you get a kick in the pants, but you're young, sort of a genius. You're gonna invent a lot of things beside the Bubble Gun." He paused and his voice dropped and he wished he could turn his head away as he added, "But right now, Julian, I need the patent more than you do."

Their eyes, on a level, were caught up. Julian said nothing.

Marshall continued, "See, I put my last buck down for that patent. You know, all those drawings cost money. I suppose you got the colonel to do it for you. I'm flat on my—" He stopped and said quickly, "I'm flat broke, but I can get some sort of job to keep myself going and when the patent goes through, I'll have a stake. I could get a real start."

If only the boy would do or say something or burst into tears or lash out at him instead of this uncomprehending stare. Yet

534

though Marshall was too guilt-ridden to see it something was awakening behind the lenses of the spectacles.

He pleaded, "Look, kid, we had a great time together. And I kept the cops off your back. You got your picture in the papers, you're a hero and when you get back to school all the kids will be envious of you."

The boy's face was no longer dead but perplexed and questioning. Marshall didn't know which was worse. He got in quickly with, "You know you had plenty of guts going off like you did—and you weren't scared like me of that hijacker." This last brought up something that had been missing and after a moment's hesitation he said, "Do you want to let me have the gun? You wouldn't be needing it now and they asked me about it upstairs."

Automatically, Julian's hand went to the pocket where the Bubble Gun used to live. Marshall's eyes followed the gesture. Julian's hand came out of his pocket empty, pulling a part of the lining with it. Then Marshall knew that for whatever reason he no longer had the Bubble Gun, but if he had he would have given it to him. And it was Marshall, not Julian, who fought back tears.

He said, "What else can I say, kid? Maybe it's a good lesson. Never trust anybody, especially a guy like me." He rose saying, "I'll let you know how things come out," and then after another hesitation, "No hard feelings, eh, Julian?"

Julian looked dumbly into Marshall's eyes and slowly shook his head to show that there were none. He felt nothing but unappeasable sorrow as only the young can experience, the grief of disillusionment and the shattering of trust.

Marshall held out his hand. "Will you shake?"

Slowly Julian put a limp hand into Marshall's and they shook. Marshall could bear it no longer. He gave the cold hand one more squeeze, strode quickly away and plunged through the revolving door.

As Marshall went out through one side of the door, Aldrin West came in the other. West almost immediately spied his son and hurried over to him. "Julian, my God, I'm glad I've found you."

The meeting, of course, was like nothing he had imagined. He had seen himself throwing his arms about the boy and hugging him hard and Julian returning the embrace. He was not prepared for the diffident person who, his face almost expressionless, greeted him with "Hello, Dad."

His father sat down beside him. "Julian, I've just seen the colonel. He told me all about you and I'm proud of you. You're the greatest son a man ever had and I've been a rotten father to you."

Julian looked surprised at this and shook his head. It had never dawned on him to evaluate his father or mother. Parents were as they were and that was that. He said, "No, you aren't . . ." But then suddenly his voice trailed off. He stopped and the strange far-away look with which West was to become familiar passed into his eyes.

West said, "Your idea is great. The colonel said it'll work."

But the look upon Julian's face was so remote that West became alarmed. "Has something gone wrong? Have you filed the papers? Now that I'm here I can help you."

Julian had been comforted by having his father there, but now all the sadness within him forced him to shake his head again. He began, "They were stol—somebody got there ahead of me. I was too late."

CHAPTER 15

They were on the jet, homeward bound. Julian had told his father the story piecemeal, except for the Top Secret part, interrupted by long silences puzzling to Aldrin West but which because of his new respect for his son he did not attempt to penetrate. West felt that there was more than a generation gap between himself and his boy. There was a mystery connected with Julian which cut him off from his son and what had really happened. There had been the newspaper account, there had been Julian's story and there was still the enigma—Julian.

The pain within Julian was always there. An unhealing wound, and it seemed that every part of the story he told his father or the questions he answered were in some way attached to it. Marshall, Marshall, Marshall.

Childhood was over. Julian stood on the threshold of young

manhood, with all the pangs of adolescence still to be suffered. He was unable to put into words his emotions of love and pain. Most difficult of all was for Julian to understand and separate the nature of his hurt, stemming not only from what had been done to him, but from what Marshall had done to himself. But speak of these things to his father? Impossible.

The view from the window of the aircraft showed the green striations of the Appalachian Range as Julian concluded the most difficult part of his narration, ". . . I guess he took it and copied it while I was asleep." And then almost immediately he felt the need to defend, and he said, "It didn't get into the paper, but he was the one who threw the grenade out the window." Then as his thoughts turned back to more recent events, he murmured half to himself, "He said he needed it more than I did." And again Aldrin West was aware of change and that it was no longer a child speaking when Julian said briefly and quietly, "I guess maybe he did."

West, however, mistook it for the helplessness of the young and supplied some adult belligerence. "Look here, Julian, we can fight it in court. I'm a witness as to when you made it. He wouldn't dare stand up to it. We can beat him."

Julian, once more lost in thought, was looking out of the window at country which was the beginning of midwestern farmlands. Then he became aware that his father had spoken to him and he replied simply, "I don't want to."

Aldrin West became confused for here again was the shell he was unable to penetrate. What shadows had fallen upon this boy? Had something too terrible to relate happened to him? He felt his own guilt come choking into his throat and was miserably frightened until common sense once more asserted itself. Julian's story had been straightforward enough. He had encountered a rascal and had been taken by him. He tried another track.

"Well, then it doesn't really matter that much. Does it? What's important is that you set out to do something and you got there by yourself. You've shown that you're a man. . . ." West had wanted to go on with this speech but it dried up against the barrier of Julian's absence once more.

Julian should have been glowing at this praise, but he wasn't. His mind had been turning back to the trip and all the times that

Marshall had been there when he needed him, and at times when he hadn't even known what it was all about and he saw once more the gay, half-amused, half-mocking expression on Marshall's face.

Julian's memory was still unreeling scenes and he suddenly laughed aloud and when his father looked at him said, "He got the truck driver to take us and then he changed me into Buffalo Bill."

West had not heard that before. He said, "What was that all about?"

But Julian was away again. He said, "Oh, nothing."

West felt himself seized by jealousy. He was Julian's father. He ought to come first with him. And yet someone else had managed to take his place. But this was ridiculous too. The boy had had an exciting adventure, a momentary relationship with an apparently attractive ex-soldier type who would be a hero to any child. He loved his son and wanted to throw his arms about his thin shoulders and hold him hard to himself and shelter him. Instead he felt himself pushed into flat sentences such as, "There's the Mississippi down there. Old Man River."

Julian said, "I know. We came over it on a bridge. Marshall said he went down it on a riverboat once. . . ."

A little later something which had been at the back of Aldrin's head ever since he had become reunited with his son, surfaced into an exclamation of surprise. "Hey, what happened to your stammer?"

Julian, without even looking up, replied, "Marshall said to cut it out."

The plane was over the Rockies and West observed, "The Great Divide."

Julian said, "Uh huh. Marshall said if you poured a glass of water over it half would go into the Pacific and the other half into the Atlantic."

West regarded his son with a sense of helplessness. He hadn't been getting through to him at all. But he had one more card to play. They would be arriving home soon. He said, "I'll tell you what we could do. Next to the trunk room we could make a lab and fix up a lathe, a drawing board or anything you need."

Julian's attention was riveted to the window and the wild moonscape of the badlands of the West, the bluffs, the escarpments and canyons, the tumbled country akin to that which carried the deepest memories for him.

". . . and we could work it out together." His father's voice broke in upon Julian's vision. He turned from the window and gave his father a half smile. "O.K., thanks. That would be great."

Aldrin had expected more enthusiasm or perhaps even physical contact from his son. They had yet to touch one another since their meeting. Julian hadn't even taken his proffered hand when they had made their way through the airport in Washington. To cover his disappointment he himself looked down out of the window over Julian's shoulder. The landscape had changed again.

West said, "We ought to be home in about an hour. Your mother will be so happy." Julian made no reply.

THERE WAS NO DOUBT but that Julian had changed and grown up. The manifestations were subtle, a slight difference in the way he wore his clothes, the sound of his footsteps, and yet he remained remote, enabling him to survive the spate of publicity that attended his return.

His father tried daily. He tried hard. His eyes had been opened to the insensitivity of his own behaviour. He had been badly frightened by Julian's escapade which might have ended in disaster. His problem was that he did not know what to do. His avenues of approach to Julian consisted of showing an exaggerated interest in his extra-curricular activities and Julian accepted this gratefully and responded. Yet Aldrin West was aware that he never penetrated the curious reserve which had fallen upon the boy since he had found him in Washington.

West did not know of one major achievement on his part, which was that he had shown Julian that he cared, and restored some of his son's trust in him by his concern over Julian's trip and above all by his crossing the continent to bring Julian home.

West was not a person with much understanding, but he thought it strange that Julian had never broken down. One would have expected a child of his age to shed tears at being robbed of the most important thing he had ever achieved. West, during the ensuing days, was often to wonder at Julian's stony-faced acceptance of things as they were. Outwardly he was a normal schoolboy. The laboratory in the basement had to be accounted a huge success, for when his homework was done Julian was always down there tinkering. But once the excitement over the adventure had subsided Julian never referred to it again and the barrier between his father and himself remained. As for his mother, she was blissfully unaware. She had her son back. She was pleased with her husband's efforts and the minor manifestations of Julian's independence were realized without too much regret.

It was several months later that Julian came home from school, entered the vestibule noisily and heard his mother's voice from above stairs. "That you, Julian? How was school?"

"Fine. I'm going down to my shop, Mom." He slung his satchel over his shoulder and went down the steps. He hurried through his lessons and thereafter became engrossed in a mechanical problem.

Due to his youth and inexperience Julian's mechanical bent was still imitative and adaptive like his transformation of a water pistol into a Bubble Gun. Now he was trying to convert a flight toy he had acquired into a toy helicopter. He had made several drawings and even one mock-up, but the activation of the blades was still a difficulty.

One of the best things about his workshop was its aloneness. His mother never came down; it was understood that he was to keep it clean himself, and did, and there with the cellar door closed and lights blazing and the stillness, except for the occasional whine of his drill, his thoughts would sometimes wander far afield and old sadnesses would be revived.

AT SIX ALDRIN WEST came home, set his briefcase down and looked casually through the letters of the late afternoon delivery. One of them brought a look of curiosity to his face and he examined both sides of it. He called out, "Julian?"

The reply came from below, "I'm down here, Dad."

West descended into Julian's workshop and asked, "Who do you know in Sheridan, Alabama?" and handed him the letter.

Julian examined it: *Julian West, 137 East View Terrace, San Diego, California*, in a wandering handwriting that gave him a strange feeling. He stood there looking at it until his father said, "Well, why don't you open it?"

Julian slit the envelope with a screwdriver from his workbench and removed the letter, and his father, looking over his shoulder, saw that it was written on the letterhead of Collins Garage, 43 Main Street, Sheridan, Alabama. Directly beneath this had been pasted a two-inch square advertisement from a mail-order toy company picturing a gun with soap bubbles emerging from the muzzle that looked very much like the one Julian had invented. The text boasted,

> "BUBBLEGAT! LOOKS LIKE THE REAL THING. BUT SHOOTS
> BUBBLES. AMAZE YOUR FRIENDS. EVERY BOY SHOULD HAVE A
> BUBBLEGAT! ORDER NOW WHILE THEY LAST. FILL OUT THE
> COUPON AND SEND $1.65 TO INCLUDE THE COST OF MAILING
> TO BUBBLEGAT, P.O. BOX 37, FORT LAUDERDALE, FLORIDA."

The man and the boy stared at this advertisement uncomprehending, then their attention was drawn to the scrawl beneath it. Julian read out loud:

> "Dear Julian, I guess somebody beat us both to it. So I was
> a rat for nothing. Like I said I blew all my dough so I am
> down here in Sheridan working in a garage. Hope you are
> O.K. Your old pal, Frank Marshall."

As Julian finished reading his chin and lower lip began to tremble and his face screwed up curiously. He placed the letter on his workbench, tears streaming from his eyes, put his face down on his arms and gave way to crying. For the first time since Washington, the emotional dam had burst, drawing out the agony which had so long lived in his heart.

Aldrin West looked at his son with amazement. "What are you crying about, son? It serves him right."

Julian raised his head only long enough to shake his head before he was seized by a fresh paroxysm of sobs.

His father groped, "Is it because somebody else thought of the Bubble Gun first? Look, it can happen to anyone. It shows you your invention was O.K."

Punctuated by sobs and half-smothered because the small head was still buried in his arms came the words, "Who cares about an old Bubble Gun. It's Marshall."

West picked up the letter and read through it again and for the first time had one of those moments of clarity that are able to sweep away stupidities and demolish all barriers between two humans. He let the letter fall upon the workbench and put a comforting arm about Julian's shoulder. He said, "Julian. I guess perhaps I understand. We'll write. Maybe we can give him a hand."

Julian lifted his head from his arms and looked up at his father standing close beside him, and in his ears rang the simple phrase that West had used in all sincerity, "Maybe we can give him a hand." Julian put his arms about his father's waist and his face against the rough pocket of his jacket and hugged him hard.

Paul Gallico

Like many of the great story-tellers of our time, Paul Gallico has his literary roots in journalism. Born in New York in 1899 of an Italian father and a Viennese mother, he was for fourteen years a leading sports columnist in the U.S.A. A tough, rangy, six-footer, interested always in complete authenticity, he even got himself knocked out once by Jack  Dempsey in a training bout while trying to find out for a projected article exactly what the boxing world was all about.

Quite suddenly, in 1936, he decided to change his entire way of life. He came to Britain, determined thereafter to earn his living as a fiction writer. Since then, with a brief interval as war correspondent in World War II, he has written innumerable internationally-successful novels, beginning with perhaps the most famous of them all, *The Snow Goose*. Several of his books have been filmed, notably *The Poseidon Adventure*, and he has written original screen plays also.

These days he lives mainly in the South of France. His interest in sport has remained undimmed, however: even at the age of seventy-five his favourite pastime is fencing, and he is a considerable expert in the art of the epée.

Picture credits: Page 271: top, photo by Peter B. Young; bottom, photo by Ian Alsop. Page 272: photo by Peter B. Young.

Acknowledgments: Page 173: from "The Modern Traveller" by H. Belloc, © 1972, quoted by permission of Gerald Duckworth & Co. Ltd. Page 184: from "The Love Song of J. Alfred Prufrock" in Collected Poems, 1909–1962 by T. S. Eliot, © 1963, quoted by permission of Faber & Faber Ltd. Pages 184–185: from "Henry King" by H. Belloc, © 1970, quoted by permission of Gerald Duckworth & Co. Ltd. Page 248: from "Whispers of Immortality" in Collected Poems, 1909–1962 by T. S. Eliot, © 1963, quoted by permission of Faber & Faber Ltd. Page 259: from "Preludes" in Collected Poems, 1909–1962 by T. S. Eliot, © 1963, quoted by permission of Faber & Faber Ltd.

V.V.80